ID0934993

THE LAND THAT TIME

FORGOT

and

THE MOON MAID

Two Science Fiction Novels
by Edgar Rice Burroughs

Illustrated by
J. ALLEN ST. JOHN

Dover Publications, Inc.
New York

This new Dover edition, first published in 1963,
is an unabridged and unaltered republication of
the following works by Edgar Rice Burroughs:

The Land That Time Forgot, first published in
1924.

The Moon Maid, first published in 1926.

Manufactured in the United States of America

Dover Publications, Inc.
180 Varick Street
New York 14, N. Y.

CONTENTS

THE LAND THAT TIME FORGOT

by

Edgar Rice Burroughs

There were all sorts and conditions of horrible
things; huge, hideous, grotesque monsters.

CONTENTS

PART I

The Land That Time Forgot

CHAPTER I

It must have been a little after three o'clock in the afternoon that it happened—the afternoon of June 3rd, 1916. It seems incredible that all that I have passed through—all those weird and terrifying experiences—should have been encompassed within so short a span as three brief months. Rather might I have experienced a cosmic cycle, with all its changes and evolutions for that which I have seen with my own eyes in this brief interval of time —things that no other mortal eye had seen before, glimpses of a world past, a world dead, a world so long dead that even in the lowest Cambrian stratum no trace of it remains. Fused with the melting inner crust, it has passed forever beyond the ken of man other than in that lost pocket of the earth whither fate has borne me and where my doom is sealed. I am here and here I must remain.

After reading this far, my interest, which already had been stimulated by the finding of the manuscript, was approaching the boiling-point. I had come to Greenland for the summer, on the advice of my physician, and was slowly being bored to extinction, as I had thoughtlessly neglected to bring sufficient reading-matter. Being an indifferent fisherman, my enthusiasm for this form of sport soon waned; yet in the absence of other forms of recreation I was now risking my life in an entirely inadequate boat off Cape Farewell at the southernmost extremity of Greenland.

Greenland! As a descriptive appellation, it is a sorry joke—but my story has nothing to do with Greenland, nothing to do with me; so I shall get through with the one and the other as rapidly as possible.

The inadequate boat finally arrived at a precarious landing, the natives, waist-deep in the surf, assisting. I was carried ashore, and while the evening meal was being prepared, I wandered to and fro along the rocky, shattered shore. Bits of surf-harried beach clove the worn granite, or whatever the rocks of Cape

Farewell may be composed of, and as I followed the ebbing tide down one of these soft stretches, I saw the thing. Were one to bump into a Bengal tiger in the ravine behind the Bimini Baths, one could be no more surprised than was I to see a perfectly good quart thermos bottle turning and twisting in the surf of Cape Farewell at the southern extremity of Greenland. I rescued it, but I was soaked above the knees doing it; and then I sat down in the sand and opened it, and in the long twilight read the manuscript, neatly written and tightly folded, which was its contents.

You have read the opening paragraph, and if you are an imaginative idiot like myself, you will want to read the rest of it; so I shall give it to you here, omitting quotation marks—which are difficult of remembrance. In two minutes you will forget me.

My home is in Santa Monica. I am, or was, junior member of my father's firm. We are shipbuilders. Of recent years we have specialized on submarines, which we have built for Germany, England, France and the United States. I know a sub as a mother knows her baby's face, and have commanded a score of them on their trial runs. Yet my inclinations were all toward aviation. I graduated under Curtiss, and after a long siege with my father obtained his permission to try for the Lafayette Escadrille. As a stepping-stone I obtained an appointment in the American ambulance service and was on my way to France when three shrill whistles altered, in as many seconds, my entire scheme of life.

I was sitting on deck with some of the fellows who were going into the American ambulance service with me, my Airedale, Crown Prince Nobbler, asleep at my feet, when the first blast of the whistle shattered the peace and security of the ship. Ever since entering the U-boat zone we had been on the lookout for periscopes, and children that we were, bemoaning the unkind fate that was to see us safely into France on the morrow without a glimpse of the dread marauders. We were young; we craved thrills, and God knows we got them that day; yet by comparison with that through which I have since passed they were as tame as a Punch-and-Judy show.

I shall never forget the ashy faces of the passengers as they stampeded for their life-belts, though there was no panic. Nobs rose with a low growl. I rose, also, and over the ship's side I saw not two hundred yards distant the periscope of a submarine, while racing toward the liner the wake of a torpedo was distinctly visible. We were aboard an American ship— which, of course, 'was not armed. We were entirely defense- less; yet without warning, we were being torpedoed.

I stood rigid, spellbound, watching the white wake of the torpedo. It struck us on the starboard side almost amidships. The vessel rocked as though the sea beneath it had been up- torn by a mighty volcano. We were thrown to the decks, bruised and stunned, and then above the ship, carrying with it fragments of steel and wood and dismembered human bodies, rose a column of water hundreds of feet into the air.

The silence which followed the detonation of the exploding torpedo was almost equally horrifying. It lasted for perhaps two seconds, to be followed by the screams and moans of the wounded, the cursing of the men and the hoarse commands of the ship's officers. They were splendid—they and their crew. Never before had I been so proud of my nationality as I was that moment. In all the chaos which followed the torpedoing of the liner no officer or member of the crew lost his head or showed in the slightest any degree of panic or fear.

While we were attempting to lower boats, the submarine emerged and trained guns on us. The officer in command or- dered us to lower our flag, but this the captain of the liner refused to do. The ship was listing frightfully to starboard, rendering the port boats useless, while half the starboard boats had been demolished by the explosion. Even while the passen- gers were crowding the starboard rail and scrambling into the few boats left to us, the submarine commenced shelling the ship. I saw one shell burst in a group of women and children, and then I turned my head and covered my eyes.

When I looked again to horror was added chagrin, for with the emerging of the U-boat I had recognized her as a product of our own shipyard. I knew her to a rivet. I had superintended her construction. I had sat in that very conning-tower and directed the efforts of the sweating crew below when first her prow clove the sunny summer waters of the Pacific; and now this creature of my brain and hand had turned *Frankenstein,* bent upon pursuing me to my death.

A second shell exploded upon the deck. One of the lifeboats, frightfully overcrowded, swung at a dangerous angle from its davits. A fragment of the shell shattered the bow tackle, and I saw the women and children and the men vomited into the sea beneath, while the boat dangled stern up for a moment from its single davit, and at last with increasing momentum dived into the midst of the struggling victims screaming upon the face of the waters.

Now I saw men spring to the rail and leap into the ocean. The deck was tilting to an impossible angle. Nobs braced himself with all four feet to keep from slipping into the scuppers and looked up into my face with a questioning whine. I stooped and stroked his head.

"Come on, boy!" I cried, and running to the side of the ship, dived headforemost over the rail. When I came up, the first thing I saw was Nobs swimming about in a bewildered sort of way a few yards from me. At sight of me his ears went flat, and his lips parted in a characteristic grin.

The submarine was withdrawing toward the north, but all the time it was shelling the open boats, three of them, loaded to the gunwales with survivors. Fortunately the small boats presented a rather poor target, which, combined with the bad marksmanship of the Germans, preserved their occupants from harm; and after a few minutes a blotch of smoke appeared upon the eastern horizon and the U-boat submerged and disappeared.

All the time the lifeboats had been pulling away from the danger of the sinking liner, and now, though I yelled at the top of my lungs, they either did not hear my appeals for help or else did not dare return to succor me. Nobs and I had gained some little distance from the ship when it rolled completely over and sank. We were caught in the suction only enough to be drawn backward a few yards, neither of us being carried beneath the surface. I glanced hurriedly about for something to which to cling. My eyes were directed toward the point at which the liner had disappeared when there came from the depths of the ocean the muffled reverberation of an explosion, and almost simultaneously a geyser of water in which were shattered lifeboats, human bodies, steam, coal, oil, and the flotsam of a liner's deck leaped high above the surface of the sea—a watery column momentarily marking the grave of another ship in this greatest cemetery of the seas.

When the turbulent waters had somewhat subsided and the sea had ceased to spew up wreckage, I ventured to swim back in search of something substantial enough to support my weight and that of Nobs as well. I had gotten well over the area of the wreck when not a half-dozen yards ahead of me a lifeboat shot bow foremost out of the ocean almost its entire length to flop down upon its keel with a mighty splash. It must have been carried far below, held to its mother ship by a single rope which finally parted to the enormous strain put upon it. In no other way can I account for its having leaped so far out of the water—a beneficent circumstance to which I doubtless owe my life, and that of another far dearer to me than my own. I say beneficent circumstance even in the face of the fact that a fate far more hideous confronts us than that which we escaped that day; for because of that circumstance I have met her whom otherwise I never should have known; I have met and loved her. At least I have had that great happiness in life; nor can Caspak, with all her horrors, expunge that which has been.

So for the thousandth time I thank the strange fate which sent that lifeboat hurtling upward from the green pit of destruction to which it had been dragged—sent it far up above the surface, emptying its water as it rose above the waves, and dropping it upon the surface of the sea, buoyant and safe.

It did not take me long to clamber over its side and drag Nobs in to comparative safety, and then I glanced around upon the scene of death and desolation which surrounded us. The sea was littered with wreckage among which floated the pitiful forms of women and children, buoyed up by their useless life-belts. Some were torn and mangled; others lay rolling quietly to the motion of the sea, their countenances composed and peaceful; others were set in hideous lines of agony or horror. Close to the boat's side floated the figure of a girl. Her face was turned upward, held above the surface by her life-belt, and was framed in a floating mass of dark and waving hair. She was very beautiful. I had never looked upon such perfect features, such a divine molding which was at the same time human—intensely human. It was a face filled with character and strength and femininity—the face of one who was created to love and to be loved. The cheeks were flushed to the hue of life and health and vitality, and yet she lay there upon the bosom of the sea, dead. I felt something rise in my throat as I looked down upon that radiant vision, and I swore that I should live to avenge her murder.

And then I let my eyes drop once more to the face upon the water, and what I saw nearly tumbled me backward into the sea, for the eyes in the dead face had opened; the lips had parted; and one hand was raised toward me in a mute appeal for succor. She lived! She was not dead! I leaned over the boat's side and drew her quickly in to the comparative safety which God had given me. I removed her life-belt and my soggy coat and made a pillow for her head. I chafed her hands and arms and feet. I worked over her for an hour, and at last I was rewarded by a deep sigh, and again those great eyes opened and looked into mine.

At that I was all embarrassment. I have never been a ladies' man; at Leland-Stanford I was the butt of the class because of my hopeless imbecility in the presence of a pretty girl; but the men liked me, nevertheless. I was rubbing one of her hands when she opened her eyes, and I dropped it as though it were a red-hot rivet. Those eyes took me in slowly from head to foot; then they wandered slowly around the horizon marked by the rising and falling gunwales of the lifeboat. They looked at Nobs and softened, and then came back to me, filled with questioning.

"I—I—" I stammered, moving away and stumbling over the next thwart. The vision smiled wanly.

"Aye-aye, sir!" she replied faintly, and again her lids drooped, and her long lashes swept the firm, fair texture of her skin.

"I hope that you are feeling better," I finally managed to say.

"Do you know," she said after a moment of silence, "I have been awake for a long time! But I did not dare open my eyes. I thought I must be dead, and I was afraid to look, for fear that I should see nothing but blackness all about me. I am afraid to die! Tell me what happened after the ship went down. I remember all that happened before—oh, but I wish that I might forget it!" A sob broke her voice. "The beasts!" she went on after a moment. "And to think that I was to have married one of them —a lieutenant in the German navy."

Presently she resumed as though she had not ceased speaking. "I went down and down and down. I thought I should never cease to sink. I felt no particular distress until I suddenly started upward at ever-increasing velocity; then my lungs seemed about to burst, and I must have lost consciousness, for I remember nothing more until I opened my eyes after listening to a torrent of invective against Germany and Germans. Tell me, please, all that happened after the ship sank."

I told her, then, as well as I could, all that I had seen—the submarine shelling the open boats and all the rest of it. She thought it marvelous that we should have been spared in so providential a manner, and I had a pretty speech upon my tongue's end, but lacked the nerve to deliver it. Nobs had come over and nosed his muzzle into her lap, and she stroked his ugly face, and at last she leaned over and put her cheek against his forehead. I have always admired Nobs; but this was the first time that it had ever occurred to me that I might wish to be Nobs. I wondered how he would take it, for he is as unused to women as I. But he took to it as a duck takes to water. What I lack of being a ladies' man Nobs certainly makes up for as a ladies' dog. The old scalawag just closed his eyes and put on one of the softest "sugar-wouldn't-melt-in-my-mouth" expressions you ever saw and stood there taking it and asking for more. It made me jealous.

"You seem fond of dogs," I said.

"I am fond of this dog," she replied.

Whether she meant anything personal in that reply I did not know; but I took it as personal and it made me feel mighty good.

As we drifted about upon that vast expanse of loneliness it is not strange that we should quickly become well acquainted. Constantly we scanned the horizon for signs of smoke, venturing guesses as to our chances of rescue; but darkness settled, and the black night enveloped us without ever the sight of a speck upon the waters.

We were thirsty, hungry, uncomfortable, and cold. Our wet garments had dried but little and I knew that the girl must be in grave danger from the exposure to a night of cold and wet upon the water in an open boat, without sufficient clothing and no food. I had managed to bail all the water out of the boat with cupped hands, ending by mopping the balance up with my handkerchief—a slow and backbreaking procedure; thus I had made a comparatively dry place for the girl to lie down low in the bottom of the boat, where the sides would protect her from the night wind, and when at last she did so, almost overcome as she was by weakness and fatigue, I threw my wet coat over her further to thwart the chill. But it was of no avail; as I sat watching her, the moonlight marking out the graceful curves of her slender young body, I saw her shiver.

"Isn't there something I can do?" I asked. "You can't lie there chilled through all night. Can't you suggest something?"

She shook her head. "We must grin and bear it," she replied after a moment.

Nobbler came and lay down on the thwart beside me, his back against my leg, and I sat staring in dumb misery at the girl, knowing in my heart of hearts that she might die before morning came, for what with the shock and the exposure, she had already gone through enough to kill almost any woman. And as I gazed down at her, so small and delicate and helpless, there was born slowly within my breast a new emotion. It had never been there before; now it will never cease to be there. It made me almost frantic in my desire to find some way to keep warm the cooling life-blood in her veins. I was cold myself, though I had almost forgotten it until Nobbler moved and I felt a new sensation of cold along my leg against which he had lain, and suddenly realized that in that one spot I had been warm. Like a great light came the understanding of a means to warm the girl. Immediately I knelt beside her to put my scheme into practice when suddenly I was overwhelmed with embarrassment. Would she permit it, even if I could muster the courage to suggest it? Then I saw her frame convulse shudderingly, her muscles reacting to her rapidly lowering temperature, and casting prudery to the winds, I threw myself down beside her and took her in my arms, pressing her body close to mine.

She drew away suddenly, voicing a little cry of fright, and tried to push me from her.

"Forgive me," I managed to stammer. "It is the only way. You will die of exposure if you are not warmed, and Nobs and I are the only means we can command for furnishing warmth." And I held her tightly while I called Nobs and bade him lie down at her back. The girl didn't struggle any more when she learned my purpose; but she gave two or three little gasps, and then she began to cry softly, burying her face on my arm, and thus she fell asleep.

CHAPTER II

TOWARD morning, I must have dozed, though it seemed to me at the time that I had lain awake for days, instead of hours. When I finally opened my eyes, it was daylight, and the girl's hair was in my face, and she was breathing normally. I thanked God for that. She had turned her head during the night so that as I opened my eyes I saw her face not an inch from mine, my lips almost touching hers.

It was Nobs who finally awoke her. He got up, stretched, turned around a few times and lay down again, and the girl opened her eyes and looked into mine. Hers went very wide at first, and then slowly comprehension came to her, and she smiled.

"You have been very good to me," she said, as I helped her to rise, though if the truth were known I was more in need of assistance than she; the circulation all along my left side seeming to be paralyzed entirely. "You have been very good to me." And that was the only mention she ever made of it; yet I know that she was thankful and that only reserve prevented her from referring to what, to say the least, was an embarrassing situation, however unavoidable.

Shortly after daylight we saw smoke apparently coming straight toward us, and after a time we made out the squat lines of a tug —one of those fearless exponents of England's supremacy of the sea that tows sailing ships into French and English ports. I stood up on a thwart and waved my soggy coat above my head. Nobs stood upon another and barked. The girl sat at my feet straining her eyes toward the deck of the oncoming boat. "They see us," she said at last. "There is a man answering your signal." She was right. A lump came into my throat—for her sake rather than for mine. She was saved, and none too soon. She could not have lived through another night upon the Channel; she might not have lived through the coming day.

The tug came close beside us, and a man on deck threw us a rope. Willing hands dragged us to the deck, Nobs scrambling nimbly aboard without assistance. The rough men were gentle as mothers with the girl. Plying us both with questions they hustled her to the captain's cabin and me to the boiler-room. They told the girl to take off her wet clothes and throw them outside the door that they might be dried, and then to slip into the captain's bunk and get warm. They didn't have to tell me to strip after I once got into the warmth of the boiler-room. In a jiffy, my clothes hung about where they might dry most quickly, and I myself was absorbing, through every pore, the welcome heat of the stifling compartment. They brought us hot soup and coffee, and then those who were not on duty sat around and helped me damn the Kaiser and his brood.

As soon as our clothes were dry, they bade us don them, as the chances were always more than fair in those waters that we should run into trouble with the enemy, as I was only too well aware. What with the warmth and the feeling of safety for the girl, and the knowledge that a little rest and food would quickly overcome the effects of her experiences of the past dismal hours, I was feeling more content than I had experienced since those three whistle-blasts had shattered the peace of my world the previous afternoon.

But peace upon the Channel has been but a transitory thing since August, 1914. It proved itself such that morning, for I had scarce gotten into my dry clothes and taken the girl's apparel to the captain's cabin when an order was shouted down into the engine-room for full speed ahead, and an instant later I heard the dull boom of a gun. In a moment I was up on deck to see an enemy submarine about two hundred yards off our port bow. She had signaled us to stop, and our skipper had ignored the order; but now she had her gun trained on us, and the second shot grazed the cabin, warning the belligerent tug-captain that it was time to obey. Once again an order went down to the engine-room, and the tug reduced speed. The U-boat ceased firing and ordered the tug to come about and approach. Our momentum had carried us a little beyond the enemy craft, but we were turning now on the arc of a circle that would bring us alongside her. As I stood watching the maneuver and wondering what was to become of us, I felt something touch my elbow and turned to see the girl standing at my side. She looked up into my face with a rueful expression. "They seem bent on our destruction," she said, "and it looks like the same boat that sunk us yesterday."

"It is," I replied. "I know her well. I helped design her and took her out on her first run."

The girl drew back from me with a little exclamation of surprise and disappointment. "I thought you were an American," she said. "I had no idea you were a—a——"

"Nor am I," I replied. "Americans have been building submarines for all nations for many years. I wish, though, that we had gone bankrupt, my father and I, before ever we turned out that *Frankenstein* of a thing."

We were approaching the U-boat at half speed now, and I could almost distinguish the features of the men upon her deck. A sailor stepped to my side and slipped something hard and cold into my hand. I did not have to look at it to know that it was a heavy pistol. "Tyke 'er an' use 'er," was all he said.

Our bow was pointed straight toward the U-boat now as I heard word passed to the engine-room for full speed ahead. Instantly I grasped the brazen effrontery of the plucky English skipper—he was going to ram five hundred tons of U-boat in the face of her trained gun. I could scarce repress a cheer. At first the boches didn't seem to grasp his intention. Evidently they thought they were witnessing an exhibition of poor seamanship, and they yelled their warnings to the tug to reduce speed and throw the helm hard to port.

We were within fifty feet of them when they awakened to the intentional menace of our maneuver. Their gun crew was off its guard; but they sprang to their piece now and sent a futile shell above our heads. Nobs leaped about and barked furiously. "Let 'em have it!" commanded the tug-captain, and instantly revolvers and rifles poured bullets upon the deck of the submersible. Two of the gun-crew went down; the others trained their piece at the water-line of the oncoming tug. The balance of those on deck replied to our small-arms fire, directing their efforts toward the man at our wheel.

I hastily pushed the girl down the companionway leading to the engine-room, and then I raised my pistol and fired my first shot at a boche. What happened in the next few seconds happened so quickly that details are rather blurred in my memory. I saw the helmsman lunge forward upon the wheel, pulling the helm around so that the tug sheered off quickly from her course, and I recall realizing that all our efforts were to be in vain, because of all the men aboard, Fate had decreed that this one should fall first to an enemy bullet. I saw the depleted gun-crew on the submarine fire their piece and I felt the shock of impact and heard the loud explosion as the shell struck and exploded in our bows.

I saw and realized these things even as I was leaping into the pilot-house and grasping the wheel, standing astride the dead body of the helmsman. With all my strength I threw the helm to starboard; but it was too late to effect the purpose of our skipper. The best I did was to scrape alongside the sub. I heard some one shriek an order into the engine-room; the boat shuddered and trembled to the sudden reversing of the engines, and our speed quickly lessened. Then I saw what that madman of a skipper planned since his first scheme had gone wrong.

With a loud-yelled command, he leaped to the slippery deck of the submersible, and at his heels came his hardy crew. I sprang from the pilot-house and followed, not to be left out in the cold when it came to strafing the boches. From the engine-room companionway came the engineer and stokers, and together we leaped after the balance of the crew and into the hand-to-hand fight that was covering the wet deck with red blood. Beside me came Nobs, silent now, and grim. Germans were emerging from the open hatch to take part in the battle on deck. At first the pistols cracked amidst the cursing of the men and the loud commands of the commander and his junior; but presently we were too indiscriminately mixed to make it safe to use our firearms, and the battle resolved itself into a hand-to-hand struggle for possession of the deck.

The sole aim of each of us was to hurl one of the opposing force into the sea. I shall never forget the hideous expression upon the face of the great Prussian with whom chance confronted me. He lowered his head and rushed at me, bellowing like a bull. With a quick side-step and ducking low beneath his outstretched arms, I eluded him; and as he turned to come back at me, I landed a blow upon his chin which sent him spinning toward the edge of the deck. I saw his wild endeavors to regain his equilibrium; I saw him reel drunkenly for an instant upon the brink of eternity and then, with a loud scream, slip into the sea. At the same instant a pair of giant arms encircled me from behind and lifted me entirely off my feet. Kick and squirm as I would, I could neither turn toward my antagonist nor free myself from his maniacal grasp. Relentlessly he was rushing me toward the side of the vessel and death. There was none to stay him, for each of my companions was more than occupied by from one to three of the enemy. For an instant I was fearful for myself, and then I saw that which filled me with a far greater terror for another.

My boche was bearing me toward the side of the submarine against which the tug still was pounding. That I should be ground to death between the two was lost upon me as I saw the girl standing alone upon the tug's deck, as I saw the stern high in air and the bow rapidly settling for the final dive, as I saw death from which I could not save her clutching at the skirts of the woman I now knew all too well that I loved.

I had perhaps the fraction of a second longer to live when I heard an angry growl behind us mingle with a cry of pain and rage from the giant who carried me. Instantly he went backward to the deck, and as he did so he threw his arms outwards to save himself, freeing me. I fell heavily upon him, but was upon my feet in the instant. As I arose, I cast a single glance at my opponent. Never again would he menace me or another, for Nobs' great jaws had closed upon his throat. Then I sprang toward the edge of the deck closest to the girl upon the sinking tug.

"Jump!" I cried. "Jump!" And I held out my arms to her. Instantly as though with implicit confidence in my ability to save her, she leaped over the side of the tug onto the sloping, slippery side of the U-boat. I reached far over to seize her hand. At the same instant the tug pointed its stern straight toward the sky and plunged out of sight. My hand missed the girl's by a fraction of an inch, and I saw her slip into the sea; but scarce had she touched the water when I was in after her.

The sinking tug drew us far below the surface; but I had seized her the moment I struck the water, and so we went down together, and together we came up—a few yards from the U-boat. The first thing I heard was Nobs barking furiously; evidently he had missed me and was searching. A single glance at the vessel's deck assured me that the battle was over and that we had been victorious, for I saw our survivors holding a handful of the enemy at pistol points while one by one the rest of the crew was coming out of the craft's interior and lining up on deck with the other prisoners.

As I swam toward the submarine with the girl, Nobs' persistent barking attracted the attention of some of the tug's crew, so that as soon as we reached the side there were hands to help us aboard. I asked the girl if she was hurt, but she assured me that she was none the worse for this second wetting; nor did she seem to suffer any from shock. I was to learn for myself that this slender and seemingly delicate creature possessed the heart and courage of a warrior.

As we joined our own party, I found the tug's mate checking up our survivors. There were ten of us left, not including the girl. Our brave skipper was missing, as were eight others. There had been nineteen of us in the attacking party and we had accounted in one way and another during the battle for sixteen Germans and had taken nine prisoners, including the commander. His lieutenant had been killed.

"Not a bad day's work," said Bradley, the mate, when he had completed his roll. "Only losing the skipper," he added, "was the worst. He was a fine man, a fine man."

Olson—who in spite of his name was Irish, and in spite of his not being Scotch had been the tug's engineer—was standing with Bradley and me. "Yis," he agreed, "it's a day's wor-rk we're after doin', but what are we goin' to be doin' wid it now we got it?"

"We'll run her into the nearest English port," said Bradley, "and then we'll all go ashore and get our V.C.'s," he concluded, laughing.

"How you goin' to run her?" queried Olson. "You can't trust these Dutchmen."

Bradley scratched his head. "I guess you're right," he admitted.

"And I don't know the first thing about a sub."

"I do," I assured him. "I know more about this particular sub than the officer who commanded her."

Both men looked at me in astonishment, and then I had to explain all over again as I had explained to the girl. Bradley and Olson were delighted. Immediately I was put in command, and the first thing I did was to go below with Olson and inspect the craft thoroughly for hidden boches and damaged machinery. There were no Germans below, and everything was intact and in ship-shape working order. I then ordered all hands below except one man who was to act as lookout. Questioning the Germans, I found that all except the commander were willing to resume their posts and aid in bringing the vessel into an English port. I believe that they were relieved at the prospect of being detained at a comfortable English prison-camp for the duration of the war after the perils and privations through which they had passed. The officer, however, assured me that he would never be a party to the capture of his vessel.

There was, therefore, nothing to do but put the man in irons. As we were preparing to put this decision into force, the girl descended from the deck. It was the first time that she or the German officer had seen each other's faces since we had boarded the U-boat. I was assisting the girl down the ladder and still retained a hold upon her arm—possibly after such support was no longer necessary—when she turned and looked squarely into the face of the German. Each voiced a sudden exclamation of surprise and dismay.

"Lys!" he cried, and took a step toward her.

The girl's eyes went wide, and slowly filled with a great horror, as she shrank back. Then her slender figure stiffened to the erectness of a soldier, and with chin in air and without a word she turned her back upon the officer.

"Take him away," I directed the two men who guarded him, "and put him in irons."

When he had gone, the girl raised her eyes to mine. "He is the German of whom I spoke," she said. "He is Baron von Schoenvorts."

I merely inclined my head. She had loved him! I wondered if in her heart of hearts she did not love him yet. Immediately I became insanely jealous. I hated Baron Friedrich von Schoenvorts with such utter intensity that the emotion thrilled me with a species of exaltation.

But I didn't have much chance to enjoy my hatred then, for

almost immediately the lookout poked his face over the hatchway and bawled down that there was smoke on the horizon, dead ahead. Immediately I went on deck to investigate, and Bradley came with me.

"If she's friendly," he said, "we'll speak her. If she's not, we'll sink her—eh, captain?"

"Yes, lieutenant," I replied, and it was his turn to smile.

We hoisted the Union Jack and remained on deck, asking Bradley to go below and assign to each member of the crew his duty, placing one Englishman with a pistol beside each German. "Half speed ahead," I commanded.

More rapidly now we closed the distance between ourselves and the stranger, until I could plainly see the red ensign of the British merchant marine. My heart swelled with pride at the thought that presently admiring British tars would be congratulating us upon our notable capture; and just about then the merchant steamer must have sighted us, for she veered suddenly toward the north, and a moment later dense volumes of smoke issued from her funnels. Then, steering a zigzag course, she fled from us as though we had been the bubonic plague. I altered the course of the submarine and set off in chase; but the steamer was faster than we, and soon left us hopelessly astern.

With a rueful smile I directed that our original course be resumed, and once again we set off toward merry England. That was three months ago, and we haven't arrived yet; nor is there any likelihood that we ever shall.

The steamer we had just sighted must have wirelessed a warning, for it wasn't half an hour before we saw more smoke on the horizon, and this time the vessel flew the white ensign of the Royal Navy and carried guns. She didn't veer to the north or anywhere else, but bore down on us rapidly. I was just preparing to signal her, when a flame flashed from her bows, and an instant later the water in front of us was thrown high by the explosion of a shell.

Bradley had come on deck and was standing beside me. "About one more of those, and she'll have our range," he said. "She doesn't seem to take much stock in our Union Jack."

A second shell passed over us, and I gave the command to change our direction, at the same time directing Bradley to go below and give the order to submerge. I passed Nobs down to him, and following, saw to the closing and fastening of the hatch.

It seemed to me that the diving-tanks never had filled so slowly. We heard a loud explosion apparently directly above us; the craft trembled to the shock, which threw us all to the deck. I expected momentarily to feel the deluge of inrushing water, but none came. Instead we continued to submerge until the manometer registered forty feet and then I knew that we were safe. Safe! I almost smiled. I had relieved Olson, who had remained in the tower at my direction, having been a member of one of the early British submarine crews, and therefore having some knowledge of the business. Bradley was at my side. He looked at me quizzically.

"What the devil are we to do?" he asked. "The merchantman will flee us; the war-vessel will destroy us; neither will believe our colors or give us a chance to explain. We will meet even a worse reception if we go nosing around a British port—mines, nets and all of it. We can't do it."

"Let's try it again when this fellow has lost the scent," I urged. "There must come a ship that will believe us."

And try it again we did, only to be almost rammed by a huge freighter. Later we were fired upon by a destroyer, and two merchantmen turned and fled at our approach. For two days we cruised up and down the Channel trying to tell some one, who would listen, that we were friends; but no one would listen. After our encounter with the first warship I had given instructions that a wireless message be sent out explaining our predicament; but to my chagrin I discovered that both sending and receiving instruments had disappeared.

"There is only one place you can go," von Schoenvorts sent word to me, "and that is Kiel. You can't land anywhere else in these waters. If you wish, I will take you there, and I can promise that you will be treated well."

"There is another place we can go," I sent back my reply, "and we will before we'll go to Germany. That place is hell."

CHAPTER III

THOSE were anxious days, during which I had but little opportunity to associate with Lys. I had given her the commander's room, Bradley and I taking that of the deck-officer, while Olson and two of our best men occupied the room ordinarily allotted to petty officers. I made Nobs' bed down in Lys' room, for I knew she would feel less alone.

Nothing of much moment occurred for a while after we left British waters behind us. We ran steadily along upon the surface, making good time. The first two boats we sighted made off as fast as they could go; and the third, a huge freighter, fired on us, forcing us to submerge. It was after this that our troubles commenced. One of the Diesel engines broke down in the morning, and while we were working on it, the forward port diving-tank commenced to fill. I was on deck at the time and noted the gradual list. Guessing at once what was happening, I leaped for the hatch and slamming it closed above my head, dropped to the centrale. By this time the craft was going down by the head with a most unpleasant list to port, and I didn't wait to transmit orders to some one else but ran as fast as I could for the valve that let the sea into the forward port diving-tank. It was wide open. To close it and to have the pump started that would empty it were the work of but a minute; but we had had a close call.

I knew that the valve had never opened itself. Some one had opened it—some one who was willing to die himself if he might at the same time encompass the death of all of us.

After that I kept a guard pacing the length of the narrow craft. We worked upon the engine all that day and night and half the following day. Most of the time we drifted idly upon the surface, but toward noon we sighted smoke due west, and having found that only enemies inhabited the world for us, I ordered that the other engine be started so that we could move out of the path of the oncoming steamer. The moment the engine started to turn, however, there was a grinding sound of tortured steel, and when it had been stopped, we found that some one had placed a cold-chisel in one of the gears.

It was another two days before we were ready to limp along, half repaired. The night before the repairs were completed, the sentry came to my room and awoke me. He was rather an intelligent fellow of the English middle class, in whom I had much confidence.

"Well, Wilson," I asked, "what's the matter now?"

He raised his finger to his lips and came closer to me. "I think I've found out who's doin' the mischief," he whispered, and nodded his head toward the girl's room. "I seen her sneakin' from the crew's room just now," he went on. "She'd been in gassin' wit' the boche commander. Benson seen her in there las' night, too, but he never said nothin' till I goes on watch tonight. Benson's sorter slow in the head, an' he never puts two an' two together till some one else has made four out of it."

If the man had come in and struck me suddenly in the face, I could have been no more surprised.

"Say nothing of this to anyone," I ordered. "Keep your eyes and ears open and report every suspicious thing you see or hear."

The man saluted and left me; but for an hour or more I tossed, restless, upon my hard bunk in an agony of jealousy and fear. Finally I fell into a troubled sleep. It was daylight when I awoke. We were steaming along slowly upon the surface, my orders having been to proceed at half speed until we could take an observation and determine our position. The sky had been overcast all the previous day and all night; but as I stepped into the centrale that morning I was delighted to see that the sun was again shining. The spirits of the men seemed improved; everything seemed propitious. I forgot at once the cruel misgivings of the past night as I set to work to take my observations.

What a blow awaited me! The sextant and chronometer had both been broken beyond repair, and they had been broken just this very night. They had been broken upon the night that Lys had been seen talking with von Schoenvorts. I think that it was this last thought which hurt me the worst. I could look the other disaster in the face with equanimity; but the bald fact that Lys might be a traitor appalled me.

I called Bradley and Olson on deck and told them what had happened, but for the life of me I couldn't bring myself to repeat what Wilson had reported to me the previous night. In fact, as I had given the matter thought, it seemed incredible that the girl could have passed through my room, in which Bradley and I slept, and that occupied by Olson and two others, and then carried on a conversation in the crew's room, in which von Schoenvorts was kept, without having been seen by more than a single man.

Bradley shook his head. "I can't make it out," he said. "One of those boches must be pretty clever to come it over us all like this; but they haven't harmed us as much as they think; there are still the extra instruments."

It was my turn now to shake a doleful head. "There are no extra instruments," I told them. "They too have disappeared as did the wireless apparatus."

Both men looked at me in amazement. "We still have the compass and the sun," said Olson. "They may be after getting the compass some night; but they's too many of us around in the daytime fer 'em to get the sun."

It was then that one of the men stuck his head up through the hatchway and seeing me, asked permission to come on deck and get a breath of fresh air. I recognized him as Benson, the man who, Wilson had said, reported having seen Lys with von Schoenvorts two nights before. I motioned him on deck and then called him to one side, asking if he had seen anything out of the way or unusual during his trick on watch the night before. The fellow scratched his head a moment and said "No," and then as though it was an afterthought, he told me that he had seen the girl in the crew's room about midnight talking with the German commander, but as there hadn't seemed to him to be any harm in that, he hadn't said anything about it. Telling him never to fail to report to me anything in the slightest out of the ordinary routine of the ship, I dismissed him.

Several of the other men now asked permission to come on deck, and soon all but those actually engaged in some necessary duty were standing around smoking and talking, all in the best of spirits. I took advantage of the absence of the men upon the deck to go below for my breakfast, which the cook was already preparing upon the electric stove. Lys, followed by Nobs, appeared as I entered the centrale. She met me with a pleasant "Good morning!" which I am afraid I replied to in a tone that was rather constrained and surly.

"Will you breakfast with me?" I suddenly asked the girl, determined to commence a probe of my own along the lines which duty demanded.

She nodded a sweet acceptance of my invitation, and together we sat down at the little table of the officers' mess.

"You slept well last night?" I asked.

"All night," she replied. "I am a splendid sleeper."

Her manner was so straightforward and honest that I could not bring myself to believe in her duplicity; yet— Thinking to surprise her into a betrayal of her guilt, I blurted out: "The chronometer and sextant were both destroyed last night; there is a traitor among us." But she never turned a hair by way of evidencing guilty knowledge of the catastrophe.

"Who could it have been?" she cried. "The Germans would be crazy to do it, for their lives are as much at stake as ours."

"Men are often glad to die for an ideal—an ideal of patriotism, perhaps," I replied; "and a willingness to martyr themselves includes a willingness to sacrifice others, even those who love them.

Women are much the same, except that they will go even further than most men—they will sacrifice everything, even honor, for love."

I watched her face carefully as I spoke, and I thought that I detected a very faint flush mounting her cheek. Seeing an opening and an advantage, I sought to follow it up.

"Take von Schoenvorts, for instance," I continued: "he would doubtless be glad to die and take us all with him, could he prevent in no other way the falling of his vessel into enemy hands. He would sacrifice anyone, even you; and if you still love him, you might be his ready tool. Do you understand me?"

She looked at me in wide-eyed consternation for a moment, and then she went very white and rose from her seat. "I do," she replied, and turning her back upon me, she walked quickly toward her room. I started to follow, for even believing what I did, I was sorry that I had hurt her. I reached the door to the crew's room just behind her and in time to see von Schoenvorts lean forward and whisper something to her as she passed; but she must have guessed that she might be watched, for she passed on.

That afternoon it clouded over; the wind mounted to a gale, and the sea rose until the craft was wallowing and rolling frightfully. Nearly everyone aboard was sick; the air became foul and oppressive. For twenty-four hours I did not leave my post in the conning tower, as both Olson and Bradley were sick. Finally I found that I must get a little rest, and so I looked about for some one to relieve me. Benson volunteered. He had not been sick, and assured me that he was a former R. N. man and had been detailed for submarine duty for over two years. I was glad that it was he, for I had considerable confidence in his loyalty, and so it was with a feeling of security that I went below and lay down.

I slept twelve hours straight, and when I awoke and discovered what I had done, I lost no time in getting to the conning-tower. There sat Benson as wide awake as could be, and the compass showed that we were heading straight into the west. The storm was still raging; nor did it abate its fury until the fourth day. We were all pretty well done up and looked forward to the time when we could go on deck and fill our lungs with fresh air. During the whole four days I had not seen the girl, as she evidently kept closely to her room; and during this time no untoward incident had occurred aboard the boat—a fact which seemed to strengthen the web of circumstantial evidence about her.

For six more days after the storm lessened we still had fairly

we took, together with an affidavit signed by Bradley, Olson, and myself, stating briefly how we had come into possession of the *U-33* and the urgency of our need for what we took. We addressed both to any British agent with the request that the owners of the *Balmen* be reimbursed; but whether or not they were, I do not know.[1]

With water, food, and oil aboard, we felt that we had obtained a new lease of life. Now, too, we knew definitely where we were, and I determined to make for Georgetown, British Guiana—but I was destined to again suffer bitter disappointment.

Six of us of the loyal crew had come on deck either to serve the gun or board the Swede during our set-to with her; and now, one by one, we descended the ladder into the centrale. I was the last to come, and when I reached the bottom, I found myself looking into the muzzle of a pistol in the hands of Baron Friedrich von Schoenvorts—I saw all my men lined up at one side with the remaining eight Germans standing guard over them.

I couldn't imagine how it had happened; but it had. Later I learned that they had first overpowered Benson, who was asleep in his bunk, and taken his pistol from him, and then had found it an easy matter to disarm the cook and the remaining two Englishmen below. After that it had been comparatively simple to stand at the foot of the ladder and arrest each individual as he descended.

The first thing von Schoenvorts did was to send for me and announce that as a pirate I was to be shot early the next morning. Then he explained that the *U-33* would cruise in these waters for a time, sinking neutral and enemy shipping indiscriminately, and looking for one of the German raiders that was supposed to be in these parts.

He didn't shoot me the next morning as he had promised, and it has never been clear to me why he postponed the execution of my sentence. Instead he kept me ironed just as he had been; then he kicked Bradley out of my room and took it all to himself.

We cruised for a long time, sinking many vessels, all but one by gunfire, but we did not come across a German raider. I was surprised to note that von Schoenvorts often permitted Benson

---

[1]Late in July, 1916, an item in the shipping news mentioned a Swedish sailing vessel, *Balmen*, Rio de Janeiro to Barcelona, sunk by a German raider sometime in June. A single survivor in an open boat was picked up off the Cape Verde Islands, in a dying condition. He expired without giving any details.

to take command; but I reconciled this by the fact that Benson appeared to know more of the duties of a submarine commander than did any of the stupid Germans.

Once or twice Lys passed me; but for the most part she kept to her room. The first time she hesitated as though she wished to speak to me; but I did not raise my head, and finally she passed on. Then one day came the word that we were about to round the Horn and that von Schoenvorts had taken it into his fool head to cruise up along the Pacific coast of North America and prey upon all sorts and conditions of merchantmen.

"I'll put the fear of God and the Kaiser into them," he said.

The very first day we entered the South Pacific we had an adventure. It turned out to be quite the most exciting adventure I had ever encountered. It fell about this way. About eight bells of the forenoon watch I heard a hail from deck, and presently the footsteps of the entire ship's company, from the amount of noise I heard at the ladder. Some one yelled back to those who had not yet reached the level of the deck: "It's the raider, the German raider *Geier!*"

I saw that we had reached the end of our rope. Below all was quiet—not a man remained. A door opened at the end of the narrow hull, and presently Nobs came trotting up to me. He licked my face and rolled over on his back, reaching for me with his big, awkward paws. Then other footsteps sounded, approaching me. I knew whose they were, and I looked straight down at the flooring. The girl was coming almost at a run—she was at my side immediately. "Here!" she cried. "Quick!" And she slipped something into my hand. It was a key—the key to my irons. At my side she also laid a pistol, and then she went on into the centrale. As she passed me, I saw that she carried another pistol for herself. It did not take me long to liberate myself, and then I was at her side. "How can I thank you?" I started; but she shut me up with a word.

"Do not thank me," she said coldly. "I do not care to hear your thanks or any other expression from you. Do not stand there looking at me. I have given you a chance to do something—now do it!" The last was a peremptory command that made me jump.

Glancing up, I saw that the tower was empty, and I lost no time in clambering up, looking about me. About a hundred yards off lay a small, swift cruiser-raider, and above her floated the German man-of-war's flag. A boat had just been lowered, and I could see it moving toward us filled with officers and men. The cruiser lay dead ahead. "My," I thought, "what a wonderful targ——"

I stopped even thinking, so surprised and shocked was I by the boldness of my imagery. The girl was just below me. I looked down at her wistfully. Could I trust her? Why had she released me at this moment? I must! I must! There was no other way. I dropped back below. "Ask Olson to step down here, please," I requested; "and don't let anyone see you ask him."

She looked at me with a puzzled expression on her face for the barest fraction of a second, and then she turned and went up the ladder. A moment later Olson returned, and the girl followed him. "Quick!" I whispered to the big Irishman, and made for the bow compartment where the torpedo-tubes are built into the boat; here, too, were the torpedoes. The girl accompanied us, and when she saw the thing I had in mind, she stepped forward and lent a hand to the swinging of the great cylinder of death and destruction into the mouth of its tube. With oil and main strength we shoved the torpedo home and shut the tube; then I ran back to the conning-tower, praying in my heart of hearts that the U-33 had not swung her bow away from the prey. No, thank God!

Never could aim have been truer. I signaled back to Olson: "Let 'er go!" The U-33 trembled from stem to stern as the torpedo shot from its tube. I saw the white wake leap from her bow straight toward the enemy cruiser. A chorus of hoarse yells arose from the deck of our own craft; I saw the officers stand suddenly erect in the boat that was approaching us, and I heard loud cries and curses from the raider. Then I turned my attention to my own business. Most of the men on the submarine's deck were standing in paralyzed fascination, staring at the torpedo. Bradley happened to be looking toward the conning-tower and saw me. I sprang on deck and ran toward him. "Quick!" I whispered. "While they are stunned, we must overcome them."

A German was standing near Bradley—just in front of him. The Englishman struck the fellow a frantic blow upon the neck and at the same time snatched his pistol from its holster. Von Schoenvorts had recovered from his first surprise quickly and had turned toward the main hatch to investigate. I covered him with my revolver, and at the same instant the torpedo struck the raider, the terrific explosion drowning the German's command to his men.

Bradley was now running from one to another of our men,

and though some of the Germans saw and heard him, they seemed too stunned for action.

Olson was below, so that there were only nine of us against eight Germans, for the man Bradley had struck still lay upon the deck. Only two of us were armed; but the heart seemed to have gone out of the boches, and they put up but half-hearted resistance. Von Schoenvorts was the worst—he was fairly frenzied with rage and chagrin, and he came charging for me like a mad bull, and as he came he discharged his pistol. If he'd stopped long enough to take aim, he might have gotten me; but his pace made him wild, so that not a shot touched me, and then we clinched and went to the deck. This left two pistols, which two of my own men were quick to appropriate. The Baron was no match for me in a hand-to-hand encounter, and I soon had him pinned to the deck and the life almost choked out of him.

A half-hour later things had quieted down, and all was much the same as before the prisoners had revolted—only we kept a much closer watch on von Schoenvorts. The *Geier* had sunk while we were still battling upon our deck, and afterward we had drawn away toward the north, leaving the survivors to the attention of the single boat which had been making its way toward us when Olson launched the torpedo. I suppose the poor devils never reached land, and if they did, they most probably perished on that cold and inhospitable shore; but I couldn't permit them aboard the *U-33*. We had all the Germans we could take care of.

That evening the girl asked permission to go on deck. She said that she felt the effects of long confinement below, and I readily granted her request. I could not understand her, and I craved an opportunity to talk with her again in an effort to fathom her and her intentions, and so I made it a point to follow her up the ladder. It was a clear, cold, beautiful night. The sea was calm except for the white water at our bows and the two long radiating swells running far off into the distance upon either hand astern, forming a great V which our propellers filled with choppy waves. Benson was in the tower, we were bound for San Diego and all looked well.

Lys stood with a heavy blanket wrapped around her slender figure, and as I approached her, she half turned toward me to see who it was. When she recognized me, she immediately turned away.

"I want to thank you," I said, "for your bravery and loyalty—you were magnificent. I am sorry that you had reason before to think that I doubted you."

"You did doubt me," she replied in a level voice. "You practically accused me of aiding Baron von Schoenvorts. I can never forgive you."

There was a great deal of finality in both her words and tone.

"I could not believe it," I said; "and yet two of my men reported having seen you in conversation with von Schoenvorts late at night upon two separate occasions—after each of which some great damage was found done us in the morning. I didn't want to doubt you; but I carried all the responsibility of the lives of these men, of the safety of the ship, of your life and mine. I had to watch you, and I had to put you on your guard against a repetition of your madness."

She was looking at me now with those great eyes of hers very wide and round.

"Who told you that I spoke with Baron von Schoenvorts at night, or any other time?" she asked.

"I cannot tell you, Lys," I replied, "but it came to me from two different sources."

"Then two men have lied," she asserted without heat. "I have not spoken to Baron von Schoenvorts other than in your presence when first we came aboard the *U-33*. And please, when you address me, remember that to others than my intimates I am Miss La Rue."

Did you ever get slapped in the face when you least expected it? No? Well, then you do not know how I felt at that moment. I could feel the hot, red flush surging up my neck, across my cheeks, over my ears, clear to my scalp. And it made me love her all the more; it made me swear inwardly a thousand solemn oaths that I would win her.

CHAPTER IV

FOR several days things went along in about the same course. I took our position every morning with my crude sextant; but the results were always most unsatisfactory. They always showed a considerable westing when I knew that we had been sailing due north. I blamed my crude instrument, and kept on. Then one afternoon the girl came to me.

"Pardon me," she said; "but were I you, I should watch this man Benson—especially when he is in charge." I asked her what she meant, thinking I could see the influence of von Schoenvorts raising a suspicion against one of my most trusted men.

"If you will note the boat's course a half-hour after Benson goes on duty," she said, "you will know what I mean, and you will understand why he prefers a night watch. Possibly, too, you will understand some other things that have taken place aboard."

Then she went back to her room, thus ending the conversation. I waited until half an hour after Benson had gone on duty, and then I went on deck, passing through the conning-tower where Benson sat, and looking at the compass. It showed that our course was north by west—that is, one point west of north, which was, for our assumed position, about right. I was greatly relieved to find that nothing was wrong, for the girl's words had caused me considerable apprehension. I was about to return to my room when a thought occurred to me that again caused me to change my mind—and, incidentally, came near proving my death-warrant.

When I had left the conning-tower little more than a half-hour since, the sea had been breaking over the port bow, and it seemed to me quite improbable that in so short a time an equally heavy sea could be deluging us from the opposite side of the ship— winds may change quickly, but not a long, heavy sea. There was only one other solution—since I left the tower, our course had been altered some eight points. Turning quickly, I climbed out upon the conning-tower. A single glance at the heavens confirmed my suspicions; the constellations which should have been dead ahead were directly starboard. We were sailing due west.

Just for an instant longer I stood there to check up my calculations—I wanted to be quite sure before I accused Benson of perfidy, and about the only thing I came near making quite sure of was death. I cannot see even now how I escaped it. I was standing on the edge of the conning-tower, when a heavy palm suddenly struck me between the shoulders and hurled me forward into space. The drop to the triangular deck forward of the conning-tower might easily have broken a leg for me, or I might have slipped off onto the deck and rolled overboard; but fate was upon my side, as I was only slightly bruised. As I came to my feet, I heard the conning-tower cover slam. There is a ladder which leads from the deck to the top of the tower. Up this I scrambled as fast as I could go; but Benson had the cover tight before I reached it.

I stood there a moment in dumb consternation. What did the fellow intend? What was going on below? If Benson was a traitor, how could I know that there were not other traitors among us? I cursed myself for my folly in going out upon the deck, and then this thought suggested another—a hideous one: who was it had really been responsible for my being here?

Thinking to attract attention from inside the craft, I again ran down the ladder and onto the small deck only to find that the steel covers of the conning-tower windows were shut, and then I leaned with my back against the tower and cursed myself for a gullible idiot.

I glanced at the bow. The sea seemed to be getting heavier, for every wave now washed completely over the lower deck. I watched them for a moment, and then a sudden chill pervaded my entire being. It was not the chill of wet clothing, or the dashing spray which drenched my face; no, it was the chill of the hand of death upon my heart. In an instant I had turned the last corner of life's highway and was looking God Almighty in the face—the *U-33* was being slowly submerged!

It would be difficult, even impossible, to set down in writing my sensations at that moment. All I can particularly recall is that I laughed, though neither from a spirit of bravado nor from hysteria. And I wanted to smoke. Lord! how I did want to smoke; but that was out of the question.

I watched the water rise until the little deck I stood on was awash, and then I clambered once more to the top of the conning-tower. From the very slow submergence of the boat I knew that Benson was doing the entire trick alone—that he was merely permitting the diving-tanks to fill and that the diving-rudders were not in use. The throbbing of the engines ceased, and in its stead came the steady vibration of the electric motors. The water was halfway up the conning-tower! I had perhaps five minutes longer on the deck. I tried to decide what I should do after I was washed away. Should I swim until exhaustion claimed me, or should I give up and end the agony at the first plunge?

From below came two muffled reports. They sounded not unlike shots. Was Benson meeting with resistance? Personally it could mean little to me, for even though my men might overcome the enemy, none would know of my predicament until long after it was too late to succor me. The top of the conning-tower was now awash. I clung to the wireless mast, while the great waves surged sometimes completely over me.

I knew the end was near and, almost involuntarily, I did that which I had not done since childhood—I prayed. After that I felt better.

I clung and waited, but the water rose no higher. Instead it receded. Now the top of the conning-tower received only the crests of the higher waves; now the little triangular deck below became visible! What had occurred within? Did Benson believe me already gone, and was he emerging because of that belief, or had he and his forces been vanquished? The suspense was more wearing than that which I had endured while waiting for dissolution. Presently the main deck came into view, and then the conning-tower opened behind me, and I turned to look into the anxious face of Bradley. An expression of relief overspread his features.

"Thank God, man!" was all he said as he reached forth and dragged me into the tower. I was cold and numb and rather all in. Another few minutes would have done for me, I am sure, but the warmth of the interior helped to revive me, aided and abetted by some brandy which Bradley poured down my throat, from which it nearly removed the membrane. That brandy would have revived a corpse.

When I got down into the centrale, I saw the Germans lined up on one side with a couple of my men with pistols standing over them. Von Schoenvorts was among them. On the floor lay Benson, moaning, and beyond him stood the girl, a revolver in one hand. I looked about, bewildered.

"What has happened down here?" I asked. "Tell me!"

Bradley replied. "You see the result, sir," he said. "It might have been a very different result but for Miss La Rue. We were all asleep. Benson had relieved the guard early in the evening; there was no one to watch him—no one but Miss La Rue. She felt the submergence of the boat and came out of her room to investigate. She was just in time to see Benson at the diving rudders. When he saw her, he raised his pistol and fired point-blank at her, but he missed and she fired—and didn't miss. The two shots awakened everyone, and as our men were armed, the result was inevitable as you see it; but it would have been very different had it not been for Miss La Rue. It was she who closed the diving-tank sea-cocks and roused Olson and me, and had the pumps started to empty them."

And there I had been thinking that through her machinations I had been lured to the deck and to my death! I could have gone on my knees to her and begged her forgiveness—or at least I could have, had I not been Anglo-Saxon. As it was, I could only remove my soggy cap and bow and mumble my appreciation. She made no reply—only turned and walked very rapidly toward her room. Could I have heard aright? Was it really a sob that came floating back to me through the narrow aisle of the *U-33*?

Benson died that night. He remained defiant almost to the last; but just before he went out, he motioned to me, and I leaned over to catch the faintly whispered words.

"I did it alone," he said. "I did it because I hate you—I hate all your kind. I was kicked out of your shipyard at Santa Monica. I was kicked out of California. I am an I.W.W. I became a German agent—not because I love them, for I hate them too—but because I wanted to injure Americans, whom I hated more. I threw the wireless apparatus overboard. I destroyed the chronometer and the sextant. I devised a scheme for varying the compass to suit my wishes. I told Wilson that I had seen the girl talking with von Schoenvorts, and I made the poor egg think he had seen her doing the same thing. I am sorry—sorry that my plans failed. I hate you."

He didn't die for a half-hour after that; nor did he speak again—aloud; but just a few seconds before he went to meet his Maker, his lips moved in a faint whisper; and as I leaned close to catch his words, what do you suppose I heard? "Now—I— lay me—down—to—sleep—" That was all; Benson was dead. We threw his body overboard.

The wind of that night brought on some pretty rough weather with a lot of black clouds which persisted for several days. We didn't know what course we had been holding, and there was no way of finding out, as we could no longer trust the compass, not knowing what Benson had done to it. The long and the short of it was that we cruised about aimlessly until the sun came out again. I'll never forget that day or its surprises. We reckoned, or rather guessed, that we were somewhere off the coast of Peru. The wind, which had been blowing fitfully from the east, suddenly veered around into the south, and presently we felt a sudden chill.

"Peru!" snorted Olson. "When were yez after smellin' iceber-rgs off Peru?"

Icebergs! "Icebergs, nothin'!" exclaimed one of the Englishmen. "Why, man, they don't come north of fourteen here in these waters."

"Then," replied Olson, "ye're sout' of fourteen, me b'y."

We thought he was crazy; but he wasn't, for that afternoon we sighted a great berg south of us, and we'd been running north, we thought, for days. I can tell you we were a discouraged lot; but we got a faint thrill of hope early the next morning when the lookout bawled down the open hatch: "Land! Land north-west by west!"

I think we were all sick for the sight of land. I know that I was; but my interest was quickly dissipated by the sudden illness of three of the Germans. Almost simultaneously they commenced vomiting. They couldn't suggest any explanation for it. I asked them what they had eaten, and found they had eaten nothing other than the food cooked for all of us. "Have you drunk anything?" I asked, for I knew that there was liquor aboard, and medicines in the same locker.

"Only water," moaned one of them. "We all drank water together this morning. We opened a new tank. Maybe it was the water."

I started an investigation which revealed a terrifying condition—some one, probably Benson, had poisoned all the remaining water on the ship. It would have been worse, though, had land not been in sight. The sight of land filled us with renewed hope.

Our course had been altered, and we were rapidly approaching what appeared to be a precipitous headland. Cliffs, seemingly rising perpendicularly out of the sea, faded away into the mist upon either hand as we approached. The land before us might have been a continent, so mighty appeared the shoreline; yet we knew that we must be thousands of miles from the nearest western land-mass—New Zealand or Australia.

We took our bearings with our crude and inaccurate instruments; we searched the chart; we cudgeled our brains; and at last it was Bradley who suggested a solution. He was in the tower and watching the compass, to which he called my attention. The needle was pointing straight toward the land. Bradley swung the helm hard to starboard. I could feel the *U-33* respond, and yet the arrow still clung straight and sure toward the distant cliffs.

"What do you make of it?" I asked him.

"Did you ever hear of Caproni?" he asked.

"An early Italian navigator?" I returned.

"Yes; he followed Cook about 1721. He is scarcely mentioned even by contemporaneous historians—probably because he got into political difficulties on his return to Italy. It was the fashion to scoff at his claims, but I recall reading one of his works—his only one, I believe—in which he described a new continent in the south seas, a continent made up of 'some strange metal' which attracted the compass; a rock-bound, inhospitable coast, without beach or harbor, which extended for hundreds of miles. He could make no landing; nor in the several days he cruised about it did he see sign of life. He called it Caprona and sailed away. I believe, sir, that we are looking upon the coast of Caprona, uncharted and forgotten for two hundred years."

"If you are right, it might account for much of the deviation of the compass during the past two days," I suggested. "Caprona has been luring us upon her deadly rocks. Well, we'll accept her challenge. We'll land upon Caprona. Along that long front there must be a vulnerable spot. We will find it, Bradley, for we must find it. We must find water on Caprona, or we must die."

And so we approached the coast upon which no living eyes had ever rested. Straight from the ocean's depths rose towering cliffs, shot with brown and blues and greens—withered moss and lichen and the verdigris of copper, and everywhere the rusty ocher of iron pyrites. The cliff-tops, though ragged, were of such uniform height as to suggest the boundaries of a great plateau, and now and again we caught glimpses of verdure topping the rocky escarpment, as though bush or jungle-land had pushed outward from a lush vegetation farther inland to signal to an unseeing world that Caprona lived and joyed in life beyond her austere and repellent coast.

But metaphor, however poetic, never slaked a dry throat. To enjoy Caprona's romantic suggestions we must have water, and so we came in close, always sounding, and skirted the shore. As close in as we dared cruise, we found fathomless depths, and always the same undented coast-line of bald cliff. As darkness threatened, we drew away and lay well off the coast all night. We had not as yet really commenced to suffer for lack of water; but I knew that it would not be long before we did, and so at the first streak of dawn I moved in again and once more took up the hopeless survey of the forbidding coast.

Toward noon we discovered a beach, the first we had seen. It was a narrow strip of sand at the base of a part of the cliff that seemed lower than any we had before scanned. At its foot, half buried in the sand, lay great boulders, mute evidence that in a bygone age some mighty natural force had crumpled Caprona's barrier at this point. It was Bradley who first called our attention to a strange object lying among the boulders above the surf.

"Looks like a man," he said, and passed his glasses to me.

I looked long and carefully and could have sworn that the thing I saw was the sprawled figure of a human being. Miss La Rue was on deck with us. I turned and asked her to go below. Without a word she did as I bade. Then I stripped, and as I did so, Nobs looked questioningly at me. He had been wont at home to enter the surf with me, and evidently he had not forgotten it.

"What are you going to do, sir?" asked Olson.

"I'm going to see what that thing is on shore," I replied. "If it's a man, it may mean that Caprona is inhabited, or it may merely mean that some poor devils were shipwrecked here. I ought to be able to tell from the clothing which is more near the truth."

"How about sharks?" queried Olson. "Sure, you ought to carry a knoife."

"Here you are, sir," cried one of the men.

It was a long slim blade he offered—one that I could carry between my teeth—and so I accepted it gladly.

"Keep close in," I directed Bradley, and then I dived over the side and struck out for the narrow beach. There was another splash directly behind me, and turning my head, I saw faithful old Nobs swimming valiantly in my wake.

The surf was not heavy, and there was no undertow, so we made shore easily, effecting an equally easy landing. The beach was composed largely of small stones worn smooth by the action of water. There was little sand, though from the deck of the _U-33_ the beach had appeared to be all sand, and I saw no evidences of mollusca or crustacea such as are common to all beaches I have previously seen. I attribute this to the fact of the smallness of the beach, the enormous depth of surrounding water and the great distance at which Caprona lies from her nearest neighbor.

As Nobs and I approached the recumbent figure farther up the beach, I was appraised by my nose that whether man or not, the thing had once been organic and alive, but that for some time it had been dead. Nobs halted, sniffed and growled. A little later he sat down upon his haunches, raised his muzzle to the heavens and bayed forth a most dismal howl. I shied a small stone at him and bade him shut up—his uncanny noise made me nervous. When I had come quite close to the thing, I still could not say whether it had been man or beast. The carcass was badly swollen and partly decomposed. There was no sign of clothing upon or about it. A fine, brownish hair covered the chest and abdomen, and the face, the palms of the hands, the feet, the shoulders and back were practically hairless. The creature must have been about the height of a fair-sized man; its features were similar to those of a man; yet had it been a man?

I could not say, for it resembled an ape no more than it did a man. Its large toes protruded laterally as do those of the semiarboreal peoples of Borneo, the Philippines and other remote regions where low types still persist. The countenance might have been that of a cross between *Pithecanthropus,* the Java ape-man, and a daughter of the Piltdown race of prehistoric Sussex. A wooden cudgel lay beside the corpse.

Now this fact set me thinking. There was no wood of any description in sight. There was nothing about the beach to suggest a wrecked mariner. There was absolutely nothing about the body to suggest that it might possibly in life have known a maritime experience. It was the body of a low type of man or a high type of beast. In neither instance would it have been of a seafaring race. Therefore I deduced that it was native to Caprona—that it lived inland, and that it had fallen or been hurled from the cliffs above. Such being the case, Caprona was inhabitable, if not inhabited, by man; but how to reach the inhabitable interior! That was the question. A closer view of the cliffs than had been afforded me from the deck of the *U-33* only confirmed my conviction that no mortal man could scale those perpendicular heights; there was not a finger-hold, not a toe-hold, upon them. I turned away baffled.

Nobs and I met with no sharks upon our return journey to the submarine. My report filled everyone with theories and speculations, and with renewed hope and determination. They all reasoned along the same lines that I had reasoned—the conclusions were obvious, but not the water. We were now thirstier than ever.

The balance of that day we spent in continuing a minute and fruitless exploration of the monotonous coast. There was not another break in the frowning cliffs—not even another minute patch of pebbly beach. As the sun fell, so did our spirits. I had tried to make advances to the girl again; but she would have none of me, and so I was not only thirsty but otherwise sad and downhearted. I was glad when the new day broke the hideous spell of a sleepless night.

The morning's search brought us no shred of hope. Caprona was impregnable—that was the decision of all; yet we kept on. It must have been about two bells of the afternoon watch that Bradley called my attention to the branch of a tree, with leaves upon it, floating on the sea. "It may have been carried down to the ocean by a river," he suggested.

"Yes," I replied, "it may have; it may have tumbled or been thrown off the top of one of these cliffs."

Bradley's face fell. "I thought of that, too," he replied, "but I wanted to believe the other."

"Right you are!" I cried. "We must believe the other until we prove it false. We can't afford to give up heart now, when we need heart most. The branch was carried down by a river, and we are going to find that river." I smote my open palm with a clenched fist, to emphasize a determination unsupported by hope. "There!" I cried suddenly. "See that, Bradley?" And I pointed at a spot closer to shore. "See that, man!" Some flowers and grasses and another leafy branch floated toward us. We both scanned the water and the coastline. Bradley evidently discovered something, or at least thought that he had. He called down for a bucket and rope, and when they were passed up to him, he lowered the former into the sea and drew it in filled with water. Of this he took a taste, and straightening up, looked into my eyes with an expression of elation—as much as to say "I told you so!"

"This water is warm," he announced, "and fresh!"

I grabbed the bucket and tasted its contents. The water was very warm, and it was fresh, but there was a most unpleasant taste to it.

"Did you ever taste water from a stagnant pool full of tadpoles?" Bradley asked.

"That's it," I exclaimed, "—that's just the taste exactly, though I haven't experienced it since boyhood; but how can water from a flowing stream taste thus, and what the dickens makes it so warm? It must be at least 70 or 80 Fahrenheit, possibly higher."

"Yes," agreed Bradley, "I should say higher; but where does it come from?"

"That is easily discovered now that we have found it," I answered. "It can't come from the ocean; so it must come from the land. All that we have to do is follow it, and soon or later we shall come upon its source."

We were already rather close in; but I ordered the *U-33's* prow turned inshore and we crept slowly along, constantly dipping up the water and tasting it to assure ourselves that we didn't get outside the fresh-water current. There was a very light offshore wind and scarcely any breakers, so that the approach to the shore was continued with little or no danger. We sounded constantly without finding bottom; yet though we were already quite close, we saw no indication of any indentation in the coast from which even a tiny brooklet might issue, and certainly no mouth of a large river such as this must necessarily be to freshen the ocean even two hundred yards from shore. The tide was running out, and this, together with the strong flow of the fresh-water current, would have prevented our going against the cliffs even had we not been under power; as it was we had to buck the combined forces in order to hold our position at all. We came up to within twenty-five feet of the sheer wall, which loomed high above us. There was no break in its forbidding face. As we watched the face of the waters and searched the cliff's face, Olson suggested that the fresh water might come from a submarine geyser. This, he said, would account for its heat; but even as he spoke a bush, covered thickly with leaves and flowers, bubbled to the surface and floated off astern.

"Flowering shrubs don't thrive in the subterranean caverns from which geysers spring," suggested Bradley.

Olson shook his head. "It beats me," he said.

"I've got it!" I exclaimed suddenly. "Look there!" And I pointed at the base of the cliff ahead of us, which the receding tide was gradually exposing to our view. They all looked, and all saw what I had seen—the top of a dark opening in the rock, through which water was pouring out into the sea. "It's the subterranean channel of an inland river," I cried. "It flows through a land covered with vegetation—and therefore a land upon which the sun shines. No subterranean caverns produce any order of plant life even remotely resembling what we have seen disgorged by this river. Beyond those cliffs lie fertile lands and fresh water—perhaps, game."

"Yis sir," said Olson, "behoind the cliffs! Ye spoke a true word, sir—behoind!"

Bradley laughed—a rather sorry laugh, though. "You might as well call our attention to the fact, sir," he said, "that science has indicated that there is fresh water and vegetation on Mars."

"Not at all," I rejoined. "A U-boat isn't constructed to navigate space, but it is designed to travel below the surface of the water."

"You'd be after sailin' into that blank pocket?" asked Olson.

"I would, Olson," I replied. "We haven't one chance for life in a hundred thousand if we don't find food and water upon Caprona. This water coming out of the cliff is not salt; but neither is it fit to drink, though each of us has drunk it. It is fair to assume that inland the river is fed by pure streams, that there are fruits and herbs and game. Shall we lie out here and die of thirst and starvation with a land of plenty possibly only a few hundred yards away? We have the means for navigating a subterranean river. Are we too cowardly to utilize this means?"

"Be afther goin' to it," said Olson.

"I'm willing to see it through," agreed Bradley.

"Then under the bottom, wi' the best o' luck an' give 'em hell!" cried a young fellow who had been in the trenches.

"To the diving-stations!" I commanded, and in less than a minute the deck was deserted, the conning-tower covers had slammed to and the *U-33* was submerging—possibly for the last time. I know that I had this feeling, and I think that most of the others did.

As we went down, I sat in the tower with the searchlight projecting its seemingly feeble rays ahead. We submerged very slowly and without headway more than sufficient to keep her nose in the right direction, and as we went down, I saw outlined ahead of us the black opening in the great cliff. It was an opening that would have admitted a half-dozen U-boats at one and the same time, roughly cylindrical in contour—and dark as the pit of perdition.

As I gave the command which sent the *U-33* slowly ahead, I could not but feel a certain uncanny presentiment of evil. Where were we going? What lay at the end of this great sewer? Had we bidden farewell forever to the sunlight and to life, or were there before us dangers even greater than those which we now faced? I tried to keep my mind from vain imagining by calling everything which I observed to the eager ears below. I was the eyes of the whole company, and I did my best not to fail them. We had advanced a hundred yards, perhaps, when our first danger confronted us. Just ahead was a sharp right-angle turn in the tunnel. I could see the river's flotsam hurtling against the rocky wall upon the left as it was driven on by the mightly current, and I feared for the safety of the *U-33* in making so sharp a turn under such adverse conditions; but there was nothing for it but to try it. I didn't warn my fellows of the danger—it could have but caused them useless apprehension, for if we were to be smashed against the rocky wall, no power on earth could avert the quick end that would come to us. I gave the command full speed ahead and went charging toward the menace. I was forced to approach the dangerous left-hand wall in order to make the turn, and I depended upon the power of the motors to carry us through the surging waters in safety. Well, we made it; but it was a narrow squeak. As we swung around, the full force of the current caught us and drove the stern against the rocks; there was a thud which sent a tremor through the whole craft, and then a moment of nasty grinding as the steel hull scraped the rock wall. I expected momentarily the inrush of waters that would seal our doom; but presently from below came the welcome word that all was well.

In another fifty yards there was a second turn, this time toward the left! but it was more of a gentle curve, and we took it without trouble. After that it was plain sailing, though as far as I could know, there might be most anything ahead of us, and my nerves were strained to the snapping-point every instant. After the second turn the channel ran comparatively straight for between one hundred and fifty and two hundred yards. The waters grew suddenly lighter, and my spirits rose accordingly. I shouted down to those below that I saw daylight ahead, and a great shout of thanksgiving reverberated through the ship. A moment later we emerged into sunlit water, and immediately I raised the periscope and looked about me upon the strangest landscape I had ever seen.

We were in the middle of a broad and now sluggish river the banks of which were lined by giant, arboraceous ferns, raising their mightly fronds fifty, one hundred, two hundred feet into the quiet air. Close by us something rose to the surface of the river and dashed at the periscope. I had a vision of wide, distended jaws, and then all was blotted out. A shiver ran down into the tower as the thing closed upon the periscope. A moment later it was gone, and I could see again. Above the trees there soared into my vision a huge thing on batlike wings—a creature large as a large whale, but fashioned more after the order of a lizard. Then again something charged the periscope and blotted out the mirror. I will confess that I was almost gasping for breath as I gave the commands to emerge. Into what sort of strange land had fate guided us?

The instant the deck was awash, I opened the conning-tower hatch and stepped out. In another minute the deck-hatch lifted, and those who were not on duty below streamed up the ladder, Olson bringing Nobs under one arm. For several minutes no one spoke; I think they must each have been as overcome by awe as was I. All about us was a flora and a fauna as strange and wonderful to us as might have been those upon a distant planet had we suddenly been miraculously transported through ether to an unknown world. Even the grass upon the nearer bank was unearthly—lush and high it grew, and each blade bore upon its tip a brilliant flower—violet or yellow or carmine or blue—making as gorgeous a sward as human imagination might conceive. But the life! It teemed. The tall, fernlike trees were alive with monkeys, snakes, and lizards. Huge insects hummed and buzzed hither and thither. Mighty forms could be seen moving upon the ground in the thick forest, while the bosom of the river wriggled with living things, and above flapped the wings of gigantic creatures such as we are taught have been extinct throughout countless ages.

"Look!" cried Olson. "Would you look at the giraffe comin' up out o' the bottom of the say?" We looked in the direction he pointed and saw a long, glossy neck surmounted by a small head rising above the surface of the river. Presently the back of the creature was exposed, brown and glossy as the water dripped from it. It turned its eyes upon us, opened its lizardlike mouth, emitted a shrill hiss and came for us. The thing must have been sixteen or eighteen feet in length and closely resembled pictures I had seen of restored plesiosaurs of the lower Jurassic. It charged us as savagely as a mad bull, and one would have thought it intended to destroy and devour the mighty U-boat, as I verily believe it did intend.

We were moving slowly up the river as the creature bore down upon us with distended jaws. The long neck was far outstretched, and the four flippers with which it swam were working with powerful strokes, carrying it forward at a rapid pace. When it reached the craft's side, the jaws closed upon one of the stanchions of the deck rail and tore it from its socket as though it had been a toothpick stuck in putty. At this exhibition of titanic strength I think we all simultaneously stepped backward, and Bradley drew his revolver and fired. The bullet struck the thing in the neck, just above its body; but instead of disabling it, merely increased its rage. Its hissing rose to a shrill scream as it raised half its body out of water onto the sloping sides of the hull of the U-33 and endeavored to scramble upon the deck to devour us. A dozen shots rang out as we who were armed drew our pistols and fired at the thing; but though struck several times, it showed no signs of succumbing and only floundered farther aboard the submarine.

I had noticed that the girl had come on deck and was standing not far behind me, and when I saw the danger to which we all were exposed, I turned and forced her toward the hatch. We had not spoken for some days, and we did not speak now; but she gave me a disdainful look, which was quite as eloquent as words, and broke loose from my grasp. I saw I could no nothing with her unless I exerted force, and so I turned with my back toward her that I might be in a position to shield her from the strange reptile should it really succeed in reaching the deck; and as I did so I saw the thing raise one flipper over the rail, dart its head forward and with the quickness of lightning seize upon one of the boches. I ran forward, discharging my pistol into the creature's body in an effort to force it to relinquish its prey; but I might as profitably have shot at the sun.

Shrieking and screaming, the German was dragged from the deck, and the moment the reptile was clear of the boat, it dived beneath the surface of the water with its terrified prey. I think we were all more or less shaken by the frightfulness of the tragedy—until Olson remarked that the balance of power now rested where it belonged. Following the death of Benson we had been nine and nine—nine Germans and nine "Allies," as we called ourselves; now there were but eight Germans. We never counted the girl to either side, I suppose because she was a girl, though we knew well enough now that she was ours.

And so Olson's remark helped to clear the atmosphere, for the Allies at least, and then our attention was once more directed toward the river, for around us there had sprung up a perfect bedlam of screams and hisses and a seething caldron of hideous reptiles, devoid of fear and filled only with hunger and with rage. They clambered, squirmed and wriggled to the deck, forcing us steadily backward, though we emptied our pistols into them. There were all sorts and conditions of horrible things—huge, hideous, grotesque, monstrous—a veritable Mesozoic nightmare. I saw that the girl was gotten below as quickly as possible, and she took Nobs with her—poor Nobs had nearly barked his head off; and I think, too, that for the first time since his littlest puppyhood he had known fear; nor can I blame him. After the girl I sent Bradley and most of the Allies and then the Germans who were on deck—von Schoenvorts being still in irons below.

The creatures were approaching perilously close before I dropped through the hatchway and slammed down the cover. Then I went into the tower and ordered full speed ahead, hoping to distance the fearsome things; but it was useless. Not only could any of them easily outdistance the *U-33*, but the futher upstream we progressed the greater the number of our besiegers, until fearful of navigating a strange river at high speed, I gave orders to reduce and moved slowly and majestically through the plunging, hissing mass. I was mighty glad that our entrance into the interior of Caprona had been inside a submarine rather than in any other form of vessel. I could readily understand how it might have been that Caprona had been invaded in the past by venturesome navigators without word of it ever reaching the outside world, for I can assure you that only by submarine could man pass up that great sluggish river, alive.

We proceeded up the river for some forty miles before darkness overtook us. I was afraid to submerge and lie on the bottom overnight for fear that the mud might not be deep enough to hold us, and as we could not hold with the anchor, I ran in close to shore, and in a brief interim of attack from the reptiles we made fast to a large tree. We also dipped up some of the river water and found it, though quite warm, a little sweeter than before. We had food enough, and with the water we were all quite refreshed; but we missed fresh meat. It had been weeks, now, since we had tasted it, and the sight of the reptiles gave me an idea—that a steak or two from one of them might not be bad eating. So I went on deck with a rifle, twenty of which were aboard the *U-33*. At sight of me a huge thing charged and climbed to the deck. I retreated to the top of the conning-tower, and when it had raised its mighty bulk to the level of the little deck on which I stood, I let it have a bullet right between the eyes.

The thing stopped then and looked at me a moment as much as to say: "Why, this thing has a stinger! I must be careful." And then it reached out its long neck and opened its mighty jaws and grabbed for me; but I wasn't there. I had tumbled backward into the tower, and I mighty near killed myself doing it. When I glanced up, that little head on the end of its long neck was coming straight down on top of me, and once more I tumbled into greater safety, sprawling upon the floor of the centrale.

Olson was looking up, and seeing what was poking about in the tower, ran for an ax; nor did he hesitate a moment when he returned with one, but sprang up the ladder and commenced chopping away at that hideous face. The thing didn't have sufficient brainpan to entertain more than a single idea at once. Though chopped and hacked, and with a bullet-hole between its eyes, it still persisted madly in its attempt to get inside the tower and devour Olson, though its body was many times the diameter of the hatch; nor did it cease its efforts until after Olson had succeeded in decapitating it. Then two men went on deck through the main hatch, and while one kept watch, the other cut a hind quarter off *Plesiosaurus Olsoni,* as Bradley dubbed the thing. Meantime Olson cut off the long neck, saying that it would make fine soup. By the time we had cleared away the blood and refuse in the tower, the cook had juicy steaks and a

At sight of me a huge thing charged and climbed to
the deck.

steaming broth upon the electric stove, and the aroma arising from P. Olsoni filled us all with a hitherto unfelt admiration for him and all his kind.

CHAPTER V

THE steaks we had that night, and they were fine; and the following morning we tasted the broth. It seemed odd to be eating a creature that should, by all the laws of paleontology, have been extinct for several million years. It gave one a feeling of newness that was almost embarrassing, although it didn't seem to embarrass our appetites. Olson ate until I thought he would burst.

The girl ate with us that night at the little officers' mess just back of the torpedo compartment. The narrow table was unfolded; the four stools were set out; and for the first time in days we sat down to eat, and for the first time in weeks we had something to eat other than the monotony of the short rations of an impoverished U-boat. Nobs sat between the girl and me and was fed with morsels of the Plesiosaurus steak, at the risk of forever contaminating his manners. He looked at me sheepishly all the time, for he knew that no well-bred dog should eat at table; but the poor fellow was so wasted from improper food that I couldn't enjoy my own meal had he been denied an immediate share in it; and anyway Lys wanted to feed him. So there you are.

Lys was coldly polite to me and sweetly gracious to Bradley and Olson. She wasn't of the gushing type, I knew; so I didn't expect much from her and was duly grateful for the few morsels of attention she threw upon the floor to me. We had a pleasant meal, with only one unfortunate occurrence—when Olson suggested that possibly the creature we were eating was the same one that ate the German. It was some time before we could persuade the girl to continue her meal, but at last Bradley prevailed upon her, pointing out that we had come upstream nearly forty miles since the boche had been seized, and that during that time we had seen literally thousands of these denizens of the river, indicating that the chances were very remote that this was the same Plesiosaur. "And anyway," he concluded, "it was only a scheme of Mr. Olson's to get all the steaks for himself."

We discussed the future and ventured opinions as to what

lay before us; but we could only theorize at best, for none of us knew. If the whole land was infested by these and similar horrid monsters, life would be impossible upon it, and we decided that we would only search long enough to find and take aboard fresh water and such meat and fruits as might be safely procurable and then retrace our way beneath the cliffs to the open sea.

And so at last we turned into our narrow bunks, hopeful, happy and at peace with ourselves, our livers and our God, to awaken the following morning refreshed and still optimistic. We had an easy time getting away—as we learned later, because the saurians do not commence to feed until late in the morning. From noon to midnight their curve of activity is at its height, while from dawn to about nine o'clock it is lowest. As a matter of fact, we didn't see one of them all the time we were getting under way, though I had the cannon raised to the deck and manned against an assault. I hoped, but I was none too sure, that shells might discourage them. The trees were full of monkeys of all sizes and shades, and once we thought we saw a manlike creature watching us from the depth of the forest.

Shortly after we resumed our course upstream, we saw the mouth of another and smaller river emptying into the main channel from the south—that is, upon our right; and almost immediately after we came upon a large island five or six miles in length; and at fifty miles there was a still larger river than the last coming in from the northwest, the course of the main stream having now changed to northeast by southwest. The water was quite free from reptiles, and the vegetation upon the banks of the river had altered to more open and parklike forest, with eucalyptus and acacia mingled with a scattering of tree ferns, as though two distinct periods of geologic time had overlapped and merged. The grass, too, was less flowering, though there were still gorgeous patches mottling the greensward; and lastly, the fauna was less multitudinous.

Six or seven miles farther, and the river widened considerably; before us opened an expanse of water to the farther horizon, and then we sailed out upon an inland sea so large that only the shore-line upon our side was visible to us. The waters all about us were alive with life. There were still a few reptiles; but there were fish by the thousands, by the millions.

The water of the inland sea was very warm, almost hot, and the atmosphere was hot and heavy above it. It seemed strange that beyond the buttressed walls of Caprona icebergs floated and the south wind was biting, for only a gentle breeze moved across the face of these living waters, and that was damp and warm. Gradually we commenced to divest ourselves of our clothing, retaining only sufficient for modesty; but the sun was not hot. It was more the heat of a steam-room than of an oven.

We coasted up the shore of the lake in a northwesterly direction, sounding all the time. We found the lake deep and the bottom rocky and steeply shelving toward the center, and once when I moved straight out from shore to take other soundings we could find no bottom whatsoever. In open spaces along the shore we caught occasional glimpses of the distant cliffs, and here they appeared only a trifle less precipitous than those which bound Caprona on the seaward side. My theory is that in a far distant era Caprona was a mighty mountain—perhaps the world's mightiest mountain—and that in some titanic eruption volcanic action blew off the entire crest, blew thousands of feet of the mountain upward and outward and onto the surrounding continent, leaving a great crater; and then, possibly, the continent sank as ancient continents have been known to do, leaving only the summit of Caprona above the sea. The encircling walls, the central lake, the hot springs which feed the lake, all point to such a conclusion, and the fauna and the flora bear indisputable evidence that Caprona was once part of some great land-mass.

As we cruised up along the coast, the landscape continued a more or less open forest, with here and there a small plain where we saw animals grazing. With my glass I could make out a species of large red deer, some antelope and what appeared to be a species of horse; and once I saw the shaggy form of what might have been a monstrous bison. Here was game a plenty! There seemed little danger of starving upon Caprona. The game, however, seemed wary; for the instant the animals discovered us, they threw up their heads and tails and went cavorting off, those farther inland following the example of the others until all were lost in the mazes of the distant forest. Only the great, shaggy ox stood his ground. With lowered head he watched us until we had passed, and then continued feeding.

About twenty miles up the coast from the mouth of the river we encountered low cliffs of sandstone, broken and tortured evidence of the great upheaval which had torn Caprona asunder in the past, intermingling upon a common level the rock formations of widely separated eras, fusing some and leaving others untouched.

We ran along beside them for a matter of ten miles, arriving off a broad cleft which led into what appeared to be another lake. As we were in search of pure water, we did not wish to overlook any portion of the coast, and so after sounding and finding that we had ample depth, I ran the *U-33* between headlands into as pretty a landlocked harbor as sailorman could care to see, with good water right up to within a few yards of the shore. As we cruised slowly along, two of the boches again saw what they believed to be a man, or manlike creature, watching us from a fringe of trees a hundred yards inland, and shortly after we discovered the mouth of a small stream emptying into the bay. It was the first stream we had found since leaving the river, and I at once made preparations to test its water. To land, it would be necessary to run the *U-33* close in to the shore, at least as close as we could, for even these waters were infested, though not so thickly, by savage reptiles. I ordered sufficient water let into the diving-tanks to lower us about a foot, and then I ran the bow slowly toward the shore, confident that should we run aground, we still had sufficient lifting force to free us when the water should be pumped out of the tanks; but the bow nosed its way gently into the reeds and touched the shore with the keel still clear.

My men were all armed now with both rifles and pistols, each having plenty of ammunition. I ordered one of the Germans ashore with a line, and sent two of my own men to guard him, for from what little we had seen of Caprona, or Caspak as we learned later to call the interior, we realized that any instant some new and terrible danger might confront us. The line was made fast to a small tree, and at the same time I had the stern anchor dropped.

As soon as the boche and his guard were aboard again, I called all hands on deck, including von Schoenvorts, and there I explained to them that the time had come for us to enter into some sort of an agreement among ourselves that would relieve us of the annoyance and embarrassment of being divided into two antagonistic parts—prisoners and captors. I told them that it was obvious our very existence depended upon our unity of action, that we were to all intent and purpose entering a new world as far from the seat and causes of our own world-war as if millions of miles of space and eons of time separated us from our past lives and habitations.

"There is no reason why we should carry our racial and political hatreds into Caprona," I insisted. "The Germans among us might kill all the English, or the English might kill the last German, without affecting in the slightest degree either the outcome of even the smallest skirmish upon the western front or the opinion of a single individual in any belligerent or neutral country. I therefore put the issue squarely to you all: shall we bury our animosities and work together with and for one another while we remain upon Caprona, or must we continue thus divided and but half armed, possibly until death has claimed the last of us? And let me tell you, if you have not already realized it, the chances are a thousand to one that not one of us ever will see the outside world again. We are safe now in the matter of food and water; we could provision the *U-33* for a long cruise; but we are practically out of fuel, and without fuel we cannot hope to reach the ocean, as only a submarine can pass through the barrier cliffs. What is your answer?" I turned toward von Schoenvorts.

He eyed me in that disagreeable way of his and demanded to know, in case they accepted my suggestion, what their status would be in event of our finding a way to escape with the *U-33*. I replied that I felt that if we had all worked loyally together we should leave Caprona upon a common footing, and to that end I suggested that should the remote possibility of our escape in the submarine develop into reality, we should then immediately make for the nearest neutral port and give ourselves into the hands of the authorities, when we should all probably be interned for the duration of the war. To my surprise he agreed that this was fair and told me that they would accept my conditions and that I could depend upon their loyalty to the common cause.

I thanked him and then addressed each one of his men individually, and each gave me his word that he would abide by all that I had outlined. It was further understood that we were to act as a military organization under military rules and discipline—I as commander, with Bradley as my first lieutenant and Olson as my second, in command of the Englishmen; while von Schoenvorts was to act as an additional second lieutenant and have charge of his own men. The four of us were to constitute a military court under which men might be tried and sentenced to punishment for infraction of military rules and discipline, even to the passing of the death-sentence.

I then had arms and ammunition issued to the Germans, and leaving Bradley and five men to guard the *U-33*, the balance of us went ashore. The first thing we did was to taste the water of the little stream—which, to our delight, we found sweet, pure and cold. This stream was entirely free from dangerous reptiles, because, as I later discovered, they become immediately dormant when subjected to a much lower temperature than 70 degrees Fahrenheit. They dislike cold water and keep as far away from it as possible. There were countless brook-trout here, and deep holes that invited us to bathe, and along the bank of the stream were trees bearing a close resemblance to ash and beech and oak, their characteristics evidently induced by the lower temperature of the air above the cold water and by the fact that their roots were watered by the water from the stream rather than from the warm springs which we afterward found in such abundance elsewhere.

Our first concern was to fill the water tanks of the U-33 with fresh water, and that having been accomplished, we set out to hunt for game and explore inland for a short distance. Olson, von Schoenvorts, two Englishmen and two Germans accompanied me, leaving ten to guard the ship and the girl. I had intended leaving Nobs behind, but he got away and joined me and was so happy over it that I hadn't the heart to send him back. We followed the stream upward through a beautiful country for about five miles, and then came upon its source in a little boulder-strewn clearing. From among the rocks bubbled fully twenty ice-cold springs. North of the clearing rose sandstone cliffs to a height of some fifty to seventy-five feet, with tall trees growing at their base and almost concealing them from our view. To the west the country was flat and sparsely wooded, and here it was that we saw our first game—a large red deer. It was grazing away from us and had not seen us when one of my men called my attention to it. Motioning for silence and having the rest of the party lie down, I crept toward the quarry, accompanied only by Whitely. We got within a hundred yards of the deer when he suddenly raised his antlered head and pricked up his great ears. We both fired at once and had the satisfaction of seeing the buck drop; then we ran forward to finish him with our knives. The deer lay in a small open space close to a clump of acacias, and we had advanced to within several yards of our kill when we both halted suddenly and simultaneously. Whitely looked at me, and I looked at Whitely, and then we both looked back in the direction of the deer.

"Blime!" he said. "Wot is hit, sir?"

"It looks to me, Whitely, like an error," I said; "some assistant god who had been creating elephants must have been temporarily transferred to the lizard-department."

"Hi wouldn't s'y that, sir," said Whitely; "it sounds blasphemous."

"It is no more blasphemous than that thing which is swiping our meat," I replied, for whatever the thing was, it had leaped upon our deer and was devouring it in great mouthfuls which it swallowed without mastication. The creature appeared to be a great lizard at least ten feet high, with a huge, powerful tail as long as its torso, mighty hind legs and short forelegs. When it had advanced from the wood, it hopped much after the fashion of a kangaroo, using its hind feet and tail to propel it, and when it stood erect, it sat upon its tail. Its head was long and thick, with a blunt muzzle, and the opening of the jaws ran back to a point behind the eyes, and the jaws were armed with long sharp teeth. The scaly body was covered with black and yellow spots about a foot in diameter and irregular in contour. These spots were outlined in red with edgings about an inch wide. The underside of the chest, body and tail were a greenish white.

"Wot s'y we pot the bloomin' bird, sir?" suggested Whitely.

I told him to wait until I gave the word; then we would fire simultaneously, he at the heart and I at the spine.

"Hat the 'eart, sir—yes, sir," he replied, and raised his piece to his shoulder.

Our shots rang out together. The thing raised its head and looked about until its eyes rested upon us; then it gave vent to a most appalling hiss that rose to the crescendo of a terrific shriek and came for us.

"Beat it, Whitely!" I cried as I turned to run.

We were about a quarter of a mile from the rest of our party, and in full sight of them as they lay in the tall grass, watching us. That they saw all that had happened was evidenced by the fact that they now rose and ran toward us, and at their head leaped Nobs. The creature in our rear was gaining on us rapidly when Nobs flew past me like a meteor and rushed straight for the frightful reptile. I tried to recall him, but he would pay no attention to me, and as I couldn't see him sacrificed, I, too, stopped and faced the monster. The creature appeared to be more impressed by Nobs than by us and our firearms, for it stopped as the Airedale dashed at it growling, and struck at him viciously with its powerful jaws.

Nobs, though, was lightning by comparison with the slow-thinking beast and dodged his opponent's thrust with ease. Then he raced to the rear of the tremendous thing and seized it by the tail. There Nobs made the error of his life. Within that mottled organ were the muscles of a Titan, the force of a dozen mighty catapults, and the owner of the tail was fully aware of

to be of a lower order than he, yet higher than that of the apes, carried heavy clubs; the others were armed only with giant muscles and fighting fangs—nature's weapons. All were males, and all were entirely naked; nor was there upon even the highest among them a sign of ornamentation.

At sight of us they turned with bared fangs and low growls to confront us. I did not wish to fire among them unless it became absolutely necessary, and so I started to lead my party around them; but the instant that the Neanderthal man guessed my intention, he evidently attributed it to cowardice upon our part, and with a wild cry he leaped toward us, waving his cudgel above his head. The others followed him, and in a minute we should have been overwhelmed. I gave the order to fire, and at the first volley six of them went down, including the Neanderthal man. The others hesitated a moment and then broke for the trees, some running nimbly among the branches, while others lost themselves to us between the boles. Both von Schoenvorts and I noticed that at least two of the higher, manlike types took to the trees quite as nimbly as the apes, while others that more nearly approached man in carriage and appearance sought safety upon the ground with the gorillas.

An examination disclosed that five of our erstwhile opponents were dead and the sixth, the Neanderthal man, was but slightly wounded, a bullet having glanced from his thick skull, stunning him. We decided to take him with us to camp, and by means of belts we managed to secure his hands behind his back and place a leash around his neck before he regained consciousness. We then retraced our steps for our meat, being convinced by our own experience that those aboard the U-33 had been able to frighten off this party with a single shell—but when we came to where we had left the deer it had disappeared.

On the return journey Whitely and I preceded the rest of the party by about a hundred yards in the hope of getting another shot at something edible, for we were all greatly disgusted and disappointed by the loss of our venison. Whitely and I advanced very cautiously, and not having the whole party with us, we fared better than on the journey out, bagging two large antelope not a half-mile from the harbor; so with our game and our prisoner we made a cheerful return to the boat, where we found that all were safe. On the shore a little north of where we lay there were the corpses of twenty of the wild creatures who had attacked Bradley and his party in our absence, and the rest of whom we had met and scattered a few minutes later.

We felt that we had taught these wild ape-men a lesson and that because of it we would be safer in the future—at least safer from them; but we decided not to abate our carefulness one whit, feeling that this new world was filled with terrors still unknown to us; nor were we wrong.

The following morning we commenced work upon our camp, Bradley, Olson, von Schoenvorts, Miss La Rue, and I having sat up half the night discussing the matter and drawing plans. We set the men at work felling trees, selecting for the purpose jarrah, a hard, weather-resisting timber which grew in profusion near by. Half the men labored while the other half stood guard, alternating each hour with an hour off at noon. Olson directed this work. Bradley, von Schoenvorts and I, with Miss La Rue's help, staked out the various buildings and the outer wall. When the day was done, we had quite an array of logs nicely notched and ready for our building operations on the morrow, and we were all tired, for after the buildings had been staked out we all fell in and helped with the logging—all but von Schoenvorts. He, being a Prussian and a gentleman, couldn't stoop to such menial labor in the presence of his men, and I didn't see fit to ask it of him, as the work was purely voluntary upon our part. He spent the afternoon shaping a swagger-stick from a branch of jarrah and talking with Miss La Rue, who had sufficiently unbent toward him to notice his existence.

We saw nothing of the wild men of the previous day, and only once were we menaced by any of the strange denizens of Caprona, when some frightful nightmare of the sky swooped down upon us, only to be driven off by a fusillade of bullets. The thing appeared to be some variety of pterodactyl, and what with its enormous size and ferocious aspect was most awe-inspiring. There was another incident, too, which to me at least was far more unpleasant than the sudden onslaught of the prehistoric reptile. Two of the men, both Germans, were stripping a felled tree of its branches. Von Schoenvorts had completed his swagger-stick, and he and I were passing close to where the two worked.

One of the men threw to his rear a small branch that he had just chopped off, and as misfortune would have it, it struck von Schoenvorts across the face. It couldn't have hurt him, for it didn't leave a mark; but he flew into a terrific rage, shouting: "Attention!" in a loud voice. The sailor immediately straightened up, faced his officer, clicked his heels together and saluted. "Pig!" roared the Baron, and struck the fellow across the face, breaking his nose. I grabbed von Schoenvorts' arm and jerked him away before he could strike again, if such had been his intention, and then he raised his little stick to strike me; but before it descended the muzzle of my pistol was against his belly and he must have seen in my eyes that nothing would suit me better than an excuse to pull the trigger. Like all his kind and all other bullies, von Schoenvorts was a coward at heart, and so he dropped his hand to his side and started to turn away; but I pulled him back, and there before his men I told him that such a thing must never again occur—that no man was to be struck or otherwise punished other than in due process of the laws that we had made and the court that we had established. All the time the sailor stood rigidly at attention, nor could I tell from his expression whether he most resented the blow his officer had struck him or my interference in the gospel of the Kaiser-breed. Nor did he move until I said to him: "Plesser, you may return to your quarters and dress your wound." Then he saluted and marched stiffly off toward the U-33.

Just before dusk we moved out into the bay a hundred yards from shore and dropped anchor, for I felt that we should be safer there than elsewhere. I also detailed men to stand watch during the night and appointed Olson officer of the watch for the entire night, telling him to bring his blankets on deck and get what rest he could. At dinner we tasted our first roast Caprona antelope, and we had a mess of greens that the cook had found growing along the stream. All during the meal von Schoenvorts was silent and surly.

After dinner we all went on deck and watched the unfamiliar scenes of a Capronian night—that is, all but von Schoenvorts. There was less to see than to hear. From the great inland lake behind us came the hissing and the screaming of countless saurians. Above we heard the flap of giant wings, while from the shore rose the multitudinous voices of a tropical jungle—of a warm, damp atmosphere such as must have enveloped the entire earth during the Paleozoic and Mesozoic eras. But here were intermingled the voices of later eras—the scream of the panther, the roar of the lion, the baying of wolves and a thunderous growling which we could attribute to nothing earthly but which one day we were to connect with the most fearsome of ancient creatures.

One by one the others went to their rooms, until the girl and I were left alone together, for I had permitted the watch to go below for a few minutes, knowing that I would be on deck. Miss

La Rue was very quiet, though she replied graciously enough to whatever I had to say that required reply. I asked her if she did not feel well.

"Yes," she said, "but I am depressed by the awfulness of it all. I feel of so little consequence—so small and helpless in the face of all these myriad manifestations of life stripped to the bone of its savagery and brutality. I realize as never before how cheap and valueless a thing is life. Life seems a joke, a cruel, grim joke. You are a laughable incident or a terrifying one as you happen to be less powerful or more powerful than some other form of life which crosses your path; but as a rule you are of no moment whatsoever to anything but yourself. You are a comic little figure hopping from the cradle to the grave. Yes, that is our trouble—we take ourselves too seriously; but Caprona should be a sure cure for that." She paused and laughed.

"You have evolved a beautiful philosophy," I said. "It fills such a longing in the human breast. It is full, it is satisfying, it is ennobling. What wondrous strides toward perfection the human race might have made if the first man had evolved it and it had persisted until now as the creed of humanity."

"I don't like irony," she said; "it indicates a small soul."

"What other sort of soul, then, would you expect from 'a comic little figure hopping from the cradle to the grave'?" I inquired. "And what difference does it make, anyway, what you like and what you don't like? You are here for but an instant, and you mustn't take yourself too seriously."

She looked up at me with a smile. "I imagine that I am frightened and blue," she said, "and I know that I am very, very homesick and lonely." There was almost a sob in her voice as she concluded. It was the first time that she had spoken thus to me. Involuntarily I laid my hand upon hers where it rested on the rail.

"I know how difficult your position is," I said; "but don't feel that you are alone. There is—is one here who—who would do anything in the world for you," I ended lamely. She did not withdraw her hand, and she looked up into my face with tears on her cheeks and I read in her eyes the thanks her lips could not voice. Then she looked away across the weird moonlit landscape and sighed. Evidently her new-found philosophy had tumbled about her ears, for she was seemingly taking herself seriously. I wanted to take her in my arms and tell her how I loved her, and had taken her hand from the rail and started to draw her toward me when Olson came blundering up on deck with his bedding.

The following morning we started building-operations in earnest, and things progressed finely. The Neanderthal man was something of a care, for we had to keep him in irons all the time, and he was mighty savage when approached; but after a time he became more docile, and then we tried to discover if he had a language. Lys spent a great deal of time talking to him and trying to draw him out; but for a long while she was unsuccessful. It took us three weeks to build all the houses, which we constructed close by a cold spring some two miles from the harbor.

We changed our plans a trifle when it came to building the palisade, for we found a rotted cliff near by where we could get all the flat building-stone we needed, and so we constructed a stone wall entirely around the buildings. It was in the form of a square, with bastions and towers at each corner which would permit an enfilading fire along any side of the fort, and was about one hundred and thirty-five feet square on the outside, with walls three feet thick at the bottom and about a foot and a half wide at the top, and fifteen feet high. It took a long time to build that wall, and we all turned in and helped except von Schoenvorts, who, by the way, had not spoken to me except in the line of official business since our encounter—a condition of armed neutrality which suited me to a T. We have just finished it, the last touches being put on today. I quit about a week ago and commenced working on this chronicle of our strange adventures, which will account for any minor errors in chronology which may have crept in; there was so much material that I may have made some mistakes, but I think they are but minor and few.

I see in reading over the last few pages that I neglected to state that Lys finally discovered that the Neanderthal man possessed a language. It is very meager, but still it is a spoken language. She has learned to speak it, and so have I, to some extent. It was he—his name he says is Am, or Ahm—who told us that this country is called Caspak. When we asked him how far it extended, he waved both arms about his head in an all-including gesture which took in, apparently, the entire universe. He is more tractable now, and we are going to release him, for he has assured us that he will not permit his fellows to harm us. He calls us Galus and says that in a short time he will be a Galu. It is not quite clear to us what he means. He says that there are many

Galus north of us, and that as soon as he becomes one he will go and live with them.

Ahm went out to hunt with us yesterday and was much impressed by the ease with which our rifles brought down antelope and deer. We have been living upon the fat of the land, Ahm having shown us the edible fruits, tubers and herbs, and twice a week we go out after fresh meat. A certain proportion of this we dry and store away, for we do not know what may come. Our drying process is really smoking. We have also dried a large quantity of two varieties of cereal which grow wild a few miles south of us. One of these is a giant Indian maize—a lofty perennial often fifty and sixty feet in height, with ears the size of a man's body and kernels as large as your fist. We have had to construct a second store house for the great quantity of this that we have gathered.

September 3, 1916: Three months ago today the torpedo from the *U-33* started me from the peaceful deck of the American liner upon the strange voyage which has ended here in Caspak. We have settled down to an acceptance of our fate, for all are convinced that none of us will ever see the outer world again. Ahm's repeated assertions that there are human beings like ourselves in Caspak have roused the men to a keen desire for exploration. I sent out one party last week under Bradley. Ahm, who is now free to go and come as he wishes, accompanied them. They marched about twenty-five miles due west, encountering many terrible beasts and reptiles and not a few manlike creatures whom Ahm sent away. Here is Bradley's report of the expedition:

Marched fifteen miles the first day, camping on the bank of a large stream which runs southward. Game was plentiful and we saw several varieties which we had not before encountered in Caspak. Just before making camp we were charged by an enormous woolly rhinoceros, which Plesser dropped with a perfect shot. We had rhinoceros-steaks for supper. Ahm called the thing "Atis." It was almost a continuous battle from the time we left the fort until we arrived at camp. The mind of man can scarce conceive the plethora of carnivorous life in this lost world; and their prey, of course, is even more abundant.

The second day we marched about ten miles to the foot of the cliffs. Passed through dense forests close to the base of the cliffs. Saw manlike creatures and a low order of ape in one band, and some of the men swore that there was a white man among them. They were inclined to attack us at first; but a volley from our rifles caused them to change their minds. We scaled the cliffs as far as we could; but near the top they are absolutely perpendicular without any sufficient cleft or protuberance to give hand or foothold. All were disappointed, for we hungered for a view of the ocean and the outside world. We even had hope that we might see and attract the attention of a passing ship. Our exploration has determined one thing which will probably be of little value to us and never heard of beyond Caprona's walls—this crater was once entirely filled with water. Indisputable evidence of this is on the face of the cliffs.

Our return journey occupied two days and was as filled with adventure as usual. We are all becoming accustomed to adventure. It is beginning to pall on us. We suffered no casualties and there was no illness.

I had to smile as I read Bradley's report. In those four days he had doubtless passed through more adventures than an African big-game hunter experiences in a lifetime, and yet he covered it all in a few lines. Yes, we are becoming accustomed to adventure. Not a day passes that one or more of us does not face death at least once. Ahm taught us a few things that have proved profitable and saved us much ammunition, which it is useless to expend except for food or in the last recourse of self-preservation. Now when we are attacked by large flying reptiles we run beneath spreading trees; when land carnivora threaten us, we climb into trees, and we have learned not to fire at any of the dinosaurs unless we can keep out of their reach for at least two minutes after hitting them in the brain or spine, or five minutes after puncturing their hearts—it takes them so long to die. To hit them elsewhere is worse than useless, for they do not seem to notice it, and we had discovered that such shots do not kill or even disable them.

September 7, 1916: Much has happened since last I wrote. Bradley is away again on another exploring expedition to the cliffs. He expects to be gone several weeks and to follow along their base in search of a point where they may be scaled. He took Sinclair, Brady, James, and Tippet with him. Ahm has disappeared. He has been gone about three days; but the most startling thing I have to record is that von Schoenvorts and Olson while out hunting the other day discovered oil about fifteen miles north of us beyond the sandstone cliffs. Olson says there is a geyser of oil there, and von Schoenvorts is making preparations to refine it. If he succeeds, we shall have the means for leaving Caspak and returning to our own world. I can scarce believe the truth of it. We are all elated to the seventh heaven of bliss. Pray God we shall not be disappointed.

I have tried on several occasions to broach the subject of my love to Lys; but she will not listen.

CHAPTER VII

October 8, 1916: This is the last entry I shall make upon my manuscript. When this is done, I shall be through. Though I may pray that it reaches the haunts of civilized man, my better judgment tells me that it will never be perused by other eyes than mine, and that even though it should, it would be too late to avail me. I am alone upon the summit of the great cliff overlooking the broad Pacific. A chill south wind bites at my marrow, while far below me I can see the tropic foliage of Caspak on the one hand and huge icebergs from the near Antarctic upon the other. Presently I shall stuff my folded manuscript into the thermos bottle I have carried with me for the purpose since I left the fort—Fort Dinosaur we named it—and hurl it far outward over the cliff-top into the Pacific. What current washes the shore of Caprona I know not; whither my bottle will be borne I cannot even guess; but I have done all that mortal man may do to notify the world of my whereabouts and the dangers that threaten those of us who remain alive in Caspak—if there be any other than myself.

About the 8th of September I accompanied Olson and von Schoenvorts to the oil-geyser. Lys came with us, and we took a number of things which von Schoenvorts wanted for the purpose of erecting a crude refinery. We went up the coast some ten or twelve miles in the *U-33*, tying up to shore near the mouth of a small stream which emptied great volumes of crude oil into the sea—I find it difficult to call this great lake by any other name. Then we disembarked and went inland about five miles, where we came upon a small lake entirely filled with oil, from the center of which a geyser of oil spouted.

On the edge of the lake we helped von Schoenvorts build his primitive refinery. We worked with him for two days until he got things fairly well started, and then we returned to Fort Dinosaur, as I feared that Bradley might return and be worried by our absence. The *U-33* merely landed those of us that were to return to the fort and then retraced its course toward the oil-well. Olson, Whitely, Wilson, Miss La Rue, and myself disembarked, while von Schoenvorts and his German crew returned to refine the oil. The next day Plesser and two other Germans came down overland for ammunition. Plesser said they had been attacked by wild men and had exhausted a great deal of ammunition. He also asked permission to get some dried meat and maize, saying that they were so busy with the work of refining that they had no time to hunt. I let him have everything he asked for, and never once did a suspicion of their intentions enter my mind. They returned to the oilwell the same day, while we continued with the multitudinous duties of camp life.

For three days nothing of moment occurred. Bradley did not return; nor did we have any word from von Schoenvorts. In the evening Lys and I went up into one of the bastion towers and listened to the grim and terrible night-life of the frightful ages of the past. Once a saber-tooth screamed almost beneath us, and the girl shrank close against me. As I felt her body against mine, all the pent love of these three long months shattered the bonds of timidity and conviction, and I swept her up into my arms and covered her face and lips with kisses. She did not struggle to free herself; but instead her dear arms crept up about my neck and drew my own face even closer to hers.

"You love me, Lys?" I cried.

I felt her head nod an affirmative against my breast. "Tell me, Lys," I begged, "tell me in words how much you love me."

Low and sweet and tender came the answer: "I love you beyond all conception."

My heart filled with rapture then, and it fills now as it has each of the countless times I have recalled those dear words, as it shall fill always until death has claimed me. I may never see her again; she may not know how I love her—she may question, she may doubt; but always true and steady and warm with the fires of love my heart beats for the girl who said that night: "I love you beyond all conception."

For a long time we sat there upon the little bench constructed for the sentry that we had not as yet thought it necessary to post in more than one of the four towers. We learned to know one another better in those two brief hours than we had in all the months that had intervened since we had been thrown together. She told me that she had loved me from the first,

and that she never had loved von Schoenvorts, their engagement having been arranged by her aunt for social reasons.

That was the happiest evening of my life; nor ever do I
expect to experience its like; but at last, as is the way of happiness, it terminated. We descended to the compound, and I
walked with Lys to the door of her quarters. There again she
kissed me and bade me good night, and then she went in and
closed the door.

I went to my own room, and there I sat by the light of one of
the crude candles we had made from the tallow of the beasts we
had killed, and lived over the events of the evening. At last I
turned in and fell asleep, dreaming happy dreams and planning
for the future, for even in savage Caspak I was bound to make
my girl safe and happy. It was daylight when I awoke. Wilson,
who was acting as cook, was up and astir at his duties in the
cook-house. The others slept; but I arose and followed by Nobs
went down to the stream for a plunge. As was our custom, I
went armed with both rifle and revolver; but I stripped and had
my swim without further disturbance than the approach of a
large hyena, a number of which occupied caves in the sandstone
cliffs north of the camp. These brutes are enormous and exceed-
ingly ferocious. I imagine they correspond with the cave-hyena of
prehistoric times. This fellow charged Nobs, whose Capronian
experiences had taught him that discretion is the better part of
valor—with the result that he dived head foremost into the
stream beside me after giving vent to a series of ferocious growls
which had no more effect upon *Hyaena spelaeus* than might a
sweet smile upon an enraged tusker. Afterward I shot the beast,
and Nobs had a feast while I dressed, for he had become quite a
raw-meat eater during our numerous hunting expeditions, upon
which we always gave him a portion of the kill.

Whitely and Olson were up and dressed when we returned,
and we all sat down to a good breakfast. I could not but wonder
at Lys' absence from the table, for she had always been one of
the earliest risers in camp; so about nine o'clock, becoming apprehensive lest she might be indisposed, I went to the door of
her room and knocked. I received no response, though I finally
pounded with all my strength; then I turned the knob and entered, only to find that she was not there. Her bed had been
occupied, and her clothing lay where she had placed it the previous night upon retiring; but Lys was gone. To say that I was
distracted with terror would be to put it mildly. Though I knew

she could not be in camp, I searched every square inch of the compound and all the buildings, yet without avail.

It was Whitely who discovered the first clue—a huge human-like footprint in the soft earth beside the spring, and indications of a struggle in the mud. Then I found a tiny handkerchief close to the outer wall. Lys had been stolen! It was all too plain. Some hideous member of the ape-man tribe had entered the fort and carried her off. While I stood stunned and horrified at the frightful evidence before me, there came from the direction of the great lake an increasing sound that rose to the volume of a shriek. We all looked up as the noise approached apparently just above us, and a moment later there followed a terrific explosion which hurled us to the ground. When we clambered to our feet, we saw a large section of the west wall torn and shattered. It was Olson who first recovered from his daze sufficiently to guess the explanation of the phenomenon.

"A shell!" he cried. "And there ain't no shells in Caspak besides what's on the U-33. The dirty boches are shellin' the fort. Come on!" and he grasped his rifle and started on a run toward the lake. It was over two miles, but we did not pause until the harbor was in view, and still we could not see the lake because of the sandstone cliffs which intervened. We ran as fast as we could around the lower end of the harbor, scrambled up the cliffs and at last stood upon their summit in full view of the lake. Far away down the coast, toward the river through which we had come to reach the lake, we saw upon the surface the outline of the U-33, black smoke vomiting from her funnel.

Von Schoenvorts had succeeded in refining the oil! The cur had broken his every pledge and was leaving us there to our fates. He had even shelled the fort as a parting compliment; nor could anything have been more truly Prussian than this leave-taking of the Baron Friedrich von Schoenvorts.

Olson, Whitely, Wilson, and I stood for a moment looking at one another. It seemed incredible that man could be so perfidious—that we had really seen with our own eyes the thing that we had seen; but when we returned to the fort, the shattered wall gave us ample evidence that there was no mistake.

Then we began to speculate as to whether it had been an ape-man or a Prussian that had abudcted Lys. From what we knew of von Schoenvorts, we would not have been surprised at anything from him; but the footprints by the spring seemed indisputable evidence that one of Caprona's undeveloped men had borne off the girl I loved.

As soon as I had assured myself that such was the case, I made my preparations to follow and rescue her. Olson, Whitely, and Wilson each wished to accompany me; but I told them that they were needed here, since with Bradley's party still absent and the Germans gone it was necessary that we conserve our force as far as might be possible.

CHAPTER VIII

IT WAS a sad leave-taking as in silence I shook hands with each of the three remaining men. Even poor Nobs appeared dejected as we quit the compound and set out upon the well-marked spoor of the abductor. Not once did I turn my eyes backward toward Fort Dinosaur. I have not looked upon it since—nor in all likelihood shall I ever look upon it again. The trail led northwest until it reached the western end of the sandstone cliffs to the north of the fort; there it ran into a well-defined path which wound northward into a country we had not as yet explored. It was a beautiful, gently rolling country, broken by occasional outcroppings of sandstone and by patches of dense forest relieved by open, parklike stretches and broad meadows whereon grazed countless herbivorous animals —red deer, aurochs, and infinite variety of antelope and at least three distinct species of horse, the latter ranging in size from a creature about as large as Nobs to a magnificent animal fourteen to sixteen hands high. These creatures fed together in perfect amity; nor did they show any great indications of terror when Nobs and I approached. They moved out of our way and kept their eyes upon us until we had passed; then they resumed their feeding.

The path led straight across the clearing into another forest, lying upon the verge of which I saw a bit of white. It appeared to stand out in marked contrast and incongruity to all its surroundings, and when I stopped to examine it, I found that it was a small strip of muslin—part of the hem of a garment. At once I was all excitement, for I knew that it was a sign left by Lys that she had been carried this way; it was a tiny bit torn from the hem of the undergarment that she wore in lieu of the nightrobes she had lost with the sinking of the liner. Crushing the bit of fabric to my lips, I pressed on even more rapidly than before, because I now knew that I was upon the right trail and that up to this point at least, Lys still had lived.

I made over twenty miles that day, for I was now hardened to fatigue and accustomed to long hikes, having spent considerable time hunting and exploring in the immediate vicinity of camp. A dozen times that day was my life threatened by fearsome creatures of the earth or sky, though I could not but note that the farther north I traveled, the fewer were the great dinosaurs, though they still persisted in lesser numbers. On the other hand the quantity of ruminants and the variety and frequency of carnivorous animals increased. Each square mile of Caspak harbored its terrors.

At intervals along the way I found bits of muslin, and often they reassured me when otherwise I should have been doubtful of the trail to take where two crossed or where there were forks, as occurred at several points. And so, as night was drawing on, I came to the southern end of a line of cliffs loftier than any I had before seen, and as I approached them, there was wafted to my nostrils the pungent aroma of wood-smoke. What could it mean? There could, to my mind, be but a single solution: man abided close by, a higher order of man than we had as yet seen, other than Ahm, the Neanderthal man. I wondered again as I had so many times that day. if it had not been Ahm who stole Lys.

Cautiously I approached the flank of the cliffs, where they terminated in an abrupt escarpment as though some allpowerful hand had broken off a great section of rock and set it upon the surface of the earth. It was now quite dark, and as I crept around the edge of the cliff, I saw at a little distance a great fire around which were many figures—apparently human figures. Cautioning Nobs to silence, and he had learned many lessons in the value of obedience since we had entered Caspak, I slunk forward, taking advantage of whatever cover I could find, until from behind a bush I could distinctly see the creatures assembled by the fire. They were human and yet not human. I should say that they were a little higher in the scale of evolution than Ahm, possibly occupying a plane of evolution between that of the Neanderthal man and what is known as the Grimaldi race. Their features were distinctly negroid, though their skins were white. A considerable portion of both torso and limbs was covered with short hair, and their physical proportions were in many respects apelike, though not so much so as were Ahm's. They carried themselves in a more erect position, although their arms were considerably longer than those of the Neanderthal man. As I watched them, I saw that they possessed a language, that they had knowledge of fire and that they carried besides the wooden club of Ahm a thing which resembled a crude stone hatchet. Evidently they were very low in the scale of humanity, but they were a step upward from those I had previously seen in Caspak.

But what interested me most was the slender figure of a dainty girl, clad only in a thin bit of muslin which scarce covered her knees—a bit of muslin torn and ragged about the lower hem. It was Lys, and she was alive and so far as I could see, unharmed. A huge brute with thick lips and prognathous jaw stood at her shoulder. He was talking loudly and gesticulating wildly. I was close enough to hear his words, which were similar to the language of Ahm, though much fuller, for there were many words I could not understand. However, I caught the gist of what he was saying—which in effect was that he had found and captured this Galu, that she was his and that he defied anyone to question his right of possession. It appeared to me, as I afterward learned was the fact, that I was witnessing the most primitive of marriage ceremonies. The assembled members of the tribe looked on and listened in a sort of dull and perfunctory apathy, for the speaker was by far the mightiest of the clan. There seemed no one to dispute his claims when he said, or rather shouted, in stentorian tones: "I am Tsa. This is my she. Who wishes her more than Tsa?"

"I do," I said in the language of Ahm, and I stepped out into the firelight before them. Lys gave a little cry of joy and started toward me, but Tsa grasped her arm and dragged her back.

"Who are you?" shrieked Tsa. "I kill! I kill! I kill!"

"The she is mine," I replied, "and I have come to claim her. I kill if you do not let her come to me." And I raised my pistol to a level with his heart. Of course the creature had no conception of the purpose of the strange little implement which I was poking toward him. With a sound that was half human and half the growl of a wild beast, he sprang toward me. I aimed at his heart and fired, and as he sprawled headlong to the ground, the others of his tribe, overcome by fright at the report of the pistol, scattered toward the cliffs—while Lys, with outstretched arms, ran toward me.

As I crushed her to me, there rose from the black night behind us and then to our right and to our left a series of frightful screams and shrieks, bellowings, roars and growls. It was the night-life of this jungle world coming into its own—the huge, carnivorous nocturnal beasts which make the nights of Caspak hideous. A shuddering sob ran through Lys' figure. "O God," she cried, "give me the strength to endure, for his sake!" I saw that she was upon the verge of a breakdown, after all that she must have passed through of fear and horror that day, and I tried to quiet and reassure her as best I might; but even to me the future looked most unpromising, for what chance of life had we against the frightful hunters of the night who even now were prowling closer to us?

Now I turned to see what had become of the tribe, and in the fitful glare of the fire I perceived that the face of the cliff was pitted with large holes into which the man-things were clambering. "Come," I said to Lys, "we must follow them. We cannot last a half-hour out here. We must find a cave." Already we could see the blazing green eyes of the hungry carnivora. I seized a brand from the fire and hurled it out into the night, and there came back an answering chorus of savage and rageful protest; but the eyes vanished for a short time. Selecting a burning branch for each of us, we advanced toward the cliffs, where we were met by angry threats.

"They will kill us," said Lys. "We may as well keep on in search of another refuge."

"They will not kill us so surely as will those others out there," I replied. "I am going to seek shelter in one of these caves; nor will the man-things prevent." And I kept on in the direction of the cliff's base. A huge creature stood upon a ledge and brandished his stone hatchet. "Come and I will kill you and take the she," he boasted.

"You saw how Tsa fared when he would have kept my she," I replied in his own tongue. "Thus will you fare and all your fellows if you do not permit us to come in peace among you out of the dangers of the night."

"Go north," he screamed. "Go north among the Galus, and we will not harm you. Some day will we be Galus; but now we are not. You do not belong among us. Go away or we will kill you. The she may remain if she is afraid, and we will keep her; but the he must depart."

"The he won't depart," I replied, and approached still nearer. Rough and narrow ledges formed by nature gave access to the upper caves. A man might scale them if unhampered and unhindered, but to clamber upward in the face of a belligerent tribe of half-men and with a girl to assist was beyond my capability.

"I do not fear you," screamed the creature. "You were close to Tsa; but I am far above you. You cannot harm me as you harmed Tsa. Go away!"

I placed a foot upon the lowest ledge and clambered upward, reaching down and pulling Lys to my side. Already I felt safer. Soon we would be out of danger of the beasts again closing in upon us. The man above us raised his stone hatchet above his head and leaped lightly down to meet us. His position above me gave him a great advantage, or at least so he probably thought, for he came with every show of confidence. I hated to do it, but there seemed no other way, and so I shot him down as I had shot down Tsa.

"You see," I cried to his fellows, "that I can kill you wherever you may be. A long way off I can kill you as well as I can kill you near by. Let us come among you in peace. I will not harm you if you do not harm us. We will take a cave high up. Speak!"

"Come, then," said one. "If you will not harm us, you may come. Take Tsa's hole, which lies above you."

The creature showed us the mouth of a black cave, but he kept at a distance while he did it, and Lys followed me as I crawled in to explore. I had matches with me, and in the light of one I found a small cavern with a flat roof and floor which followed the cleavage of the strata. Pieces of the roof had fallen at some long-distant date, as was evidenced by the depth of the filth and rubble in which they were embedded. Even a superficial examination revealed the fact that nothing had ever been attempted that might have improved the livability of the cavern; nor, should I judge, had it ever been cleaned out. With considerable difficulty I loosened some of the larger pieces of broken rock which littered the floor and placed them as a barrier before the doorway. It was too dark to do more than this. I then gave Lys a piece of dried meat, and sitting inside the entrance, we dined as must have some of our ancient forbears at the dawning of the age of man, while from below the open diapason of the savage night rose weird and horrifying to our ears. In the light of the great fire still burning we could see huge, skulking forms, and in the blacker background countless flaming eyes.

Lys shuddered, and I put my arm around her and drew her to me; and thus we sat throughout the hot night. She told me of her abduction and of the fright she had undergone, and together we thanked God that she had come through unharmed, because the great brute had dared not pause along the danger-infested way. She said that they had but just reached the cliffs when I arrived, for on several occasions her captor had been forced to take to the trees with her to escape the clutches of some hungry cave-lion or saber-tooth tiger, and that twice they had been obliged to remain for considerable periods before the beasts had retired.

Nobs, by dint of much scrambling and one or two narrow escapes from death, had managed to follow us up the cliff and was now curled between me and the doorway, having devoured a piece of the dried meat, which he seemed to relish immensely. He was the first to fall asleep; but I imagine we must have followed suit soon, for we were both tired. I had laid aside my ammunition-belt and rifle, though both were close beside me; but my pistol I kept in my lap beneath my hand. However, we were not disturbed during the night, and when I awoke, the sun was shining on the tree-tops in the distance. Lys' head had drooped to my breast, and my arm was still about her.

Shortly afterward Lys awoke, and for a moment she could not seem to comprehend her situation. She looked at me and then turned and glanced at my arm about her, and then she seemed quite suddenly to realize the scantiness of her apparel and drew away, covering her face with her palms and blushing furiously. I drew her back toward me and kissed her, and then she threw her arms about my neck and wept softly in mute surrender to the inevitable.

It was an hour later before the tribe began to stir about. We watched them from our "apartment," as Lys called it. Neither men nor women wore any sort of clothing or ornaments, and they all seemed to be about of an age; nor were there any babies or children among them. This was, to us, the strangest and most inexplicable of facts, but it recalled to us that though we had seen many of the lesser developed wild people of Caspak, we had never yet seen a child or an old man or woman.

After a while they became less suspicious of us and then quite friendly in their brutish way. They picked at the fabric of our clothing, which seemed to interest them, and examined my rifle and pistol and the ammunition in the belt around my waist. I showed them the thermos-bottle, and when I poured a little water from it, they were delighted, thinking that it was a spring which I carried about with me—a never-failing source of water supply.

One thing we both noticed among their other characteristics: they never laughed nor smiled; and then we remembered that Ahm had never done so, either. I asked them if they knew Ahm; but they said they did not.

One of them said: "Back there we may have known him." And he jerked his head to the south.

"You came from back there?" I asked. He looked at me in surprise.

"We all come from there," he said. "After a while we go there." And this time he jerked his head toward the north. "Be Galus," he concluded.

Many times now had we heard this reference to becoming Galus. Ahm had spoken of it many times. Lys and I decided that it was a sort of original religious conviction, as much a part of them as their instinct for self-preservation—a primal acceptance of a hereafter and a holier state. It was a brilliant theory, but it was all wrong. I know it now, and how far we were from guessing the wonderful, the miraculous, the gigantic truth which even yet I may only guess at—the thing that sets Caspak apart from all the rest of the world far more definitely than her isolated geographic position or her impregnable barrier of giant cliffs. If I could live to return to civilization, I should have meat for the clergy and the layman to chew upon for years—and for the evolutionists, too.

After breakfast the men set out to hunt, while the women went to a large pool of warm water covered with a green scum and filled with billions of tadpoles. They waded in to where the water was about a foot deep and lay down in the mud. They remained there from one to two hours and then returned to the cliff. While we were with them, we saw this same thing repeated every morning; but though we asked them why they did it we could get no reply which was intelligible to us. All they vouchsafed in way of explanation was the single word *Ata*. They tried to get Lys to go in with them and could not understand why she refused. After the first day I went hunting with the men, leaving my pistol and Nobs with Lys, but she never had to use them, for no reptile or beast ever approached the pool while the women were there—nor, so far as we know, at other times. There was no spoor of wild beast in the soft mud along the banks, and the water certainly didn't look fit to drink.

This tribe lived largely upon the smaller animals which they bowled over with their stone hatchets after making a wide circle about their quarry and driving it so that it had to pass close to one of their number. The little horses and the smaller antelope they secured in sufficient numbers to support life, and they also ate numerous varieties of fruits and vegetables. They never brought in more than sufficient food for their immediate needs; but why bother? The food problem of Caspak is not one to cause worry to her inhabitants.

The fourth day Lys told me that she thought she felt equal to attempting the return journey on the morrow, and so I set out for the hunt in high spirits, for I was anxious to return to the fort and learn if Bradley and his party had returned and what had been the result of his expedition. I also wanted to relieve their minds as to Lys and myself, as I knew that they must already have given us up for dead. It was a cloudy day, though warm, as it always is in Caspak. It seemed odd to realize that just a few miles away winter lay upon the storm-tossed ocean, and that snow might be falling all about Caprona; but no snow could ever penetrate the damp, hot atmosphere of the great crater.

We had to go quite a bit farther than usual before we could surround a little bunch of antelope, and as I was helping drive them, I saw a fine red deer a couple of hundred yards behind me. He must have been asleep in the long grass, for I saw him rise and look about him in a bewildered way, and then I raised my gun and let him have it. He dropped, and I ran forward to finish him with the long thin knife, which one of the men had given me; but just as I reached him, he staggered to his feet and ran on for another two hundred yards—when I dropped him again. Once more was this repeated before I was able to reach him and cut his throat; then I looked around for my companions, as I wanted them to come and carry the meat home; but I could see nothing of them. I called a few times and waited, but there was no response and no one came. At last I became disgusted, and cutting off all the meat that I could conveniently carry, I set off in the direction of the cliffs. I must have gone about a mile before the truth dawned upon me—I was lost, hopelessly lost.

The entire sky was still completely blotted out by dense clouds; nor was there any landmark visible by which I might have taken my bearings. I went on in the direction I thought was south but which I now imagine must have been about due north, without detecting a single familiar object. In a dense wood I suddenly stumbled upon a thing which at first filled me with hope and later with the most utter despair and dejection. It was a little mound of new-turned earth sprinkled with flowers long since withered, and at one end was a flat slab of sandstone stuck in the ground. It was a grave, and it meant for me that I had at last stumbled into a country inhabited by human beings. I would find them; they would direct me to the cliffs; perhaps they would accompany me and take us back with them to their abodes—to the abodes of men and women like ourselves. My hopes and my imagination ran riot in the few yards I had to cover to reach that lonely grave and stoop that I might read the rude characters scratched upon the simple headstone. This is what I read:

HERE LIES JOHN TIPPET
ENGLISHMAN
KILLED BY TYRANNOSAURUS
10 SEP., A. D. 1916
R. I. P.

Tippet! It seemed incredible. Tippet lying here in this gloomy wood! Tippet dead! He had been a good man, but the personal loss was not what affected me. It was the fact that this silent grave gave evidence that Bradley had come this far upon his expedition and that he too probably was lost, for it was not our intention that he should be long gone. If I had stumbled upon the grave of one of the party, was it not within reason to believe that the bones of the others lay scattered somewhere near?

CHAPTER IX

As I stood looking down upon that sad and lonely mound, wrapped in the most dismal of reflections and premonitions, I was suddenly seized from behind and thrown to earth. As I fell, a warm body fell on top of me, and hands grasped my arms and legs. When I could look up, I saw a number of giant figures pinioning me down, while others stood about surveying me. Here again was a new type of man—a higher type than the primitive tribe I had just quitted. They were a taller people, too, with better-shaped skulls and more intelligent faces. There were less of the ape characteristics about their features, and less of the negroid, too. They carried weapons, stone-shod spears, stone knives, and hatchets—and they wore ornaments and breechcloths

—the former of feathers worn in their hair and the latter made of a single snake-skin cured with the head on, the head depending to their knees.

Of course I did not take in all these details upon the instant of my capture, for I was busy with other matters. Three of the warriors were sitting upon me, trying to hold me down by main strength and awkwardness, and they were having their hands full in the doing, I can tell you. I don't like to appear conceited, but I may as well admit that I am proud of my strength and the science that I have acquired and developed in the directing of it—that and my horsemanship I always have been proud of. And now, that day, all the long hours that I had put into careful study, practice and training brought me in two or three minutes a full return upon my investment. Californians, as a rule, are familiar with jujutsu, and I especially had made a study of it for several years, both at school and in the gym of the Los Angeles Athletic Club, while recently I had had, in my employ, a Jap who was a wonder at the art.

It took me just about thirty seconds to break the elbow of one of my assailants, trip another and send him stumbling backward among his fellows, and throw the third completely over my head in such a way that when he fell his neck was broken. In the instant that the others of the party stood in mute and inactive surprise, I unslung my rifle—which, carelessly, I had been carrying across my back; and when they charged, as I felt they would, I put a bullet in the forehead of one of them. This stopped them all temporarily—not the death of their fellow, but the report of the rifle, the first they had ever heard. Before they were ready to attack me again, one of them spoke in a commanding tone to his fellows, and in a language similar but still more comprehensive than that of the tribe to the south, as theirs was more complete than Ahm's. He commanded them to stand back and then he advanced and addressed me.

He asked me who I was, from whence I came and what my intentions were. I replied that I was a stranger in Caspak, that I was lost and that my only desire was to find my way back to my companions. He asked where they were and I told him toward the south somewhere, using the Caspakian phrase which, literally translated, means "toward the beginning." His surprise showed upon his face before he voiced it in words. "There are no Galus there," he said. "You have lied. The Galus have turned you out."

"I tell you," I said angrily, "that I am from another country,

far from Caspak, far beyond the high cliffs. I do not know who
the Galus may be; I have never seen them. This is the farthest
north I have been. Look at me—look at my clothing and my
weapons. Have you ever seen a Galu or any other creature in
Caspak who possessed such things?"

He had to admit that he had not, and also that he was much
interested in me, my rifle and the way I had handled his
three warriors. Finally he became half convinced that I was telling him the truth and offered to aid me if I would show him
how I had thrown the man over my head and also make him a
present of the "bang-spear," as he called it. I refused to give him
my rifle, but promised to show him the trick he wished to
learn if he would guide me in the right direction. He told me
that he would do so tomorrow, that it was too late today and
that I might come to their village and spend the night with them.
I was loath to lose so much time; but the fellow was obdurate,
and so I accompanied them. The two dead men they left
where they had fallen, nor gave them a second glance—thus
cheap is life upon Caspak.

These people also were cave-dwellers, but their caves showed
the result of a higher intelligence that brought them a step nearer
to civilized man than the tribe next "toward the beginning."
The interiors of their caverns were cleared of rubbish, though
still far from clean, and they had pallets of dried grasses covered
with the skins of leopard, lynx, and bear, while before the entrances were barriers of stone and small, rudely circular stone
ovens. The walls of the cavern to which I was conducted were
covered with drawings scratched upon the sandstone. There were
the outlines of the giant red deer, of mammoths, of tigers and
other beasts. Here, as in the last tribe, there were no children or
any old people. The men of this tribe had two names, or rather
names of two syllables, and their language contained words
of two syllables; whereas in the tribe of Tsa the words were
all of a single syllable, with the exception of a very few like
Atis and *Galus*. The chief's name was To-jo, and his house-
hold consisted of seven females and himself. These women
were much more comely, or rather less hideous than those of
Tsa's people; one of them, even, was almost pretty, being less
hairy and having a rather nice skin, with high coloring.

They were all much interested in me and examined my clothing and equipment carefully, handling and feeling and smelling
of each article. I learned from them that their people were
known as Band-lu, or spear-men; Tsa's race was called Sto-lu—

hatchet-men. Below these in the scale of evolution came the Bo-lu, or club-men, and then the Alus, who had no weapons and no language. In that word I recognized what to me seemed the most remarkable discovery I had made upon Caprona, for unless it were mere coincidence, I had come upon a word that had been handed down from the beginning of spoken language upon earth, been handed down for millions of years, perhaps, with little change. It was the sole remaining thread of the ancient woof of a dawning culture which had been woven when Caprona was a fiery mount upon a great land-mass teeming with life. It linked the unfathomable then to the eternal now. And yet it may have been pure coincidence; my better judgment tells me that it is coincidence that in Caspak the term for speechless man is *Alus*, and in the outer world of our own day it is *Alalus*.

The comely woman of whom I spoke was called So-ta, and she took such a lively interest in me that To-jo finally objected to her attentions, emphasizing his displeasure by knocking her down and kicking her into a corner of the cavern. I leaped between them while he was still kicking her, and obtaining a quick hold upon him, dragged him screaming with pain from the cave. There I made him promise not to hurt the she again, upon pain of worse punishment. So-ta gave me a grateful look; but To-jo and the balance of his women were sullen and ominous.

Later in the evening So-ta confided to me that she was soon to leave the tribe.

"So-ta soon be Kro-lu," she confided in a low whisper. I asked her what a Kro-lu might be, and she tried to explain, but I do not yet know if I understood her. From her gestures I deduced that the Kro-lus were a people who were armed with bows and arrows, had vessels in which to cook their food and huts of some sort in which they lived, and were accompanied by animals. It was all very fragmentary and vague, but the idea seemed to be that the Kro-lus were a more advanced people than the Band-lus. I pondered a long time upon all that I had heard, before sleep came to me. I tried to find some connection between these various races that would explain the universal hope which each of them harbored that some day they would become Galus. So-ta had given me a suggestion; but the resulting idea was so weird that I could scarce even entertain it; yet it coincided with Ahm's expressed hope, with the various steps in evolution I had noted in the several tribes I had encountered and with the range of type represented in each tribe. For example, among the Band-lu were such types as So-ta, who seemed to me to be the highest in the scale of evolution, and To-jo, who was just a shade nearer the ape, while there were others who had flatter noses, more prognathous faces and hairier bodies. The question puzzled me. Possibly in the outer world the answer to it is locked in the bosom of the Sphinx. Who knows? I do not.

Thinking the thoughts of a lunatic or a dope-fiend, I fell asleep; and when I awoke, my hands and feet were securely tied and my weapons had been taken from me. How they did it without awakening me I cannot tell you. It was humiliating, but it was true. To-jo stood above me. The early light of morning was dimly filtering into the cave.

"Tell me," he demanded, "how to throw a man over my head and break his neck, for I am going to kill you, and I wish to know this thing before you die."

Of all the ingenuous declarations I have ever heard, this one copped the proverbial bun. It struck me as so funny that, even in the face of death, I laughed. Death, I may remark here, had, however, lost much of his terror for me. I had become a disciple of Lys' fleeting philosophy of the valuelessness of human life. I realized that she was quite right—that we were but comic figures hopping from the cradle to the grave, of interest to practically no other created thing than ourselves and our few intimates.

Behind To-jo stood So-ta. She raised one hand with the palm toward me—the Caspakian equivalent of a negative shake of the head.

"Let me think about it," I parried, and To-jo said that he would wait until night. He would give me a day to think it over; then he left, and the women left—the men for the hunt, and the women, as I later learned from So-ta, for the warm pool where they immersed their bodies as did the shes of the Sto-lu. "Ata," explained So-ta, when I questioned her as to the purpose of this matutinal rite; but that was later.

I must have lain there bound and uncomfortable for two or three hours when at last So-ta entered the cave. She carried a sharp knife—mine, in fact, and with it she cut my bonds.

"Come!" she said. "So-ta will go with you back to the Galus. It is time that So-ta left the Band-lu. Together we will go to the Kro-lu, and after that the Galus. To-jo will kill you tonight. He will kill So-ta if he knows that So-ta aided you. We will go together."

"I will go with you to the Kro-lu," I replied, "but then I must return to my own people 'toward the beginning.'"

"You cannot go back," she said. "It is forbidden. They would kill you. Thus far have you come—there is no returning."

"But I must return," I insisted. "My people are there. I must return and lead them in this direction."

She insisted, and I insisted; but at last we compromised. I was to escort her as far as the country of the Kro-lu and then I was to go back after my own people and lead them north into a land where the dangers were fewer and the people less murderous. She brought me all my belongings that had been filched from me—rifle, ammunition, knife, and thermos bottle, and then hand in hand we descended the cliff and set off toward the north.

For three days we continued upon our way, until we arrived outside a village of thatched huts just at dusk. So-ta said that she would enter alone; I must not be seen if I did not intend to remain, as it was forbidden that one should return and live after having advanced this far. So she left me. She was a dear girl and a stanch and true comrade—more like a man than a woman. In her simple barbaric way she was both refined and chaste. She had been the wife of To-jo. Among the Kro-lu she would find another mate after the manner of the strange Caspakian world; but she told me very frankly that whenever I returned, she would leave her mate and come to me, as she preferred me above all others. I was becoming a ladies' man after a lifetime of bashfulness!

At the outskirts of the village I left her without even seeing the sort of people who inhabited it, and set off through the growing darkness toward the south. On the third day I made a detour westward to avoid the country of the Band-lu, as I did not care to be detained by a meeting with To-jo. On the sixth day I came to the cliffs of the Sto-lu, and my heart beat fast as I approached them, for here was Lys. Soon I would hold her tight in my arms again; soon her warm lips would merge with mine. I felt sure that she was still safe among the hatchet people, and I was already picturing the joy and the love-light in her eyes when she should see me once more as I emerged from the last clump of trees and almost ran toward the cliffs.

It was late in the morning. The women must have returned from the pool; yet as I drew near, I saw no sign of life whatever. "They have remained longer," I thought; but when I was quite close to the base of the cliffs, I saw that which dashed my hopes and my happiness to earth. Strewn along the ground were a score of mute and horrible suggestions of what had taken place during my absence—bones picked clean of flesh, the bones of manlike creatures, the bones of many of the tribe of Sto-lu; nor in any cave was there sign of life.

Closely I examined the ghastly remains fearful each instant that I should find the dainty skull that would shatter my happiness for life; but though I searched diligently, picking up every one of the twenty-odd skulls, I found none that was not the skull of a creature but slightly removed from the ape. Hope, then, still lived. For another three days I searched north and south, east and west for the hatchetmen of Caspak; but never a trace of them did I find. It was raining most of the time now, and the weather was as near cold as it ever seems to get on Caprona.

. At last I gave up the search and set off toward Fort Dinosaur. For a week—a week filled with the terrors and dangers of a primeval world—I pushed on in the direction I thought was south. The sun never shone; the rain scarcely ever ceased falling. The beasts I met with were fewer in number but infinitely more terrible in temper; yet I lived on until there came to me the realization that I was hopelessly lost, that a year of sunshine would not again give me my bearings; and while I was cast down by this terrifying knowledge, the knowledge that I never again could find my Lys, I stumbled upon another grave—the grave of William James, with its little crude headstone and its scrawled characters recording that he had died upon the 13th of September—killed by a saber-tooth tiger.

I think that I almost gave up then. Never in my life have I felt more hopeless or helpless or alone. I was lost. I could not find my friends. I did not even know that they still lived; in fact, I could not bring myself to believe that they did. I was sure that Lys was dead. I wanted myself to die, and yet I clung to life —useless and hopeless and harrowing a thing as it had become. I clung to life because some ancient, reptilian forbear had clung to life and transmitted to me through the ages the most powerful motive that guided his minute brain—the motive of self-preservation.

At last I came to the great barrier-cliffs; and after three days of mad effort—of maniacal effort—I scaled them. I built crude ladders; I wedged sticks in narrow fissures; I chopped toe-holds and finger-holds with my long knife; but at last I scaled them. Near the summit I came upon a huge cavern. It is the abode of some mighty winged creature of the Triassic—or rather it was. Now it is mine. I slew the thing and took its abode. I reached the summit and looked out upon the broad gray terrible Pacific of the far-southern winter. It was cold up there. It is cold here to-day; yet here I sit watching, watching, watching for the thing I know will never come—for a sail.

CHAPTER X

ONCE a day I descend to the base of the cliff and hunt, and fill my stomach with water from a clear cold spring. I have three gourds which I fill with water and take back to my cave against the long nights. I have fashioned a spear and a bow and arrow, that I may conserve my ammunition, which is running low. My clothes are worn to shreds. Tomorrow I shall discard them for leopard-skins which I have tanned and sewn into a garment strong and warm. It is is cold up here. I have a fire burning, and I sit bent over it while I write; but I am safe here. No other living creature ventures to the chill summit of the barrier cliffs. I am safe, and I am alone with my sorrows and my remembered joys—but without hope. It is said that hope springs eternal in the human breast; but there is none in mine.

I am about done. Presently I shall fold these pages and push them into my thermos bottle. I shall cork it and screw the cap down tight, and then I shall hurl it as far out into the sea as my strength will permit. The wind is off-shore; the tide is running out; perhaps it will be carried into one of those numerous ocean-currents which sweep perpetually from pole to pole and from continent to continent, to be deposited at last upon some in-habited shore. If fate is kind and this does happen, then, *for God's sake, come and get me!*

It was a week ago that I wrote the preceding paragraph, which I thought would end the written record of my life upon Caprona. I had paused to put a new point on my quill and stir the crude ink (which I made by crushing a black variety of berry and mixing it with water) before attaching my signature, when faintly from the valley far below came an unmistakable sound which brought me to my feet, trembling with excitement, to peer eagerly downward from my dizzy ledge. How full of meaning that sound was to me you may guess when I tell you that it was the report of a firearm! For a moment my gaze traversed the landscape beneath until it was caught and held by four figures near the base of the cliff—a human figure held at bay by three hyaenodons, those ferocious and blood-thirsty wild dogs of the Eocene. A fourth beast lay dead or dying near by.

I couldn't be sure, looking down from above as I was; but yet I trembled like a leaf in the intuitive belief that it was Lys, and my judgment served to confirm my wild desire, for whoever it was carried only a pistol, and thus had Lys been armed. The first wave of sudden joy which surged through me was short-lived in the face of the swift-following conviction that the one who fought below was already doomed. Luck and only luck it must have been which had permitted that first shot to lay low one of the savage creatures, for even such a heavy weapon as my pistol is entirely inadequate against even the lesser carnivora of Caspak. In a moment the three would charge! a futile shot would but tend more greatly to enrage the one it chanced to hit; and then the three would drag down the little human figure and tear it to pieces.

And maybe it was Lys! My heart stood still at the thought, but mind and muscle responded to the quick decision I was forced to make. There was but a single hope—a single chance—and I took it. I raised my rifle to my shoulder and took careful aim. It was a long shot, a dangerous shot, for unless one is accustomed to it, shooting from a considerable altitude is most deceptive work. There is, though, something about marksmanship which is quite beyond all scientific laws.

Upon no other theory can I explain my marksmanship of that moment. Three times my rifle spoke—three quick, short syllables of death. I did not take conscious aim; and yet at each report a beast crumpled in its tracks!

From my ledge to the base of the cliff is a matter of several thousand feet of dangerous climbing; yet I venture to say that the first ape from whose loins my line has descended never could have equaled the speed with which I literally dropped down the face of that rugged escarpment. The last two hundred feet is over a steep incline of loose rubble to the valley bottom, and I had just reached the top of this when there arose to my ears an agonized cry—"Bowen! Bowen! Quick, my love, quick!"

I had been too much occupied with the dangers of the descent to glance down toward the valley; but that cry which told me that it was indeed Lys, and that she was again in danger, brought my eyes quickly upon her in time to see a hairy, burly brute seize her and start off at a run toward the near-by wood. From rock to rock, chamoislike, I leaped downward toward the valley, in pursuit of Lys and her hideous abductor.

He was heavier than I by many pounds, and so weighted by the burden he carried that I easily overtook him; and at last he turned, snarling, to face me. It was Kho of the tribe of Tsa, the hatchet-men. He recognized me, and with a low growl he threw Lys aside and came for me. "The she is mine," he cried. "I kill! I kill!"

I had had to discard my rifle before I commenced the rapid descent of the cliff, so that now I was armed only with a hunting knife, and this I whipped from its scabbard as Kho leaped toward me. He was a mighty beast, mightily muscled, and the urge that has made males fight since the dawn of life on earth filled him with blood-lust and the thirst to slay; but not one whit less did it fill me with the same primal passions. Two abysmal beasts sprang at each other's throats that day beneath the shadow of earth's oldest cliffs—the man of now and the man-thing of the earliest, forgotten then, imbued by the same deathless passion that has come down unchanged through all the epochs, periods and eras of time from the beginning, and which shall continue to the incalculable end—woman, the imperishable Alpha and Omega of life.

Kho closed and sought my jugular with his teeth. He seemed to forget the hatchet dangling by its aurochs-hide thong at his hip, as I forgot, for the moment, the dagger in my hand. And I doubt not but that Kho would easily have bested me in an encounter of that sort had not Lys' voice awakened within my momentarily reverted brain the skill and cunning of reasoning man. "Bowen!" she cried. "Your knife! Your knife!"

It was enough. It recalled me from the forgotten eon to which my brain had flown and left me once again a modern man battling with a clumsy, unskilled brute. No longer did my jaws snap at the hairy throat before me; but instead my knife sought and found a space between two ribs over the savage heart. Kho voiced a single horrid scream, stiffened spasmodically and sank to the earth. And Lys threw herself into my arms. All the fears and sorrows of the past were wiped away, and once again I was the happiest of men.

With some misgivings I shortly afterward cast my eyes upward toward the precarious ledge which ran before my cave, for it seemed to me quite beyond all reason to expect a dainty modern belle to essay the perils of that frightful climb. I asked her if she thought she could brave the ascent, and she laughed gayly in my face.

"Watch!" she cried, and ran eagerly toward the base of the

cliff. Like a squirrel she clambered swiftly aloft, so that I was forced to exert myself to keep pace with her. At first she frightened me; but presently I was aware that she was quite as safe here as was I. When we finally came to my ledge and I again held her in my arms, she recalled to my mind that for several weeks she had been living the life of a cave-girl with the tribe of hatchet-men. They had been driven from their former caves by another tribe which had slain many and carried off quite half the females, and the new cliffs to which they had flown had proven far higher and more precipitous, so that she had become, through necessity, a most practiced climber.

She told me of Kho's desire for her, since all his females had been stolen and of how her life had been a constant nightmare of terror as she sought by night and by day to elude the great brute. For a time Nobs had been all the protection she required; but one day he disappeared—nor has she seen him since. She believes that he was deliberately made away with; and so do I, for we both are sure that he never would have deserted her. With her means of protection gone, Lys was now at the mercy of the hatchet-man; nor was it many hours before he had caught her at the base of the cliff and seized her; but as he bore her triumphantly aloft toward his cave, she had managed to break loose and escape him.

"For three days he has pursued me," she said, "through this horrible world. How I have passed through in safety I cannot guess, nor how I have always managed to outdistance him; yet I have done it, until just as you discovered me. Fate was kind to us, Bowen."

I nodded my head in assent and crushed her to me. And then we talked and planned as I cooked antelope-steaks over my fire, and we came to the conclusion that there was no hope of rescue, that she and I were doomed to live and die upon Caprona. Well, it might be worse! I would rather live here always with Lys than to live elsewhere without her; and she, dear girl, says the same of me; but I am afraid of this life for her. It is a hard, fierce, dangerous life, and I shall pray always that we shall be rescued from it—for her sake.

That night the clouds broke, and the moon shone down upon our little ledge; and there, hand in hand, we turned our faces toward heaven and plighted our troth beneath the eyes of God. No human agency could have married us more sacredly than we are wed. We are man and wife, and we are content. If God wills it, we shall live out our lives here. If He wills otherwise, then this manuscript which I shall now consign to the inscrutable forces of the sea shall fall into friendly hands. However, we are each without hope. And so we say good-bye in this, our last message to the world beyond the barrier cliffs.

(*Signed*) BOWEN J. TYLER, JR.

LYS LA R. TYLER.

PART II

The People That Time Forgot

The Adventures of Thomas Billings

CHAPTER I

I AM forced to admit that even though I had traveled a long distance to place Bowen Tyler's manuscript in the hands of his father, I was still a trifle skeptical as to its sincerity, since I could not but recall that it had not been many years since Bowen had been one of the most notorious practical jokers of his alma mater. The truth was that as I sat in the Tyler library at Santa Monica I commenced to feel a trifle foolish and to wish that I had merely forwarded the manuscript by express instead of bearing it personally, for I confess that I do not enjoy being laughed at. I have a well-developed sense of humor—when the joke is not on me.

Mr Tyler, Sr., was expected almost hourly. The last steamer in from Honolulu had brought information of the date of the expected sailing of his yacht *Toreador*, which was now twenty-four hours overdue. Mr. Tyler's assistant secretary, who had been left at home, assured me that there was no doubt but that the *Toreador* had sailed as promised, since he knew his employer well enough to be positive that nothing short of an act of God would prevent his doing what he had planned to do. I was also aware of the fact that the sending apparatus of the *Toreador's* wireless equipment was sealed, and that it would only be used in event of dire necessity. There was, therefore, nothing to do but wait, and we waited.

We discussed the manuscript and hazarded guesses concerning it and the strange events it narrated. The torpedoing of the liner upon which Bowen J. Tyler, Jr., had taken passage for France to join the American Ambulance was a well-known fact, and I had further substantiated by wire to the New York office of the owners, that a Miss La Rue had been booked for passage. Further, neither she nor Bowen had been mentioned among the list of survivors; nor had the body of either of them been recovered.

Their rescue by the English tug was entirely probable; the capture of the enemy *U-33* by the tug's crew was not beyond the range of possibility; and their adventures during the perilous cruise which the treachery and deceit of Benson extended until they found themselves in the waters of the far South Pacific with depleted stores and poisoned water-casks, while bordering upon the fantastic, appeared logical enough as narrated, event by event, in the manuscript.

Caprona has always been considered a more or less mythical land, though it is vouched for by an eminent navigator of the eighteenth century; but Bowen's narrative made it seem very real, however many miles of trackless ocean lay between us and it. Yes, that narrative had us guessing. We were agreed that it was most improbable; but neither of us could say that anything which it contained was beyond the range of possibility. The weird flora and fauna of Caspak were as possible under the thick, warm atmospheric conditions of the superheated crater as they were in the Mesozoic era under almost exactly similar conditions, which were then probably world-wide. The assistant secretary had heard of Caproni and his discoveries, but admitted that he never had taken much stock in the one nor the other. We were agreed that the one statement most difficult of explanation was that which reported the entire absence of human young among the various tribes with which Tyler had had intercourse. This was the one irreconcilable statement of the manuscript. A world of adults! It was impossible.

We speculated upon the probable fate of Bradley and his party of English sailors. Tyler had found the graves of two of them; how many more might have perished! And Miss La Rue—could a young girl long have survived the horrors of Caspak after having been separated from all of her own kind? The assistant secretary wondered if Nobs still was with her, and then we both smiled at this tacit acceptance of the truth of the whole uncanny tale.

"I suppose I'm a fool," remarked the assistant secretary; "but by George, I can't help believing it, and I can see that girl now, with the big Airedale at her side protecting her from the terrors of a million years ago. I can visualize the entire scene—the apelike Grimaldi men huddled in their filthy caves; the huge pterodactyls soaring through the heavy air upon their batlike wings; the mighty dinosaurs moving their clumsy hulks beneath the dark shadows of pre-glacial forests—the dragons which we considered myths until science taught us that they were the true recollections of the first man, handed down through countless ages by word of mouth from father to son out of the unrecorded dawn of humanity."

"It is stupendous—if true," I replied. "And to think that possibly they are still there—Tyler and Miss La Rue—surrounded by hideous dangers, and that possibly Bradley still lives, and some of his party! I can't help hoping all the time that Bowen and the girl have found the others; the last that Bowen knew of them, there were six left, all told—the mate Bradley, the engineer Olson, and Wilson, Whitely, Brady and Sinclair. There might be some hope for them if they could join forces; but separated, I'm afraid they couldn't last long.

"If only they hadn't let the German prisoners capture the *U-33*! Bowen should have had better judgment than to have trusted them at all. The chances are von Schoenvorts succeeded in getting safely back to Kiel and is strutting around with an Iron Cross this very minute. With a large supply of oil from the wells they discovered in Caspak, with plenty of water and ample provisions, there is no reason why they couldn't have negotiated the submerged tunnel beneath the barrier cliffs and made good their escape."

"I don't like 'em," said the assistant secretary; "but sometimes you got to hand it to 'em."

"Yes," I growled, "and there's nothing I'd enjoy more than *handing it to them!*" And then the telephone-bell rang.

The assistant secretary answered, and as I watched him, I saw his jaw drop and his face go white. "My God!" he exclaimed as he hung up the receiver as one in a trance. "It can't be!"

"What?" I asked.

"Mr. Tyler is dead," he answered in a dull voice. "He died at sea, suddenly, yesterday."

The next ten days were occupied in burying Mr Bowen J. Tyler, Sr., and arranging plans for the succor of his son. Mr. Tom Billings, the late Mr. Tyler's secretary, did it all. He is force, energy, initiative and good judgment combined and personified. I never have beheld a more dynamic young man. He handled lawyers, courts and executors as a sculptor handles his modeling clay. He formed, fashioned and forced them to his will. He had been a classmate of Bowen Tyler at college, and a fraternity brother, and before that he had been an impoverished and improvident cow-puncher on one of the great Tyler ranches. Tyler, Sr., had picked him out of thousands of employees and made him; or rather Tyler had given him the opportunity, and then Billings had made himself. Tyler, Jr., as good a judge of men as his father, had taken him into his friendship, and between the two of them they had turned out a man who would have died for a Tyler as quickly as he would have for his flag. Yet there was none of the sycophant or fawner in Billings; ordinarily I do not wax enthusiastic about men, but this man Billings comes as close to my conception of what a regular man should be as any I have ever met. I venture to say that before Bowen J. Tyler sent him to college he had never heard the word *ethics,* and yet I am equally sure that in all his life he never has transgressed a single tenet of the code of ethics of an American gentleman.

Ten days after they brought Mr. Tyler's body off the *Toreador,* we steamed out into the Pacific in search of Caprona. There were forty in the party, including the master and crew of the *Toreador;* and Billings the indomitable was in command. We had a long and uninteresting search for Caprona, for the old map upon which the assistant secretary had finally located it was most inaccurate. When its grim walls finally rose out of the ocean's mists before us, we were so far south that it was a question as to whether we were in the South Pacific or the Antarctic. Bergs were numerous, and it was very cold.

All during the trip Billings had steadfastly evaded questions as to how we were to enter Caspak after we had found Caprona. Bowen Tyler's manuscript had made it perfectly evident to all that the subterranean outlet of the Caspakian river was the only means of ingress or egress to the crater world beyond the impregnable cliffs. Tyler's party had been able to navigate this channel because their craft had been a submarine; but the *Toreador* could as easily have flown over the cliffs as sailed under them. Jimmy Hollis and Colin Short whiled away many an hour inventing schemes for surmounting the obstacle presented by the barrier cliffs, and making ridiculous wagers as to which one Tom Billings had in mind; but immediately we were all assured that we had raised Caprona, Billings called us together.

"There was no use in talking about these things," he said, "until we found the island. At best it can be but conjecture on our part until we have been able to scrutinize the coast closely. Each of us has formed a mental picture of the Capronian sea-coast from Bowen's manuscript, and it is not likely that any two of these pictures resemble each other, or that any of them resembles the coast as we shall presently find it. I have in view three plans for scaling the cliffs, and the means for carrying out each is in the hold. There is an electric drill with plenty of waterproof cable to reach from the ship's dynamos to the cliff-top when the *Toreador* is anchored at a safe distance from shore, and there is sufficient half-inch iron rod to build a ladder from the base to the top of the cliff. It would be a long, arduous and dangerous work to bore the holes and insert the rungs of the ladder from the bottom upward; yet it can be done.

"I also have a life-saving mortar with which we might be able to throw a line over the summit of the cliffs; but this plan would necessitate one of us climbing to the top with the chances more than even that the line would cut at the summit, or the hooks at the upper end would slip.

"My third plan seems to me the most feasible. You all saw a number of large, heavy boxes lowered into the hold before we sailed. I know you did, because you asked me what they contained and commented upon the large letter 'H' which was painted upon each box. These boxes contain the various parts of a hydro-aeroplane. I purpose assembling this upon the strip of beach described in Bowen's manuscript—the beach where he found the dead body of the apelike man—provided there is sufficient space above high water; otherwise we shall have to assemble it on deck and lower it over the side. After it is assembled, I shall carry tackle and ropes to the cliff-top, and then it will be comparatively simple to hoist the search-party and its supplies in safety. Or I can make a sufficient number of trips to land the entire party in the valley beyond the barrier; all will depend, of course, upon what my first reconnaissance reveals."

That afternoon we steamed slowly along the face of Caprona's towering barrier.

"You see now," remarked Billings as we craned our necks to scan the summit thousands of feet above us, "how futile it would have been to waste our time in working out details of a plan to surmount those." And he jerked his thumb toward the cliffs. "It would take weeks, possibly months, to construct a ladder to the top. I had no conception of their formidable height. Our mortar would not carry a line halfway to the crest of the lowest point. There is no use discussing any plan other than the hydro-aeroplane. We'll find the beach and get busy."

Late the following morning the lookout announced that he could discern surf about a mile ahead; and as we approached, we all saw the line of breakers broken by a long sweep of rolling surf upon a narrow beach. The launch was lowered, and five of us made a landing, getting a good ducking in the ice-cold waters in the doing of it; but we were rewarded by the finding of the clean-picked bones of what might have been the skeleton of a high order of ape or a very low order of man, lying close to the base of the cliff. Billings was satisfied, as were the rest of us, that this was the beach mentioned by Bowen, and we further found that there was ample room to assemble the seaplane.

Billings, having arrived at a decision, lost no time in acting, with the result that before mid-afternoon we had landed all the large boxes marked *"H"* upon the beach, and were busily engaged in opening them. Two days later the plane was assembled and tuned. We loaded tackles and ropes, water, food and ammunition in it, and then we each implored Billings to let us be the one to accompany him. But he would take no one. That was Billings; if there was any especially difficult or dangerous work to be done, that one man could do, Billings always did it himself. If he needed assistance, he never called for volunteers —just selected the man or men he considered best qualified for the duty. He said that he considered the principles underlying all volunteer service fundamentally wrong, and that it seemed to him that calling for volunteers reflected upon the courage and loyalty of the entire command.

We rolled the plane down to the water's edge, and Billings mounted the pilot's seat. There was a moment's delay as he assured himself that he had everything necessary. Jimmy Hollis went over his armament and ammunition to see that nothing had been omitted. Besides pistol and rifle, there was the machine-gun mounted in front of him on the plane, and ammunition for all three. Bowen's account of the terrors of Caspak had impressed us all with the necessity for proper means of defense.

At last all was ready. The motor was started, and we pushed the plane out into the surf. A moment later, and she was skimming seaward. Gently she rose from the surface of the water, executed a wide spiral as she mounted rapidly, circled once far above us and then disappeared over the crest of the cliffs. We all stood silent and expectant, our eyes glued upon the towering summit above us. Hollis, who was now in command, consulted his wrist-watch at frequent intervals.

"Gad," exclaimed Short, "we ought to be hearing from him pretty soon!"

Hollis laughed nervously. "He's been gone only ten minutes," he announced.

"Seems like an hour," snapped Short. "What's that? Did you hear that? He's firing! It's the machine-gun! Oh, Lord; and here we are as helpless as a lot of old ladies ten thousand miles away! We can't do a thing. We don't know what's happening. Why didn't he let one of us go with him?"

Yes, it was the machine-gun. We could hear it distinctly for at least a minute. Then came silence. That was two weeks ago. We have had no sign nor signal from Tom Billings since.

CHAPTER II

I'LL NEVER forget my first impressions of Caspak as I circled in, high over the surrounding cliffs. From the plane I looked down through a mist upon the blurred landscape beneath me. The hot, humid atmosphere of Caspak condenses as it is fanned by the cold Antarctic air-currents which sweep across the crater's top, sending a tenuous ribbon of vapor far out across the Pacific. Through this the picture gave one the suggestion of a colossal impressionistic canvas in greens and browns and scarlets and yellows surrounding the deep blue of the inland sea—just blobs of color taking form through the tumbling mist.

I dived close to the cliffs and skirted them for several miles without finding the least indication of a suitable landing-place; and then I swung back at a lower level, looking for a clearing close to the bottom of the mighty escarpment; but I could find none of sufficient area to insure safety. I was flying pretty low by this time, not only looking for landing places but watching the myriad life beneath me. I was down pretty well toward the south end of the island, where an arm of the lake reaches far inland, and I could see the surface of the water literally black with creatures of some sort. I was too far up to recognize individuals, but the general impression was of a vast army of amphibious monsters. The land was almost equally alive with crawling, leaping, running, flying things. It was one of the latter which nearly did for me while my attention was fixed upon the weird scene below.

The first intimation I had of it was the sudden blotting out of the sunlight from above, and as I glanced quickly up, I saw a most terrific creature swooping down upon me. It must have been fully eighty feet long from the end of its long, hideous beak to the tip of its thick, short tail, with an equal spread of wings. It was coming straight for me and hissing frightfully—I could hear it above the whir of the propeller. It was coming straight down toward the muzzle of the machine-gun and I let it have it right in the breast; but still it came for me, so that I had to dive and turn, though I was dangerously close to earth.

The thing didn't miss me by a dozen feet, and when I rose, it wheeled and followed me, but only to the cooler air close to the level of the cliff-tops; there it turned again and dropped. Something—man's natural love of battle and the chase, I presume— impelled me to pursue it, and so I too circled and dived. The moment I came down into the warm atmosphere of Caspak, the creature came for me again, rising above me so that it might swoop down upon me. Nothing could better have suited my armament, since my machine-gun was pointed upward at an angle of about 45° and could not be either depressed or elevated by the pilot. If I had brought some one along with me, we could have raked the great reptile from almost any position, but as the creature's mode of attack was always from above, he always found me ready with a hail of bullets. The battle must have lasted a minute or more before the thing suddenly turned completely over in the air and fell to the ground.

Bowen and I roomed together at college, and I learned a lot from him outside my regular course. He was a pretty good scholar despite his love of fun, and his particular hobby was paleontology. He used to tell me about the various forms of animal and vegetable life which had covered the globe during former eras, and so I was pretty well acquainted with the fishes, amphibians, reptiles, and mammals of paleolithic times. I knew that the thing that had attacked me was some sort of ptero- dactyl which should have been extinct millions of years ago. It was all that I needed to realize that Bowen had exaggerated nothing in his manuscript.

Having disposed of my first foe, I set myself once more to search for a landing-place near to the base of the cliffs beyond which my party awaited me. I knew how anxious they would be for word from me, and I was equally anxious to relieve their minds and also to get them and our supplies well within Caspak, so that we might set off about our business of finding and rescu- ing Bowen Tyler; but the pterodactyl's carcass had scarcely fallen before I was surrounded by at least a dozen of the hideous things, some large, some small, but all bent upon my destruc- tion. I could not cope with them all, and so I rose rapidly from among them to the cooler strata wherein they dared not follow; and then I recalled that Bowen's narrative distinctly indicated that the farther north one traveled in Caspak, the fewer were

The thing didn't miss me by a dozen feet.

the terrible reptiles which rendered human life impossible at the southern end of the island.

There seemed nothing now but to search out a more northerly landing-place and then return to the *Toreador* and transport my companions, two by two, over the cliffs and deposit them at the rendezvous. As I flew north, the temptation to explore overcame me. I knew that I could easily cover Caspak and return to the beach with less petrol than I had in my tanks; and there was the hope, too, that I might find Bowen or some of his party. The broad expanse of the inland sea lured me out over its waters, and as I crossed, I saw at either extremity of the great body of water an island—one to the south and one to the north; but I did not alter my course to examine either closely, leaving that to a later time.   *99043*

The further shore of the sea revealed a much narrower strip of land between the cliffs and the water than upon the western side; but it was a hillier and more open country. There were splendid landing-places, and in the distance, toward the north, I thought I descried a village; but of that I was not positive. However, as I approached the land, I saw a number of human figures apparently pursuing one who fled across a broad expanse of meadow. As I dropped lower to have a better look at these people, they caught the whirring of my propellers and looked aloft. They paused an instant—pursuers and pursued; and then they broke and raced for the shelter of the nearest wood. Almost instantaneously a huge bulk swooped down upon me, and as I looked up, I realized that there were flying reptiles even in this part of Caspak. The creature dived for my right wing so quickly that nothing but a sheer drop could have saved me. I was already close to the ground, so that my maneuver was extremely dangerous; but I was in a fair way of making it successfully when I saw that I was too closely approaching a large tree. My effort to dodge the tree and the pterodactyl at the same time resulted disastrously. One wing touched an upper branch; the plane tipped and swung around, and then, out of control, dashed into the branches of the tree, where it came to rest, battered and torn, forty feet above the ground.

Hissing loudly, the huge reptile swept close above the tree in which my plane had lodged, circled twice over me and then flapped away toward the south. As I guessed then and was to learn later, forests are the surest sanctuary from these hideous creatures, which, with their enormous spread of wing and their great weight, are as much out of place among trees as is a seaplane.

For a minute or so I clung there to my battered flyer, now useless beyond redemption, my brain numbed by the frightful catastrophe that had befallen me. All my plans for the succor of Bowen and Miss La Rue had depended upon this craft, and in a few brief minutes my own selfish love of adventure had wrecked their hopes and mine. And what effect it might have upon the future of the balance of the rescuing expedition I could not even guess. Their lives, too, might be sacrificed to my suicidal foolishness. That I was doomed seemed inevitable; but I can honestly say that the fate of my friends concerned me more greatly than did my own.

Beyond the barrier cliffs my party was even now nervously awaiting my return. Presently apprehension and fear would claim them—and they would never know! They would attempt to scale the cliffs—of that I was sure; but I was not so positive that they would succeed; and after a while they would turn back, what there were left of them, and go sadly and mournfully upon their return-journey to home. Home! I set my jaws and tried to forget the word, for I knew that I should never again see home.

And what of Bowen and his girl? I had doomed them too. They would never even know that an attempt had been made to rescue them. If they still lived, they might some day come upon the ruined remnants of this great plane hanging in its lofty sepulcher and hazard vain guesses and be filled with wonder; but they would never know; and I could not but be glad that they would not know that Tom Billings had sealed their death-warrants by his criminal selfishness.

All these useless regrets were getting me in a bad way; but at last I shook myself and tried to put such things out of my mind and take hold of conditions as they existed and do my level best to wrest victory from defeat. I was badly shaken up and bruised, but considered myself mighty lucky to escape with my life. The plane hung at a precarious angle, so that it was with difficulty and considerable danger that I climbed from it into the tree and then to the ground.

My predicament was grave. Between me and my friends lay an island sea fully sixty miles wide at this point, and an estimated land-distance of some three hundred miles around the northern end of the sea, through such hideous dangers as I am perfectly free to admit had me pretty well buffaloed. I had seen quite enough of Caspak this day to assure me that Bowen had in no way exaggerated its perils. As a matter of fact, I am inclined to believe that he had become so accustomed to them before he started upon his manuscript that he rather slighted them. As I stood there beneath that tree—a tree which should have been part of a coal-bed countless ages since—and looked out across a sea teeming with frightful life—life which should have been fossil before God conceived of Adam—I would not have given a minim of stale beer for my chances of ever seeing my friends or the outside world again; yet then and there I swore to fight my way as far through this hideous land as circumstances would permit. I had plenty of ammunition, an automatic pistol and a heavy rifle—the latter one of twenty added to our equipment on the strength of Bowen's description of the huge beasts of prey which ravaged Caspak. My greatest danger lay in the hideous reptilia whose low nervous organizations permitted their carnivorous instincts to function for several minutes after they had ceased to live.

But to these things I gave less thought than to the sudden frustration of all our plans. With the bitterest of thoughts I condemned myself for the foolish weakness that had permitted me to be drawn from the main object of my flight into premature and useless exploration. It seemed to me then that I must be totally eliminated from further search for Bowen, since, as I estimated it, the three hundred miles of Caspakian territory I must traverse to reach the base of the cliffs beyond which my party awaited me were practically impassable for a single individual unaccustomed to Caspakian life and ignorant of all that lay before him. Yet I could not give up hope entirely. My duty lay clear before me; I must follow it while life remained to me, and so I set forth toward the north.

The country through which I took my way was as lovely as it was unusual—I had almost said unearthly, for the plants, the trees, the blooms were not of the earth that I knew. They were larger, the colors more brilliant and the shapes startling, some almost to grotesqueness, though even such added to the charm and romance of the landscape as the giant cacti render weirdly beautiful the waste spots of the sad Mohave. And over all the sun shone huge and round and red, a monster sun above a monstrous world, its light dispersed by the humid air of Caspak —the warm, moist air which lies sluggish upon the breast of this great mother of life, Nature's mightiest incubator.

All about me, in every direction, was life. It moved through the tree-tops and among the boles; it displayed itself in widening and intermingling circles upon the bosom of the sea; it leaped above the surface; it rose majestic and terrible from the depths; I could hear it in a dense wood at my right, the murmur of it rising and falling in ceaseless volumes of sound, riven at intervals by a horrid scream or a thunderous roar which shook the earth; and always I was haunted by that inexplicable sensation that unseen eyes were watching me, that soundless feet dogged my trail. I am neither nervous nor high-strung; but the burden of responsibility upon me weighed heavily, so that I was more cautious than is my wont. I turned often to right and left and rear lest I be surprised, and I carried my rifle at the ready in my hand. Once I could have sworn that among the many creatures dimly perceived amidst the shadows of the wood I saw a human figure dart from one cover to another, but I could not be sure.

For the most part I skirted the wood, making occasional detours rather than enter those forbidding depths of gloom, though many times I was forced to pass through arms of the forest which extended to the very shore of the inland sea. There was so sinister a suggestion in the uncouth sounds and the vague glimpses of moving things within the forest, of the menace of strange beasts and possibly still stranger men, that I always breathed more freely when I had passed once more into open country.

I had traveled northward for perhaps an hour, still haunted by the conviction that I was being stalked by some creature which kept always just hidden among the trees and shrubbery to my right and a little to my rear, when for the hundredth time I was attracted by a sound from that direction, and turning, saw some animal running rapidly through the forest toward me. There was no longer any effort on its part at concealment; it came on through the underbrush swiftly, and I was confident that whatever it was, it had finally gathered the courage to charge me boldly. Before it finally broke into plain view, I became aware that it was not alone, for a few yards in its rear a second thing thrashed through the leafy jungle. Evidently I was to be attacked in force by a pair of hunting beasts or men.

And then through the last clump of waving ferns broke the figure of the foremost creature, which came leaping toward me on light feet as I stood with my rifle to my shoulder covering the point at which I had expected it would emerge. I must have looked foolish indeed if my surprise and consternation were in any way reflected upon my countenance as I lowered my rifle and gazed incredulous at the lithe figure of the girl speeding swiftly in my direction. But I did not have long to stand thus with lowered weapon, for as she came, I saw her cast an affrighted glance over her shoulder, and at the same moment there broke from the jungle at the same spot at which I had seen her, the hugest cat I had ever looked upon.

At first I took the beast for a saber-tooth tiger, as it was quite the most fearsome-appearing beast one could imagine; but it was not that dread monster of the past, though quite formidable enough to satisfy the most fastidious thrill-hunter. On it came, grim and terrible, its baleful eyes glaring above its distended jaws, its lips curled in a frightful snarl which exposed a whole mouthful of formidable teeth. At sight of me it had abandoned its impetuous rush and was now sneaking slowly toward us; while the girl, a long knife in her hand, took her stand bravely at my left and a little to my rear. She had called something to me in a strange tongue as she raced toward me, and now she spoke again; but what she said I could not then, of course, know —only that her tones were sweet, well modulated and free from any suggestion of panic.

Facing the huge cat, which I now saw was an enormous panther, I waited until I could place a shot where I felt it would do the most good, for at best a frontal shot at any of the large carnivora is a ticklish matter. I had some advantage in that the beast was not charging; its head was held low and its back exposed; and so at forty yards I took careful aim at its spine at the junction of neck and shoulders. But at the same instant, as though sensing my intention, the great creature lifted its head and leaped forward in full charge. To fire at that sloping forehead I knew would be worse than useless, and so I quickly shifted my aim and pulled the trigger, hoping against hope that the soft-nosed bullet and the heavy charge of powder would have sufficient stopping effect to give me time to place a second shot.

In answer to the report of the rifle I had the satisfaction of seeing the brute spring into the air, turning a complete somersault; but it was up again almost instantly, though in the brief second that it took it to scramble to its feet and get its bearings, it exposed its left side fully toward me, and a second bullet went crashing through its heart. Down it went for the second time— and then up and at me. The vitality of these creatures of Caspak is one of the marvelous features of this strange world and bespeaks the low nervous organization of the old paleolithic life which has been so long extinct in other portions of the world.

I put a third bullet into the beast at three paces, and then I thought that I was done for; but it rolled over and stopped at my feet, stone dead. I found that my second bullet had torn its heart almost completely away, and yet it had lived to charge ferociously upon me, and but for my third shot would doubtless have slain me before it finally expired—or as Bowen Tyler so quaintly puts it, before it knew that it was dead.

With the panther quite evidently conscious of the fact that dissolution had overtaken it, I turned toward the girl, who was regarding me with evident admiration and not a little awe, though I must admit that my rifle claimed quite as much of her attention as did I. She was quite the most wonderful animal that I have ever looked upon, and what few of her charms her apparel hid, it quite effectively succeeded in accentuating. A bit of soft, undressed leather was caught over her left shoulder and beneath her right breast, falling upon her left side to her hip and upon the right to a metal band which encircled her leg above the knee and to which the lowest point of the hide was attached. About her waist was a loose leather belt, to the center of which was attached the scabbard belonging to her knife. There was a single armlet between her right shoulder and elbow, and a series of them covered her left forearm from elbow to wrist. These, I learned later, answer the purpose of a shield against knife attack when the left arm is raised in guard across the breast or face.

Her masses of heavy hair were held in place by a broad metal band which bore a large triangular ornament directly in the center of her forehead. This ornament appeared to be a huge turquoise, while the metal of all her ornaments was beaten, virgin gold, inlaid in intricate design with bits of mother-of-pearl and tiny pieces of stone of various colors. From the left shoulder depended a leopard's tail, while her feet were shod with sturdy little sandals. The knife was her only weapon. Its blade was of iron, the grip was wound with hide and protected by a guard of three out-bowing strips of flat iron, and upon the top of the hilt was a knob of gold.

I took in much of this in the few seconds during which we stood facing each other, and I also observed another salient feature of her appearance: she was frightfully dirty! Her face and limbs and garment were streaked with mud and perspiration, and yet even so, I felt that I had never looked upon so perfect and beautiful a creature as she. Her figure beggars description, and equally so, her face. Were I one of these writer-fellows, I should probably say that her features were Grecian, but being neither a writer nor a poet I can do her greater justice by saying that she combined all of the finest lines that one sees in the typical American girl's face rather than the pronounced sheeplike physiognomy of the Greek goddess. No, even the dirt couldn't hide that fact; she was beautiful beyond compare.

As we stood looking at each other, a slow smile came to her face, parting her symmetrical lips and disclosing a row of strong white teeth.

"*Galu?*" she asked with rising inflection.

And remembering that I read in Bowen's manuscript that Galu seemed to indicate a higher type of man, I answered by pointing to myself and repeating the word. Then she started off on a regular catechism, if I could judge by her inflection, for I certainly understood no word of what she said. All the time the girl kept glancing toward the forest, and at last she touched my arm and pointed in that direction.

Turning, I saw a hairy figure of a manlike thing standing watching us, and presently another and another emerged from the jungle and joined the leader until there must have been at least twenty of them. They were entirely naked. Their bodies were covered with hair, and though they stood upon their feet without touching their hands to the ground, they had a very apelike appearance, since they stooped forward and had very long arms and quite apish features. They were not pretty to look upon with their close-set eyes, flat noses, long upper lips and pro-truding yellow fangs.

"*Alus!*" said the girl.

I had reread Bowen's adventures so often that I knew them almost by heart, and so I now knew that I was looking upon the last remnant of that ancient man-race—the Alus of a forgotten period—the speechless man of antiquity.

"*Kazor!*" cried the girl, and at the same moment the Alus came jabbering toward us. They made strange growling, barking noises, as with much baring of fangs they advanced upon us. They were armed only with nature's weapons—powerful muscles and giant fangs; yet I knew that these were quite sufficient to overcome us had we nothing better to offer in defense, and so I drew my pistol and fired at the leader. He dropped like a stone, and the others turned and fled. Once again the girl smiled her slow smile and stepping closer, caressed the barrel of my automatic. As she did so, her fingers came in contact with mine, and a sudden thrill ran through me, which I attributed to the fact that it had been so long since I had seen a woman of any sort or kind.

She said something to me in her low, liquid tones; but I could not understand her, and then she pointed toward the north and started away. I followed her, for my way was north too; but had it been south I still should have followed, so hungry was I for human companionship in this world of beasts and reptiles and half-men.

We walked along, the girl talking a great deal and seeming mystified that I could not understand her. Her silvery laugh rang merrily when I in turn essayed to speak to her, as though my language was the quaintest thing she ever had heard. Often after fruitless attempts to make me understand she would hold her palm toward me, saying, *"Galu!"* and then touch my breast or arm and cry, *"Alu, alu!"* I knew what she meant, for I had learned from Bowen's narrative the negative gesture and the two words which she repeated. She meant that I was no Galu, as I claimed, but an Alu, or speechless one. Yet every time she said this she laughed again, and so infectious were her tones that I could only join her. It was only natural, too, that she should be mystified by my inability to comprehend her or to make her comprehend me, for from the club-men, the lowest human type in Caspak to have speech, to the golden race of Galus, the tongues of the various tribes are identical except for amplifications in the rising scale of evolution. She, who is a Galu, can understand one of the Bo-lu and make herself understood to him, or to a hatchet-man, a spear-man or an archer. The Ho-lus, or apes, the Alus and myself were the only creatures of human semblance with which she could hold no converse; yet it was evident that her intelligence told her that I was neither Ho-lu nor Alu, neither anthropoid ape nor speechless man.

Yet she did not despair, but set out to teach me her language; and had it not been that I worried so greatly over the fate of Bowen and my companions of the *Toreador,* I could have wished the period of instruction prolonged.

I never have been what one might call a ladies' man, though I like their company immensely, and during my college days and since have made various friends among the sex. I think that I rather appeal to a certain type of girl for the reason that I never make love to them; I leave that to the numerous others who do it infinitely better than I could hope to, and take my pleasure

Then she pointed toward the North, and started
away.

out of girls' society in what seem to be more rational ways—dancing, golfing, boating, riding, tennis, and the like. Yet in the company of this half-naked little savage I found a new pleasure that was entirely distinct from any that I ever had experienced. When she touched me, I thrilled as I had never before thrilled in contact with another woman. I could not quite understand it, for I am sufficiently sophisticated to know that this is a symptom of love and I certainly did not love this filthy little barbarian with her broken, unkempt nails and her skin so besmeared with mud and the green of crushed foliage that it was difficult to say what color it originally had been. But if she was outwardly uncouth, her clear eyes and strong white, even teeth, her silvery laugh and her queenly carriage, bespoke an innate fineness which dirt could not quite successfully conceal.

The sun was low in the heavens when we came upon a little river which emptied into a large bay at the foot of low cliffs. Our journey so far had been beset with constant danger, as is every journey in this frightful land. I have not bored you with a recital of the wearying successions of attacks by the multitude of creatures which were constantly crossing our path or deliberately stalking us. We were always upon the alert; for here, to paraphrase, eternal vigilance is indeed the price of life.

I had managed to progress a little in the acquisition of a knowledge of her tongue, so that I knew many of the animals and reptiles by their Caspakian names, and trees and ferns and grasses. I knew the words for *sea* and *river* and *cliff*, for *sky* and *sun* and *cloud*. Yes, I was getting along finely, and then it occurred to me that I didn't know my companion's name; so I pointed to myself and said, "Tom," and to her and raised my eyebrows in interrogation. The girl ran her fingers into that mass of hair and looked puzzled. I repeated the action a dozen times.

"Tom," she said finally in that clear, sweet, liquid voice. "Tom!"

I had never thought much of my name before; but when she spoke it, it sounded to me for the first time in my life like a mighty nice name, and then she brightened suddenly and tapped her own breast and said: "Ajor!"

"Ajor!" I repeated, and she laughed and struck her palms together.

Well, we knew each other's names now, and that was some satisfaction. I rather liked hers—Ajor! And she seemed to like mine, for she repeated it.

So we came to the cliffs beside the little river where it empties into the bay with the great inland sea beyond. The cliffs were weather-worn and rotted, and in one place a deep hollow ran back beneath the overhanging stone for several feet, suggesting shelter for the night. There were loose rocks strewn all about with which I might build a barricade across the entrance to the cave, and so I halted there and pointed out the place to Ajor, trying to make her understand that we would spend the night here.

As soon as she grasped my meaning, she assented with the Caspakian equivalent of an affirmative nod, and then touching my rifle, motioned me to follow her to the river. At the bank she paused, removed her belt and dagger, dropping them to the ground at her side; then unfastening the lower edge of her garment from the metal leg-band to which it was attached, slipped it off her left shoulder and let it drop to the ground around her feet. It was done so naturally, so simply and so quickly that it left me gasping like a fish out of water. Turning, she flashed a smile at me and then dived into the river, and there she bathed while I stood guard over her. For five or ten minutes she splashed about, and when she emerged her glistening skin was smooth and white and beautiful. Without means of drying herself, she simply ignored what to me would have seemed a necessity, and in a moment was arrayed in her simple though effective costume.

It was now within an hour of darkness, and as I was nearly famished, I led the way back about a quarter of a mile to a low meadow where we had seen antelope and small horses a short time before. Here I brought down a young buck, the report of my rifle sending the balance of the herd scampering for the woods, where they were met by a chorus of hideous roars as the carnivora took advantage of their panic and leaped among them.

With my hunting-knife I removed a hind-quarter, and then we returned to camp. Here I gathered a great quantity of wood from fallen trees, Ajor helping me; but before I built a fire, I also gathered sufficient loose rock to build my barricade against the frightful terrors of the night to come.

I shall never forget the expression upon Ajor's face as she saw me strike a match and light the kindling beneath our camp-fire. It was such an expression as might transform a mortal face with awe as its owner beheld the mysterious workings of divinity. It was evident that Ajor was quite unfamiliar with modern methods of fire-making. She had thought my rifle and pistol wonderful; but these tiny slivers of wood which from a magic rub brought flame to the camp hearth were indeed miracles to her.

As the meat roasted above the fire, Ajor and I tried once again to talk; but though copiously filled with incentive, gestures and sounds, the conversation did not flourish notably. And then Ajor took up in earnest the task of teaching me her language. She commenced, as I later learned, with the simplest form of speech known to Caspak or for that matter to the world—that employed by the Bo-lu. I found it far from difficult, and even though it was a great handicap upon my instructor that she could not speak my language, she did remarkably well and demonstrated that she possessed ingenuity and intelligence of a high order.

After we had eaten, I added to the pile of firewood so that I could replenish the fire before the entrance to our barricade, believing this as good a protection against the carnivora as we could have; and then Ajor and I sat down before it, and the lesson proceeded, while from all about us came the weird and awesome noises of the Caspakian night—the moaning and the coughing and roaring of the tigers, the panthers and the lions, the barking and the dismal howling of wolf, jackal and hyaeno-don, the shrill shrieks of stricken prey and the hissing of the great reptiles; the voice of man alone was silent.

But though the voice of this choir-terrible rose and fell from far and near in all directions, reaching at times such a tremendous volume of sound that the earth shook to it, yet so engrossed was I in my lesson and in my teacher that often I was deaf to what at another time would have filled me with awe. The face and voice of the beautiful girl who leaned so eagerly toward me as she tried to explain the meaning of some word or correct my pronunciation of another quite entirely occupied my every faculty of perception. The firelight shone upon her animated features and sparkling eyes; it accentuated the graceful motions of her gesturing arms and hands; it sparkled from her white teeth and from her golden ornaments, and glistened on the smooth firmness of her perfect skin. I am afraid that often I was more occupied with admiration of this beautiful animal than with a desire for knowledge; but be that as it may, I nevertheless learned much that evening, though part of what I learned had naught to do with any new language.

Ajor seemed determined that I should speak Caspakian as quickly as possible, and I thought I saw in her desire a little of that all-feminine trait which has come down through all the ages from the first lady of the world—curiosity. Ajor desired that I should speak her tongue in order that she might satisfy a curiosity concerning me that was filling her to a point where she was in danger of bursting; of that I was positive. She was a regular little animated question-mark. She bubbled over with interrogations which were never to be satisfied unless I learned to speak her tongue. Her eyes sparkled with excitement; her hand flew in expressive gestures; her little tongue raced with time; yet all to no avail. I could say *man* and *tree* and *cliff* and *lion* and a number of other words in perfect Caspakian; but such a vocabulary was only tantalizing; it did not lend itself well to a very general conversation, and the result was that Ajor would wax so wroth that she would clench her little fists and beat me on the breast as hard as ever she could, and then she would sink back laughing as the humor of the situation captured her.

She was trying to teach me some verbs by going through the actions herself as she repeated the proper word. We were very much engrossed—so much so that we were giving no heed to what went on beyond our cave—when Ajor stopped very suddenly, crying: *"Kazor!"* Now she had been trying to teach me that *ju* meant *stop*; so when she cried *Kazor* and at the same time stopped, I thought for a moment that this was part of my lesson—for the moment I forgot that *kazor* means *beware*. I therefore repeated the word after her; but when I saw the expression in her eyes as they were directed past me and saw her point toward the entrance to the cave, I turned quickly—to see a hideous face at the small aperture leading out into the night. It was the fierce and snarling countenance of a gigantic bear. I have hunted silver-tips in the White Mountains of Arizona and thought them quite the largest and most formidable of big game; but from the appearance of the head of this awful creature I judged that the largest grizzly I had ever seen would shrink by comparison to the dimensions of a Newfoundland dog.

Our fire was just within the cave, the smoke rising through the apertures between the rocks that I had piled in such a way that they arched inward toward the cliff at the top. The opening by means of which we were to reach the outside was barricaded with a few large fragments which did not by any means close it entirely; but through the apertures thus left no large animal could gain ingress. I had depended most, however, upon our fire, feeling that none of the dangerous nocturnal beasts of prey would venture close to the flames. In this, however, I was quite

evidently in error, for the great bear stood with his nose not
a foot from the blaze, which was now low, owing to the fact that
I had been so occupied with my lesson and my teacher that I
had neglected to replenish it.

Ajor whipped out her futile little knife and pointed to my
rifle. At the same time she spoke in a quite level voice entirely
devoid of nervousness or any evidence of fear or panic. I knew
she was exhorting me to fire upon the beast; but this I did not
wish to do other than as a last resort, for I was quite sure that
even my heavy bullets would not more than further enrage
him—in which case he might easily force an entrance to our cave.

Instead of firing, I piled some more wood upon the fire, and
as the smoke and blaze arose in the beast's face, it backed away,
growling most frightfully; but I still could see two ugly points of
light blazing in the outer darkness and hear its growls rumbling
terrifically without. For some time the creature stood there
watching the entrance to our frail sanctuary while I racked my
brains in futile endeavor to plan some method of defense or
escape. I knew full well that should the bear make a determined
effort to get at us, the rocks I had piled as a barrier would come
tumbling down about his giant shoulders like a house of cards,
and that he would walk directly in upon us.

Ajor, having less knowledge of the effectiveness of firearms
than I, and therefore greater confidence in them, entreated
me to shoot the beast; but I knew that the chance that I could
stop it with a single shot was most remote, while that I should
but infuriate it was real and present; and so I waited for what
seemed an eternity, watching those devilish points of fire glaring
balefully at us, and listening to the ever-increasing volume of
those seismic growls which seemed to rumble upward from the
bowels of the earth, shaking the very cliffs beneath which we
cowered, until at last I saw that the brute was again approaching
the aperture. It availed me nothing that I piled the blaze high
with firewood, until Ajor and I were near to roasting; on came
that mighty engine of destruction until once again the hideous
face yawned its fanged yawn directly within the barrier's opening. It stood thus a moment, and then the head was withdrawn.
I breathed a sigh of relief, the thing had altered its intention
and was going on in search of other and more easily procurable
prey; the fire had been too much for it.

But my joy was short-lived, and my heart sank once again
as a moment later I saw a mighty paw insinuated into the opening—a paw as large around as a large dish-pan. Very gently the

paw toyed with the great rock that partly closed the entrance, pushed and pulled upon it and then very deliberately drew it outward and to one side. Again came the head, and this time much farther into the cavern; but still the great shoulders would not pass through the opening. Ajor moved closer to me until her shoulder touched my side, and I thought I felt a slight tremor run through her body, but otherwise she gave no indication of fear. Involuntarily I threw my left arm about her and drew her to me for an instant. It was an act of reassurance rather than a caress, though I must admit that again and even in the face of death I thrilled at the contact with her; and then I released her and threw my rifle to my shoulder, for at last I had reached the conclusion that nothing more could be gained by waiting. My only hope was to get as many shots into the creature as I could before it was upon me. Already it had torn away a second rock and was in the very act of forcing its huge bulk through the opening it had now made.

So now I took careful aim between its eyes; my right fingers closed firmly and evenly upon the small of the stock, drawing back my trigger-finger by the muscular action of the hand. The bullet could not fail to hit its mark! I held my breath lest I swerve the muzzle a hair by my breathing. I was as steady and cool as I ever had been upon a target-range, and I had the full consciousness of a perfect hit in anticipation; I knew that I could not miss. And then, as the bear surged forward toward me, the hammer fell—futilely, upon an imperfect cartridge.

Almost simultaneously I heard from without a perfectly hellish roar; the bear gave voice to a series of growls far transcending in volume and ferocity anything that he had yet essayed and at the same time backed quickly from the cave. For an instant I couldn't understand what had happened to cause this sudden retreat when his prey was practically within his clutches. The idea that the harmless clicking of the hammer had frightened him was too ridiculous to entertain. However, we had not long to wait before we could at least guess at the cause of the diversion, for from without came mingled growls and roars and the sound of great bodies thrashing about until the earth shook. The bear had been attacked in the rear by some other mighty beast, and the two were now locked in a titanic struggle for supremacy. With brief respites, during which we could hear the labored breathing of the contestants, the battle continued for the better part of an hour until the sounds of combat grew gradually less and finally ceased entirely.

At Ajor's suggestion, made by signs and a few of the words we knew in common, I moved the fire directly to the entrance to the cave so that a beast would have to pass directly through the flames to reach us, and then we sat and waited for the victor of the battle to come and claim his reward; but though we sat for a long time with our eyes glued to the opening, we saw no sign of any beast.

At last I signed to Ajor to lie down, for I knew that she must have sleep, and I sat on guard until nearly morning, when the girl awoke and insisted that I take some rest; nor would she be denied, but dragged me down as she laughingly menaced me with her knife.

CHAPTER III

When I awoke, it was daylight, and I found Ajor squatting before a fine bed of coals roasting a large piece of antelope-meat. Believe me, the sight of the new day and the delicious odor of the cooking meat filled me with renewed happiness and hope that had been all but expunged by the experience of the previous night; and perhaps the slender figure of the bright-faced girl proved also a potent restorative. She looked up and smiled at me, showing those perfect teeth, and dimpling with evident happiness—the most adorable picture that I had ever seen. I recall that it was then I first regretted that she was only a little untutored savage and so far beneath me in the scale of evolution.

Her first act was to beckon me to follow her outside, and there she pointed to the explanation of our rescue from the bear—a huge saber-tooth tiger, its fine coat and its flesh torn to ribbons, lying dead a few paces from our cave, and beside it, equally mangled, and disemboweled, was the carcass of a huge cave-bear. To have had one's life saved by a saber-tooth tiger, and in the twentieth century into the bargain, was an experience that was to say the least unique; but it had happened—I had the proof of it before my eyes.

So enormous are the great carnivora of Caspak that they must feed perpetually to support their giant thews, and the result is that they will eat the meat of any other creature and will attack anything that comes within their ken, no matter how formidable the quarry. From later observation—I mention this as worthy the attention of paleontologists and naturalists—I came to the conclusion that such creatures as the cave-bear, the cave-lion and the saber-tooth tiger, as well as the larger carnivorous reptiles make, ordinarily, two kills a day—one in the morning and one after nightfall. They immediately devour the entire carcass, after which they lie up and sleep for a few hours. Fortunately their numbers are comparatively few; otherwise there would be no other life within Caspak. It is their very voracity that keeps their numbers down to a point which permits other forms of life to persist, for even in the season of love the great males often turn upon their own mates and devour them, while both males and females occasionally devour their young. How the human and semihuman races have managed to survive during all the countless ages that these conditions must have existed here is quite beyond me.

After breakfast Ajor and I set out once more upon our northward journey. We had gone but a little distance when we were attacked by a number of apelike creatures armed with clubs. They seemed a little higher in the scale than the Alus. Ajor told me they were Bo-lu, or club-men. A revolver-shot killed one and scattered the others; but several times later during the day we were menaced by them, until we had left their country and entered that of the Sto-lu, or hatchet-men. These people were less hairy and more manlike; nor did they appear so anxious to destroy us. Rather they were curious, and followed us for some distance examining us most closely. They called out to us, and Ajor answered them; but her replies did not seem to satisfy them, for they gradually became threatening, and I think they were preparing to attack us when a small deer that had been hiding in some low brush suddenly broke cover and dashed across our front. We needed meat, for it was near one o'clock and I was getting hungry; so I drew my pistol and with a single shot dropped the creature in its tracks. The effect upon the Bo-lu was electrical. Immediately they abandoned all thoughts of war, and turning, scampered for the forest which fringed our path.

That night we spent beside a little stream in the Sto-lu country. We found a tiny cave in the rock bank, so hidden away that only chance could direct a beast of prey to it, and after we had eaten of the deer-meat and some fruit which Ajor gathered, we crawled into the little hole, and with sticks and stones which I had gathered for the purpose I erected a strong barricade inside the entrance. Nothing could reach us without swimming and wading through the stream, and I felt quite secure from attack. Our quarters were rather cramped. The ceiling was so low that we could not stand up, and the floor so narrow that it was with difficulty that we both wedged into it together; but we were very tired, and so we made the most of it; and so great was the feeling of security that I am sure I fell asleep as soon as I had stretched myself beside Ajor.

During the three days wich followed, our progress was exasperatingly slow. I doubt if we made ten miles in the entire three days. The country was hideously savage, so that we were forced to spend hours at a time in hiding from one or another of the great beasts which menaced us continually. There were fewer reptiles; but the quantity of carnivora seemed to have increased, and the reptiles that we did see were perfectly gigantic. I shall never forget one enormous specimen which we came upon browsing upon water-reeds at the edge of the great sea. It stood well over twelve feet high at the rump, its highest point, and with its enormously long tail and neck it was somewhere between seventy-five and a hundred feet in length. Its head was ridiculously small; its body was unarmored, but its great bulk gave it a most formidable appearance. My experience of Caspakian life led me to believe that the gigantic creature would but have to see us to attack us, and so I raised my rifle and at the same time drew away toward some brush which offered concealment; but Ajor only laughed, and picking up a stick, ran toward the great thing, shouting. The little head was raised high upon the long neck as the animal stupidly looked here and there in search of the author of the disturbance. At last its eyes discovered tiny little Ajor, and then she hurled the stick at the diminutive head. With a cry that sounded not unlike the bleat of a sheep, the colossal creature shuffled into the water and was soon submerged.

As I slowly recalled my collegiate studies and paleontological readings in Bowen's text-books, I realized that I had looked upon nothing less than a diplodocus of the Upper Jurassic; but how infinitely different was the true, live thing from the crude restorations of Hatcher and Holland! I had had the idea that the diplodocus was a land-animal, but evidently it is partially amphibious. I have seen several since my first encounter, and in each case the creature took to the sea for concealment as soon as it was disturbed. With the exception of its gigantic tail, it has no weapon of defense; but with this appendage it can lash so terrific a blow as to lay low even a giant cave-bear, stunned and broken. It is a stupid, simple, gentle beast—one of the few

the cliff which seemed ideal for our purpose. It opened upon a narrow ledge where we could build our cook-fire; the opening was so small that we had to lie flat and wriggle through it to gain ingress, while the interior was high-ceiled and spacious. I lighted a faggot and looked about; but as far as I could see, the chamber ran back into the cliff.

Laying aside my rifle, pistol and heavy ammunition-belt, I left Ajor in the cave while I went down to gather firewood. We already had meat and fruits which we had gathered just before reaching the cliffs, and my canteen was filled with fresh water. Therefore all we required was fuel, and as I always saved Ajor's strength when I could, I would not permit her to accompany me. The poor girl was very tired; but she would have gone with me until she dropped, I know, so loyal was she. She was the best comrade in the world, and sometimes I regretted and sometimes I was glad that she was not of my own caste, for had she been, I should unquestionably have fallen in love with her. As it was, we traveled together like two boys, with huge respect for each other but no softer sentiment.

There was little timber close to the base of the cliffs, and so I was forced to enter the wood some two hundred yards distant. I realize now how foolhardy was my act in such a land as Caspak, teeming with danger and with death; but there is a certain amount of fool in every man; and whatever proportion of it I own must have been in the ascendant that day, for the truth of the matter is that I went down into those woods absolutely defenseless; and I paid the price, as people usually do for their indiscretions. As I searched around in the brush for likely pieces of firewood, my head bowed and my eyes upon the ground, I suddenly felt a great weight hurl itself upon me. I struggled to my knees and seized my assailant, a huge, naked man—naked except for a breechcloth of snake-skin, the head hanging down to the knees. The fellow was armed with a stone-shod spear, a stone knife and a hatchet. In his black hair were several gay-colored feathers. As we struggled to and fro, I was slowly gaining advantage of him, when a score of his fellows came running up and overpowered me.

They bound my hands behind me with long rawhide thongs and then surveyed me critically. I found them fine-looking specimens of manhood, for the most part. There were some among them who bore a resemblance to the Sto-lu and were hairy; but the majority had massive heads and not unlovely features. There was little about them to suggest the ape, as in the Sto-lu, Bo-lu and Alus. I expected them to kill me at once, but they did not. Instead they questioned me; but it was evident that they did not believe my story, for they scoffed and laughed.

"The Galus have turned you out," they cried. "If you go back to them, you will die. If you remain here, you will die. We shall kill you; but first we shall have a dance and you shall dance with us—the dance of death."

It sounded quite reassuring! But I knew that I was not to be killed immediately, and so I took heart. They led me toward the cliffs, and as we approached them, I glanced up and was sure that I saw Ajor's bright eyes peering down upon us from our lofty cave; but she gave no sign if she saw me; and we passed on, rounded the end of the cliffs and proceeded along the opposite face of them until we came to a section literally honeycombed with caves. All about, upon the ground and swarming the ledges before the entrances, were hundreds of members of the tribe. There were many women but no babes or children, though I noticed that the females had better developed breasts than any that I had seen among the hatchet-men, the club-men, the Alus or the apes. In fact, among the lower orders of Caspakian man the female breast is but a rudimentary organ, barely suggested in the apes and Alus, and only a little more defined in the Bo-lu and Sto-lu, though always increasingly so until it is found about half developed in the females of the spear-men; yet never was there an indication that the females had suckled young; nor were there any young among them. Some of the Band-lu women were quite comely. The figures of all, both men and women, were symmetrical though heavy, and though there were some who verged strongly upon the Sto-lu type, there were others who were positively handsome and whose bodies were quite hairless. The Alus are all bearded, but among the Bo-lu the beard disappears in the women. The Sto-lu men show a sparse beard, the Band-lu none; and there is little hair upon the bodies of their women.

The members of the tribe showed great interest in me, especially in my clothing, the like of which, of course, they never had seen. They pulled and hauled upon me, and some of them struck me; but for the most part they were not inclined to brutality. It was only the hairier ones, who most closely resembled the Sto-lu, who maltreated me. At last my captors led me into a great cave in the mouth of which a fire was burning. The floor was littered with filth, including the bones of many animals, and the atmosphere reeked with the stench of human bodies and putrefying flesh. Here they fed me, releasing my arms, and I ate of half-cooked aurochs steak and a stew which may have been made of snakes, for many of the long, round pieces of meat suggested them most nauseatingly.

The meal completed, they led me well within the cavern, which they lighted with torches stuck in various crevices, in the light of which I saw, to my astonishment, that the walls were covered with paintings and etchings. There were aurochs, red deer, saber-tooth tiger, cave-bear, hyaenodon and many other examples of the fauna of Caspak done in colors, usually of four shades of brown, or scratched upon the surface of the rock. Often they were superimposed upon each other until it required careful examination to trace out the various outlines. But they all showed a rather remarkable aptitude for delineation which further fortified Bowen's comparisons between these people and the extinct Cro-Magnons whose ancient art is still preserved in the caverns of Niaux and Le Portel. The Band-lu, however, did not have the bow and arrow, and in this respect they differ from their extinct progenitors, or descendants, of Western Europe.

Should any of my friends chance to read the story of my adventures upon Caprona, I hope they will not be bored by these diversions, and if they are, I can only say that I am writing my memoirs principally for my own edification and therefore setting down those things which interested me particularly at the time. I have no desire that the general public should ever have access to these pages; but it is possible that my friends may, and also certain savants who are interested; and to them, while I do not apologize for my philosophizing, I humbly explain that they are witnessing the gropings of a finite mind after the infinite, the search for explanations of the inexplicable.

In a far recess of the cavern my captors bade me halt. Again my hands were secured, and this time my feet as well. During the operation they questioned me, and I was mighty glad that the marked similarity between the various tribal tongues of Caspak enabled us to understand each other perfectly, even though they were unable to believe or even to comprehend the truth of my origin and the circumstances of my advent in Caspak; and finally they left me saying that they would come for me before the dance of death upon the morrow. Before they departed with their torches, I saw that I had not been conducted to the farthest extremity of the cavern, for a dark and gloomy corridor led beyond my prison room into the heart of the cliff.

I could not but marvel at the immensity of this great underground grotto. Already I had traversed several hundred yards of it, from many points of which other corridors diverged. The whole cliff must be honeycombed with apartments and passages of which this community occupied but a comparatively small part, so that the possibility of the more remote passages being the lair of savage beasts that had other means of ingress and egress than that used by the Band-lu filled me with dire forebodings.

I believe that I am not ordinarily hysterically apprehensive; yet I must confess that under the conditions with which I was confronted, I felt my nerves to be somewhat shaken. On the morrow I was to die some sort of nameless death for the diversion of a savage horde, but the morrow held fewer terrors for me than the present, and I submit to any fair-minded man if it is not a terrifying thing to lie bound hand and foot in the Stygian blackness of an immense cave peopled by unknown dangers in a land overrun by hideous beasts and reptiles of the greatest ferocity. At any moment, perhaps at this very moment, some silent-footed beast of prey might catch my scent where it luired in some contiguous passage, and might creep stealthily upon me. I craned my neck about, and stared through the inky darkness for the twin spots of blazing hate which I knew would herald the coming of my executioner. So real were the imaginings of my overwrought brain that I broke into a cold sweat in absolute conviction that some beast was close before me; yet the hours dragged, and no sound broke the gravelike stillness of the cavern.

During that period of eternity many events of my life passed before my mental vision, a vast parade of friends and occurrences which would be blotted out forever on the morrow. I cursed myself for the foolish act which had taken me from the search-party that so depended upon me, and I wondered what progress, if any, they had made. Were they still beyond the barrier cliffs, awaiting my return? Or had they found a way into Caspak? I felt that the latter would be the truth, for the party was not made up of men easily turned from a purpose. Quite probable it was that they were already searching for me; but that they would ever find a trace of me I doubted. Long since, had I come to the conclusion that it was beyond human prowess to circle the shores of the inland sea of Caspak in the face of the myriad menaces which lurked in every shadow by day and by night. Long since, had I given up any hope of reaching the point where I had made my entry into the country, and so I was now equally convinced that our entire expedition had been worse than futile before ever it was conceived, since Bowen J. Tyler and his wife could not by any possibility have survived during all these long months; no more could Bradley and his party of seamen be yet in existence. If the superior force and equipment of my party enabled them to circle the north end of the sea, they might some day come upon the broken wreck of my plane hanging in the great tree to the south; but long before that, my bones would be added to the litter upon the floor of this mighty cavern.

And through all my thoughts, real and fanciful, moved the image of a perfect girl, clear-eyed and strong and straight and beautiful, with the carriage of a queen and the supple, undulating grace of a leopard. Though I loved my friends, their fate seemed of less importance to me than the fate of this little barbarian stranger for whom, I had convinced myself many a time, I felt no greater sentiment than passing friendship for a fellow-wayfarer in this land of horrors. Yet I so worried and fretted about her and her future that at last I quite forgot my own predicament, though I still struggled intermittently with my bonds in vain endeavor to free myself; as much, however, that I might hasten to her protection as that I might escape the fate which had been planned for me. And while I was thus engaged and had for the moment forgotten my apprehensions concerning prowling beasts, I was startled into tense silence by a distinct and unmistakable sound coming from the dark corridor farther toward the heart of the cliff—the sound of padded feet moving stealthily in my direction.

I believe that never before in all my life, even amidst the terrors of childhood nights, have I suffered such a sensation of extreme horror as I did that moment in which I realized that I must lie bound and helpless while some horrid beast of prey crept upon me to devour me in that utter darkness of the Bandlu pits of Caspak. I reeked with cold sweat, and my flesh crawled—I could feel it crawl. If ever I came nearer to abject cowardice, I do not recall the instance; and yet it was not that I was afraid to die, for I had long since given myself up as lost— a few days of Caspak must impress anyone with the utter nothingness of life. The waters, the land, the air teem with it, and always it is being devoured by some other form of life. Life is the cheapest thing in Caspak, as it is the cheapest thing on earth and, doubtless, the cheapest cosmic production. No, I was not afraid to die; in fact, I prayed for death, that I might be relieved of the frightfulness of the interval of life which remained to me—the waiting, the awful waiting, for that fearsome beast to reach me and to strike.

Presently it was so close that I could hear its breathing, and then it touched me and leaped quickly back as though it had come upon me unexpectedly. For long moments no sound broke the sepulchral silence of the cave. Then I heard a movement on the part of the creature near me, and again it touched me, and I felt something like a hairless hand pass over my face and down until it touched the collar of my flannel shirt. And then, subdued, but filled with pent emotion, a voice cried: "Tom!"

I think I nearly fainted, so great was the reaction. "Ajor!" I managed to say. "Ajor, my girl, can it be you?"

"Oh, Tom!" she cried again in a trembly little voice and flung herself upon me, sobbing softly. I had not known that Ajor could cry.

As she cut away my bonds, she told me that from the entrance to our cave she had seen the Band-lu coming out of the forest with me, and she had followed until they took me into the cave, which she had seen was upon the opposite side of the cliff in which ours was located; and then, knowing that she could do nothing for me until after the Band-lu slept, she had hastened to return to our cave. With difficulty she had reached it, after having been stalked by a cave-lion and almost seized. I trembled at the risk she had run.

It had been her intention to wait until after midnight, when most of the carnivora would have made their kills, and then attempt to reach the cave in which I was imprisoned and rescue me. She explained that with my rifle and pistol—both of which she assured me she could use, having watched me so many times—she planned upon frightening the Band-lu and forcing them to give me up. Brave little girl! She would have risked her life willingly to save me. But some time after she reached our cave she heard voices from the far recesses within, and immediately concluded that we had but found another entrance to the caves which the Band-lu occupied upon the other face of the cliff. Then she had set out through those winding passages and in total darkness had groped her way, guided solely by a marvelous sense of direction, to where I lay. She had had to proceed with utmost caution lest she fall into some abyss in the darkness, and in truth she had thrice come upon sheer drops and had been forced to take the most frightful risks to pass them. I shudder even now as I contemplate what this girl passed through for my sake and how she enhanced her peril in loading herself down with the weight of my arms and ammunition and the awkwardness of the long rifle which she was unaccustomed to bearing.

I could have knelt and kissed her hand in reverence and gratitude; nor am I ashamed to say that that is precisely what I did after I had been freed from my bonds and heard the story of her trials. Brave little Ajor! Wonder-girl out of the dim, unthinkable past! Never before had she been kissed; but she seemed to sense something of the meaning of the new caress, for she leaned forward in the dark and pressed her own lips to my forehead. A sudden urge surged through me to seize her and strain her to my bosom and cover her hot young lips with the kisses of a real love, but I did not do so, for I knew that I did not love her; and to have kissed her thus, with passion, would have been to inflict a great wrong upon her who had offered her life for mine.

No, Ajor should be as safe with me as with her own mother, if she had one, which I was inclined to doubt, even though she told me that she had once been a babe and hidden by her mother. I had come to doubt if there was such a thing as a mother in Caspak, a mother such as we know. From the Bo-lu to the Kro-lu there is no word which corresponds with our word *mother*. They speak of *ata* and *cor sva jo,* meaning *reproduction* and *from the beginning*, and point toward the south; but no one has a mother.

After considerable difficulty we gained what we thought was our cave, only to find that it was not, and then we realized that we were lost in the labyrinthine mazes of the great cavern. We retraced our steps and sought the point from which we had started, but only succeeded in losing ourselves the more. Ajor was aghast—not so much from fear of our predicament; but that she should have failed in the functioning of that wonderful sense she possessed in common with most other creatures Caspakian, which makes it possible for them to move unerringly from place to place without compass or guide.

Hand in hand we crept along, searching for an opening into the outer world, yet realizing that at each step we might be burrowing more deeply into the heart of the great cliff, or circling futilely in the vague wandering that could end only in death. And the darkness! It was almost palpable, and utterly depressing. I had matches, and in some of the more difficult

places I struck one; but we couldn't afford to waste them, and so
we groped our way slowly along, doing the best we could to
keep to one general direction in the hope that it would eventually lead us to an opening into the outer world. When I struck
matches, I noticed that the walls bore no paintings; nor was
there other sign that man had penetrated this far within the
cliff, nor any spoor of animals of other kinds.

It would be difficult to guess at the time we spent wandering
through those black corridors, climbing steep ascents, feeling
our way along the edges of bottomless pits, never knowing at
what moment we might be plunged into some abyss and always haunted by the ever-present terror of death by starvation
and thirst. As difficult as it was, I still realized that it might
have been infinitely worse had I had another companion than
Ajor—courageous, uncomplaining, loyal little Ajor! She was tired
and hungry and thirsty, and she must have been discouraged;
but she never faltered in her cheerfulness. I asked her if she
was afraid, and she replied that here the Wieroo could not get
her, and that if she died of hunger, she would at least die with
me, and she was quite content that such should be her end. At
the time I attributed her attitude to something akin to a dog-
like devotion to a new master who had been kind to her. I can
take oath to the fact that I did not think it was anything more.

Whether we had been imprisoned in the cliff for a day or a
week I could not say; nor even now do I know. We became very
tired and hungry; the hours dragged; we slept at least twice, and
then we rose and stumbled on, always weaker and weaker.
There were ages during which the trend of the corridors was
always upward. It was heartbreaking work for people in the
state of exhaustion in which we then were, but we clung tenaciously to it. We stumbled and fell; we sank through pure
physical inability to retain our feet; but always we managed to
rise at last and go on. At first, wherever it had been possible,
we had walked hand in hand lest we become separated, and later,
when I saw that Ajor was weakening rapidly, we went side by
side, I supporting her with an arm about her waist. I still retained the heavy burden of my armament; but with the rifle
slung to my back, my hands were free. When I too showed indisputable evidences of exhaustion, Ajor suggested that I lay
aside my arms and ammunition; but I told her that as it would
mean certain death for me to traverse Caspak without them, I
might as well take the chance of dying here in the cave with

them, for there was the other chance that we might find our way to liberty.

There came a time when Ajor could no longer walk, and then it was that I picked her up in my arms and carried her. She begged me to leave her, saying that after I found an exit, I could come back and get her; but she knew, and she knew that I knew, that if ever I did leave her, I could never find her again. Yet she insisted. I barely had sufficient strength to take a score of steps at a time; then I would have to sink down and rest for five or ten minutes. I don't know what force urged me on and kept me going in the face of an absolute conviction that my efforts were utterly futile. I counted us already as good as dead; but still I dragged myself along until the time came that I could no longer rise, but could only crawl along a few inches at a time, dragging Ajor beside me. Her sweet voice, now almost inaudible from weakness, implored me to abandon her and save myself— she seemed to think only of me. Of course I couldn't have left her there alone, no matter how much I might have desired to do so; but the fact of the matter was that I didn't desire to leave her. What I said to her then came very simply and naturally to my lips. It couldn't very well have been otherwise, I imagine, for with death so close, I doubt if people are much inclined to heroics. "I would rather not get out at all, Ajor," I said to her, "than to get out without you." We were resting against a rocky wall, and Ajor was leaning against me, her head on my breast. I could feel her press closer to me, and one hand stroked my arm in a weak caress; but she didn't say anything, nor were words necessary.

After a few minutes' more rest, we started on again upon our utterly hopeless way; but I soon realized that I was weakening rapidly, and presently I was forced to admit that I was through. "It's no use, Ajor," I said, "I've come as far as I can. It may be that if I sleep, I can go on again after;" but I knew that that was not true, and that the end was near. "Yes, sleep," said Ajor. "We will sleep together—forever."

She crept close to me as I lay on the hard floor and pillowed her head upon my arm. With the little strength which remained to me, I drew her up until our lips touched, and then I whispered: "Good-bye!" I must have lost consciousness almost immediately, for I recall nothing more until I suddenly awoke out of a troubled sleep, during which I dreamed that I was drowning, to find the cave lighted by what appeared to be diffused daylight, and a tiny trickle of water running down the corridor and forming a puddle in the little depression in which it chanced that Ajor and I lay. I turned my eyes quickly upon Ajor, fearful for what the light might disclose; but she still breathed, though very faintly. Then I searched about for an explanation of the light, and soon discovered that it came from about a bend in the corridor just ahead of us and at the top of a steep incline; and instantly I realized that Ajor and I had stumbled by night almost to the portal of salvation. Had chance taken us a few yards further, up either of the corridors which diverged from ours just ahead of us, we might have been irrevocably lost; we might still be lost; but at least we could die in the light of day, out of the horrid blackness of this terrible cave.

I tried to rise, and found that sleep had given me back a portion of my strength; and then I tasted the water and was further refreshed. I shook Ajor gently by the shoulder; but she did not open her eyes, and then I gathered a few drops of water in my cupped palm and let them trickle between her lips. This revived her so that she raised her lids, and when she saw me, she smiled.

"What happened?" she asked. "Where are we?"

"We are at the end of the corridor," I replied, "and daylight is coming in from the outside world just ahead. We are saved, Ajor!"

She sat up then and looked about, and then, quite womanlike, she burst into tears. It was the reaction, of course; and then too, she was very weak. I took her in my arms and quieted her as best I could, and finally, with my help, she got to her feet; for she, as well as I, had found some slight recuperation in sleep. Together we staggered upward toward the light, and at the first turn we saw an opening a few yards ahead of us and a leaden sky beyond—a leaden sky from which was falling a drizzling rain, the author of our little, trickling stream which had given us drink when we were most in need of it.

The cave had been damp and cold; but as we crawled through the aperture, the muggy warmth of the Caspakian air caressed and comforted us; even the rain was warmer than the atmosphere of those dank corridors. We had water now, and warmth, and I was sure that Caspak would soon offer us meat or fruit; but as we came to where we could look about, we saw that we were upon the summit of the cliffs, where there seemed little reason to expect game. However, there were trees, and among them we soon descried edible fruits with which we broke our long fast.

CHAPTER IV

WE SPENT two days upon the cliff-top, resting and recuperating. There was some small game which gave us meat, and the little pools of rainwater were sufficient to quench our thirst. The sun came out a few hours after we emerged from the cave, and in its warmth we soon cast off the gloom which our recent experiences had saddled upon us.

Upon the morning of the third day we set out to search for a path down to the valley. Below us, to the north, we saw a large pool lying at the foot of the cliffs, and in it we could discern the women of the Band-lu lying in the shallow waters, while beyond and close to the base of the mighty barrier-cliffs there was a large party of Band-lu warriors going north to hunt. We had a splendid view from our lofty cliff-top. Dimly, to the west, we could see the farther shore of the inland sea, and southwest the large southern island loomed distinctly before us. A little east of north was the northern island, which Ajor, shuddering, whispered was the home of the Wieroo—the land of Oo-oh. It lay at the far end of the lake and was barely visible to us, being fully sixty miles away.

From our elevation, and in a clearer atmosphere, it would have stood out distinctly; but the air of Caspak is heavy with moisture, with the result that distant objects are blurred and indistinct. Ajor also told me that the mainland east of Oo-oh was her land—the land of the Galu. She pointed out the cliffs at its southern boundary, which mark the frontier, south of which lies the country of Kro-lu—the archers. We now had but to pass through the balance of the Band-lu territory and that of the Kro-lu to be within the confines of her own land; but that meant traversing thirty-five miles of hostile country filled with every imaginable terror, and possibly many beyond the powers of imagination. I would certainly have given a lot for my plane at that moment, for with it, twenty minutes would have landed us within the confines of Ajor's country.

We finally found a place where we could slip over the edge of the cliff onto a narrow ledge which seemed to give evidence of being something of a game-path to the valley, though it apparently had not been used for some time. I lowered Ajor

at the end of my rifle and then slid over myself, and I am free
to admit that my hair stood on end during the process, for the
drop was considerable and the ledge appallingly narrow, with
a frightful drop sheer below down to the rocks at the base
of the cliff; but with Ajor there to catch and steady me, I made
it all right, and then we set off down the trail toward the valley.
There were two or three more bad places, but for the most
part it was an easy descent, and we came to the highest of
the Band-lu caves without further trouble. Here we went
more slowly, lest we should be set upon by some member of the
tribe.

We must have passed about half the Band-lu cave-levels
before we were accosted, and then a huge fellow stepped out in
front of me, barring our further progress.

"Who are you?" he asked; and then he recognized me and I
him, for he had been one of those who had led me back into
the cave and bound me the night that I had been captured.
From me his gaze went to Ajor. He was a fine-looking man with
clear, intelligent eyes, a good forehead and superb physique—
by far the highest type of Caspakian I had yet seen, barring
Ajor, of course.

"You are a true Galu," he said to Ajor, "but this man is of
a different mold. He has the face of a Galu, but his weapons
and the strange skins he wears upon his body are not of the
Galus nor of Caspak. Who is he?"

"He is Tom," replied Ajor succinctly.

"There is no such people," asserted the Band-lu quite truth-
fully, toying with his spear in a most suggestive manner.

"My name is Tom," I explained, "and I am from a country
beyond Caspak." I thought it best to propitiate him if possible,
because of the necessity of conserving ammunition as well as to
avoid the loud alarm of a shot which might bring other Band-lu
warriors upon us. "I am from America, a land of which you
never heard, and I am seeking others of my countrymen who
are in Caspak and from whom I am lost. I have no quarrel
with you or your people. Let us go our way in peace."

"You are going there?" he asked, and pointed toward the
north.

"I am," I replied.

He was silent for several minutes, apparently weighing some
thought in his mind. At last he spoke. "What is that?" he asked.
"And what is that?" He pointed first to my rifle and then to my
pistol.

"They are weapons," I replied, "weapons which kill at a great distance." I pointed to the women in the pool beneath us. "With this," I said, tapping my pistol, "I could kill as many of those women as I cared to, without moving a step from where we now stand."

He looked his incredulity, but I went on. "And with this"— I weighed my rifle at the balance in the palm of my right hand —"I could slay one of those distant warriors." And I waved my left hand toward the tiny figures of the hunters far to the north.

The fellow laughed. "Do it," he cried derisively, "and then it may be that I shall believe the balance of your strange story."

"But I do not wish to kill any of them," I replied. "Why should I?"

"Why not?" he insisted. "They would have killed you when they had you prisoner. They would kill you now if they could get their hands on you, and they would eat you into the bargain. But I know why you do not try it—it is because you have spoken lies; your weapon will not kill at a great distance. It is only a queerly wrought club. For all I know, you are nothing more than a lowly Bo-lu."

"Why should you wish me to kill your own people?" I asked.

"They are no longer my people," he replied proudly. "Last night, in the very middle of the night, the call came to me. Like that it came into my head"—and he struck his hands together smartly once—"that I had risen. I have been waiting for it and expecting it for a long time; today I am a Kro-lu. Today I go out into the *coslupak*" (unpeopled country, or literally, no man's land) "between the Band-lu and the Kro-lu, and there I fashion my bow and my arrows and my shield; there I hunt the red deer for the leathern jerkin which is the badge of my new estate. When these things are done, I can go to the chief of the Kro-lu, and he dare not refuse me. That is why you may kill those low Band-lu if you wish to live, for I am in a hurry."

"But why do you wish to kill me?" I asked.

He looked puzzled and finally gave it up. "I do not know," he admitted. "It is the way in Caspak. If we do not kill, we shall be killed, therefore it is wise to kill first whomever does not belong to one's own people. This morning I hid in my cave till the others were gone upon the hunt, for I knew that they would know at once that I had become a Kro-lu and would kill me. They will kill me if they find me in the *coslupak;*

so will the Kro-lu if they come upon me before I have won my Kro-lu weapons and jerkin. You would kill me if you could, and that is the reason I know that you speak lies when you say that your weapons will kill at a great distance. Would they, you would long since have killed me. Come! I have no more time to waste in words. I will spare the woman and take her with me to the Kro-lu, for she is comely." And with that he advanced upon me with raised spear.

My rifle was at my hip at the ready. He was so close that I did not need to raise it to my shoulder, having but to pull the trigger to send him into Kingdom Come whenever I chose; but yet I hesitated. It was difficult to bring myself to take a human life. I could feel no enmity toward this savage barbarian who acted almost as wholly upon instinct as might a wild beast, and to the last moment I was determined to seek some way to avoid what now seemed inevitable. Ajor stood at my shoulder, her knife ready in her hand and a sneer on her lips at his suggestion that he would take her with him.

Just as I thought I should have to fire, a chorus of screams broke from the women beneath us. I saw the man halt and glance downward, and following his example my eyes took in the panic and its cause. The women had, evidently, been quitting the pool and slowly returning toward the caves, when they were confronted by a monstrous cave-lion which stood directly between them and their cliffs in the center of the narrow path that led down to the pool among the tumbled rocks. Screaming, the women were rushing madly back to the pool.

"It will do them no good," remarked the man, a trace of excitement in his voice. "It will do them no good, for the lion will wait until they come out and take as many as he can carry away; and there is one there," he added, a trace of sadness in his tone, "whom I hoped would soon follow me to the Kro-lu. Together have we come up from the beginning." He raised his spear above his head and poised it ready to hurl downward at the lion. "She is nearest to him," he muttered. "He will get her and she will never come to me among the Kro-lu, or ever thereafter. It is useless! No warrior lives who could hurl a weapon so great a distance."

But even as he spoke, I was leveling my rifle upon the great brute below; and as he ceased speaking, I squeezed the trigger. My bullet must have struck to a hair the point at which I had aimed, for it smashed the brute's spine back of his shoulders and tore on through his heart, dropping him dead in his tracks. For a moment the women were as terrified by the report of the rifle as they had been by the menace of the lion; but when they saw that the loud noise had evidently destroyed their enemy, they came creeping cautiously back to examine the carcass.

The man, toward whom I had immediately turned after firing, lest he should pursue his threatened attack, stood staring at me in amazement and admiration.

"Why," he asked, "if you could do that, did you not kill me long before?"

"I told you," I replied, "that I had no quarrel with you. I do not care to kill men with whom I have no quarrel."

But he could not seem to get the idea through his head. "I can believe now that you are not of Caspak," he admitted, "for no Caspakian would have permitted such an opportunity to escape him." This, however, I found later to be an exaggeration, as the tribes of the west coast and even the Kro-lu of the east coast are far less bloodthirsty than he would have had me believe. "And your weapon!" he continued. "You spoke true words when I thought you spoke lies." And then, suddenly: "Let us be friends!"

I turned to Ajor. "Can I trust him?" I asked.

"Yes," she replied. "Why not? Has he not asked to be friends?"

I was not at the time well enough acquainted with Caspakian ways to know that truthfulness and loyalty are two of the strongest characteristics of these primitive people. They are not sufficiently cultured to have become adepts in hypocrisy, treason and dissimulation. There are, of course, a few exceptions.

"We can go north together," continued the warrior. "I will fight for you, and you can fight for me. Until death will I serve you, for you have saved So-al, whom I had given up as dead." He threw down his spear and covered both his eyes with the palms of his two hands. I looked inquiringly toward Ajor, who explained as best she could that this was the form of the Caspakian oath of allegiance. "You need never fear him after this," she concluded.

"What should I do?" I asked.

"Take his hands down from before his eyes and return his spear to him," she explained.

I did as she bade, and the man seemed very pleased. I then asked what I should have done had I not wished to accept his friendship. They told me that had I walked away, the moment that I was out of sight of the warrior we would have become deadly enemies again. "But I could so easily have killed him as he stood there defenseless!" I exclaimed.

"Yes," replied the warrior, "but no man with good sense blinds his eyes before one whom he does not trust."

It was rather a decent compliment, and it taught me just how much I might rely on the loyalty of my new friend. I was glad to have him with us, for he knew the country and was evidently a fearless warrior. I wished that I might have recruited a battalion like him.

As the women were now approaching the cliffs, To-mar the warrior suggested that we make our way to the valley before they could intercept us, as they might attempt to detain us and were almost certain to set upon Ajor. So we hastened down the narrow path, reaching the foot of the cliffs but a short distance ahead of the women. They called after us to stop; but we kept on at a rapid walk, not wishing to have any trouble with them, which could only result in the deaths of some of them.

We had proceeded about a mile when we heard some one behind us calling To-mar by name, and when we stopped and looked around, we saw a woman running rapidly toward us. As she approached nearer, I could see that she was a very comely creature, and like all her sex that I had seen in Caspak, apparently young.

"It is So-al!" exclaimed To-mar. "Is she mad that she follows me thus?"

In another moment the young woman stopped, panting, before us. She paid not the slightest attention to Ajor or me; but devouring To-mar with her sparkling eyes, she cried: "I have risen! I have risen!"

"So-al!" was all that the man could say.

"Yes," she went on, "the call came to me just before I quit the pool; but I did not know that it had come to you. I can see it in your eyes, To-mar, my To-mar! We shall go on together!" And she threw herself into his arms.

It was a very affecting sight, for it was evident that these two had been mates for a long time and that they had each thought that they were about to be separated by that strange law of evolution which holds good in Caspak and which was slowly unfolding before my incredulous mind. I did not then comprehend even a tithe of the wondrous process, which goes on eternally within the confines of Caprona's barrier cliffs nor am I any too sure that I do even now.

To-mar explained to So-al that it was I who had killed the cave-lion and saved her life, and that Ajor was my woman and thus entitled to the same loyalty which was my due.

At first Ajor and So-al were like a couple of stranger cats on a back fence but soon they began to accept each other under something of an armed truce, and later became fast friends. So-al was a mighty fine-looking girl, built like a tigress as to strength and sinuosity, but withal sweet and womanly. Ajor and I came to be very fond of her, and she was, I think, equally fond of us. To-mar was very much of a man—a savage, if you will, but none the less a man.

Finding that traveling in company with To-mar made our journey both easier and safer, Ajor and I did not continue on our way alone while the novitiates delayed their approach to the Kro-lu country in order that they might properly fit themselves in the matter of arms and apparel, but remained with them. Thus we became well acquainted—to such an extent that we looked forward with regret to the day when they took their places among their new comrades and we should be forced to continue upon our way alone. It was a matter of much concern to To-mar that the Kro-lu would undoubtedly not receive Ajor and me in a friendly manner, and that consequently we should have to avoid these people.

It would have been very helpful to us could we have made friends with them, as their country abutted directly upon that of the Galus. Their friendship would have meant that Ajor's dangers were practically passed, and that I had accomplished fully one-half of my long journey. In view of what I had passed through, I often wondered what chance I had to complete that journey in search of my friends. The further south I should travel on the west side of the island, the more frightful would the dangers become as I neared the stamping-grounds of the more hideous reptilia and the haunts of the Alus and the Ho-lu, all of which were at the southern half of the island; and then if I should not find the members of my party, what was to become of me? I could not live for long in any portion of Caspak with which I was familiar; the moment my ammunition was exhausted, I should be as good as dead.

There was a chance that the Galus would receive me; but even Ajor could not say definitely whether they would or no, and even provided that they would, could I retrace my steps from *the beginning*, after failing to find my own people, and return to the far nothern land of Galus? I doubted it. However, I was learning from Ajor, who was more or less of a fatalist, a philosophy which was as necessary in Caspak to peace of mind as is faith to the devout Christian of the outer world.

CHAPTER V

WE WERE sitting before a little fire inside a safe grotto one night shortly after we had quit the cliff-dwellings of the Band-lu, when So-al raised a question which it had never occurred to me to propound to Ajor. She asked her why she had left her own people and how she had come so far south as the country of the Alus, where I had found her.

At first Ajor hesitated to explain; but at last she consented, and for the first time I heard the complete story of her origin and experiences. For my benefit she entered into greater detail of explanation than would have been necessary had I been a native Caspakian.

"I am a *cos-ata-lo*," commenced Ajor, and then she turned toward me. "A *cos-ata-lo*, my Tom, is a woman" (*lo*) "who did not come from an egg and thus on up *from the beginning*" (*cor sva jo*). "I was a babe at my mother's breast. Only among the Galus are such, and then but infrequently. The Wieroo get most of us; but my mother hid me until I had attained such size that the Wieroo could not readily distinguish me from one who had come up from the beginning. I knew both my mother and my father, as only such as I may. My father is high chief among the Galus. His name is Jor, and both he and my mother came up from the beginning; but one of them, probably my mother, had completed the seven cycles" (approximately seven hundred years), "with the result that their offspring might be *cos-ata-lo*, or born as are all the children of your race, my Tom, as you tell me is the fact. I was therefore apart from my fellows in that my children would probably be as I, of a higher state of evolution, and so I was sought by the men of my people; but none of them appealed to me. I cared for none. The most persistent was Du-seen, a huge warrior of whom my father stood in considerable fear, since it was quite possible that Du-seen could wrest from him his chieftainship of the Galus. He has a large following of the newer Galus, those most recently come up from the Kro-lu, and as this class is usually much more powerful numerically than the older Galus, and as Du-seen's ambition knows no bounds, we have for a long time been expecting him to find some excuse for a break with Jor the High Chief, my father.

"A further complication lay in the fact that Du-seen wanted me, while I would have none of him, and then came evidence to my father's ears that he was in league with the Wieroo; a hunter, returning late at night, came trembling to my father, saying that he had seen Du-seen talking with a Wieroo in a lonely spot far from the village, and that plainly he had heard the words: 'If you will help me, I will help you—I will deliver into your hands all *cos-ata-lo* among the Galus, now and hereafter; but for that service you must slay Jor the High Chief and bring terror and confusion to his followers.'

"Now, when my father heard this, he was angry; but he was also afraid—afraid for me, who am *cos-ata-lo*. He called me to him and told me what he had heard, pointing out two ways in which we might frustrate Du-seen. The first was that I go to Du-seen as his mate, after which he would be loath to give me into the hands of the Wieroo or to further abide by the wicked compact he had made—a compact which would doom his own offspring, who would doubtless be as am I, their mother. The alternative was flight until Du-seen should have been overcome and punished. I chose the latter and fled toward the south. Beyond the confines of the Galu country is little danger from the Wieroo, who seek ordinarily only Galus of the highest orders. There are two excellent reasons for this: One is that from the beginning of time jealousy has existed between the Wieroo and the Galus as to which constituted the higher order and therefore which would eventually dominate the world. It seems generally conceded that that race which first reaches a point of evolution which permits them to produce young of their own species and of both sexes must dominate all other creatures. The Wieroo first began to produce their own kind—after which evolution from Galu to Wieroo ceased gradually until now it is unknown; but the Wieroo produce only males—which is why they steal our female young, and by stealing *cos-ata-lo* they increase their own chances of eventually reproducing both sexes and at the same time lessen ours. Already the Galus produce both male and female; but so carefully do

the Wieroo watch us that few of the males ever grow to manhood, while even fewer are the females that are not stolen away.
It is indeed a strange condition, for while our greatest enemies
hate and fear us, they dare not exterminate us, knowing that
they too would become extinct but for us.

"Ah, but could we once get a start, I am sure that when all
were true *cos-ata-lo* there would have been evolved at last
the true dominant race before which all the world would be
forced to bow."

Ajor always spoke of the world as though nothing existed
beyond Caspak. She could not seem to grasp the truth of my
origin or the fact that there were countless other peoples outside
her stern barrier-cliffs. She apparently felt that I came from an
entirely different world. Where it was and how I came to Caspak from it were matters quite beyond her with which she refused to trouble her pretty head.

"Well," she continued, "and so I ran away to hide, intending
to pass the cliffs to the south of Galu and find a retreat in the
Kro-lu country. It would be dangerous, but there seemed no
other way.

"The third night I took refuge in a large cave in the cliffs
at the edge of my own country; upon the following day I would
cross over into the Kro-lu country, where I felt that I should
be reasonably safe from the Wieroo, though menaced by countless other dangers. However, to a *cos-ata-lo* any fate is preferable
to that of falling into the clutches of the frightful Wieroo,
from whose land none returns.

"I had been sleeping peacefully for several hours when I
was awakened by a slight noise within the cavern. The moon
was shining brightly, illumining the entrance, against which I
saw silhouetted the dread figure of a Wieroo. There was no
escape. The cave was shallow, the entrance narrow. I lay
very still, hoping against hope that the creature had but
paused here to rest and might soon depart without discovering
me; yet all the while I knew that he came seeking me.

"I waited, scarce breathing, watching the thing creep stealthily
toward me, its great eyes luminous in the darkness of the cave's
interior, and at last I knew that those eyes were directed upon
me, for the Wieroo can see in the darkness better than even the
lion or the tiger. But a few feet separated us when I sprang
to my feet and dashed madly toward my menacer in a vain effort
to dodge past him and reach the outside world. It was madness,
of course, for even had I succeeded temporarily, the Wieroo

would have but followed and swooped down upon me from above. As it was, he reached forth and seized me, and though I struggled, he overpowered me. In the duel his long, white robe was nearly torn from him, and he became very angry, so that he trembled and beat his wings together in his rage.

"He asked me my name; but I would not answer him, and that angered him still more. At last he dragged me to the entrance of the cave, lifted me in his arms, spread his great wings and leaping into the air, flapped dismally through the night. I saw the moonlit landscape sliding away beneath me, and then we were out above the sea and on our way to Oo-oh, the country of the Wieroo.

"The dim outlines of Oo-oh were unfolding below us when there came from above a loud whirring of giant wings. The Wieroo and I glanced up simultaneously, to see a pair of huge *jo-oos*" (flying reptiles—pterodactyls) "swooping down upon us. The Wieroo wheeled and dropped almost to sea-level, and then raced southward in an effort to outdistance our pursuers. The great creatures, notwithstanding their enormous weight, are swift on their wings; but the Wieroo are swifter. Even with my added weight, the creature that bore me maintained his lead, though he could not increase it. Faster than the fastest wind we raced through the night, southward along the coast. Sometimes we rose to great heights, where the air was chill and the world below but a blur of dim outlines; but always the jo-oos stuck close behind us.

"I knew that we had covered a great distance, for the rush of the wind by my face attested the speed of our progress, but I had no idea where we were when at last I realized that the Wieroo was weakening. One of the jo-oos gained on us and succeeded in heading us, so that my captor had to turn in to-ward the coast. Further and further they forced him to the left; lower and lower he sank. More labored was his breathing, and weaker the stroke of his once powerful wings. We were not ten feet above the ground when they overtook us, and at the edge of a forest. One of them seized the Wieroo by his right wing, and in an effort to free himself, he loosed his grasp upon me, dropping me to earth. Like a frightened *ecca* I leaped to my feet and raced for the sheltering sanctuary of the forest, where I knew neither could follow or seize me. Then I turned and looked back to see two great reptiles tear my abductor asunder and devour him on the spot.

"I was saved; yet I felt that I was lost. How far I was from the country of the Galus I could but guess; nor did it seem probable that I ever could make my way in safety to my native land.

"Day was breaking; soon the carnivora would stalk forth for their first kill; I was armed only with my knife. About me was a strange landscape—the flowers, the trees, the grasses, even, were different from those of my northern world, and presently there appeared before me a creature fully as hideous as the Wieroo—a hairy man-thing that barely walked erect. I shuddered, and then I fled. Through the hideous dangers that my forbears had endured in the earlier stages of their human evolution I fled; and always pursuing was the hairy monster that had discovered me. Later he was joined by others of his kind. They were the speechless men, the Alus, from whom you rescued me, my Tom. From then on, you know the story of my adventures, and from the first, I would endure them all again because they led me to you!"

It was very nice of her to say that, and I appreciated it. I felt that she was a mighty nice little girl whose friendship anyone might be glad to have; but I wished that when she touched me, those peculiar thrills would not run through me. It was most discomforting, because it reminded me of love; and I knew that I never could love this half-baked little barbarian. I was very much interested in her account of the Wieroo, which up to this time I had considered a purely mythological creature; but Ajor shuddered so at even the veriest mention of the name that I was loath to press the subject upon her, and so the Wieroo still remained a mystery to me.

While the Wieroo interested me greatly, I had little time to think about them, as our waking hours were filled with the necessities of existence—the constant battle for survival which is the chief occupation of Caspakians. To-mar and So-al were now about fitted for their advent into Kro-lu society and must therefore leave us, as we could not accompany them without incurring great danger ourselves and running the chance of endangering them; but each swore to be always our friend and assured us that should we need their aid at any time we had but to ask it; nor could I doubt their sincerity, since we had been so instrumental in bringing them safely upon their journey toward the Kro-lu village.

This was our last day together. In the afternoon we should separate, To-mar and So-al going directly to the Kro-lu village, while Ajor and I made a detour to avoid a conflict with the archers. The former both showed evidence of nervous apprehension as the time approached for them to make their entry into the village of their new people, and yet both were very proud and happy. They told us that they would be well received as additions to a tribe always are welcomed, and the more so as the distance from the beginning increased, the higher tribes or races being far weaker numerically than the lower. The southern end of the island fairly swarms with the Ho-lu, or apes; next above these are the Alus, who are slightly fewer in numbers than the Ho-lu; and again there are fewer Bo-lu than Alus, and fewer Sto-lu than Bo-lu. Thus it goes until the Kro-lu are fewer in number than any of the others; and here the law reverses, for the Galus outnumber the Kro-lu. As Ajor explained it to me, the reason for this is that as evolution practically ceases with the Galus, there is no loss among them on this score, for even the *cos-ata-lo* are still considered Galus and remain with them. And Galus come up both from the west and east coasts. There are, too, fewer carnivorous reptiles at the north end of the island, and not so many of the great and ferocious members of the cat family as take their hideous toll of life among the races further south.

By now I was obtaining some idea of the Caspakian scheme of evolution, which partly accounted for the lack of young among the races I had so far seen. Coming up from the beginning, the Caspakian passes, during a single existence, through the various stages of evolution, or at least many of them, through which the human race has passed during the countless ages since life first stirred upon a new world; but the question which continued to puzzle me was: What creates life at the beginning, *cor sva jo?*

I had noticed that as we traveled northward from the Alus' country the land had gradually risen until we were now several hundred feet above the level of the inland sea. Ajor told me that the Galu country was still higher and considerably colder, which accounted for the scarcity of reptiles. The change in form and kinds of the lower animals was even more marked than the evolutionary stages of man. The diminutive *ecca,* or small horse, became a rough-coated and sturdy little pony in the Kro-lu country. I saw a greater number of small lions and tigers, though many of the huge ones still persisted, while the woolly mammoth was more in evidence, as were several varieties of the Labyrinthodonta. These creatures, from which God save me, I should have expected to find further south;

but for some unaccountable reason they gain their greatest bulk in the Kro-lu and Galu countries, though fortunately they are rare. I rather imagine that they are a very early form of life which is rapidly nearing extinction in Caspak, though where-ever they are found, they constitute a menace to all forms of life.

It was mid-afternoon when To-mar and So-al bade us good-bye. We were not far from the Kro-lu village; in fact, we had approached it much closer than we had intended, and now Ajor and I were to make a detour toward the sea while our companions went directly in search of the Kro-lu chief.

Ajor and I had gone perhaps a mile or two and were just about to emerge from a dense wood when I saw that ahead of us which caused me to draw back into concealment, at the same time pushing Ajor behind me. What I saw was a party of Band-lu warriors—large, fierce-appearing men. From the di-rection of their march I saw that they were returning to their caves, and that if we remained where we were, they would pass without discovering us.

Presently Ajor nudged me. "They have a prisoner," she whispered. "He is a Kro-lu."

And then I saw him, the first fully developed Kro-lu I had seen. He was a fine-looking savage, tall and straight, with a regal carriage. To-mar was a handsome fellow; but this Kro-lu showed plainly in his every physical attribute a higher plane of evolution. While To-mar was just entering the Kro-lu sphere, this man, it seemed to me, must be close indeed to the next stage of his development, which would see him an envied Galu.

"They will kill him?" I whispered to Ajor.

"The dance of death," she replied, and I shuddered, so recently had I escaped the same fate. It seemed cruel that one who must have passed safely up through all the frightful stages of human evolution within Caspak, should die at the very foot of his goal. I raised my rifle to my shoulder and took careful aim at one of the Band-lu. If I hit him, I would hit two, for another was directly behind the first.

Ajor touched my arm. "What would you do?" she asked. "They are all our enemies."

"I am going to save him from the dance of death," I re-plied, "enemy or no enemy," and I squeezed the trigger. At the report, the two Band-lu lunged forward upon their faces. I handed my rifle to Ajor, and drawing my pistol, stepped out in full view of the startled party. The Band-lu did not run away as had some of the lower orders of Caspakians at the sound of the rifle. Instead, the moment they saw me, they let out a series of demoniac war-cries, and raising their spears above their heads, charged me.

The Kro-lu stood silent and statuesque, watching the proceedings. He made no attempt to escape, though his feet were not bound and none of the warriors remained to guard him. There were ten of the Band-lu coming for me. I dropped three of them with my pistol as rapidly as a man might count to three, and then my rifle spoke close to my left shoulder, and another of them stumbled and rolled over and over upon the ground. Plucky little Ajor! She had never fired a shot before in all her life, though I had taught her to sight and aim and how to squeeze the trigger instead of pulling it. She had practiced these new accomplishments often, but little had I thought they would make a marksman of her so quickly.

With six of their fellows put out of the fight so easily, the remaining six sought cover behind some low bushes and commenced a council of war. I wished that they would go away, as I had no ammunition to waste, and I was fearful that should they institute another charge, some of them would reach us, for they were already quite close. Suddenly one of them rose and launched his spear. It was the most marvelous exhibition of speed I have ever witnessed. It seemed to me that he had scarce gained an upright position when the weapon was halfway upon its journey, speeding like an arrow toward Ajor. And then it was, with that little life in danger, that I made the best shot I have ever made in my life. I took no conscious aim; it was as though my subconscious mind, impelled by a stronger power even than that of self-preservation, directed my hand. Ajor was in danger! Simultaneously with the thought my pistol flew to position, a streak of incandescent powder marked the path of the bullet from its muzzle; and the spear, its point shattered, was deflected from its path. With a howl of dismay the six Band-lu rose from their shelter and raced away toward the south.

I turned toward Ajor. She was very white and wide-eyed, for the clutching fingers of death had all but seized her; but a little smile came to her lips and an expression of great pride to her eyes. "My Tom!" she said, and took my hand in hers. That was all—"My Tom!" and a pressure of the hand. Her Tom! Something stirred within my bosom. Was it exaltation or was it consternation? Impossible! I turned away almost brusquely.

"Come!" I said, and strode off toward the Kro-lu prisoner. The Kro-lu stood watching us with stolid indifference. I presume that he expected to be killed; but if he did, he showed no outward sign of fear. His eyes, indicating his greatest interest, were fixed upon my pistol or the rifle which Ajor still carried. I cut his bonds with my knife. As I did so, an expression of surprise tinged and animated the haughty reserve of his countenance. He eyed me quizzically.

"What are you going to do with me?" he asked.

"You are free," I replied. "Go home, if you wish."

"Why don't you kill me?" he inquired. "I am defenseless."

"Why should I kill you? I have risked my life and that of this young lady to save your life. Why, therefore, should I now take it?" Of course, I didn't say "young lady" as there is no Caspakian equivalent for that term; but I have to allow myself considerable latitude in the translation of Caspakian conversations. To speak always of a beautiful young girl as a "she" may be literal; but it seems far from gallant.

The Kro-lu concentrated his steady, level gaze upon me for at least a full minute. Then he spoke again.

"Who are you, man of strange skins?" he asked. "Your she is Galu; but you are neither Galu nor Kro-lu nor Band-lu, nor any other sort of man which I have seen before. Tell me from whence comes so mighty a warrior and so generous a foe."

"It is a long story," I replied; "but suffice it to say that I am not of Caspak. I am a stranger here, and—let this sink in—I am not a foe. I have no wish to be an enemy of any man in Caspak, with the possible exception of the Galu warrior Du-seen."

"Du-seen!" he exclaimed. "You are an enemy of Du-seen? And why?"

"Because he would harm Ajor," I replied. "You know him?"

"He cannot know him," said Ajor. "Du-seen rose from the Kro-lu long ago, taking a new name, as all do when they enter a new sphere. He cannot know him, as there is no intercourse between the Kro-lu and the Galu."

The warrior smiled. "Du-seen rose not so long ago," he said, "that I do not recall him well, and recently he has taken it upon himself to abrogate the ancient laws of Caspak; he has had intercourse with the Kro-lu. Du-seen would be chief of the Galus, and he has come to the Kro-lu for help."

Ajor was aghast. The thing was incredible. Never had Kro-lu and Galu had friendly relations; by the savage laws of Caspak they were deadly enemies, for only so can the several races maintain their individuality.

"Will the Kro-lu join him?" asked Ajor. "Will they invade the country of Jor my father?"

"The younger Kro-lu favor the plan," replied the warrior, "since they believe they will thus become Galus immediately. They hope to span the long years of change through which they must pass in the ordinary course of events and at a single stride become Galus. We of the older Kro-lu tell them that though they occupy the land of the Galu and wear the skins and ornaments of the golden people, still they will not be Galus till the time arrives that they are ripe to rise. We also tell them that even then they will never become a true Galu race, since there will still be those among them who can never rise. It is all right to raid the Galu country occasionally for plunder, as our people do; but to attempt to conquer it and hold it is madness. For my part, I have been content to wait until the call came to me. I feel that it cannot now be long."

"What is your name?" asked Ajor.

"Chal-az," replied the man.

"You are chief of the Kro-lu?" Ajor continued.

"No, it is Al-tan who is chief of the Kro-lu of the east," answered Chal-az.

"And he is against this plan to invade my father's country?"

"Unfortunately he is rather in favor of it," replied the man, "since he has about come to the conclusion that he is *batu*. He has been chief ever since before I came up from the Band-lu, and I can see no change in him in all those years. In fact, he still appears to be more Band-lu than Kro-lu. However, he is a good chief and a mighty warrior, and if Du-seen persuades him to his cause, the Galus may find themselves under a Kro-lu chieftain before long—Du-seen as well as the others, for Al-tan would never consent to occupy a subordinate position, and once he plants a victorious foot in Galu, he will not withdraw it without a struggle."

I asked them what *batu* meant, as I had not before heard the word. Literally translated, it is equivalent to *through, finished, done-for,* as applied to an individual's evolutionary progress in Caspak, and with this information was developed the interesting fact that not every individual is capable of rising through every stage to that of Galu. Some never progress beyond the

Alu stage; others stop as Bo-lu, as Sto-lu, as Band-lu or as
Kro-lu. The Ho-lu of the first generation may rise to become
Alus; the Alus of the second generation may become Bo-lu,
while it requires three generations of Bo-lu to become Band-lu,
and so on until the Kro-lu's parent on one side must be of the
sixth generation.

It was not entirely plain to me even with this explanation,
since I couldn't understand how there could be different generations of peoples who apparently had no offspring. Yet I
was commencing to get a slight glimmer of the strange laws
which govern propagation and evolution in this weird land.
Already I knew that the warm pools which always lie close
to every tribal abiding-place were closely linked with the Caspakian scheme of evolution, and that the daily immersion of
the females in the greenish slimy water was in response to some
natural law, since neither pleasure nor cleanliness could be derived from what seemed almost a religious rite. Yet I was still
at sea; nor, seemingly, could Ajor enlighten me, since she was
compelled to use words which I could not understand and
which it was impossible for her to explain the meanings of.

As we stood talking, we were suddenly startled by a commotion in the bushes and among the boles of the trees surrounding us, and simultaneously a hundred Kro-lu warriors
appeared in a rough circle about us. They greeted Chal-az
with a volley of questions as they approached slowly from all
sides, their heavy bows fitted with long, sharp arrows. Upon
Ajor and me they looked with covetousness in the one instance
and suspicion in the other; but after they had heard Chal-az's
story, their attitude was more friendly. A huge savage did all
the talking. He was a mountain of a man, yet perfectly pro-
portioned.

"This is Al-tan the chief," said Chal-az by way of introduction. Then he told something of my story, and Al-tan asked me
many questions of the land from which I came. The warriors
crowded around close to hear my replies, and there were many
expressions of incredulity as I spoke of what was to them another world, of the yacht which had brought me over vast
waters, and of the plane that had borne me Jo-oo-like over
the summit of the barrier-cliffs. It was the mention of the hydro-aeroplane which precipitated the first outspoken skepticism,
and then Ajor came to my defense.

"I saw it with my own eyes!" she exclaimed. "I saw him

flying through the air in battle with a Jo-oo. The Alus were chasing me, and they saw and ran away."

"Whose is this she?" demanded Al-tan suddenly, his eyes fixed fiercely upon Ajor.

For a moment there was silence. Ajor looked up at me, a hurt and questioning expression on her face. "Whose she is this?" repeated Al-tan.

"She is mine," I replied, though what force it was that impelled me to say it I could not have told; but an instant later I was glad that I had spoken the words, for the reward of Ajor's proud and happy face was reward indeed.

Al-tan eyed her for several minutes and then turned to me. "Can you keep her?" he asked, just the tinge of a sneer upon his face.

I laid my palm upon the grip of my pistol and answered that I could. He saw the move, glanced at the butt of the automatic where it protruded from its holster, and smiled. Then he turned and raising his great bow, fitted an arrow and drew the shaft far back. His warriors, supercilious smiles upon their faces, stood silently watching him. His bow was the longest and the heaviest among them all. A mighty man indeed must he be to bend it; yet Al-tan drew the shaft back until the stone point touched his left forefinger, and he did it with consummate ease. Then he raised the shaft to the level of his right eye, held it there for an instant and released it. When the arrow stopped, half its length protruded from the opposite side of a six-inch tree fifty feet away. Al-tan and his warriors turned toward me with expressions of immense satisfaction upon their faces, and then, apparently for Ajor's benefit, the chieftain swaggered to and fro a couple of times, swinging his great arms and his bulky shoulders for all the world like a drunken prize-fighter at a beach dance-hall.

I saw that some reply was necessary, and so in a single motion, I drew my gun, dropped it on the still quivering arrow and pulled the trigger. At the sound of the report, the Kro-lu leaped back and raised their weapons; but as I was smiling, they took heart and lowered them again, following my eyes to the tree; the shaft of their chief was gone, and through the bole was a little round hole marking the path of my bullet. It was a good shot if I do say it myself, "as shouldn't"; but necessity must have guided that bullet; I simply *had* to make a good shot, that I might immediately establish my position among those savage and warlike Caspakians of the sixth sphere. That it had its effect was immediately noticeable, but I am none too sure that it helped my cause with Al-tan. Whereas he might have condescended to tolerate me as a harmless and interesting curiosity, he now, by the change in his expression, appeared to consider me in a new and unfavorable light. Nor can I wonder, knowing this type as I did, for had I not made him ridiculous in the eyes of his warriors, beating him at his own game? What king, savage or civilized, could condone such impudence? Seeing his black scowls, I deemed it expedient, especially on Ajor's account, to terminate the interview and continue upon our way; but when I would have done so, Al-tan detained us with a gesture, and his warriors pressed around us.

"What is the meaning of this?" I demanded, and before Al-tan could reply, Chal-az raised his voice in our behalf.

"Is this the gratitude of a Kro-lu chieftain, Al-tan," he asked, "to one who has served you by saving one of your warriors from the enemy—saving him from the death dance of the Band-lu?"

Al-tan was silent for a moment, and then his brow cleared, and the faint imitation of a pleasant expression struggled for existence as he said: "The stranger will not be harmed. I wished only to detain him that he may be feasted tonight in the village of Al-tan the Kro-lu. In the morning he may go his way. Al-tan will not hinder him."

I was not entirely reassured; but I wanted to see the interior of the Kro-lu village, and anyway I knew that if Al-tan intended treachery I would be no more in his power in the morning than I now was—in fact, during the night I might find opportunity to escape with Ajor, while at the instant neither of us could hope to escape unscathed from the encircling warriors. Therefore, in order to disarm him of any thought that I might entertain suspicion as to his sincerity, I promptly and courteously accepted his invitation. His satisfaction was evident, and as we set off toward his village, he walked beside me, asking many questions as to the country from which I came, its peoples and their customs. He seemed much mystified by the fact that we could walk abroad by day or night without fear of being devoured by wild beasts or savage reptiles, and when I told him of the great armies which we maintained, his simple mind could not grasp the fact that they existed solely for the slaughtering of human beings.

"I am glad," he said, "that I do not dwell in your country among such savage peoples. Here, in Caspak, men fight with

friendly crowd of curious warriors and women, to whom Chal-az generously explained the service we had rendered him, whereupon they showered us with the most well-meant attentions, for Chal-az, it seemed, was a most popular member of the tribe. Necklaces of lion and tiger-teeth, bits of dried meat, finely tanned hides and earthen pots, beautifully decorated, they thrust upon us until we were loaded down, and all the while Al-tan glared balefully upon us, seemingly jealous of the attentions heaped upon us because we had served Chal-az.

At last we reached a hut that they set apart for us, and there we cooked our meat and some vegetables the women brought us, and had milk from cows—the first I had had in Caspak— and cheese from the milk of wild goats, with honey and thin bread made from wheat flour of their own grinding, and grapes and the fermented juice of grapes. It was quite the most wonderful meal I had eaten since I quit the *Toreador* and Bowen J. Tyler's colored chef, who could make pork-chops taste like chicken, and chicken taste like heaven.

CHAPTER VI

AFTER dinner I rolled a cigaret and stretched myself at ease upon a pile of furs before the doorway, with Ajor's head pillowed in my lap and a feeling of great content pervading me. It was the first time since my plane had topped the barriercliffs of Caspak that I had felt any sense of peace or security. My hand wandered to the velvet cheek of the girl I had claimed as mine, and to her luxuriant hair and the golden fillet which bound it close to her shapely head. Her slender fingers groping upward sought mine and drew them to her lips, and then I gathered her in my arms and crushed her to me, smothering her mouth with a long, long kiss. It was the first time that passion had tinged my intercourse with Ajor. We were alone, and the hut was ours until morning.

But now from beyond the palisade in the direction of the main gate came the hallooing of men and the answering calls and queries of the guard. We listened. Returning hunters, no doubt. We heard them enter the village amidst the barking dogs. I have forgotten to mention the dogs of the Kro-lu. The village swarmed with them, gaunt, wolflike creatures that guarded the herd by day when it grazed without the palisade, ten dogs to a cow. By night the cows were herded in an outer inclosure roofed against the onslaughts of the carnivorous cats; and the dogs, with the exception of a few, were brought into the village; these few well-tested brutes remained with the herd. During the day they fed plentifully upon the beasts of prey which they killed in protection of the herd, so that their keep amounted to nothing at all.

Shortly after the commotion at the gate had subsided, Ajor and I arose to enter the hut, and at the same time a warrior appeared from one of the twisted alleys which, lying between the irregularly placed huts and groups of huts, form the streets of the Kro-lu village. The fellow halted before us and addressed me, saying that Al-tan desired my presence at his hut. The wording of the invitation and the manner of the messenger threw me entirely off my guard, so cordial was the one and respectful the other, and the result was that I went willingly, telling Ajor that I would return presently. I had laid my arms and ammunition aside as soon as we had taken over the hut, and I left them with Ajor now, as I had noticed that aside from their hunting-knives the men of Kro-lu bore no weapons about the village streets. There was an atmosphere of peace and security within that village that I had not hoped to experience within Caspak, and after what I had passed through, it must have cast a numbing spell over my faculties of judgment and reason. I had eaten of the lotus-flower of safety; dangers no longer threatened for they had ceased to be.

The messenger led me through the labyrinthine alleys to an open plaza near the center of the village. At one end of this plaza was a long hut, much the largest that I had yet seen, before the door of which were many warriors. I could see that the interior was lighted and that a great number of men were gathered within. The dogs about the plaza were as thick as fleas, and those I approached closely evinced a strong desire to devour me, their noses evidently apprising them of the fact that I was of an alien race, since they paid no attention whatever to my companion. Once inside the council-hut, for such it appeared to be, I found a large concourse of warriors seated, or rather squatted, around the floor. At one end of the oval space which the warriors left down the center of the room stood Al-tan and another warrior whom I immediately recognized as a Galu, and then I saw that there were many Galus present. About the walls were a number of flaming torches stuck in holes in a clay plaster which evidently served the purpose of preventing the inflammable wood and grasses of which the hut was composed from being ignited by the flames. Lying about among the warriors or wandering restlessly to and fro were a number of savage dogs.

The warriors eyed me curiously as I entered, especially the Galus, and then I was conducted into the center of the group and led forward toward Al-tan. As I advanced, I felt one of the dogs sniffing at my heels, and of a sudden a great brute leaped upon my back. As I turned to thrust it aside before its fangs found a hold upon me, I beheld a huge Airedale leaping frantically about me. The grinning jaws, the half-closed eyes, the back-laid ears spoke to me louder than might the words of man that here was no savage enemy but a joyous friend, and then I recognized him, and fell to one knee and put my arms about his neck while he whined and cried with joy. It was Nobs, dear old Nobs, Bowen Tyler's Nobs, who had loved me next to his master.

"Where is the master of this dog?" I asked, turning toward Al-tan.

The chieftain inclined his head toward the Galu standing at his side. "He belongs to Du-seen the Galu," he replied.

"He belongs to Bowen J. Tyler, Jr., of Santa Monica," I retorted, "and I want to know where his master is."

The Galu shrugged. "The dog is mine," he said. "He came to me *cor-sva-jo*, and he is unlike any dog in Caspak, being kind and docile and yet a killer when aroused. I would not part with him. I do not know the man of whom you speak."

So this was Du-seen! This was the man from whom Ajor had fled. I wondered if he knew that she was here. I wondered if they had sent for me because of her; but after they had commenced to question me, my mind was relieved; they did not mention Ajor. Their interest seemed centered upon the strange world from which I had come, my journey to Caspak and my intentions now that I had arrived. I answered them frankly as I had nothing to conceal and assured them that my only wish was to find my friends and return to my own country. In the Galu Du-seen and his warriors I saw something of the explanation of the term "golden race" which is applied to them, for their ornaments and weapons were either wholly of beaten gold or heavily decorated with the precious metal. They were a very imposing set of men—tall and straight and handsome. About their heads were bands of gold like that which Ajor wore, and from their left shoulders depended the leopard-tails of the Galus. In addition to the deer-skin tunic which constituted the major portion of their apparel, each carried a light blanket of barbaric yet beautiful design—the first evidence of weaving I had seen in Caspak. Ajor had had no blanket, having lost it during her flight from the attentions of Du-seen; nor was she so heavily incrusted with gold as these male members of her tribe.

The audience must have lasted fully an hour when Al-tan signified that I might return to my hut. All the time Nobs had lain quietly at my feet; but the instant that I turned to leave, he was up and after me. Du-seen called to him; but the terrier never even so much as looked in his direction. I had almost reached the doorway leading from the council-hall when Al-tan rose and called after me. "Stop!" he shouted. "Stop, stranger! The beast of Du-seen the Galu follows you."

"The dog is not Du-seen's," I replied. "He belongs to my friend, as I told you, and he prefers to stay with me until his master is found." And I turned again to resume my way. I had taken but a few steps when I heard a commotion behind me, and at the same moment a man leaned close and whispered "Kazor!" close to my ear— kazor, the Caspakian equivalent of beware. It was To-mar. As he spoke, he turned quickly away as though loath to have others see that he knew me, and at the same instant I wheeled to discover Du-seen striding rapidly after me. Al-tan followed him, and it was evident that both were angry.

Du-seen, a weapon half drawn, approached truculently. "The beast is mine," he reiterated. "Would you steal him?"

"He is not yours nor mine," I replied, "and I am not stealing him. If he wishes to follow you, he may; I will not interfere; but if he wishes to follow me, he shall; nor shall you prevent." I turned to Al-tan. "Is not that fair?" I demanded. "Let the dog choose his master."

Du-seen, without waiting for Al-tan's reply, reached for Nobs and grasped him by the scruff of the neck. I did not interfere, for I guessed what would happen; and it did. With a savage growl Nobs turned like lightning upon the Galu, wrenched loose from his hold and leaped for his throat. The man stepped back and warded off the first attack with a heavy blow of his fist, immediately drawing his knife with which to meet the Airedale's return. And Nobs would have returned, all right, had not I spoken to him. In a low voice I called him to heel. For just an instant he hesitated, standing there trembling and with bared fangs, glaring at his foe; but he was well trained and had been out with me quite as much as he had with Bowen—in fact, I had had most to do with his early training; then he walked slowly and very stiff-legged to his place behind me.

Du-seen, red with rage, would have had it out with the two of us had not Al-tan drawn him to one side and whispered in his ear—upon which, with a grunt, the Galu walked straight back to the opposite end of the hall, while Nobs and I continued upon our way toward the hut and Ajor. As we passed out into the village plaza, I saw Chal-az—we were so close to one another that I could have reached out and touched him— and our eyes met; but though I greeted him pleasantly and paused to speak to him, he brushed past me without a sign of recognition. I was puzzled at his behavior, and then I recalled that To-mar, though he had warned me, had appeared not to wish to seem friendly with me. I could not understand their attitude, and was trying to puzzle out some sort of explanation, when the matter was suddenly driven from my mind by the report of a firearm. Instantly I broke into a run, my brain in a whirl of forebodings, for the only firearms in the Kro-lu country were those I had left in the hut with Ajor.

That she was in danger I could not but fear, as she was now something of an adept in the handling of both the pistol and rifle, a fact which largely eliminated the chance that the shot had come from an accidentally discharged firearm. When I left the hut, I had felt that she and I were safe among friends; no thought of danger was in my mind; but since my audience with Al-tan, the presence and bearing of Du-seen and the strange attitude of both To-mar and Chal-az had each contributed toward arousing my suspicions, and now I ran along the narrow, winding alleys of the Kro-lu village with my heart fairly in my mouth.

I am endowed with an excellent sense of direction, which has been greatly perfected by the years I have spent in the mountains and upon the plains and deserts of my native state, so that it was with little or no difficulty that I found my way back to the hut in which I had left Ajor. As I entered the doorway, I called her name aloud. There was no response. I drew a box of matches from my pocket and struck a light, and as the flame flared up, a half-dozen brawny warriors leaped upon me from as many directions; but even in the brief instant that the flare lasted, I saw that Ajor was not within the

THE PEOPLE THAT TIME FORGOT

hut, and that my arms and ammunition had been removed. As the six men leaped upon me, an angry growl burst from behind them. I had forgotten Nobs. Like a demon of hate he sprang among those Kro-lu fighting-men, tearing, rending, ripping with his long tusks and his mighty jaws. They had me down in an instant, and it goes without saying that the six of them could have kept me there had it not been for Nobs; but while I was struggling to throw them off, Nobs was springing first upon one and then upon another of them until they were so put to it to preserve their hides and their lives from him that they could give me only a small part of their attention. One of them was assiduously attempting to strike me on the head with his stone hatchet; but I caught his arm and at the same time turned over upon my belly, after which it took but an instant to get my feet under me and rise suddenly.

As I did so, I kept a grip upon the man's arm, carrying it over one shoulder. Then I leaned suddenly forward and hurled my antagonist over my head to a nasty fall at the opposite side of the hut. In the dim light of the interior I saw that Nobs had already accounted for one of the others—one who lay very quiet upon the floor—while the four remaining upon their feet were striking at him with knives and hatchets.

Running to the side of the man I had just put out of the fighting, I seized his hatchet and knife, and in another moment was in the thick of the argument. I was no match for these savage warriors with their own weapons and would soon have gone down to ignominious defeat and death had it not been for Nobs, who alone was a match for the four of them. I never saw any creature so quick upon its feet as was that great Airedale, nor such frightful ferocity as he manifested in his attacks. It was as much the latter as the former which contributed to the undoing of our enemies, who, accustomed though they were to the ferocity of terrible creatures, seemed awed by the sight of this strange beast from another world battling at the side of his equally strange master. Yet they were no cowards, and only by teamwork did Nobs and I overcome them at last. We would rush for a man, simultaneously, and as Nobs leaped for him upon one side, I would strike at his head with the stone hatchet from the other.

As the last man went down, I heard the running of many feet approaching us from the direction of the plaza. To be captured now would mean death; yet I could not attempt to leave the village without first ascertaining the whereabouts of Ajor and releasing her if she were held a captive. That I could escape the village I was not at all sure; but of one thing I was positive; that it would do neither Ajor nor myself any service to remain where I was and be captured; so with Nobs, bloody but happy, following at heel, I turned down the first alley and slunk away in the direction of the northern end of the village.

Friendless and alone, hunted through the dark labyrinths of this savage community, I seldom have felt more helpless than at that moment; yet far transcending any fear which I may have felt for my own safety was my concern for that of Ajor. What fate had befallen her? Where was she, and in whose power? That I should live to learn the answers to these queries I doubted; but that I should face death gladly in the attempt—of that I was certain. And why? With all my concern for the welfare of my friends who had accompanied me to Caprona, and of my best friend of all, Bowen J. Tyler, Jr., I never yet had experienced the almost paralyzing fear for the safety of any other creature which now threw me alternately into a fever of despair and into a cold sweat of apprehension as my mind dwelt upon the fate of one bit of half-savage femininity of whose very existence even I had not dreamed a few short weeks before.

What was this hold she had upon me? Was I bewitched, that my mind refused to function sanely, and that judgment and reason were dethroned by some mad sentiment which I steadfastly refused to believe was love? I had never been in love. I was not in love now—the very thought was preposterous. How could I, Thomas Billings, the right-hand man of the late Bowen J. Tyler, Sr., one of America's foremost captains of industry and the greatest man in California, be in love with a—a—the word stuck in my throat; yet by my own American standards Ajor could be nothing else; at home, for all her beauty, for all her delicately tinted skin, little Ajor by her apparel, by the habits and customs and manners of her people, by her life, would have been classed a *squaw*. Tom Billings in love with a squaw! I shuddered at the thought.

And then there came to my mind, in a sudden, brilliant flash upon the screen of recollection the picture of Ajor as I had last seen her, and I lived again the delicious moment in which we had clung to one another, lips smothering lips, as I left her to go to the council hall of Al-tan; and I could have kicked myself for the snob and the cad that my thoughts had proven me—me, who had always prided myself that I was neither the one nor the other!

These things ran through my mind as Nobs and I made our way through the dark village, the voices and footsteps of those who sought us still in our ears. These and many other things, nor could I escape the incontrovertible fact that the little figure round which my recollections and my hopes entwined themselves was that of Ajor—beloved barbarian! My reveries were broken in upon by a hoarse whisper from the black interior of a hut past which we were making our way. My name was called in a low voice, and a man stepped out beside me as I halted with raised knife. It was Chal-az.

"Quick!" he warned. "In here! It is my hut, and they will not search it."

I hesitated, recalling his attitude of a few minutes before; and as though he had read my thoughts, he said quickly: "I could not speak to you in the plaza without danger of arousing suspicions which would prevent me aiding you later, for word had gone out that Al-tan had turned against you and would destroy you—this was after Du-seen the Galu arrived."

I followed him into the hut, and with Nobs at our heels we passed through several chambers into a remote and windowless apartment where a small lamp sputtered in its unequal battle with the inky darkness. A hole in the roof permitted the smoke from the burning oil egress; yet the atmosphere was far from lucid. Here Chal-az motioned me to a seat upon a furry hide spread upon the earthen floor.

"I am your friend," he said. "You saved my life; and I am no ingrate as is the *batu* Al-tan. I will serve you, and there are others here who will serve you against Al-tan and this renegade Galu, Du-seen."

"But where is Ajor?" I asked, for I cared little for my own safety while she was in danger.

"Ajor is safe, too," he answered. "We learned the designs of Al-tan and Du-seen. The latter, learning that Ajor was here, demanded her; and Al-tan promised that he should have her; but when the warriors went to get her, To-mar went with them. Ajor tried to defend herself. She killed one of the warriors, and then To-mar picked her up in his arms when the others had taken her weapons from her. He told the others to look after the wounded man, who was really already dead, and to seize you upon your return, and that he, To-mar, would bear Ajor to Al-tan; but instead of bearing her to Al-tan, he took her to his own hut, where she now is with So-al, To-mar's she. It all happened very quickly. To-mar and I were in the council-hut when Du-seen attempted to take the dog from you. I was seeking To-mar for this work. He ran out immediately and accompanied the warriors to your hut while I remained to watch what went on within the council-hut and to aid you if you needed aid. What has happened since you know."

I thanked him for his loyalty and then asked him to take me to Ajor; but he said that it could not be done, as the village streets were filled with searchers. In fact, we could hear them passing to and fro among the huts, making inquiries, and at last Chal-az thought it best to go to the doorway of his dwelling, which consisted of many huts joined together, lest they enter and search.

Chal-az was absent for a long-time—several hours which seemed an eternity to me. All sounds of pursuit had long since ceased, and I was becoming uneasy because of his protracted absence when I heard him returning through the other apartments of his dwelling. He was perturbed when he entered that in which I awaited him, and I saw a worried expression upon his face.

"What is wrong?" I asked. "Have they found Ajor?"

"No," he replied; "but Ajor has gone. She learned that you had escaped them and was told that you had left the village, believing that she had escaped too. So-al could not detain her. She made her way out over the top of the palisade, armed only with her knife."

"Then I must go," I said, rising. Nobs rose and shook himself. He had been dead asleep when I spoke.

"Yes," agreed Chal-az, "you must go at once. It is almost dawn. Du-seen leaves at daylight to search for her." He leaned close to my ear and whispered: "There are many to follow and help you. Al-tan has agreed to aid Du-seen against the Galus of Jor; but there are many of us who have combined to rise against Al-tan and prevent this ruthless desecration of the laws and customs of the Kro-lu and of Caspak. We will rise as Luata has ordained that we shall rise, and only thus. No *batu* may win to the estate of a Galu by treachery and force of arms while Chal-az lives and may wield a heavy bow and a sharp spear with true Kro-lus at his back!"

"I hope that I may live to aid you," I replied. "If I had my weapons and my ammunition, I could do much. Do you know where they are?"

"No," he said, "they have disappeared." And then: "Wait! You cannot go forth half armed, and garbed as you are. You are going into the Galu country, and you must go as a Galu. Come!" And without waiting for a reply, he led me into another apartment, or to be more explicit, another of the several huts which formed his cellular dwelling.

Here was a pile of skins, weapons and ornaments. "Remove your strange apparel," said Chal-az, "and I will fit you out as a true Galu. I have slain several of them in the raids of my early days as a Kro-lu, and here are their trappings."

I saw the wisdom of his suggestion, and as my clothes were by now so ragged as to but half conceal my nakedness, I had no regrets in laying them aside. Stripped to the skin, I donned the red-deerskin tunic, the leopard-tail, the golden fillet, armlets and leg-ornaments of a Galu, with the belt, scabbard and knife, the shield, spear, bow and arrow and the long rope which I learned now for the first time is the distinctive weapon of the Galu warrior. It is a rawhide rope, not dissimilar to those of the Western plains and cow-camps of my youth. The *honda* is a golden oval about which is braided the rawhide, making a heavy and accurate weight for the throwing of the noose. This heavy *honda*, Chal-az explained, is used as a weapon, being thrown with great force and accuracy at an enemy and then coiled in for another cast. In hunting and in battle, they use both the noose and the *honda*. If several warriors surround a single foeman or quarry, they rope it with the noose from several sides; but a single warrior against a lone antagonist will attempt to brain his foe with the metal oval.

I could not have been more pleased with any weapon, short of a rifle, which he could have found for me, since I have been adept with the rope from early childhood; but I must confess that I was less favorably inclined toward my apparel. In so far as the sensation was concerned, I might as well have been entirely naked, so short and light was the tunic. When I asked Chal-az for the Caspakian name for rope, he told me *ga*, and for the first time I understood the derivation of the word *Galu*, which means ropeman.

Entirely outfitted I would not have known myself, so strange was my garb and my armament. Upon my back were slung my bow, arrows, shield, and short spear; from the center of my girdle depended my knife; at my right hip was my stone hatchet; and at my left hung the coils of my long rope. By reaching my right hand over my left shoulder, I could seize the spear or arrows; my left hand could find my bow over my right shoulder, while a veritable contortionist-act was necessary to place my shield in front of me and upon my left arm. The shield, long and oval, is utilized more as back-armor than as a defense against frontal attack, for the close-set armlets of gold upon the left forcarm are principally depended upon to ward off knife, spear, hatchet, or arrow from in front; but against the greater carnivora and the attacks of several human antagonists, the shield is utilized to its best advantage and carried by loops upon the left arm.

Fully equipped, except for a blanket, I followed Chal-az from his domicile into the dark and deserted alleys of Kro-lu. Silently we crept along, Nobs silent at heel, toward the nearest portion of the palisade. Here Chal-az bade me farewell, telling me that he hoped to see me soon among the Galus, as he felt that "the call soon would come" to him. I thanked him for his loyal assistance and promised that whether I reached the Galu country or not, I should always stand ready to repay his kindness to me, and that he could count on me in the revolution against Al-tan.

CHAPTER VII

To RUN up the inclined surface of the palisade and drop to the ground outside was the work of but a moment, or would have been but for Nobs. I had to put my rope about him after we reached the top, lift him over the sharpened stakes and lower him upon the outside. To find Ajor in the unknown country to the north seemed rather hopeless; yet I could do no less than try, praying in the meanwhile that she would come through unscathed and in safety to her father.

As Nobs and I swung along in the growing light of the coming day, I was impressed by the lessening numbers of savage beasts the farther north I traveled. With the decrease among the carnivora, the herbivora increased in quantity, though anywhere in Caspak they are sufficiently plentiful to furnish ample food for the meat-eaters of each locality. The wild cattle, antelope, deer, and horses I passed showed changes in evolution from their cousins farther south. The kine were smaller and less shaggy, the horses larger. North of the Kro-lu village I saw a small band of the latter of about the size of those of our old Western plains—such as the Indians bred in former days and to a lesser extent even now. They were fat and sleek, and I looked upon them with covetous eyes and with thoughts that any old cowpuncher may well imagine I might entertain after having hoofed it for weeks; but they were wary, scarce permitting me to approach within bow-and-arrow range, much less within roping distance; yet I still had hopes which I never discarded.

Twice before noon we were stalked and charged by man-eaters; but even though I was without firearms, I still had ample protection in Nobs, who evidently had learned something of Caspakian hunt rules under the tutorage of Du-seen or some other Galu, and of course a great deal more by experience. He always was on the alert for dangerous foes, invariably warning me by low growls of the approach of a large carnivorous animal long before I could either see or hear it, and then when the thing appeared, he would run snapping at its heels, drawing the charge away from me until I found safety in some tree; yet never did the wily Nobs take an unnecessary chance of a mauling. He would dart in and away so quickly that not even the lightninglike movements of the great cats could reach him. I have seen him tantalize them thus until they fairly screamed in rage.

The greatest inconvenience the hunters caused me was the delay, for they have a nasty habit of keeping one treed for an hour or more if balked in their designs; but at last we came in sight of a line of cliffs running east and west across our path as far as the eye could see in either direction, and I knew that we had reached the natural boundary which marks the line between the Kro-lu and Galu countries. The southern face of these cliffs loomed high and forbidding, rising to an altitude of some two hundred feet, sheer and precipitous, without a break that the eye could perceive. How I was to find a crossing I could not guess. Whether to search to the east toward the still loftier barrier-cliffs fronting upon the ocean, or westward in the direction of the inland sea was a question which baffled me. Were there many passes or only one? I had no way of knowing. I could but trust to chance. It never occurred to me that Nobs had made the crossing at least once, possibly a greater number of times, and that he might lead me to the pass; and so it was with no idea of assistance that I appealed to him as a man alone with a dumb brute so often does.

"Nobs," I said, "how the devil are we going to cross those cliffs?"

I do not say that he understood me, even though I realize that an Airedale is a mighty intelligent dog; but I do swear that he seemed to understand me, for he wheeled about, barking joyously, and trotted off toward the west; and when I didn't follow him, he ran back to me, barking furiously, and at last taking hold of the calf of my leg in an effort to pull me along in the direction he wished me to go. Now, as my legs were naked and Nob's jaws are much more powerful than he realizes, I gave in and followed him, for I knew that I might as well go west as east, as far as any knowledge I had of the correct direction went.

We followed the base of the cliffs for a considerable distance. The ground was rolling and tree-dotted and covered with grazing animals, alone, in pairs and in herds—a motley aggregation of the modern and extinct herbivora of the world. A huge woolly mastodon stood swaying to and fro in the shade of a giant fern— a mighty bull with enormous upcurving tusks. Near him grazed an aurochs bull with a cow and calf, close beside a lone rhinoceros asleep in a dust-hole. Deer, antelope, bison, horses, sheep, and goats were all in sight at the same time, and at a little distance a giant megatherium reared up on its huge tail and massive hind feet to tear the leaves from a tall tree. The forgotten past rubbed flanks with the present—while Tom Billings, modern of the moderns, passed in the garb of a pre-Glacial man, and before him trotted a creature of a breed scarce sixty years old. Nobs was a parvenu; but it failed to worry him.

As we neared the inland sea we saw more flying reptiles and several great amphibians, but none of them attacked us. As we were topping a rise in the middle of the afternoon, I saw something that brought me to a sudden stop. Calling Nobs in a whisper, I cautioned him to silence and kept him at heel while I threw myself flat and watched, from behind a sheltering shrub, a body of warriors approaching the cliff from the south. I could see that they were Galus, and I guessed that Du-seen led them. They had taken a shorter route to the pass and so had overhauled me. I could see them plainly, for they were no great distance away, and I saw with relief that Ajor was not with them.

The cliffs before them were broken and ragged, those coming from the east overlapping the cliffs from the west. Into the defile formed by this overlapping the party filed. I could see them climbing upward for a few minutes, and then they disappeared from view. When the last of them had passed from sight, I rose and bent my steps in the direction of the pass—the same pass toward which Nobs had evidently been leading me. I went warily as I approached it, for fear the party might have halted to rest.

If they hadn't halted, I had no fear of being discovered, for I had seen that the Galus marched without point, flankers or rear guard; and when I reached the pass and saw a narrow, one-man trail leading upward at a stiff angle, I wished that I were chief of the Galus for a few weeks. A dozen men could hold off forever in that narrow pass all the hordes which might be brought up from the south; yet there it lay entirely unguarded.

The Galus might be a great people in Caspak; but they were pitifully inefficient in even the simpler forms of military tactics. I was surprised that even a man of the Stone Age should be so lacking in military perspicacity. Du-seen dropped far below par in my estimation as I saw the slovenly formation of his troop as it passed through an enemy country and entered the domain of the chief against whom he had risen in revolt; but Du-seen must have known Jor the chief and known that Jor would not be waiting for him at the pass. Nevertheless he took unwarranted chances. With one squad of a home-guard company I could have conquered Caspak.

Nobs and I followed to the summit of the pass, and there we saw the party defiling into the Galu country, the level of which was not, on an average, over fifty feet below the summit of the cliffs and about a hundred and fifty feet above the adjacent Kro-lu domain. Immediately the landscape changed. The trees, the flowers and the shrubs were of a hardier type, and I realized that at night the Galu blanket might be almost a necessity. Acacia and eucalyptus predominated among the trees; yet there were ash and oak and even pine and fir and hemlock. The tree-life was riotous. The forests were dense and peopled by enormous trees. From the summit of the cliff I could see forests rising hundreds of feet above the level upon which I stood, and even at the distance they were from me I realized that the boles were of gigantic size.

At last I had come to the Galu country. Though not conceived in Caspak, I had indeed come up *cor-sva-jo*—from the beginning I had come up through the hideous horrors of the lower Caspakian spheres of evolution, and I could not but feel something of the elation and pride which had filled To-mar and So-al when they realized that the call had come to them and they were about to rise from the estate of Band-lus to that of Kro-lus. I was glad that I was not *batu*.

But where was Ajor? Though my eyes searched the wide landscape before me, I saw nothing other than the warriors of Du-seen and the beasts of the fields and the forests. Surrounded by forests, I could see wide plains dotting the country as far as the eye could reach; but nowhere was a sign of a small Galu she—the beloved she whom I would have given my right hand to see.

Nobs and I were hungry; we had not eaten since the preceding night, and below us was game—deer, sheep, anything that a hungry hunter might crave; so down the steep trail we made our way, and then upon my belly with Nobs crouching low behind me, I crawled toward a small herd of red deer feeding at the edge of a plain close beside a forest. There was ample cover, what with solitary trees and dotting bushes, so that I found no difficulty in stalking up wind to within fifty feet of my quarry—a large, sleek doe unaccompanied by a fawn. Greatly then did I regret my rifle. Never in my life had I shot an arrow; but I knew how it was done, and fitting the shaft to my string, I aimed carefully and let drive. At the same instant I called to Nobs and leaped to my feet.

The arrow caught the doe full in the side, and in the same moment Nobs was after her. She turned to flee with the two of us pursuing her, Nobs with his great fangs bared and I with my short spear poised for a cast. The balance of the herd sprang quickly away; but the hurt doe lagged, and in a moment Nobs was beside her and had leaped at her throat. He had her down when I came up, and I finished her with my spear. It didn't take me long to have a fire going and a steak broiling, and while I was preparing for my own feast, Nobs was filling himself with raw venison. Never have I enjoyed a meal so heartily.

For two days I searched fruitlessly back and forth from the inland sea almost to the barrier cliffs for some trace of Ajor, and always I trended northward; but I saw no sign of any human being, not even the band of Galu warriors under Du-seen; and then I commenced to have misgivings. Had Chal-az spoken the truth to me when he said that Ajor had quit the village of the Kro-lu? Might he not have been acting upon the orders of Al-tan, in whose savage bosom might have lurked some small spark of shame that he had attempted to do to death one who had befriended a Kro-lu warrior—a guest who had brought no harm upon the Kro-lu race—and thus have sent me out upon a fruitless mission in the hope that the wild beasts would do what Al-tan hesitated to do? I did not know; but the more I thought upon it, the more convinced I became that Ajor had not quitted the Kro-lu village; but if not, what had brought Du-seen forth without her? There was a puzzler, and once again I was all at sea.

On the second day of my experience of the Galu country I

came upon a bunch of as magnificent horses as it has ever been my lot to see. They were dark bays with blazed faces and perfect surcingles of white about their barrels. Their forelegs were white to the knees. In height they stood almost sixteen hands, the mares being a trifle smaller than the stallions, of which there were three or four in this band of a hundred, which comprised many colts and half-grown horses. Their markings were almost identical, indicating a purity of strain that might have persisted since long ages ago. If I had coveted one of the little ponies of the Kro-lu country, imagine my state of mind when I came upon these magnificent creatures! No sooner had I espied them than I determined to possess one of them; nor did it take me long to select a beautiful young stallion—a four-year-old, I guessed him.

The horses were grazing close to the edge of the forest in which Nobs and I were concealed, while the ground between us and them was dotted with clumps of flowering brush which offered perfect concealment. The stallion of my choice grazed with a filly and two yearlings a little apart from the balance of the herd and nearest to the forest and to me. At my whispered "Charge!" Nobs flattened himself to the ground, and I knew that he would not again move until I called him, unless danger threatened me from the rear. Carefully I crept forward toward my unsuspecting quarry, coming undetected to the concealment of a bush not more than twenty feet from him. Here I quietly arranged my noose, spreading it flat and open upon the ground.

To step to one side of the bush and throw directly from the ground, which is the style I am best in, would take but an instant, and in that instant the stallion would doubtless be under way at top speed in the opposite direction. Yet I felt that I could accomplish it, and especially so if the animal would but turn for a moment in my direction. Then he would have to wheel about when I surprised him, and in doing so, he would most certainly rise slightly upon his hind feet and throw up his head, presenting a perfect target for my noose as he pivoted.

Yes, I had it beautifully worked out, and I waited until he should turn in my direction. At last it became evident that he was doing so, when apparently without cause, the filly raised her head, neighed and started off at a trot in the opposite direction, immediately followed, of course, by the colts and my stallion. It looked for a moment as though my last hope was blasted; but presently their fright, if fright it was, passed, and they resumed grazing again a hundred yards farther on. This time there was no bush within fifty feet of them, and I was at a loss as to how to get within safe roping-distance. Anywhere under forty feet I am an excellent roper, at fifty feet I am fair; but over that I knew it would be but a matter of luck if I succeeded in getting my noose about that beautiful arched neck.

As I stood debating the question in my mind, I was almost upon the point of making the attempt at the long throw. I had plenty of rope, this Galu weapon being fully sixty feet long. How I wished for the collies from the ranch! At a word they would have circled this little bunch and driven it straight down to me; and then it flashed into my mind that Nobs had run with those collies all one summer, that he had gone down to the pasture with them after the cows every evening and done his part in driving them back to the milking-barn, and had done it intelligently; but Nobs had never done the thing alone, and it had been a year since he had done it at all. However, the chances were more in favor of my foozling the long throw than that Nobs would fall down in his part if I gave him the chance.

Having come to a decision, I had to creep back to Nobs and get him, and then with him at my heels return to a large bush near the four horses. Here we could see directly through the bush, and pointing the animals out to Nobs I whispered: "Fetch 'em, boy!"

In an instant he was gone, circling wide toward the rear of the quarry. They caught sight of him almost immediately and broke into a trot away from him; but when they saw that he was apparently giving them a wide berth they stopped again, though they stood watching him, with high-held heads and quivering nostrils. It was a beautiful sight. And then Nobs turned in behind them and trotted slowly back toward me. He did not bark, nor come rushing down upon them, and when he had come closer to them, he proceeded at a walk. The splendid creatures seemed more curious than fearful, making no effort to escape until Nobs was quite close to them; then they trotted slowly away, but at right angles.

And now the fun and trouble commenced. Nobs, of course, attempted to turn them, and he seemed to have selected the stallion to work upon, for he paid no attention to the others, having intelligence enough to know that a lone dog could run his legs off before he could round up four horses that didn't wish to be rounded up. The stallion, however, had notions of his own about being headed, and the result was as pretty a race as one would care to see. Gad, how that horse could run! He seemed to flatten out and shoot through the air with the very minimum of exertion, and at his forefoot ran Nobs, doing his best to turn him. He was barking now, and twice he leaped high against the stallion's flank; but this cost too much effort and always lost him ground, as each time he was hurled heels over head by the impact; yet before they disappeared over a rise in the ground I was sure that Nobs' persistence was bearing fruit; it seemed to me that the horse was giving way a trifle to the right. Nobs was between him and the main herd, to which the yearlings and filly had already fled.

As I stood waiting for Nobs' return, I could not but speculate upon my chances should I be attacked by some formidable beast. I was some distance from the forest and armed with weapons in the use of which I was quite untrained, though I had practiced some with the spear since leaving the Kro-lu country. I must admit that my thoughts were not pleasant ones, verging almost upon cowardice, until I chanced to think of little Ajor alone in this same land and armed only with a knife! I was immediately filled with shame; but in thinking the matter over since, I have come to the conclusion that my state of mind was influenced largely by my approximate nakedness. If you have never wandered about in broad daylight garbed in a bit of red-deer skin of inadequate length, you can have no conception of the sensation of futility that overwhelms one. Clothes, to a man accustomed to wearing clothes, impart a certain self-confidence; lack of them induces panic.

But no beast attacked me, though I saw several menacing forms passing through the dark aisles of the forest. At last I commenced to worry over Nobs' protracted absence and to fear that something had befallen him. I was coiling my rope to start out in search of him, when I saw the stallion leap into view at almost the same spot behind which he had disappeared, and at his heels ran Nobs. Neither was running so fast or furiously as when last I had seen them.

The horse, as he approached me, I could see was laboring hard; yet he kept gamely to his task, and Nobs, too. The splendid fellow was driving the quarry straight toward me. I crouched behind my bush and laid my noose in readiness to throw. As the two approached my hiding-place, Nobs reduced his speed, and the stallion, evidently only too glad of the respite, dropped into a trot. It was at this gait that he passed me; my rope-hand flew forward; the *honda*, well down, held the noose open, and the beautiful bay fairly ran his head into it.

Instantly he wheeled to dash off at right angles. I braced myself with the rope around my hip and brought him to a sudden stand. Rearing and struggling, he fought for his liberty while Nobs, panting and with lolling tongue, came and threw himself down near me. He seemed to know that his work was done and that he had earned his rest. The stallion was pretty well spent, and after a few minutes of struggling he stood with feet far spread, nostrils dilated and eyes wide, watching me as I edged slowly toward him, taking in the slack of the rope as I advanced. A dozen times he reared and tried to break away; but always I spoke soothingly to him, and after an hour of effort I succeeded in reaching his head and stroking his muzzle. Then I gathered a handful of grass and offered it to him, and always I talked to him in a quiet and reassuring voice.

I had expected a battle royal; but on the contrary I found his taming a matter of comparative ease. Though wild, he was gentle to a degree, and of such remarkable intelligence that he soon discovered that I had no intention of harming him. After that, all was easy. Before that day was done, I had taught him to lead and to stand while I stroked his head and flanks, and to eat from my hand, and had the satisfaction of seeing the light of fear die in his large, intelligent eyes.

The following day I fashioned a hackamore from a piece which I cut from the end of my long Galu rope, and then I mounted him fully prepared for a struggle of titanic proportions in which I was none too sure that he would not come off victor; but he never made the slightest effort to unseat me, and from then on his education was rapid. No horse ever learned more quickly the meaning of the rein and the pressure of the knees. I think he soon learned to love me, and I know that I loved him; while he and Nobs were the best of pals. I called him Ace. I had a friend who was one in the French flying-corps, and when Ace let himself out, he certainly flew.

I cannot explain to you, nor can you understand, unless you too are a horseman, the exhilarating feeling of well-being which pervaded me from the moment that I commenced riding Ace. I was a new man, imbued with a sense of superiority that led me to feel that I could go forth and conquer all Caspak single-handed. Now, when I needed meat, I ran it down on Ace and roped it, and when some great beast with which we could not cope threatened us, we galloped away to safety; but for the most part the creatures we met looked upon us in terror, for Ace and I in combination presented a new and unusual beast beyond their experience and ken.

For five days I rode back and forth across the southern end of the Galu country without seeing a human being; yet all the time I was working slowly toward the north, for I had determined to comb the territory thoroughly in search of Ajor; but on the fifth day as I emerged from a forest, I saw some distance ahead of me a single small figure pursued by many others. Instantly I recognized the quarry as Ajor. The entire party was fully a mile away from me, and they were crossing my path at right angles, Ajor a few hundred yards in advance of those who followed her. One of her pursuers was far in advance of the others, and was gaining upon her rapidly. With a word and a pressure of the knees I sent Ace leaping out into the open, and with Nobs running close alongside, we raced toward her.

At first none of them saw us; but as we neared Ajor, the pack behind the foremost pursuer discovered us and set up such a howl as I never before have heard. They were all Galus, and I soon recognized the foremost as Du-seen. He was almost upon Ajor now, and with a sense of terror such as I had never before experienced, I saw that he ran with his knife in his hand and that his intention was to slay rather than capture. I could not understand it; but I could only urge Ace to gather speed, and most nobly did the wondrous creature respond to my demands. If ever a four-footed creature approximated flying, it was Ace that day.

Du-seen, intent upon his brutal design, had as yet not noticed us. He was within a pace of Ajor when Ace and I dashed between them, and I, leaning down to the left, swept my little barbarian into the hollow of an arm and up to the withers of my glorious Ace. We had snatched her from the very clutches of Du-seen, who halted, mystified and raging. Ajor, too, was mystified, as we had come up from diagonally behind her so that she had no idea that we were near until she was swung to Ace's back. The little savage turned with drawn knife to stab me, thinking that I was some new enemy, when her eyes found my face and she recognized me. With a little sob she threw her arms about my neck, gasping: "My Tom! My Tom!"

And then Ace sank suddenly into thick mud to his belly, and Ajor and I were thrown far over his head. He had run into one of those numerous springs which cover Caspak. Sometimes they are little lakes, again but tiny pools, and often mere quagmires of mud, as was this one overgrown with lush grasses which effectually hid its treacherous identity. It is a wonder that Ace did not break a leg, so fast was he going when he fell; but he didn't, though with four good legs he was unable to wallow from the mire. Ajor and I had sprawled face down into the covering grasses and so had not sunk deeply; but when we tried to rise, we found that there was not footing, and presently we saw that Du-seen and his followers were coming down upon us. There was no escape. It was evident that we were doomed.

"Slay me!" begged Ajor. "Let me die at thy loved hands rather than beneath the knife of this hateful thing, for he will kill me. He has sworn to kill me. Last night he captured me, and when later he would have had his way with me, I struck him with my fists and with my knife I stabbed him, and then I escaped, leaving him raging in pain and thwarted desire. Today they searched for me and found me; and as I fled, Du-seen ran after me crying that he would slay me. Kill me, my Tom, and then fall upon thine own spear, for they will kill you horribly if they take you alive."

I couldn't kill her—not at least until the last moment; and I told her so, and that I loved her, and that until death came, I would live and fight for her.

Nobs had followed us into the bog and had done fairly well at first, but when he neared us, he too sank to his belly and could only flounder about. We were in this predicament when Du-seen and his followers approached the edge of the horrible swamp. I saw that Al-tan was with him and many other Kro-lu warriors. The alliance against Jor the chief had, therefore, been consummated, and this horde was already marching upon the Galu city. I sighed as I thought how close I had been to saving not only Ajor but her father and his people from defeat and death.

Beyond the swamp was a dense wood. Could we have reached this, we would have been safe; but it might as well have been a hundred miles away as a hundred yards across that hidden lake of sticky mud. Upon the edge of the swamp Du-seen and his horde halted to revile us. They could not reach us with their hands; but at a command from Du-seen they fitted arrows to their bows, and I saw that the end had come. Ajor huddled close to me, and I took her in my arms. "I love you, Tom," she said, "only you." Tears came to my eyes then, not tears of self-pity for my predicament, but tears from a heart filled with a great love—a heart that sees the sun of its life and its love setting even as it rises.

The renegade Galus and their Kro-lu allies stood waiting for the word from Du-seen that would launch that barbed avalanche of death upon us, when there broke from the wood beyond the

swamp the sweetest music that ever fell upon the ears of man—
the sharp staccato of at least two score rifles fired rapidly at will.
Down went the Galu and Kro-lu warriors like tenpins before
that deadly fusillade.

What could it mean? To me it meant but one thing, and that
was that Hollis and Short and the others had scaled the cliffs and
made their way north to the Galu country upon the opposite side
of the island in time to save Ajor and me from almost certain
death. I didn't have to have an introduction to them to know
that the men who held those rifles were the men of my own
party; and when, a few minutes later, they came forth from their
concealment, my eyes verified my hopes. There they were, every
man-jack of them; and with them were a thousand straight,
sleek warriors of the Galu race; and ahead of the others came
two men in the garb of Galus. Each was tall and straight and
wonderfully muscled; yet they differed as Ace might differ from
a perfect specimen of another species. As they approached the
mire, Ajor held forth her arms and cried, "Jor, my chief! My
father!" and the elder of the two rushed in knee-deep to rescue
her, and then the other came closer and looked into my face,
and his eyes went wide, and mine too, and I cried: "Bowen! For
heaven's sake, Bowen Tyler!"

It was he. My search was ended. Around me were all my company and the man we had searched a new world to find. They
cut saplings from the forest and laid a road into the swamp
before they could get us all out, and then we marched back to
the city of Jor the Galu chief, and there was great rejoicing when
Ajor came home again mounted upon the glossy back of the
stallion Ace.

Tyler and Hollis and Short and all the rest of us Americans
nearly worked our jaws loose on the march back to the village,
and for days afterward we kept it up. They told me how they
had crossed the barrier cliffs in five days, working twenty-four
hours a day in three eight-hour shifts with two reliefs to each
shift alternating half-hourly. Two men with electric drills driven
from the dynamos aboard the *Toreador* drilled two holes four
feet apart in the face of the cliff and in the same horizontal
plane. The holes slanted slightly downward. Into these holes the
iron rods brought as a part of our equipment and for just this
purpose were inserted, extending about a foot beyond the face
of the rock, across these two rods a plank was laid, and then the
next shift, mounting to the new level, bored two more holes five
feet above the new platform, and so on.

During the nights the searchlights from the *Toreador* were kept playing upon the cliff at the point where the drills were working, and at the rate of ten feet an hour the summit was reached upon the fifth day. Ropes were lowered, blocks lashed to trees at the top, and crude elevators rigged, so that by the night of the fifth day the entire party, with the exception of the few men needed to man the *Toreador*, were within Caspak with an abundance of arms, ammunition and equipment.

From then on, they fought their way north in search of me, after a vain and perilous effort to enter the hideous reptile-infested country to the south. Owing to the number of guns among them, they had not lost a man; but their path was strewn with the dead creatures they had been forced to slay to win their way to the north end of the island, where they had found Bowen and his bride among the Galus of Jor.

The reunion between Bowen and Nobs was marked by a frantic display upon Nobs' part, which almost stripped Bowen of the scanty attire that the Galu custom had vouchsafed him. When we arrived at the Galu city, Lys La Rue was waiting to welcome us. She was Mrs. Tyler now, as the master of the *Toreador* had married them the very day that the search-party had found them, though neither Lys nor Bowen would admit that any civil or religious ceremony could have rendered more sacred the bonds with which God had united them.

Neither Bowen nor the party from the *Toreador* had seen any sign of Bradley and his party. They had been so long lost now that any hopes for them must be definitely abandoned. The Galus had heard rumors of them, as had the Western Kro-lu and Band-lu; but none had seen aught of them since they had left Fort Dinosaur months since.

We rested in Jor's village for a fortnight while we prepared for the southward journey to the point where the *Toreador* was to lie offshore in wait for us. During these two weeks Chal-az came up from the Kro-lu country, now a full-fledged Galu. He told us that the remnants of Al-tan's party had been slain when they attempted to reenter Kro-lu. Chal-az had been made chief, and when he rose, had left the tribe under a new leader whom all respected.

Nobs stuck close to Bowen; but Ace and Ajor and I went out upon many long rides through the beautiful north Galu country. Chal-az had brought my arms and ammunition up from Kro-lu with him; but my clothes were gone; nor did I miss them once I became accustomed to the free attire of the Galu.

At last came the time for our departure; upon the following morning we were to set out toward the south and the *Toreador* and dear old California. I had asked Ajor to go with us; but Jor her father had refused to listen to the suggestion. No pleas could swerve him from his decision: Ajor, the *cos-ata-lo,* from whom might spring a new and greater Caspakian race, could not be spared. I might have any other she among the Galus; but Ajor —no!

The poor child was heartbroken; and as for me, I was slowly realizing the hold that Ajor had upon my heart and wondering how I should get along without her. As I held her in my arms that last night, I tried to imagine what life would be without her, for at last there had come to me the realization that I loved her—loved my little barbarian; and as I finally tore myself away and went to my own hut to snatch a few hours' sleep before we set off upon our long journey on the morrow, I consoled myself with the thought that time would heal the wound and that back in my native land I should find a mate who would be all and more to me than little Ajor could ever be—a woman of my own race and my own culture.

Morning came more quickly than I could have wished. I rose and breakfasted, but saw nothing of Ajor. It was best, I thought, that I go thus without the harrowing pangs of a last farewell. The party formed for the march, an escort of Galu warriors ready to accompany us. I could not even bear to go to Ace's corral and bid him farewell. The night before, I had given him to Ajor, and now in my mind the two seemed inseparable.

And so we marched away, down along the street flanked with its stone houses and out through the wide gateway in the stone wall which surrounds the city and on across the clearing toward the forest through which we must pass to reach the northern boundary of Galu, beyond which we would turn south. At the edge of the forest I cast a last backward glance at the city which held my heart, and beside the massive gateway I saw that which brought me to a sudden halt. It was a little figure leaning against one of the great upright posts upon which the gates swing—a crumpled little figure; and even at this distance I could see its shoulders heave to the sobs that racked it. It was the last straw.

Bowen was near me. "Good-bye, old man," I said. "I'm going back."

He looked at me in surprise. "Good-bye, old man," he said, and grasped my hand. "I thought you'd do it in the end."

And then I went back and took Ajor in my arms and kissed the tears from her eyes and a smile to her lips while together we watched the last of the Americans disappear into the forest.

PART III

Out of Time's Abyss

The Tale of Bradley

CHAPTER I

THIS IS the tale of Bradley after he left Fort Dinosaur upon the west coast of the great lake that is in the center of the island.

Upon the fourth day of September, 1916, he set out with four companions, Sinclair, Brady, James, and Tippet, to search along the base of the barrier cliffs for a point at which they might be scaled.

Through the heavy Caspakian air, beneath the swollen sun, the five men marched northwest from Fort Dinosaur, now waist-deep in lush, jungle grasses starred with myriad gorgeous blooms, now across open meadow-land and parklike expanses and again plunging into dense forests of eucalyptus and acacia and giant arboreous ferns with feathered fronds waving gently a hundred feet above their heads.

About them upon the ground, among the trees and in the air over them moved and swung and soared the countless forms of Caspak's teeming life. Always were they menaced by some frightful thing and seldom were their rifles cool, yet even in the brief time they had dwelt upon Caprona they had become callous to danger, so that they swung along laughing and chatting like soldiers on a summer hike.

"This reminds me of South Clark Street," remarked Brady, who had once served on the traffic squad in Chicago; and as no one asked him why, he volunteered that it was "because it's no place for an Irishman."

"South Clark Street and heaven have something in common, then," suggested Sinclair. James and Tippet laughed, and then a hideous growl broke from a dense thicket ahead and diverted their attention to other matters.

"One of them behemoths of 'Oly Writ," muttered Tippet as they came to a halt and with guns ready awaited the almost inevitable charge.

"Hungry lot o' beggars, these," said Bradley; "always trying to eat everything they see."

For a moment no further sound came from the thicket. "He

may be feeding now," suggested Bradley. "We'll try to go around him. Can't waste ammunition. Won't last forever. Follow me." And he set off at right angles to their former course, hoping to avert a charge. They had taken a dozen steps, perhaps, when the thicket moved to the advance of the thing within it, the leafy branches parted, and the hideous head of a gigantic bear emerged.

"Pick your trees," whispered Bradley. "Can't waste ammunition."

The men looked about them. The bear took a couple of steps forward, still growling menacingly. He was exposed to the shoulders now. Tippet took one look at the monster and bolted for the nearest tree; and then the bear charged. He charged straight for Tippet. The other men scattered for the various trees they had selected—all except Bradley. He stood watching Tippet and the bear. The man had a good start and the tree was not far away; but the speed of the enormous creature behind him was something to marvel at, yet Tippet was in a fair way to make his sanctuary when his foot caught in a tangle of roots and down he went, his rifle flying from his hand and falling several yards away. Instantly Bradley's piece was at his shoulder, there was a sharp report answered by a roar of mingled rage and pain from the carnivore. Tippet attempted to scramble to his feet.

"Lie still!" shouted Bradley. "Can't waste ammunition."

The bear halted in its tracks, wheeled toward Bradley and then back again toward Tippet. Again the former's rifle spit angrily, and the bear turned again in his direction. Bradley shouted loudly. "Come on, you behemoth of Holy Writ!" he cried. "Come on, you duffer! Can't waste ammunition." And as he saw the bear apparently upon the verge of deciding to charge him, he encouraged the idea by backing rapidly away, knowing that an angry beast will more often charge one who moves than one who lies still.

And the bear did charge. Like a bolt of lightning he flashed down upon the Englishman. "Now run!" Bradley called to Tippet and himself turned in flight toward a near-by tree. The other men, now safely ensconced upon various branches, watched the race with breathless interest. Would Bradley make it? It seemed scarce possible. And if he didn't! James gasped at the thought. Six feet at the shoulder stood the frightful mountain of blood-mad flesh and bone and sinew that was bearing down with the speed of an express train upon the seemingly slow-moving man.

It all happened in a few seconds; but they were seconds that seemed like hours to the men who watched. They saw Tippet leap to his feet at Bradley's shouted warning. They saw him run, stooping to recover his rifle as he passed the spot where it had fallen. They saw him glance back toward Bradley, and then they saw him stop short of the tree that might have given him safety and turn back in the direction of the bear. Firing as he ran, Tippet raced after the great cave bear—the monstrous thing that should have been extinct ages before—ran for it and fired even as the beast was almost upon Bradley. The men in the trees scarcely breathed. It seemed to them such a futile thing for Tippet to do, and Tippet of all men! They had never looked upon Tippet as a coward—there seemed to be no cowards among that strangely assorted company that Fate had gathered together from the four corners of the earth—but Tippet was considered a cautious man. Overcautious, some thought him. How futile he and his little pop-gun appeared as he dashed after that living engine of destruction! But, oh, how glorious! It was some such thought as this that ran through Brady's mind, though articulated it might have been expressed otherwise, albeit more forcefully.

Just then it occurred to Brady to fire and he, too, opened upon the bear, but at the same instant the animal stumbled and fell forward, though still growling most fearsomely. Tippet never stopped running or firing until he stood within a foot of the brute, which lay almost touching Bradley and was already struggling to regain its feet. Placing the muzzle of his gun against the bear's ear, Tippet pulled the trigger. The creature sank limply to the ground and Bradley scrambled to his feet.

"Good work, Tippet," he said. "Mightily obliged to you— awful waste of ammunition, really."

And then they resumed the march and in fifteen minutes the encounter had ceased even to be a topic of conversation.

For two days they continued upon their perilous way. Already the cliffs loomed high and forbidding close ahead without sign of break to encourage hope that somewhere they might be scaled. Late in the afternoon the party crossed a small stream of warm water upon the sluggishly moving surface of which floated countless millions of tiny green eggs surrounded by a light scum of the same color, though of a darker shade. Their past experience of Caspak had taught them that they might expect to come upon a stagnant pool of warm water if they followed the stream to its source; but there they were almost certain to find some of

that was not moved by some species of terror or awe. Then Brady spoke again in an almost inaudible voice. "Holy Mother protect us—it's a banshee!"

Bradley, always cool almost to indifference in the face of danger, felt a strange, creeping sensation run over his flesh, as slowly, not a hundred feet above them, the thing flapped itself across the sky, its huge, round eyes glaring down upon them. And until it disappeared over the tops of the trees of a near-by wood the five men stood as though paralyzed, their eyes never leaving the weird shape; nor never one of them appearing to recall that he grasped a loaded rifle in his hands.

With the passing of the thing came the reaction. Tippet sank to the ground and buried his face in his hands. "Oh, Gord," he moaned. "Tyke me away from this orful plice." Brady, recovered from the first shock, swore loud and luridly. He called upon all the saints to witness that he was unafraid and that anybody with half an eye could have seen that the creature was nothing more than "one av thim flyin' alligators" that they all were familiar with.

"Yes," said Sinclair with fine sarcasm, "we've saw so many of them with white shrouds on 'em."

"Shut up, you fool!" growled Brady. "If you know so much, tell us what it was after bein' then."

Then he turned toward Bradley. "What was it, sor, do you think?" he asked.

Bradley shook his head. "I don't know," he said. "It looked like a winged human being clothed in a flowing white robe. Its face was more human than otherwise. That is the way it looked to me; but what it really was I can't even guess, for such a creature is as far beyond my experience or knowledge as it is beyond yours. All that I am sure of is that whatever else it may have been, it was quite material—it was no ghost; rather just another of the strange forms of life which we have met here and with which we should be accustomed by this time."

Tippet looked up. His face was still ashy. "Yer cawn't tell me," he cried. "Hi seen hit. Blime, Hi seen hit. Hit was ha dead man flyin' through the hair. Didn't Hi see 'is heyes? Oh, Gord! Didn't Hi see 'em?"

"It didn't look like any beast or reptile to me," spoke up Sinclair. "It was lookin' right down at me when I looked up and I saw its face plain as I see yours. It had big round eyes that looked all cold and dead, and its cheeks were sunken in deep, and I could see its yellow teeth behind thin, tight-drawn lips—

like a man who had been dead a long while, sir," he added, turning toward Bradley.

"Yes!" James had not spoken since the apparition had passed over them, and now it was scarce speech which he uttered—rather a series of articulate gasps. "Yes—dead—a—long—while. It —means something. It—come—for some—one. For one—of us. One—of—us is—goin'—to die. I'm goin' to die!" he ended in a wail.

"Come! Come!" snapped Bradley. "Won't do. Won't do at all. Get to work, all of you. Waste of time. Can't waste time."

His authoritative tones brought them all up standing, and presently each was occupied with his own duties; but each worked in silence and there was no singing and no bantering such as had marked the making of previous camps. Not until they had eaten and to each had been issued the little ration of smoking tobacco allowed after each evening meal did any sign of a relaxation of taut nerves appear. It was Brady who showed the first signs of returning good spirits. He commenced humming "It's a Long Way to Tipperary" and presently to voice the words, but he was well into his third song before anyone joined him, and even then there seemed a dismal note in even the gayest of tunes.

A huge fire blazed in the opening of their rocky shelter that the prowling carnivora might be kept at bay; and always one man stood on guard, watchfully alert against a sudden rush by some maddened beast of the jungle. Beyond the fire, yellow-green spots of flame appeared, moved restlessly about, disappeared and reappeared, accompanied by a hideous chorus of screams and growls and roars as the hungry meat-eaters hunting through the night were attracted by the light or the scent of possible prey.

But to such sights and sounds as these the five men were become callous. They sang or talked as unconcernedly as they might have done in the barroom of some public-house at home.

Sinclair was standing guard. The others were listening to Brady's description of traffic congestion at the Rush Street bridge during the rush hour at night. The fire crackled cheerily. The owners of the yellow-green eyes raised their frightful chorus to the heavens. Conditions seemed again to have returned to normal. And then, as though the hand of Death had reached out and touched them all, the five men tensed into sudden rigidity.

Above the nocturnal diapason of the teeming jungle sounded a dismal flapping of wings and overhead, through the thick night, a shadowy form passed across the diffused light of the flaring camp-fire. Sinclair raised his rifle and fired. An eerie wail floated down from above and the apparition, whatever it might have been, was swallowed by the darkness. For several seconds the listening men heard the sound of those dismally flapping wings lessening in the distance until they could no longer be heard.

Bradley was the first to speak. "Shouldn't have fired, Sinclair," he said; "can't waste ammunition." But there was no note of censure in his tone. It was as though he understood the nervous reaction that had compelled the other's act.

"I couldn't help it, sir," said Sinclair. "Lord, it would take an iron man to keep from shootin' at that awful thing. Do you believe in ghosts, sir?"

"No," replied Bradley. "No such things."

"I don't know about that," said Brady. "There was a woman murdered over on the prairie near Brighton—her throat was cut from ear to ear, and—"

"Shut up," snapped Bradley.

"My gran'daddy used to live down Coppington wy," said Tippet. "They were a hold ruined castle on a 'ill near by, hand at midnight they used to see pale blue lights through the windows an' 'ear—"

"Will you close your hatch!" demanded Bradley. "You fools will have yourselves scared to death in a minute. Now go to sleep."

But there was little sleep in camp that night until utter exhaustion overtook the harassed men toward morning; nor was there any return of the weird creature that had set the nerves of each of them on edge.

The following forenoon the party reached the base of the barrier cliffs and for two days marched northward in an effort to discover a break in the frowning abutment that raised its rocky face almost perpendicularly above them, yet nowhere was there the slightest indication that the cliffs were scalable.

Disheartened, Bradley determined to turn back toward the fort, as he already had exceeded the time decided upon by Bowen Tyler and himself for the expedition. The cliffs for many miles had been trending in a northeasterly direction, indicating to Bradley that they were approaching the northern extremity of the island. According to the best of his calculations they had made sufficient easting during the past two days to have brought them to a point almost directly north of Fort Dinosaur and as nothing could be gained by retracing their steps along the base of the cliffs he decided to strike due south through the unexplored country between them and the fort.

That night (September 9, 1916), they made camp a short distance from the cliffs beside one of the numerous cool springs that are to be found within Caspak, oftentimes close beside the still more numerous warm and hot springs which feed the many pools. After supper the men lay smoking and chatting among themselves. Tippet was on guard. Fewer night prowlers threatened them, and the men were commenting upon the fact that the farther north they had traveled the smaller the number of all species of animal life became, though it was still present in what would have seemed appalling plenitude in any other part of the world. The diminution in reptilian life was the most noticeable change in the fauna of northern Caspak. Here, however, were forms they had not met elsewhere, several of which were of gigantic proportions.

According to their custom all, with the exception of the man on guard, sought sleep early, nor, once disposed upon the ground for slumber, were they long in finding it. It seemed to Bradley that he had scarcely closed his eyes when he was brought to his feet, wide awake, by a piercing scream which was punctuated by the sharp report of a rifle from the direction of the fire where Tippet stood guard. As he ran toward the man, Bradley heard above him the same uncanny wail that had set every nerve on edge several nights before, and the dismal flapping of huge wings. He did not need to look up at the white-shrouded figure winging slowly away into the night to know that their grim visitor had returned.

The muscles of his arm, reacting to the sight and sound of the menacing form, carried his hand to the butt of his pistol; but after he had drawn the weapon, he immediately returned it to its holster with a shrug.

"What for?" he muttered. "Can't waste ammunition." Then he walked quickly to where Tippet lay sprawled upon his face. By this time James, Brady and Sinclair were at his heels, each with his rifle in readiness.

"Is he dead, sir?" whispered James as Bradley kneeled beside the prostrate form.

Bradley turned Tippet over on his back and pressed an ear close to the other's heart. In a moment he raised his head. "Fainted," he announced. "Get water. Hurry!" Then he loosened Tippet's shirt at the throat and when the water was brought,

threw a cupful in the man's face. Slowly Tippet regained consciousness and sat up. At first he looked curiously into the faces
of the men about him; then an expression of terror overspread
his features. He shot a startled glance up into the black void
above and then burying his face in his arms began to sob like a
child.

"What's wrong, man?" demanded Bradley. "Buck up! Can't
play cry-baby. Waste of energy. What happened?"

"Wot 'appened, sir!" wailed Tippet. "Oh, Gord, sir! Hit came
back. Hit came for me, sir. Right hit did, sir; strite hat me, sir;
hand with long w'ite 'ands it clawed for me. Oh, Gord! Hit almost caught me, sir. Hi'm has good as dead; Hi'm a marked man;
that's wot Hi ham. Hit was a-goin' for to carry me horf, sir."

"Stuff and nonsense," snapped Bradley. "Did you get a good
look at it?"

Tippet said that he did—a much better look than he wanted.
The thing had almost clutched him, and he had looked straight
into its eyes—"dead heyes in a dead face," he had described them.

"Wot was it after bein', do you think?" inquired Brady.

"Hit was Death," moaned Tippet, shuddering, and again a
pall of gloom fell upon the little party.

The following day Tippet walked as one in a trance. He never
spoke except in reply to a direct question, which more often
than not had to be repeated before it could attract his attention. He insisted that he was already a dead man, for if the
thing didn't come for him during the day he would never live
through another night of agonized apprehension, waiting for
the frightful end that he was positive was in store for him. "I'll
see to that," he said, and they all knew that Tippet meant
to take his own life before darkness set in.

Bradley tried to reason with him, in his short, crisp way, but
soon saw the futility of it; nor could he take the man's weapons
from him without subjecting him to almost certain death from
any of the numberless dangers that beset their way.

The entire party was moody and glum. There was none of the
bantering that had marked their intercourse before, even in the
face of blighting hardships and hideous danger. This was a new
menace that threatened them, something that they couldn't explain; and so, naturally, it aroused within them superstitious
fear which Tippet's attitude only tended to augment. To add
further to their gloom, their way led through a dense forest,
where, on account of the underbrush, it was difficult to make
even a mile an hour. Constant watchfulness was required to

avoid the many snakes of various degrees of repulsiveness and enormity that infested the wood; and the only ray of hope they had to cling to was that the forest would, like the majority of Caspakian forests, prove to be of no considerable extent.

Bradley was in the lead when he came suddenly upon a grotesque creature of Titanic proportions. Crouching among the trees, which here commenced to thin out slightly, Bradley saw what appeared to be an enormous dragon devouring the carcass of a mammoth. From frightful jaws to the tip of its long tail it was fully forty feet in length. Its body was covered with plates of thick skin which bore a striking resemblance to armor-plate. The creature saw Bradley almost at the same instant that he saw it and reared up on its enormous hind legs until its head towered a full twenty-five feet above the ground. From the cavernous jaws issued a hissing sound of a volume equal to the escaping steam from the safety-valves of half a dozen locomotives, and then the creature came for the man.

"Scatter!" shouted Bradley to those behind him; and all but Tippet heeded the warning. The man stood as though dazed, and when Bradley saw the other's danger, he too stopped and wheeling about sent a bullet into the massive body forcing its way through the trees toward him. The shot struck the creature in the belly where there was no protecting armor, eliciting a new note which rose in a shrill whistle and ended in a wail. It was then that Tippet appeared to come out of his trance, for with a cry of terror he turned and fled to the left. Bradley, seeing that he had as good an opportunity as the others for escape, now turned his attention to extricating himself; and as the woods seemed dense on the right, he ran in that direction, hoping that the close-set boles would prevent pursuit on the part of the great reptile. The dragon paid no further attention to him, however, for Tippet's sudden break for liberty had attracted its attention; and after Tippet it went, bowling over small trees, uprooting underbrush and leaving a wake behind it like that of a small tornado.

Bradley, the moment he had discovered the thing was pursuing Tippet, had followed it. He was afraid to fire for fear of hitting the man, and so it was that he came upon them at the very moment that the monster lunged its great weight forward upon the doomed man. The sharp, three-toed talons of the forelimbs seized poor Tippet, and Bradley saw the unfortunate fellow lifted high above the ground as the creature again reared up on its hind legs, immediately transferring Tippet's body to its gaping jaws, which closed with a sickening, crunching sound as Tippet's bones cracked beneath the great teeth.

Bradley half raised his rifle to fire again and then lowered it with a shake of his head. Tippet was beyond succor—why waste a bullet that Caspak could never replace? If he could now escape the further notice of the monster it would be a wiser act than to throw his life away in futile revenge. He saw that the reptile was not looking in his direction, and so he slipped noiselessly behind the bole of a large tree and thence quietly faded away in the direction he believed the others to have taken. At what he considered a safe distance he halted and looked back. Half hidden by the intervening trees he still could see the huge head and the massive jaws from which protruded the limp legs of the dead man. Then, as though struck by the hammer of Thor, the creature collapsed and crumpled to the ground. Bradley's single bullet, penetrating the body through the soft skin of the belly, had slain the Titan.

A few minutes later, Bradley found the others of the party. The four returned cautiously to the spot where the creature lay and after convincing themselves that it was quite dead, came close to it. It was an arduous and gruesome job extricating Tippet's mangled remains from the powerful jaws, the men working for the most part silently.

"It was the work of the banshee all right," muttered Brady. "It warned poor Tippet, it did."

"Hit killed him, that's wot hit did, hand hit'll kill some more of us," said James, his lower lip trembling.

"If it was a ghost," interjected Sinclair, "and I don't say as it was; but if it was, why, it could take on any form it wanted to. It might have turned itself into this thing, which ain't no natural thing at all, just to get poor Tippet. If it had of been a lion or something else humanlike it wouldn't look so strange; but this here thing ain't humanlike. There ain't no such thing an' never was."

"Bullets don't kill ghosts," said Bradley, "so this couldn't have been a ghost. Furthermore, there are no such things. I've been trying to place this creature. Just succeeded. It's a tyrannosaurus. Saw picture of skeleton in magazine. There's one in New York Natural History Museum. Seems to me it said it was found in place called Hell Creek somewhere in western North America. Supposed to have lived about six million years ago."

"Hell Creek's in Montana," said Sinclair. "I used to punch cows in Wyoming, an' I've heard of Hell Creek. Do you s'pose

that there thing's six million years old?" His tone was skeptical.
"No," replied Bradley; "but it would indicate that the island
of Caprona has stood almost without change for more than six
million years."

The conversation and Bradley's assurance that the creature
was not of supernatural origin helped to raise a trifle the spirits
of the men; and then came another diversion in the form of
ravenous meat-eaters attracted to the spot by their uncanny sense
of smell which had apprised them of the presence of flesh, killed
and ready for the eating.

It was a constant battle while they dug a grave and consigned
all that was mortal of John Tippet to his last, lonely resting-
place. Nor would they leave then; but remained to fashion a
rude headstone from a crumbling out-cropping of sandstone
and to gather a mass of the gorgeous flowers growing in such
great profusion around them and heap the new-made grave
with bright blooms. Upon the headstone Sinclair scratched in
rude characters the words:

HERE LIES JOHN TIPPET
ENGLISHMAN
KILLED BY TYRANNOSAURUS
10 SEPT. A. D. 1916
R. I. P.

and Bradley repeated a short prayer before they left their comrade forever.

For three days the party marched due south through forests
and meadow-land and great park-like areas where countless herbivorous animals grazed—deer and antelope and bos and the
little *ecca*, the smallest species of Caspakian horse, about the
size of a rabbit. There were other horses, too; but all were
small, the largest being not above eight hands in height. Preying
continually upon the herbivora were the meat-eaters, large and
small—wolves, hyaenodons, panthers, lions, tigers, and bear as
well as several large and ferocious species of reptilian life.

On September twelfth the party scaled a line of sandstone
cliffs which crossed their route toward the south; but they crossed
them only after an encounter with the tribe that inhabited the
numerous caves which pitted the face of the escarpment. That
night they camped upon a rocky plateau which was sparsely
wooded with jarrah, and here once again they were visited by

the weird, nocturnal apparition that had already filled them with a nameless terror.

As on the night of September ninth the first warning came from the sentinel standing guard over his sleeping companions. A terror-stricken cry punctuated by the crack of a rifle brought Bradley, Sinclair and Brady to their feet in time to see James, with clubbed rifle, battling with a white-robed figure that hovered on widespread wings on a level with the Englishman's head. As they ran, shouting, forward, it was obvious to them that the weird and terrible apparition was attempting to seize James; but when it saw the others coming to his rescue, it desisted, flapping rapidly upward and away, its long, ragged wings giving forth the peculiarly dismal notes which always characterized the sound of its flying.

Bradley fired at the vanishing menacer of their peace and safety; but whether he scored a hit or not, none could tell, though, following the shot, there was wafted back to them the same piercing wail that had on other occasions frozen their marrow.

Then they turned toward James, who lay face downward upon the ground, trembling as with ague. For a time he could not even speak, but at last regained sufficient composure to tell them how the thing must have swooped silently upon him from above and behind as the first premonition of danger he had received was when the long, clawlike fingers had clutched him beneath either arm. In the mêlée his rifle had been discharged and he had broken away at the same instant and turned to defend himself with the butt. The rest they had seen.

From that instant James was an absolutely broken man. He maintained with shaking lips that his doom was sealed, that the thing had marked him for its own, and that he was as good as dead, nor could any amount of argument or raillery convince him to the contrary. He had seen Tippet marked and claimed, and now he had been marked. Nor were his constant reiterations of this belief without effect upon the rest of the party. Even Bradley felt depressed, though for the sake of the others he managed to hide it beneath a show of confidence he was far from feeling.

And on the following day William James was killed by a saber-tooth tiger—September 13, 1916. Beneath a jarrah tree on the stony plateau on the northern edge of the Sto-lu country in the land that Time forgot, he lies in a lonely grave marked by a rough headstone.

Southward from his grave marched three grim and silent men. To the best of Bradley's reckoning they were some twenty-five miles north of Fort Dinosaur, and that they might reach the fort on the following day, they plodded on until darkness overtook them. With comparative safety fifteen miles away, they made camp at last; but there was no singing now and no joking. In the bottom of his heart each prayed that they might come safely through just this night, for they knew that during the morrow they would make the final stretch, yet the nerves of each were taut with strained anticipation of what gruesome thing might flap down upon them from the black sky, marking another for its own. Who would be the next?

As was their custom, they took turns at guard, each man doing two hours and then arousing the next. Brady had gone on from eight to ten, followed by Sinclair from ten to twelve, then Bradley had been awakened. Brady would stand the last guard from two to four, as they had determined to start the moment that it became light enough to insure comparative safety upon the trail.

The snapping of a twig aroused Brady out of a dead sleep, and as he opened his eyes, he saw that it was broad daylight and that at twenty paces from him stood a huge lion. As the man sprang to his feet, his rifle ready in his hand, Sinclair awoke and took in the scene in a single swift glance. The fire was out and Bradley was nowhere in sight. For a long moment the lion and the men eyed one another. The latter had no mind to fire if the beast minded its own affairs—they were only too glad to let it go its way if it would; but this lion was of a different mind.

Suddenly the long tail snapped stiffly erect, and as though it had been attached to two trigger fingers the two rifles spoke in unison, for both men knew this signal only too well—the immediate forerunner of a deadly charge. As the brute's head had been raised, his spine had not been visible; and so they did what they had learned by long experience was best to do. Each covered a front leg, and as the tail snapped aloft, fired. With a hideous roar the mighty flesh-eater lurched forward to the ground with both front legs broken. It was an easy accomplishment in the instant before the beast charged—after, it would have been well-nigh an impossible feat. Brady stepped close in and finished him with a shot in the base of the brain lest his terrific roarings should attract his mate or others of their kind.

Then the two men turned and looked at one another. "Where is Lieutenant Bradley?" asked Sinclair. They walked to the fire.

Only a few smoking embers remained. A few feet away lay Bradley's rifle. There was no evidence of a struggle. The two men circled about the camp twice and on the last lap Brady stopped and picked up an object which had lain about ten yards beyond the fire—it was Bradley's cap. Again the two looked questioningly at one another, and then, simultaneously, both pairs of eyes swung upward and searched the sky. A moment later Brady was examining the ground about the spot where Bradley's cap had lain. It was one of those little barren, sandy stretches that they had found only upon this stony plateau. Brady's own footsteps showed as plainly as black ink upon white paper; but his was the only foot that had marred the smooth, windswept surface—there was no sign that Bradley had crossed the spot *upon the surface of the ground,* and yet his cap lay well toward the center of it.

Breakfastless and with shaken nerves the two survivors plunged madly into the long day's march. Both were strong, courageous, resourceful men; but each had reached the limit of human nerve endurance and each felt that he would rather die than spend another night in the hideous open of that frightful land. Vivid in the mind of each was a picture of Bradley's end, for though neither had witnessed the tragedy, both could imagine almost precisely what had occurred. They did not discuss it—they did not even mention it—yet all day long the thing was upper-most in the mind of each and mingled with it a similar picture with himself as victim should they fail to make Fort Dinosaur before dark.

And so they plunged forward at reckless speed, their clothes, their hands, their faces torn by the retarding underbrush that reached forth to hinder them. Again and again they fell; but be it to their credit that the one always waited and helped the other and that into the mind of neither entered the thought or the temptation to desert his companion—they would reach the fort together if both survived, or neither would reach it.

They encountered the usual number of savage beasts and rep-tiles; but they met them with a courageous recklessness born of desperation, and by virtue of the very madness of the chances they took, they came through unscathed and with the minimum of delay.

Shortly after noon they reached the end of the plateau. Before them was a drop of two hundred feet to the valley beneath. To the left, in the distance, they could see the waters of the great inland sea that covers a considerable portion of the area of the

crater island of Caprona and at a little lesser distance to the
south of the cliffs they saw a thin spiral of smoke arising above
the tree-tops.

The landscape was familiar—each recognized it immediately
and knew that that smoky column marked the spot where Dinosaur had stood. Was the fort still there, or did the smoke arise
from the smoldering embers of the building they had helped to
fashion for the housing of their party? Who could say!

Thirty precious minutes that seemed as many hours to the
impatient men were consumed in locating a precarious way
from the summit to the base of the cliffs that bounded the
plateau upon the south, and then once again they struck off
upon level ground toward their goal. The closer they approached
the fort the greater became their apprehension that all would
not be well. They pictured the barracks deserted or the small
company massacred and the buildings in ashes. It was almost in
a frenzy of fear that they broke through the final fringe of jungle
and stood at last upon the verge of the open meadow a half-mile
from Fort Dinosaur.

"Lord!" ejaculated Sinclair. "They are still there!" And he
fell to his knees, sobbing.

Brady trembled like a leaf as he crossed himself and gave silent
thanks, for there before them stood the sturdy ramparts of Dinosaur and from inside the inclosure rose a thin spiral of smoke
that marked the location of the cook-house. All was well, then,
and their comrades were preparing the evening meal!

Across the clearing they raced as though they had not already
covered in a single day a trackless, primeval country that might
easily have required two days by fresh and untired men. Within
hailing distance they set up such a loud shouting that presently
heads appeared above the top of the parapet and soon answering shouts were rising from within Fort Dinosaur. A moment
later three men issued from the inclosure and came forward to
meet the survivors and listen to the hurried story of the eleven
eventful days since they had set out upon their expedition to
the barrier cliffs. They heard of the deaths of Tippet and James
and of the disappearance of Lieutenant Bradley, and a new
terror settled upon Dinosaur.

Olson, the Irish engineer, with Whitely and Wilson constituted the remnants of Dinosaur's defenders, and to Brady and
Sinclair they narrated the salient events that had transpired
since Bradley and his party had marched away on September
4th. They told them of the infamous act of Baron Friedrich von

Schoenvorts and his German crew who had stolen the *U-33*, breaking their parole, and steaming away toward the subterranean opening through the barrier cliffs that carried the waters of the inland sea into the open Pacific beyond; and of the cowardly shelling of the fort.

They told of the disappearance of Miss La Rue in the night of September 11th, and of the departure of Bowen Tyler in search of her, accompanied only by his Airedale, Nobs. Thus of the original party of eleven Allies and nine Germans that had constituted the company of the *U-33* when she left English waters after her capture by the crew of the English tug there were but five now to be accounted for at Fort Dinosaur. Benson, Tippet, James, and one of the Germans were known to be dead. It was assumed that Bradley, Tyler and the girl had already succumbed to some of the savage denizens of Caspak, while the fate of the Germans was equally unknown, though it might readily be believed that they had made good their escape. They had had ample time to provision the ship and the refining of the crude oil they had discovered north of the fort could have insured them an ample supply to carry them back to Germany.

CHAPTER II

WHEN Bradley went on guard at midnight, September 14th, his thoughts were largely occupied with rejoicing that the night was almost spent without serious mishap and that the morrow would doubtless see them all safely returned to Fort Dinosaur. The hopefulness of his mood was tinged with sorrow by recollection of the two members of his party who lay back there in the savage wilderness and for whom there would never again be a homecoming.

No premonition of impending ill cast gloom over his anticipations for the coming day, for Bradley was a man who, while taking every precaution against possible danger, permitted no gloomy forebodings to weigh down his spirit. When danger threatened, he was prepared; but he was not forever courting disaster, and so it was that when, about one o'clock in the morning of the fifteenth, he heard the dismal flapping of giant wings overhead, he was neither surprised nor frightened but fully prepared for an attack he had known might reasonably be expected.

The sound seemed to come from the south, and presently, low

above the trees in that direction, the man made out a dim, shadowy form circling slowly about. Bradley was a brave man, yet so keen was the feeling of revulsion engendered by the sight and sound of that grim, uncanny shape that he distinctly felt the gooseflesh rise over the surface of his body, and it was with difficulty that he refrained from following an instinctive urge to fire upon the nocturnal intruder. Better, far better would it have been had he given in to the insistent demand of his subconscious mentor; but his almost fanatical obsession to save ammunition proved now his undoing, for while his attention was riveted upon the thing circling before him and while his ears were filled with the beating of its wings, there swooped silently out of the black night behind him another weird and ghostly shape. With its huge wings partly closed for the dive and its white robe fluttering in its wake, the apparition swooped down upon the Englishman.

So great was the force of the impact when the thing struck Bradley between the shoulders that the man was half stunned. His rifle flew from his grasp; he felt clawlike talons of great strength seize him beneath his arms and sweep him off his feet; and then the thing rose swiftly with him, so swiftly that his cap was blown from his head by the rush of air as he was borne rapidly upward into the inky sky and the cry of warning to his companions was forced back into his lungs.

The creature wheeled immediately toward the east and was at once joined by its fellow, who circled them once and then fell in behind them. Bradley now realized the strategy that the pair had used to capture him and at once concluded that he was in the power of reasoning beings closely related to the human race if not actually of it.

Past experience suggested that the great wings were a part of some ingenious mechanical device, for the limitations of the human mind, which is always loath to accept aught beyond its own little experience, would not permit him to entertain the idea that the creatures might be naturally winged and at the same time of human origin. From his position Bradley could not see the wings of his captor, nor in the darkness had he been able to examine those of the second creature closely when it circled before him. He listened for the purr of a motor or some other telltale sound that would prove the correctness of his theory. However, he was rewarded with nothing more than the constant flap-flap.

Presently, far below and ahead, he saw the waters of the inland sea, and a moment later he was borne over them. Then his captor did that which proved beyond doubt to Bradley that he was in the hands of human beings who had devised an almost perfect scheme of duplicating, mechanically, the wings of a bird—the thing spoke to its companion and in a language that Bradley partially understood, since he recognized words that he had learned from the savage races of Caspak. From this he judged that they were human, and being human, he knew that they could have no natural wings—for who had ever seen a human being so adorned! Therefore their wings must be mechanical. Thus Bradley reasoned—thus most of us reason; not by what might be possible; but by what has fallen within the range of our experience.

What he heard them say was to the effect that having covered half the distance the burden would now be transferred from one to the other. Bradley wondered how the exchange was to be accomplished. He knew that those giant wings would not permit the creatures to approach one another closely enough to effect the transfer in this manner; but he was soon to discover that they had other means of doing it.

He felt the thing that carried him rise to a greater altitude, and below he glimpsed momentarily the second white-robed figure; then the creature above sounded a low call, it was answered from below, and instantly Bradley felt the clutching talons release him; gasping for breath, he hurtled downward through space.

For a terrifying instant, pregnant with horror, Bradley fell; then something swooped for him from behind, another pair of talons clutched him beneath the arms, his downward rush was checked within another hundred feet, and close to the surface of the sea he was again borne upward. As a hawk dives for a songbird on the wing, so this great, human bird had dived for Bradley. It was a harrowing experience, but soon over, and once again the captive was being carried swiftly toward the east and what fate he could not even guess.

It was immediately following his transfer in mid-air that Bradley made out the shadowy form of a large island far ahead, and not long after, he realized that this must be the intended destination of his captors. Nor was he mistaken. Three quarters of an hour from the time of his seizure his captors dropped gently to earth in the strangest city that human eye had ever rested upon. Just a brief glimpse of his immediate surroundings was vouchsafed Bradley before he was whisked into the interior of one of the buildings; but in that momentary glance he saw strange piles

of stone and wood and mud fashioned into buildings of all
conceivable sizes and shapes, sometimes piled high on top of one
another, sometimes standing alone in an open courtway, but
usually crowded and jammed together, so that there were no
streets or alleys between them other than a few which ended
almost as soon as they began. The principal doorways appeared
to be in the roofs, and it was through one of these that Bradley
was inducted into the dark interior of a low-ceiled room. Here
he was pushed roughly into a corner where he tripped over a
thick mat, and there his captors left him. He heard them moving
about in the darkness for a moment, and several times he saw
their large luminous eyes glowing in the dark. Finally these
disappeared and silence reigned, broken only by the breathing of
the creatures which indicated to the Englishman that they were
sleeping somewhere in the same apartment.

It was now evident that the mat upon the floor was intended
for sleeping purposes and that the rough shove that had sent
him to it had been a rude invitation to repose. After taking stock
of himself and finding that he still had his pistol and ammunition, some matches, a little tobacco, a canteen full of water and
a razor, Bradley made himself comfortable upon the mat and
was soon asleep, knowing that an attempted escape in the darkness without knowledge of his surroundings would be predoomed
to failure.

When he awoke, it was broad daylight, and the sight that
met his eyes made him rub them again and again to assure
himself that they were really open and that he was not dreaming.
A broad shaft of morning light poured through the open doorway in the ceiling of the room which was about thirty feet
square, or roughly square, being irregular in shape, one side
curving outward, another being indented by what might have
been the corner of another building jutting into it, another al-
coved by three sides of an octagon, while the fourth was serpen-
tine in contour. Two windows let in more daylight, while two
doors evidently gave ingress to other rooms. The walls were
partially ceiled with thin strips of wood, nicely fitted and finished, partially plastered and the rest covered with a fine, woven
cloth. Figures of reptiles and beasts were painted without regard
to any uniform scheme here and there upon the walls. A striking
feature of the decorations consisted of several engaged columns
set in the walls at no regular intervals, the capitals of each supporting a human skull the cranium of which touched the ceiling, as though the latter was supported by these grim reminders

either of departed relatives or of some hideous tribal rite—
Bradley could not but wonder which.

Yet it was none of these things that filled him with greatest
wonder—no, it was the figures of the two creatures that had
captured him and brought him hither. At one end of the room
a stout pole about two inches in diameter ran horizontally
from wall to wall some six or seven feet from the floor, its ends
securely set in two of the columns. Hanging by their knees from
this perch, their heads downward and their bodies wrapped in
their huge wings, slept the creatures of the night before—like
two great, horrid bats they hung, asleep.

As Bradley gazed upon them in wide-eyed astonishment, he
saw plainly that all his intelligence, all his acquired knowledge
through years of observation and experience were set at naught
by the simple evidence of the fact that stood out glaringly before
his eyes—the creatures' wings were not mechanical devices but
as natural appendages, growing from their shoulder-blades, as
were their arms and legs. He saw, too, that except for their wings
the pair bore a strong resemblance to human beings, though
fashioned in a most grotesque mold.

As he sat gazing at them, one of the two awoke, separated his
wings to release his arms that had been folded across his breast,
placed his hands upon the floor, dropped his feet and stood
erect. For a moment he stretched his great wings slowly, solemnly
blinking his large, round eyes. Then his gaze fell upon Bradley.
The thin lips drew back tightly against yellow teeth in a grimace
that was nothing but hideous. It could not have been termed a
smile, and what emotion it registered the Englishman was at a
loss to guess. No expression whatever altered the steady gaze of
those large, round eyes; there was no color upon the pasty,
sunken cheeks. A death's head grimaced as though a man long
dead raised his parchment-covered skull from an old grave.

The creature stood about the height of an average man but
appeared much taller from the fact that the joints of his long
wings rose fully a foot above his hairless head. The bare arms
were long and sinewy, ending in strong, bony hands with clawlike fingers—almost talonlike in their suggestiveness. The white
robe was separated in front, revealing skinny legs and the further
fact that the thing wore but the single garment, which was of
fine, woven cloth. From crown to sole the portions of the body
exposed were entirely hairless, and as he noted this, Bradley also
noted for the first time the cause of much of the seeming ex-
pressionlessness of the creature's countenance—it had neither

eye-brows nor lashes. The ears were small and rested flat against the skull, which was noticeably round, though the face was quite flat. The creature had small feet, beautifully arched and plump, but so out of keeping with every other physical attribute it possessed as to appear ridiculous.

After eying Bradley for a moment the thing approached him. "Where from?" it asked.

"England," replied Bradley, as briefly.

"Where is England and what?" pursued the questioner.

"It is a country far from here," answered the Englishman.

"Are your people *cor-sva-jo* or *cos-ata-lu?*"

"I do not understand you," said Bradley; "and now suppose you answer a few questions. Who are you? What country is this? Why did you bring me here?"

Again the sepulchral grimace. "We are Wieroos. Luata is our father. Caspak is ours. This, our country, is called Oo-oh. We brought you here for (literally) Him Who Speaks for Luata to gaze upon and question. He would know from whence you came and why; but principally if you be *cos-ata-lu.*"

"And if I am not *cos*—whatever you call the bloomin' beast— what of it?"

The Wieroo raised his wings in a very human shrug and waved his bony claws toward the human skulls supporting the ceiling. His gesture was eloquent; but he embellished it by remarking, "And possibly if you are."

"I'm hungry," snapped Bradley.

The Wieroo motioned him to one of the doors which he threw open, permitting Bradley to pass out onto another roof on a level lower than that upon which they had landed earlier in the morning. By daylight the city appeared even more re- markable than in the moonlight, though less weird and unreal. The houses of all shapes and sizes were piled about as a child might pile blocks of various forms and colors. He saw now that there were what might be called streets or alleys, but they ran in baffling turns and twists, nor ever reached a destination, al- ways ending in a dead wall where some Wieroo had built a house across them.

Upon each house was a slender column supporting a human skull. Sometimes the columns were at one corner of the roof, sometimes at another, or again they rose from the center or near the center, and the columns were of varying heights, from that of a man to those which rose twenty feet above their roofs. The skulls were, as a rule, painted—blue or white, or in combinations of both colors. The most effective were painted blue with the teeth white and the eye-sockets rimmed with white.

There were other skulls—thousands of them—tens, hundreds of thousands. They rimmed the eaves of every house, they were set in the plaster of the outer walls and at no great distance from where Bradley stood rose a round tower built entirely of human skulls. And the city extended in every direction as far as the Englishman could see.

All about him Wieroos were moving across the roofs or winging through the air. The sad sound of their flapping wings rose and fell like a solemn dirge. Most of them were appareled all in white, like his captors; but others had markings of red or blue or yellow slashed across the front of their robes.

His guide pointed toward a doorway in an alley below them. "Go there and eat," he commanded, "and then come back. You cannot escape. If any question you, say that you belong to Fosh-bal-soj. There is the way." And this time he pointed to the top of a ladder which protruded above the eaves of the roof near-by. Then he turned and reentered the house.

Bradley looked about him. No, he could not escape—that seemed evident. The city appeared interminable, and beyond the city, if not a savage wilderness filled with wild beasts, there was the broad inland sea infested with horrid monsters. No wonder his captor felt safe in turning him loose in Oo-oh—he wondered if that was the name of the country or the city and if there were other cities like this upon the island.

Slowly he descended the ladder to the seemingly deserted alley which was paved with what appeared to be large, round cobblestones. He looked again at the smooth, worn pavement, and a rueful grin crossed his features—the alley was paved with skulls. "The City of Human Skulls," mused Bradley. "They must have been collectin' 'em since Adam," he thought, and then he crossed and entered the building through the doorway that had been pointed out to him.

Inside he found a large room in which were many Wieroos seated before pedestals the tops of which were hollowed out so that they resembled the ordinary bird drinking- and bathing-fonts so commonly seen on suburban lawns. A seat protruded from each of the four sides of the pedestals—just a flat board with a support running from its outer end diagonally to the base of the pedestal.

As Bradley entered, some of the Wieroos espied him, and a dismal wail arose. Whether it was a greeting or a threat, Bradley did not know. Suddenly from a dark alcove another Wieroo rushed out toward him. "Who are you?" he cried. "What do you want?"

"Fosh-bal-soj sent me here to eat," replied Bradley.

"Do you belong to Fosh-bal-soj?" asked the other.

"That appears to be what he thinks," answered the Englishman.

"Are you *cos-ata-lu?*" demanded the Wieroo.

"Give me something to eat or I'll be all of that," replied Bradley.

The Wieroo looked puzzled. "Sit here, *jaal-lu,*" he snapped, and Bradley sat down unconscious of the fact that he had been insulted by being called a hyena-man, an appellation of contempt in Caspak.

The Wieroo had seated him at a pedestal by himself, and as he sat waiting for what was next to transpire, he looked about him at the Wieroo in his immediate vicinity. He saw that in each font was a quantity of food, and that each Wieroo was armed with a wooden skewer, sharpened at one end, with which they carried solid portions of food to their mouths. At the other end of the skewer was fastened a small clam-shell. This was used to scoop up the smaller and softer portions of the repast into which all four of the occupants of each table dipped impartially. The Wieroo leaned far over their food, scooping it up rapidly and with much noise, and so great was their haste that a part of each mouthful always fell back into the common dish; and when they choked, by reason of the rapidity with which they attempted to bolt their food, they often lost it all. Bradley was glad that he had a pedestal all to himself.

Soon the keeper of the place returned with a wooden bowl filled with food. This he dumped into Bradley's "trough," as he already thought of it. The Englishman was glad that he could not see into the dark alcove or know what were all the ingredients that constituted the mess before him, for he was very hungry.

After the first mouthful he cared even less to investigate the antecedents of the dish, for he found it peculiarly palatable. It seemed to consist of a combination of meat, fruits, vegetables, small fish and other undistinguishable articles of food all seasoned to produce a gastronomic effect that was at once baffling and delicious.

When he had finished, his trough was empty, and then he commenced to wonder who was to settle for his meal. As he waited for the proprietor to return, he fell to examining the dish from which he had eaten and the pedestal upon which it rested. The font was of stone worn smooth by long-continued use, the four outer edges hollowed and polished by the contact of the countless Wieroo bodies that had leaned against them for how long a period of time Bradley could not even guess. Everything about the place carried the impression of hoary age. The carved pedestals were black with use, the wooden seats were worn hollow, the floor of stone slabs was polished by the contact of possibly millions of naked feet and worn away in the aisles between the pedestals so that the latter rested upon little mounds of stone several inches above the general level of the floor.

Finally, seeing that no one came to collect, Bradley arose and started for the doorway. He had covered half the distance when he heard the voice of mine host calling to him. "Come back, *jaal-lu*," screamed the Wieroo; and Bradley did as he was bid. As he approached the creature which stood now behind a large, flat-topped pedestal beside the alcove, he saw lying upon the smooth surface something that almost elicited a gasp of astonishment from him—a simple, common thing it was, or would have been almost anywhere in the world but Caspak—a square bit of paper!

And on it, in a fine hand, written compactly, were many strange hieroglyphics! These remarkable creatures, then, had a written as well as a spoken language and besides the art of weaving cloth possessed that of paper-making. Could it be that such grotesque beings represented the highest culture of the human race within the boundaries of Caspak? Had natural selection produced during the countless ages of Caspakian life a winged monstrosity that represented the earthly pinnacle of man's evolution?

Bradley had noted something of the obvious indications of a gradual evolution from ape to spear-man as exemplified by the several overlapping races of Alalus, club-men and hatchet-men that formed the connecting links between the two extremes with which he had come in contact. He had heard of the Kro-lus and the Galus—reputed to be still higher in the plane of evolution—and now he had indisputable evidence of a race possessing refinements of civilization eons in advance of the spear-men. The conjectures awakened by even a momentary consideration of the possibilities involved became at once as wildly bizarre as the insane imaginings of a drug addict.

As these thoughts flashed through his mind, the Wieroo held out a pen of bone fixed to a wooden holder and at the same time made a sign that Bradley was to write upon the paper. It was difficult to judge from the expressionless features of the Wieroo what was passing in the creature's mind; but Bradley could not but feel that the thing cast a supercilious glance upon him as much as to say, "Of course you do not know how to write, you poor, low creature; but you can make your mark."

Bradley seized the pen and in a clear, bold hand wrote: "John Bradley, England." The Wieroo showed evidences of consternation as it seized the piece of paper and examined the writing with every mark of incredulity and surprise. Of course it could make nothing of the strange characters; but it evidently accepted them as proof that Bradley possessed knowledge of a written language of his own, for following the Englishman's entry it made a few characters of its own.

"You will come here again just before Lua hides his face behind the great cliff," announced the creature, "unless before that you are summoned by Him Who Speaks for Luata, in which case you will not have to eat any more."

"Reassuring cuss," thought Bradley as he turned and left the building.

Outside were several of the Wieroos that had been eating at the pedestals within. They immediately surrounded him, asking all sorts of questions, plucking at his garments, his ammunition-belt and his pistol. Their demeanor was entirely different from what it had been within the eating-place and Bradley was to learn that a house of food was sanctuary for him, since the stern laws of the Wieroos forbade altercations within such walls. Now they were rough and threatening, as with wings half spread they hovered about him in menacing attitudes, barring his way to the ladder leading to the roof from whence he had descended; but the Englishman was not one to brook interference for long. He attempted at first to push his way past them, and then when one seized his arm and jerked him roughly back, Bradley swung upon the creature and with a heavy blow to the jaw felled it.

Instantly pandemonium reigned. Loud wails arose, great wings opened and closed with a loud, beating noise and many clawlike hands reached forth to clutch him. Bradley struck to right and left. He dared not use his pistol for fear that once they discovered its power he would be overcome by weight of numbers and relieved of possession of what he considered his trump card, to be reserved until the last moment that it might be used to aid in his escape, for already the Englishman was planning, though almost hopelessly, such an attempt.

A few blows convinced Bradley that the Wieroos were arrant cowards and that they bore no weapons, for after two or three had fallen beneath his fists the others formed a circle about him, but at a safe distance, and contented themselves with threatening and blustering, while those whom he had felled lay upon the pavement without trying to arise, the while they moaned and wailed in lugubrious chorus.

Again Bradley strode toward the ladder, and this time the circle parted before him; but no sooner had he ascended a few rungs than he was seized by one foot and an effort made to drag him down. With a quick backward glance the Englishman, clinging firmly to the ladder with both hands, drew up his free foot and with all the strength of a powerful leg planted a heavy shoe squarely in the flat face of the Wieroo that held him. Shrieking horribly, the creature clapped both hands to its face and sank to the ground while Bradley clambered quickly the remaining distance to the roof, though no sooner did he reach the top of the ladder than a great flapping of wings beneath him warned him that the Wieroos were rising after him. A moment later they swarmed about his head as he ran for the apartment in which he had spent the early hours of the morning after his arrival.

It was but a short distance from the top of the ladder to the doorway, and Bradley had almost reached his goal when the door flew open and Fosh-bal-soj stepped out. Immediately the pursuing Wieroos demanded punishment of the *jaal-lu* who had so grievously maltreated them. Fosh-bal-soj listened to their complaints and then with a sudden sweep of his right hand seized Bradley by the scruff of the neck and hurled him sprawling through the doorway upon the floor of the chamber.

So sudden was the assault and so surprising the strength of the Wieroo that the Englishman was taken completely off his guard. When he arose, the door was closed, and Fosh-bal-soj was standing over him, his hideous face contorted into an expression of rage and hatred.

"Hyena, snake, lizard!" he screamed. "You would dare lay your low, vile, profaning hands upon even the lowliest of the Wieroos—the sacred, chosen of Luata!"

Bradley was mad, and so he spoke in a very low, calm voice while a half-smile played across his lips; but his cold, gray eyes were unsmiling. "What you did to me just now," he said. "—I am going to kill you for that," and even as he spoke, he launched himself at the throat of Fosh-bal-soj. The other Wieroo that had been asleep when Bradley left the chamber had departed, and the two were alone. Fosh-bal-soj displayed little of the cowardice of those that had attacked Bradley in the alleyway; but that may have been because he had so slight opportunity, for Bradley had him by the throat before he could utter a cry and with his right hand struck him heavily and repeatedly upon his face and over his heart—ugly, smashing, short-arm jabs of the sort that take the fight out of a man in quick time.

But Fosh-bal-soj was of no mind to die passively. He clawed and struck at Bradley while with his great wings he attempted to shield himself from the merciless rain of blows, at the same time searching for a hold upon his antagonist's throat. Presently he succeeded in tripping the Englishman, and together the two fell heavily to the floor, Bradley underneath, and at the same instant the Wieroo fastened his long talons about the other's windpipe.

Fosh-bal-soj was possessed of enormous strength and he was fighting for his life. The Englishman soon realized that the battle was going against him. Already his lungs were pounding painfully for air as he reached for his pistol. It was with difficulty that he drew it from its holster, and even then, with death staring him in the face, he thought of his precious ammunition. "Can't waste it," he thought; and slipping his fingers to the barrel he raised the weapon and struck Fosh-bal-soj a terrific blow between the eyes. Instantly the clawlike fingers released their hold, and the creature sank limply to the floor beside Bradley, who lay for several minutes gasping painfully in an effort to regain his breath.

When he was able, he rose and leaned close over the Wieroo, lying silent and motionless, his wings drooping limply and his great, round eyes staring blankly toward the ceiling. A brief examination convinced Bradley that the thing was dead, and with the conviction came an overwhelming sense of the dangers which must now confront him; but how was he to escape?

His first thought was to find some means for concealing the evidence of his deed and then to make a bold effort to escape. Stepping to the second door he pushed it gently open and peered in upon what seemed to be a store room. In it was a litter of cloth such as the Wieroos' robes were fashioned from, a number of chests painted blue and white, with white hieroglyphics painted in bold strokes upon the blue and blue hieroglyphics upon the white. In one corner was a pile of human skulls reaching almost to the ceiling and in another a stack of dried Wieroo wings. The chamber was as irregularly shaped as the other and had but a single window and a second door at the further end, but was without the exit through the roof and, most important of all, there was no creature of any sort in it.

As quickly as possible Bradley dragged the dead Wieroo through the doorway and closed the door; then he looked about for a place to conceal the corpse. One of the chests was large enough to hold the body if the knees were bent well up, and with this idea in view Bradley approached the chest to open it. The lid was made in two pieces, each being hinged at an opposite end of the chest and joining nicely where they met in the center of the chest, making a snug, well-fitting joint. There was no lock. Bradley raised one half the cover and looked in. With a smothered "By Jove!" he bent closer to examine the contents—the chest was about half filled with an assortment of golden trinkets. There were what appeared to be bracelets, anklets and brooches of virgin gold.

Realizing that there was no room in the chest for the body of the Wieroo, Bradley turned to seek another means of concealing the evidence of his crime. There was a space between the chests and the wall, and into this he forced the corpse, piling the discarded robes upon it until it was entirely hidden from sight; but now how was he to make good his escape in the bright glare of that early Spring day?

He walked to the door at the far end of the apartment and cautiously opened it an inch. Before him and about two feet away was the blank wall of another building. Bradley opened the door a little farther and looked in both directions. There was no one in sight to the left over a considerable expanse of roof-top, and to the right another building shut off his line of vision at about twenty feet. Slipping out, he turned to the right and in a few steps found a narrow passageway between two buildings. Turning into this he passed about half its length when he saw a Wieroo appear at the opposite end and halt. The creature was not looking down the passageway; but at any moment it might turn its eyes toward him, when he would be immediately discovered.

To Bradley's left was a triangular niche in the wall of one of the houses, and into this he dodged, thus concealing himself from the sight of the Wieroo. Beside him was a door painted a vivid yellow and constructed after the same fashion as the other Wieroo doors he had seen, being made up of countless narrow strips of wood from four to six inches in length laid on in patches of about the same width, the strips in adjacent patches never running in the same direction. The result bore some resemblance to a crazy patchwork quilt, which was heightened when, as in one of the doors he had seen, contiguous patches were painted different colors. The strips appeared to have been bound together and to the underlying framework of the door with gut or fiber and also glued, after which a thick coating of paint had been applied. One edge of the door was formed of a straight, round pole about two inches in diameter that protruded at top and bottom, the projections setting in round holes in both lintel and sill and forming the axis upon which the door swung. An eccentric disk upon the inside face of the door engaged a slot in the frame when it was desired to secure the door against intruders.

As Bradley stood flattened against the wall waiting for the Wieroo to move on, he heard the creature's wings brushing against the sides of the buildings as it made its way down the narrow passage in his direction. As the yellow door offered the only means of escape without detection, the Englishman decided to risk whatever might lie beyond it, and so, boldly pushing it in, he crossed the threshold and entered a small apartment.

As he did so, he heard a muffled ejaculation of surprise, and turning his eyes in the direction from whence the sound had come, he beheld a wide-eyed girl standing flattened against the opposite wall, an expression of incredulity upon her face. At a glance he saw that she was of no race of humans that he had come in contact with since his arrival upon Caprona— there was no trace about her form or features of any relationship to those low orders of men, nor was she appareled as they—or, rather, she did not entirely lack apparel as did most of them.

A soft hide fell from her left shoulder to just below her left hip on one side and almost to her right knee on the other, a loose girdle was about her waist, and golden ornaments such as he had seen in the blue-and-white chest encircled her arms and legs, while a golden fillet with a triangular diadem bound her heavy hair above her brows. Her skin was white as from long confinement within doors; but it was clear and fine. Her figure, but partially concealed by the soft deerskin, was all curves of symmetry and youthful grace, while her features might easily have been the envy of the most feted of Continental beauties.

If the girl was surprised by the sudden appearance of Bradley, the latter was absolutely astounded to discover so wondrous a creature among the hideous inhabitants of the City of Human Skulls. For a moment the two looked at one another in unconcealed consternation, and then Bradley spoke, using, to the best of his poor ability, the common tongue of Caspak.

"Who are you," he asked, "and from where do you come? Do not tell me that you are a Wieroo."

"No," she replied, "I am no Wieroo." And she shuddered slightly as she pronounced the word. "I am a Galu; but who and what are you? I am sure that you are no Galu, from your garments; but you are like the Galus in other respects. I know that you are not of this frightful city, for I have been here for almost ten moons, and never have I seen a male Galu brought hither before, nor are there such as you and I, other than prisoners in the land of Oo-oh, and these are all females. Are you a prisoner, then?"

He told her briefly who and what he was, though he doubted if she understood, and from her he learned that she had been a prisoner there for many months; but for what purpose he did not then learn, as in the midst of their conversation the yellow door swung open and a Wieroo with a robe slashed with yellow entered.

At sight of Bradley the creature became furious. "Whence came this reptile?" it demanded of the girl. "How long has it been here with you?"

"It came through the doorway just ahead of you," Bradley answered for the girl.

The Wieroo looked relieved. "It is well for the girl that this is so," it said, "for now only you will have to die." And stepping to the door the creature raised its voice in one of those uncanny, depressing wails.

The Englishman looked toward the girl. "Shall I kill it?" he asked, half drawing his pistol. "What is best to do?—I do not wish to endanger you."

The Wieroo backed toward the door. "Defiler!" it screamed. "You dare threaten one of the sacred chosen of Luata!"

"Do not kill him," cried the girl, "for then there could be no hope for you. That you are here, alive, shows that they may not intend to kill you at all, and so there is a chance for you if you do not anger them; but touch him in violence and your bleached skull will top the loftiest pedestal of Oo-oh."

"And what of you?" asked Bradley.

"I am already doomed," replied the girl; "I am *cos-ata-lo.*"

Cos-ata-lo! cos-ata-lu! What did these phrases mean that they were so oft repeated by the denizens of Oo-oh? *Lu* and *lo,* Bradley knew to mean man and woman; *ata* was employed variously to indicate life, eggs, young, reproduction and kindred subjects; *cos* was a negative; but in combination they were meaningless to the European.

"Do you mean they will kill you?" asked Bradley.

"I but wish that they would," replied the girl. "My fate is to be worse than death—in just a few nights more, with the coming of the new moon."

"Poor she-snake!" snapped the Wieroo. "You are to become sacred above all other shes. He Who Speaks for Luata has chosen you for himself. Today you go to his temple"—the Wieroo used a phrase meaning literally High Place—"where you will receive the sacred commands."

The girl shuddered and cast a sorrowful glance toward Bradley. "Ah," she sighed, "if I could but see my beloved country once again!"

The man stepped suddenly close to her side before the Wieroo could interpose and in a low voice asked her if there was no way by which he might encompass her escape. She shook her head sorrowfully. "Even if we escaped the city," she replied, "there is the big water between the island of Oo-oh and the Galu shore."

"And what is beyond the city, if we could leave it?" pursued Bradley.

"I may only guess from what I have heard since I was brought here," she answered; "but by reports and chance remarks I take it to be a beautiful land in which there are but few wild beasts and no men, for only the Wieroos live upon this island and they dwell always in cities of which there are three, this being the largest. The others are at the far end of the island, which is about three marches from end to end and at its widest point about one march."

From his own experience and from what the natives on the mainland had told him, Bradley knew that ten miles was a good day's march in Caspak, owing to the fact that at most points it was a trackless wilderness and at all times travelers were beset by hideous beasts and reptiles that greatly impeded rapid progress.

The two had spoken rapidly but were now interrupted by the advent through the opening in the roof of several Wieroos who had come in answer to the alarm it of the yellow slashing had uttered.

"This *jaal-lu*," cried the offended one, "has threatened me. Take its hatchet from it and make it fast where it can do no harm until He Who Speaks for Luata has said what shall be done with it. It is one of those strange creatures that Fosh-bal-soj discovered first above the Band-lu country and followed back toward the beginning. He Who Speaks for Luata sent Fosh-bal-soj to fetch him one of the creatures, and here it is. It is hoped that it may be from another world and hold the secret of the *cos-ata-lus.*"

The Wieroos approached boldly to take Bradley's "hatchet" from him, their leader having indicated the pistol hanging in its holster at the Englishman's hip, but the first one went reeling backward against his fellows from a blow to the chin which Bradley followed up with a rush and the intention to clean up the room in record time; but he had reckoned without the opening in the roof. Two were down and a great wailing and moaning was arising when reinforcements appeared from above. Bradley did not see them; but the girl did, and though she cried out a warning, it came too late for him to avoid a large Wieroo who dived headforemost for him, striking him between the shoulders and bearing him to the floor. Instantly a dozen more were piling on top of him. His pistol was wrenched from its holster and he was securely pinioned down by the weight of numbers.

At a word from the Wieroo of the yellow slashing, who evidently was a person of authority, one left and presently returned with fiber ropes with which Bradley was tightly bound.

"Now bear him to the Blue Place of Seven Skulls," directed the chief Wieroo, "and one take the word of all that has passed to Him Who Speaks for Luata."

Each of the creatures raised a hand, the back against its face, as though in salute. One seized Bradley and carried him through the yellow doorway to the roof from whence it rose upon its widespread wings and flapped off across the roof-tops of Oo-oh with its heavy burden clutched in its long talons.

Below him Bradley could see the city stretching away to a distance on every hand. It was not as large as he had imagined, though he judged that it was at least three miles square. The houses were piled in indescribable heaps, sometimes to a height of a hundred feet. The streets and alleys were short and crooked and there were many areas where buildings had been wedged in so closely that no light could possibly reach the lowest tiers, the entire surface of the ground being packed solidly with them.

The colors were varied and startling, the architecture amazing. Many roofs were cup or saucer-shaped with a small hole in the center of each, as though they had been constructed to catch rain-water and conduct it to a reservoir beneath; but nearly all the others had the large opening in the top that Bradley had seen used by these flying men in lieu of doorways. At all levels were the myriad poles surmounted by grinning skulls; but the two most prominent features of the city were the round tower of human skulls that Bradley had noted earlier in the day and another and much larger edifice near the center of the city. As they approached it, Bradley saw that it was a huge building rising a hundred feet in height from the ground and that it stood alone in the center of what might have been called a plaza in some other part of the world. Its various parts, however, were set together with the same strange irregularity that marked the architecture of the city as a whole; and it was capped by an enormous saucer-shaped roof which projected far beyond the eaves, having the appearance of a colossal Chinese coolie hat, inverted.

The Wieroo bearing Bradley passed over one corner of the open space about the large building, revealing to the Englishman grass and trees and running water beneath. They passed the building and about five hundred yards beyond the creature alighted on the roof of a square, blue building surmounted by seven poles bearing seven skulls. This then, thought Bradley, is the Blue Place of Seven Skulls.

Over the opening in the roof was a grated covering, and this the Wieroo removed. The thing then tied a piece of fiber rope to one of Bradley's ankles and rolled him over the edge of the opening. All was dark below and for an instant the Englishman came as near to experiencing real terror as he had ever come in his life before. As he rolled off into the black abyss he felt the rope tighten about his ankle and an instant later he was stopped with a sudden jerk to swing pendulumlike, head downward. Then the creature lowered away until Bradley's

The skinny arms now embraced his neck, holding the teeth to his throat against all his efforts to dislodge the thing. Weak as it was it had strength enough for this in its mad efforts to eat. Mumbling as it worked, it repeated again and again, "Food! Food! There is a way out!" until Bradley thought those two expressions alone would drive him mad.

And all but mad he was as with a final effort backed by almost maniacal strength he tore his wrists from the confining bonds and grasping the repulsive thing upon his breast hurled it halfway across the room. Panting like a spent hound Bradley worked at the thongs about his ankles while the maniac lay quivering and mumbling where it had fallen. Presently the Englishman leaped to his feet—freer than he had ever before felt in all his life, though he was still hopelessly a prisoner in the Blue Place of Seven Skulls.

With his back against the wall for support, so weak the reaction left him, Bradley stood watching the creature upon the floor. He saw it move and slowly raise itself to its hands and knees, where it swayed to and fro as its eyes roved about in search of him; and when at last they found him, there broke from the drawn lips the mumbled words: "Food! Food! There is a way out!" The pitiful supplication in the tones touched the Englishman's heart. He knew that this could be no Wieroo, but possibly once a man like himself who had been cast into this pit of solitary confinement with this hideous result that might in time be his fate, also.

And then, too, there was the suggestion of hope held out by the constant reiteration of the phrase, "There is a way out." Was there a way out? What did this poor thing know? "Who are you and how long have you been here?" Bradley suddenly demanded.

For a moment the man upon the floor made no response, then mumblingly came the words: "Food! Food!"

"Stop!" commanded the Englishman—the injunction might have been barked from the muzzle of a pistol. It brought the man to a sitting posture, his hands off the ground. He stopped swaying to and fro and appeared to be startled into an attempt to master his faculties of concentration and thought.

Bradley repeated his questions sharply.

"I am An-Tak, the Galu," replied the man. "Luata alone knows how long I have been here—maybe ten moons, maybe ten moons three times"—it was the Caspakian equivalent of thirty. "I was young and strong when they brought me here.

Now I am old and very weak. I am *cos-ata-lu*—that is why they have not killed me. If I tell them the secret of becoming *cos-ata-lu* they will take me out; but how can I tell them that which Luata alone knows?"

"What is *cos-ata-lu?*" demanded Bradley.

"Food! Food! There is a way out!" mumbled the Galu.

Bradley strode across the floor, seized the man by his shoulders and shook him.

"Tell me," he cried, "what is *cos-ata-lu?*"

"Food!" whimpered An-Tak.

Bradley bethought himself. His haversack had not been taken from him. In it besides his razor and knife were odds and ends of equipment and a small quantity of dried meat. He tossed a small strip of the latter to the starving Galu. An-Tak seized upon it and devoured it ravenously. It instilled new life in the man.

"What is *cos-ata-lu?*" insisted Bradley again.

An-Tak tried to explain. His narrative was often broken by lapses of concentration during which he reverted to his plaintive mumbling for food and recurrence to the statement that there was a way out; but by firmness and patience the Englishman drew out piece-meal a more or less lucid exposition of the remarkable scheme of evolution that rules in Caspak. In it he found explanations of the hitherto inexplicable. He discovered why he had seen no babes or children among the Caspakian tribes with which he had come in contact; why each more northerly tribe evinced a higher state of development than those south of them; why each tribe included individuals ranging in physical and mental characteristics from the highest of the next lower race to the lowest of the next higher, and why the women of each tribe immersed themselves mornings for an hour or more in the warm pools near which the habitations of their people always were located; and, too, he discovered why those pools were almost immune from the attacks of carnivorous animals and reptiles.

He learned that all but those who were *cos-ata-lu* came up *cor-sva-jo,* or *from the beginning.* The egg from which they first developed into tadpole form was deposited, with millions of others, in one of the warm pools and with it a poisonous serum that the carnivora instinctively shunned. Down the warm stream from the pool floated the countless billions of eggs and tadpoles, developing as they drifted slowly toward the sea. Some became tadpoles in the pool, some in the sluggish stream and some not until they reached the great inland sea. In the next stage they became fishes or reptiles, An-Tak was not positive which, and in this form, always developing, they swam far to the south, where, amid the rank and teeming jungles, some of them evolved into amphibians. Always there were those whose development stopped at the fish stage, others whose development ceased when they became reptiles, while by far the greater proportion formed the food supply of the ravenous creatures of the deep.

Few indeed were those that eventually developed into baboons and then apes, which was considered by Caspakians the real beginning of evolution. From the egg, then, the individual developed slowly into a higher form, just as the frog's egg develops through various stages from a fish with gills to a frog with lungs. With that thought in mind Bradley discovered that it was not difficult to believe in the possibility of such a scheme—there was nothing new in it.

From the ape the individual, if it survived, slowly developed into the lowest order of man—the Alu—and then by degrees to Bo-lu, Sto-lu, Band-lu, Kro-lu and finally to Galu. And in each stage countless millions of other eggs were deposited in the warm pools of the various races and floated down to the great sea to go through a similar process of evolution outside the womb as develops our own young within; but in Caspak the scheme is much more inclusive, for it combines not only individual development but the evolution of species and genera. If an egg survives it goes through all the stages of development that man has passed through during the unthinkable eons since life first moved upon the earth's face.

The final stage—that which the Galus have almost attained and for which all hope—is *cos-ata-lu,* which, literally, means no-egg-man, or one who is born directly as are the young of the outer world of mammals. Some of the Galus produce *cos-ata-lu* and *cos-ata-lo* both; the Wieroos only *cos-ata-lu*—in other words all Wieroos are born male, and so they prey upon the Galus for their women and sometimes capture and torture the Galu men who are *cos-ata-lu* in an endeavor to learn the secret which they believe will give them unlimited power over all other denizens of Caspak.

No Wieroos come up from the beginning—all are born of Wieroo fathers and Galu mothers who are *cos-ata-lo,* and there are very few of the latter owing to the long and precarious stages of development. Seven generations of the same ancestor must come up from the beginning before a *cos-ata-lu* child may be born; and when one considers the frightful dangers that surround the vital spark from the moment it leaves the warm pool where it has been deposited to float down to the sea amid the voracious creatures that swarm the surface and the deeps and the almost equally unthinkable trials of its efforts to survive after it once becomes a land animal and starts northward through the horrors of the Caspakian jungles and forests, it is plainly a wonder that even a single babe has ever been born to a Galu woman.

Seven cycles it requires before the seventh Galu can complete the seventh danger-infested circle since its first Galu ancestor achieved the state of Galu. For ages before, the ancestors of this first Galu may have developed from a Band-lu or Bo-lu egg without ever once completing the whole circle—that is from a Galu egg, back to a fully developed Galu.

Bradley's head was whirling before he even commenced to grasp the complexities of Caspakian evolution; but as the truth slowly filtered into his understanding—as gradually it became possible for him to visualize the scheme, it appeared simpler. In fact, it seemed even less difficult of comprehension than that with which he was familiar.

For several minutes after An-Tak ceased speaking, his voice having trailed off weakly into silence, neither spoke again. Then the Galu recommenced his, "Food! Food! There is a way out!" Bradley tossed him another bit of dried meat, waiting patiently until he had eaten it, this time more slowly.

"What do you mean by saying there is a way out?" he asked.

"He who died here just after I came, told me," replied An-Tak. "He said there was a way out, that he had discovered it but was too weak to use his knowledge. He was trying to tell me how to find it when he died. Oh, Luata, if he had lived but a moment more!"

"They do not feed you here?" asked Bradley.

"No, they give me water once a day—that is all."

"But how have you lived, then?"

"The lizards and the rats," replied An-Tak. "The lizards are not so bad; but the rats are foul to taste. However, I must eat them or they would eat me, and they are better than nothing; but of late they do not come so often, and I have not had a lizard for a long time. I shall eat though," he mumbled. "I shall eat now, for you cannot remain awake forever." He laughed, a cackling, dry laugh. "When you sleep, An-Tak will eat."

It was horrible. Bradley shuddered. For a long time each sat in silence. The Englishman could guess why the other made no sound—he awaited the moment that sleep should overcome his victim. In the long silence there was borne upon Bradley's ears a faint, monotonous sound as of running water. He listened intently. It seemed to come from far beneath the floor.

"What is that noise?" he asked. "That sounds like water running through a narrow channel."

"It is the river," replied An-Tak. "Why do you not go to sleep? It passes directly beneath the Blue Place of Seven Skulls. It runs through the temple grounds, beneath the temple and under the city. When we die, they will cut off our heads and throw our bodies into the river. At the mouth of the river await many large reptiles. Thus do they feed. The Wieroos do likewise with their own dead, keeping only the skulls and the wings. Come, let us sleep."

"Do the reptiles come up the river into the city?" asked Bradley.

"The water is too cold—they never leave the warm water of the great pool," replied An-Tak.

"Let us search for the way out," suggested Bradley.

An-Tak shook his head. "I have searched for it all these moons," he said. "If I could not find it, how would you?"

Bradley made no reply but commenced a diligent examination of the walls and floor of the room, pressing over each square foot and tapping with his knuckles. About six feet from the floor he discovered a sleeping-perch near one end of the apartment. He asked An-Tak about it, but the Galu said that no Wieroo had occupied the place since he had been incarcerated there. Again and again Bradley went over the floor and walls as high up as he could reach. Finally he swung himself to the perch, that he might examine at least one end of the room all the way to the ceiling.

In the center of the wall close to the top, an area about three feet square gave forth a hollow sound when he rapped upon it. Bradley felt over every square inch of that area with the tips of his fingers. Near the top he found a small round hole a trifle larger in diameter than his forefinger, which he immediately stuck into it. The panel, if such it was, seemed about an inch thick, and beyond it his finger encountered nothing. Bradley crooked his finger upon the opposite side of the panel and pulled toward him, steadily but with considerable force. Suddenly the panel flew inward, nearly precipitating the man to the floor. It was hinged at the bottom, and when lowered the outer edge rested upon the perch, making a little platform parallel with the floor of the room.

Beyond the opening was an utterly dark void. The Englishman leaned through it and reached his arm as far as possible into the blackness but touched nothing. Then he fumbled in his haversack for a match, a few of which remained to him. When he struck it, An-Tak gave a cry of terror. Bradley held the light far into the opening before him and in its flickering rays saw the top of a ladder descending into a black abyss below. How far down it extended he could not guess; but that he should soon know definitely he was positive.

"You have found it! You have found the way out!" screamed An-Tak. "Oh Luata! And now I am too weak to go. Take me with you! Take me with you!"

"Shut up!" admonished Bradley. "You will have the whole flock of birds around our heads in a minute, and neither of us will escape. Be quiet, and I'll go ahead. If I find a way out, I'll come back and help you, if you'll promise not to try to eat me up again."

"I promise," cried An-Tak. "Oh, Luata! How could you blame me? I am half crazed by hunger and long confinement and the horror of the lizards and the rats and the constant waiting for death."

"I know," said Bradley simply. "I'm sorry for you, old top. Keep a stiff upper lip." And he slipped through the opening, found the ladder with his feet, closed the panel behind him, and started downward into the darkness.

Below him rose more and more distinctly the sound of running water. The air felt damp and cool. He could see nothing of his surroundings and felt nothing but the smooth, worn sides and rungs of the ladder down which he felt his way cautiously lest a broken rung or a misstep should hurl him downward.

As he descended thus slowly, the ladder seemed interminable and the pit bottomless, yet he realized when at last he reached the bottom that he could not have descended more than fifty feet. The bottom of the ladder rested on a narrow ledge paved with what felt like large round stones, but what he knew from experience to be human skulls. He could not but marvel as to where so many countless thousands of the things had come from, until he paused to consider that the infancy of Caspak dated doubtlessly back into remote ages, far beyond what the outer world considered the beginning of earthly time. For all these eons the Wieroos might have been collecting human skulls from their enemies and their own dead—enough to have built an entire city of them.

Feeling his way along the narrow ledge, Bradley came presently to a blank wall that stretched out over the water swirling beneath him, as far as he could reach. Stooping, he groped about with one hand, reaching down toward the surface of the water, and discovered that the bottom of the wall arched above the stream. How much space there was between the water and the arch he could not tell, nor how deep the former. There was only one way in which he might learn these things, and that was to lower himself into the stream. For only an instant he hesitated, weighing his chances. Behind him lay almost certainly the horrid fate of An-Tak; before him nothing worse than a comparatively painless death by drowning. Holding his haversack above his head with one hand he lowered his feet slowly over the edge of the narrow platform. Almost immediately he felt the swirling of cold water about his ankles, and then with a silent prayer he let himself drop gently into the stream.

Great was Bradley's relief when he found the water no more than waist deep and beneath his feet a firm, gravel bottom. Feeling his way cautiously he moved downward with the current, which was not so strong as he had imagined from the noise of the running water.

Beneath the first arch he made his way, following the winding curvatures of the right-hand wall. After a few yards of progress his hand came suddenly in contact with a slimy thing clinging to the wall—a thing that hissed and scuttled out of reach. What it was, the man could not know; but almost instantly there was a splash in the water just ahead of him and then another.

On he went, passing beneath other arches at varying distances, and always in utter darkness. Unseen denizens of this great sewer, disturbed by the intruder, splashed into the water ahead of him and wriggled away. Time and again his hand touched them and never for an instant could he be sure that at the next step some gruesome thing might not attack him. He had strapped his haversack about his neck, well above the surface of the water, and in his left hand he carried his knife. Other precautions there were none to take.

The monotony of the blind trail was increased by the fact that from the moment he had started from the foot of the ladder he had counted his every step. He had promised to return for An-Tak if it proved humanly possible to do so, and he knew that in the blackness of the tunnel he could locate the foot of the ladder in no other way.

He had taken two hundred and sixty-nine steps—afterward he knew that he should never forget that number—when something bumped gently against him from behind. Instantly he wheeled about and with knife ready to defend himself stretched forth his right hand to push away the object that now had lodged against his body. His fingers feeling through the darkness came in contact with something cold and clammy—they passed to and fro over the thing until Bradley knew that it was the face of a dead man floating upon the surface of the stream. With an oath he pushed his gruesome companion out into mid-stream to float on down toward the great pool and the awaiting scavengers of the deep.

At his four hundred and thirteenth step another corpse bumped against him—how many had passed him without touching he could not guess; but suddenly he experienced the sensation of being surrounded by dead faces floating along with him, all set in hideous grimaces, their dead eyes glaring at this profaning alien who dared intrude upon the waters of this river of the dead—a horrid escort, pregnant with dire forebodings and with menace.

Though he advanced very slowly, he tried always to take steps of about the same length; so that he knew that though considerable time had elapsed, yet he had really advanced no more than four hundred yards when ahead he saw a lessening of the pitch-darkness, and at the next turn of the stream his surroundings became vaguely discernible. Above him was an arched roof and on either hand walls pierced at intervals by apertures covered with wooden doors. Just ahead of him in the roof of the aqueduct was a round, black hole about thirty inches in diameter. His eyes still rested upon the opening when there shot downward from it to the water below the naked body of a human being which almost immediately rose to the surface again and floated off down the stream. In the dim light Bradley saw that it was a dead Wieroo from which the wings and head had been removed. A moment later another headless body floated past, recalling what An-Tak had told him of the skull-collecting customs of the Wieroo. Bradley wondered how it happened that the first corpse he had encountered in the stream had not been similarly mutilated.

The farther he advanced now, the lighter it became. The number of corpses was much smaller than he had imagined, only two more passing him before, at six hundred steps, or about five hundred yards, from the point he had taken to the stream, he came to the end of the tunnel and looked out upon sunlit water, running between grassy banks.

One of the last corpes to pass him was still clothed in the white robe of a Wieroo, blood-stained over the headless neck that it concealed.

Drawing closer to the opening leading into the bright daylight, Bradley surveyed what lay beyond. A short distance before him a large building stood in the center of several acres of grass and tree-covered ground, spanning the stream which disappeared through an opening in its foundation wall. From the large saucer-shaped roof and the vivid colorings of the various heterogeneous parts of the structure he recognized it as the temple past which he had been borne to the Blue Place of Seven Skulls.

To and fro flew Wieroos, going to and from the temple. Others passed on foot across the open grounds, assisting themselves with their great wings, so that they barely skimmed the earth. To leave the mouth of the tunnel would have been to court instant discovery and capture; but by what other avenue he might escape, Bradley could not guess, unless he retraced his steps up the stream and sought egress from the other end of the city. The thought of traversing that dark and horror-ridden tunnel for perhaps miles he could not entertain—there must be some other way. Perhaps after dark he could steal through the temple grounds and continue on downstream until he had come beyond the city; and so he stood and waited until his limbs became almost paralyzed with cold, and he knew that he must find some other plan for escape.

A half-formed decision to risk an attempt to swim under water to the temple was crystallizing in spite of the fact that any chance Wieroo flying above the stream might easily see him, when again a floating object bumped against him from behind and lodged across his back. Turning quickly he saw that the thing was what he had immediately guessed it to be—a headless and wingless Wieroo corpse. With a grunt of disgust he was about to push it from him when the white garment enshrouding it suggested a bold plan to his resourceful brain. Grasping the corpse by an arm he tore the garment from it and then let the body float downward toward the temple. With great care he draped the robe about him; the bloody blotch that had covered the severed neck he arranged about his own head. His haversack he rolled as tightly as possible and stuffed beneath his coat over his breast. Then he fell gently to the surface of the stream and lying upon his back floated downward with the current and out into the open sunlight.

Through the weave of the cloth he could distinguish large objects. He saw a Wieroo flap dismally above him; he saw the banks of the stream float slowly past; he heard a sudden wail upon the right-hand shore, and his heart stood still lest his ruse had been discovered; but never by a move of a muscle did he betray that aught but a cold lump of clay floated there upon the bosom of the water, and soon, though it seemed an eternity to him, the direct sunlight was blotted out, and he knew that he had entered beneath the temple.

Quickly he felt for bottom with his feet and as quickly stood erect, snatching the bloody, clammy cloth from his face. On both sides were blank walls and before him the river turned a sharp corner and disappeared. Feeling his way cautiously forward he approached the turn and looked around the corner. To his left was a low platform about a foot above the level of the stream, and onto this he lost no time in climbing, for he was soaked from head to foot, cold and almost exhausted.

As he lay resting on the skull-paved shelf, he saw in the center of the vault above the river another of those sinister round holes through which he momentarily expected to see a headless corpse shoot downward in its last plunge to a watery grave. A few feet along the platform a closed door broke the blankness of the wall. As he lay looking at it and wondering what lay beyond, his mind filled with fragments of many wild schemes of escape, it opened and a white-robed Wieroo stepped out upon the platform. The creature carried a large wooden basin filled with rubbish. Its eyes were not upon Bradley, who drew himself to a squatting position and crouched as far back in the corner of the niche in which the platform was set as he could force himself. The Wieroo stepped to the edge of the platform and dumped the rubbish into the stream. If it turned away from him as it started to retrace its steps to the doorway, there was a small chance that it might not see him; but if it turned toward him there was none at all. Bradley held his breath.

The Wieroo paused a moment, gazing down into the water, then it straightened up and turned toward the Englishman. Bradley did not move. The Wieroo stopped and stared intently at him. It approached him questioningly. Still Bradley remained as though carved of stone. The creature was directly in front of him. It stopped. There was no chance on earth that it would not discover what he was.

With the quickness of a cat, Bradley sprang to his feet and with all his great strength, backed by his heavy weight, struck the Wieroo upon the point of the chin. Without a sound the thing crumpled to the platform, while Bradley, acting almost instinctively to the urge of the first law of nature, rolled the inanimate body over the edge into the river.

Then he looked at the open doorway, crossed the platform and peered within the apartment beyond. What he saw was a large room, dimly lighted, and about the sides rows of wooden vessels stacked one upon another. There was no Wieroo in sight, so the Englishman entered. At the far end of the room was another door, and as he crossed toward it, he glanced into some of the vessels, which he found were filled with dried fruits, vegetables and fish. Without more ado he stuffed his pockets and his haversack full, thinking of the poor creature awaiting his return in the gloom of the Place of Seven Skulls.

When night came, he would return and fetch An-Tak this far at least; but in the meantime it was his intention to reconnoiter in the hope that he might discover some easier way out of the city than that offered by the chill, black channel of the ghastly river of corpses.

Beyond the farther door stretched a long passageway from which closed doorways led into other parts of the cellars of the temple. A few yards from the storeroom a ladder rose from the corridor through an aperture in the ceiling. Bradley paused at the foot of it, debating the wisdom of further investigation against a return to the river; but strong within him was the spirit of exploration that has scattered his race to the four corners of the earth. What new mysteries lay hidden in the chambers above? The urge to know was strong upon him though his better judgment warned him that the safer course lay in retreat. For a moment he stood thus, running his fingers through his hair; then he cast discretion to the winds and began the ascent.

In conformity with such Wieroo architecture as he had already observed, the well through which the ladder rose continually varied in form and size, being now circular, now oval, rectangular or polyhedrical and occasionally canted at an angle from the perpendicular. At more or less regular stages it was pierced by apertures closed by doors, none of which he could open until he had climbed fully fifty feet from the river level. Here he discovered a door already ajar opening into a large, circular chamber, the walls and floors of which were covered with the skins of wild beasts and with rugs of many colors; but what interested him most was the occupants of the room—a Wieroo, and a girl of human proportions. She was standing with her back against a column which rose from the center of the apartment from floor to ceiling—a hollow column about forty inches in diameter in which he could see an opening some thirty inches across. The girl's side was toward Bradley, and her face averted, for she was watching the Wieroo, who was now advancing slowly toward her, talking as he came.

Bradley could distinctly hear the words of the creature, who was urging the girl to accompany him to another Wieroo city. "Come with me," he said, "and you shall have your life; remain here and He Who Speaks for Luata will claim you for his own; and when he is done with you, your skull will bleach at the top of a tall staff while your body feeds the reptiles at the mouth of the River of Death. Even though you bring into the world a female Wieroo, your fate will be the same if you do not escape him, while with me you shall have life and food and none shall harm you."

He was quite close to the girl when she replied by striking him in the face with all her strength. "Until I am slain," she cried, "I shall fight against you all." From the throat of the Wieroo issued that dismal wail that Bradley had heard so often in the past—it was like a scream of pain smothered to a groan—and then the thing leaped upon the girl, its face working in hideous grimaces as it clawed and beat at her to force her to the floor.

The Englishman was upon the point of entering to defend her when a door at the opposite side of the chamber opened to admit a huge Wieroo clothed entirely in red. At sight of the two struggling upon the floor the newcomer raised his voice in a shriek of rage. Instantly the Wieroo who was attacking the girl leaped to his feet and faced the other.

"I heard," screamed he who had just entered the room. "I heard, and when He Who Speaks for Luata shall have heard—" He paused and made a suggestive movement of a forefinger across his throat.

"He shall not hear," returned the first Wieroo as, with a powerful motion of his great wings, he launched himself upon the red-robed figure. The latter dodged the first charge, drew a wicked-looking, curved blade from beneath its red robe, spread its wings and dived for its antagonist. Beating their wings, wailing and groaning, the two hideous things sparred for position.

The white-robed one being unarmed sought to grasp the other by the wrist of its knife-hand and by the throat, while the latter hopped around on its dainty white feet, seeking an opening for a mortal blow. Once it struck and missed, and then the other rushed in and clinched, at the same time securing both the holds it sought. Immediately the two commenced beating at each other's heads with the joints of their wings, kicking with their soft, puny feet and biting, each at the other's face.

In the meantime the girl moved about the room, keeping out of the way of the duelists, and as she did so, Bradley caught a glimpse of her full face and immediately recognized her as the girl of the place of the yellow door. He did not dare intervene now until one of the Wieroo had overcome the other, lest the two should turn upon him at once, when the chances were fair that he would be defeated in so unequal a battle as the curved blade of the red Wieroo would render it, and so he waited, watching the white-robed figure slowly choking the life from him of the red robe. The protruding tongue and the popping eyes proclaimed that the end was near and a moment later the red robe sank to the floor of the room, the curved blade slipping from nerveless fingers. For an instant longer the victor clung to the throat of his defeated antagonist and then he rose, dragging the body after him, and approached the central column. Here he raised the body and thrust it into the aperture where Bradley saw it drop suddenly from sight. Instantly there flashed into his memory the circular openings in the roof of the river vault and the corpses he had seen drop from them to the water beneath.

As the body disappeared, the Wieroo turned and cast about the room for the girl. For a moment he stood eying her. "You saw," he muttered, "and if you tell them, He Who Speaks for Luata will have my wings severed while still I live and my head will be severed and I shall be cast into the River of Death, for thus it happens even to the highest who slay one of the red robe. You saw, and you must die!" he ended with a scream as he rushed upon the girl.

Bradley waited no longer. Leaping into the room he ran for the Wieroo, who had already seized the girl, and as he ran, he stooped and picked up the curved blade. The creature's back was toward him as, with his left hand, he seized it by the neck. Like a flash the great wings beat backward as the creature turned, and Bradley was swept from his feet, though he still retained his hold upon the blade. Instantly the Wieroo was upon him. Bradley lay slightly raised upon his left elbow, his right arm free, and as the thing came close, he cut at the hideous face with all the strength that lay within him. The blade struck at the junction of the neck and torso and with such force as to completely decapitate the Wieroo, the hideous head dropping to the floor and the body falling forward upon the Englishman.

Pushing it from him he rose to his feet and faced the wide-eyed girl.

"Luata!" she exclaimed. "How came you here?"

Bradley shrugged. "Here I am," he said; "but the thing now is to get out of here—both of us."

The girl shook her head. "It cannot be," she stated sadly.

"That is what I thought when they dropped me into the Blue Place of Seven Skulls," replied Bradley. "Can't be done. I did it. —Here! You're mussing up the floor something awful, you." This last to the dead Wieroo as he stooped and dragged the corpse to the central shaft, where he raised it to the aperture and let it slip into the tube. Then he picked up the head and tossed it after the body. "Don't be so glum," he admonished the former as he carried it toward the well; "smile!"

"But how can he smile?" questioned the girl, a half-puzzled, half-frightened look upon her face. "He is dead."

"That's so," admitted Bradley, "and I suppose he does feel a bit cut up about it."

The girl shook her head and edged away from the man—toward the door.

"Come!" said the Englishman. "We've got to get out of here. If you don't know a better way than the river, it's the river then."

The girl still eyed him askance. "But how could he smile when he was dead?"

Bradley laughed aloud. "I thought we English were supposed to have the least sense of humor of any people in the world," he cried; "but now I've found one human being who hasn't any. Of course you don't know half I'm saying; but don't worry, little girl; I'm not going to hurt you, and if I can get you out of here, I'll do it."

Even if she did not understand all he said, she at least read something in his smiling countenance—something which reassured her. "I do not fear you," she said; "though I do not understand all that you say even though you speak my own tongue and use words that I know. But as for escaping"—she sighed— "alas, how can it be done?"

"I escaped from the Blue Place of Seven Skulls," Bradley reminded her. "Come!" And he turned toward the shaft and the ladder that he had ascended from the river. "We cannot waste time here."

The girl followed him; but at the doorway both drew back, for from below came the sound of some one ascending. Bradley tiptoed to the door and peered cautiously into the well; then he stepped back beside the girl. "There are half a dozen of them coming up; but possibly they will pass this room."

"No," she said, "they will pass directly through this room—they are on their way to Him Who Speaks for Luata. We may be able to hide in the next room—there are skins there beneath which we may crawl. They will not stop in that room; but they may stop in this one for a short time—the other room is blue."

"What's that got to do with it?" demanded the Englishman.

"They fear blue," she replied. "In every room where murder has been done you will find blue—a certain amount for each murder. When the room is all blue, they shun it. This room has much blue; but evidently they kill mostly in the next room, which is now all blue."

"But there is blue on the outside of every house I have seen," said Bradley.

"Yes," assented the girl, "and there are blue rooms in each of those houses—when all the rooms are blue then the whole outside of the house will be blue as is the Blue Place of Seven Skulls. There are many such here."

"And the skulls with blue upon them?" inquired Bradley. "Did they belong to murderers?"

"They were murdered—some of them; those with only a small amount of blue were murderers—known murderers. All Wieroos are murderers. When they have committed a certain number of murders without being caught at it, they confess to Him Who Speaks for Luata and are advanced, after which they wear robes with a slash of some color—I think yellow comes first. When they reach a point where their entire robe is of yellow, they discard it for a white robe with a red slash; and when one wins a complete red robe, he carries such a long, curved knife as you have in your hand; after that comes the blue slash on a white robe, and then, I suppose, an all blue robe. I have never seen such a one."

As they talked in low tones they had moved from the room of the death shaft into an all blue room adjoining, where they sat down together in a corner with their backs against a wall and drew a pile of hides over themselves. A moment later they heard a number of Wieroos enter the chamber. They were talking together as they crossed the floor, or the two could not have heard them. Halfway across the chamber they halted as the door toward which they were advancing opened and a dozen others of their kind entered the apartment.

Bradley could guess all this by the increased volume of sound and the dismal greetings; but the sudden silence that almost immediately ensued he could not fathom, for he could not know that from beneath one of the hides that covered him protruded one of his heavy army shoes, or that some eighteen large Wieroos with robes either solid red or slashed with red or blue were standing gazing at it. Nor could he hear their stealthy approach.

The first intimation he had that he had been discovered was when his foot was suddenly seized, and he was yanked violently from beneath the hides to find himself surrounded by menacing blades. They would have slain him on the spot had not one clothed all in red held them back, saying that He Who Speaks for Luata desired to see this strange creature.

As they led Bradley away, he caught an opportunity to glance back toward the hides to see what had become of the girl, and, to his gratification, he discovered that she still lay concealed beneath the hides. He wondered if she would have the nerve to attempt the river trip alone and regretted that now he could not accompany her. He felt rather all in, himself, more so than he had at any time since he had been captured by the Wieroo, for there appeared not the slightest cause for hope in his present predicament. He had even dropped the curved blade beneath the hides when he had been jerked so violently from their fancied security. It was almost in a spirit of resigned hopelessness that he quietly accompanied his captors through various chambers and corridors toward the heart of the temple.

CHAPTER IV

THE farther the group progressed, the more barbaric and the more sumptuous became the decoration. Hides of leopard and tiger predominated, apparently because of their more beautiful markings, and decorative skulls became more and more numerous. Many of the latter were mounted in precious metals and set with colored stones and priceless gems, while thick upon the hides that covered the walls were golden ornaments similar to those worn by the girl and those which had filled the chests he had examined in the storeroom of Fosh-bal-soj, leading the

Englishman to the conviction that all such were spoils of war or theft, since each piece seemed made for personal adornment, while in so far as he had seen, no Wieroo wore ornaments of any sort.

And also as they advanced the more numerous became the Wieroos moving hither and thither within the temple. Many now were the solid red robes and those that were slashed with blue—a veritable hive of murderers.

At last the party halted in a room in which were many Wieroos who gathered about Bradley questioning his captors and examining him and his apparel. One of the party accompanying the Englishman spoke to a Wieroo that stood beside a door leading from the room. "Tell Him Who Speaks for Luata," he said, "that Fosh-bal-soj we could not find; but that in returning we found this creature within the temple, hiding. It must be the same that Fosh-bal-soj captured in the Sto-lu country during the last darkness. Doubtless He Who Speaks for Luata would wish to see and question this strange thing."

The creature addressed turned and slipped through the doorway, closing the door after it, but first depositing its curved blade upon the floor without. Its post was immediately taken by another, and Bradley now saw that at least twenty such guards loitered in the immediate vicinity. The doorkeeper was gone but for a moment, and when he returned, he signified that Bradley's party was to enter the next chamber; but first each of the Wieroos removed his curved weapon and laid it upon the floor. The door was swung open, and the party, now reduced to Bradley and five Wieroos, was ushered across the threshold into a large, irregularly shaped room in which a single, giant Wieroo whose robe was solid blue sat upon a raised dais.

The creature's face was white with the whiteness of a corpse, its dead eyes entirely expressionless, its cruel, thin lips tight-drawn against yellow teeth in a perpetual grimace. Upon either side of it lay an enormous, curved sword, similar to those with which some of the other Wieroos had been armed, but larger and heavier. Constantly its clawlike fingers played with one or the other of these weapons.

The walls of the chamber as well as the floor were entirely hidden by skins and woven fabrics. Blue predominated in all the colorations. Fastened against the hides were many pairs of Wieroo wings, mounted so that they resembled long, black shields. Upon the ceiling were painted in blue characters a bewildering series of hieroglyphics, and upon pedestals set against the walls or standing out well within the room were many human skulls. As the Wieroos approached the figure upon the dais, they leaned far forward, raising their wings above their heads and stretching their necks as though offering them to the sharp swords of the grim and hideous creature.

"O Thou Who Speakest for Luata!" exclaimed one of the party. "We bring you the strange creature that Fosh-bal-soj captured and brought hither at thy command."

So this then was the godlike figure that spoke for divinity! This arch-murderer was the Caspakian representative of God on earth! His blue robe announced him the one and the seeming humility of his minions the other. For a long minute he glared at Bradley. Then he began to question him—from whence he came and how, the name and description of his native country, and a hundred other queries.

"Are you *cos-ata-lu?*" the creature asked.

Bradley replied that he was and that all his kind were, as well as every living thing in his part of the world.

"Can you tell me the secret?" asked the creature.

Bradley hesitated and then, thinking to gain time, replied in the affirmative.

"What is it?" demanded the Wieroo, leaning far forward and exhibiting every evidence of excited interest.

Bradley leaned forward and whispered: "It is for your ears alone; I will not divulge it to others, and then only on condition that you carry me and the girl I saw in the place of the yellow door near to that of Fosh-bal-soj back to her own country."

The thing rose in wrath, holding one of its swords above its head.

"Who are you to make terms for Him Who Speaks for Luata?" it shrilled. "Tell me the secret or die where you stand!"

"And if I die now, the secret goes with me," Bradley reminded him. "Never again will you get the opportunity to question another of my kind who knows the secret." Anything to gain time, to get the rest of the Wieroos from the room, that he might plan some scheme for escape and put it into effect.

The creature turned upon the leader of the party that had brought Bradley.

"Is the thing with weapons?" it asked.

"No," was the response.

"Then go; but tell the guard to remain close by," commanded the high one.

The Wieroos salaamed and withdrew, closing the door behind

them. He Who Speaks for Luata grasped a sword nervously in his right hand. At his left side lay the second weapon. It was evident that he lived in constant dread of being assassinated. The fact that he permitted none with weapons within his presence and that he always kept two swords at his side pointed to this.

Bradley was racking his brain to find some suggestion of a plan whereby he might turn the situation to his own account. His eyes wandered past the weird figure before him; they played about the walls of the apartment as though hoping to draw inspiration from the dead skulls and the hides and the wings, and then they came back to the face of the Wieroo god, now working in anger.

"Quick!" screamed the thing. "The secret!"

"Will you give me and the girl our freedom?" insisted Bradley.

For an instant the thing hesitated, and then it grumbled "Yes." At the same instant Bradley saw two hides upon the wall directly back of the dais separate and a face appear in the opening. No change of expression upon the Englishman's countenance betrayed that he had seen aught to surprise him, though surprised he was for the face in the aperture was that of the girl he had but just left hidden beneath the hides in another chamber. A white and shapely arm now pushed past the face into the room, and in the hand, tightly clutched, was the curved blade, smeared with blood, that Bradley had dropped beneath the hides at the moment he had been discovered and drawn from his concealment.

"Listen, then," said Bradley in a low voice to the Wieroo. "You shall know the secret of *cos-ata-lu* as well as do I; but none other may hear it. Lean close—I will whisper it into your ear."

He moved forward and stepped upon the dais. The creature raised its sword ready to strike at the first indication of treachery, and Bradley stooped beneath the blade and put his ear close to the gruesome face. As he did so, he rested his weight upon his hands, one upon either side of the Wieroo's body, his right hand upon the hilt of the spare sword lying at the left of Him Who Speaks for Luata.

"This then is the secret of both life and death," he whispered, and at the same instant he grasped the Wieroo by the right wrist and with his own right hand swung the extra blade in a sudden vicious blow against the creature's neck before the thing could give even a single cry of alarm; then without waiting an instant Bradley leaped past the dead god and vanished behind the hides that had hidden the girl.

Wide-eyed and panting the girl seized his arm. "Oh, what have you done?" she cried. "He Who Speaks for Luata will be avenged by Luata. Now indeed must you die. There is no escape, for even though we reached my own country Luata can find you out."

"Bosh!" exclaimed Bradley, and then: "But you were going to knife him yourself."

"Then I alone should have died," she replied.

Bradley scratched his head. "Neither of us is going to die," he said; "at least not at the hands of any god. If we don't get out of here though, we'll die right enough. Can you find your way back to the room where I first came upon you in the temple?"

"I know the way," replied the girl; "but I doubt if we can go back without being seen. I came hither because I only met Wieroos who knew that I am supposed now to be in the temple; but you could go nowhere without being discovered."

Bradley's ingenuity had come up against a stone wall. There seemed no possibility of escape. He looked about him. They were in a small room where lay a litter of rubbish—torn bits of cloth, old hides, pieces of fiber rope. In the center of the room was a cylindrical shaft with an opening in its face. Bradley knew it for what it was. Here the arch-fiend dragged his victims and cast their bodies into the river of death far below. The floor about the opening in the shaft and the sides of the shaft were clotted thick with a dried, dark brown substance that the Englishman knew had once been blood. The place had the appearance of having been a veritable shambles. An odor of decaying flesh permeated the air.

The Englishman crossed to the shaft and peered into the opening. All below was dark as pitch; but at the bottom he knew was the river. Suddenly an inspiration and a bold scheme leaped to his mind. Turning quickly he hunted about the room until he found what he sought—a quantity of the rope that lay strewn here and there. With rapid fingers he unsnarled the different lengths, the girl helping him, and then he tied the ends together until he had three ropes about seventy-five feet in length. He fastened these together at each end and without a word secured one of the ends about the girl's body beneath her arms.

"Don't be frightened," he said at length, as he led her toward the opening in the shaft. "I'm going to lower you to the river, and then I'm coming down after you. When you are safe below, give two quick jerks upon the rope. If there is danger there and you want me to draw you up into the shaft, jerk once. Don't be afraid—it is the only way."

"I am not afraid," replied the girl, rather haughtily Bradley thought, and herself climbed through the aperture and hung by her hands waiting for Bradley to lower her.

As rapidly as was consistent with safety, the man paid out the rope. When it was about half out, he heard loud cries and wails suddenly arise within the room they had just quitted. The slaying of their god had been discovered by the Wieroos. A search for the slayer would begin at once.

Lord! Would the girl never reach the river? At last, just as he was positive that searchers were already entering the room behind him, there came two quick tugs at the rope. Instantly Bradley made the rest of the strands fast about the shaft, slipped into the black tube and began a hurried descent toward the river. An instant later he stood waist deep in water beside the girl. Impulsively she reached toward him and grasped his arm. A strange thrill ran through him at the contact; but he only cut the rope from about her body and lifted her to the little shelf at the river's side.

"How can we leave here?" she asked.

"By the river," he replied; "but first I must go back to the Blue Place of Seven Skulls and get the poor devil I left there. I'll have to wait until after dark, though, as I cannot pass through the open stretch of river in the temple gardens by day."

"There is another way," said the girl. "I have never seen it; but often I have heard them speak of it—a corridor that runs beside the river from one end of the city to the other. Through the gardens it is below ground. If we could find an entrance to it, we could leave here at once. It is not safe here, for they will search every inch of the temple and the grounds."

"Come," said Bradley. "We'll have a look for it, anyway." And so saying he approached one of the doors that opened onto the skull-paved shelf.

They found the corridor easily, for it paralleled the river, separated from it only by a single wall. It took them beneath the gardens and the city, always through inky darkness. After they had reached the other side of the gardens, Bradley counted his steps until he had retraced as many as he had taken coming down the stream; but though they had to grope their way along, it was a much more rapid trip than the former.

When he thought he was about opposite the point at which he had descended from the Blue Place of Seven Skulls, he sought and found a doorway leading out onto the river; and then, still in the blackest darkness, he lowered himself into the stream and felt up and down upon the opposite side for the little shelf and the ladder. Ten yards from where he had emerged he found them, while the girl waited upon the opposite side.

To ascend to the secret panel was the work of but a minute. Here he paused and listened lest a Wieroo might be visiting the prison in search of him or the other inmate; but no sound came from the gloomy interior. Bradley could not but muse upon the joy of the man on the opposite side when he should drop down to him with food and a new hope for escape. Then he opened the panel and looked into the room. The faint light from the grating above revealed the pile of rags in one corner; but if the man lay beenath them, he made no response to Bradley's low greeting.

The Englishman lowered himself to the floor of the room and approached the rags. Stooping he lifted a corner of them. Yes, there was the man asleep. Bradley shook him—there was no response. He stooped lower and in the dim light examined An-Tak; then he stood up with a sigh. A rat leaped from beneath the coverings and scurried away. "Poor devil!" muttered Bradley.

He crossed the room to swing himself to the perch preparatory to quitting the Blue Place of Seven Skulls forever. Beneath the perch he paused. "I'll not give them the satisfaction," he growled. "Let them believe that he escaped."

Returning to the pile of rags he gathered the man into his arms. It was difficult work raising him to the high perch and dragging him through the small opening and thus down the ladder; but presently it was done, and Bradley had lowered the body into the river and cast it off. "Good-bye, old top!" he whispered.

A moment later he had rejoined the girl and hand in hand they were following the dark corridor upstream toward the farther end of the city. She told him that the Wieroos seldom frequented these lower passages, as the air here was too chill for them; but occasionally they came, and as they could see quite as well by night as by day, they would be sure to discover Bradley and the girl.

"If they come close enough," she said, "we can see their eyes shining in the dark—they resemble dull splotches of light. They glow, but do not blaze like the eyes of the tiger or the lion."

The man could not but note the very evident horror with which she mentioned the creatures. To him they were uncanny; but she had been used to them for a year almost, and probably all her life she had either seen or heard of them constantly.

"Why do you fear them so?" he asked. "It seems more than any ordinary fear of the harm they can do you."

She tried to explain; but the nearest he could gather was that she looked upon the Wieroo almost as supenatural beings. "There is a legend current among my people that once the Wieroo were unlike us only in that they possessed rudimentary wings. They lived in villages in the Galu country, and while the two peoples often warred, they held no hatred for one another. In those days each race came up from the beginning and there was great rivalry as to which was the higher in the scale of evolution. The Wieroo developed the first *cos-ata-lu;* but they were always male—never could they reproduce woman. Slowly they commenced to develop certain attributes of the mind which, they considered, placed them upon a still higher level and which gave them many advantages over us, seeing which they thought only of mental development—their minds became like the stars and the rivers, moving always in the same manner, never varying. They called this *tas-ad,* which means doing everything the right way, or, in other words, the Wieroo way. If foe or friend, right or wrong, stood in the way of *tas-ad,* then it must be crushed.

"Soon the Galus and the lesser races of men came to hate and fear them. It was then that the Wieroos decided to carry *tas-ad* into every part of the world. They were very warlike and very numerous, although they had long since adopted the policy of slaying all those among them whose wings did not show advanced development.

"It took ages for all this to happen—very slowly came the different changes; but at last the Wieroos had wings that they could use. But by reason of always making war upon their neighbors they were hated by every creature of Caspak, for no one wanted their *tas-ad,* and so they used their wings to fly to this island when the other races turned against them and threatened to kill them all. So cruel had they become and so bloodthirsty that they no longer had hearts that beat with love or sympathy; but their very cruelty and wickedness kept them from conquering the other races, since they were also cruel and wicked to one another, so that no Wieroo trusted another.

"Always were they slaying those above them that they might rise in power and possessions, until at last came one more powerful that the others with a *tas-ad* all his own. He gathered about him a few of the most terrible Wieroos, and among them they made laws which took from all but these few Wieroos every weapon they possessed.

"Now their *tas-ad* has reached a high plane among them. They make many wonderful things that we cannot make. They think great thoughts, no doubt, and still dream of greatness to come, but their thoughts and their acts are regulated by ages of custom —they are all alike—and they are most unhappy."

As the girl talked, the two moved steadily along the dark passageway beside the river. They had advanced a considerable distance when there sounded faintly from far ahead the muffled roar of falling water, which increased in volume as they moved forward until at last it filled the corridor with a deafening sound. Then the corridor ended in a blank wall; but in a niche to the right was a ladder leading aloft, and to the left was a door opening onto the river. Bradley tried the latter first and as he opened it, felt a heavy spray against his face. The little shelf outside the doorway was wet and slippery, the roaring of the water tremendous. There could be but one explanation—they had reached a waterfall in the river, and if the corridor actually terminated here, their escape was effectually cut off, since it was quite evidently impossible to follow the bed of the river and ascend the falls.

As the ladder was the only alternative, the two turned toward it and, the man first, began the ascent, which was through a well similar to that which had led him to the upper floors of the temple. As he climbed, Bradley felt for openings in the sides of the shaft; but he discovered none below fifty feet. The first he came to was ajar, letting a faint light into the well. As he paused, the girl climbed to his side, and together they looked through the crack into a low-ceiled chamber in which were several Galu women and an equal number of hideous little replicas of the full-grown Wieroos with which Bradley was now quite familiar.

He could feel the body of the girl pressed close to his tremble as her eyes rested upon the inmates of the room, and involuntarily his arm encircled her shoulders as though to protect her from some danger which he sensed without recognizing.

"Poor things," she whispered. "This is their horrible fate—to be imprisoned here beneath the surface of the city with their hideous offspring whom they hate as they hate the fathers. A Wieroo keeps his children thus hidden until they are full-grown lest they be murdered by their fellows. The lower rooms of the city are filled with many such as these."

Several feet above was a second door beyond which they found a small room stored with food in wooden vessels. A grated window in one wall opened above an alley, and through it they could see that they were just below the roof of the building. Darkness was coming, and at Bradley's suggestion they decided to remain hidden here until after dark and then to ascend to the roof and reconnoiter.

Shortly after they had settled themselves they heard something descending the ladder from above. They hoped that it would continue on down the well and fairly held their breath as the sound approached the door to the storeroom. Their hearts sank as they heard the door open and from between cracks in the vessels behind which they hid saw a yellow-slashed Wieroo enter the room. Each recognized him immediately, the girl indicating the fact of her own recognition by a sudden pressure of her fingers on Bradley's arm. It was the Wieroo of the yellow slashing whose abode was the place of the yellow door in which Bradley had first seen the girl.

The creature carried a wooden bowl which it filled with dried food from several of the vessels; then it turned and quit the room. Bradley could see through the partially open doorway that it descended the ladder. The girl told him that it was taking the food to the women and the young below, and that while it might return immediately, the chances were that it would remain for some time.

"We are just below the place of the yellow door," she said. "It is far from the edge of the city; so far that we may not hope to escape if we ascend to the roofs here."

"I think," replied the man, "that of all the places in Oo-oh this will be the easiest to escape from. Anyway, I want to return to the place of the yellow door and get my pistol if it is there."

"It is still there," replied the girl. "I saw it placed in a chest where he keeps the things he takes from his prisoners and victims."

"Good!" exclaimed Bradley. "Now come, quickly." And the two crossed the room to the well and ascended the ladder a short distance to its top where they found another door that opened into a vacant room—the same in which Bradley had first met the girl. To find the pistol was a matter of but a moment's search on the part of Bradley's companion; and then, at the Englishman's signal, she followed him to the yellow door.

It was quite dark without as the two entered the narrow passage between two buildings. A few steps brought them undiscovered to the doorway of the storeroom where lay the body of Fosh-bal-soj. In the distance, toward the temple, they could hear sounds as of a great gathering of Wieroos—the peculiar, uncanny wailing rising above the dismal flapping of countless wings.

"They have heard of the killing of Him Who Speaks for Luata," whispered the girl. "Soon they will spread in all directions searching for us."

"And will they find us?"

"As surely as Lua gives light by day," she replied; "and when they find us, they will tear us to pieces, for only the Wieroos may murder—only they may practice *tas-ad.*"

"But they will not kill you," said Bradley. "You did not slay him."

"It will make no difference," she insisted. "If they find us together they will slay us both."

"Then they won't find us together," announced Bradley decisively. "You stay right here—you won't be any worse off than before I came—and I'll get as far as I can and account for as many of the beggars as possible before they get me. Good-bye! You're a mighty decent little girl. I wish that I might have helped you."

"No," she cried. "Do not leave me. I would rather die. I had hoped and hoped to find some way to return to my own country. I wanted to go back to An-Tak, who must be very lonely without me; but I know that it can never be. It is difficult to kill hope, though mine is nearly dead. Do not leave me."

"An-Tak!" Bradley repeated. "You loved a man called An-Tak?"

"Yes," replied the girl. "An-Tak was away, hunting, when the Wieroo caught me. How he must have grieved for me! He also was *cos-ata-lu,* twelve moons older than I, and all our lives we have been together."

Bradley remained silent. So she loved An-Tak. He hadn't the heart to tell her than An-Tak had died, or how.

At the door of Fosh-bal-soj's storeroom they halted to listen. No sound came from within, and gently Bradley pushed open the door. All was inky darkness as they entered; but presently their eyes became accustomed to the gloom that was partially relieved by the soft starlight without. The Englishman searched and found those things for which he had come—two robes, two pairs of dead wings and several lengths of fiber rope. One pair of the wings he adjusted to the girl's shoulders by means of the rope. Then he draped the robe about her, carrying the cowl over her head.

He heard her gasp of astonishment when she realized the ingenuity and boldness of his plan; then he directed her to adjust the other pair of wings and the robe upon him. Working with strong, deft fingers she soon had the work completed, and the two stepped out upon the roof, to all intent and purpose genuine Wieroos. Besides his pistol Bradley carried the sword of the slain Wieroo prophet, while the girl was armed with the small blade of the red Wieroo.

Side by side they walked slowly across the roofs toward the north edge of the city. Wieroos flapped above them and several times they passed others walking or sitting upon the roofs. From the temple still rose the sounds of commotion, now pierced by occasional shrill screams.

"The murderers are abroad," whispered the girl. "Thus will another become the tongue of Luata. It is well for us, since it keeps them too busy to give the time for searching for us. They think that we cannot escape the city, and they know that we cannot leave the island—and so do I."

Bradley shook his head. "If there is any way, we will find it," he said.

"There is no way," replied the girl.

Bradley made no response, and in silence they continued until the outer edge of roofs was visible before them. "We are almost there," he whispered.

The girl felt for his fingers and pressed them. He could feel hers trembling as he returned the pressure, nor did he relinquish her hand; and thus they came to the edge of the last roof.

Here they halted and looked about them. To be seen attempting to descend to the ground below would be to betray the fact that they were not Wieroos. Bradley wished that their wings were attached to their bodies by sinew and muscle rather than by ropes of fiber. A Wieroo was flapping far overhead. Two more stood near a door a few yards distant. Standing between these and one of the outer pedestals that supported one of the numerous skulls Bradley made one end of a piece of rope fast about the pedestal and dropped the other end to the ground outside the city. Then they waited.

It was an hour before the coast was entirely clear and then a moment came when no Wieroo was in sight. "Now!" whispered Bradley; and the girl grasped the rope and slid over the edge of the roof into the darkness below. A moment later Bradley felt two quick pulls upon the rope and immediately followed to the girl's side.

Across a narrow clearing they made their way and into a wood beyond. All night they walked, following the river upward toward its source, and at dawn they took shelter in a thicket beside the stream. At no time did they hear the cry of a carnivore, and though many startled animals fled as they approached, they were not once menaced by a wild beast. When Bradley expressed surprise at the absence of the fiercer beasts that are so numerous upon the mainland of Caprona, the girl explained the reason that is contained in one of their ancient legends.

"When the Wieroos first developed wings upon which they could fly, they found this island devoid of any life other than a few reptiles that live either upon land or in the water and these only close to the coast. Requiring meat for food the Wieroos carried to the island such animals as they wished for that purpose. They still occasionally bring them, and this with the natural increase keeps them provided with flesh."

"As it will us," suggested Bradley.

The first day they remained in hiding, eating only the dried food that Bradley had brought with him from the temple storeroom, and the next night they set out again up the river, continuing steadily on until almost dawn, when they came to low hills where the river wound through a gorge—it was little more than a rivulet now, the water clear and cold and filled with fish similar to brook trout though much larger. Not wishing to leave the stream the two waded along its bed to a spot where the gorge widened between perpendicular bluffs to a wooded acre of level land. Here they stopped, for here also the stream ended. They had reached its source—many cold springs bubbling up from the center of a little natural amphitheater in the hills and forming a clear and beautiful pool overshadowed by trees upon one side and bounded by a little clearing upon the other.

With the coming of the sun they saw they had stumbled upon a place where they might remain hidden from the Wieroos for a long time and also one that they could defend against these winged creatures, since the trees would shield them from an attack from above and also hamper the movements of the creatures should they attempt to follow them into the wood.

For three days they rested here before trying to explore the neighboring country. On the fourth, Bradley stated that he was going to scale the bluffs and learn what lay beyond. He told the girl that she should remain in hiding; but she refused to be left, saying that whatever fate was to be his, she intended to share it, so that he was at last forced to permit her to come with him. Through woods at the summit of the bluff they made their way toward the north and had gone but a short distance when the wood ended and before them they saw the waters of the inland sea and dimly in the distance the coveted shore.

The beach lay some two hundred yards from the foot of the hill on which they stood, nor was there a tree nor any other form of shelter between them and the water as far up and down the coast as they could see. Among other plans Bradley had thought of constructing a covered raft upon which they might drift to the mainland; but as such a contrivance would necessarily be of considerable weight, it must be built in the water of the sea, since they could not hope to move it even a short distance overland.

"If this wood was only at the edge of the water," he sighed.

"But it is not," the girl reminded him, and then: "Let us make the best of it. We have escaped from death for a time at least. We have food and good water and peace and each other. What more could we have upon the mainland?"

"But I thought you wanted to get back to your own country!" he exclaimed.

She cast her eyes upon the ground and half turned away. "I do," she said, "yet I am happy here. I could be little happier there."

Bradley stood in silent thought. "We have food and good water and peace and *each other!*" he repeated to himself. He turned then and looked at the girl, and it was as though in the days that they had been together this was the first time that he had really seen her. The circumstances that had thrown them together, the dangers through which they had passed, all the weird and horrible surroundings that had formed the background of his knowledge of her had had their effect—she had been but the companion of an adventure; her self-reliance, her endurance, her loyalty, had been only what one man might expect of another, and he saw that he had unconsciously assumed an attitude toward her that he might have assumed toward a man. Yet there had been a difference—he recalled now the strange sensation of elation that had thrilled him upon the occasions when the girl had pressed his hand in hers, and the depression that had followed her announcement of her love for An-tak.

He took a step toward her. A fierce yearning to seize her and crush her in his arms, swept over him, and then there flashed upon the screen of recollection the picture of a stately hall set amidst broad gardens and ancient trees and of a proud old man with beetling brows—an old man who held his head very high— and Bradley shook his head and turned away again.

They went back then to their little acre, and the days came and went, and the man fashioned spear and bow and arrows and hunted with them that they might have meat, and he made hooks of fish-bone and caught fishes with wondrous flies of his own invention; and the girl gathered fruits and cooked the flesh and the fish and made beds of branches and soft grasses. She cured the hides of the animals he killed and made them soft by much pounding. She made sandals for herself and for the man and fashioned a hide after the manner of those worn by the warriors of her tribe and made the man wear it, for his own garments were in rags.

She was always the same—sweet and kind and helpful—but always there was about her manner and her expression just a trace of wistfulness, and often she sat and looked at the man when he did not know it, her brows puckered in thought as though she were trying to fathom and to understand him.

In the face of the cliff, Bradley scooped a cave from the rotted granite of which the hill was composed, making a shelter for them against the rains. He brought wood for their cook-fire which they used only in the middle of the day—a time when there was little likelihood of Wieroos being in the air so far from their city—and then he learned to bank it with earth in such a way that the embers held until the following noon without giving off smoke.

Always he was planning on reaching the mainland, and never a day passed that he did not go to the top of the hill and look out across the sea toward the dark, distant line that meant for him comparative freedom and possibly reunion with his comrades. The girl always went with him, standing at his side and watching the stern expression on his face with just a tinge of sadness on her own.

"You are not happy," she said once.

"I should be over there with my men," he replied. "I do not know what may have happened to them."

"I want you to be happy," she said quite simply; "but I should be very lonely if you went away and left me here."

He put his hand on her shoulder. "I would not do that, little girl," he said gently. "If you cannot go with me, I shall not go. If either of us must go alone, it will be you."

Her face lighted to a wondrous smile. "Then we shall not be separated," she said, "for I shall never leave you as long as we both live."

"Throw aside your weapons," Bradley commanded. After a moment's hesitation they obeyed.

"Now approach!" A great plan—the only plan—had suddenly come to him like an inspiration.

The Wieroos came closer and halted at his command. Bradley turned to the girl. "There is rope in the shelter," he said. "Fetch it!"

She did as he bid, and then he directed her to fasten one end of a fifty-foot length to the ankle of one of the Wieroos and the opposite end to the second. The creatures gave evidence of great fear, but they dared not attempt to prevent the act.

"Now go out into the clearing," said Bradley, "and remember that I am walking close behind and that I will shoot the nearer one should either attempt to escape—that will hold the other until I can kill him as well."

In the open he halted them. "The girl will get upon the back of the one in front," announced the Englishman. "I will mount the other. She carries a sharp blade, and I carry this weapon that you know kills easily at a distance. If you disobey in the slightest the instructions that I am about to give you, you shall both die. That we must die with you, will not deter us. If you obey, I promise to set you free without harming you.

"You will carry us due west, depositing us upon the shore of the mainland—that is all. It is the price of your lives. Do you agree?"

Sullenly the Wieroos acquiesced. Bradley examined the knots that held the rope to their ankles, and finding them secure directed the girl to mount the back of the leading Wieroo, himself climbing upon the other. Then he gave the signal for the two to rise together. With loud flapping of the powerful wings the creatures took to the air, circling once before they topped the trees upon the hill and then taking a course due west over the waters of the sea.

Nowhere about them could Bradley see signs of other Wieroos, nor of those other menaces which he had feared might bring disaster to his plans for escape—the huge, winged reptilia that are so numerous above the southern areas of Caspak and which are often seen, though in lesser numbers, farther north.

Nearer and nearer loomed the mainland—a broad, parklike expanse stretching inland to the foot of a low plateau spread out before them. The little dots in the foreground became grazing herds of deer and antelope and bos; a huge woolly rhinoceros wallowed in a mudhole to the right, and beyond, a mighty mammoth culled the tender shoots from a tall tree. The roars and screams and growls of giant carnivora came faintly to their ears. Ah, this was Caspak. With all of its dangers and its primal savagery it brought a fullness to the throat of the Englishman as to one who sees and hears the familiar sights and sounds of home after a long absence. Then the Wieroos dropped swiftly downward to the flower-starred turf that grew almost to the water's edge, the fugitives slipped from their backs, and Bradley told the red-robed creatures they were free to go.

When he had cut the ropes from their ankles they rose with that uncanny wailing upon their lips that always brought a shudder to the Englishman, and upon dismal wings they flapped away toward frightful Oo-oh.

When the creatures had gone, the girl turned toward Bradley. "Why did you have them bring us here?" she asked. "Now we are far from my country. We may never live to reach it, as we are among enemies who, while not so horrible, will kill us just as surely as would the Wieroos should they capture us, and we have before us many marches through lands filled with savage beasts."

"There were two reasons," replied Bradley. "You told me that there are two Wieroo cities at the eastern end of the island. To have passed near either of them might have been to have brought about our heads hundreds of the creatures from whom we could not possibly have escaped. Again, my friends must be near this spot—it cannot be over two marches to the fort of which I have told you. It is my duty to return to them. If they still live we shall find a way to return you to your people."

"And you?" asked the girl.

"I escaped from Oo-oh," replied Bradley. "I have accomplished the impossible once, and so I shall accomplish it again—I shall escape from Caspak."

He was not looking at her face as he answered her, and so he did not see the shadow of sorrow that crossed her countenance. When he raised his eyes again, she was smiling.

"What you wish, I wish," said the girl.

Southward along the coast they made their way following the beach, where the walking was best, but always keeping close enough to trees to insure sanctuary from the beasts and reptiles that so often menaced them. It was late in the afternoon when the girl suddenly seized Bradley's arm and pointed straight ahead along the shore. "What is that?" she whispered. "What strange reptile is it?"

Bradley looked in the direction her slim forefinger indicated. He rubbed his eyes and looked again, and then he seized her wrist and drew her quickly behind a clump of bushes.

"What is it?" she asked.

"It is the most frightful reptile that the waters of the world have ever known," he replied. "It is a German U-boat!"

An expression of amazement and understanding lighted her features. "It is the thing of which you told me," she exclaimed, "—the thing that swims under the water and carries men in its belly!"

"It is," replied Bradley.

"Then why do you hide from it?" asked the girl. "You said that now it belonged to your friends."

"Many months have passed since I knew what was going on among my friends," he replied. "I cannot know what has befallen them. They should have been gone from here in this vessel long since, and so I cannot understand why it is still here. I am going to investigate first before I show myself. When I left, there were more Germans on the *U-33* than there were men of my own party at the fort, and I have had sufficient experience of Germans to know that they will bear watching—if they have not been properly watched since I left."

Making their way through a fringe of wood that grew a few yards inland the two crept unseen toward the U-boat which lay moored to the shore at a point which Bradley now recognized as being near the oil-pool north of Dinosaur. As close as possible to the vessel they halted, crouching low among the dense vegetation, and watched the boat for signs of human life about it. The hatches were closed—no one could be seen or heard. For five minutes Bradley watched, and then he determined to board the submarine and investigate. He had risen to carry his decision into effect when there suddenly broke upon his ear, uttered in loud and menacing tones, a volley of German oaths and expletives among which he heard *Englische schweinhunde* repeated several times. The voice did not come from the direction of the U-boat; but from inland. Creeping forward Bradley reached a spot where, through the creepers hanging from the trees, he could see a party of men coming down toward the shore.

He saw Baron Friedrich von Schoenvorts and six of his men— all armed—while marching in a little knot among them were Olson, Brady, Sinclair, Wilson, and Whitely.

Bradley knew nothing of the disappearance of Bowen Tyler and Miss La Rue, nor of the perfidy of the Germans in shelling the fort and attempting to escape in the *U-33;* but he was in no way surprised at what he saw before him.

The little party came slowly onward, the prisoners staggering beneath heavy cans of oil, while Schwartz, one of the German noncommissioned officers cursed and beat them with a stick of wood, impartially. Von Schoenvorts walked in the rear of the column, encouraging Schwartz and laughing at the discomfiture of the Britishers. Dietz, Heinz, and Klatz also seemed to enjoy the entertainment immensely; but two of the men—Plesser and Hindle—marched with eyes straight to the front and with scowling faces.

Bradley felt his blood boil at sight of the cowardly indignities being heaped upon his men, and in the brief span of time occupied by the column to come abreast of where he lay hidden he made his plans, foolhardy though he knew them. Then he drew the girl close to him. "Stay here," he whispered. "I am going out to fight those beasts; but I shall be killed. Do not let them see you. Do not let them take you alive. They are more cruel, more cowardly, more bestial than the Wieroos."

The girl pressed close to him, her face very white. "Go, if that is right," she whispered; "but if you die, I shall die, for I cannot live without you."

He looked sharply into her eyes. "Oh!" he ejaculated. "What an idiot I have been! Nor could I live without you, little girl." And he drew her very close and kissed her lips. "Good-bye." He disengaged himself from her arms and looked again in time to see that the rear of the column had just passed him. Then he rose and leaped quickly and silently from the jungle.

Suddenly Von Schoenvorts felt an arm thrown about his neck and his pistol jerked from its holster. He gave a cry of fright and warning, and his men turned to see a half-naked white man holding their leader securely from behind and aiming a pistol at them over his shoulder.

"Drop those guns!" came in short, sharp syllables and perfect German from the lips of the newcomer. "Drop them or I'll put a bullet through the back of von Schoenvorts' head."

The Germans hesitated for a moment, looking first toward von Schoenvorts and then to Schwartz, who was evidently second in command, for orders.

"It's the English pig, Bradley," shouted the latter, "and he's alone—go and get him!"

"Go yourself," growled Plesser. Hindle moved close to the side of Plesser and whispered something to him. The latter nodded. Suddenly von Schoenvorts wheeled about and seized Bradley's pistol arm with both hands. "Now!" he shouted. "Come and take him, quick!"

Schwartz and three others leaped forward; but Plesser and Hindle held back, looking questioningly toward the English prisoners. Then Plesser spoke. "Now is your chance, *Engländer*," he called in low tones. "Seize Hindle and me and take our guns from us—we will not fight hard."

Olson and Brady were not long in acting upon the suggestion. They had seen enough of the brutal treatment von Schoenvorts accorded his men and the especially venomous attentions he had taken great enjoyment in according Plesser and Hindle to understand that these two might be sincere in a desire for revenge. In another moment the two Germans were unarmed and Olson and Brady were running to the support of Bradley; but already it seemed too late.

Von Schoenvorts had managed to drag the Englishman around so that his back was toward Schwartz and the other advancing Germans. Schwartz was almost upon Bradley with gun clubbed and ready to smash down upon the Englishman's skull. Brady and Olson were charging the Germans in the rear with Wilson, Whitely, and Sinclair supporting them with bare fists. It seemed that Bradley was doomed when, apparently out of space, an arrow whizzed, striking Schwartz in the side, passing halfway through his body to crumple him to earth. With a shriek the man fell, and at the same time Olson and Brady saw the slim figure of a young girl standing at the edge of the jungle coolly fitting another arrow to her bow.

Bradley had now succeeded in wresting his arm free from von Schoenvorts' grip and in dropping the latter with a blow from the butt of his pistol. The rest of the English and Germans were engaged in a hand-to-hand encounter, Plesser and Hindle standing aside from the mêlée and urging their comrades to surrender and join with the English against the tyranny of von Schoenvorts. Heinz and Klatz, possibly influenced by their exhortation, were putting up but a half-hearted resistance; but Dietz, a huge, bearded, bull-necked Prussian, yelling like a maniac, sought to exterminate the *Englische schweinhunde* with his bayonet, fearing to fire his piece lest he kill some of his comrades.

It was Olson who engaged him, and though unused to the long German rifle and bayonet, he met the bull-rush of the Hun with the cold, cruel precision and science of English bayonet-fighting. There was no feinting, no retiring and no parrying that was not also an attack. Bayonet-fighting today is not a pretty thing to see—it is no artistic fencing-match in which men give and take—it is slaughter inevitable and quickly over. Dietz lunged once madly at Olson's throat. A short point, with just a twist of the bayonet to the left sent the sharp blade over the Englishman's left shoulder. Instantly he stepped close in, dropped his rifle through his hands and grasped it with both close below the muzzle and with a short, sharp jab sent his blade up beneath Dietz's chin clear to the brain. So quickly was the thing done and so quick the withdrawal that Olson had wheeled to take on another adversary before the German's corpse had toppled to the ground.

But there were no more adversaries to take on. Heinz and Klatz had thrown down their rifles and with hands above their heads- were crying "Kamerad! Kamerad!" at the tops of their voices. Von Schoenvorts still lay where he had fallen. Plesser and Hindle were explaining to Bradley that they were glad of the outcome of the fight, as they could no longer endure the brutality of the U-boat commander.

The remainder of the men were looking at the girl who now advanced slowly, her bow ready, when Bradley turned toward her and held out his hand.

"Co-Tan," he said, "unstring your bow—these are my friends, and yours." And to the Englishmen: "This is Co-Tan. You who saw her save me from Schwartz know a part of what I owe her."

The rough men gathered about the girl, and when she spoke to them in broken English, with a smile upon her lips enhancing the charm of her irresistible accent, each and every one of them promptly fell in love with her and constituted himself henceforth her guardian and her slave.

A moment later the attention of each was called to Plesser by a volley of invective. They turned in time to see the man running toward von Schoenvorts who was just rising from the ground. Plesser carried a rifle with bayonet fixed, that he had snatched from the side of Dietz's corpse. Von Schoenvorts' face was livid with fear, his jaws working as though he would call for help; but no sound came from his blue lips.

"You struck me," shrieked Plesser. "Once, twice, three times, you struck me, pig. You murdered Schwerke—you drove him insane by your cruelty until he took his own life. You are only one of your kind—they are all like you from the Kaiser down. I wish that you were the Kaiser. Thus would I do!" And he lunged his bayonet through von Schoenvorts' chest. Then he let his rifle fall with the dying man and wheeled toward Bradley. "Here I am," he said. "Do with me as you like. All my life I have been kicked and cuffed by such as that, and yet always have I gone out when they commanded, singing, to give up my life if need be to keep them in power. Only lately have I come to know what a fool I have been. But now I am no longer a fool, and besides, I am avenged and Schwerke is avenged, so you can kill me if you wish. Here I am."

"If I was after bein' the king," said Olson, "I'd pin the V. C. on your noble chist; but bein' only an Irishman with a Swede name, for which God forgive me, the bist I can do is shake your hand."

"You will not be punished," said Bradley. "There are four of you left—if you four want to come along and work with us, we will take you; but you will come as prisoners."

"It suits me," said Plesser. "Now that the captain-lieutenant is dead you need not fear us. All our lives we have known nothing but to obey his class. If I had not killed him, I suppose I would be fool enough to obey him again; but he is dead. Now we will obey you—we must obey some one."

"And you?" Bradley turned to the other survivors of the original crew of the U-33. Each promised obedience.

The two dead Germans were buried in a single grave, and then the party boarded the submarine and stowed away the oil.

Here Bradley told the men what had befallen him since the night of September 14th when he had disappeared so mysteriously from the camp upon the plateau. Now he learned for the first time that Bowen J. Tyler, Jr., and Miss La Rue had been missing even longer than he and that no faintest trace of them had been discovered.

Olson told him of how the Germans had returned and waited in ambush for them outside the fort, capturing them that they might be used to assist in the work of refining the oil and later in manning the U-33, and Plesser told briefly of the experiences of the German crew under von Schoenvorts since they had escaped from Caspak months before—of how they lost their bearings after having been shelled by ships they had attempted to speak farther north and how at last with provisions gone and fuel almost exhausted they had sought and at last found, more by accident than design, the mysterious island they had once been so glad to leave behind.

"Now," announced Bradley, "we'll plan for the future. The

boat has fuel, provisions and water for a month, I believe you said, Plesser; there are ten of us to man it. We have a last sad duty here—we must search for Miss La Rue and Mr. Tyler. I say a sad duty because we know that we shall not find them; but it is none the less our duty to comb the shore-line, firing signal shells at intervals, that we at least may leave at last with full knowledge that we have done all that men might do to locate them."

None dissented from this conviction, nor was there a voice raised in protest against the plan to at least make assurance doubly sure before quitting Caspak forever.

And so they started, cruising slowly up the coast and firing an occasional shot from the gun. Often the vessel was brought to a stop, and always there were anxious eyes scanning the shore for an answering signal. Late in the afternoon they caught sight of a number of Band-lu warriors; but when the vessel approached the shore and the natives realized that human beings stood upon the back of the strange monster of the sea, they fled in terror before Bradley could come within hailing distance.

That night they dropped anchor at the mouth of a sluggish stream whose warm waters swarmed with millions of tiny tad-polelike organisms—minute human spawn starting on their pre-carious journey from some inland pool toward "the beginning" —a journey which one in millions, perhaps, might survive to complete. Already almost at the inception of life they were being greeted by thousands of voracious mouths as fish and reptiles of many kinds fought to devour them, the while other and larger creatures pursued the devourers, to be, in turn, preyed upon by some other of the countless forms that inhabit the deeps of Cap-rona's frightful sea.

The second day was practically a repetition of the first. They moved very slowly with frequent stops, and once they landed in the Kro-lu country to hunt. Here they were attacked by the bow-and-arrow men, whom they could not persuade to palaver with them. So belligerent were the natives that it became necessary to fire into them in order to escape their persistent and ferocious attentions.

"What chance," asked Bradley, as they were returning to the boat with their game, "could Tyler and Miss La Rue have had among such as these?"

But they continued on their fruitless quest, and the third day, after cruising along the shore of a deep inlet, they passed a line of lofty cliffs that formed the southern shore of the inlet and rounded a sharp promontory about noon. Co-Tan and Bradley were on deck alone, and as the new shoreline appeared beyond the point, the girl gave an exclamation of joy and seized the man's hand in hers.

"Oh, look!" she cried. "The Galu country! The Galu country! It is my country that I never thought to see again."

"You are glad to come again, Co-Tan?" asked Bradley.

"Oh, so glad!" she cried. "And you will come with me to my people? We may live here among them, and you will be a great warrior—oh, when Jor dies you may even be chief, for there is none so mighty as my warrior. You will come?"

Bradley shook his head. "I cannot, little Co-Tan," he answered. "My country needs me, and I must go back. Maybe some day I shall return. You will not forget me, Co-Tan?"

She looked at him in wide-eyed wonder. "You are going away from me?" she asked in a very small voice. "You are going away from Co-Tan?"

Bradley looked down upon the little bowed head. He felt the soft cheek against his bare arm; and he felt something else there too—hot drops of moisture that ran down to his very finger-tips and splashed upon the deck—tiny little splashes, but each one wrung from a woman's heart.

He bent low and raised the tear-stained face to his own. "No, Co-Tan," he said, "I am not going away from you—for you are going with me. You are going back to my own country to be my wife. Tell me that you will, Co-Tan." And he bent still lower yet from his height and kissed her lips. Nor did he need more than the wonderful new light in her eyes to tell him that she would go to the end of the world with him if he would but take her. And then the gun-crew came up from below again to fire a signal shot, and the two were brought down from the high heaven of their new happiness to the scarred and weather-beaten deck of the *U-33*.

An hour hour later the vessel was running close in by a shore of wondrous beauty beside a parklike meadow that stretched back a mile inland to the foot of a plateau when Whitely called attention to a score of figures clambering downward from the elevation to the lowland below. The engines were reversed and the boat brought to a stop while all hands gathered on deck to watch the little party coming toward them across the meadow.

"They are Galus," cried Co-Tan; "they are my own people. Let me speak to them lest they think we come to fight them. Put me ashore, my man, and I will go and meet them."

The nose of the U-boat was run close in to the steep bank; but when Co-Tan would have run forward alone, Bradley seized her hand and held her back. "I will go with you, Co-Tan," he said; and together they advanced to meet the oncoming party.

There were about twenty warriors moving forward in a thin line, as our infantry advance as skirmishers. Bradley could not but notice the marked difference between this formation and the moblike methods of the lower tribes he had come in contact with, and he commented upon it to Co-Tan.

"Galu warriors always advance into battle thus," she said. "The lesser people remain in a huddled group where they can scarce use their weapons the while they present so big a mark to us that our spears and arrows cannot miss them; but when they hurl theirs at our warriors, if they miss the first man, there is no chance that they will kill some one behind him.

"Stand still now," she cautioned, "and fold your arms. They will not harm us then."

Bradley did as he was bid, and the two stood with arms folded as the line of warriors approached. When they had come within some fifty yards, they halted and one spoke. "Who are you and from whence do you come?" he asked; and then Co-Tan gave a little, glad cry and sprang forward with outstretched arms.

"Oh, Tan!" she exclaimed. "Do you not know your little Co-Tan?"

The warrior stared, incredulous, for a moment, and then he, too, ran forward and when they met, took the girl in his arms. It was then that Bradley experienced to the full a sensation that was new to him—a sudden hatred for the strange warrior before him and a desire to kill without knowing why he would kill. He moved quickly to the girl's side and grasped her wrist.

"Who is this man?" he demanded in cold tones.

Co-Tan turned a surprised face toward the Englishman and then of a sudden broke forth into a merry peal of laughter. "This is my father, Brad-lee," she cried.

"And who is Brad-lee?" demanded the warrior.

"He is my man," replied Co-Tan simply.

"By what right?" insisted Tan.

And then she told him briefly of all that she had passed through since the Wieroos had stolen her and of how Bradley had rescued her and sought to rescue An-Tak, her brother.

"You are satisfied with him?" asked Tan.

"Yes," replied the girl proudly.

It was then that Bradley's attention was attracted to the edge of the plateau by a movement there, and looking closely he saw a horse bearing two figures sliding down the steep declivity. Once at the bottom, the animal came charging across the meadowland at a rapid run. It was a magnificent animal— a great bay stallion with a white-blazed face and white forelegs to the knees, its barrel encircled by a broad surcingle of white; and as it came to a sudden stop beside Tan, the Englishman saw that it bore a man and a girl—a tall man and a girl as beautiful as Co-Tan. When the girl espied the latter, she slid from the horse and ran toward her, fairly screaming for joy.

The man dismounted and stood beside Tan. Like Bradley he was garbed after the fashion of the surrounding warriors; but there was a subtle difference between him and his companion. Possibly he detected a similar difference in Bradley, for his first question was, "From what country?" and though he spoke in Galu Bradley thought he detected an accent.

"England," replied Bradley.

A broad smile lighted the newcomer's face as he held out his hand. "I am Tom Billings of Santa Monica, California," he said. "I know all about you, and I'm mighty glad to find you alive."

"How did you get here?" asked Bradley. "I thought ours was the only party of men from the outer world ever to enter Caprona."

"It was, until we came in search of Bowen J. Tyler, Jr.," replied Billings. "We found him and sent him home with his bride; but I was kept a prisoner here."

Bradley's face darkened—then they were not among friends after all. "There are ten of us down there on a German sub with small-arms and a gun," he said quickly in English. "It will be no trick to get away from these people."

"You don't know my jailer," replied Billings, "or you'd not be so sure. Wait, I'll introduce you." And then turning to the girl who had accompanied him he called her by name. "Ajor," he said, "permit me to introduce Lieutenant Bradley; Lieutenant, Mrs. Billings—my jailer!"

The Englishman laughed as he shook hands with the girl. "You are not as good a soldier as I," he said to Billings. "Instead of being taken prisoner myself I have taken one—Mrs. Bradley, this is Mr. Billings."

Ajor, quick to understand, turned toward Co-Tan. "You are going back with him to his country?" she asked. Co-Tan admitted it.

"You dare?" asked Ajor. "But your father will not permit it—Jor, my father, High Chief of the Galus, will not permit it, for like me you are *cos-ata-lo*. Oh, CoTan, if we but could! How I would love to see all the strange and wonderful things of which my Tom tells me!"

Bradley bent and whispered in her ear. "Say the word and you may both go with us."

Billings heard and speaking in English, asked Ajor if she would go.

"Yes," she answered, "if you wish it; but you know, my Tom, that if Jor captures us, both you and Co-Tan's man will pay the penalty with your lives—not even his love for me nor his admiration for you can save you."

Bradley noticed that she spoke in English—broken English like Co-Tan's but equally appealing. "We can easily get you aboard the ship," he said, "on some pretext or other, and then we can steam away. They can neither harm nor detain us, nor will we have to fire a shot at them."

And so it was done, Bradley and Co-Tan taking Ajor and Billings aboard to "show" them the vessel, which almost immediately raised anchor and moved slowly out into the sea.

"I hate to do it," said Billings. "They have been fine to me. Jor and Tan are splendid men and they will think me an ingrate; but I can't waste my life here when there is so much to be done in the outer world."

As they steamed down the island sea past the island of Oo-oh, the stories of their adventures were retold, and Bradley learned that Bowen Tyler and his bride had left the Galu country but a fortnight before and that there was every reason to believe that the *Toreador* might still be lying in the Pacific not far off the subterranean mouth of the river which emitted Caprona's heated waters into the ocean.

Late in the second day, after running through swarms of hideous reptiles, they submerged at the point where the river entered beneath the cliffs and shortly after rose to the sunlit surface of the Pacific; but nowhere as far as they could see was sign of another craft. Down the coast they steamed toward the beach where Billings had made his crossing in the hydro-aeroplane and just at dusk the lookout announced a light dead ahead. It proved to be aboard the *Toreador*, and a half-hour later there was such a reunion on the deck of the trig little yacht as no one there had ever dreamed might be possible. Of the Allies there were only Tippet and James to be mourned, and no one mourned any of the German dead nor Benson, the traitor, whose ugly story was first told in Bowen Tyler's manuscript.

Tyler and the rescue party had but just reached the yacht that afternoon. They had heard, faintly, the signal shots fired by the *U-33* but had been unable to locate their direction and so had assumed that they had come from the guns of the *Toreador*.

It was a happy party that sailed north toward sunny, southern California, the old *U-33* trailing in the wake of the *Toreador* and flying with the latter the glorious Stars and Stripes beneath which she had been born in the shipyard at Santa Monica. Three newly married couples, their bonds now duly solemnized by the master of the ship, joyed in the peace and security of the untracked waters of the South Pacific and the unique honeymoon which, had it not been for stern duty ahead, they could have wished protracted till the end of time.

And so they came one day to dock at the shipyard which Bowen Tyler now controlled, and here the *U-33* still lies while those who passed so many eventful days within and because of her, have gone their various ways.

THE MOON MAID

by

Edgar Rice Burroughs

CONTENTS

PART III

THE RED HAWK

Being the Story of Julian 20th

PART I

The Moon Maid

The Moon Maid

THE MESSAGE FROM MARS

I MET him in the Blue Room of the Transoceanic Liner *Harding* the night of Mars Day—June 10, 1967. I had been wandering about the city for several hours prior to the sailing of the flier watching the celebration, dropping in at various places that I might see as much as possible of scenes that doubltess will never again be paralleled—a world gone mad with joy. There was only one vacant chair in the Blue Room and that at a small table at which he was already seated alone. I asked his permission and he graciously invited me to join him, rising as he did so, his face lighting with a smile that compelled my liking from the first.

I had thought that Victory Day, which we had celebrated two months before, could never be eclipsed in point of mad national enthusiasm, but the announcement that had been made this day appeared to have had even a greater effect upon the minds and imaginations of the people.

The more than half-century of war that had continued almost uninterruptedly since 1914 had at last terminated in the absolute domination of the Anglo-Saxon race over all the other races of the World, and practically for the first time since the activities of the human race were preserved for posterity in any enduring form no civilized, or even semi-civilized, nation maintained a battle line upon any portion of the globe. War was at an end—definitely and forever. Arms and ammunition were being dumped into the five oceans; the vast armadas of the air were being scrapped or converted into carriers for purposes of peace and commerce.

The peoples of all nations had celebrated—victors and vanquished alike—for they were tired of war. At least they thought that they were tired of war; but were they? What else did they know? Only the oldest of men could recall even a semblance of world peace, the others knew nothing but war. Men had been born and lived their lives and died with their grandchildren clustered about them—all with the alarms of war ringing constantly in their ears. Perchance the little area of their activities was never actually encroached upon by the iron-shod hoof of battle; but always somewhere war endured, now receding like the salt tide only to return again; until there arose that great tidal wave of human emotion in 1959 that swept the entire world for eight bloody years, and receding, left peace upon a spent and devastated world.

Two months had passed—two months during which the world appeared to stand still, to mark time, to hold its breath. What now? We have peace, but what shall we do with it? The leaders of thought and of action are trained for but one condition—war. The reaction brought despondency—our nerves, accustomed to the constant stimulus of excitement, cried out against the monotony of peace, and yet no one wanted war again. We did not know what we wanted.

And then came the announcement that I think saved a world from madness, for it directed our minds along a new line to the contemplation of a fact far more engrossing than prosaic wars and equally as stimulating to the imagination and the nerves—intelligible communication had at last been established with Mars!

Generations of wars had done their part to stimulate scientific research to the end that we might kill one another more expeditiously, that we might transport our youth more quickly to their shallow graves in alien soil, that we might transmit more secretly and with greater celerity our orders to slay our fellow men. And always, generation after generation, there had been those few who could detach their minds from the contemplation of massacre and looking forward to a happier era concentrate their talents and their energies upon the utilization of scientific achievement for the betterment of mankind and the rebuilding of civilization.

Among these was that much ridiculed but devoted coterie who had clung tenaciously to the idea that communication could be established with Mars. The hope that had been growing for a hundred years had never been permitted to die, but had been transmitted from teacher to pupil with ever-growing enthusiasm, while the people scoffed as, a hundred years before, we are told, they scoffed at the experimenters with *flying machines*, as they chose to call them.

About 1940 had come the first reward of long years of toil and hope, following the perfection of an instrument which accurately indicated the direction and distance of the focus of any radio-activity with which it might be attuned. For several years prior to this all the more highly sensitive receiving instruments had recorded a series of three dots and three dashes which began at precise intervals of twenty-four hours and thirty-seven minutes and continued for approximately fifteen minutes. The new instrument indicated conclusively that these signals, if they were signals, originated always at the same distance from the Earth and in the same direction as the point in the universe occupied by the planet Mars.

It was five years later before a sending apparatus was evolved that bade fair to transmit its waves from Earth to Mars. At first their own message was repeated—three dots and three dashes. Although the usual interval of time had not elapsed since we had received their daily signal, ours was immediately answered. Then we sent a message consisting of five dots and two dashes, alternating. Immediately they replied with five dots and two dashes and we knew beyond peradventure of a doubt that we were in communication with the Red Planet, but it required twenty-two years of unremitting effort, with the most brilliant intellects of two worlds concentrated upon it, to evolve and perfect an intelligible system of inter-communication between the two planets.

Today, this tenth of June, 1967, there was published broadcast to the world the first message from Mars. It was dated Helium, Barsoom, and merely extended greetings to a sister world and wished us well. But it was the beginning.

The Blue Room of *The Harding* was, I presume, but typical of every other gathering place in the civilized world. Men and women were eating, drinking, laughing, singing and talking. The flier was racing through the air at an altitude of little over a thousand feet. Its engines, motivated wirelessly from power plants thousands of miles distant, drove it noiselessly and swiftly along its overnight pathway between Chicago and Paris.

I had of course crossed many times, but this instance was unique because of the epoch-making occasion which the passengers were celebrating, and so I sat at the table longer than usual, watching my fellow diners, with, I imagine, a slightly indulgent smile upon my lips, since—I mention it in no spirit of egotism—it had been my high privilege to assist in the consummation of a hundred years of effort that had borne fruit that day. I looked around at my fellow diners and then back to my table companion.

He was a fine looking chap, lean and bronzed—one need not have noted the Air Corps overseas service uniform, the Admiral's stars and anchors or the wound stripes to have guessed that he was a fighting man; he looked it, every inch of him, and there were a full seventy-two inches.

We talked a little—about the great victory and the message from Mars, of course, and though he often smiled I noticed an occasional shadow of sadness in his eyes and once, after a particularly mad outburst of pandemonium on the part of the celebrators, he shook his head, remarking: "Poor devils!" and then: "It is just as well—let them enjoy life while they may. I envy them their ignorance."

"What do you mean," I asked.

He flushed a little and then smiled. "Was I speaking aloud?" he asked.

I repeated what he had said and he looked steadily at me for a long minute before he spoke again. "Oh, what's the use!" he exclaimed, almost petulantly; "you wouldn't understand and of course you wouldn't believe. I do not understand it myself; but I have to believe because I know—I know from personal observation. God! if you could have seen what I have seen."

"Tell me," I begged; but he shook his head dubiously.

"Do you realize that there is no such thing as Time?" he asked suddenly—"That man has invented Time to suit the limitations of his finite mind, just as he has named another thing, that he can neither explain nor understand, Space?"

"I have heard of such a theory," I replied; "but I neither believe nor disbelieve—I simply do not know."

I thought I had him started and so I waited as I have read in fiction stories is the proper way to entice a strange narrative from its possessor. He was looking beyond me and I imagined that the expression of his eyes denoted that he was witnessing again the thrilling scenes of the past. I must have been wrong, though—in fact I was quite sure of it when he next spoke.

"If that girl isn't careful," he said, "the thing will upset and give her a nasty fall—she is much too near the edge."

I turned to see a richly dressed and much dishevelled young lady busily dancing on a table-top while her friends and the surrounding diners cheered her lustily.

My companion arose. "I have enjoyed your company immensely," he said, "and I hope to meet you again. I am going to look for a place to sleep now—they could not give me a stateroom—I don't seem to be able to get enough sleep since they sent me back." He smiled.

"Miss the gas shells and radio bombs, I suppose," I remarked.

"Yes," he replied, "just as a convalescent misses smallpox."

"I have a room with two beds," I said. "At the last minute my secretary was taken ill. I'll be glad to have you share the room with me."

He thanked me and accepted my hospitality for the night—the following morning we would be in Paris.

As we wound our way among the tables filled with laughing, joyous diners, my companion paused beside that at which sat the young woman who had previously attracted his attention. Their eyes met and into hers came a look of puzzlement and half-recognition. He smiled frankly in her face, nodded and passed on.

"You know her, then?" I asked.

"I shall—in two hundred years," was his enigmatical reply.

We found my room, and there we had a bottle of wine and some little cakes and a quiet smoke and became much better acquainted.

It was he who first reverted to the subject of our conversation in the Blue Room.

"I am going to tell you," he said, "what I have never told another; but on the condition that if you retell it you are not to use my name. I have several years of this life ahead of me and I do not care to be pointed out as a lunatic. First let me say that I do not try to explain anything, except that I do not believe prevision to be a proper explanation. I have actually *lived* the experiences I shall tell you of, and that girl we saw dancing on the table tonight lived them with me; but she does not know it. If you care to, you can keep in mind the theory that there is no such thing as Time—just keep it in mind—you cannot understand it, or at least I cannot. Here goes."

CHAPTER I

THE FLIGHT OF "THE BARSOOM"

"I HAD intended telling you my story of the days of the twenty-second century, but it seems best, if you are to understand it, to tell first the story of my great-great-grandfather who was born in the year 2000."

I must have looked up at him quizzically, for he smiled and shook his head as one who is puzzled to find an explanation suited to the mental capacity of his auditor.

"My great-great-grandfather was, in reality, the great-great-grandson of my previous incarnation which commenced in 1896. I married in 1916, at the age of twenty. My son Julian was born in 1917. I never saw him. I was killed in France in 1918—on Armistice Day.

"I was again reincarnated in my son's son in 1937. I am thirty years of age. My son was born in 1970—that is the son of my 1937 incarnation—and his son, Julian 5th, in whom I again returned to Earth, in the year 2000. I see you are confused, but please remember my injunction that you are to try to keep in mind the theory that there is no such thing as Time. It is now the year 1967 yet I recall distinctly every event of my life that occurred in four incarnations—the last that I recall being that which had its origin in the year 2100. Whether I actually skipped three generations that time or through some caprice of Fate I am merely unable to visualize an intervening incarnation, I do not know.

"My theory of the matter is that I differ only from my fellows in that I can recall the events of many incarnations, while they can recall none of theirs other than a few important episodes of that particular one they are experiencing; but perhaps I am wrong. It is of no importance. I will tell you the story of Julian 5th who was born in the year 2000, and then, if we have time and you yet are interested, I will tell you of the torments during the harrowing days of the twenty-second century, following the birth of Julian 9th in 2100."

I will try to tell the story in his own words in so far as I can recall them, but for various reasons, not the least of which is that I am lazy, I shall omit superfluous quotation marks—that is, with your permission, of course.

My name is Julian. I am called Julian 5th. I come of an illustrious family—my great-great-grandfather, Julian 1st, a major at twenty-two, was killed in France early in The Great War. My great-grandfather, Julian 2nd, was killed in battle in Turkey in 1938. My grandfather, Julian 3rd, fought continuously from his sixteenth year until peace was declared in his thirtieth year. He died in 1992 and during the last twenty-five years of his life was an Admiral of the Air, being transferred at the close of the war to command of the International Peace Fleet, which patrolled and policed the world. He also was killed in line of duty, as was my father who succeeded him in the service.

At sixteen I graduated from the Air School and was detailed to the International Peace Fleet, being the fifth generation of my line to wear the uniform of my country. That was in 2016, and I recall that it was a matter of pride to me that it rounded out the full century since Julian 1st graduated from West Point, and that during that one hundred years no adult male of my line had ever owned or worn civilian clothes.

Of course there were no more wars, but there still was fighting. We had the pirates of the air to contend with and occasionally some of the uncivilized tribes of Russia, Africa and central Asia required the attention of a punitive expedition. However, life seemed tame and monotonous to us when we read of the heroic deeds of our ancestors from 1914 to 1967, yet none of us wanted war. It had been too well schooled into us that we must not think of war, and the International Peace Fleet so effectively prevented all preparation for war that we all knew there could never be another. There wasn't a firearm in the world other than those with which we were armed, and a few of ancient design that were kept as heirlooms, or in museums, or that were owned by savage tribes who could procure no ammunition for them, since we permitted none to be manufactured. There was not a gas shell nor a radio bomb, nor any engine to discharge or project one; and there wasn't a big gun of any calibre in the world. I veritably believed that a thousand men equipped with the various engines of destruction that had reached their highest efficiency at the close of the war in 1967 could have conquered the world; but there were not a thousand men so armed—there never could be a thousand men so equipped anywhere upon the face of the Earth. The International Peace Fleet was equipped and manned to prevent just such a calamity.

But it seems that Providence never intended that the world should be without calamities. If man prevented those of possible internal origin there still remained undreamed of external sources over which he had no control. It was one of these which was to prove our undoing. Its seed was sown thirty-three years before I was born, upon that historic day, June 10th, 1967, that Earth received her first message from Mars, since which the two planets have remained in constant friendly communication, carrying on a commerce of reciprocal enlightenment. In some branches of the arts and sciences the Martians, or Barsoomians, as they call themselves, were far in advance of us, while in others we had progressed more rapidly than they. Knowledge was thus freely exchanged to the advantage of both worlds. We learned of their history and customs and they of ours, though they had for ages already known much more of us than we of them. Martian news held always a prominent place in our daily papers from the first.

They helped us most, perhaps, in the fields of medicine and aeronautics, giving us in one, the marvelous healing lotions of Barsoom and in the other, knowledge of the Eighth Ray, which is more generally known on Earth as the Barsoomian Ray, which is now stored in the buoyancy tanks of every air craft and has made obsolete those ancient types of plane that depended upon momentum to keep them afloat.

That we ever were able to communicate intelligibly with them is due to the presence upon Mars of that deathless Virginian, John Carter, whose miraculous transportation to Mars occurred March 4th, 1866, as every school child of the twenty-first century knows. Had not the little band of Martian scientists, who sought so long to communicate with Earth, mistakenly formed themselves into a secret organization for political purposes, messages might have been exchanged between the two planets nearly half a century before they were, and it was not until they finally called upon John Carter that the present inter-planetary code was evolved.

Almost from the first the subject which engrossed us all the most was the possibility of an actual exchange of visits between Earth Men and Barsoomians. Each planet hoped to be the first to achieve this, yet neither withheld any information that would aid the other in the consummation of the great fact. It was a generous and friendly rivalry which about the time of my graduation from the Air School seemed, in theory at least, to be almost ripe for successful consummation by one or the other. We had the Eighth Ray, the motors, the oxygenating devices, the insulating processes—everything to insure the safe and certain transit of a specially designed air craft to Mars, were Mars the only other inhabitant of space. But it was not and it was the other planets and the Sun that we feared.

In 2015 Mars had dispatched a ship for Earth with a crew of five men provisioned for ten years. It was hoped that with good luck the trip might be made in something less than five years, as the craft had developed an actual trial speed of one thousand miles per hour. At the time of my graduation the ship was already off its course almost a million miles and generally conceded to be hopelessly lost. Its crew, maintaining constant radio communication with both Earth and Mars, still hoped for success, but the best informed upon both worlds had given them up.

We had had a ship about ready at the time of the sailing of the Martians, but the government at Washington had forbidden the venture when it became apparent that the Barsoomian ship was doomed—a wise decision, since our vessel was no better equipped than theirs. Nearly ten years elapsed before anything further was accomplished in the direction of assuring any greater hope of success for another interplanetary venture into space, and this was directly due to the discovery made by a former classmate of mine, Lieutenant Commander Orthis, one of the most brilliant men I have ever known, and at the same time one of the most unscrupulous, and, to me at least, the most obnoxious.

We had entered the Air School together—he from New York and I from Illinois—and almost from the first day we had seemed to discover a mutual antagonism that, upon his part at least, must have been considerably strengthened by numerous unfortunate occurrences during our four years beneath the same roof. In the first place he was not popular with either the cadets, the instructors, or the officers of the school, while I was most fortunate in this respect. In those various fields of athletics in which he considered himself particularly expert, it was always I, unfortunately, who excelled him and kept him from major honors. In the class room he outshone us all—even the instructors were amazed at the brilliancy of his intellect—and yet as we passed from grade to grade I often topped him in the final examinations. I ranked him always as a cadet officer, and upon graduation I took a higher grade among the new ensigns than he—a rank that had many years before been discontinued, but which had recently been revived.

From then on I saw little of him, his services confining him principally to land service, while mine kept me almost constantly in the air in all parts of the world. Occasionally I heard of him —usually something unsavory; he had married a nice girl and abandoned her—there had been talk of an investigation of his accounts—and the last that there was a rumor that he was affiliated with a secret order that sought to overthrow the government. Some things I might believe of Orthis, but not this.

And during these nine years since graduation, as we had drifted apart in interests, so had the breach between us been widened by constantly increasing difference in rank. He was a Lieutenant Commander and I a Captain, when in 2024 he announced the discovery and isolation of the Eighth Solar Ray, and within two months those of the Moon, Mercury, Venus and Jupiter. The Eighth Barsoomian and the Eighth Earthly Rays had already been isolated, and upon Earth the latter erroneously called by the name of the former.

Orthis' discoveries were hailed upon two planets as the key to actual travel between the Earth and Barsoom, since by means of these several rays the attraction of the Sun and the planets, with the exception of Saturn, Uranus and Neptune, could be definitely overcome and a ship steer a direct and unimpeded course through space to Mars. The effect of the pull of the three farther planets was considered negligible, owing to their great distance from both Mars and Earth.

Orthis wanted to equip a ship and start at once, but again government intervened and forbade what it considered an unnecessary risk. Instead Orthis was ordered to design a small radio operated flier, which would carry no one aboard, and which it was believed could be automatically operated for at least half the distance between the two planets. After his designs were completed, you may imagine his chagrin, and mine as well, when I was detailed to supervise construction, yet I will say that Orthis hid his natural emotions well and gave me perfect cooperation in the work we were compelled to undertake together, and which was as distasteful to me as to him. On my part I made it as easy for him as I could, working with him rather than over him.

It required but a short time to complete the experimental ship and during this time I had an opportunity to get a still better

permitted us to construct a little world, which moved at will through space—a little world inhabited by five souls.

Had it not been for Orthis' presence I could have looked forward to a reasonably pleasurable voyage, for West and Jay were extremely likeable fellows and sufficiently mature to be companionable, while young Norton, the ensign, though but seventeen years of age, endeared himself to all of us from the very start of the voyage by his pleasant manners, his consideration and his willingness in the performance of his duties. There were three staterooms aboard *The Barsoom*, one of which I occupied alone, while West and Orthis had the second and Jay and Norton the third. West and Jay were lieutenants and had been classmates at the air school. They would of course have preferred to room together, but could not unless I commanded it or Orthis requested it. Not wishing to give Orthis any grounds for offense I hesitated to make the change, while Orthis, never having thought a considerate thought or done a considerate deed in his life, could not, of course, have been expected to suggest it. We all messed together, West, Jay and Norton taking turns at preparing the meals. Only in the actual operation of the ship were the lines of rank drawn strictly. Otherwise we associated as equals, nor would any other arrangement have been endurable upon such an undertaking, which required that we five be practically imprisoned together upon a small ship for a period of not less than five years. We had books and writing materials and games, and we were, of course, in constant radio communication with both Earth and Mars, receiving continuously the latest news from both planets. We listened to opera and oratory and heard the music of two worlds, so that we were not lacking for entertainment. There was always a certain constraint in Orthis' manner toward me, yet I must give him credit for behaving outwardly admirably. Unlike the others we never exchanged pleasantries with one another, nor could I, knowing as I did that Orthis hated me, and feeling for him personally the contempt that I felt because of his character. Intellectually he commanded my highest admiration, and upon intellectual grounds we met without constraint or reserve, and many were the profitable dis cussions we had during the first days of what was to prove a very brief voyage.

It was about the second day that I noticed with some surprise that Orthis was exhibiting a friendly interest in Norton. It had never been Orthis' way to make friends, but I saw that he and Norton were much together and that each seemed to derive a great deal of pleasure from the society of the other. Orthis was a good talker. He knew his profession thoroughly, and was an inventor and scientist of high distinction. Norton, though but a boy, was himself the possessor of a fine mind. He had been honor-man in his graduating class, heading the list of ensigns for that year, and I could not help but notice that he was drinking in every word along scientific lines that Orthis vouchsafed.

We had been out about six days when Orthis came to me and suggested, that inasmuch as West and Jay had been classmates and chums that they be permitted to room together and that he had spoken to Norton who had said that he would be agreeable to the change and would occupy West's bunk in Orthis' stateroom. I was very glad of this for it now meant that my subordinates would be paired off in the most agreeable manner, and as long as they were contented, I knew that the voyage from that standpoint at least would be more successful. I was, of course, a trifle sorry to see a fine boy like Norton brought under the influence of Orthis, yet I felt that what little danger might result would be offset by the influence of West and Jay and myself or counterbalanced by the liberal education which five years' constant companionship with Orthis would be to any man with whom Orthis would discuss freely the subjects of which he was master.

We were beginning to feel the influence of the Moon rather strongly. At the rate we were traveling we would pass closest to it upon the twelfth day, or about the 6th of January, 2026.

Our course would bring us within about twenty thousand miles of the Moon, and as we neared it I believe that the sight of it was the most impressive thing that human eye had ever gazed upon before. To the naked eye it loomed large and magnificent in the heavens, appearing over ten times the size that it does to terrestrial observers, while our powerful glasses brought its weird surface to such startling proximity that one felt that he might reach out and touch the torn rocks of its tortured mountains.

This nearer view enabled us to discover the truth or falsity of the theory that has been long held by some scientists that there is a form of vegetation upon the surface of the Moon. Our eyes were first attracted by what appeared to be movement upon the surface of some of the valleys and in the deeper ravines of the mountains. Norton exclaimed that there were creatures there, moving about, but closer observation revealed the fact of the existence of a weird fungus-like vegetation which grew so rapidly that we could clearly discern the phenomena. From the several days' observation which we had at close range we came to the conclusion that the entire life span of this vegetation is encompassed in a single sidereal month. From the spore it developed in the short period of a trifle over twenty-seven days into a mighty plant that is sometimes hundreds of feet in height. The branches are angular and grotesque, the leaves broad and thick, and in the plants which we discerned the seven primary colors were distinctly represented. As each portion of the Moon passed slowly into shadow the vegetation first drooped, then wilted, then crumbled to the ground, apparently disintegrating almost immediately into a fine, dust-like powder—at least in so far as our glasses revealed, it quite disappeared entirely. The movement which we discerned was purely that of rapid growth, as there is no wind upon the surface of the Moon. Both Jay and Orthis were positive that they discerned some form of animal life, either insect or reptilian. These I did not myself see, though I did perceive many of the broad, flat leaves which seemed to have been partially eaten, which certainly strengthened the theory that there is other than vegetable life upon our satellite.

I presume that one of the greatest thrills that we experienced in this adventure, that was to prove a veritable Pandora's box of thrills, was when we commenced to creep past the edge of the Moon and our eyes beheld for the first time that which no other human eyes had ever rested upon—portions of that two-fifths of the Moon's surface which is invisible from the Earth.

We had looked with awe upon Mare Crisium and Lacus Somniorum, Sinus Roris, Oceanus Procellarum and the four great mountain ranges. We had viewed at close range the volcanoes of Opollonius, Secchi, Borda, Tycho and their mates, but all these paled into insignificance as there unrolled before us the panorama of the vast unknown.

I cannot say that it differed materially from that portion of the Moon that is visible to us—it was merely the glamour of mystery which had surrounded it since the beginning of time that lent to it its thrill for us. Here we observed other great mountain ranges and wide undulating plains, towering volcanoes and mighty craters and the same vegetation with which we were now become familiar.

We were two days past the Moon when our first trouble developed. Among our stores were one hundred and twenty quarts of spirits per man, enough to allow us each a liberal two ounces per day for a period of five years. Each night, before dinner, we

had drunk to the President in a cocktail which contained a single
ounce of spirits, the idea being to conserve our supply in the
event of our journey being unduly protracted as well as to have
enough in the event that it became desirable fittingly to celebrate
any particular occasion.

Toward the third meal hour of the thirteenth day of the
voyage Orthis entered the messroom noticeably under the influence of liquor.

History narrates that under the regime of prohibition drunkenness was common and that it grew to such proportions as to
become a national menace, but with the repeal of the Prohibition
Act, nearly a hundred years ago, the habit of drinking to excess
abated, so that it became a matter of disgrace for any man to
show his liquor, and in the service it was considered as reprehen-
sible as cowardice in action. There was therefore but one thing
for me to do. I ordered Orthis to his quarters.

He was drunker than I had thought him, and he turned upon
me like a tiger.

"You damned cur," he cried. "All my life you have stolen
everything from me; the fruits of all my efforts you have garnered
by chicanery and trickery, and even now, were we to reach Mars,
it is you who would be lauded as the hero—not I whose labor
and intellect have made possible this achievement. But by God
we will not reach Mars. Not again shall you profit by my efforts.
You have gone too far this time, and now you dare to order me
about like a dog and an inferior—I, whose brains have made you
what you are."

I held my temper, for I saw that the man was unaccountable
for his words. "Go to your quarters, Orthis," I repeated my command. "I will talk with you again in the morning."

West and Jay and Norton were present. They seemed momentarily paralyzed by the man's condition and gross insubordination. Norton, however, was the first to recover. Jumping quickly
to Orthis' side he laid his hand upon his arm. "Come, sir," he
said, and to my surprise Orthis accompanied him quietly to their
stateroom.

During the voyage we had continued the fallacy of night and
day, gauging them merely by our chronometers, since we moved
always through utter darkness, surrounded only by a tiny nebula
of light, produced by the sun's rays impinging upon the radiation from our insulating generator. Before breakfast, therefore,
on the following morning I sent for Orthis to come to my stateroom. He entered with a truculent swagger, and his first words

indicated that if he had not continued drinking, he had at least been moved to no regrets for his unwarranted attack of the previous evening.

"Well," he said, "what in hell are you going to do about it?"

"I cannot understand your attitude, Orthis," I told him. "I have never intentionally injured you. When orders from government threw us together I was as much chagrined as you. Association with you is as distasteful to me as it is to you. I merely did as you did—obeyed orders. I have no desire to rob you of anything, but that is not the question now. You have been guilty of gross insubordination and of drunkenness. I can prevent a repetition of the latter by confiscating your liquor and keeping it from you during the balance of the voyage, and an apology from you will atone for the former. I shall give you twenty-four hours to reach a decision. If you do not see fit to avail yourself of my clemency, Orthis, you will travel to Mars and back again in irons. Your decision now and your behavior during the balance of the voyage will decide your fate upon our return to Earth. And I tell you, Orthis, that if I possibly can do so I shall use the authority which is mine upon this expedition and expunge from the log the record of your transgressions last night and this morning. Now go to your quarters; your meals will be served there for twenty-four hours and at the end of that time I shall receive your decision. Meanwhile your liquor will be taken from you."

He gave me an ugly look, turned upon his heel and left my stateroom.

Norton was on watch that night. We were two days past the Moon. West, Jay and I were asleep in our staterooms, when suddenly Norton entered mine and shook me violently by the shoulder.

"My God, Captain," he cried, "come quick. Commander Orthis is destroying the engines."

I leaped to my feet and followed Norton amidships to the engine-room, calling to West and Jay as I passed their stateroom. Through the bull's-eye in the engine-room door, which he had locked, we could see Orthis working over the auxiliary generator which was to have proven our salvation in an emergency, since by means of it we could overcome the pull of any planet into the sphere of whose influence we might be carried. I breathed a sigh of relief as my eyes noted that the main battery of engines was functioning properly, since, as a matter of fact, we had not expected to have to rely at all upon the auxiliary generator, having stored sufficient quantities of the Eighth Ray of the various heavenly bodies by which we might be influenced, to carry us safely throughout the entire extent of the long voyage. West and Jay had joined us by this time, and I now called to Orthis, commanding him to open the door. He did something more to the generator and then arose, crossed the engine-room directly to the door, unbolted it and threw the door open. His hair was dishevelled, his face drawn, his eyes shining with a peculiar light, but withal his expression denoted a drunken elation that I did not at the moment understand.

"What have you been doing here, Orthis?" I demanded. "You are under arrest, and supposed to be in your quarters."

"You'll see what I've been doing," he replied truculently, "and it's done—it's done—it can't ever be undone. I've seen to that."

I grabbed him roughly by the shoulder. "What do you mean? Tell me what you have done, or by God I will kill you with my own hands," for I knew, not only from his words but from his expression, that he had accomplished something which he considered very terrible.

The man was a coward and he quailed under my grasp. "You wouldn't dare to kill me," he cried, "and it don't make any difference, for we'll all be dead in a few hours. Go and look at your damned compass."

CHAPTER II

THE HEART OF THE MOON

NORTON, whose watch it was, had already hurried toward the pilot room where were located the controls and the various instruments. This room, which was just forward of the engine-room, was in effect a circular conning-tower which projected about twelve inches above the upper hull. The entire circumference of this twelve inch superstructure was set with small ports of thick crystal glass.

As I turned to follow Norton I spoke to West. "Mr. West," I said, "you and Mr. Jay will place Lieutenant Commander Orthis in irons immediately. If he resists, kill him."

As I hurried after Norton I heard a volley of oaths from Orthis and a burst of almost maniacal laughter. When I reached the pilot house I found Norton working very quietly with the controls. There was nothing hysterical in his movements, but his face was absolutely ashen.

"What is wrong, Mr. Norton?" I asked. But as I looked at the compass simultaneously I read my answer there before he spoke. We were moving at right angles to our proper course.

"We are falling toward the Moon, sir," he said, "and she does not respond to her control."

"Shut down the engines," I ordered, "they are only accelerating our fall."

"Aye, aye, sir," he replied.

"The Lunar Eighth Ray tank is of sufficient capacity to keep us off the Moon," I said. "If it has not been tampered with, we should be in no danger of falling to the Moon's surface."

"If it has not been tampered with, sir; yes, sir, that is what I have been thinking."

"But the gauge here shows it full to capacity," I reminded him.

"I know, sir," he replied, "but if it were full to capacity, we should not be falling so rapidly."

Immediately I fell to examining the gauge, almost at once discovering that it had been tampered with and the needle set permanently to indicate a maximum supply. I turned to my companion.

"Mr. Norton," I said, "please go forward and investigate the Lunar Eighth Ray tank, and report back to me immediately."

The young man saluted and departed. As he approached the tank it was necessary for him to crawl through a very restricted place beneath the deck.

In about five minutes Norton returned. He was not so pale as he had been, but he looked very haggard.

"Well?" I inquired as he halted before me.

"The exterior intake valve has been opened, sir," he said, "the rays were escaping into space. I have closed it, sir."

The valve to which he referred was used only when the ship was in dry dock, for the purpose of refilling the buoyancy tank, and, because it was so seldom used and as a further precaution against accident, the valve was placed in an inaccessible part of the hull where there was absolutely no likelihood of its being accidentally opened.

Norton glanced at the instrument. "We are not falling quite so rapidly now," he said.

"Yes," I replied, "I had noted that, and I have also been able to adjust the Lunar Eighth Ray gauge—it shows that we have about half the original pressure."

"Not enough to keep us from going aground," he commented. "No, not here, where there is no atmosphere. If the Moon had an atmosphere we could at least keep off the surface if we wished to. As it is, however, I imagine that we will be able to make a safe landing, though, of course that will do us little good. You understand, I suppose, Mr. Norton, that this is practically the end."

He nodded. "It will be a sad blow to the inhabitants of two worlds," he remarked, his entire forgetfulness of self indicating the true nobility of his character.

"It is a sad report to broadcast," I remarked, "but it must be done, and at once. You will, please, send the following message to the Secretary of Peace:

"U. S. S. *The Barsoom*, January 6, 2026, about twenty thousand miles off the Moon. Lieutenant Commander Orthis, while under the influence of liquor, has destroyed auxiliary engine and opened exterior intake valve Lunar Eighth Ray buoyancy tank. Ship sinking rapidly. Will keep you—"

Norton who had seated himself at the radio desk leaped suddenly to his feet and turned toward me. "My God, sir," he cried, "he has destroyed the radio outfit also. We can neither send nor receive."

A careful examination revealed the fact that Orthis had so cleverly and completely destroyed the instruments that there was no hope of repairing them. I turned to Norton.

"We are not only dead, Norton, but we are buried, as well."

I smiled as I spoke and he answered me with a smile that betokened his utter fearlessness of death.

"I have but one regret, sir," he said, "and that is that the world will never know that our failure was not due to any weakness of our machinery, ship or equipment."

"That is, indeed, too bad," I replied, "for it will retard transportation between the two worlds possibly a hundred years— maybe forever."

I called to West and Jay who by this time had placed Orthis in irons and confined him to his stateroom. When they came I told them what had happened, and they took it as coolly as did Norton. Nor was I surprised, for these were fine types selected from the best of that splendid organization which officered the International Peace Fleet.

Together we immediately made a careful inspection of the ship, which revealed no further damage than that which we had already discovered, but which was sufficient as we well knew, to preclude any possibility of our escaping from the pull of the Moon.

"You gentlemen realize our position as well as I," I told them. "Could we repair the auxiliary generator we might isolate the Lunar Eighth Ray, refill our tank, and resume our voyage. But the diabolical cleverness with which Lieutenant Commander Orthis has wrecked the machine renders this impossible. We might fight away from the surface of the Moon for a considerable period, but in the end it would avail us nothing. It is my plan, therefore, to make a landing. In so far as the actual lunar conditions are concerned, we are confronted only by a mass of theories, many of which are conflicting. It will, therefore, be at least a matter of consuming interest to us to make a landing upon this dead world where we may observe it closely, but there is also the possibility, remote, I grant you, that we may discover conditions there which may in some manner alleviate our position. At least we can be no worse off. To live for fifteen years cooped in the hull of this dead ship is unthinkable. I may speak only for myself, but to me it would be highly preferable to die immediately than to live on thus, knowing that there was no hope of rescue. Had Orthis not destroyed the radio outfit we could have communicated with Earth and another ship been outfitted and sent to our rescue inside a year. But now we cannot tell them, and they will never know our fate. The emergency that has arisen has, however, so altered conditions that I do not feel warranted in taking this step without consulting you gentlemen. It is a matter now largely of the duration of our lives. I cannot proceed upon the mission upon which I have been dispatched, nor can I return to Earth. I wish, therefore, that you would express yourselves freely concerning the plan which I have outlined."

West, who was the senior among them, was naturally the one to reply first. He told me that he was content to go wherever I led, and Jay and Norton in turn signified a similar willingness to abide by whatever decision I might reach. They also assured me that they were as keen to explore the surface of the Moon at close range as I, and that they could think of no better way of spending the remainder of their lives than in the acquisition of new experiences and the observation of new scenes.

"Very well, Mr. Norton," I said, "you will set your course directly toward the Moon."

Aided by lunar gravity our descent was rapid.

As we plunged through space at a terrific speed, the satellite seemed to be leaping madly toward us, and at the end of fifteen hours I gave orders to slack off and brought the ship almost to a stop about nine thousand feet above the summit of the higher lunar peaks. Never before had I gazed upon a more awe-inspiring scene than that presented by those terrific peaks towering five miles above the broad valleys at their feet. Sheer cliffs of three and four thousand feet were nothing uncommon, and all was rendered weirdly beautiful by the variegated colors of the rocks and the strange prismatic hues of the rapidly-growing vegetation upon the valley floors. From our lofty elevation above the peaks we could see many craters of various dimensions, some of which were huge chasms, three and four miles in diameter. As we descended slowly we drifted directly over one of these abysses, into the impenetrable depths of which we sought to strain our eyesight. Some of us believed that we detected a faint luminosity far below, but of that we could not be certain. Jay thought it might be the reflected light from the molten interior. I was confident that had this been the case there would have been a considerable rise of temperature as we passed low across the mouth of the crater.

At this altitude we made an interesting discovery. There is an atmosphere surrounding the Moon. It is extremely tenuous, but yet it was recorded by our barometer at an altitude of about fifteen hundred feet above the highest peak we crossed. Doubtless in the valleys and deep ravines, where the vegetation thrived, it is denser, but that I do not know, since we never landed upon the surface of the Moon. As the ship drifted we presently noted that it was taking a circular course paralleling the rim of the huge volcanic crater above which we were descending. I immediately gave orders to alter our course since, as we were descending constantly, we should presently be below the rim of the crater and, being unable to rise, be hopelessly lost in its huge maw.

It was my plan to drift slowly over one of the larger valleys as we descended, and make a landing amidst the vegetation which we perceived growing in riotous profusion and movement beneath us. But when West, whose watch it now was, attempted to alter the course of the ship, he found that it did not respond. Instead it continued to move slowly in a great circle around the inside rim of the crater. At the moment of this discovery we were not much more than five hundred feet above the summit of the volcano, and we were constantly, though slowly, dropping. West looked up at us, smiled, and shook his head.

"It is no use, sir," he said, addressing me. "It is about all over, sir, and there won't even be any shouting. We seem to be caught in what one might call a lunar whirlpool, for you will have noticed, sir, that our circles are constantly growing smaller."

"Our speed does not seem to be increasing," I remarked, "as would follow were we approaching the vortex of a true whirlpool."

"I think I can explain it, sir," said Norton. "It is merely due to the action of the Lunar Eighth Ray which still remains in the forward buoyancy tank. Its natural tendency is to push itself away from the Moon, which, as far as we are concerned, is represented by the rim of this enormous crater. As each portion of the surface repels us in its turn we are pushed gently along in a lessening circle, because, as we drop nearer the summit of the peak the greater the reaction of the Eighth Lunar Ray. If I am not mistaken in my theory our circle will cease to narrow after we have dropped beneath the rim of the crater."

"I guess you are right, Norton," I said. "At least it is a far more tenable theory than that we are being sucked into the vortex of an enormous whirlpool. There is scarcely enough atmosphere for that, it seems to me."

As we dropped slowly below the rim of the crater the tenability of Norton's theory became more and more apparent, for presently, though our speed increased slightly, the diameter of our circular course remained constant, and, at a little greater depth, our speed as well. We were descending now at the rate of a little over ten miles an hour, the barometer recording a constantly increasing atmospheric pressure, though nothing approximating that necessary to the support of life upon Earth. The temperature rose slightly, but not alarmingly. From a range of twenty-five or thirty below zero, immediately after we had entered the shadow of the crater's interior, it rose gradually to zero at a point some one hundred and twenty-five miles below the summit of the giant extinct volcano that had engulfed us.

During the next ten miles our speed diminished rapidly, until we suddenly realized that we were no longer falling, but that our motion had been reversed and we were rising. Up we went for approximately eight miles, when suddenly we began to fall again. Again we fell, but this time for only six miles, when our motion was reversed and we rose again a distance of about four miles. This see-sawing was continued until we finally came to rest at about what we estimated was a distance of some one hundred and thirty miles below the summit of the crater. It was quite dark, and we had only our instruments to tell us of what was happening to the ship, the interior of which was, of course, brilliantly illuminated and comfortably warm.

Now below us, and now above us, for the ship had rolled completely over each time we had passed the point at which we came finally to rest, we had noted the luminosity that Norton had first observed from above the mouth of the crater. Each of us had been doing considerable thinking, and at last young Norton could contain himself no longer.

"I beg your pardon, sir," he said deferentially, "but won't you tell us what you think of it; what your theory is as to where we are and why we hang here in mid-air, and why the ship rolled over every time we passed this point?"

"I can only account for it," I replied, "upon a single and rather preposterous hypothesis, which is that the Moon is a hollow sphere, with a solid crust some two hundred and fifty miles in thickness. Gravity is preventing us from rising above the point where we now are, while centrifugal force keeps us from falling."

The others nodded. They too had been forced to accept the same apparently ridiculous theory, since there was none other that could explain our predicament. Norton had walked across the room to read the barometer which he had rather neglected while the ship had been performing her eccentric antics far below the surface of the Moon. I saw his brows knit as he glanced at it, and then I saw him studying it carefully, as though to assure himself that he had made no mistake in the reading. Then he turned toward us.

"There must be something wrong with this instrument, sir," he said. "It is registering pressure equivalent to that at the Earth's surface."

I walked over and looked at the instrument. It certainly was registering the pressure that Norton had read, nor did there seem to be anything wrong with the instrument.

"There is a way to find out," I said. "We can shut down the insulating generator and open an air-cock momentarily. It won't take five seconds to determine whether the barometer is correct or not." It was, of course, in some respects a risky proceeding, but with West at the generator, Jay at the air-cock and Norton at the pump I knew that we would be reasonably safe, even if there proved to be no atmosphere without. The only danger lay in the chance that we were hanging in a poisonous gas of the same density as the earthly atmosphere, but as there was no particular incentive to live in the situation in which we were, we each felt that no matter what chance we might take it would make little difference in the eventual outcome of our expedition.

I tell you that it was a very tense moment as the three men took their posts to await my word of command. If we had indeed discovered a true atmosphere beneath the surface of the Moon, what more might we not discover? If it were an atmosphere, we could propel the ship in it, and we could, if nothing more, go out on deck to breathe fresh air. It was arranged that at my word of command West was to shut off the generator, Jay to open the air-cock, and Norton to start the pump. If fresh air failed to enter through the tube Jay was to give the signal, whereupon Norton would reverse the pump, West start the generator, and immediately Jay would close the air-cock again.

As Jay was the only man who was to take a greater chance than the others, I walked over and stood beside him, placing my nostrils as close to the air-cock as his. Then I gave the word of command. Everything worked perfectly and an instant later a rush of fresh, cold air was pouring into the hull of *The Barsoom*. West and Norton had been watching the effects upon our faces closely, so that they knew almost as soon as we did that the result of our test had been satisfactory. We were all smiles, though just why we were so happy I am sure none of us could have told. Possibly it was just because we had found a condition that was identical with an earthly condition, and though we might never see our world again we could at least breathe air similar to hers.

I had them start the motors again then, and presently we were moving in a great spiral upward toward the interior of the Moon. Our progress was very slow, but as we rose the temperature rose slowly, too, while the barometer showed a very-slightly-decreasing atmospheric pressure. The luminosity, now above us, increased as we ascended, until finally the sides of the great well through which we were passing became slightly illuminated.

All this time Orthis had remained in irons in his stateroom. I had given instructions that he was to be furnished food and water, but no one was to speak to him, and I had taken Norton into my stateroom with me. Knowing Orthis to be a drunkard, a traitor and a potential murderer I had no sympathy whatsoever for him. I had determined to court-martial him and did not intend to spend the few remaining hours or years of my life cooped up in a small ship with him, and I knew that the verdict of any court, whether composed of the remaining crew of *The Barsoom* or appointed by the Judge Advocate General of the

Navy, could result in but one thing, and that was death for
Orthis. I had left the matter, however, until we were not pressed
with other matters of greater importance, and so he still lived,
though he shared neither in our fears, our hopes, nor our joys.

About twenty-six hours after we entered the mouth of the
crater at the surface of the Moon we suddenly emerged from its
opposite end to look upon a scene that was as marvelous and
weird, by comparison with the landscape upon the surface of
the Moon, as the latter was in comparison with that of our own
Earth. A soft, diffused light revealed to us in turn mountains,
valleys and sea, the details of which were more slowly encompassed by our minds. The mountains were as rugged as those
upon the surface of the satellite, and appeared equally as lofty.
They were, however, clothed with verdure almost to their summits, at least a few that were within our range of vision. And
there were forests, too—strange forests, of strange trees, so unearthly in appearance as to suggest the weird phantasmagoria of
a dream.

We did not rise much above five hundred feet from the opening of the well through which we had come from outer space
when I descried an excellent landing place and determined to
descend. This was readily accomplished, and we made a safe
landing close to a large forest and near the bank of a small
stream. Then we opened the forward hatch and stepped out
upon the deck of *The Barsoom,* the first Earth Men to breathe
the air of Luna. It was, according to Earth time, eleven A.M.,
January 8, 2026.

I think that the first thing which engaged our interest and
attention was the strange, and then, to us, unaccountable luminosity which pervaded the interior of the Moon. Above us were
banks of fleecy clouds, the undersurfaces of which appeared to be
lighted from beneath, while, through breaks in the cloud banks
we could discern a luminous firmament beyond, though nowhere
was there any suggestion of a central incandescent orb radiating
light and heat as does our sun. The clouds themselves cast no
shadows upon the ground, nor, in fact, were there any well-defined shadows even directly beneath the hull of the ship or
surrounding the forest trees which grew close at hand. The
shadows were vague and nebulous, blending off into nothingness
at their edges. We ourselves cast no more shadows upon the deck
of *The Barsoom* than would have been true upon a cloudy day
on Earth. Yet the general illumination surrounding us approximated that of a very slightly hazy Earth day. This peculiar lunar

light interested us profoundly, but it was some time before we discovered the true explanation of its origin. It was of two kinds, emanating from widely different sources, the chief of which was due to the considerable radium content of the internal lunar soil, and principally of the rock forming the loftier mountain ranges, the radium being so combined as to diffuse a gentle perpetual light which pervaded the entire interior of the Moon. The secondary source was sunlight, which penetrated to the interior of the Moon through the hundreds of thousands of huge craters penetrating the lunar crust. It was this sunlight which carried heat to the inner world, maintaining a constant temperature of about eighty degrees Fahrenheit.

Centrifugal force, in combination with the gravity of the Moon's crust, confined the internal lunar atmosphere to a blanket which we estimated at about fifty miles in thickness over the inner surface of this buried world. This atmosphere rarefies rapidly as one ascends the higher peaks, with the result that these are constantly covered with perpetual snow and ice, sending great glaciers down mighty gorges toward the central seas. It is this condition which has probably prevented the atmosphere, confined as it is within an almost solid sphere, from becoming superheated, through the unthinkable ages that this condition must have existed. The Earth seasons are reflected but slightly in the Moon, there being but a few degrees difference between summer and winter. There are, however, periodic windstorms, which recur with greater or less regularity once each sidereal month, due, I imagine, to the unequal distribution of crater openings through the crust of the Moon, a fact which must produce an unequal absorption of heat at various times and in certain localities. The natural circulation of the lunar atmosphere, affected as it is by the constantly-changing volume and direction of the sun's rays, as well as the great range of temperature between the valleys and the ice-clad mountain peaks, produces frequent storms of greater or less violence. High winds are accompanied by violent rains upon the lower levels and blinding snowstorms among the barren heights above the vegetation line. Rains which fall from low-hanging clouds are warm and pleasant; those which come from high clouds are cold and disagreeable, yet however violent or protracted the storm, the illumination remains practically constant—there are never any dark, lowering days within the Moon, nor is there any night.

CHAPTER III

HUMAN QUADRUPEDS

OF course we did not reach all these conclusions in a few moments, but I have given them here merely as the outcome of our deductions following a considerable experience within the Moon. Several miles from the ship rose foothills which climbed picturesquely toward the cloudy heights of the loftier mountains behind them, and as we looked in the direction of these latter, and then out across the forest, there was appreciable to us a strangeness that at first we could not explain, but which we later discovered was due to the fact that there was no horizon, the distance that one could see being dependent solely upon one's power of vision. The general effect was of being in the bottom of a tremendous bowl, with sides so high that one might not see the top.

The ground about us was covered with rank vegetation of pale hues—lavenders, violets, pinks and yellows predominating. Pink grasses which became distinctly flesh-color at maturity grew in abundance, and the stalks of most of the flowering plants were of this same peculiar hue. The flowers themselves were often of highly complex form, of pale and delicate shades, of great size and rare beauty. There were low shrubs that bore a berry-like fruit, and many of the trees of the forest carried fruit of considerable size and of a variety of forms and colors. Norton and Jay were debating the possible edibility of some of these, but I gave orders that no one was to taste them until we had had an opportunity to learn by analysis or otherwise those varieties that were non-poisonous.

There was aboard *The Barsoom* a small laboratory equipped especially for the purpose of analyzing the vegetable and mineral products of Mars according to earthly standards, as well as other means of conducting research work upon our sister planet. As we had sufficient food aboard for a period of fifteen years, there was no immediate necessity for eating any of the lunar fruit, but I was anxious to ascertain the chemical properties of the water since the manufacture of this necessity was slow, laborious and expensive. I therefore instructed West to take a sample from the stream and subject it to laboratory tests, and the others I ordered below for sleep.

They were rather more keen to set out upon a tour of exploration, nor could I blame them, but as none of us had slept for rather better than forty-eight hours I considered it of importance that we recuperate our vital forces against whatever contingency might confront us in this unknown world. Here were air, water and vegetation—the three prime requisites for the support of animal life—and so I judged it only reasonable to assume that animal life existed within the Moon. If it did exist, it might be in some highly predatory form, against which it would tax our resources to the utmost to defend ourselves. I insisted, therefore, upon each of us obtaining his full quota of sleep before venturing from the safety of *The Barsoom*.

We already had seen evidences of life of a low order, both reptile and insect, or perhaps it would be better to describe the latter as flying reptiles, as they later proved to be—toad-like creatures with the wings of bats, that flitted among the fleshy boughs of the forest, emitting plaintive cries. Upon the ground near the ship we had seen but a single creature, though the moving grasses had assured us that there were others there aplenty. The thing that we had seen had been plainly visible to us all and may be best described as a five-foot snake with four frog-like legs, and a flat head with a single eye in the center of the forehead. Its legs were very short, and as it moved along the ground it both wriggled like a true snake and scrambled with its four short legs. We watched it to the edge of the river and saw it dive in and disappear beneath the surface.

"Silly looking beggar," remarked Jay, "and devilish unearthly."

"I don't know about that," I returned. "He possessed nothing visible to us that we are not familiar with on Earth. Possibly he was assembled after a slightly different plan from any Earth creature; but aside from that he is familiar to us, even to his amphibious habits. And these flying toads, too; what of them? I see nothing particularly remarkable about them. We have just as strange forms on Earth, though nothing precisely like these. Mars, too, has forms of animal and vegetable life peculiar to herself, yet nothing the existence of which would be impossible upon Earth, and she has, as well, human forms almost identical with our own. You see what I am trying to suggest?"

"Yes, sir," replied Jay; "that there may be human life similar to our own within the Moon."

"I see no reason to be surprised should we discover human beings here," I said; "nor would I be surprised to find a reasoning creature of some widely divergent form. I would be surprised, however, were we to find no form analogous to the human race of Earth."

"That is, a dominant race with well developed reasoning faculties?" asked Norton.

"Yes, and it is because of this possibility that we must have sleep and keep ourselves fit, since we may not know the disposition of these creatures, provided they exist, nor the reception that they will accord us. And so, Mr. Norton, if you will get a receptacle and fetch some water from the stream we will leave Mr. West on watch to make his analysis and the rest of us will turn in."

Norton went below and returned with a glass jar in which to carry the water and the balance of us lined the rail with our service revolvers ready in the event of an emergency as he went over the side. None of us had walked more than a few steps since coming on deck after our landing. I had noticed a slightly peculiar sensation of buoyancy, but in view of the numerous other distractions had given it no consideration. As Norton reached the bottom of the ladder and set foot on lunar soil I called to him to make haste. Just in front of him was a low bush and beyond it lay the river, about thirty feet distant. In response to my command he gave a slight leap to clear the bush and, to our amazement as well as to his own consternation, rose fully eighteen feet into the air, cleared a space of fully thirty-five feet and lit in the river.

"Come!" I said to the others, wishing them to follow me to Norton's aid, and sprang for the rail; but I was too impetuous. I never touched the rail, but cleared it by many feet, sailed over the intervening strip of land, and disappeared beneath the icy waters of the lunar river. How deep it was I do not know; but at least it was over my head. I found myself in a sluggish, yet powerful current, the water seeming to move much as a heavy oil moves to the gravity of Earth. As I came to the surface I saw Norton swimming strongly for the bank and a second later Jay emerged not far from me. I glanced quickly around for West, whom I immediately perceived was still on the deck of *The Barsoom*, where, of course, it was his duty to remain, since it was his watch.

The moment that I realized that my companions were all safe I could not repress a smile, and then Norton and Jay commenced to laugh, and we were still laughing when we pulled ourselves from the stream a short distance below the ship.

"Get your sample, Norton?" I asked.

"I still have the container, sir," he replied, and indeed he had clung to it throughout his surprising adventure, as Jay and I, fortunately, had clung to our revolvers. Norton removed the cap from the bottle and dipped the latter into the stream. Then he looked up at me and smiled.

"I think we have beaten Mr. West to it, sir," he said. "It seems like very good water, sir, and when I struck it I was so surprised that I must have swallowed at least a quart."

"I tested a bit of it myself," I replied. "As far as we three are concerned, Mr. West's analysis will not interest us if he discovers that lunar water contains poisonous matter, but for his own protection we will let him proceed with his investigation."

"It is strange, sir," remarked Jay, "that none of us thought of the natural effects of the lesser gravity of the Moon. We have discussed the matter upon many occasions, as you will recall, yet when we faced the actual condition we gave it no consideration whatsoever."

"I am glad," remarked Norton, "that I did not attempt to jump the river—I should have been going yet. Probably landed on the top of some mountain."

As we approached the ship I saw West awaiting us with a most serious and dignified mien; but when he saw that we were all laughing he joined us, telling us after we reached the deck, that he had never witnessed a more surprising or ludicrous sight in his life.

We went below then and after closing and securing the hatch, three of us repaired to our bunks, while West with the sample of lunar water went to the laboratory. I was very tired and slept soundly for some ten hours, for it was the middle of Norton's watch before I awoke.

The only important entry upon the log since I had turned in was West's report of the results of his analysis of the water, which showed that it was not only perfectly safe for drinking purposes but unusually pure, with an extremely low saline content.

I had been up about a half an hour when West came to me, saying that Orthis requested permission to speak to me. Twenty-four hours before, I had been fairly well determined to bring Orthis to trial and execute him immediately, but that had been when I had felt that we were all hopelessly doomed to death on his account. Now, however, with a habitable world beneath our

feet, surrounded by conditions almost identical with those which
existed upon Earth, our future looked less dark, and because of
this I found myself in a quandary as to what course of action to
pursue in the matter of Orthis' punishment. That he deserved
death there was no question, but when men have faced death so
closely and escaped, temporarily at least, I believe that they must
look upon life as a most sacred thing and be less inclined to deny
life to others. Be that as it may, the fact remains that having sent
for Orthis in compliance with his request I received him in a
mood of less stern and uncompromising justice than would have
been the case twenty-four hours previous. When he had been
brought to my stateroom and stood before me, I asked him what
he wished to say to me. He was entirely sober now and bore himself with a certain dignity that was not untinged with humility.

"I do not know what has occurred since I was put in irons, as
you have instructed the others not to speak to me or answer my
questions. I know, of course, however, that the ship is at rest and
that pure air is circulating through it, and I have heard the
hatch raised and footsteps upon the upper deck. From the time
that has elapsed since I was placed under arrest I know that the
only planet upon which we have had time to make a landing is
the Moon, and so I may guess that we are upon the surface of the
Moon. I have had ample time to reflect upon my actions. That I
was intoxicated is, of course, no valid excuse, and yet it is the
only excuse that I have to offer. I beg, sir, that you will accept
the assurance of my sincere regret of the unforgivable things that
I have done, and that you will permit me to live and atone for
my wrongdoings, for if we are indeed upon the surface of the
Moon it may be that we can ill spare a single member of our
small party. I throw myself, sir, entirely upon your mercy, but
beg that you will give me another chance."

Realizing my natural antipathy for the man and wishing most
sincerely not to be influenced against him because of it, I let his
plea influence me against my better judgment with the result
that I promised him that I would give the matter careful consideration, discuss it with the others, and be influenced largely
by their decision. I had him returned to his stateroom then and
sent for the other members of the party. With what fidelity my
memory permitted I repeated to them in Orthis' own words his
request for mercy.

"And now, gentlemen," I said, "I would like to have your
opinions in the matter. It is of as much moment to you as to me,
and under the peculiar circumstances in which we are placed, I

prefer in so far as possible to defer wherever I can to the judgment of the majority. Whatever my final action, the responsibility will be mine. I do not seek to divide that, and it may be that I shall act contrary to the wishes of the majority in some matters, but in this one I really wish to abide by your desires because of the personal antagonism that has existed between Lieutenant Commander Orthis and myself since boyhood."

I knew that none of these men liked Orthis, yet I knew, too, that they would approach the matter in a spirit of justice tempered by mercy, and so I was not at all surprised when one after another they assured me that they would be glad if I would give the man another opportunity.

Again I sent for Orthis, and after explaining to him that inasmuch as he had given me his word to commit no disloyal act in the future I should place him on parole, his eventual fate depending entirely upon his own conduct; then had his irons removed and told him that he was to return to duty. He seemed most grateful and assured us that we would never have cause to regret our decision. Would to God that instead of freeing him I had drawn my revolver and shot him through the heart!

We were all pretty well rested up by this time, and I undertook to do a little exploring in the vicinity of the ship, going out for a few hours each day with a single companion, leaving the other three upon the ship. I never went far afield at first, confining myself to an area some five miles in diameter between the crater and the river. Upon both sides of the latter, below where the ship had landed, was a considerable extent of forest. I ventured into this upon several occasions and once, just about time for us to return to the ship, I came upon a well-marked trail in the dust of which were the imprints of three-toed feet. Each day I set the extreme limit of time that I would absent myself from the ship with instructions that two of those remaining aboard should set out in search of me and my companion, should we be absent over the specified number of hours. Therefore, I was unable to follow the trail the day upon which I discovered it, since we had scarcely more than enough time to make a brief examination of the tracks if we were to reach the ship within the limit I had allowed.

It chanced that Norton was with me that day and in his quiet way was much excited by our discovery. We were both positive that the tracks had been made by a four-footed animal, something that weighed between two hundred and fifty and three hundred pounds. How recently it had been used we could scarcely estimate, but the trail itself gave every indication of being a very old one. I was sorry that we had no time to pursue the animal which had made the tracks but determined that upon the following day I should do so. We reached the ship and told the others what we had discovered. They were much interested and many and varied were the conjectures as to the nature of the animals whose tracks we had seen.

After Orthis had been released from arrest Norton had asked permission to return to the former's stateroom. I had granted his request and the two had been very much together ever since. I could not understand Norton's apparent friendship for this man, and it almost made me doubt the young ensign. One day I was to learn the secret of this intimacy, but at the time I must confess that it puzzled me considerably and bothered me not a little, for I had taken a great liking to Norton and disliked to see him so much in the company of a man of Orthis' character.

Each of the men had now accompanied me on my short excursions of exploration with the exception of Orthis. Inasmuch as his parole had fully reinstated him among us in theory at least, I could not very well discriminate against him and leave him alone of all the others aboard ship as I pursued my investigations of the surrounding country.

The day following our discovery of the trail, I accordingly invited him to accompany me, and we set out early, each armed with a revolver and a rifle. I advised West, who automatically took command of the ship during my absence, that we might be gone considerably longer than usual and that he was to feel no apprehension and send out no relief party unless we should be gone a full twenty-four hours, as I wished to follow up the spoor we had discovered, learn where the trail led and have a look at the animal that had made it.

I led the way directly to the spot at which we had found the trail, about four miles down river from the ship and apparently in the heart of dense forest.

The flying-toads darted from tree to tree about us, uttering their weird and plaintive cries, while upon several occasions, as in the past, we saw four-legged snakes such as we had seen upon the day of our landing. Neither the toads nor the snakes bothered us, seeming only to wish to avoid us.

Just before we came upon the trail, both Orthis and I thought we heard the sound of footsteps ahead of us—something similar to that made by a galloping animal—and when we came upon the trail a moment later it was apparent to both of us that dust was hanging in the air and slowly settling on the vegetation nearby. Something, therefore, had passed over the trail but a minute or two before we arrived. A brief examination of the spoor revealed the fact that it had been made by a three-toed animal whose direction of travel was to our right and toward the river, at this point some half mile from us.

I could not help but feel considerable inward excitement, and I was sorry that one of the others had not been with me, for I never felt perfectly at ease with Orthis. I had done considerable hunting in various parts of the world where wild game still exists but I had never experienced such a thrill as I did at the moment that I undertook to stalk this unknown beast upon an unknown trail in an unknown world. Where the trail would lead me, what I should find upon it, I never knew from one step to another, and the lure of it because of that was tremendous. The fact that there were almost nine million square miles of this world for me to explore, and that no Earth Man had ever before set foot upon an inch of it, helped a great deal to compensate for the fact that I knew I could never return to my own Earth again.

The trail led to the edge of the river which at this point was very wide and shallow. Upon the opposite shore, I could see the trail again directly opposite and I knew therefore that this was a ford. Without hesitating, I stepped into the river, and as I did so I glanced to my left to see stretching before me as far as my eyes could reach a vast expanse of water. Here then I had stumbled upon the mouth of the river and, beyond, a lunar sea.

The land upon the opposite side of the river was rolling and grass-covered, but in so far as I could see, almost treeless. As I turned my eyes from the sea back toward the opposite shore, I saw that which caused me to halt in my tracks, cock my rifle and issue a cautious warning to Orthis for silence, for there before us upon a knoll stood a small horse-like animal.

It would have been a long shot, possibly five hundred yards, and I should have preferred to have come closer but there was no chance to do that now, for we were in the middle of the river in plain view of the animal which stood there watching us intently. I had scarcely raised my rifle, however, ere it wheeled and disappeared over the edge of the knoll upon which it had been standing.

"What did it look like to you, Orthis?" I asked my companion.

"It was a good ways off," he replied, "and I only just got my binoculars on it as it disappeared, but I could have sworn that it wore a harness of some sort. It was about the size of a small pony, I should say, but it didn't have a pony's head."

"It appeared tailless to me," I remarked.

"I saw no tail," said Orthis, "nor any ears or horns. It was a devilish funny looking thing. I don't understand it. There was something about it—" he paused. "My God, sir, there was something about it that looked human."

"It gave me that same impression, too, Orthis, and I doubt if I should have fired had I been able to cover it, for just at the instant that I threw my rifle to my shoulder I felt that same strange impression that you mention. There was something human about the thing."

As we talked, we had been moving on across the ford which we found an excellent one, the water at no time coming to our waists while the current was scarcely appreciable. Finally, we stepped out on the opposite shore and a moment later, far to the left, we caught another glimpse of the creature that we had previously seen. It stood upon a distant knoll, evidently watching us.

Orthis and I raised our binoculars to our eyes almost simultaneously and for a full minute we examined the thing as it stood there, neither of us speaking, and then we dropped our glasses and looked at each other.

"What do you make of it, sir?" he asked.

I shook my head. "I don't know what to make of it, Orthis," I replied; "but I should swear that I was looking straight into a human face, and yet the body was that of a quadruped."

"There can be no doubt of it, sir," he replied, "and this time one could see the harness and the clothing quite plainly. It appears to have some sort of a weapon hanging at its left side. Did you notice it, sir?"

"Yes, I noticed it, but I don't understand it."

A moment longer we stood watching the creature until it turned and galloped off, disappearing behind the knoll on which it had stood. We decided to follow the trail which led in a southerly direction, feeling reasonably assured that we were more likely to come in contact with the creature or others similar to it upon the trail than off of it. We had gone but a short distance when the trail approached the river again, which puzzled me at the time somewhat, as we had gone apparently directly away from the river since we had left the ford, but after we had gone some mile and a half, we found the explanation, since we came again to another ford while on beyond we saw the river emptying into the sea and realized that we had crossed an island lying in the mouth of the river.

I was hesitating as to whether to make the crossing and continue along the trail or to go back and search the island for the strange creature we had discovered. I rather hoped to capture it, but since I had finally descried its human face, I had given up all intention of shooting it unless I found that it would be necessary to do so in self defense. As I stood there, rather undecided, our attention was attracted back to the island by a slight noise, and as we looked in the direction of the disturbance, we saw five of the creatures eyeing us from high land a quarter of a mile away. When they saw that they were discovered they galloped boldly toward us. They had come a short distance only, when they stopped again upon a high knoll, and then one of them raised his face toward the sky and emitted a series of piercing howls. Then they came on again toward us nor did they pause until they were within fifty feet of us, when they came to a sudden halt.

CHAPTER IV

IN THE HANDS OF THE VA-GAS

Our first view of the creatures proved beyond a question of a doubt that they were in effect human quadrupeds. The faces were very broad, much broader than any human faces that I have ever seen, but their profiles were singularly like those of the ancient North American Indians. Their bodies were covered with a garment with short legs that ended above the knees, and which was ornamented about the collar and also about the bottom of each leg with a rather fanciful geometric design. About the barrel of each was a surcingle and connected with it by a backstrap was something analogous to a breeching in Earth horse harness. Where the breeching straps crossed on either side, was a small circular ornament, and there was a strap resembling a trace leading from this forward to the collar, passing beneath a quite large, circular ornament, which appeared to be supported by the surcingle. Smaller straps, running from these two ornaments upon the left side, supported a sheath in which was carried what appeared to be a knife of some description. And upon the right side a short spear was carried in a boot, similarly suspended from the two ornaments, much as the carbine of our ancient Earth cavalry was carried. The spear, which was about six feet long, was of peculiar design, having a slender, well-shaped head, from the base of which a crescent-shaped arm curved backward from one side, while upon the side opposite the crescent was a short, sharp point at right angles to the median line of the weapon.

For a moment we stood there eyeing each other, and from their appearance I judged that they were as much interested in us as we were in them. I noticed that they kept looking beyond us, across the river toward the mainland. Presently, I turned for a glance in the same direction, and far away beyond a thin forest I saw a cloud of dust which seemed to be moving rapidly toward us. I called Orthis' attention to it.

"Reinforcements," I said. "That is what that fellow was calling for when he screamed. I think we had better try conclusions with the five before any more arrive. We will try to make friends first, but if we are unsuccessful we must fight our way back toward the ship at once."

Accordingly, I stepped forward toward the five with a smile upon my lips and my hand outstretched. I knew of no other way in which to carry to them an assurance of our friendliness. At the same time, I spoke a few words in English in a pleasant and conciliatory tone. Although I knew that my words would be meaningless to them, I hoped that they would catch their intent from my inflection.

Immediately upon my advance, one of the creatures turned and spoke to another, indicating to us for the first time that they possessed a spoken language. Then he turned and addressed me in a tongue that was, of course, utterly meaningless to me; but if he had misinterpreted my action, I could not misunderstand that which accompanied his words, for he reared up on his hind feet and simultaneously drew his spear and a wicked-looking, short-bladed sword or dagger, his companions at the same time following his example, until I found myself confronted by an array of weapons backed by scowling, malignant faces. Their leader uttered a single word which I interpreted as meaning halt, and so I halted.

I pointed to Orthis and to myself, and then to the trail along which we had come, and then back in the direction of the ship. I was attempting to tell them that we wished to go back whence we had come. Then I turned to Orthis.

"Draw your revolver," I said, "and follow me. If they interfere we shall have to shoot them. We must get out of this before the others arrive."

As we turned to retrace our steps along the trail, the five dropped upon all fours, still holding their weapons in their forepaws, and galloped quickly to a position blocking our way.

"Stand aside," I yelled, and fired my pistol above their heads. From their actions, I judged that they had never before heard the report of a firearm, for they stood an instant in evident surprise, and then wheeled and galloped off for about a hundred yards, where they turned and halted again, facing us. They were still directly across our trail, and Orthis and I moved forward determinedly toward them. They were talking among themselves, and at the same time watching us closely.

When we had arrived at a few yards from them, I again threatened them with my pistol, but they stood their ground, evidently reassured by the fact that the thing that I held in my hand, though it made a loud noise, inflicted no injury. I did not want to shoot one of them if I could possibly avoid it, so I kept on toward them, hoping that they would make way for us; but instead they reared again upon their hind feet and threatened us with their weapons.

Just how formidable their weapons were, I could not, of course, determine; but I conjectured that if they were at all adept in its use, their spear might be a very formidable thing indeed. I was within a few feet of them now, and their attitude was more war-like than ever, convincing me that they had no intention of permitting us to pass peacefully.

Their features, which I could now see distinctly, were hard, fierce, and cruel in the extreme. Their leader seemed to be addressing me, but, of course, I could not understand him; but when, at last, standing there upon his hind feet, with evidently as much ease as I stood upon my two legs, he carried his spear back in a particularly menacing movement, I realized that I must act and act quickly.

I think the fellow was just on the point of launching his spear at me, when I fired. The bullet struck him square between the eyes, and he dropped like a log, without a sound. Instantly, the others wheeled again and galloped away, this time evincing speed that was almost appalling, clearing spaces of a hundred feet in a single bound, even though handicapped, as they must have been, by the weapons which they clutched in their forepaws.

A glance behind me showed the dust-cloud rapidly approaching the river, upon the mainland, and calling to Orthis to follow me, I ran rapidly along the trail which led back in the direction of the ship.

The four Moon creatures retreated for about half a mile, and then halted and faced us. They were still directly in our line of retreat, and there they stood for a moment, evidently discussing their plans. We were nearing them rapidly, for we had discovered that we, too, could show remarkable speed, when retarded by gravity only one-sixth of that of Earth. To clear forty feet at a jump was nothing, our greatest difficulty lying in a tendency to leap to too great heights, which naturally resulted in cutting down our horizontal distance. As we neared the four, who had taken their stand upon the summit of a knoll, I heard a great splashing in the river behind us, and turning, saw that their reinforcements were crossing the ford, and would soon be upon us. There appeared to be fully a hundred of them, and our case looked hopeless indeed, unless we could manage to pass the four ahead of us, and reach the comparative safety of the forest beyond the first ford.

"Commence firing, Orthis," I said. "Shoot to kill. Take the two at the left as your targets, and I'll fire at the two at the right. We had better halt and take careful aim, as we cannot afford to waste ammunition."

We came to a stop about twenty-five yards from the foremost creature, which is a long pistol shot; but they were standing still upon the crest of a knoll, distinctly outlined against the sky, and were such a size as to present a most excellent target. Our shots rang out simultaneously. The creature at the left, at which Orthis had aimed, leaped high into the air, and fell to the ground, where it lay kicking convulsively. The one at the right uttered a piercing shriek, clutched at its breast, and dropped dead. Then Orthis and I charged the remaining two, while behind us we heard loud weird cries and the pounding of galloping feet. The two before us did not retreat this time, but came to meet us, and we halted and fired. This time they were so close that we could not miss them, and the last of our original lunar foemen lay dead before us.

We ran then, ran as neither of us had imagined human beings ever could run. I know that I covered over fifty feet in many a leap, but by comparison with the speed of the things behind us, we might have been standing still. They fairly flew over the lavender sward, indicating that those, which we had first seen, had at no time extended themselves in an effort to escape us. I venture to say that some of them leaped fully three hundred feet at a time, and now, at every bound, they emitted fierce and terrible yells, which I assumed to be their war cry, intended to intimidate us.

"It's no use, Orthis," I said to my companion. "We might as well make our stand here and fight it out. We cannot reach the ford. They are too fast for us."

We stopped then, and faced them, and when they saw we were going to make a stand, they circled and halted about a hundred yards distant, entirely surrounding us. We had killed five of their fellows, and I knew we could hope for no quarter. We were evidently confronted by a race of fierce and warlike creatures, the appearance of which, at least, gave no indication of the finer characteristics that are so much revered among humankind upon Earth. After a good look at one of them, I could not imagine the creature harboring even the slightest conception of the word mercy, and I knew that if we ever escaped that fierce cordon, it would be by fighting our way through it.

"Come," I said to Orthis, "straight through for the ford," and turning again in that direction, I started blazing away with my pistol as I walked slowly along the trail. Orthis was at my side, and he, too, fired as rapidly as I. Each time our weapons spoke, a Moon Man fell. And now, they commenced to circle us at a run, much as the savage Indians of the western plains circled the parked wagon trains of our long-gone ancestors in North America. They hurled spears at us, but I think the sound of our revolvers and the effect of the shots had to some measure unnerved them, for their aim was poor and we were not, at any time, seriously menaced.

As we advanced slowly, firing, we made many hits, but I was horrified to see that every time one of the creatures fell, the nearest of his companions leaped upon him and cut his throat from ear to ear. Some of them had only to fall to be dispatched by his fellows. A bullet from Orthis' weapon shattered the hind leg of one of them, bringing him to the ground. It was, of course, not a fatal wound, but the creature had scarcely gone down, when the nearest to him sprang forward, and finished him. And thus we walked slowly toward the ford, and I commenced to have hope that we might reach it and make our escape. If our antagonists had been less fearless, I should have been certain of it, but they seemed almost indifferent to their danger, evidently counting upon their speed to give them immunity from our bullets. I can assure you that they presented most difficult targets, moving as they did in great leaps and bounds. It was probably more their number than our accuracy that permitted us the hits we made.

We were almost at the ford when the circle suddenly broke, and then formed a straight line parallel to us, the leader swinging his spear about his head, grasping the handle at its extreme end. The weapon moved at great speed, in an almost horizontal plane. I was wondering at the purpose of his action, when I saw that three or four of those directly in the rear of him had commenced to swing their spears in a similar manner. There was something strangely menacing about it that filled me with alarm. I fired at the leader and missed, and at the report of my pistol, a half dozen of them let go of their swift whirling spears, and an instant later, I realized the purpose of their strange maneuver; for the heavy weapons shot toward us, butts first, with the speed of lightning, the crescent-like hooks catching us around a leg, an arm and the neck, hurling us backward to the ground, and each time we essayed to rise, we were struck again, until we finally lay there, bruised and half stunned, and wholly at the mercy of our antagonists, who galloped forward quickly, stripping our weapons from us. Those who had hurled their spears at us recovered them, and then they all gathered about, examining us, and jabbering among themselves.

Presently, the leader spoke to me, prodding me with the sharp point of his spear. I took it that he wanted me to arise, and I tried to do so, but I was pretty much all in and fell back each time I essayed to obey. Then he spoke to two of his followers, who lifted me and laid me across the back of a third. There I was fastened in a most uncomfortable position by means of leather straps which were taken from various parts of the harnesses of several of the creatures. Orthis was similarly lashed to another of them, whereupon they moved slowly back in the direction from which they had come, stopping, as they went, to collect the bodies of their dead, which were strapped to the backs of others of their companions. The fellow upon whom I rode had several well-defined gaits, one of which, a square trot, was the acme of torture for me, since I was bruised and hurt and had been placed across him face down, upon my belly; but inasmuch as this gait must have been hard, too, upon him, while thus saddled with a burden, he used it but little, for which I was tremendously thankful. When he changed to a single-foot, which, fortunately for me, he often did, I was much less uncomfortable.

As we crossed the ford toward the mainland, it was with difficulty that I kept from being drowned, since my head dragged in
the water for a considerable distance and I was mighty glad when
we came out again on shore. The thing that bore me was con-
sistently inconsiderate of me, bumping me against others, and
against the bodies of their slain that were strapped to the backs
of his fellows. He was apparently quite tireless, as were the
others, and we often moved for what seemed many miles at a
fast run. Of course, my lunar weight was equivalent to only
about thirty pounds on Earth while our captors seemed fully
as well-muscled as a small earthly horse, and as we later learned,
were capable of carrying heavy burdens.

How long we were on the march, I do not know, for where it
is always daylight and there is no sun nor other means of measuring time, one may only guess at its duration, the result being
influenced considerably by one's mental and physical sensations
during the period. Judged by these considerations, then, we
might have been on the trail for many hours, for I was not only
most uncomfortable in body, but in mind as well. However that
may be, I know only that it was a terrible journey; that we
crossed rivers twice after reaching the mainland, and came at
last to our destination, amid low hills, where there was a level,
parklike space, dotted with weird trees. Here the straps were
loosened, and we were dumped upon the ground, more dead
than alive, and immediately surrounded by great numbers of
creatures who were identical with those who had captured us.

When I was finally able to sit up and look about, I saw that
we were at the threshold of a camp or village, consisting of a
number of rectangular huts, with high-peaked roofs, thatched
or rather shingled, with the broad, round leaves of the trees that
grew about.

We saw now for the first time the females and the young. The
former were similar to the males, except that they were of
lighter build, and they were far more numerous. They had
udders, with from four to six teats, and many of them were
followed by numerous progeny, several that I saw having as
high as six young in a litter. The young were naked, but the
females wore a garment similar to that worn by the males, except that it was less ornate, as was their harness and other trappings. From the way the women and children rushed upon us as
we were unloaded in camp, I felt that they were going to tear
us to pieces, and I really believe they would have had not our
captors prevented. Evidently the word was passed that we were

not to be injured, for after the first rush they contented themselves with examining us, and sometimes feeling of us or our clothing, the while they discussed us, but with the bodies of those who were slain, it was different, for when they discovered these where they had been unloaded upon the ground, they fell upon them and commenced to devour them, the warriors joining them in the gruesome and terrible feast. Orthis and I understood now that they had cut the throats of their fellows to let the blood, in anticipation of the repast to come.

As we came to understand them and the conditions under which they lived, many things concerning them were explained. For example, at least two-thirds of the young that are born are males, and yet there are only about one-sixth as many adult males, as there are females. They are naturally carnivorous, but with the exception of one other creature upon which they prey, there is no animal in that part of the interior lunar world with which I am familiar, that they may eat with safety. The flying-toad and the walking snake and the other reptilia are poisonous, and they dare not eat them. The time had been, I later learned, possibly, however, ages before, when many other animals roamed the surface of the inner Moon, but all had become extinct except our captors and another creature, of which we, at the time of our capture, knew nothing, and these two preyed upon one another, while the species which was represented by those into whose hands we had fallen, raided the tribes and villages of their own kind for food, and ate their own dead, as we had already seen. As it was the females to whom they must look for the production of animal food, they did not kill these of their own species and never ate the body of one. Enemy women of their own kind, whom they captured, they brought to their villages, each warrior adding to his herd the individuals that he captured. As only the males are warriors, and as no one will eat the flesh of a female, the mortality among the males is, accordingly, extremely high, accounting for the vastly greater number of adult females. The latter are very well treated, as the position of a male in a community is dependent largely upon the size of his herd.

The principal mortality among the females results from three causes—raids by the other flesh-eating species which inhabit the inner lunar world, quarrels arising from jealousy among themselves, and death while bringing forth their young, especially during lean seasons when their warriors have been defeated in battle and have been unable to furnish them with flesh.

These creatures eat fruit and herbs and nuts as well as meat, but they do not thrive well upon these things exclusively. Their existence, therefore, is dependent upon the valor and ferocity of their males whose lives are spent in making raids and forays against neighboring tribes and in defending their own villages against invaders.

As Orthis and I sat watching the disgusting orgy of cannibalism about us, the leader of the party that had captured us came toward us from the center of the village, and speaking a single word, which I later learned meant come, he prodded us with his spear point until finally we staggered to our feet. Repeating the word, then, he started back into the village.

"I guess he wants us to follow him, Orthis," I said. And so we fell in behind the creature, which was evidently what he desired, for he nodded his head, and stepped on in the direction that he had taken, which led toward a very large hut—by far the largest in the village.

In the side of the hut presented to us there seemed to be but a single opening, a large door covered by a heavy hanging, which our conductor thrust aside as we entered the interior with him. We found ourselves in a large room, without any other opening whatsoever, save the doorway through which we had entered, and over which the hanging had again been drawn, yet the interior was quite light, though not so much so as outside, but there were no means for artificial lighting apparent. The walls were covered with weapons and with the skulls and other bones of creatures similar to our captors, though Orthis and I both noticed a few skulls much narrower than the others and which, from their appearance, might have been the human skulls of Earth Men, though in discussing it later, we came to the conclusion that they were the skulls of the females and the young of the species, whose faces are not so wide as the adult male.

Lying upon a bed of grasses at the opposite side of the room was a large male whose skin was of so much deeper lavender hue than the others that we had seen, as to almost suggest a purple. The face, though badly disfigured by scars, and grim and ferocious in the extreme, was an intelligent one, and the instant that I looked into those eyes, I knew that we were in the presence of a leader. Nor was I wrong, for this was the chief or king of the tribe into whose clutches Fate had thrown us.

A few words passed between the two, and then the chief arose and came toward us. He examined us very critically, our clothing seeming to interest him tremendously. He tried to talk with

us, evidently asking us questions, and seemed very much disgusted when it became apparent to him that we could not understand him, nor he us, for Orthis and I spoke to one another
several times, and once or twice addressed him. He gave some
instructions to the fellow who had brought us, and we were
taken out again, and to another hut, to which there was presently
brought a portion of the carcass of one of the creatures we had
killed before we were captured. I could not eat any of it, however, and neither could Orthis; and after a while, by signs and
gestures, we made them understand that we wished some other
kind of food, with the result that a little later, they brought us
fruit and vegetables, which were more palatable and, as we were
to discover later, sufficiently nutritious to carry us along and
maintain our strength.

I had become thirsty, and by simulating drinking, I finally
succeeded in making plain to them my desire in that direction,
with the result that they led us out to a little stream which ran
through the village, and there we quenched our thirst.

We were still very weak and sore from the manhandling
we had received, but we were both delighted to discover that we
were not seriously injured, nor were any of our bones broken.

CHAPTER V

A LUNAR STORM

SHORTLY after we arrived at the village, they took away our
watches, our pocket-knives, and everything that we possessed of
a similar nature, and which they considered as curiosities. The
chief wore Orthis' wristwatch above one fore-paw and mine
above the other, but as he did not know how to wind them, nor
the purpose for which they were intended, they did him or us
no good. The result was, however, that it was now entirely impossible for us to measure time in any way, and I do not know,
even to this day, how long we were in this strange village. We
ate when we were hungry, and slept when we were tired. It was
always daylight; and it seemed that there were always raiding
parties going out or returning, so that flesh was plentiful, and
we became rather reconciled to our fate, in so far as the immediate danger of being eaten was concerned, but why they kept us

alive, as we had slain so many of their fellows, I could not understand.

It must have been immediately after we arrived that they made an attempt to teach us their language. Two females were detailed for this duty. We were given unlimited freedom within certain bounds, which were well indicated by the several sentries which constantly watched from the summit of hills surrounding the village. Past these we could not go, nor do I know that we had any particular desire to do so, since we realized only too well that there would be little chance of our regaining the ship should we escape the village, inasmuch as we had not the remotest idea in what direction it lay.

Our one hope lay in learning their language, and then utilizing our knowledge in acquiring some definite information as to the surrounding country and the location of *The Barsoom*.

It did not seem to take us very long to learn their tongue, though, of course, I realize that it may really have been months. Almost before we knew it, we were conversing freely with our captors. When I say freely, it is possible that I exaggerate a trifle, for though we could understand them fairly well, it was with difficulty that we made ourselves understood, yet we managed it some way, handicapped as we were by the peculiarities of the most remarkable language of which I have any knowledge.

It is a very difficult language to speak, and as a written language, would be practically impossible. For example, there is their word *gu-e-ho*, for which Orthis and I discovered twenty-seven separate and distinct meanings, and that there are others I have little or no doubt. Their speech is more aptly described as song, the meaning of each syllable being governed by the note in which it is sung. They speak in five notes, which we may describe as A, B, C, D and E. *Gu* sung in A means something radically different from *gu* sung in E, and again if *gu* is sung in A, followed by *e* in G, it means something other than if *gu* had been sung in D followed by *e* in A.

Fortunately for us, there are no words of over three syllables, and most of them consist of only one or two, or we should have been entirely lost. The resulting speech, however, is extremely beautiful, and Orthis used to say that if he closed his eyes, he could imagine himself living constantly in grand opera.

The chief's name, as we learned, was Ga-va-go; the name of the tribe or village was No-vans, while the race to which they belonged was known as Va-gas.

When I felt that I had mastered the language sufficiently well to make myself at least partially understood, I asked to speak to Ga-va-go, and shortly thereafter, I was taken to him.

"You have learned our speech?" he asked.

I nodded in the affirmative. "I have," I said, "and I have come to ask why we are held captives and what you intend to do with us. We did not come to seek a quarrel with you. We wish only to be friends, and to be allowed to go our way in peace."

"What manner of creature are you," he asked, "and where do you come from?"

I asked him if he had ever heard of the Sun or the stars or the other planets or any worlds outside his own, and he replied that he had not, and that there were no such things.

"But there are, Ga-va-go," I said, "and I and my companion are from another world, far, far outside your own. An accident brought us here. Give us back our weapons, and let us go."

He shook his head negatively.

"Where you come from, do you eat one another?" he asked.

"No," I replied, "we do not."

"Why?" he asked, and I saw his eyes narrow as he awaited my reply.

Was it mental telepathy or just luck that put the right answer in my mouth, for somehow, intuitively, I seemed to grasp what was in the creature's mind.

"Our flesh is poison," I said, "those who eat it die."

He looked at me then for a long time, with an expression upon his face which I could not interpret. It may have been that he doubted my word, or again, it may have been that my reply confirmed his suspicion, I do not know; but presently he asked me another question.

"Are there many like you in the land where you live?"

"Millions upon millions," I replied.

"And what do they eat?"

"They eat fruits and vegetables and the flesh of animals," I answered.

"What animals?" he asked.

"I have seen no animals here like them," I replied, "but there are many kinds unlike us, so that we do not have to eat flesh of our own race."

"Then you have all the flesh that you want?"

"All that we can eat," I replied. "We raise these animals for their flesh."

"Where is your country?" he demanded. "Take me to it."

I smiled. "I cannot take you to it," I said. "It is upon another world."

It was quite evident that he did not believe me, for he scowled at me ferociously.

"Do you wish to die?" he demanded.

I told him that I had no such longing.

"Then you will lead me to your country," he said, "where there is plenty of flesh for everyone. You may think about it until I send for you again. Go!" And thus he dismissed me. Then he sent for Orthis, but what Orthis told him, I never knew exactly, for he would not tell me, and as our relations, even in our captivity, were far from friendly, I did not urge him to any confidences. I had occasion to notice, however, that from that time Ga-va-go indicated a marked preference for Orthis, and the latter was often called to his hut.

I was momentarily expecting to be summoned into Ga-va-go's presence, and learn my fate, when he discovered that I could not lead him to my country, where flesh was so plentiful. But at about this time we broke camp, and in the press of other matters, he evidently neglected to take any further immediate action in my case, or at least, so I thought, until I later had reason to suspect that he felt that he need no longer depend upon me to lead him to this land of milk and honey.

The Va-gas are a nomadic race, moving hither and thither, either as they are pressed by some foes, or till their victories have frightened away the other tribes from their vicinity, in either of which events, they march in search of fresh territory. The move that we made now was necessitated by the fact that all the other tribes nearby had fled before the ferocity of the No-vans, whose repeated and successful raids had depleted the villages of their neighbors and filled them with terror.

The breaking of camp was a wonderfully simple operation. All their few belongings, consisting of extra clothing, trappings, weapons, and their treasured skulls and bones of victims, were strapped to the backs of the women. Orthis and I each bestrode a warrior detailed by Ga-va-go for the purpose of transporting us, and we filed out of the village, leaving the huts behind.

Ga-va-go, with a half-dozen warriors, galloped far ahead. Then came a strong detachment of warriors, with the women folks behind them, another detachment of warriors following in the rear of the women and children, while others rode upon either flank. A mile or so in the rear, came three warriors, and there were two or three scattered far out on either flank. Thus we moved, thoroughly protected against surprise, regulating our speed by that of the point with which Ga-va-go traveled.

Because of the women and the children, we moved more slowly than warriors do when on the march alone, when they seldom, if ever, travel slower than a trot, and more generally, at a fast gallop. We moved along a well-worn trail, passing several deserted villages, from which the prey of the No-vans had fled. We crossed many rivers, for the lunar world is well watered. We skirted several lakes, and at one point of high ground, I saw, far at our left, the waters of what appeared to be a great ocean.

There was never a time when Orthis and I were not plentifully supplied with food, for there is an abundance of it growing throughout all the territory we crossed, but the No-vans had been without flesh for several days and were, in consequence, mad with hunger, as the fruits and vegetables which they ate seemed not to satisfy them at all.

We were moving along at a brisk trot when, without warning, we were struck by a sudden gust of wind that swept, cold and refreshing, down from some icy mountain fastness. The effect upon the No-vans was electrical. I would not have had to understand their language to realize that they were terrified. They looked apprehensively about and increased their speed as though endeavoring to overtake Ga-va-go, who was now far ahead with the point. A moment later a dash of rain struck us, and then it was every man for himself and the devil take the hindmost, as they broke into a wild stampede to place themselves close to their chief. Their hysterical flight was like the terrorized rush of wild cattle. They jostled and tripped one another, and stumbled and fell and were trampled upon, in their haste to escape.

Old Ga-va-go had stopped with his point, and was waiting for us. Those who accompanied him seemed equally terrified with the rest, but evidently they did not dare run until Ga-va-go gave the word. I think, however, that they all felt safer when they were close to him, for they had a great deal of confidence in him, yet they were still pretty badly frightened, and it would not have taken much to have set them off again into another rout. Ga-va-go waited until the last of the rearguard straggled in, and then he set off directly toward the mountains, the entire tribe moving in a compact mass, though they might have fallen easy prey to an ambush or any sudden attack. They knew, however, what I half guessed, that knowing that their enemies were as terrified of the storm as they, there was little danger of their being attacked—none whatever, in fact.

We came at last to a hillside covered with great trees which offered some protection from both the wind and the rain, which had now arisen to the proportion of a hurricane.

As we came to a halt, I slipped from the back of the warrior who had been carrying me, and found myself beside one of the women who had taught Orthis and me the language of the Va-gas.

"Why is everyone so terrified?" I asked her.

"It is Zo-al," she whispered, fearfully. "He is angry."

"Who is Zo-al?" I asked.

She looked at me in wide-eyed astonishment. "Who is Zo-al!" she repeated. "They told me that you said that you came from another world, and I can well believe it, when you ask, who is Zo-al?"

"Well, who is he?" I insisted.

"He is a great beast," she whispered. "He is everywhere. He lives in all the great holes in the ground, and when he is angry, he comes forth and makes the water fall and the air run away. We know that there is no water up there," and she pointed toward the sky. "But when Zo-al is angry, he makes water fall from where there is no water, so mighty is Zo-al, and he makes the air to run away so that the trees fall before it as it rushes past, and huts are knocked flat or carried high above the ground. And then, O terror of terrors, he makes a great noise, before which mighty warriors fall upon the ground and cover up their ears. We have angered Zo-al, and he is punishing us, and I do not dare to ask him not to send the big noise."

It was at that instant that there broke upon my ears the most terrific detonation that I have ever heard. So terrific was it that I thought my ear drums had burst, and simultaneously, a great ball of fire seemed to come rolling down from the mountain heights above us.

The woman, covering her ears, shuddered, and when she saw the ball of fire, she voiced a piercing shriek.

"The light that devours!" she cried. "When that comes too, it is the end, for then is Zo-al mad with rage."

The ground shook to the terrifying noise, and though the ball of fire did not pass close to us, still could I feel the heat of it even as it went by at a distance, leaving a trail of blackened and smoking vegetation in its rear. What flames there were, the torrential rain extinguished almost immediately. It must have traveled about ten miles, down toward the sea, across rolling hills and level valleys, when suddenly it burst, the explosion being followed by a report infinitely louder than that which I had first heard. An earthquake could scarce have agitated the ground more terrifyingly than did this peal of lunar thunder.

I had witnessed my first lunar electrical storm, and I did not wonder that the inhabitants of this strange world were terrified by it. They attribute these storms, as they do all their troubles. to Zo-al, a great beast, which is supposed to dwell in the depth of the lunar craters, the lower ends of which open into the interior lunar world. As we cowered there among the trees, I wondered if they were not afraid that the wind would blow the forest down and crush them, and I asked the woman who stood beside me.

"Yes," she said, "that often happens, but more often does it happen that if one is caught in a clearing, the air that runs away picks him up and carries him along to drop him from a great height upon the hard ground. The trees bend before they break, and those who watch are warned, and they escape destruction if they are quick. When the wind that runs seizes one, there is no escape."

"It seems to me," I said, "that it would have been safer if Ga-va-go had led us into one of those sheltered ravines," and I indicated a gorge in the hillside at our right.

"No," she said, "Ga-va-go is wise. He led us to the safest spot. We are sheltered from the air that runs away, and perhaps a little from the light that devours, nor can the waters that drown reach us here, for presently they will fill that ravine full."

Nor was she wrong. Rushing down from the hillside, the water poured in torrents into the ravine, and presently, though it must have been twenty or thirty feet deep, it was filled almost to overflowing. Whoever had sought refuge there, would have been drowned and washed away to the big ocean far below. It was evident that Ga-va-go had not been actuated solely by blind terror, though I came to know that he must have felt terror, for these terrible electrical storms alone can engender it in the breasts of these fearless and ferocious people.

The storm must have lasted for a considerable time; how long, of course, I do not know, but some idea of its duration may be gained by the fact that I became hungry and ate of the fruit of the trees, which sheltered us, at least six times, and slept twice. We were soaked to the skin and very cold, for the rain evidently came from a great altitude. During the entire storm, the No-vans scarcely moved from their positions beneath the trees, with their backs toward the storm, where they stood with lowered heads like cattle. We experienced twelve detonations of the ground-shaking thunder, and witnessed six manifestations of the light that devours. Trees had fallen all about us, and as far as we could see, the grasses lay flat and matted upon the ground. They told me that storms of the severity of this were infrequent, though rain and wind, accompanied by electrical manifestations, might be expected at any season of the year—I use that expression from habit, for one can scarcely say that there are any well-marked seasonal changes within the Moon that could indicate corresponding divisions of time as upon the Earth. From what I was able to gather from observation and from questioning the Vagas, lunar vegetation reproduces itself entirely independent of any seasonal restrictions, the frequency and temperature of the rains having, seemingly, the greatest influence in the matter. A period of drought and cold rains retards growth and germination, while frequent warm rains have an opposite effect, the result being that you find vegetation of the same variety in all stages of development, growing side by side—blossoms upon one tree, fruit upon another, and the dry seed-pods upon a third. Not even, therefore, by the growth of plant life, might one measure time within the Moon, and the period of gestation among the Va-gas is similarly irregular, being affected by the physical condition of the female as well as by climatic conditions, I imagine. When the tribe is well-fed, and the weather warm, the warriors victorious, and the minds of the women at peace, they bring forth their young in an incredibly short period. On the other hand, a period of cold, or of hunger, and of long marches, following defeat, induces an opposite result. It seems to me that the females nurse their young for a very short period of time, for they grow rapidly, and as soon as their molars are through, and they can commence eating meat, they are weaned. They are devilish little rascals, their youthful exuberance finding its outlet in acts of fiendish cruelty. As they are not strong enough to inflict their tortures on adults they perpetrate them upon one another, with the result that the weaker are often killed, after they are weaned and have left the protection of their savage mothers. Of course, they tried to play some of their fiendish tricks on Orthis and myself, but after we had knocked a few of them down, they left us severely alone.

During the storm, they huddled, shivering and cold, against the adults. Possibly I should be ashamed to say it, but I felt no pity for them, and rather prayed that they would all be chilled to death, so hateful and wantonly cruel were they. As they become adults, they are less wanton in their atrocities, though no less cruel, their energies, however, being intelligently directed upon the two vital interests of their lives—procuring flesh and women.

Shortly after the rain ceased, the wind began to abate, and as I was cold, cramped and uncomfortable, I walked out into the open, in search of exercise that would stimulate my circulation and warm me again. As I walked briskly to and fro, looking here and there at the evidences of the recent storm, my glance chanced to rise toward the sky, and there I saw what appeared at first to be a huge bird, a few hundred feet above the forest in which we had sought shelter. It was flapping its great wings weakly and seemed to be almost upon the verge of exhaustion, and though I could see that it was attempting to fly back in the direction of the mountains, the force of the wind was steadily carrying it in the direction of the lowlands and the sea. Presently it would be directly above me, and as it drew nearer, I knit my brows in puzzlement, for except for its wings, and what appeared to be a large hump upon its back, its form bore a striking resemblance to that of a human being.

Some of the No-vans evidently saw me looking upwards thus interestedly, and prompted by curiosity, joined me. When they saw the creature flying weakly overhead, they set up a great noise, until presently all the tribe had run into the open and were looking up at the thing above us.

The wind was lessening rapidly, but it still was strong enough to carry the creature gently toward us, and at the same time I perceived that whatever it was, it was falling slowly to the ground, or more correctly, sinking slowly.

"What is it?" I asked of the warrior standing beside me.

"It is a U-ga," he replied. "Now shall we eat."

I had seen no birds in the lunar world, and as I knew they would not eat the flying reptiles, I guessed that this must be some species of bird life, but as it dropped closer, I became more and more convinced that it was a winged human being, or at least a winged creature with human form.

As it fluttered toward the ground, the No-vans ran along to meet it, waiting for it to fall within reach. As they did so, Ga-va-go called to them to bring the creature to him alive and unharmed.

I was about a hundred yards from the spot, when the poor thing finally fell into their clutches. They dragged it to the ground roughly, and a moment later I was horrified to see them tear its wings from it and the hump from its back. There was a great deal of grumbling at Ga-va-go's order, as following the storm and their long fast, the tribe was ravenously hungry. "Flesh, flesh!" they growled. "We are hungry. Give us flesh!" But Ga-va-go paid no attention to them, standing to one side beneath a tree, awaiting the prisoner that they were bringing toward him.

CHAPTER VI

AN EXODUS AND A BATTLE

ORTHIS, who was becoming the almost constant companion of the chief, was standing beside the latter, while I was twenty-five or thirty yards away, and directly between Ga-va-go and the warriors who were approaching with the prisoner, who would of necessity have to pass close beside me. I remained where I was, therefore, in order to get a better look at it, which was rather difficult because it was almost entirely surrounded by No-vans. However as they came opposite me, there was a little break momentarily in the ranks, and I had my first opportunity, though brief, for a closer observation of the captive; and my comprehension was almost staggered by what my eyes revealed to me, for there before me, was as perfectly formed a human female as I had ever seen. By earthly standards, she appeared a girl of about eighteen, with hair of glossy blackness, that suggested more the raven's wing than aught else and a skin of almost marble whiteness, slightly tinged with a creamy shade. Only in the color of her skin did she differ from earthly women in appearance except that she seemed far more beautiful than they. Such perfection of features seemed almost unbelievable. Had I seen her first posed motionless, I could have sworn that she was chiseled from marble, yet there was nothing cold about her appearance. She fairly radiated life and feeling. If my first impression had been startling, it was nothing to the effect that was produced when she turned her eyes full upon me. Her black brows were two thin, penciled arches, beneath which were dark wells of light, vying in blackness with her raven hair. On either cheek was just the faintest suggestion of a deeper cream, and to think that these hideous creatures saw in that form divine only flesh to eat! I shuddered at the thought and then my eyes met hers and I saw an expression of incredulity and surprise registered in those liquid orbs. She half-turned her head as she was dragged past, that she might have a further look at me, for doubtless she was as surprised to see a creature like me as I was to see her.

Involuntarily I started forward. Whether there was an appeal for succor in those eyes I do not know, but at least they aroused within me instantly, that natural instinct of a human male to protect the weak. And so it was that I was a little behind her and to her right, when she was halted before Ga-va-go.

The savage Va-gas' chieftain eyed her coldly, while from all sides there arose cries of "Give us flesh! Give us flesh! We are hungry!" to which Ga-va-go paid not the slightest attention.

"From whence come you, U-ga?" he demanded.

Her head was high, and she eyed him with cold dignity as she replied, "From Laythe."

The No-van raised his brows. "Ah," he breathed, "from Laythe. The flesh of the women from Laythe is good," and he licked his thin lips.

The girl narrowed her eyes, and tilted her chin a bit higher. "Rympth!" she ejaculated, disgustedly.

As rympth is the name of the four-legged snake of Va-nah, the inner lunar world, and considered the lowest and most disgusting of created things, she could not well have applied a more opprobrious epithet to the No-van chieftain, but if it had been her intent to affront him, his expression gave no indication that she had succeeded.

"Your name?" he asked.

"Nah-ee-lah," she replied.

"Nah-ee-lah," he repeated. "Ah, you are the daughter of Sagroth, Jemadar of Laythe."

She nodded in indifferent affirmation, as though aught he might say was a matter of perfect indifference to her.

"What do you expect us to do with you?" asked Ga-va-go, a question which suggested a cat playing with a mouse before destroying it.

"What can I expect of the Va-gas, other than that they will kill me and eat me?" she replied.

A roar of savage assent arose from the creatures surrounding her. Ga-va-go flashed a quick look of anger and displeasure at his people.

"Do not be too sure of that," he snapped. "This be little more than a meal for Ga-va-go alone. It would but whet the appetite of the tribe."

"There are two more," suggested a bold warrior, close beside me, pointing at me and at Orthis.

"Silence!" roared Ga-va-go. "Since when did you become chief of the No-vans?"

"We can starve without a chief," muttered the warrior who had spoken, and from two or three about him arose grumblings of assent.

Swift, at that, Ga-va-go reared upon his hind feet, and in the same motion, drew and hurled his spear, the sharp point penetrating the breast of the malcontent, piercing his heart. As the creature fell, the warrior closest to him slit his throat, while another withdrew Ga-va-go's spear from the corpse, and returned it to the chief.

"Divide the carcass among you," commanded the chief, "and whosoever thinks that there is not enough, let him speak as that one spoke, and there shall be more flesh to eat."

Thus did Ga-va-go, chief of the No-vans, hold the obedience of his savage tribesmen. There was no more muttering then, but I saw several cast hungry eyes at me—hungry, angry eyes that boded me no good.

In what seemed an incredibly short space of time, the carcass of the slain warrior had been divided and devoured, and once again we set out upon the march, in search of new fields to conquer, and fresh flesh to eat.

Now Ga-va-go sent scouts far in advance of the point, for we were entering territory which he had not invaded for a long time, a truth which was evidenced by the fact that there were only about twenty warriors in the tribe, besides Ga-va-go, who were at all familiar with the territory. Naturally quarrelsome and disagreeable, the No-vans were far from pleasant companions upon that memorable march, since they had not recovered from the fright and discomforts of the storm and, in addition, were ravenously hungry. I imagine that none, other than Ga-va-go, could have held them. What his purpose was in preserving the three prisoners, that would have made such excellent food for the tribe, I did not know. However, we were not slain, though I judged the fellow who carried me, would much sooner have eaten me, and to vent his spite upon me he trotted as much as he could, and I can assure you that he had the most devilishly execrable trot I ever sat. I felt that he was rather running the thing into the ground, for he had an easy rack, which would have made it much more comfortable for both of us, and inasmuch as I knew that I was safe as long as I was under Ga-va-go's protection, I made up my mind to teach the fellow a lesson, which I finally did, although almost as much to my discomfort as his, by making no effort to ease myself upon his back so that at every step I rose high and came down hard upon him, sitting as far back as possible so as to pound his kidneys painfully. It made him very angry and he threatened me with all kinds of things if I didn't desist, but I only answered by suggesting that he take an easier gait, which at last he was forced to do.

Orthis was riding ahead with Ga-va-go, who as usual led the point, while the new prisoner astride a No-van warrior was with the main body, as was I.

Once the warriors that we bestrode paced side by side, and I saw the girl eyeing me questioningly. She seemed much interested in the remnants of my uniform, which must have differed greatly from any clothing she had seen in her own world. It seemed that she spoke and understood the same language that Ga-va-go used, and so at last I made bold to address her.

"It is unfortunate," I said, "that you have fallen into the hands of these creatures. I wish that I might be of service to you, but I also am a prisoner."

She acknowledged my speech with a slight inclination of her head, and at first I thought that she was not going to reply, but finally looking me full in the face she asked, "What are you?"

"I am one of the inhabitants of the planet Earth."

"Where is that, and what is planet?" she asked, for I had had to use the Earth word, since there is no word of similar meaning in the language of the Va-gas.

"You know, of course," I said, "that space outside of Va-nah is filled with other worlds. The closest to Va-nah is Earth, which is many, many times larger than your world. It is from Earth that I come."

She shook her head. "I do not understand," she said. She closed her eyes, and waved her hands with a gesture that might have included the universe. "All, all, is rock," she said, "except here in the center of everything, in this space we call Va-nah. All else is rock."

I suppressed a smile at the vast egotism of Va-nah, but yet how little different is it from many worldlings, who conceive that the entire cosmos exists solely for the inhabitants of Earth. I even know men in our own enlightened twenty-first century, who insist that Mars is not inhabited and that the messages that are purported to come from our sister planet, are either the evidences of a great world hoax, or the voice of the devil luring people from belief in the true God.

"Did you ever see my like in Va-nah?" I asked her.

"No," she replied, "I never did, but I have not been to every part of Va-nah. Va-nah is a very great world, and there are many corners of it of which I know nothing."

"I am not of Va-nah," I told her again, "I am from another world far, far away"; and then I tried to explain something of the universe to her—of the sun and the planets and their satellites, but I saw that it was as far beyond her as are the conceptions of eternity and space beyond the finite mind of Earth Men. She simply couldn't get it, that was all. To her, everything was solid rock that we know as space. She thought for a long time, though, and then she said, "Ah, perhaps after all there may be other worlds than Va-nah. The great Hoos, those vast holes that lead into the eternal rock, may open into other worlds like Va-nah. I have heard that theory discussed, but no one in Va-nah believes it. It is true, then!" she exclaimed brightly, "and you come from another world like Va-nah. You came through one of the Hoos, did you not?"

"Yes, I came through one of the Hoos," I replied—the word means hole in the Va-gas tongue—"but I did not come from a world like Va-nah. Here you live upon the inside of a hollow sphere. We Earth Men live upon the outside of a similar though much larger sphere."

"But what holds it up?" she cried, laughing. It was the first time that she had laughed, and it was a very contagious laugh, and altogether delightful. Although I knew that it would probably be useless, I tried to explain the whole thing to her, commencing with the nebular hypothesis, and winding up with the relations that exist between the Moon and the Earth. If I didn't accomplish anything else, I at least gave her something to distract her mind from her grave predicament, and to amuse her temporarily, for she laughed often at some of my statements. I had never seen so gay and vivacious a creature, nor one so entirely beautiful as she. The single, sleeveless, tunic-like garment that she wore, fell scarcely to her knees and as she bestrode the No-van warrior, it often flew back until her thighs, even, were exposed. Her figure was divinely perfect, its graceful contours being rather accentuated than hidden by the diaphanous material of her dainty covering; but when she laughed, she exposed two rows of even white teeth that would be the envy of the most beautiful of Earth Maids.

"Suppose," she said, "that I should take a handful of gravel and throw it up in the air. According to your theory the smaller would all commence to revolve about the larger and they would go flying thus wildly around in the air forever, but that is not what would happen. If I threw a handful of gravel into the air it would fall immediately to the ground again, and if the worlds you tell me of were cast thus into the air, they too would fall, just as the gravel falls."

It was useless, but I had known that from the beginning. What would be more interesting would be to question her, and that I had wished to do for some time, but she always put me off with a pretty gesture and a shake of her head, insisting that I answer some of her questions instead, but this time I insisted.

"Tell me, please," I asked, "how you came to the spot where you were captured, how you flew, and what became of your wings, and why, when they tore them from you, it did not injure you?"

She laughed at that quite merrily.

"The wings do not grow upon us," she explained, "we make them and fasten them upon our arms."

"Then you can support yourself in the air with wings fastened to your arms?" I demanded, incredulously.

"Oh, no," she said, "the wings we use simply for propelling ourselves through the air. In a bag, upon our backs, we carry a gas that is lighter than air. It is this gas which supports us, and we carry it in such quantities as to maintain a perfect equilibrium, so that we may float at any altitude, or with our wings rise or fall gently; but as I hovered over Laythe, came the air that runs, and seizing me with its strong arms bore me off across the surface of Va-nah. Futilely I fought against it until I was spent and weak, and then it dropped me into the clutches of the Va-gas, for the gas in my bag had become depleted. It was not intended to carry me aloft for any great length of time."

She had used a word which, when I questioned her, she explained so that I understood that it meant time, and I asked her what she meant by it and how she could measure it, since I had seen no indication of the Va-gas having any conception of a measurable aspect of duration.

Nah-ee-lah explained to me that the Va-gas, who were a lower order, had no means of measuring time, but that the U-ga, the race to which she belonged, had always been able to compute time through their observation of the fact that during certain periods the bottoms of the hoos, or craters, were illuminated, and for another period they were dark, and so they took as a unit of measure the total period from the beginning of this light in a certain crater to its beginning again, and this they called a *ula,* which corresponds with a sidereal month. By mechanical means they divide this into a hundred parts, called *ola,* the duration of each of which is about six hours and thirty-two minutes earth time. Ten ulas make a *keld,* which one might call the lunar year of about two hundred and seventy-two days earth time.

I asked her many questions and took great pleasure in her answers, for she was a bright, intelligent girl, and although I saw many evidences of regal dignity about her, yet her manner toward me was most natural and unaffected, and I could not help but feel that she occupied a position of importance among her own people.

Our conversation was suddenly interrupted, however, by a messenger from the point, who came racing back at tremendous speed, carrying word from Ga-va-go that the scouts were signaling that they had discovered a large village, and that the warriors were to prepare to fight.

Immediately we moved up rapidly to Ga-va-go, and then we all advanced toward the scout who could be seen upon a knoll far ahead. We were cautioned to silence, and as we moved at a brisk canter over the soft, pale lavender vegetation of the inner Moon, the feet of the Va-gas giving forth no sound, the picture presented to my earthly eyes was weird and mysterious in the extreme.

When we reached the scout, we learned that the village was situated just beyond a low ridge not far distant, so Ga-va-go gave orders that the women, the children, and the three prisoners should remain under a small guard where we were until they had topped the ridge, when we were to advance to a position where we might overlook the village, and if the battle was against the No-vans we could retreat to a point which he indicated to the warriors left to guard us. This was to be the rendezvous, for following defeat the Va-gas warriors scatter in all directions, thus preventing any considerable body of them being attacked and destroyed by a larger body of the pursuing enemy.

As we stood there upon the knoll, watching Ga-va-go and his savage warriors galloping swiftly toward the distant ridge, I could not but wonder that the inhabitants of the village which they were about to attack had not placed sentinels along the ridge to prevent just such a surprise as this, but when I questioned one of the warriors who had been left to guard us, he said that not all the Va-gas tribes were accustomed to posting sentinels when they felt themselves reasonably safe from attack. It had always been Ga-va-go's custom, however, and to it they attributed his supremacy among the other Va-gas tribes over a large territory.

"After a tribe has made a few successful raids and returned victorious, they are filled with pride," the warrior explained to me, "and presently they begin to think that no one dares to attack them and then they grow careless, and little by little the custom of posting sentinels drops into disuse. The very fact that they have no sentinels indicates that they are a large, powerful and successful tribe. We shall feed well for a long time."

The very idea of the thought that was passing through his mind was repellent in the extreme, and I fairly shuddered when I contemplated the callousness with which this creature spoke of the coming orgy, in which he hoped to devour flesh of his own kind.

Presently we saw our force disappear beyond the ridge, and then we too, advanced, and as we moved forward there came suddenly to us from the distance the fierce and savage war cry of the No-vans and a moment later it was answered by another no less terrible, rising from the village beyond the ridge. Our guards hastened us then, to greater speed, until, at a full run, we mounted the steep slope of the ridge and halted upon its crest.

Below us lay a broad valley, and in the center a long, beautiful lake, the opposite shore of which was clothed in forest while that nearest us was open and park-like, dotted here and there with beautiful trees, and in this open space we descried a large village.

The ferocity of the scene below us was almost indescribable. The No-vans warriors were circling the village at a rapid run, attempting to keep the enemy in a compact mass within, where it would present a better target for their spears. Already the ground was dotted with corpses. There were no wounded, for whenever one fell the nearest to him whether friend or foe cut his throat, since the victors would devour them all without partiality. The females and the young had taken refuge in the huts, from the doorways of which they watched the progress of the battle. The defenders attempted repeatedly to break through the circling No-vans. The warriors with whom I had been talking told me

that if they were successful the females and the young would
follow them through the break scattering in all directions, while
their warriors attempted to encircle the No-vans. It was almost
immediately evident that the advantage lay with the force that
succeeded in placing this swift-moving circle about its enemy,
and keeping the enemy within it until they had been dispatched,
for those in the racing circle presented a poor target, while the
compact mass of warriors milling in the center could scarce be
missed.

Following several unsuccessful attempts to break through
the ring of savage foemen the defenders suddenly formed
another smaller ring within, and moving in the opposite direction to the No-vans, raced in a rapid circle. No longer did they
cast spears at the enemy, but contented themselves with leaping
and bounding at a rapid gait. At first it seemed to me that they
had lost their heads with terror, but at last I realized that they
were executing a strategic maneuver which demonstrated both
cunning and high discipline. In the earlier stages of the battle
each side had depended for its weapons upon those hurled by the
opposing force, but now the defenders hurled no weapons, and
it became apparent that the No-vans would soon no longer have
spears to cast at them. The defenders were also lessening their
casualties by moving in a rapid circle in a direction opposite to
that taken by the attackers, but it must have required high courage and considerable discipline to achieve this result since it is
difficult in the extreme to compel men to present themselves
continuously as living targets for a foe while they themselves are
permitted to inflict no injury upon the enemy.

Ga-va-go apparently was familiar with the ruse, for suddenly
he gave a loud cry which was evidently a command. Instantaneously, his entire force wheeled in their tracks and raced in the
opposite direction paralleling the defenders of the village, and
immediately thereafter cast their remaining spears at comparatively easy targets.

The defenders, who were of the tribe called Lu-thans, wheeled
instantly to reverse the direction of their flight. Those wounded
in the sudden onslaught stumbled and fell, tripping and im-
peding the others, with the result that for an instant they were
a tangled mass, without order or formation. Then it was that
Ga-va-go and his No-vans leaped in upon them with their short,
wicked sword-daggers. At once the battle resolved itself into a
ferocious and bloody hand-to-hand conflict, in which daggers and
teeth and three-toed paws each did their share to inflict injury

upon an antagonist. In their efforts to escape a blow, or to place themselves in an advantageous position, many of the combatants leaped high into the air, sometimes between thirty and forty feet. Their shrieks and howls were continuous and piercing. Corpses lay piled so thick as to impede the movements of the warriors, and the ground was slippery with blood, yet on and on they fought, until it seemed that not a single one would be left alive.

"It is almost over," remarked the warrior at my side. "See, there are two or three No-vans now attacking each Lu-than."

It was true, and I saw that the battle could last but a short time. As a matter of fact it ended almost immediately, the remaining Lu-thans suddenly attempting to break away and scatter in different directions. Some of them succeeded in escaping, possibly twenty but I am sure that there were not more than that, and the rest fell.

Ga-va-go and his warriors did not pursue the few who had escaped, evidently considering that it was not worth the effort, since there were not enough of them to menace the village, and there was already plenty of meat lying fresh and warm upon the ground.

We were summoned now, and as we filed down into the village, great was the rejoicing of our females and young.

Guards were placed over the women and children of the defeated Lu-thans, and then at a signal from Ga-va-go, the No-vans fell upon the spoils of war. It was a revolting spectacle, as mothers devoured their sons, and wives, their husbands. I do not care to dwell upon it.

When the victors had eaten their fill, the prisoners were brought forth under heavy guard, and divided by the Va-gas between the surviving No-vans warriors. There was no favoritism shown in the distribution of the prisoners, except that Ga-va-go was given first choice, and received also those that remained after as nearly equal a distribution as possible had been made. I had expected that the male children would be killed, but they were not, being inducted into the tribe upon an equal footing with those that had been born into it.

Being capable of no sentiments of either affection or loyalty, it is immaterial to these creatures to what tribe they belong, but once inducted into a tribe, the instinct of self-preservation holds them to it, since they would be immediately slain by the members of any other tribe.

I learned shortly after this engagement that Ga-va-go had lost fully half his warriors, and that this was one of the most important battles that the tribe had ever fought. The spoils, however, had been rich, for they had taken over ten thousand women and fully fifty thousand young, and great quantities of weapons, harness, and apparel.

The flesh that they could not eat was wrapped up and buried, and I was told that it would remain in excellent condition almost indefinitely.

CHAPTER VII

THE MOON MAID ESCAPES

AFTER occupying the new village, Orthis and I were separated, he being assigned a hut close to Ga-va-go, while I was placed in another section of the village. If I could have been said to have been on good terms with any of the terrible creatures of the tribe, it was with the woman who had taught me the language of the Va-gas, and it was from her that I learned why Orthis was treated with such marked distinction by Ga-va-go, whom, it seemed, he had promised to lead to the land of our origin, where, he had assured the savage chieftain, he would find flesh in abundance.

Nah-ee-lah was confined in still another part of the village, and I only saw her occasionally, for it was evident that Ga-va-go wished to keep the prisoners separated. Upon one occasion when I met her at the shore of the lake I asked her why it was that they had not slain and eaten her, and she told me that when Ga-va-go had discovered her identity, and that her father was a Jemadar, a ruler of a great city, he had sent messengers with an offer to return Nah-ee-lah for a ransom of one hundred young women of the city of Laythe.

"Do you think your father will send the ransom?" I asked.

"I do not know," she replied. "I do not see how they are going to get a message to him, for ordinarily, my race kills the Va-gas on sight. They may succeed, however, but even so, it is possible that my father will not send the ransom. I would not wish him to. The daughters of my father's people are as dear to them, as am I to him. It would be wrong to give a hundred of the daughters of Laythe in return for one, even though she be the daughter of the Jemadar."

We had drunk, and were returning toward our huts when, wishing to prolong our conversation and to be with this pleasant companion while I might, I suggested that we walk farther into the woods and gather fruit. Nah-ee-lah signified her willingness, and together we strolled out of the village into the denser woods at its rear, where we found a particularly delicious fruit growing in abundance. I gathered some and offered it to her, but she refused, thanking me, saying that she had but just eaten.

"Do they bring the fruit to you," I asked, "or do you have to come and gather it yourself?"

"What fruit I eat I gather," she replied, "but they bring me flesh. It is of that which I have just eaten, and so I do not care for fruit now."

"Flesh!" I exclaimed. "What kind of flesh?"

"The flesh of the Va-gas, of course," she replied. "What other flesh might a U-ga eat?"

I fear that I ill-concealed my surprise and disgust at the thought that the beautiful Nah-ee-lah ate of the flesh of the Va-gas.

"You, too, eat of the flesh of these creatures?" I demanded.

"Why not?" she asked. "You eat flesh, do you not, in your own country. You have told me that you raise beasts solely for their flesh."

"Yes," I replied, "that is true, but we eat only the flesh of lower orders; we do not eat the flesh of humans."

"You mean that you do not eat the flesh of your own species," she said.

"Yes," I replied, "that is what I mean."

"Neither do I," she said. "The Va-gas are not of the same species as the U-ga. They are a lower order, just as are the creatures whose flesh you eat in your own country. You have told me of beef, and of mutton, and of pork, which you have described as creatures that run about on four legs, like the Va-gas. What is the difference, then, between the eating of the flesh of pork and beef or mutton, and the eating of Va-gas, who are low creatures also?"

"But they have human faces!" I cried, "and a spoken language."

"You had better learn to eat them," she said, "otherwise you will eat no flesh in Va-nah."

The more I thought about it the more reason I saw in her

point of view. She was right. She was no more transgressing any natural law in eating the flesh of the Va-gas than do we, eating the flesh of cattle. To her the Va-gas were less than cattle. They were dangerous and hated enemies. The more I analyzed the thing, the more it seemed to me that we humans of the earth were more surely transgressing a natural law by devouring our domestic animals, many of which we learned to love, than were the U-ga of Va-nah in devouring the flesh of their four-footed foes, the Va-gas. Upon our earthly farms we raise calves and sheep and little pigs, and oftentimes we become greatly attached to individuals and they to us. We gain their confidence, and they have implicit trust in us, and yet, when they are of the right age, we slay and devour them. Presently it did not seem either wrong or unnatural that Nah-ee-lah should eat the flesh of the Va-gas, but as for myself, I could never do it, nor ever did.

We had left the forest, and were returning to the village to our huts when, near the large hut occupied by Ga-va-go, we came suddenly upon Orthis. At the sight of us together he scowled.

"If I were you," he said to me, "I would not associate with her too much. It may arouse the displeasure of Ga-va-go."

It was the first time that Orthis had spoken to me since we had occupied this village. I did not like his tone or his manner.

"You will please to mind your own business, Orthis," I said to him, and continued on with Nah-ee-lah. I saw the man's eyes narrow malignantly, and then he turned, and entered the hut of Ga-va-go, the chief of the No-vans.

Every time I went to the river, I had to pass in the vicinity of Nah-ee-lah's hut. It was a little out of my way, but I always made the slight detour in the hope of meeting her, though I had never entered her hut nor called for her, since she had never invited me and realizing her position, I did not wish to intrude. I was of course ignorant of the social customs of her people, and feared offending her accidentally.

It chanced that the next time that I walked down to the lake shore, following our stroll in the woods, I made my usual detour that I might pass by the hut of Nah-ee-lah. As I came near I heard voices, one of which I recognized as that of Nah-ee-lah, and the other, a man's voice. The girl's tones were angry and imperious.

"Leave my presence, creature!" were the first words that I could distinguish, and then the man's voice.

"Come," he said, ingratiatingly. "Let us be friends. Come to

my hut, and you will be safe, for Ga-va-go is my friend." The
voice was the voice of Orthis.

"Go!" she ordered him again. "I would as soon lie with Ga-va-
go as with you."

"Know then," cried Orthis, angrily, "that you will go, whether
you wish it or not, for Ga-va-go has given you to me. Come!" and
then he must have seized her, for I heard her cry out, "How dare
you lay hands upon me, Nah-ee-lah, princess of Laythe!"

I was close beside the entrance to the hut now, and I did not
wait to hear any more, but thrusting the hanging aside entered.
There they were, in the center of the single room, Orthis struggling to drag the girl toward the opening while she resisted and
struck at him. Orthis' back was toward me and he did not know
that there was another in the hut until I had stepped up behind
him and grasping him roughly by the shoulder, had jerked him
from the girl and swung him about facing me.

"You cad," I said; "get out of here before I kick you out, and
don't ever let me hear of you molesting this girl again."

His eyes narowed, and he looked at me with an ugly light in
them. "Since boyhood, you have cheated me out of all that I
wished. You ruined my life on earth, but now, conditions are
reversed. The tables are turned. Believe me, then, when I tell
you that if you interfere with me you sign your own death warrant. It is only by my favor that you live at all. If I gave the word
Ga-va-go would destroy you at once. Go then to your hut and
stop your meddling in the affairs of others—a habit that you
developed in a most flagrant degree on Earth, but which will
avail you nothing here within the Moon. The woman is mine.
Ga-va-go has given her to me. Even if her father should fail to
send the ransom her life shall be spared as long as I desire her.
Your interference then can only result in your death, and do her
no good, for provided you are successful in keeping me from her,
you would be but condemning her to death in the event that her
father does not send the ransom, and Ga-va-go has told me that
there is little likelihood of that, since it is scarcely possible that
his messengers will be able to deliver Ga-va-go's demands to
Sagroth."

"You have heard him," I said, turning to the girl. "What are
your wishes in the matter? Perhaps he speaks the truth."

"I have no doubt but that he speaks the truth," she replied,
"but know, strangers, that the honor of a princess of Laythe is
dearer than her life."

"Very well, Orthis," I said to the man. "You have heard her. Now get out."

He was almost white with anger, and for a moment I thought that he was going to attack me, but he was ever a coward, and contenting himself with giving me a venomous look, he walked from the hut without another word.

I turned to Nah-ee-lah, after the hanging had dropped behind Orthis. "It is too bad," I said, "that with all your suffering at the hands of the Va-gas, you should also be annoyed by one who is practically of your own species."

"Your kindness more than compensates," she replied graciously. "You are a brave man, and I am afraid that you are going to suffer for your protection of me. This man is powerful. He has made wonderful promises to Ga-va-go. He is going to teach him how to use the strange weapons that you brought from your own world. The woman who brings me my meat told me of all this, and that the tribe is much excited by the promises that your friend has made to Ga-va-go. He will teach them to make the weapons, such as you slew their warriors with, so that they will be invincible, and may go abroad in Va-nah slaying all who oppose them and even raiding the cities of the U-ga. He has told them that he will lead them to the strange thing which brought you from your world to Va-nah, and that there they will find other weapons, like those that you carried, and having the noise which they make, and the things with which they kill. All these he says they may have, and that later he will build other things, such as brought you from your world to Va-nah, and he will take Ga-va-go and all the No-vans to what you call Earth."

"If there is any man in the universe who might do it, it is he," I replied, "but there is little likelihood that he can do it. He is merely deceiving Ga-va-go in the hope of prolonging his own life, against the possibility that an opportunity to escape will develop, in which event he will return to our ship and our friends. He is a bad man though, Nah-ee-lah, and you must be careful of him. There is a vacant hut near yours, and I will come and live in it. There is no use in asking Ga-va-go, for if he is friendly with Orthis, he will not permit me to make the change. If you ever need me, call 'Julian' as loud as you can, and I will come."

"You are very good," she said. "You are like the better men of Laythe, the high nobles of the court of the Jemadar, Sagroth, my father. They too are honorable men, to whom a woman may look for protection, but there are no others in all Va-nah since the Kalkars arose thousands of kelds ago, and destroyed the power of the nobles and the Jemadars, and all the civilization that was Va-nah's. Only in Laythe, have we preserved a semblance of the old order. I wish I might take you to Laythe, for there you would be safe and happy. You are a brave man. It is strange that you are not married."

I was upon the point of making some reply, when the hangings at the doorway parted, and a No-van warrior entered. Behind him were three others. They were walking erect, with drawn spears.

"Here he is," said the leader, and then, addressing me, "Come!"

"Why?" I asked. "What do you want of me?"

"Is it for you to question," he demanded, "when Ga-va-go commands?"

"He has sent for me?" I asked.

"Come!" repeated the leader, and an instant later they had hooked their spears about my arms and neck and none too gently they dragged me from the hut. I had something of a presentiment that this was to be the end. At the doorway I half turned to glance back at the girl. She was standing wide-eyed and tense, watching them drag me away.

"Good-bye—Julian," she said. "We shall never meet again for there is none to carry our souls to a new incarnation."

"We are not dead yet," I called back, "and remember if you need me call me," and then the hanging dropped behind us, and she was shut off from my vision.

They did not take me to my own hut, but to another, not far distant from Nah-ee-lah's, and there they bound my hands and feet with strips of leather and threw me upon the ground. Afterwards they left me, dropping the hanging before the entrance. I did not think that they would eat me, for Orthis had joined with me in explaining to Ga-va-go and the others that our flesh was poisonous, and though they may have questioned the veracity of our statements, nevertheless I was quite sure that they would not risk the chance of our having told the truth.

The Va-gas obtain their leather by curing the hides of their dead. The better portions they use for their trappings and harness. The other portions they cut into thin strips, which they use in lieu of rope. Most of this is very strong, but some of it is not, especially that which is improperly cured.

The warriors who had been sent to seize me had scarcely left the hut before I commenced working with my bonds in an attempt to loosen or break them. I exerted all my strength in the

effort, until I became sure that those which held my hands were
stretching. The effort, however, was very tiring, and I had to
stop often and rest. I do not know how long I worked at them,
but it must have been a very long time before I became convinced that however much they gave they were not going to
break. Just what I intended to do with my freedom I do not
know, since there was little or no chance that I might escape
from the village. Perpetual daylight has its disadvantages, and
this was one of them, that there was no concealing nocturnal
darkness during which I might sneak away from the village
unseen.

As I lay resting after my exertions, I suddenly became aware
of a strange, moaning sound from without, and then the hut
shook, and I realized that another storm had come. Soon after I
heard the beat of rain drops on the roof, and then a staggering,
deafening peal of lunar thunder. As the storm waxed in violence,
I could imagine the terror of the No-vans, nor even in my plight
could I resist the desire to smile at their discomfiture. I knew
that they must all be hiding in their huts, and again I renewed
my efforts to break the bonds at my wrists, but all to no avail;
and then suddenly, above the moaning of the wind and the beating of the rain, there came distinctly to my ears in a clear, full
voice, a single word: "Julian!"

"Nah-ee-lah," I thought. "She needs me. What are they doing
to her?" There flashed quickly before my mental vision a dozen
scenes, in each of which I saw the divine figure of the Moon
Maid, the victim of some fiendish brutality. Now she was being
devoured by Ga-va-go; now some of the females were tearing her
to pieces, and again the warriors were piercing that beautiful
skin with their cruel spears; or it was Orthis, come to claim
Ga-va-go's gift. It was this last thought, I think, which turned me
almost mad, giving to my muscles the strength of a dozen men. I
have always been accounted a powerful man, but in the instant
that that sweet voice came across the storm to find me, and my
imagination pictured her in the clutches of Orthis, something
within moved me to Herculean efforts far transcending aught
that I had previously achieved. As though they had been cotton
twine now, the leather bonds at my wrists snapped asunder, and
an instant later those at my ankles were torn away, and I was
upon my feet. I sprang to the door and into the open, where I
found myself in a maelstrom of wind and rain. In two bounds I
had cleared the space between the hut in which I had been
confined and that occupied by Nah-ee-lah, had torn the hanging

aside, and had sprung into the interior; and there I beheld the materialization of my last vision—there was Orthis, one arm about the slender body of the girl pinning her arms close to her side, while his other hand was at her throat, choking her and pressing her slowly backward across his knees toward the ground.

He was facing the door this time, and saw me enter, and as he realized who it was, he hurled the girl roughly from him and rose to meet me. For once in his life he seemed to know no fear, and I think that what with his passion for the girl, and the hatred he felt for me, and the rage that my interference must have engendered, he was momentarily insane, for he suddenly leaped upon me like a madman, and for an instant I came near going down beneath his blows—but only for an instant, and then I caught him heavily upon the chin with my left fist, and again, full in the face with my right, and though he was a splendid boxer, he was helpless in my hands. Neither of us had a weapon, or one of us certainly would have been killed in short order. As it was I tried to kill him with my bare fists, and at last, when he had fallen for the dozenth time, and I had picked him up and held him upon his feet and struck him repeatedly again and again, and he no longer moved I was sure that he was dead, and it was with a feeling of relief and of satisfaction in a duty well performed that I looked down upon his lifeless body. Then I turned to Nah-ee-lah.

"Come," I said, "there has been given to us this chance for escape. Never again may such a fortuitous combination of circumstances arise. The Va-gas will be hiding in their huts, crouching in terror of the storm. I do not know whither we may fly, but wherever it be, we can be in no greater danger than we are here."

She shuddered a little at the thought of going out into the terrors of the storm. Though not so fearful of it as the ignorant Va-gas, she still feared the wrath of the elements, as do all the inhabitants of Va-nah, but she did not hesitate, and as I stretched out a hand, she placed one of hers within it, and together we stepped out into the swirling rain and wind.

CHAPTER VIII

INTO THE MOUTH OF THE CRATER

NAH-EE-LAH and I passed through the village of the No-vans un-detected, since the people of Ga-va-go were cowering in their huts, terror-stricken by the storm. The girl led me immediately to high ground and upward along a barren ridge toward the high mountains in the distance. I could see that she was afraid though she tried to hide it from me, putting on a brave front that I was sure she was far from feeling. My respect for her increased, as I have always respected courage, and I believe that it requires the highest courage to do that which fills one with fear. The man who performs heroic acts without fear is less brave than he who overcomes his cowardice.

Realizing her fear I retained her hand in mine, that the contact might impart to her a little of the confidence that I felt, now that I was temporarily at least out of the clutches of the Va-gas.

We had reached the ridge above the village when the thought that we were weaponless and without means of protection overwhelmed me. I had been in so much of a hurry to escape the village that I had overlooked this very vital consideration. I spoke to Nah-ee-lah about it, telling her that I had best return to the village and make an effort to regain possession of my own weapons and ammunition. She tried to dissuade me, telling me that such an attempt was foredoomed to failure and prophesying that I would be recaptured.

"But we cannot cross this savage world of yours, Nah-ee-lah, without means of protection," I urged. "We do not know at what minute some fierce creature may confront us—think how helpless we shall be without weapons with which to defend ourselves."

"There are only the Va-gas," she said, "to fear in this part of Va-nah. We know no other dangerous beast, except the tor-ho. They are seldom seen. Against the Va-gas your weapons would be useless, as you already have discovered. The risk of meeting a tor-ho is infinitely less than that which you will incur if you attempt to enter Ga-va-go's hut to secure your weapons. You simply could not do it and escape, for doubtless the dwelling of the Chief is crowded with warriors."

I was compelled, finally, to admit the wisdom of her reasoning and to forego an attempt to secure my rifle and pistol, though I can assure you that I felt lost without them, especially when thus venturing forth into a new world so strange to me as Va-nah, and so savage. As a matter of fact, from what I gleaned from Nah-ee-lah, there was but a single spot upon the entire inner lunar world where she and I could hope to be even reasonably free from danger, and that was her native city of Laythe. Even there I should have enemies, she told me, for her race is ever suspicious of strangers; but the friendship of the princess would be my protection, she assured me with a friendly pressure of the hand.

The rain and wind must have persisted for a considerable time, for when it was finally over and we looked back through a clear atmosphere we found that a low range of mountains lay between us and the distant sea. We had crossed these and were upon a plateau at the foot of the higher peaks. The sea looked very far away indeed, and we could not even guess at the location of the No-vans village from which we had escaped.

"Do you think they will pursue us?" I asked her.

"Yes," she said; "they will try to find us, but it will be like looking for a raindrop in the ocean. They are creatures of the low-lands—I am of the mountains. Down there," and she pointed into the valley, "they might find me easily, but in my own mountains—no."

"We are near Laythe?" I asked.

"I do not know. Laythe is hard to find—it is well hidden. It is for this reason that it exists at all. Its founders were pursued by the Kalkars, and had they not found an almost inaccessible spot they would have been discovered and slain long before they could have constructed an impregnable city."

She led me then straight into the mighty mountains of the Moon, past the mouths of huge craters that reached through the lunar crust to the surface of the satellite, along the edges of yawning chasms that dropped three, four, yes, sometimes five miles, sheer into frightful gorges, and then out upon vast plateaus, but ever upward toward the higher peaks that seemed to topple above us in the distance. The craters, as a rule, lay in the deep gorges, but some we found upon the plateaus, and even a few opened into the summits of mountain peaks as do those upon the outer surface of planets. Those in the low places were, I believe, the openings through which the original molten lunar core was vomited forth by the surface volcanoes upon the outer crust.

Nah-ee-lah told me that the secret entrance to Laythe lay just below the lip of one of these craters, and it was this she sought. To me the quest seemed hopeless, for as far as the eye could reach lay naught but an indescribable jumble of jagged peaks, terrific gorges and bottomless craters. Yet always the girl seemed to find a way among or about them—instinctively, apparently, she found trails and footholds where there were no trails and where a chamois might have been hard put to it to find secure footing.

In these higher altitudes we found a vegetation that differed materially from that which grew in the lowlands. Edible fruits and berries were, however, still sufficiently plentiful to keep us reasonably well supplied with food. When we were tired we usually managed to find a cave in which we could rest in comparative security, and when it was possible to do so Nah-ee-lah always insisted upon barricading the entrance with rocks, since there was always the danger, she told me, of our being attacked by tor-hos. These bloodthirsty creatures while rare, were nevertheless very much to be feared, since not only were they voracious meat eaters and of such a savage disposition that they attacked nearly everything they saw in wanton ferocity, but even a minor wound inflicted by their fangs or talons often proved fatal, because of the fact that their principal diet was the poisonous flesh of the rympth and the flying toad. I tried to get Nah-ee-lah to describe the creature to me, but inasmuch as there was no creature with which we were both familiar that she might compare it with, I learned little more from her than that it stood between eighteen inches and two feet in height, had long, sharp fangs, four legs and was hairless.

As an aid to climbing, as well as to give me some means of protection, I broke a stout and rather heavy branch from one of the mountain trees, the wood of which was harder than any that I had seen growing in the lowlands. To roam a strange and savage world armed only with a wooden stick seemed to me the height of rashness, but there was no alternative until the time arrived when I might find the materials with which to fashion more formidable weapons. I had in mind a bow and arrows and was constantly on the lookout for wood which I considered adapted to the former, and I also determined to forego my cane for a spear whenever the material for the making of one came to hand. I had little time, however, for such things, as it seemed that when we were not sleeping we were constantly upon the move, Nah-ee-lah becoming more and more impatient to find her native city as the chances for so doing lessened—and it seemed to me that they were constantly lessening. While I was quite sure that she had no more idea where Laythe lay than I, yet we stumbled on and on and on, through the most stupendous mountain ranges that the mind of man can conceive, nor ever, apparently, did Nah-ee-lah discover a single familiar landmark upon which to hang a shred of hope that eventually we might come upon Laythe.

I never saw such a sanguine and hopeful person as Nah-ee-lah. It was her constant belief that Laythe lay just beyond the next mountain, in spite of the fact that she was invariably mistaken— which seemed never to lessen the exuberance of her enthusiasm for the next guess—which I knew beforehand was going to be a wrong guess.

Once just after we had rounded the shoulder of a mountain we came upon a little strip of level land clinging to the side of a mighty peak. I was in the lead—a position which I tried always to take when it was not absolutely necessary for Nah-ee-lah to go ahead in order to find a trail. As I came around the shoulder of the mountain, and in full sight of the little level area, I was positive that I saw a slight movement among some bushes at my right about halfway along one side of the little plain.

As we came abreast of the spot, upon which I kept my eye, there broke upon our ears the most hideous scream that I have ever heard, and simultaneously there leaped from the concealment of the bushes a creature about the size of a North American mountain lion, though quite evidently a reptile and probably a tor-ho, as such it proved to be. There was something about the head and face which suggested the cat family to me, yet there was really no resemblance between it and any of the earthly felines. It came at me with those terrible curved fangs bared and bristling and as it came it emitted the most terrifying sounds—I have called them screams, because that word more nearly describes them than any other, and yet they were a combination of shrieks and moans—the most blood-curdling that I have ever heard.

Nah-ee-lah grasped my arm. "Run!" she cried, "run." But I shook her loose and stood my ground. I wanted to run, that I will admit, but where to? The creature was covering the ground at tremendous speed and our only avenue of escape was the narrow trail over which we had just come, which clung precariously to the side of a perpendicular cliff. And so I stood there waiting, my feeble stick grasped in both hands. Just what I expected to do with it I scarcely knew until the tor-ho was upon me. Then I swung for its head as a batter swings for a pitched ball. I struck it square upon the nose—a terrific blow that not only stopped it, but felled it. I could hear the bones crushing beneath the impact of my crude weapon and I thought that I had done for the thing with that single blow, but I did not know the tremendous vitality of the creature. Almost instantly it was up and at me again, and again I struck it, this time upon the side of the head, and again I heard bones crush and again it fell heavily to the ground.

What appeared to be cold blood was oozing slowly from its wounded face as it came at me for the third time, its eyes glaring hideously, its broken jaws agape to seize me, while its shrieks and moans rose to a perfect frenzy of rage and pain. It reared up and struck at me with its talons now, but I met it again with my bludgeon and this time I broke a fore leg.

How long I fought that awful thing I cannot even guess. Time and time again it charged me furiously and each time, though often by but a miracle of fortune, I managed to keep it from closing, and each blow that I delivered crushed and maimed it a little more, until at last it was nothing but a bleeding wreck of pulp, still trying to crawl toward me upon its broken legs and seize me and drag me down with its broken, toothless jaws. Even then it was with the greatest difficulty that I killed it, that I might put it out of its misery.

Rather exhausted, I turned to look for Nah-ee-lah, and much to my surprise, I found her standing directly behind me.

"I thought you had run away," I said.

"No," she said, "you did not run and so I did not, but I never thought that you would be able to kill it."

"You thought that it would kill me, then?" I asked.

"Certainly," she replied. "Even now I cannot understand how you were able to overcome a tor-ho with that pitiful little stick of wood."

"But if you thought I was going to be killed," I insisted, "why was it that you did not seek safety in flight?"

"If you had been killed I should not have cared to live," she said simply.

I did not exactly understand her attitude and scarcely knew what reply to make.

"It was very foolish of you," I said at last, rather blunderingly, "and if we are attacked again you must run and save yourself."

She looked at me for a moment with a peculiar expression

upon her face which I could not interpret and then turned and resumed her way in the direction in which we had been traveling when our journey had been interrupted by the tor-ho. She did not say anything, but I felt that I had offended her and I was sorry. I did not want her falling in love with me, though, and according to earthly standards, her statement that she would rather die than live without me might naturally have been interpreted as a confession of love. The more I thought of it, however, as we moved along in silence, the more possible it seemed to me that her standards might differ widely from mine and that I was only proving myself to be an egotistical ass in assuming that Nah-ee-lah loved me. I wished that I might explain matters to her, but it is one of those things that is rather difficult to explain, and I realized that it might be made much worse if I attempted to do so.

We had been such good friends and our fellowship had been so perfect that the apparently strained silence which existed between us was most depressing. Nah-ee-lah had always been a talkative little person and always gay and cheerful, even under the most trying conditions.

I was rather tired out after my encounter with the tor-ho and should have liked to stop for a rest, but I did not suggest it, neither did Nah-ee-lah, and so we continued on our seemingly interminable way, though, almost exhausted as I was, I dropped some little distance behind my beautiful guide.

She was quite out of sight ahead of me upon the winding trail when suddenly I heard her calling my name aloud. I answered her as, simultaneously, I broke into a run, for I did not know but what she might be in danger, though her voice did not sound at all like it. She was only a short distance ahead and when I came in sight of her I saw her standing at the edge of a mighty crater. She was facing me and she was smiling.

"Oh, Julian," she cried, "I have found it. I am home and we are safe at last."

"I am glad, Nah-ee-lah," I said. "I have been much worried on account of the dangers to which you have been constantly subjected, as well as because of a growing fear that you would never be able to find Laythe."

"Oh, my!" she exclaimed, "I knew that I would find it. If I had to hunt through every mountain range in Va-nah I would have found it."

"You are quite sure that this is the crater where lies the entrance to Laythe?" I asked her.

"There is no doubt of it, Julian," she replied, and she pointed downward over the lip of the crater toward a narrow ledge which lay some twenty feet below and upon which I saw what appeared to be the mouth of a cave opening into the crater.

"But, how are we going to reach it?" I asked.

"It may be difficult," she replied, "but we will find a way."

"I hope so, Nah-ee-lah," I said, "but without a rope or wings I do not see how we are going to accomplish it."

"In the mouth of the tunnel," explained Nah-ee-lah, "there are long poles, each of which has a hook at one end. Ages ago there were no other means of ingress or egress to the city and those who came out to hunt or for any other purpose came through this long tunnel from the city, and from the ledge below they raised their poles and placed the hooked ends over the rim of the crater, after which it was a simple matter to clamber up or down the poles as they wished; but it has been long since these tunnels were used by the people of Va-nah, who had no further need of them after the perfection of the flying wings which you saw me using when I was captured by the Va-gas."

"If they used poles, so may we," I said, "since there are plenty of young trees growing close to the rim of the crater. The only difficulty will be in felling one of them."

"We can do that," said Nah-ee-lah, "if we can find some sharp fragments of stone. It will be slow work, but it can be done," and she started immediately to hunt for a fragment with a cutting edge. I joined her in the search and it was not long before we had discovered several pieces of obsidian with rather sharp edges. We then started to work upon a young tree about four inches in diameter that grew almost straight for a height of some thirty feet.

Cutting the tree down with our bits of lava glass was tedious work, but finally it was accomplished, and we were both much elated when the tree toppled and fell to the ground. Cutting away the branches occupied almost as long a time, but that, too, was finally accomplished. The next problem which confronted us was that of making the top of the pole secure enough to hold while we descended to the ledge before the mouth of the tunnel. We had no rope and nothing with which to fashion one, other than my garments, which I was loth to destroy, inasmuch as in these higher altitudes it was often cold. Presently, however, I hit upon a plan which, if Nah-ee-lah's muscles and my nerves withstood the strain it put upon them, bade fair to assure the success of our undertaking. I lowered the larger end of the pole over the side of the crater until the butt rested upon the ledge before the mouth of the tunnel. Then I turned to Nah-ee-lah.

"Lie down flat at full length, Nah-ee-lah," I directed her, "and hold this pole securely with both hands. You will only have to keep it from toppling to the sides or outward, and to that, I think, your strength is equal. While you hold it, I will descend to the mouth of the tunnel and raise one of the regular hooked poles which you say should be deposited there. If they are not, I believe that I can hold our own pole securely from below while you descend." She looked over into the vast abyss below and shuddered. "I can hold it at the top," she said, "if the bottom does not slip from the ledge."

"That is a chance that I shall have to take," I replied, "but I will descend very carefully and I think there will be little danger upon that score."

I could see, upon a more careful examination of the ledge below, that there was some danger of an accident such as she suggested.

Nah-ee-lah took her position as I had directed and lay grasping the pole securely in both hands at the rim of the crater, which was absolutely perpendicular at this point, and I prepared to make the perilous descent.

I can assure you that my sensations were far from pleasurable as I looked over into that awful abyss. The crater itself was some four or five miles in diameter, and, as I had every reason to suspect, extended fully two hundred and fifty miles through the lunar crust to the surface of the Moon. It was one of the most impressive moments of my life as I clung balancing upon the edge of that huge orifice, gazing into the silent, mysterious depths below. And then I seized the pole very gently and lowered myself over the edge.

"Courage, Julian!" whispered Nah-ee-lah; "I shall hold very tight."

"I shall be quite safe, Nah-ee-lah," I assured her. "I must be safe, for if I am not, how are you to reach the ledge and Laythe?"

As I descended very slowly I tried not to think at all, but to exclude from my mind every consideration of the appalling depths beneath me. I could not have been more than two feet from the ledge when the very thing that we both tried so hard to guard against transpired—a splintered fragment of the pole's butt crumpled beneath my weight and that slight jar was just sufficient to start the base of my precarious ladder sliding toward the edge of the narrow projection upon which I had rested it, and beyond which lay eternity. Above me I heard a slight scream and then the pole slipped from the ledge and I felt myself falling.

It was over in an instant. My feet struck the ledge and I threw myself within the mouth of the tunnel. And then, above me, I heard Nah-ee-lah's voice crying in agonized tones:

"Julian! Julian! I am falling!"

Instantly I sprang to my feet and peered upward from the mouth of the tunnel upon a sight that froze my blood, so horrifying did it seem, for there above me, still clinging to the pole, hung Nah-ee-lah, her body, with the exception of her legs, completely over the edge of the crater. Just as I looked up she dropped the pole and although I made a grab for it I missed it and it fell past me into the maw of the crater.

"Julian! Julian! You are safe!" she cried; "I am glad of that. It terrified me so when I thought you were falling and I tried my best to hold the pole, but your weight dragged me over the edge of the crater. Good-bye, Julian, I cannot hold on much longer."

"You must, Nah-ee-lah!" I cried; "do not forget the hooked poles that you told me of. I will find one and have you down in no time." And even as I spoke I turned and dove into the tunnel; but my heart stood still at the thought that the poles might not be there. My first glance revealed only the bare rock of walls and floor and ceiling and no hooked poles in sight. I sprang quickly farther into the tunnel which turned abruptly a few yards ahead of me and just around the bend my eyes were gladdened by the sight of a dozen or more of the poles which Nah-ee-lah had described. Seizing one of them, I ran quickly back to the entrance. I was almost afraid to look up, but as I did so I was rewarded by the sight of Nah-ee-lah's face smiling down at me—she could smile even in the face of death, could Nah-ee-lah.

"Just a moment more, Nah-ee-lah!" I cried to her, as I raised the pole and caught the hook upon the crater's rim. There were small protuberances on either side of the pole for its entire length, which made climbing it comparatively simple.

"Make haste, Julian!" she cried, "I am slipping."

It wasn't necessary for her to tell me to make haste. I think that I never did anything more quickly in my life than I climbed that pole, but I reached her not an instant too soon, for even as my arm slipped about her, her hold upon the ledge above gave way, and she came down head foremost upon me. I had no difficulty in catching her and supporting her weight. My only fear was that the hook above might not sustain the added weight under the strain of her falling body. But it held, and I blessed the artisan who had made it thus strong.

A moment later I had descended to the mouth of the tunnel and drawn Nah-ee-lah into the safety of its interior. My arm was still around her and hers about me as she stood there sobbing upon my breast. She was utterly relaxed and her supple body felt so helpless against me that there was suddenly aroused within me a feeling such as I had never experienced before—a rather indescribable feeling, yet one which induced, seemingly, an irresistible and ridiculous desire to go forth and slay whole armies of men in protection of this little Moon Maid. It must have been a sudden mental reversion to some ancient type of crusading ancestor of the Middle Ages—some knight in armor from whose loins I had sprung, transmitting to me his own flamboyant, yet none the less admirable, chivalry. The feeling rather surprised me, for I have always considered myself more or less practical and hard-headed. But more sober thought finally convinced me that it was but a nervous reaction from the thrilling moments through which we had both just passed, coupled with her entire helplessness and dependence upon me. Be that as it may, I disengaged her arms from about my neck as gently and as quickly as I could and lowered her carefully to the floor of the tunnel, so that she sat with her back leaning against one of the walls.

"You are very brave, Julian," she said, "and very strong."

"I am afraid I am not very brave," I told her. "I am almost weak from fright even now—I was so afraid that I would not reach you in time, Nah-ee-lah."

"It is the brave man who is afraid after the danger is past," she said. "He has no time to think of fear until after the happening is all over. You may have been afraid for me, Julian, but you could not have been afraid for yourself, or otherwise you would not have taken the risk of catching me as I fell. Even now I cannot understand how you were able to hold me."

"Perhaps," I reminded her, "I am stronger than the men of Va-nah, for my earthly muscles are accustomed to overcoming a gravity six times as great as that upon your world. Had this same accident happened upon Earth I might not have been able to hold you when you fell."

CHAPTER IX

THE FIGHT WITH THE KALKARS

THE tunnel in which I found myself and along which Nah-ee-lah led me toward the city of Laythe was remarkable in several particulars. It was largely of natural origin, seemingly consisting of a series of caves which may have been formed by bubbles in the cooling lava of the original molten flow and which had later been connected by man to form a continuous subterranean corridor. The caves themselves were usually more or less spherical in shape and the debris from the connecting passageways had been utilized to fill the bottoms of them to the level of the main floor of the passageway. The general trend of the tunnel was upward from the point at which we had entered it, and there was a constant draught of air rushing along it in the same direction in which we were moving, assuring me that it was undoubtedly well ventilated for its full length. The walls and ceiling were coated with a substance of which radium was evidently one of the ingredients, since even after we had lost sight of the entrance the passageway was well illuminated. We had been moving along in silence for quite a little distance when I finally addressed Nah-ee-lah.

"It must seem good," I said, "to travel again this familiar tunnel of your native city. I know how happy I should be were I thus approaching my own birthplace."

"I am glad to be returning to Laythe," she said, "for many reasons, but for one I am sorry, and as for this passageway it is scarcely more familiar to me than to you, since I have traversed it but once before in my life and that when I was a little girl and came here with my father and his court upon the occasion of his periodical inspection of the passageway, which is now practically never used."

"If you are not familiar with the tunnel," I asked, "are you sure that there is no danger of our going astray at some fork or branch?"

"There is but the one passageway," she replied, "which leads from the crater to Laythe."

"And how long is the tunnel?" I asked. "Will we soon enter the city?"

"No," she replied, "it is a great distance from the crater to Laythe."

We had covered some little distance at this time, possibly five or six miles, and she had scarcely ceased speaking when a turn in the passageway led us into a cave of larger proportions than any through which we had previously passed and from the opposite side of which two passageways diverged.

"I thought there were no branches," I remarked.

"I do not understand it," she said. "There is no branch from the tunnel of Laythe."

"Could it be possible that we are in the wrong tunnel?" I asked, "and that this does not lead to Laythe?"

"A moment before I should have been sure that we were in the right tunnel," she replied, "but now, Julian, I do not know, for never had I heard of any branch of our own tunnel."

We had crossed the cave and were standing between the openings of the two divergent passageways.

"Which one shall we take?" I asked, but again she shook her head.

"I do not know," she replied.

"Listen!" I cautioned her. "What was that?" For I was sure that I had heard a sound issuing from one of the tunnels.

We stood peering into an aperture which revealed about a hundred yards of the passageway before an abrupt turn hid the continuation of it from our view. We could hear what now resolved itself into the faint sound of voices approaching us along the corridor, and then quite suddenly the figure of a man appeared around the corner of the turn. Nah-ee-lah leaped to one side out of sight, drawing me with her.

"A Kalkar!" she whispered. "Oh, Julian, if they find us we are lost."

"If there is only one of them I can take care of him," I said.

"There will be more than one," she replied; "there will be many."

"Then, let us return the way we came and make our way to the top of the crater's rim before they discover us. We can throw their hooked poles into the crater, including the one which we use to ascend from the mouth of the tunnel, thus effectually preventing any pursuit."

"We cannot cross this room again to the tunnel upon the opposite side without being apprehended," she replied. "Our only hope is in hiding in this other tunnel until they have passed and trusting to chance that we meet no one within it."

"Come, then," I said. "I dislike the idea of flying like a scared rabbit, but neither would there be any great wisdom in facing armed men without a single weapon of defense."

Even as we had whispered thus briefly together, we found the voices from the other tunnel had increased and I thought that I noted a tone of excitement in them, though the speakers were still too far away for us to undertsand their words. We moved swiftly up the branch tunnel, Nah-ee-lah in the lead, and after passing the first turn we both felt comparatively safe, for Nah-ee-lah was sure that the men who had interrupted our journey were a party of hunters on their way to the outer world by means of the crater through which we had entered the tunnel and that they would not come up the branch in which we were hiding. Thus believing, we halted after we were safely out of sight and hearing of the large cave we had just left.

"That man was a Kalkar," said Nah-ee-lah, "which means that we are in the wrong tunnel and that we must retrace our steps and continue our search for Laythe upon the surface of the ground." Her voice sounded tired and listless, as though hope had suddenly deserted her brave heart. We were standing shoulder to shoulder in the narrow corridor and I could not resist the impulse to place an arm about her and comfort her.

"Do not despair, Nah-ee-lah," I begged her; "we are no worse off than we have been and much better off than before we escaped the Va-gas of Ga-va-go. Then do you not recall that you mentioned one drawback to your return to Laythe—that you might be as well off here as there? What was the reason, Nah-ee-lah?"

"Ko-tah wants me in marriage," she replied. "Ko-tah is very powerful. He expects one day to be Jemadar of Laythe. This he cannot be while I live unless he marries me."

"Do you wish to marry him?" I asked.

"No," she said; "not now. Before—" she hesitated—"before I left Laythe I did not care so very much; but now I know that I cannot wed with Ko-tah."

"And your father," I continued, "what of him—will he insist that you marry Ko-tah?"

"He cannot do otherwise," replied Nah-ee-lah, "for Ko-tah is very powerful. If my father refuses to permit me to marry him Ko-tah may overthrow him, and when my father is dead, should I still refuse to marry Ko-tah he may slay me, also, and then become Jemadar easily, for the blood of Jemadars flows in his veins."

"It appears to me, Nah-ee-lah, that you will be about as badly off at home as anywhere else in Va-nah. It is too bad that I cannot take you to my own Earth, where you would be quite safe, and I am sure, happy."

"I wish that you might, Julian," she replied simply.

I was about to reply when she placed slim fingers upon my lips. "Hush, Julian!" she whispered, "they are following us up this corridor. Come quickly, we must escape before they overtake us," and so saying, she turned and ran quickly along the corridor which led neither of us knew whither.

But we were soon to find out, for we had gone but a short distance when we came to the tunnel's end in a large circular chamber, at one end of which was a rostrum upon which were a massive, elaborately carved desk and a chair of similar design. Below the rostrum were arranged other chairs in rows, with a broad aisle down the center. The furniture, though of peculiar design and elaborately carved with strange figures of unearthly beasts and reptiles, was not, for all of that, markedly dissimilar to articles of the same purpose fabricated upon Earth. The chairs had four legs, high backs and broad arms, seeming to have been designed equally for durability, service, and comfort.

I glanced quickly around the apartment, as we first entered, only taking in the details later, but I saw that there was no other opening than the one through which we had entered.

"We will have to wait here, Nah-ee-lah," I said. "Perhaps, though, all will be well—the Kalkars may prove friendly."

She shook her head negatively. "No," she said, "they will not be friendly."

"What will they do to us?" I asked.

"They will make slaves of us," she replied, "and we shall spend the balance of our lives working almost continuously until we drop with fatigue under the cruelest of taskmakers, for the Kalkars hate us of Laythe and will hesitate at nothing that will humiliate or injure us."

She had scarcely ceased speaking when there appeared in the entrance of the cave the figure of a man about my own height dressed in a tunic similar to Nah-ee-lah's but evidently made of leather. He carried a knife slung in a scabbard depending from a shoulder belt, and in his right hand he grasped a slender lance. His eyes were close set upon either side of a prominent, hooked nose. They were watery, fishy, blue eyes, and the hair growing profusely above his low forehead was flaxen in color. His physique was admirable, except for a noticeable stoop. His feet were very large and his gait awkward when he moved. Behind him I could see the heads and shoulders of others. They stood there grinning at us for a moment, most malevolently, it seemed to me, and then they entered the cave—a full dozen of them. There were several types, with eyes and hair of different colors, the former ranging from blue to brown, the latter from light blond to almost black.

As they emerged from the mouth of the tunnel they spread out and advanced slowly toward us. We were cornered like rats in a trap. How I longed for the feel of my automatic at my hip! I envied them their slender spears and their daggers. If I could have but these I might have a chance at least to take Nah-ee-lah out of their clutches and save her from the hideous fate of slavery among the Kalkars, for I had guessed what such slavery would mean to her from the little that she had told me, and I had guessed, too, that she would rather die than submit to it. For my own part, life held little for me; I had long since definitely given up any hope of ever returning to my own world, or of finding the ship and being re-united with West and Jay and Norton. There came upon me at that moment, however, a sense of appreciation of the fact that since we had left the village of the No-vans I had been far from unhappy, nor could I attribute this to aught else than the companionship of Nah-ee-lah—a realization that convinced me that I should be utterly miserable were she to be taken from me now. Was I to submit supinely then, to capture and slavery for myself and worse than death for Nah-ee-lah, with the assurance of consequent separation from her? No. I held up my hand as a signal for the advancing Kalkars to halt.

"Stop!" I commanded. "Before you advance farther I wish to know your intentions toward us. We entered this tunnel, mistaking it for that which led to the city of my companion. Permit us to depart in peace and all will be well."

"All will be well, anyway," replied the leader of the Kalkars. "You are a strange creature, such as I have never before seen in Va-nah. Of you we know nothing except that you are not of the Kalkars, and therefore an enemy of the Kalkars, but this other is from Laythe."

"You will not permit us to go in peace, then?" I demanded.

He laughed sneeringly. "Nor in any other way," he said.

I had been standing in the aisle, with my hand upon one of

the chairs near the rostrum and now I turned to Nah-ee-lah who was standing close beside me.

"Come," I said to her, "follow me; stay close behind me."

Several of the Kalkars were coming down the main aisle toward us, and as I turned toward them from speaking to Nah-ee-lah, I raised the chair which my hand had been resting upon, and swinging it quickly around my head hurled it full in the face of the leader. As he went down Nah-ee-lah and I ran forward, gaining a little toward the opening of the tunnel, and then without pausing I hurled another chair and a third and a fourth, in rapid succession. The Kalkars tried to bring us down with their lances, but they were so busy dodging chairs that they could not cast their weapons accurately, and even those few which might otherwise have struck us were warded off by my rather remarkable engines of defense.

There had been four Kalkars advancing toward us down the center aisle. The balance of the party had divided, half of it circling the cave to the left and the other half to the right, with the evident intention of coming up the center aisle from behind us. This maneuver had started just before I commenced hurling chairs at the four directly in front of us, and now when those who had intended to take us from the rear discovered that we were likely to make our way through to the tunnel's entrance, some of them sprang toward us along the passageways between the chairs, which necessitated my turning and devoting a moment's attention to them. One huge fellow was in the lead, coming across the backs of the chairs leaping from seat to seat; and being the closest to me, he was naturally my first target. The chairs were rather heavy and the one that I let drive at him caught him full in the chest with an impact that brought a howl from him and toppled him over across the backs of the chairs behind him, where he hung limp and motionless. Then I turned my attention again to those before us, all of whom had fallen before my massive ammunition. Three of them lay still, but one of them had scrambled to his feet and was in the very act of casting his lance as I looked. I stopped the weapon with a chair and as the fellow went down I caught a glimpse of Nah-ee-lah from the corners of my eyes as she snatched the lance from the first Kalkar who had fallen and hurled it at someone behind me. I heard a scream of rage and pain and then I turned in time to see another of the Kalkars fall almost at my feet, the lance imbedded in his heart.

The way before us was temporarily open, while the Kalkars

behind us had paused, momentarily, at least, in evident consternation at the havoc I wrought with these unseemly weapons against which they had no defense.

"Get two knives and two lances from those who have fallen," I cried to Nah-ee-lah, "while I hold these others back."

She did as I bade, and slowly we backed toward the mouth of the tunnel. My chairs had accounted for half our enemies when at last we stood in the opening, each armed with a lance and a knife.

"Now, run, Nah-ee-lah, as you never ran before," I whispered to my companion. "I can hold them off until you have reached the mouth of the tunnel and clambered to the rim of the crater. If I am lucky, I will follow you."

"I will not leave you, Julian," she replied, "we will go together or not at all."

"But you must, Nah-ee-lah," I insisted, "it is for you that I have been fighting them. What difference can it make in my fate where I am when in Va-nah—all here are my enemies."

She laid her hand gently upon my arm. "I will not leave you, Julian," she repeated, "and that is final."

The Kalkars within the room were now advancing toward us menacingly.

"Halt!" I cried to them, "you see what fate your companions have met, because you would not let us go in peace. That is all we ask. I am armed now and it will be death to any who follow us."

They paused and I saw them whispering together as Nah-ee-lah and I backed along the corridor, a turn in which soon shut them from our view. Then we wheeled and ran like deer along the winding passageway. I did not feel very safe from capture at any time, but at least I breathed a sigh of relief after we had passed the chamber from which the Kalkars had run us into the *cul-de-sac*, and we had seen no sign of any other of their kind. We heard no sound of pursuit, but that in itself meant nothing, since the Kalkars are shod with soft leather sandals, the material for which, like all their other leather trappings, is made of the skins of Va-gas and of the prisoners from Laythe.

As we came to the pile of hooked poles which marked the last turn before the entrance of the tunnel I breathed an inward sigh of relief. Stooping, I gathered them all in my arms, and then we ran on to the opening into the crater, where I cast all but one of the poles into the abyss. That which I retained I hooked over the lip of the crater and then turning to Nah-ee-lah, I bade her ascend.

"You should have saved two of the poles," she said, "and then we could have ascended together; but I will make haste and you can follow me immediately, for we do not know but that they are pursuing us. I cannot imagine that they will let us escape thus easily."

Even as she spoke I heard the soft patter of sandal shod feet up the corridor.

"Make haste, Nah-ee-lah," I cried; "they come!"

Climbing a pole is slow work at best, but when one is suspended over the brink of a bottomless chasm and is none too sure of the security of the hook that is holding the pole above, one must needs move cautiously. Yet, even so, Nah-ee-lah scrambled upward so rapidly as to fill me with apprehension for her safety. Nor were my fears entirely groundless, for, standing in the mouth of the tunnel, where I could keep one eye upon Nah-ee-lah and the other toward the turn around which my pursuers would presently come in view, I saw the girl's hands grasp the rim of the crater at the very instant that the hook came loose and the pole dropped past me into the abyss. I might have caught it as it fell, but my whole mind was fixed upon Nah-ee-lah and her grave danger. Would she be able to draw herself upward, or would she fall? I saw her straining frantically to raise her body above the edge of the volcano, and then from up the corridor behind me came an exultant cry and I turned to face a brawny Kalkar who was racing toward me.

CHAPTER X

THE KALKAR CITY

Now, indeed, did I have reason to curse the stupidity that had permitted me to cast into the abyss all of the hooked poles save one, since even this one was now lost to me and I was utterly without means of escape from the tunnel.

As the fellow approached me at a rapid run I hurled my lance, but being unaccustomed to the weapon, I missed, and then he was upon me, dropping his own lance as he leaped for me, for it was evidently his desire to take me alive and unharmed. I thought that I was going to have him now, for I believed that I was more than a match for him, but there are tricks in every method of attack and this lunar warrior was evidently well schooled in his own methods of offense. He scarcely seemed to touch me, and yet he managed to trip me and push me simultaneously so that I fell heavily backward to the ground and turning a little sideways as I fell, I must have struck my head against the side of the tunnel, for that is the last that I remember until I regained consciousness in the very cave that Nah-ee-lah and I had reached when we saw the first of the Kalkars. I was surrounded by a party of eight of the Kalkars, two of whom were half carrying, half dragging me. I learned later that in the fight before the rostrum I had killed four of their number.

The fellow who had captured me was in very good humor, doubtless because of his success, and when he discovered that I had regained consciousness he started to converse with me.

"You thought that you could escape from Gapth, did you?" he cried, "but never; you might escape from the others, but not from me—no, not from Gapth."

"I did the principal thing that I desired to do," I replied, wishing to learn if Nah-ee-lah had escaped.

"What is that?" demanded Gapth.

"I succeeded in accomplishing the escape of my companion," I replied.

He made a wry face at that. "If Gapth had been there a moment earlier she would not have escaped, either," he said, and by that I knew that she had escaped, unless she had fallen back into the crater; and I was amply repaid for my own capture if it had won freedom for Nah-ee-lah.

"Although I did not escape this time," I said, "I shall next time."

He laughed a nasty laugh. "There will be no next time," he said, "for we are taking you to the city, and once there, there is no escape, for this is the only avenue by which you can reach the outer world and once within the city you never can retrace your steps to the mouth of the tunnel."

I was not so sure of that, myself, for my sense of direction and that of location are very well developed within me. The degree of perfection attained in orientation by many officers of the International Peace Fleet has been described as almost miraculous, and even among such as these my ability in this line was a matter of comment. I was glad, therefore, that the fellow had warned me, since now I should be particularly upon the watch for each slightest scrap of information that would fix in my memory whatever route I might be led over. From the cave in which I regained consciousness there was but a single route to the mouth of the tunnel, but from here on into the city I must watch every turn and fork and crossing and draw upon the tablets of my memory an accurate and detailed map of the entire route.

"We do not even have to confine our prisoners," continued Gapth, "after we have so marked them that their ownership may always be determined."

"How do you mark them?" I asked.

"With heated irons we make the mark of the owner here," and he touched my forehead just above my eyes.

"Pleasant," I thought to myself, and then aloud: "Shall I belong to you?"

"I do not know," he replied, "but you will belong to whomever The Twentyfour allot you."

We moved on after we left the cave for a considerable period of time in silence. I was busy making mental notes of every salient feature that might be useful to me in retracing my steps, but I found nothing other than a winding and gently ascending corridor, without crossings or branches until we reached the foot of a long flight of stone steps at the summit of which we emerged into a large chamber in the walls of which there must have been at least a dozen doorways, where, to my great disappointment, I was immediately blindfolded. They whirled me around then, but evidently it was done perfunctorily, since it was exactly one full turn and I was halted in my tracks facing precisely in the same direction that I had been before. This I was positive of, for our powers of orientation are often tested in this way in the air service. Then they marched me straight forward across the room through a doorway directly opposite that at which I had entered the chamber. I could tell when we left the larger chamber and entered the corridor from the different sound which our footsteps made. We advanced along this corridor ninety-seven paces, when we turned abruptly to the right and at the end of thirty-three paces emerged into another chamber, as I could easily tell again from the sound of our footsteps the instant we crossed the threshold. They led me about this chamber a couple of times with the evident intention of bewildering me, but in this they did not succeed, for when they turned again into a corridor I knew that it was the same corridor from which I had just emerged and that I was retracing my steps.

This time they took me back thirty-three paces and then turned abruptly to the right. I could not but smile to myself when I realized that we were now continuing directly along the same corridor as that which we had entered immediately after they had first blindfolded me, their little excursion through the short corridor into the second chamber having been but a ruse to bewilder me. A moment later, at the foot of a flight of steps they removed the blind, evidently satisfied that there was now no chance of my being able to retrace my steps and find the main tunnel leading to the crater, while, as a matter of fact, I could easily have retraced every foot of it blindfolded.

From here on we climbed interminable stairways, passed through numerous corridors and chambers, all of which were illuminated by the radium-bearing substance which coated their walls and ceilings, and then we emerged suddenly upon a terrace into the open air, and I obtained my first view of a lunar city. It was built around a crater, and the buildings were terraced back from the rim, the terraces being generally devoted to the raising of garden truck and the principal fruit-bearing trees and shrubs. The city extended upward several hundred feet, the houses, as I learned later, being built one upon another, the great majority of them, therefore, being without windows looking upon the outer world.

I was led along the terrace for a short distance, and during this brief opportunity for observation I deduced that the cultivated terraces lay upon the roofs of the tier of buildings next below. To my right I could see the terraced steps extending downward to the rim of the crater. Nearly all the terraces were covered with vegetation, and in numerous places I saw what appeared to be Va-gas feeding upon the plants, and this I later learned was the fact, and that the Kalkars, when they are able to capture members of the race of Va-gas, keep them in captivity and breed them as we breed cattle, for their flesh. It is necessary, to some extent, to change the diet of the Va-gas almost exclusively to vegetation, though this diet is supplemented by the flesh of the Kalkars, and their Laythean slaves who die, the Va-gas thus being compelled to serve the double purpose of producing flesh for the Kalkars and acting as their scavengers as well.

Upon my left were the faces of buildings, uniformly two stories in height, with an occasional slender tower rising fifteen, twenty or sometimes as high as thirty feet from the terraced roofs above. It was into one of these buildings that my captors led me after we had proceeded a short distance along the terrace, and I found myself in a large apartment in which were a number of male Kalkars, and at a desk facing the entrance a large, entirely bald man who appeared to be of considerable age. To this person I was led by Gapth, who narrated my capture and the escape of Nah-ee-lah.

The fellow before whom I had been brought questioned me briefly. He made no comment when I told him that I was from another world, but he examined my garments rather carefully and then after a moment turned to Gapth.

"We will hold him for questioning by The Twentyfour," he said. "If he is not of Va-nah he is neither Kalkar nor Laythean, and consequently, he must be flesh of a lower order and therefore may be eaten." He paused a moment and fell to examining a large book which seemed to be filled with plans upon which strange hieroglyphics appeared. He turned over several leaves, and finally coming evidently to the page he sought, he ran a forefinger slowly over it until it came to rest near the center of the plat. "You may confine him here," he said to Gapth, "in chamber eight of the twenty-fourth section, at the seventh elevation, and you will produce him upon orders from the Twentyfour when next they meet," and then to me: "It is impossible for you to escape from the city, but if you attempt it, it may be difficult for us to find you again immediately and when we do you will be tortured to death as an example to other slaves. Go!"

I went; following Gapth and the others who had conducted me to the presence of this creature. They led me back into the very corridor from which we had emerged upon the terrace and then straight into the heart of that amazing pile for fully half a mile, where they shoved me roughly into an apartment at the right of the corridor with the admonition that I stay there until I was wanted.

I found myself in a dimly lighted, rectangular room, the air of which was very poor, and at the first glance I discovered that I was not alone, for upon a bench against the opposite wall sat a man. He looked up as I entered and I saw that his features were very fine and that he had black hair like Nah-ee-lah. He looked at me for a moment with a puzzled expression in his eyes and then he addressed me.

"You, too, are a slave?" he asked.

"I am not a slave," I replied, "I am a prisoner."

"It is all the same," he said; "but from whence come you? I have never seen your like before in Va-nah."

"I do not come from Va-nah," I replied, and then I briefly explained my origin and how I came to be in his world. He did not understand me, I am sure, for though he seemed to be, and really was, highly intelligent, he could not conceive of any condition concerning which he had had no experience and in this way he did not differ materially from intelligent and highly educated Earth Men.

"And you," I asked, at length—"you are not a Kalkar? From whence come you?"

"I am from Laythe," he replied. "I fell outside the city and was captured by one of their hunting parties."

"Why all this enmity," I asked, "between the men of Laythe and the Kalkars—who are the Kalkars, anyway?"

"You are not of Va-nah," he said, "that I can see, or you would not ask these questions. The Kalkars derive their name from a corruption of a word meaning The Thinkers. Ages ago we were one race, a prosperous people living at peace with all the world of Va-nah. The Va-gas we bred for flesh, as we do today within our own city of Laythe and as the Kalkars do within their city. Our cities, towns and villages covered the slopes of the mountains and stretched downward to the sea. No corner of the three oceans but knew our ships, and our cities were joined together by a network of routes along which passed electrically driven trains"—he did not use the word trains, but an expression which might be literally translated as ships of the land—"while other great carriers flew through the air. Our means of communication between distant points were simplified by science through the use of electrical energy, with the result that those who lived in one part of Va-nah could talk with those who lived in any other part of Va-nah, though it were to the remotest ends of the world. There were ten great divisions, each ruled by its Jemadar, and each division vied with all the others in the service which it rendered to its people. There were those who held high positions and those who held low; there were those who were rich and those who were poor, but the favors of the state were distributed equally among them, and the children of the poor had the same opportunities for education as the children of the rich, and there it was that our troubles first started. There is a saying among us that 'no learning is better than a little,' and I can well believe this true when I consider the history of my world, where, as the masses became a little educated, there developed among them a small coterie that commenced to find fault with everyone who had achieved greater learning or greater power than they. Finally, they organized themselves into a secret society called the Thinkers, but known more accurately to the rest of Va-nah as those who thought that they thought. It is a long story, for it covers a great period of time, but the result was that, slowly at first, and later rapidly, The Thinkers, who did more talking than thinking, filled the people with dissatisfaction, until at last they arose and took over the government and commerce of the entire world. The Jemadars were overthrown and the ruling class driven from power, the majority of them being murdered, though some managed to escape, and it was these, my ancestors, who founded the city of Laythe. It is believed that there are other similar cities in remote parts of Va-nah inhabited by the descendants of the Jemadar and noble classes, but Laythe is the only one of which we have knowledge. The Thinkers would not work, and the result was that both government and commerce fell into rapid decay. They not only had neither the training nor the intelligence to develop new things, but they could not carry out the old that had been developed for them. The arts and sciences languished and died with commerce and government, and Va-nah fell back into barbarism. The Va-gas saw their chance and threw off the yoke that had held them through countless ages. As the Kalkars had driven the noble class into the lofty mountains, so the Va-gas drove the Kalkars. Practically every vestige of the ancient culture and commercial advancement of Va-nah has been wiped from the face of the world. The Laytheans have held their own for many centuries, but their numbers have not increased.

"Many generations elapsed before the Laytheans found sanctuary in the city of Laythe, and during that period they, too, lost all touch with the science and advancement and the culture of the past. Nor was there any way in which to rebuild what the Kalkars had torn down, since they had destroyed every written record and every book in every library in Va-nah. And so occupied are both races in eking out a precarious existence that there is little likelihood that there will ever again be any advancement made along these lines—it is beyond the intellectual powers of the Kalkars, and the Laytheans are too weak numerically to accomplish aught."

"It does look hopeless," I said, "almost as hopeless as our situation. There is no escape, I imagine, from this Kalkar city, is there?"

"No," he said, "none whatever. There is only one avenue and we are so confused when we are brought into the city that it would be impossible for us to find our way out again through this labyrinth of corridors and chambers."

"And if we did win our way to the outer world we would be as bad off, I presume, for we could never find Laythe, and sooner or later would be recaptured by the Kalkars or taken by the Vagas. Am I not right?"

"No," he said, "you are not right. If I could reach the rim of the crater beyond this city I could find my way to Laythe. I know the way well, for I am one of Ko-tah's hunters and am thoroughly familiar with the country for great distances in all directions from Laythe."

So this was one of Ko-tah's men. I was glad, indeed, that I had not mentioned Nah-ee-lah or told him of her possible escape, or of my acquaintance with her.

"And who is Ko-tah?" I asked, feigning ignorance.

"Ko-tah is the most powerful noble of Laythe," he replied, "some day he will be Jemadar, for now that Nah-ee-lah, the Princess, is dead, and Sagroth, the Jemadar, grows old, it will not be long before there is a change."

"And if the Princess should return to Laythe," I asked, "would Ko-tah still become Jemadar then, upon the death of Sagroth?"

"He would become Jemadar in any event," replied my companion, "for had the Princess not been carried off by the air that runs away, Ko-tah would have married her, unless she refused, in which event she might have died—people do die, you know."

"You feel no loyalty, then," I asked, "for your old Jemadar, Sagroth, or for his daughter, the Princess?"

"On the contrary, I feel every loyalty toward them, but like many others, I am afraid of Ko-tah, for he is very powerful and we know that sooner or later he will become ruler of Laythe. That is why so many of the high nobles have attached themselves to him—it is not through love of Ko-tah, but through fear that he recruits his ranks."

"But the Princess!" I exclaimed, "would the nobles not rally to her defense?"

"What would be the use?" he asked. "We of Laythe do but exist in the narrow confines of our prison city. There is no great future to which we may look forward in this life, but future incarnations may hold for us a brighter prospect. It is no cruelty, then, to kill those who exist now under the chaotic reign of anarchy which has reduced Va-nah to a wilderness."

I partially caught his rather hopeless point of view and realized that the fellow was not bad or disloyal at heart, but like all his race, reduced to a state of hopelessness that was the result of ages of retrogression to which they could see no end.

"I can find the way to the mouth of the tunnel where it opens into the crater," I told him. "But how can we reach it unarmed through a city populated with our enemies who would slay us on sight?"

"There are never very many people in the chambers or corridors far removed from the outer terraces, and if we were branded upon the forehead, as accepted slaves are, and your apparel was not so noticeable, we might possibly reach the tunnel without weapons."

"Yes," I said, "my clothes are a handicap. They would immediately call attention to us; yet, it is worth risking, for I know that I can find my way back to the crater and I should rather die than remain a slave of the Kalkars."

The truth of the matter was that I was not prompted so much by abhorrence of the fate that seemed in store for me, as by a desire to learn if Nah-ee-lah had escaped. I was constantly haunted by the horrid fear that her hold upon the rim of the crater had given and that she had fallen into the abyss below. Gapth had thought that she had escaped, but I knew that she might have fallen without either of us having seen her, since the pole up which she had clambered had been fastened a little beyond the opening of the tunnel, so that, had her hold become loosened, she would not have fallen directly past the aperture. The more I thought of it, the more anxious I became to reach Laythe and institute a search for her.

While we were still discussing our chances of escape, two slaves brought us food in the shape of raw vegetables and fruit. I scanned them carefully for weapons, but they had none, a circumstance to which they may owe their lives. I could have used their garments, had they been other than slaves, but I had hit upon a bolder plan than this and must wait patiently for a favorable opportunity to put it into practice.

After eating I became sleepy and was about to stretch out upon the floor of our prison when my companion, whose name was Moh-goh, told me that there was a sleeping apartment adjoining the room in which we were, that had been set apart for us.

The doorway leading to the sleeping chamber was covered by heavy hangings, and as I parted them and stepped into the adjoining chamber, I found myself in almost total darkness, the walls and ceiling of this room not having been treated with the illuminating coating used in the corridors and apartments which they wished to maintain in a lighted condition. I later learned that all their sleeping apartments were thus naturally dark. In one corner of the room was a pile of dried vegetation which I discovered must answer the purpose of mattress and covering, should I require any. However, I was not so particular, as I had been accustomed to only the roughest of fare since I had left my luxurious stateroom aboard *The Barsoom*. How long I slept I do not know, but I was awakened by Moh-goh calling me. He was leaning over me, shaking me by the shoulder.

"You are wanted," he whispered. "They have come to take us before The Twentyfour."

"Tell them to go to the devil," I said, for I was very sleepy and only half awake. Of course, he did not know what devil meant, but evidently he judged from my tone that my reply was disrespectful to the Kalkars.

"Do not anger them," he said, "it will only make your fate the harder. When The Twentyfour command, all must obey."

"Who are The Twentyfour?" I demanded.

"They compose the committee that rules this Kalkar city."

I was thoroughly awakened now and rose to my feet, following him into the adjoining chamber, where I saw two Kalkar warriors standing impatiently awaiting us. As I saw them a phrase leaped to my brain and kept repeating itself: "There are but two, there are but two."

They were across the room from us, standing by the entrance, and Moh-goh was close to me.

"There are but two," I whispered to him in a low voice, "you take one and I will take the other. Do you dare?"

"I will take the one at the right," he replied, and together we advanced across the room slowly toward the unsuspecting warriors. The moment that we were in reach of them we leaped for them simultaneously. I did not see how Moh-goh attacked his man, for I was busy with my own, though it took me but an instant to settle him, for I struck him a single terrific blow upon the chin and as he fell I leaped upon him, wresting his dagger from its scabbard and plunging it into his heart before he could regain his senses from the stunning impact of my fist. Then I turned to assist Moh-goh, only to discover that he needed no assistance, but was already arising from the body of his antagonist, whose throat was cut from ear to ear with his own weapon.

"Quick!" I cried to Moh-goh, "drag them into the sleeping apartment before we are discovered"; and a moment later we had deposited the two corpses in the dimly lighted apartment adjoining.

"We will leave the city as Kalkar warriors," I said, commencing to strip the accoutrements and garments from the man I had slain.

Moh-goh grinned. "Not a bad idea," he said. "If you can find the route to the crater it is possible that we may yet escape."

It took us but a few moments to effect the change, and after we had hidden the bodies beneath the vegetation that had served as a bed and stepped out into the other chamber, where we could have a good look at one another, we realized that if we were not too closely scrutinized we might pass safely through the corridors beneath the Kalkar city, for the Kalkars are a mongrel breed, comprising many divergent types. My complexion, which differed outrageously from that of either the Kalkars or the Laytheans, constituted our greatest danger, but we must take the chance, and at least we were armed.

"Lead the way," said Moh-goh, "and if you can find the crater I can assure you that I can find Laythe."

"Very good," I said, "come," and stepping into the corridor I moved off confidently in the direction that I knew I should find the passageways and stairs along which I had been conducted from the crater tunnel. I was as confident of success as though I were traversing the most familiar precinct of my native city.

We traveled a considerable distance without meeting anyone, and at last reached the chamber in which I had been blindfolded. As we entered it I saw fully a score of Kalkars lolling upon benches or lying upon vegetation that was piled upon the floor. They looked up as we entered, and at the same time Moh-goh stepped in front of me.

"Who are you and where are you going?" demanded one of the Kalkars.

"By order of The Twentyfour," said Moh-goh, and stepped into the room. Instantly I realized that he did not know in which direction to go, and that by his hesitancy all might be lost.

"Straight ahead, straight across the room," I whispered to him, and he stepped out briskly in the direction of the entrance to the tunnel. Fortunately for us, the chamber was not brilliantly lighted, and the Kalkars were at the far end of it; otherwise they must certainly have discovered my deception, at least, since any sort of close inspection would have revealed the fact that I was not of Va-nah. However, they did not halt us, though I was sure that I saw one of them eyeing me suspiciously, and I venture to say that I took the last twenty steps without drawing a breath.

It was quickly over, however, and we had entered the tunnel which now led without further confusing ramifications directly to the crater.

"We were fortunate," I said to Moh-goh.

"That we were," he replied.

In silence, then, that we might listen for pursuit, or for the sound of Kalkars ahead of us, we hastened rapidly along the descending passageway toward the mouth of the tunnel where it opened into the crater; and at last, as we rounded the last turn and I saw the light of day ahead of me, I breathed a deep sigh of relief, though almost simultaneously my happiness turned to despair at the sudden recollection that there were no hooked poles here to assist us to the summit of the crater wall. What were we to do?

"Moh-goh," I said, turning to my companion as we halted at the end of the tunnel, "there are no poles with which to ascend. I had forgotten it, but in order to prevent the Kalkars from ascending after me, I threw all but one into the abyss, and that one slipped from the rim and was lost also, just as my pursuers were about to seize me."

I had not told Moh-goh that I had had a companion, since it would be difficult to answer any questions he might propound on the subject without revealing the identity of Nah-ee-lah.

"Oh, we can overcome that," replied my companion. "We have these two spears, which are extremely stout, and inasmuch as we shall have plenty of time, we can easily arrange them in some way that will permit us to ascend to the summit of the crater. It is very fortunate that we were not pursued."

The Kalkar's spears had a miniature crescent-shaped hook at the base of their point similar to the larger ones effected by the Va-gas. Moh-goh thought that we could fasten the two spears securely together and then catch the small hook of the upper one upon the rim of the crater, testing its hold thoroughly before either of us attempted to ascend. Beneath his tunic he wore a rope coiled around his waist which he explained to me was a customary part of the equipment of all Laytheans. It was his idea to tie one end of this around the waist of whichever of us ascended first, the other going as far back into the tunnel as possible and bracing himself, so that in the event that the climber fell, he would be saved from death, though I figured that he would get a rather nasty shaking up and some bad bruises, under the best of circumstances.

I volunteered to go first and began fastening one end of the rope securely about my waist while Moh-goh made the two spears fast together with a short length that he had cut from the other end. He worked rapidly, with deft, nimble fingers, and seemed to know pretty well what he was doing. In the event that I reached the summit in safety, I was to pull up the spears and then haul Moh-goh up by the rope.

Having fastened the rope to my satisfaction, I stood as far out upon the ledge before the entrance to the tunnel as I safely could, and with my back toward the crater looked up at the rim twenty feet above me, in a vain attempt to select from below, if possible, a reasonably secure point upon which to hook the spear. As I stood thus upon the edge of eternity, steadying myself with one hand against the tunnel wall, there came down to me from out of the tunnel a noise which I could not mistake. Moh-goh heard it, too, and looked at me, with a rueful shake of his head and a shrug of his shoulders.

"Everything is against us, Earth Man," he said, for this was the name he had given me when I told him what my world was called.

CHAPTER XI

LAYTHE

THE pursuers were not yet in sight, but I knew from the nearness of the sound of approaching footsteps that it would be impossible to complete the splicing of the spears, to find a secure place for the hook above, and for me to scramble upward to the rim of the crater and haul Moh-goh after me before they should be upon us. Our position looked almost hopeless. I could think of no avenue of escape, and yet I tried, and as I stood there with bent head, my eyes cast upon the floor of the tunnel, they fell upon the neatly coiled rope lying at my feet, one end of which was fastened securely about my waist. Instantly there flashed into my mind a mad inspiration. I glanced up at the overhanging rim above me. Could I do it? There was a chance—the lesser gravity of the Moon placed the thing within the realm of

possibility, and yet by all earthly standards it was impossible. I
did not wait, I could not wait, for had I given the matter any
thought I doubt that I would have had the nerve to attempt it.
Behind me lay a cavern opening into the depths of space, into
which I should be dashed if my mad plan failed; but, what of
it? Better death than slavery. I stooped low, then, and concen-
trating every faculty upon absolute coordination of mind and
muscles, I leaped straight upward with all the strength of my
legs.

And in that instant during which my life hung in the balance,
of what did I think? Of home, of Earth, of the friends of my
childhood? No—of a pale and lovely face, with great, dark eyes
and a perfect forehead, surmounted by a wealth of raven hair. It
was the image of Nah-ee-lah, the Moon Maid, that I would have
carried with me into eternity, had I died that instant.

But, I did not die. My leap carried me above the rim of the
crater, where I lunged forward and fell sprawling, my arms and
upper body upon the surface of the ground. Instantly I turned
about and lying upon my belly, seized the rope in both hands.

"Quick, Moh-goh!" I cried to my companion below; "make
the rope fast about you, keep hold of the spears and I will drag
you up!"

"Pull away," he answered me instantly, "I have no time to
make the rope fast about me. They are almost upon me, pull
away and be quick about it."

I did as he bade, and a moment later his hands grasped the
rim of the crater and with my assistance he gained the top, dragging the spears after him. For a moment he stood there in silence
looking at me with a most peculiar expression upon his face;
then he shook his head.

"I do not understand, yet," he said, "how you did it, but it
was very wonderful."

"I scarcely expected to accomplish it in safety, myself," I replied, "but anything is better than slavery."

From below us came the voices of the Kalkars in angry altercation. Moh-goh picked up a fragment of rock, and leaning over
the edge of the crater, threw it down among them. "I got one,"
he said, turning to me with a laugh, "he tumbled off into nothing; they hate that. They believe that there is no reincarnation
for those who fall into a crater."

"Do you think that they will try to follow us?" I asked.

"No," he said, "they will be afraid to use their hooked poles
here for a long time, lest we should be in the neighborhood and

shove them off into the crater. I will drop another rock down if any of them are in sight and then we will go upon our way. I do not fear them here in the hills, anyway. There is always plenty of broken stone upon the level places, and we of Laythe are trained to use it most effectively—almost as far as I can throw, I can score a hit."

The Kalkars had withdrawn into the tunnel, so Moh-goh lost his opportunity to despatch another, and presently turned away from the crater and set out into the mountains, I following close behind.

I can assure you that I felt much better, now that I was armed with a spear and a knife, and as we walked I practiced casting stones, at Moh-goh's suggestion and under his instruction, until I became rather proficient in the art.

I shall not weary you with a narration of our journey to Laythe. How long it took, I do not know. It may have consumed a day, a week, or a month, for time seemed quite a meaningless term in Va-nah, but at length, after clambering laboriously from the bottom of a deep gorge, we stood upon the edge of a rolling plateau, and at some little distance beheld what at first appeared to be a cone-shaped mountain, rising fully a mile into the air above the surface of the plateau.

"There," cried Moh-goh, "is Laythe! The crater where lies the entrance to the tunnel leading to the city is beyond it."

As we approached the city, the base of which we must skirt in order to reach the crater beyond, I was able to obtain a better idea of the dimensions and methods of construction of this great interior lunar city, the base of which was roughly circular and about six miles in diameter, ranging from a few hundred to a thousand feet above the level of the plateau. The base of the city appeared to be the outer wall of an ancient extinct volcano, the entire summit of which had been blown off during some terrific eruption of a bygone age. Upon this base the ancient Laytheans had commenced the construction of their city, the houses of which rose one upon another as did those of the Kalkar city from which we had just escaped. The great age of Laythe was attested by the tremendous height to which these superimposed buildings had arisen, the loftiest wall of Laythe now rising fully a mile above the floor of the plateau. Narrow terraces encircled the periphery of the towering city, and as we approached more closely I saw doors and windows opening upon the terraces and figures moving to and fro, the whole resembling closely an enormous hive of bees. When we had reached a point near the base of the city, I saw that we had been discovered, for directly above us there were people at various points who were unquestionably looking down at us and commenting upon us.

"They have seen us from above," I said to Moh-goh, "why don't you hail them?"

"They take us for Kalkars," he replied. "It is easier for us to enter the city by way of the tunnel, where I shall have no difficulty in establishing my identity."

"If they think we are Kalkars," I said, "will they not attack us?"

"No," he replied, "Kalkars often pass Laythe. If they do not try to enter the city, we do not molest them."

"Your people fear them, then?" I asked.

"It practically amounts to that," he replied. "They greatly outnumber us, perhaps a thousand to one, and as they are without justice, mercy or honor we try not to antagonize them unnecessarily."

We came at length to the mouth of the crater, and here Moh-goh looped his rope about the base of a small tree growing close to the rim and slipped down to the opening of the tunnel directly beneath. I followed his example, and when I was beside him Moh-goh pulled the rope in, coiled it about his waist, and we set off along the passageway leading toward Laythe.

After my long series of adventures with unfriendly people in Va-nah, I had somewhat the sensation of one returning home after a long absence, for Moh-goh had assured me that the people of Laythe would receive me well and that I should be treated as a friend. He even assured me that he would procure for me a good berth in the service of Ko-tah. My greatest regret now was for Nah-ee-lah, and that she was not my companion, instead of Moh-goh. I was quite sure that she was lost, for had she escaped falling back into the crater outside the Kalkar city, I doubted that she could successfully have found her way to Laythe. My heart had been heavy since we had been separated, and I had come to realize that the friendship of this little Moon Maid had meant a great deal more to me than I had thought. I could scarcely think of her now without a lump coming into my throat, for it seemed cruel, indeed, that one so young and lovely should have met so untimely an end.

The distance between the crater and the city of Laythe is not great, and presently we came directly out upon the lower terrace within the city. This terrace is at the very rim of the crater around which Laythe is built. And here we ran directly into the arms of a force of about fifty warriors.

Moh-goh emerged from the tunnel with his spear grasped in both hands high above his head, the point toward the rear, and I likewise, since he had cautioned me to do so. So surprised were the warriors to see any creatures emerge from this tunnel, which had been so long disused, that we were likely to have been slain before they realized that we had come before them with the signal of peace.

The guard that is maintained at the inner opening of the tunnel is considered by the Laytheans as more or less of an honorary assignment, the duties of which are performed perfunctorily.

"What do you here, Kalkars?" exclaimed the commander of the guard.

"We are not Kalkars," replied my companion. "I am Moh-goh the Paladar, and this be my friend. Can it be that you, Ko-vo the Kamadar, do not know me?"

"Ah!" cried the commander of the guard, "it is, indeed, Moh-goh the Paladar. You have been given up as lost."

"I was lost, indeed, had it not been for this, my friend," replied Moh-goh, nodding his head in my direction. "I was captured by the Kalkars and incarcerated in City No. 337."

"You escaped from a Kalkar city?" exclaimed Ko-vo, in evident incredulity. "That is impossible. It never has been accomplished."

"But we did accomplish it," replied Moh-goh, "thanks to my friend here," and then he narrated briefly to Ko-vo the details of our escape.

"It scarce seems possible," commented the Laythean, when Moh-goh had completed his narrative, "and what may be the name of your friend, Moh-goh, and from what country did you say he came?"

"He calls himself Ju-lan-fit," replied Moh-goh, for that was as near as he could come to the pronunciation of my name. And so it was that as Ju-lan-fit I was known to the Laytheans as long as I remained among them. They thought that fifth, which they pronounced "fit," was a title similar to one of those which always followed the name of its possessor in Laythe, as Sagroth the Jemadar, or Emperor; Ko-vo the Kamadar, a title which corresponds closely to that of the English Duke; and Moh-goh the Paladar, or Count. And so, to humor them, I told them that it meant the same as their Javadar, or Prince. I was thereafter

placing myself in the camp of the enemy I might serve the father of Nah-ee-lah, I was justified in so doing.

I found myself in a rather peculiar position in the palace of Ko-tah, since I was supposed to know little or nothing of internal condition in Laythe, and yet had learned from both Nah-ee-lah and Moh-goh a great deal concerning the intrigues and politics of this lunar city. For example, I was not supposed to know of the existence of Nah-ee-lah. Not even did Moh-goh know that I had heard of her; and so until her name was mentioned, I could ask no questions concerning her, though I was anxious indeed, to discover if by any miracle of chance, she had returned in safety to Laythe, or if aught had been learned concerning her fate.

Ko-tah held me in conversation for a considerable period of time, asking many questions concerning Earth and my voyage from that planet to the Moon. I knew that he was skeptical, and yet he was a man of such intelligence as to realize that there must be something in the Universe beyond his understanding or his knowledge. His eyes told him that I was not a native of Va-nah, and his ears must have corroborated the testimony of his eyes, for try as I would, I never was able to master the Va-nahan language so that I could pass for a native.

At the close of our interview Ko-tah announced that Moh-goh would also remain in quarters in the palace, suggesting that if it was agreeable to me, my companion should share my apartments with me.

"Nothing would give me greater pleasure, Ko-tah the Java-dar," I said, "than to have my good friend, Moh-goh the Paladar, always with me."

"Excellent!" exclaimed Ko-tah. "You must both be fatigued. Go, therefore, to your apartments and rest. Presently I will repair to the palace of the Jemadar with my court, and you will be notified in sufficient time to prepare yourselves to accompany me."

The audience was at an end, and we were led by nobles of Ko-tah's palace to our apartments, which lay upon the second floor in pleasant rooms overlooking the terraces down to the brink of the great, yawning crater below.

Until I threw myself upon the soft mattress that served as a bed for me, I had not realized how physically exhausted I had been. Scarcely had I permitted myself to relax in the luxurious ease which precedes sleep ere I was plunged into profound slumber, which must have endured for a considerable time, since when I awoke I was completely refreshed. Moh-goh was already up and in the bath, a marble affair fed by a continuous supply of icy water which originated among the ice-clad peaks of the higher mountains behind Laythe. The bather had no soap, but used rough fibre gloves with which he rubbed the surface of his skin until it glowed. These baths rather took one's breath away, but amply repaid for the shock by the sensation of exhilaration and well being which resulted from them.

In addition to private baths in each dwelling, each terrace supported a public bath, in which men, women and children disported themselves, recalling to my mind the ancient Roman baths which earthly history records.

The baths of the Jemadar which I was later to see in the palace of Sagroth were marvels of beauty and luxury. Here, when the Emperor entertains, his guests amuse themselves by swimming and diving, which, from what I have been able to judge, are the national sports of the Laytheans. The Kalkars care less for the water, while the Va-gas only enter it through necessity.

I followed Moh-goh in the bath, in which my first sensation was that I was freezing to death. While we were dressing a messenger from Ko-tah summoned us to his presence, with instructions that we were to be prepared to accompany him to the palace of Sagroth the Jemadar.

CHAPTER XII

KO-TAH THREATENS THE PRINCESS

THE palace of the Emperor stands, a magnificent pile, upon the loftiest terrace of Laythe, extending completely around the enormous crater. There are but three avenues leading to it from the terraces below—three magnificent stairways, each of which may be closed by enormous gates of stone, apparently wrought from huge slabs and intricately chiselled into marvelous designs, so that at a distance they present the appearance of magnificent lacework. Each gate is guarded by a company of fifty warriors, their tunics bearing the imperial design in a large circle over the left breast.

The ceremony of our entrance to the imperial terrace was most gorgeous and impressive. Huge drums and trumpets blared forth a challenge as we reached the foot of the stairway which we were to ascend to the palace. High dignitaries in gorgeous trappings came down the steps to meet us, as if to formally examine the credentials of Ko-tah and give official sanction to his entrance. We were then conducted through the gateway across a broad terrace beautifully landscaped and ornamented by statuary that was most evidently the work of finished artists. These works of art comprised both life size and heroic figures of individuals and groups, and represented for the most part historic or legendary figures and events of the remote past, though there were also likenesses of all the rulers of Laythe, up to and including Sagroth the present Jemadar.

Upon entering the palace we were led to a banquet hall, where we were served with food, evidently purely in accordance with ancient court ceremonial, since there was little to eat and the guests barely tasted of that which was presented to them. This ceremony consumed but a few minutes of Earth time, following which we were conducted through spacious hallways to the throne room of the Jemadar, an apartment of great beauty and considerable size. Its decorations and lines were simple, almost to severity, yet suggesting regal dignity and magnificence. Upon a dais at the far end of the room were three thrones, that in the center being occupied by a man whom I knew at once to be Sagroth, while upon either side sat a woman.

Ko-tah advanced and made his obeisance before his ruler, and after the exchange of a few words between them Ko-tah returned and conducted me to the foot of Sagroth's throne.

I had been instructed that it was in accordance with court etiquette that I keep my eyes upon the ground until I had been presented and Sagroth had spoken to me, and that then I should be introduced to the Jemadav, or Empress, when I might raise my eyes to her, also, and afterward to the occupant of the third throne when I should be formally presented to her.

Sagroth spoke most graciously to me, and as I raised my eyes I saw before me a man of great size and evident strength of character. He was by far the most regal appearing individual my eyes had ever rested upon, while his low, well modulated, yet powerful voice accentuated the majesty of his mien. It was he who presented me to his Jemadav, whom I discovered to be a creature fully as regal in appearance as her imperial mate, and although doubtless well past middle age, still possessing remarkable beauty, in which was to be plainly noted Nah-ee-lah's resemblance to her mother.

Again I lowered my eyes as Sagroth presented me to the occupant of the third throne.

"Ju-lan the Javadar," he repeated the formal words of the presentation, "raise your eyes to the daughter of Laythe, Nah-ee-lah the Nonovar."

As my eyes, filled doubtless with surprise and incredulity, shot to the face of Nah-ee-lah, I was almost upon the verge of an exclamation of the joy and happiness which I felt in seeing her again and in knowing that she was safely returned to her parents and her city once more. But as my eyes met hers the exuberance of my spirit was as effectually and quickly checked by her cold glance and haughty mien as if I had received a blow in the face.

There was no hint of recognition in Nah-ee-lah's expression. She nodded coldly in acknowledgment of the presentation and then let her eyes pass above my head toward the opposite end of the throne room. My pride was hurt, and I was angry, but I would not let her see how badly I was hurt. I have always prided myself upon my control, and so I know that then I hid my emotion and turned once more to Sagroth, as though I had received from his daughter the Nonovar precisely the favor that I had a right to expect. If the Jemadar had noticed aught peculiar in either Nah-ee-lah's manner or mine, he gave no hint of it. He spoke again graciously to me and then dismissed me, with the remark that we should meet again later.

Having withdrawn from the throne room, Ko-tah informed me that following the audience I should have an opportunity to meet Sagroth less formally, since he had commanded that I remain in the palace as his guest during the meal which followed.

"It is a mark of distinction," said Ko-tah, "but remember, Ju-lan the Javadar, that you have accepted the friendship of Ko-tah and are his ally."

"Do not embroil me in the political intrigues of Laythe," I replied. "I am a stranger, with no interest in the internal affairs of your country, for the reason that I have no knowledge of them."

"One is either a friend or an enemy," replied Ko-tah.

"I am not sufficiently well acquainted to be accounted either," I told him; "nor shall I choose my friends in Laythe until I am better acquainted, nor shall another choose them for me."

"You are a stranger here," said Ko-tah. "I speak in your best interests, only. If you would succeed here; aye, if you would live, even, you must choose quickly and you must choose correctly. I, Ko-tah the Javadar, have spoken."

"I choose my own friends," I replied, "according to the dictates of my honor and my heart. I, Ju-lan the Javadar, have spoken."

He bowed low in acquiescence, and when he again raised his eyes to mine I was almost positive from the expression in them that his consideration of me was marked more by respect than resentment.

"We shall see," was all that he said, and withdrew, leaving me to the kindly attention of some of the gentlemen of Sagroth's court who had been standing at a respectful distance out of ear-shot of Ko-tah and myself. These men chatted pleasantly with me for some time until I was bidden to join Sagroth in another part of the palace.

I found myself now with a man who had evidently thrown off the restraint of a formal audience, though without in the slightest degree relinquishing either his dignity or his majesty. He spoke more freely and his manner was more democratic. He asked me to be seated, nor would he himself sit until I had, a point of Laythean court etiquette which made a vast impression on me, since it indicated that the first gentleman of the city must also be the first in courtesy. He put question after question to me concerning my own world and the means by which I had been transported to Va-nah.

"There are fragmentary, extremely fragmentary, legends handed down from extreme antiquity which suggest that our remote ancestors had some knowledge concerning the other worlds of which you speak," he said, "but these have been considered always the veriest of myths. Can it be possible that, after all, they are based upon truth?"

"The remarkable part of them," I suggested, "is that they exist at all, since it is difficult to understand how any knowledge of the outer Universe could ever reach to the buried depths of Va-nah."

"No, not by any means," he said, "if what you tell me is the truth, for our legends bear out the theory that Va-nah is located in the center of an enormous globe and that our earliest progenitors lived upon the outer surface of this globe, being forced at last by some condition which the legends do not even suggest, to find their way into this inner world."

I shook my head. It did not seem possible.

"And, yet," he said, noting the doubt that my expression evidently betrayed, "you yourself claim to have reached Va-nah from a great world far removed from our globe which you call the Moon. If you reached us from another world, is it then so difficult to believe that those who preceded us reached Va-nah from the outer crust of this Moon? It is almost an historic certainty," he continued, "that our ancestors possessed great ships which navigated the air. As you entered Va-nah by means of a similar conveyance, may not they have done likewise?"

I had to admit that it was within the range of possibilities, and in so doing, to avow that the Moon Men of antiquity had been millions of years in advance of their brethren of the Earth.

But, after all, was it such a difficult conclusion to reach when one considers the fact that the Moon, being smaller, must have cooled more rapidly than Earth, and therefore, provided that it had an atmosphere, have been habitable to man ages before man could have lived upon our own planet?

We talked pleasantly upon many subjects for some time, and then, at last, Sagroth arose.

"We will join the others at the tables now," he said, and as he led the way from the apartment in which we had been conversing alone, stone doors opened before us as by magic, indicating that the Jemadar of Laythe was not only well served, but well protected, or possibly well spied upon.

After we emerged from the private audience, guards accompanied us, some preceding the Jemadar and some following, and thus we moved in semi-state through several corridors and apartments until we came out upon a balcony upon the second floor of the palace overlooking the terraces and the crater.

Here, along the rail of the balcony, were numerous small tables, each seating two, all but two of the tables being occupied by royal and noble retainers and their women. As the Jemadar entered, these all arose, facing him respectfully, and simultaneously through another entrance, came the Jemadav and Nah-ee-lah.

They stood just within the room, waiting until Sagroth and I crossed to them. While we were doing so, Sagroth very courteously explained the procedure I was to follow.

"You will place yourself upon the Nonovar's left," he concluded, "and conduct her to her table precisely as I conduct the Jemadav."

Nah-ee-lah's head was high as I approached her and she vouchsafed me only the merest inclination of it in response to my respectful salutation. In silence we followed Sagroth and his Empress to the tables reserved for us. The balance of the company remained standing until, at a signal from Sagroth, we all took our seats. It was necessary for me to watch the others closely, as I knew nothing concerning the social customs of Laythe, but when I saw that conversation had become general I glanced at Nah-ee-lah.

"The Princess of Laythe so soon forgets her friends?" I asked.

"The Princess of Laythe never forgets her friends," she replied.

"I know nothing of your customs here," I said, "but in my world even royalty may greet their friends with cordiality and seeming pleasure."

"And here, too," she retorted.

I saw that something was amiss, that she seemed to be angry with me, but the cause I could not imagine. Perhaps she thought I had deserted her at the entrance to the tunnel leading to the Kalkar city. But no, she must have guessed the truth. What then, could be the cause of her cold aloofness, who, the last that I had seen of her, had been warm with friendship?

"I wonder," I said, trying a new tack, "if you were as surprised to see me alive as I you. I had given you up for lost, Nah-ee-lah, and I had grieved more than I can tell you. When I saw you in the audience chamber I could scarce repress myself, but when I saw that you did not wish to recognize me, I could only respect your desires."

She made no reply, but turned and looked out the window across the terraces and the crater to the opposite side of Laythe. She was ice, who had been almost fire. No longer was she little Nah-ee-lah, the companion of my hardships and dangers. No longer was she friend and confidante, but a cold and haughty Princess, who evidently looked upon me with disfavor. Her attitude outraged all the sacred tenets of friendship, and I was angered.

"Princess," I said, "if it is customary for Laytheans thus to cast aside the sacred bonds of friendship, I should do as well to be among the Va-gas or the Kalkars."

"The way to either is open," she replied haughtily. "You are not a prisoner in Laythe."

Thereafter conversation languished and expired, as far at least, as Nah-ee-lah and I were concerned, and I was more than relieved when the unpleasant function was concluded.

Two young nobles took me in charge, following the meal; as it seemed that I was to remain as a guest in the palace for awhile, and as I expressed a desire to see as much of the imperial residence as I might be permitted to, they graciously conducted me upon a tour of inspection. We went out upon the outer terraces which overlooked the valleys and the mountains, and never in my life have I looked upon a landscape more majestic or inspiring. The crater of Laythe, situated upon a broad plateau entirely surrounded by lofty mountains, titanic peaks that would dwarf our Alps into insignificance and reduce the Himalayas to foothills, lowered far into the distance upon the upper side, the iceclad summits of those more distant seemed to veritably topple above us, while a thousand feet below us the pinks and lavenders of the weird lunar vegetation lay like a soft carpet upon the gently undulating surface of the plateau.

But my guides seemed less interested in the scenery than in me. They plied me with questions continually, until I was more anxious to be rid of them than aught else that I could think of. They asked me a little concerning my own world and what I thought of Laythe, and if I found the Princess Nah-ee-lah charming, and my opinion of the Emperor Sagroth. My answers must have been satisfactory, for presently they came very close to me and one of them whispered:

"You need not fear to speak in our presence. We, too, are friends and followers of Ko-tah."

"The Devil!" I thought. "They are bound to embroil me in their petty intrigues. What do I care for Sagroth or Ko-tah or"— and then my thoughts reverted to Nah-ee-lah. She had treated me cruelly. Her cold aloofness and her almost studied contempt had wounded me, yet I could not say to myself that Nah-ee-lah was nothing to me. She had been my friend and I had been hers, and I should remain her friend to my dying day. Perhaps, then, if these people were bound to draw me into their political disputes, I might turn their confidences into profit for Nah-ee-lah. I had never told them that I was a creature of Ko-tah's, for I was not, nor had I ever told Ko-tah that I was an enemy to Sagroth; in fact, I had led him to believe the very opposite. And so I gave these two an evasive answer which might have meant anything, and they chose to interpret it as meaning that I was one of them. Well, what could I do? It was not my fault if they insisted upon deceiving themselves, and Nah-ee-lah might yet need the friendship that she had scorned.

"Has Sagroth no loyal followers, then," I asked, "that you are all so sure of the success of the *coup d'état* that Ko-tah plans?"

"Ah, you know about it then!" cried one of them. "You are in the confidence of the Javadar."

I let them think that I was. It could do no harm, at least.

"Did he tell you when it was to happen?" asked the other.

"Perhaps, already I have said too much," I replied. "The confidences of Ko-tah are not to be lightly spread about."

"You are right," said the last speaker. "It is well to be discreet, but let us assure you, Ju-lan the Javadar, that we are equally in the confidence and favor of Ko-tah with any of those who serve him; otherwise, he would not have entrusted us with a portion of the work which must be done within the very palace of the Jemadar."

"Have you many accomplices here?" I asked.

"Many," he replied, "outside of the Jemadar's guards. They remain loyal to Sagroth. It is one of the traditions of the organization, and they will die for him, to a man and," he added with a shrug, "they shall die, never fear. When the time arrives and the signal is given, each member of the guard will be set upon by two of Ko-tah's faithful followers."

I do not know how long I remained in the City of Laythe. Time passed rapidly, and I was very happy after I returned to the dwelling of Moh-goh. I swam and dived with them and their friends in the baths upon our terrace, and also in those of Ko-tah. I learned to use the flying wings that I had first seen upon Nah-ee-lah the day that she fell exhausted into the clutches of the Va-gas, and many were the lofty and delightful excursions we took into the higher mountains of the Moon, when Moh-goh or his friends organized pleasure parties for the purpose. Constantly surrounded by people of culture and refinement, by brave men and beautiful women, my time so filled with pleasurable activities that I made no effort to gauge it. I felt that I was to spend the balance of my life here, and I might as well get from it all the pleasure that Laythe could afford.

I did not see Nah-ee-lah during all this time, and though I still heard a great deal concerning the conspiracy against Sagroth, I presently came to attach but little importance to what I did hear, after I learned that the conspiracy had been on foot for over thirteen kelds, or approximately about ten earthly years, and seemed, according to my informers, no nearer consummation than it ever had been in the past.

Time does not trouble these people much, and I was told that it might be twenty kelds before Ko-tah took action, though on the other hand, he might strike within the next ola.

There was an occurrence during this period which aroused my curiosity, but concerning which Moh-goh was extremely reticent. Upon one of the occasions that I was a visitor in Ko-tah's palace, I was passing through a little used corridor in going from one chamber to another, when just ahead of me a door opened and a man stepped out in front of me. When he heard my footsteps behind him he turned and looked at me, and then stepped quickly back into the apartment he had just left and closed the door hurriedly behind him. There would have been nothing particularly remarkable in that, had it not been for the fact that the man was not a Laythean, but unquestionably a Kalkar.

Believing that I had discovered an enemy in the very heart of Laythe, I leaped forward, and throwing open the door, followed into the apartment into which the man had disappeared. To my astonishment, I found myself confronted by six men, three of whom were Kalkars, while the other three were Laytheans, and among the latter I instantly recognized Ko-tah, himself. He flushed angrily as he saw me, but before he could speak I bowed and explained my action.

"I crave your pardon, Javadar," I said. "I thought that I saw an enemy of Laythe in the heart of your palace, and that by apprehending him I should serve you best"; and I started to withdraw from the chamber.

"Wait," he said. "You did right, but lest you misunderstand their presence here, I may tell you that these three are prisoners."

"I realized that at once when I saw you, Javadar," I replied, though I knew perfectly that he had lied to me; and then I backed from the room, closing the door after me.

I spoke to Moh-goh about it the next time that I saw him.

"You saw nothing, my friend," he said. "Remember that—you saw nothing."

"If you mean that it is none of my business, Moh-goh," I replied, "I perfectly agree with you, and you may rest assured that I shall not meddle in affairs that do not concern me."

However, I did considerable thinking upon the matter, and possibly I went out of my way a little more than one should who is attending strictly to his own business, that I might keep a little in touch with the course of the conspiracy, for no matter what I had said to Moh-goh, no matter how I attempted to convince myself that it did not interest me, the truth remained that anything that affected in any way the fate of Nah-ee-lah transcended in interest any event which might transpire within Vanah, in so far as I was concerned.

The unobtrusive espionage which I practiced bore fruit, to the extent that it permitted me to know that on at least three other occasions delegations of Kalkars visited Ko-tah.

The fact that this ancient palace of the Prince of Laythe was a never-ending source of interest to me aided me in my self-imposed task of spying upon the conspirators, for the retainers of Ko-tah were quite accustomed to see me in out-of-the-way corridors and passages, oftentimes far from the inhabited portions of the building.

Upon the occasion of one of these tours I had descended to a lower terrace, along an ancient stone stairway which wound spirally downward and had discovered a dimly lighted room in which were stored a number of ancient works of art. I was quietly examining these, when I heard voices in an adjoining chamber.

"Upon no other conditions will he assist you, Javadar," said the speaker, whose voice I first heard.

"His demands are outrageous," replied a second speaker. "I refuse to consider them. Laythe is impregnable. He can never take it." The voice was that of Ko-tah.

"You do not know him, Laythean," replied the other. "He has given us engines of destruction with which we can destroy any city in Va-nah. He will give you Laythe. Is that not enough?"

"But he will be Jemadar of Jemadars and rule us all!" exclaimed Ko-tah. "The Jemadar of Laythe can be subservient to none."

"If you do not accede he will take Laythe in spite of you and reduce you to the status of a slave."

"Enough, Kalkar!" cried Ko-tah, his voice trembling with rage. "Be gone! Tell your master that Ko-tah refuses his base demands."

"You will regret it, Laythean," replied the Kalkar, "for you do not know what this creature has brought from another world in knowledge of war and the science of destruction of human life."

"I do not fear him," snapped Ko-tah, "my swords are many, my spearmen are well trained. Be gone, and do not return until your master is ready to sue with Ko-tah for an alliance."

I heard receding footsteps then, and following that, a silence which I thought indicated that all had left the chamber, but presently I heard Ko-tah's voice again.

"What think you of it?" he asked. And then I heard the voice of a third man, evidently a Laythean, replying:

"I think that if there is any truth in the fellow's assertions, we may not too quickly bring about the fall of Sagroth and place you upon the throne of Laythe, for only thus may we stand united against a common outside enemy."

"You are right," replied the Javadar. "Gather our forces. We shall strike within the ola."

I wanted to hear more, but they passed out of the chamber then, and their voices became only a subdued murmur which quickly trailed off into silence. What should I do? Within six hours Ko-tah would strike at the power of Sagroth, and I well knew what that would mean to Nah-ee-lah; either marriage with the new Jemadar, or death, and I guessed that the proud Princess would choose the latter in preference to Ko-tah.

CHAPTER XIII

KO-TAH IS KILLED

As rapidly as I could I made my way from the palace of Ko-tah, and upward, terrace by terrace, toward the palace of the Jemadar. I had never presented myself at Sagroth's palace since Nah-ee-lah had so grievously offended me. I did not even know the customary procedure to follow to gain an audience with the Emperor, but nevertheless I came boldly to the carven gates and demanded to speak with the officer in command of the guards. When he came I told him that I desired to speak either with Sagroth or the Princess Nah-ee-lah at once, upon a matter of the most urgent importance.

"Wait," he said, "and I will take your message to the Jemadar."

He was gone for what seemed to me a very long time, but at last he returned, saying that Sagroth would see me at once, and I was conducted through the gates and into the palace toward the small audience chamber in which Sagroth had once received me so graciously. As I was ushered into the room I found myself facing both Sagroth and Nah-ee-lah. The attitude of the Jemadar seemed apparently judicial, but that of the Princess was openly hostile.

"What are you doing here, traitor?" she demanded, without waiting for Sagroth to speak, and at the same instant a door upon the opposite side of the room burst open and three warriors leaped into the apartment with bared swords. They wore the livery of Ko-tah, and I knew instantly the purpose for which they had come. Drawing my own sword, I leaped forward.

"I have come to defend the life of the Jemadar and his Princess," I cried, as I sprang between them and the advancing three. "What means this?" demanded Sagroth. "How dare you enter the presence of your Jemadar with drawn sword?"

"They are the assassins of Ko-tah come to slay you!" I cried. "Defend yourself, Sagroth of Laythe!" And with that, I tried to engage the three until help arrived.

I am no novice with the sword. The art of fencing has been one of my chief diversions since my cadet days in the Air School, and I did not fear the Laytheans, though I knew that, even were they but mediocre swordsmen, I could not for long withstand the assaults of three at once. But upon this point I need not have concerned myself, for no sooner had I spoken than Sagroth's sword leaped from its scabbard, and placing himself at my side, he fought nobly and well in defense of his life and his honor.

One of our antagonists merely tried to engage me while the other two assassinated the Jemadar. And so, seeing that he was playing me, and that I could do with him about as I pleased if I did not push him too hard, I drove him back a few steps until I was close at the side of one of those who engaged Sagroth. Then before any could know my intention, I wheeled and lunged my sword through the heart of one of those who opposed the father of Nah-ee-lah. So quickly had I disengaged my former antagonist, so swift my lunge, that I had recovered and was ready to meet the renewed assaults of the first who had engaged me almost before he realized what had happened.

It was man against man, now, and the odds were even. I had no opportunity to watch Sagroth, but from the ring of steel on steel, I knew that the two were bitterly engaged. My own man kept me well occupied. He was a magnificent swordsman, but he was only fighting for his life; I was fighting for more—for my life and for my honor, too, since after the word "traitor" that Nah-ee-lah had hurled at me, I had felt that I must redeem myself in her eyes. I did not give any thought at all to the question as to just why I should care what Nah-ee-lah the Moon Maid thought of me, but something within me reacted mightily to the contempt that she had put into that single word.

I could catch an occasional glimpse of her standing there behind the massive desk at which her father had sat upon the first occasion of my coming to this chamber. She stood there very tense, her wide eyes fixed upon me in evident incredulity.

I had almost worn my man down and we were fighting now so that I was facing Nah-ee-lah, with my back toward the doorway through which the three assassins had entered. Sagroth must have been more than holding his own, too, for I could see his opponent slowly falling back before the older man's assaults. And then there broke above the clang of steel a girl's voice—Nah-ee-lah's—raised in accents of fear.

"Julian, beware! Behind you! Behind you!"

At the instant of her warning the eyes of my antagonist left mine, which, for his own good, they never should have done, and passed in a quick glance over my shoulder at something or someone behind me. His lack of concentration cost him his life. I saw my opening the instant that it was made, and with a quick lunge I passed my blade through his heart. Whipping it out again, I wheeled to face a dozen men springing into the chamber. They paid no attention to me, but leaped toward Sagroth, and before I could prevent he went down with half a dozen blades through his body.

Upon the opposite side of the desk from us was another doorway directly behind Nah-ee-lah, and in the instant that she saw Sagroth fall, she called to me in a low voice: "Come, Julian, quick! Or we, too, are lost."

Realizing that the Jemadar was dead and that it would be folly to remain and attempt to fight this whole roomful of warriors, I leaped the desk and followed Nah-ee-lah through the doorway beyond. There was a cry, then, from someone within the room, to stop us, but Nah-ee-lah wheeled and slammed the door in their faces as they rushed forward, fastened it upon our side and then turned to me.

"Julian," she said, "how can you ever forgive me? You who have risked your life for the Jemadar, my father, in spite of the contemptible treatment that in my ignorance I have accorded you?"

"I could have explained," I said, "but you would not let me. Appearances were against me, and so I cannot blame you for thinking as you did."

"It was wicked of me not to listen to you, Julian, but I thought that Ko-tah had won you over, as he has won over even some of the staunchest friends of Sagroth."

"You might have known, Nah-ee-lah, that, even could I have been disloyal to your father, I never could have been disloyal to his daughter."

"I did not know," she said. "How could I?"

There suddenly came over me a great desire to take her in my arms and cover those lovely lips with kisses. I could not tell why this ridiculous obsession had seized upon me, nor why, of a sudden, I became afraid of little Nah-ee-lah, the Moon Maid. I must have looked very foolish indeed, standing there looking at her, and suddenly I realized how fatuous I must appear, and so I shook myself and laughed.

"Come, Nah-ee-lah," I said, "we must not remain here. Where can I take you, that you will be safe?"

"Upon the outer terrace there may be some of the loyal guards," she replied, "but if Ko-tah has already taken the palace, flight will be useless."

"From what I know of the conspiracy, it will be useless," I replied, "for the service of Sagroth and his palace is rotten with the spies and retainers of the Javadar."

"I feared as much," she said. "The very men who came to assassinate Sagroth wore the imperial livery less than an ola since."

"Are there none, then, loyal to you?" I asked her.

"The Jemadar's guard is always loyal," she said, "but they number scarce a thousand men."

"How may we summon them?" I asked.

"Let us go to the outer terraces and if there are any of them there we can congregate the balance, or as many of them as Ko-tah has left alive."

"Come, then," I said, "let us hasten"; and together, hand in hand, we ran along the corridors of the Jemadar's palace to the outer terraces of the highest tier of Laythe. There we found a hundred men, and when we had told them of what had happened within the palace they drew their swords and, surrounding Nah-ee-lah, they shouted:

"To the death for Nah-ee-lah, Jemadav of Laythe!"

They wanted to remain there and protect her, but I told them that there would be nothing gained by that, that sooner or later they would be overwhelmed by far greater numbers, and the cause of Nah-ee-lah lost.

"Send a dozen men," I said to their commander, "to rally all of the loyal guards that remain alive. Tell them to come to the throne room, ready to lay down their lives for the new Jemadav, and then let the dozen continue on out into the city, rallying the people to the protection of Nah-ee-lah. As for us, we will accompany her immediately to the throne room, and there, place her upon the throne and proclaim her ruler of Laythe. A hundred men may hold the throne room for a long time, if we reach it before Ko-tah reaches it with his forces."

The officer looked at Nah-ee-lah questioningly.

"Your command, Jemadav?" he inquired.

"We will follow the plan of Ju-lan the Javadar," she replied.

Immediately a dozen warriors were dispatched to rally the Imperial Guard and arouse the loyal citizens of the city to the protection of their new Jemadav, while the balance of us conducted Nah-ee-lah by a short course toward the throne room.

As we entered the great chamber at one end, Ko-tah and a handful of warriors came in at the other, but we had the advantage, in that we entered through a doorway directly behind the throne and upon the dais.

"Throw your men upon the main entrance," I called to the officer of the guard, "and hold it until reenforcements come"; and then, as the hundred raced the length of the throne room toward the surprised and enraged Ko-tah, I led Nah-ee-lah to the central throne and seated her upon it. Then stepping forward, I raised my hand for silence.

"The Jemadar Sagroth is dead!" I cried. "Behold Nah-ee-lah, the Jemadav of Laythe!"

"Stop!" cried Ko-tah, "she may share the throne with me, but she may not possess it alone."

"Take that traitor!" I called to the loyal guard, and they rushed forward, evidently glad to do my bidding. But Ko-tah did not wait to be taken. He was accompanied by only a handful of men, and when he saw that the guard really intended to seize him and realized that he would be given short shrift at the hands of Nah-ee-lah and myself, he turned and fled. But I knew he would come back, and come back he did, though not until after the majority of the Jemadav's guard had gathered within the throne room.

He came with a great concourse of warriors, and the fighting was furious, but he might have brought a million men against our thousand and not immediately have overcome us, since only a limited number could fight at one time in the entrance way to the throne room. Already the corpses lay stacked as high as a man's head, yet no single member of Ko-tah's forces had crossed the threshold.

How long the fight was waged I do not know, but it must have been for a considerable time, since I know that our men fought in relays and rested many times, and that food was brought from other parts of the palace to the doorway behind the throne, and there were times when Ko-tah's forces withdrew and rested and recuperated, but always they came back in greater number, and eventually I realized we must be worn down by the persistence of their repeated attacks.

And then there arose slowly a deep-toned sound, at first we could not interpret. It rose and fell in increasing volume, until finally we knew that it was the sound of human voices, the voices of a great mob—of a mighty concourse of people and that it was sweeping toward us slowly and resistlessly.

Closer and closer it approached the palace as it rose, terrace upon terrace, toward the lofty pinnacle of Laythe. The fighting at the entrance to the throne room had almost ceased. Both sides were worn down almost to utter exhaustion, and now we but stood upon our arms upon either side of the wall of corpses that lay between us, our attention centered upon the sound of the growling multitude that was sweeping slowly upward toward us.

"They come," cried one of Nah-ee-lah's nobles, "to acclaim the new Jemadav and to tear the minions of Ko-tah the traitor to pieces!"

He spoke in a loud voice that was easily audible to Ko-tah and his retainers in the corridors without.

"They come to drag the spawn of Sagroth from the throne!" cried one of Ko-tah's followers. And then from the throne came the sweet, clear voice of Nah-ee-lah:

"Let the people's will be done," she said, and thus we stood, awaiting the verdict of the populace. Nor had we long to wait, for presently we realized that they had reached the palace terrace and entered the building itself. We could hear the shouting horde moving through the corridors and chambers, and finally the muffled bellowing resolved itself into articulate words:

"Sagroth is no more! Rule, Ko-tah, Jemadar of Laythe!"

I turned in consternation toward Nah-ee-lah. "What does it mean?" I cried. "Have the people turned against you?"

"Ko-tah's minions have done their work well during these many kelds," said the commander of the Jemadav's guard, who stood upon the upper steps of the dais, just below the throne. "They have spread lies and sedition among the people which not even Sagroth's just and kindly reign could overcome."

"Let the will of the people be done," repeated Nah-ee-lah.

"It is the will of fools betrayed by a scoundrel," cried the commander of the guard. "While there beats a single heart beneath the tunic of a guardsman of the Jemadav, we shall fight for Nah-ee-lah, Empress of Laythe."

Ko-tah's forces, now augmented by the rabble, were pushing their way over the corpses and into the throne room, so that we were forced to join the defenders, that we might hold them off while life remained to any of us. When the commander of the guard saw me fighting at his side he asked me to return to Nah-ee-lah. "We must not leave the Jemadav alone," he said. "Return and remain at her side, Ju-lan the Javadar, and when the last of us has fallen, drive your dagger into her heart."

I shuddered and turned back toward Nah-ee-lah. The very thought of plunging my dagger into that tender bosom fairly nauseated me. There must be some other way, and yet, what other means of escape could there be for Nah-ee-lah, who preferred death to the dishonor of surrender to Ko-tah, the murderer of her father? As I reached Nah-ee-lah's side, and turned again to face the entrance to the throne room, I saw that the warriors of Ko-tah were being pushed into the chamber by the mob behind them and that our defenders were being overwhelmed by the great number of their antagonists. Ko-tah, with a half dozen warriors, had been carried forward, practically without volition, by the press of numbers in their rear, and even now, with none to intercept him, was running rapidly up the broad center aisle toward the throne. Some of those in the entrance way saw him, and as he reached the foot of the steps leading to the dais, a snarling cry arose:

"Ko-tah the Jemadar!"

With bared sword, the fellow leaped toward me where I stood alone between Nah-ee-lah and her enemies.

"Surrender, Julian!" she cried. "It is futile to oppose them. You are not of Laythe. Neither duty nor honor impose upon you the necessity of offering your life for one of us. Spare him, Ko-tah!" she cried to the advancing Javadar, "and I will bow to the will of the people and relinquish the throne to you."

"Ko-tah the traitor shall never sit upon the throne of Nah-ee-lah!" I exclaimed, and leaping forward, I engaged the Prince of Laythe.

His warriors were close behind him, and it behooved me to work fast, and so I fought as I had never guessed that it lay within me to fight, and at the instant that the rabble broke through the remaining defenders and poured into the throne room of the Jemadars of Laythe, I slipped my point into the heart of Ko-tah. With a single piercing shriek, he threw his hands above his head and toppled backward down the steps to lie dead at the foot of the throne he had betrayed.

For an instant the silence of death reigned in the great chamber. Friend and foe stood alike in the momentary paralysis of shocked surprise.

That tense, breathless silence had endured for but a moment, when it was shattered by a terrific detonation. We felt the palace tremble and rock. The assembled mob looked wildly about, their eyes filled with fear and questioning. But before they could voice a question, another thunderous report burst upon our startled ears, and then from the city below the palace there arose the shrieks and screams of terrified people. Again the palace trembled, and a great crack opened in one of the walls of the throne room. The people saw it, and in an instant their anger against the dynasty of Sagroth was swallowed in the mortal terror which they felt for their own safety. With shrieks and screams they turned and bolted for the doorway. The weaker were knocked down and trampled upon. They fought with fists and swords and daggers, in their mad efforts to escape the crumbling building. They tore the clothing from one another, as each sought to drag back his fellow, that he might gain further in the race for the outer world.

And as the rabble fought, Nah-ee-lah and I stood before the throne of Laythe, watching them, while below us the few remaining members of the Jemadav's guard stood viewing in silent contempt the terror of the people.

Explosion after explosion followed one another in rapid succession. The people had fled. The palace was empty, except for that handful of us faithful ones who remained within the throne room.

"Let us go," I said to Nah-ee-lah, "and discover the origin of these sounds, and the extent of the damage that is being done."

"Come," she said, "here is a short corridor to the inner terrace, where we may look down upon the entire city of Laythe." And then, turning to the commander of the guard, she said: "Proceed, please, to the palace gates, and secure them against the return of our enemies, if they have by this time all fled from the palace grounds."

The officer bowed, and followed by the few heroic survivors of the Jemadav's guard, he left by another corridor for the palace gates, while I followed Nah-ee-lah up a stairway that led to the roof of the palace.

Coming out upon the upper terrace, we made our way quickly to the edge overlooking the city and the crater. Below us a shrieking multitude ran hither and thither from terrace to terrace, while, now here and now there, terrific explosions occurred that shattered age-old structures and carried debris high into the air. Many terraces showed great gaps and tumbled ruins where other explosions had occurred and smoke and flames were rising from a dozen portions of the city.

But an instant it took me to realize that the explosions were caused by something that was being dropped into the city from above, and as I looked up I saw a missile describing an arc above the palace, past which it hurtled to a terrace far below, and at once I realized that the missile had originated outside the city. Turning quickly, I ran across the terrace to the outer side which overlooked the plateau upon which the city stood. I could not repress an exclamation of astonishment at the sight that greeted my eyes, for the surface of the plateau was alive with warriors. Nah-ee-lah had followed me and was standing at my elbow. "The Kalkars," she said. "They have come again to reduce Laythe. It has been long since they attempted it, many generations ago, but what is it, Julian, that causes the great noise and the destruction and the fires within Laythe?"

"It is this which fills me with surprise," I said, "and not the presence of the Kalkar warriors. Look! Nah-ee-lah," and I pointed to a knoll lying at the verge of the plateau, where, unless my eyes deceived me badly, there was mounted a mortar which was hurling shells into the city of Laythe. "And there, and there," I continued, pointing to other similar engines of destruction mounted at intervals. "The city is surrounded with them, Nah-ee-lah. Have your people any knowledge of such engines of warfare or of high explosives?" I demanded.

"Only in our legends are such things mentioned," she replied. "It has been ages since the inhabitants of Va-nah lost the art of manufacturing such things."

As we stood there talking, one of the Jemadav's guards emerged from the palace and approached us.

"Nah-ee-lah, Jemadav," he cried, "there is one here who craves audience with you and who says that if you listen to him you may save your city from destruction."

"Fetch him," replied Nah-ee-lah. "We will receive him here." We had but a moment to wait when the guardsman returned with one of Ko-tah's captains.

"Nah-ee-lah, Jemadav," he cried, when she had given him permission to speak, "I come to you with a message from one who is Jemadar of Jemadars, ruler of all Va-nah. If you would save your city and your people, listen well."

The girl's eyes narrowed. "You are speaking to your Jemadav, fellow," she said. "Be careful, not only of your words, but of your tone."

"I come but to save you," replied the man sullenly. "The Kalkars have discovered a great leader, and they have joined together from many cities to overthrow Laythe. My master does not wish to destroy this ancient city, and there is but one simple condition upon which he will spare it."

"Name your condition," said Nah-ee-lah.

"If you will wed him, he will make Laythe the capital of Va-nah, and you shall rule with him as Jemadav of Jemadavs."

Nah-ee-lah's lips curled in scorn. "And who is the presumptuous Kalkar that dares aspire to the hand of Nah-ee-lah?" she demanded.

"He is no Kalkar, Jemadav," replied the messenger. "He is one from another world, who says that he knows you well and that he has loved you long."

"His name," snapped Nah-ee-lah impatiently.

"He is called Or-tis, Jemadar of Jemadars."

Nah-ee-lah turned toward me with elevated brows and a smile of comprehension upon her face.

"Or-tis," she repeated.

"Now I understand, my Jemadav," I said, "and I am commencing to have some slight conception of the time that must have elapsed since I first landed within Va-nah, for even since our escape from the Va-gas Orthis has had time to discover the Kalkars and ingratiate himself among them, to conspire with them for the overthrow of Laythe, and to manufacture explosives and shells and the guns which are reducing Laythe this moment. Even had I not heard the name, I might have guessed that it was Or-this, for it is all so like him—ingrate, traitor, cur."

"Go back to your master," she said to the messenger, "and tell him that Nah-ee-lah, Jemadav of Laythe, would as leave mate with Ga-va-go the Va-gas as with him, and that Laythe will be happier destroyed and her people wiped from the face of Va-nah than ruled by such a beast. I have spoken. Go."

The fellow turned and left us, being accompanied from Nah-ee-lah's presence by the guardsman who had fetched him, and whom Nah-ee-lah commanded to return as soon as he had conducted the other outside the palace gates. Then the girl turned to me:

"O, Julian, what shall I do? How may I combat these terrible forces that you have brought to Va-nah from another world?"

I shook my head. "We, too, could manufacture both guns and

ammunition to combat him, but now we have not the time, since Laythe will be reduced to a mass of ruins before we could even make a start. There is but one way, Nah-ee-lah, and that is to send your people—every fighting man that you can gather, and the women, too, if they can bear arms, out upon the plateau in an effort to overwhelm the Kalkars and destroy the guns."

She stood and thought for a long time, and presently the officer of the guard returned and halted before her, awaiting her commands. Slowly she raised her head and looked at him.

"Go into the city," she said, "and gather every Laythean who can carry a sword, a dagger, or a lance. Tell them to assemble on the inner terraces below the castle, and that I, Nah-ee-lah their Jemadav, will address them. The fate of Laythe rests with you. Go."

CHAPTER XIV

BACK TO "THE BARSOOM"

THE city was already in flames in many places, and though the people fought valiantly to extinguish them, it seemed to me that they but spread the more rapidly with each succeeding minute. And then, as suddenly as it had commenced, the bombardment ceased. Nah-ee-lah and I crossed over to the outer edge of the terrace to see if we could note any new movement by the enemy, nor did we have long to wait. We saw a hundred ladders raised as if by magic toward the lowest terrace, which rose but a bare two hundred feet above the base of the city. The men who carried the ladders were not visible to us when they came close to the base of the wall, but I guessed from the distant glimpses that I caught of the ladders as they were rushed forward by running men that here, again, Orthis' earthly knowledge and experience had come to the assistance of the Kalkars, for I was sure that only some form of extension ladder could be successfully used to reach even the lowest terrace.

When I saw their intention I ran quickly down into the palace and out upon the terrace before the gates, where the remainder of the guard were stationed, and there I told them what was happening and urged them to hasten the people to the lowest terrace to repulse the enemy before they had secured a foothold upon the city. Then I returned to Nah-ee-lah, and together we watched the outcome of the struggle, but almost from the first I realized that Laythe was doomed, for before any of her defenders could reach the spot, fully a thousand Kalkars had clambered to the terrace, and there they held their own while other thousands ascended in safety to the city.

We saw the defenders rush forth to attack them, and for a moment, so impetuous was their charge, I thought that I had been wrong and that the Kalkars might yet be driven from Laythe. Fighting upon the lower outer terrace far beneath us was a surging mass of shouting warriors. The Kalkars were falling back before the impetuous onslaught of the Laytheans.

"They have not the blood in their veins," whispered Nah-ee-lah, clinging tightly to my arm. "One noble is worth ten of them. Watch them. Already are they fleeing."

And so it seemed, and the rout of the Kalkars appeared almost assured, as score upon score of them were hurled over the edge of the terrace, to fall mangled and bleeding upon the ground hundreds of feet below.

But suddenly a new force seemed to be injected into the strife. I saw a stream of Kalkars emerging above the edge of the lower terrace—new men clambering up the ladders from the plateau below, and as they came they shouted something which I could not understand, but the other Kalkars seemed to take heart and made once more the semblance of a stand against the noble Laytheans, and I saw one, the leader of the newcomers, force his way into the battling throng. And then I saw him raise his hand above his head and hurl something into the midst of the compact ranks of the Laytheans.

Instantly there was a terrific explosion and a great, bloody gap lay upon the terrace where an instant before a hundred of the flower of the fighting men of Laythe had been so gloriously defending their city and their honor.

"Grenades," I exclaimed. "Hand grenades!"

"What is it, Julian? What is it that they are doing down there?" cried Nah-ee-lah. "They are murdering my people."

"Yes, Nah-ee-lah, they are murdering your people, and well may Va-nah curse the day that Earth Men set foot upon your world."

"I do not understand, Julian," she said.

"This is the work of Orthis," I said, "who has brought from Earth the knowledge of diabolical engines of destruction. He first shelled the city with what must have been nothing more than crude mortars, for it is impossible that he has had the time to construct the machinery to build any but the simplest of guns. Now his troops are hurling hand grenades among your men. There is no chance, Nah-ee-lah, for the Laytheans to successfully pit their primitive weapons against the modern agents of destruction which Orthis has brought to bear against them. Laythe must surrender or be destroyed."

Nah-ee-lah laid her head upon my shoulder and wept softly. "Julian," she said at last, "this is the end, then. Take me to the Jemadav, my mother, please, and then you must go and make your peace with your fellow Earth Man. It is not right that you, a stranger, who have done so much for me, should fall with me and Laythe."

"The only peace I can make with Orthis, Nah-ee-lah," I replied, "is the peace of death. Orthis and I may not live together again in the same world."

She was crying very softly, sobbing upon my shoulder, and I put my arm about her in an effort to quiet her.

"I have brought you only suffering and danger, and now death, Julian," she said, "when you deserve naught but happiness and peace."

I suddenly felt very strange and my heart behaved wretchedly, so that when I attempted to speak it pounded so that I could say nothing and my knees shook beneath me. What had come over me? Could it be possible that already Orthis had loosed his poison gas? Then, at last, I managed to gather myself together.

"Nah-ee-lah," I said, "I do not fear death if you must die, and I do not seek happiness except with you."

She looked up suddenly, her great, tear-dimmed eyes wide and gazing deep into mine.

"You mean—Julian? You mean—?"

"I mean, Nah-ee-lah, that I love you," I replied, though I must have stumbled through the words in a most ridiculous manner, so frightened was I.

"Ah, Julian," she sighed, and put her arms about my neck.

"And you, Nah-ee-lah!" I exclaimed incredulously, as I crushed her to me, "can it be that you return my love?"

"I have loved you always," she replied. "From the very first, almost—way back when we were prisoners together in the Novans village. You Earth Men must be very blind, my Julian. A Laythean would have known it at once, for it seemed to me that upon a dozen occasions I almost avowed my love openly to you."

"Alas, Nah-ee-lah! I must have been very blind, for I had not guessed until this minute that you loved me."

"Now," she said, "I do not care what happens. We have one another, and if we die together, doubtless we shall live together in a new incarnation."

"I hope so," I said, "but I should much rather be sure of it and live together in this."

"And I, too, Julian, but that is impossible."

We are walking now through the corridors of the palace toward the chamber occupied by her mother, but we did not find her there and Nah-ee-lah became apprehensive as to her safety. Hurriedly we searched through other chambers of the palace, until at last we came to the little audience chamber in which Sagroth had been slain, and as we threw open the door I saw a sight that I tried to hide from Nah-ee-lah's eyes as I drew her around in an effort to force her back into the corridor. Possibly she guessed what impelled my action, for she shook her head and murmured: "No, Julian; whatever it is I must see it." And then she pushed her way gently past me and we stood together upon the threshold, looking at the harrowing sight which the interior of the room displayed.

There were the bodies of the assassins Sagroth and I had slain, and the dead Jemadar, too, precisely as he had fallen, while across his breast lay the body of Nah-ee-lah's mother, a dagger self-thrust through her heart. For just a moment Nah-ee-lah stood there looking at them in silence, as though in prayer, and then she turned wearily away and left the chamber, closing the door behind her. We walked on in silence for some time, ascending the stairway back to the upper terrace. Upon the inner side, the flames were spreading throughout the city, roaring like a mighty furnace and vomiting up great clouds of smoke, for though the Laythean terraces are supported by tremendous arches of masonry, yet there is much wood used in the interior construction of the buildings, while the hangings and the furniture are all inflammable.

"We had no chance to save the city," said Nah-ee-lah, with a sigh. "Our people, called from their normal duties by the false Ko-tah, were leaderless. The fire fighters, instead of being at their posts, were seeking the life of their Jemadar. Unhappy day! Unhappy day!"

"You think they could have stopped the fire?" I asked.

"The little ponds, the rivulets, the waterfalls, the great public baths and the tiny lakes that you see upon every terrace were all built with fire protection in mind. It is easy to divert their waters and flood any tier of buildings. Had my people been at their posts, this, at least, could not have happened."

As we stood watching the flames we suddenly saw people emerging in great numbers upon several of the lower terraces. They were evidently in terrified flight, and then others appeared upon terraces above them—Kalkars who hurled hand grenades amongst the Laytheans beneath them. Men, women, and children ran hither and thither, shrieking and crying and seeking for shelter, but from the buildings behind them, rushing them outward upon the terraces, came other Kalkars with hand grenades. The fires hemmed the people of Laythe upon either side and the Kalkars attacked them from the rear and from above. The weaker fell and were trodden to death, and I saw scores fall upon their own lances or drive daggers into the hearts of their loved ones.

The massacre spread rapidly around the circumference of the city and the Kalkars drove the people from the upper terraces downward between the raging fires which were increasing until the mouth of the great crater was filled with roaring flames and smoke. In the occasional gaps we could catch glimpses of the holocaust beneath us.

A sudden current of air rising from the crater lifted the smoke pall high for a moment, revealing the entire circumference of the crater, the edge of which was crowded with Laytheans. And then I saw a warrior from the opposite side leap upon the surrounding wall that bordered the lower terrace at the edge of the yawning crater. He turned and called aloud some message to his fellows, and then wheeling, threw his arms above his head and leaped outward into the yawning, bottomless abyss. Instantly the others seemed to be inoculated with the infection of his mad act. A dozen men leaped to the wall and dove head foremost into the crater. The thing spread slowly at first, and then with the rapidity of a prairie fire, it ran around the entire circle of the city. Women hurled their children in and then leaped after them. The multitude fought one with another for a place upon the wall from which they might cast themselves to death. It was a terrible —an awe-inspiring sight.

Nah-ee-lah covered her eyes with her hands. "My poor people!" she cried. "My poor people!" And far below her, by the thousands now, they were hurling themselves into eternity, while above them the screaming Kalkars hurled hand grenades among them and drove the remaining inhabitants of Laythe, terrace by terrace, down toward the crater's rim.

Nah-ee-lah turned away. "Come, Julian," she said, "I cannot look, I cannot look." And together we walked across the terrace to the outer side of the city.

Almost directly beneath us upon the next terrace was a palace gate and as we reached a point where we could see it, I was horrified to see that the Kalkars had made their way up the outer terraces to the very palace walls. The Jemadav's guard was standing there ready to defend the palace against the invaders. The great stone gates would have held indefinitely against spears and swords, but even the guardsmen must have guessed that their doom was already sealed and that these gates, that had stood for ages, an ample protection to the Jemadars of Laythe, were about to fall, as the Kalkars halted fifty yards away, and from their ranks a single individual stepped forth a few paces.

As my eyes alighted upon him I seized Nah-ee-lah's arm. "Orthis!" I cried. "It is Orthis." At the same instant the man's eyes rose above the gates and fell upon us. A nasty leer curled his lips as he recognized us.

"I come to claim my bride," he cried, in a voice that reached us easily, "and to balance my account with you, at last," and he pointed a finger at me.

In his right hand he held a large, cylindrical object, and as he ceased speaking he hurled it at the gates precisely as a baseball pitcher pitches a swift ball.

The missile struck squarely at the bottom of the gates. There was a terrific explosion, and the great stone portals crumbled, shattered into a thousand fragments. The last defense of the Empress of Laythe had fallen, and with it there went down in bloody death at least half the remaining members of her loyal guard.

Instantly the Kalkars rushed forward, hurling hand grenades among the survivors of the guard.

Nah-ee-lah turned toward me and put her arms about my neck. "Kiss me once more, Julian," she said, "and then the dagger."

"Never, never, Nah-ee-lah!" I cried. "I cannot do it."

"But I can!" she exclaimed, and drew her own from its sheath at her hip.

I seized her wrist. "Not that, Nah-ee-lah!" I cried. "There must be some other way." And then there came to me a mad inspiration. "The wings!" I cried. "Where are they kept? The last of your people have been destroyed. Duty no longer holds you here. Let us escape, even if it is only to frustrate Orthis' plans and deny him the satisfaction of witnessing our death."

"But where can we go?" she asked.

"We may at least choose our own manner of death," I replied, "far from Laythe and far from the eyes of an enemy who would gloat over our undoing."

"You are right, Julian. We still have a little time, for I doubt if Orthis or his Kalkars can quickly find the stairway leading to this terrace." And then she led me quickly to one of the many towers that rise above the palace. Entering it, we ascended a spiral staircase to a large chamber at the summit of the tower. Here were kept the imperial wings. I fastened Nah-ee-lah's to her and she helped me with mine, and then from the pinnacle of the tower we arose above the buring city of Laythe and flew rapidly toward the distant lowlands and the sea. It was in my mind to search out, if possible, the location of *The Barsoom,* for I still entertained the mad hope that my companions yet lived—if I did, why not they?

The heat above the city was almost unendurable and the smoke suffocating, yet we passed through it, so that almost immediately we were hidden from the view of that portion of the palace from which we had arisen, with the result that when Orthis and his Kalkars finally found their way to the upper terrace, as I have no doubt they did, we had disappeared—whither they could not know.

We flew and drifted with the wind across the mountainous country toward the plains and the sea, it being my intention upon reaching the latter to follow the coast line until I came to a river marked by an island at its mouth. From that point I knew that I could reach the spot where *The Barsoom* had landed.

Our long flight must have covered a considerable period of time, since it was necessary for us to alight and rest many times and to search for food. We met, fortunately, with no mishaps, and upon the several occasions when we were discovered by roving bands of Va-gas we were able to soar far aloft and escape them easily. We came at length, however, to the sea, the coast of which I followed to the left, but though we passed the mouths of many rivers, I discovered none that precisely answered the description of that which I sought.

It was borne in upon me at last that our quest was futile, but where we were to find a haven of safety neither of us could guess. The gas in our bags was losing its buoyancy and we had no means wherewith to replenish it. It would still maintain us for a short time, but how long neither of us knew, other than that it had not nearly the buoyancy that it originally possessed.

Off the coast we had seen islands almost continuously and I suggested to Nah-ee-lah that we try to discover one upon which grew the fruits and nuts and vegetables necessary for our subsistence, and where we might also have a constant supply of fresh water.

I discovered that Nah-ee-lah knew little about these islands, practically nothing in fact, not even as to whether they were inhabited; but we determined to explore one, and to this end we selected an island of considerable extent that lay about ten miles off shore. We reached it without difficulty and circled slowly above it, scrutinizing its entire area carefully. About half of it was quite hilly, but the balance was rolling and comparatively level. We discovered three streams and two small lakes upon it, and an almost riotous profusion of vegetable growth, but nowhere did we discern the slightest indication that it was inhabited. And so at last, feeling secure, we made our landing upon the plain, close to the beach.

It was a beautiful spot, a veritable Garden of Eden, where we two might have passed the remainder of our lives in peace and security, for though we later explored it carefully, we found not the slightest evidence that it had ever known the foot of man.

Together we built a snug shelter against the storms. Together we hunted for food, and during our long periods of idleness we lay upon the soft sward beside the beach, and to pass the time away, I taught Nah-ee-lah my own language.

It was a lazy, indolent, happy life that we spent upon this enchanted isle, and yet, though we were happy in our love, each of us felt the futility of our existence, where our lives must be spent in useless idleness.

We had, however, given up definitely hope for any other form of existence. And thus we were lying one time, as was our wont after eating, stretched in luxurious ease upon our backs on the soft lunar grasses, I with my eyes closed, when Nah-ee-lah suddenly grasped me by the arm.

"Julian," she cried, "what is it? Look!"

I opened my eyes, to find her sitting up and gazing into the sky toward the mainland, a slim forefinger indicating the direction of the object that had attracted her attention and aroused her surprised interest.

As my eyes rested upon the thing her pointing finger indicated, I leaped to my feet with an exclamation of incredulity, for there, sailing parallel with the coast at an altitude of not more than a thousand feet, was a ship, the lines of which I knew as I had known my mother's face. It was *The Barsoom.*

Grasping Nah-ee-lah by the arm, I dragged her to her feet. "Come, quick, Nah-ee-lah!" I cried, and urged her rapidly toward our hut, where we had stored the wings and the gas bags which we had never thought to use again, yet protected carefully, though why we knew not.

There was still gas in the bags—enough to support us in the air, with the assistance of our wings, but to fly thus for long distances would have been most fatiguing, and there was even a question as to whether we could cross the ten miles of sea that lay between us and the mainland; yet I was determined to attempt it. Hastily we donned the wings and bags, and rising together, flapped slowly in the direction of the mainland.

The Barsoom was cruising slowly along a line that would cross ours before we could reach the shore, but I hoped that they would sight us and investigate.

We flew as rapidly as I dared, for I could take no chances upon exhausting Nah-ee-lah, knowing that it would be absolutely impossible for me to support her weight and my own, with our depleted gas bags. There was no way in which I could signal to *The Barsoom.* We must simply fly toward her. That was the best that we could do, and finally, try though we would, I realized that we should be too late to intercept her and that unless they saw us and changed their course, we should not come close enough to hail them. To see my friends passing so near, and yet to be unable to apprise them of my presence filled me with melancholy. Not one of the many vicissitudes and dangers through which I had passed since I left Earth depressed me more than the sight of *The Barsoom* forging slowly past us without speaking. I saw her change her course then and move inland still further from us, and I could not but dwell upon our unhappy condition, since now we might never again be able to reach the safety of our island, there being even a question as to whether the gas bags would support us to the mainland.

They did, however, and there we alighted and rested, while *The Barsoom* sailed out of sight toward the mountains.

"I shall not give it up, Nah-ee-lah," I cried. "I am going to follow *The Barsoom* until we find it, or until we die in the attempt. I doubt if we ever can reach the island again, but we can make short flights here on land, and by so doing, we may overtake my ship and my companions."

hospitality and for your generous interest," and he held out his
hand toward me.

"But the story of Julian 9th," I insisted, "am I never to hear
that?"

"If we meet again, yes," he promised, with a smile.

"I shall hold you to it," I told him.

"If we meet again," he repeated, and departed, closing the
stateroom door after him.

PART II

The Moon Men

Being the Story of Julian 9th

THE CONQUEST

IT was two years after I had first met him aboard the liner *Harding* that I came across him again. I had just been appointed Secretary of Commerce. He came to my office in Washington on official business during March, 1969. I invited him to my home for dinner and it was later in the evening that I importuned him for the promised story of Julian 9th.

He laughed good naturedly. "Very well," he exclaimed, "here goes!"

Let me preface this story, as I did the other that I told you on board the liner *Harding* two years ago, with the urgent request that you attempt to keep constantly in mind the theory that there is no such thing as time—that there is no past and no future —that there is only *now*, there never has been anything but *now*, and there never will be anything but *now*. It is a theory analogous to that which stipulates that there is no such thing as space.

I have told you of the attempt made to reach Mars in *The Barsoom* and of how it was thwarted by Lieutenant Commander Orthis. That was in the year 2026.

The son that was born to Julian 5th and the Princess Nah-ee-lah in 2036 was the great-grandfather of Julian 9th for whose story you have asked me, and in whom I lived again in the twenty-second century.

For some reason no further attempts were made to reach Mars with whom we had been in radio communication for seventy years. Possibly it was due to the rise of a religious cult which preached against all forms of scientific progress and which by political pressure was able to mold and influence several successive weak administrations of a notoriously weak party that had had its origin nearly a century before in a group of peace-at-any-price men.

In the year 2050 the blow fell. Lieutenant Commander Orthis, after twenty-four years upon the Moon, returned to Earth with one hundred thousand Kalkars and a thousand Va-gas. In a thousand great ships they came, bearing arms and ammunition and strange, new engines of destruction fashioned by the brilliant mind of the arch villain of the universe. No one but Orthis could have done it. No one but Orthis would have done it. It had been he who had perfected the engines that had made *The Barsoom* possible, and after he had become the dominant force among the Kalkars of the Moon and had aroused their imaginations with tales of the great, rich world lying ready and unarmed within easy striking distance of them, it had been an easy thing to enlist their labor in the building of the ships and the manufacture of the countless accessories necessary to the successful accomplishment of the great adventure. The Moon furnished all the needed materials, the Kalkars furnished the labor, and Orthis the knowledge, the brains and the leadership. Ten years had been devoted to the spreading of his propaganda and the winning over of The Thinkers, or Kalkars, and then fourteen years were required to build and outfit the fleet.

Five days before they arrived astronomers detected the fleet as minute specks upon the eye-pieces of their telescopes. There was much speculation, but it was Julian 5th alone who guessed the truth. He warned the governments at London and Washington, but though he was then in command of the International Peace Fleet, his appeals were treated with levity and ridicule. He knew Orthis and so he knew that it was easily within the man's ability to construct a fleet, and he also knew that only for one purpose would Orthis return to Earth with so great a number of ships. It meant war, and the Earth had nothing but a handful of cruisers wherewith to defend herself—there were not available in all the world twenty-five thousand organized fighting men, nor equipment for more than half again that number.

The inevitable occurred. Orthis seized London and Washington simultaneously. His well-armed forces met with practically no resistance. There could be no resistance, for there was nothing wherewith to resist. It was a criminal offense to possess firearms. Even edged weapons with blades over six inches long were barred by law. Military training, except for the chosen few of the International Peace Fleet, had been banned for years. And against this pitiable state of disarmament and unpreparedness was brought a force of a hundred thousand well-armed, seasoned warriors with engines of destruction that were unknown to Earth Men. A description of one alone will suffice to explain the utter hopelessness of the cause of the Earth Men.

This instrument, of which the invaders brought but one, was mounted upon the deck of their flag ship and was operated by Orthis in person. It was an invention of his own which no Kalkar understood or could operate. Briefly, it was a device for the generation of radio-activity at any desired vibratory rate and for the directing of the resultant emanations upon any given object within its effective range. We do not know what Orthis called it, but the Earth Men of that day knew it as an electronic rifle.

It was quite evidently a recent invention, and therefore in some respects crude, but be that as it may, its effects were sufficiently deadly to permit Orthis to practically wipe out the entire International Peace Fleet in less than thirty days, as rapidly as the various ships came within range of the electronic rifle. To the layman, the visual effects induced by this weird weapon were appalling and nerve shattering. A mighty cruiser vibrant with life and power might sail majestically to engage the flag ship of the Kalkars, when, as by magic, every aluminum part of the cruiser would vanish as mist before the sun, and as nearly ninety percent of a Peace Fleet cruiser, including the hull, was constructed of aluminum, the result may be imagined—one moment there was a great ship forging through the air, her flags and pennants flying in the wind, her band playing, her officers and men at their quarters—the next a mass of engines, polished wood, cordage, flags and human beings hurtling earthward to extinction.

It was Julian 5th who discovered the secret of this deadly weapon and that it accomplished its destruction by projecting upon the ships of the Peace Fleet the vibratory rate of radio-activity identical with that of aluminum, with the result that, thus excited, the electrons of the attacked substance increased their own vibratory rate to a point that they became dissipated again into their elemental and invisible state—in other words, aluminum was transmuted into something else that was as invisible and intangible as ether. Perhaps it was ether.

Assured of the correctness of his theory, Julian 5th withdrew in his own flag ship to a remote part of the world, taking with him the few remaining cruisers of the Fleet. Orthis searched for them for months, but it was not until the close of the year 2050 that the two fleets met again and for the last time. Julian 5th had by this time perfected the plan for which he had gone into hiding, and he now faced the Kalkar fleet and his old enemy,

Orthis, with some assurance of success. His flag ship moved at the head of the short column that contained the remaining hope of a world and Julian 5th stood upon her deck beside a small and innocent looking box mounted upon a stout tripod.

Orthis moved to meet him—he would destroy the ships one by one as he approached them. He gloated at the easy victory that lay before him. He directed the electronic rifle at the flag ship of his enemy and touched a button. Suddenly his brows knitted. What was this? He examined the rifle. He held a piece of aluminum before its muzzle and saw the metal disappear. The mechanism was operating, but the ships of the enemy did not disappear. Then he guessed the truth, for his own ship was now but a short distance from that of Julian 5th, and he could see that the hull of the latter was entirely coated with a grayish substance that he sensed at once for what it was—an insulating material that rendered the aluminum parts of the enemy's fleet immune from the invisible fire of his rifle.

Orthis' scowl changed to a grim smile. He turned two dials upon a control box connected with the weapon and again pressed the button. Instantly the bronze propellers of the Earth Men's flag ship vanished in thin air, together with numerous fittings and parts above decks. Similarly went the exposed bronze parts of the balance of The International Peace Fleet, leaving a squadron of drifting derelicts at the mercy of the foe.

Julian 5th's flag ship was at that time but a few fathoms from that of Orthis. The two men could plainly see one another's features. Orthis' expression was savage and gloating, that of Julian 5th sober and dignified.

"You thought to beat me, then!" jeered Orthis. "God, but I have waited and labored and sweated for this day. I have wrecked a world to best you, Julian 5th, to best you and to kill you, but to let you know first that I am going to kill you—to kill you in such a way that man was never before killed, as no other brain than mine could conceive of killing. You insulated your aluminum parts, thinking thus to thwart me, but you did not know— your feeble intellect could not know—that as easily as I destroyed aluminum I can, by the simplest of adjustments, attune this weapon to destroy any one of a hundred different substances and among them human flesh or human bone. That is what I am going to do now, Julian 5th. First I am going to dissipate the bony structure of your frame. It will be done painlessly—it may not even result in instant death, and I am hoping that it will not. For I want you to know the power of a real intellect—the intellect from which you stole the fruits of its efforts for a life time; but not again, Julian 5th, for today you die—first your bones, then your flesh, and after you, your men, and after them your spawn, the son that the woman I loved bore you; but she— she shall belong to me! Take that memory to hell with you!" and he turned toward the dials beside his lethal weapon.

But Julian 5th placed a hand upon the little box resting upon the strong tripod before him, and he it was who touched a button before Orthis had touched his. Instantly the electronic rifle vanished beneath the very eyes of Orthis, and at the same time the two ships touched and Julian 5th had leaped the rail to the enemy deck and was running toward his arch enemy.

Orthis stood gazing horrified, at the spot where the greatest invention of his giant intellect had stood but an instant before, and then he looked up at Julian 5th approaching him and cried out horribly.

"Stop!" he screamed. "Always, all our lives you have robbed me of the fruits of my efforts. Somehow you have stolen the secret of this, my greatest invention, and now you have destroyed it. May God in heaven——"

"Yes," cried Julian 5th, "and I am going to destroy you, unless you surrender to me with all your force."

"Never!" almost screamed the man, who seemed veritably demented, so hideous was his rage. "Never! This is the end, Julian 5th, for both of us." Even as he uttered the last word, he threw a lever mounted upon a controlboard before him. There was a terrific explosion, and both ships, bursting into flame, plunged meteor-like into the ocean beneath.

Thus went Julian 5th and Orthis to their deaths, carrying with them the secret of the terrible destructive force that the latter had brought with him from the Moon; but the Earth was already undone. It lay helpless before its conquerors. What the outcome might have been had Orthis lived, may only remain conjecture. Possibly he would have brought order out of the chaos he had created and instituted a reign of reason. Earth Men would at least have had the advantage of his wonderful intellect and his power to rule the ignorant Kalkars that he had transported from the Moon.

There might even have been some hope had the Earth Men banded together against the common enemy, but this they did not do. Elements who had been discontented with this or that phase of government joined issues with the invaders. The lazy, the inefficient, the defective, who ever place the blame for their failures upon the shoulders of the successful, swarmed to the banners of the Kalkars in whom they sensed kindred souls.

Political factions, labor and capital each saw, or thought they saw, an opportunity for advantage to themselves in one way or another that was inimical to the interests of the others. The Kalkar fleets returned to the Moon for more Kalkars until it was estimated that seven millions of them were being transported to Earth each year.

Julian 6th, with Nah-ee-lah, his Moon Maid mother, lived, as did Or-tis, the son of Orthis, but my story is not to be of them, but of Julian 9th, who was born just a century after the birth of Julian 5th.

Julian 9th will tell his own story.

CHAPTER I

THE FLAG

I was born in the teivos of Chicago, January 1, 2100, to Julian 8th and Elizabeth James. My father and mother were not married, as marriages had long since become illegal. I was called Julian 9th. My parents were of the rapidly diminishing intellectual class and could both read and write. This learning they imparted to me, although it was very useless learning—it was their religion. Printing was a lost art, and the last of the public libraries had been destroyed almost a hundred years before I reached maturity, so there was little or nothing to read, while to have a book in one's possession was to brand one as of the hated intellectuals, arousing the scorn and derision of the Kalkar rabble and the suspicion and persecution of the lunar authorities who ruled us.

The first twenty years of my life were uneventful. As a boy I played among the crumbling ruins of what must once have been a magnificent city. Pillaged, looted and burned half a hundred times, Chicago still reared the skeletons of some mighty edifices above the ashes of her former greatness. As a youth, I regretted the departed romance of the long gone days of my forefathers when the Earth Men still retained sufficient strength to battle for existence. I deplored the quiet stagnation of my own time with only an occasional murder to break the monotony of our black existence. Even the Kalkar Guard, stationed on the shore of the great lake, seldom harassed us, unless there came an urgent call from higher authorities for an additional tax collection, for we fed them well and they had the pick of our women and young girls—almost, but not quite, as you shall see.

The commander of the guard had been stationed here for years, and we considered ourselves very fortunate in that he was too lazy and indolent to be cruel or oppressive. His tax collectors were always with us on market days; but they did not exact so much that we had nothing left for ourselves, as ref- ugees from Milwaukee told us was the case there. I recall one poor devil from Milwaukee who staggered into our market place of a Saturday. He was nothing more than a bag of bones, and he told us that fully ten thousand people had died of starva- tion the preceding month in his teivos. The word teivos is ap- plied impartially to a district and to the administrative body that misadministers its affairs. No one knows what the word really means, though my mother has told me that her grand- father said that it came from another world, the Moon, like Kash Guard, which also means nothing in particular—one soldier is a Kash Guard, ten thousand soldiers are a Kash Guard. If a man comes with a piece of paper upon which something is written that you are not supposed to be able to read and kills your grandmother or carries off your sister, you say: "The Kash Guard did it."

Three Saturdays a month, the tax collectors were in the market places appraising our wares, and on the last Saturday they col- lected one per cent of all we had bought or sold during the month. Nothing had any fixed value—today you might haggle half an hour in trading a pint of beans for a goat skin, and next week if you wanted beans the chances were more than excellent that you would have to give four or five goat skins for a pint, and the tax collectors took advantage of that—they appraised on the basis of the highest market values for the month.

My father had a few long-haired goats—they were called Montana goats; but he said they really were Angoras, and Mother used to make cloth from their fleece. With the cloth, the milk, and the flesh from our goats we lived very well, having also a small vegetable garden beside our house; but there were some necessities that we must purchase in the market place, it being against the law to barter in private, as the tax collectors would then have known nothing about a man's income.

After supper one night Father and I went out and milked the goats and saw that the sheds were secured for the night against the dogs. It seems as though they become more numer- ous and more bold each year. They run in packs now where there were only individuals when I was a little boy, and it is scarce safe for a grown man to travel an unfrequented locality at night. We are not permitted to have firearms in our possession, nor even bows and arrows, so we cannot exterminate them, and they seem to realize our weakness, coming close in among the houses and pens at night. They are large brutes—fearless and powerful. There is one pack more formidable than the others which Father says appears to carry a strong strain of collie and Airedale blood—the members of this pack are large, cunning, and ferocious, and are becoming a terror to the city—we call them the hellhounds.

After we returned to the house with the milk, Jim Thompson and his woman, Mollie Sheehan, came over. They live up the river about half a mile, on the next farm, and are our best friends. They are the only people that Father and Mother really trust, so when we are all together alone we speak our minds very freely. It seemed strange to me, even as a boy, that such big, strong men as Father and Jim should be afraid to express their real views to anyone, and though I was born and reared in an atmosphere of suspicion and terror, I could never quite reconcile myself to the attitude of servility and cowardice which marked us all.

And yet I knew that my father was no coward. He was a fine looking man, tall and wonderfully muscled, and I have seen him fight with men and with dogs. Once he defended Mother against a Kash Guard, and with his bare hands he killed the armed soldier. He lies in the center of the goat pen now, his rifle, bayonet, and ammunition wrapped in many thicknesses of oiled cloth beside him. We left no trace and were never even suspected; but we know where there is a rifle, a bayonet, and ammunition.

Jim had had trouble with Soor, the new tax collector, and was very angry. Jim was a big man, and like Father, was always smooth shaven as were nearly all Americans, as we called those whose people had lived here long before the Great War. The others—the true Kalkars—grew no beards. Their ancestors had come from the Moon many years before. They had come in strange ships year after year, but finally, one by one, their ships had been lost, and as none of them knew how to build others or the engines that operated them, the time came when no more Kalkars could come from the Moon to Earth.

Jim was terribly mad. He said that he couldn't stand it much longer—that he would rather be dead than live in such an awful world; but I was accustomed to such talk—I had heard it since infancy. Life was a hard thing—just work, work, work for a scant existence over and above the income tax. No pleasures—few conveniences or comforts; absolutely no luxuries—and worst of all, no hope. It was seldom that anyone smiled—anyone in our class—and the grown-ups never laughed. As children we laughed—

a little; not much. It is hard to kill the spirit of childhood; but the brotherhood of man had almost done it.

Father placed his hand upon Jim's shoulder. "We must not weaken, my friend," he said. "I often feel the same way," and then he walked quickly across the room to the fireplace and removed a stone above the rough, wooden mantel. Reaching his hand into the aperture behind, he turned toward us. "But cowed and degraded as I have become," he cried, "thank God I still have a spark of manhood left—I have had the strength to defy them as my fathers defied them—I have kept this that has been handed down to me—kept it for my son to hand down to his son—and I have taught him to die for it as his forefathers died for it and as I would die for it, gladly."

He drew forth a small bundle of fabric, and holding the upper corners between the fingers of his two hands he let it unfold before us—an oblong cloth of alternate red and white stripes with a blue square in one corner, upon which were sewn many little white stars.

Jim and Mollie and Mother rose to their feet and I saw Mother cast an apprehensive glance toward the doorway. For a moment they stood thus in silence, looking with wide eyes upon the thing that Father held, and then Jim walked slowly toward it, and kneeling, took the edge of it in his great, horny fingers and pressed it to his lips. The candle upon the rough table, sputtering in the spring wind that waved the goat skin at the window, cast its feeble rays upon them.

"It is The Flag, my son," said Father to me. "It is Old Glory—the flag of your fathers—the flag that made the world a decent place to live in. It is death to possess it; but when I am gone, take it and guard it as our family has guarded it since the regiment that carried it came back from the Argonne."

I felt tears filling my eyes—why, I could not have told them—and I turned away to hide them—turned toward the window and there, beyond the waving goat skin, I saw a face in the outer darkness. I have always been quick of thought and of action; but I never thought or moved more quickly in my life than I did in the instant following my discovery of the face in the window. With a single movement I swept the candle from the table, plunging the room into utter darkness, and leaping to my father's side I tore The Flag from his hands and thrust it back into the aperture above the mantel. The stone lay upon the mantel itself, nor did it take me but a moment to grope for it and find it in the dark—an instant more and it was replaced in its niche.

So ingrained were apprehension and suspicion in the human mind that the four in the room with me sensed intuitively something of the cause of my act, and when I had hunted for the candle, found it and relighted it they were standing, tense and motionless, where I had last seen them. They did not ask me a question, for if they suspicioned correctly they knew that we must not talk upon the subject. Father was the first to speak.

"You were very careless and clumsy, Julian," he said. "If you wanted the candle, why did you not pick it up carefully instead of rushing at it so? But that is always your way—you are constantly knocking things over." He raised his voice a trifle as he spoke; but it was a lame attempt at deception and he knew it, as did we. If the man who owned the face in the dark heard his words he must have known it as well.

As soon as I had relighted the candle I went into the kitchen and out the back door and then, keeping close in the black shadow of the house, I crept around toward the front, for I wanted to learn, if I could, who it was who had looked in upon that scene of high treason. The night was moonless but clear, and I could see quite a distance in every direction as our house stood in a fair sized clearing close to the river. Southeast of us the path wound upward across the approach to an ancient bridge, long since destroyed by raging mobs or rotted away—I do not know which—and presently I saw the figure of a man silhouetted against the starlit sky as he topped the approach. The man carried a laden sack upon his back. This fact was to some extent reassuring, as it suggested that the eavesdropper was himself upon some illegal mission and that he could ill afford to be too particular of the actions of others. I have seen many men carrying sacks and bundles at night—I have carried them myself. It is the only way often, in which a man may save enough from the tax collector on which to live and support his family.

I did not follow the man, being sure that he was one of our own class; but turned back toward the house where I found the four talking in low whispers, nor did any of us raise his voice again that evening.

It must have been three-quarters of an hour later, as Jim and Mollie were preparing to leave, that there came a knock upon the door, which immediately swung open before an invitation to enter could be given. We looked up to see Peter Johansen smiling at us. I never liked Peter. He was a long, lanky man who smiled with his mouth; but never with his eyes. I didn't like the way he used to look at Mother when he thought no one was observing him, nor his habit of changing women every year or two—that was too much like the Kalkars. I always felt toward Peter as I had as a child when, barefooted, I stepped unknowingly upon a snake in the deep grass.

Father greeted the newcomer with a pleasant "Welcome, Brother Johansen"; but Jim only nodded his head and scowled, for Peter had a habit of looking at Mollie as he did at Mother, and both women were beautiful. I think I never saw a more beautiful woman than my mother, and as I grew older and learned more of men and the world I marveled that Father had been able to keep her, and too, I understood why she never went abroad, but stayed always closely about the house and farm. I never knew her to go to the market place as did most of the other women. But I was twenty now and worldly wise and so I knew what I had not known as a little child.

"What brings you out so late, Brother Johansen?" I asked. We always used the prescribed "Brother" to those of whom we were not sure. I hated the word—to me a brother meant an enemy as it did to all our class and I guess to every class—even the Kalkars.

"I followed a stray pig," replied Peter to my question. "He went in that direction," and he waved a hand toward the market place. As he did so something tumbled from beneath his coat —something that his arm had held there. It was an empty sack. Immediately I knew who it was who owned the face in the dark beyond our goat skin hanging. Peter snatched the sack from the floor in ill-concealed confusion, and then I saw the expression of his cunning face change as he held it toward Father.

"Is this yours, Brother Julian?" he asked. "I found it just before your door and thought that I would stop and ask."

"No," said I, not waiting for Father to speak, "it is not ours— it must belong to the man I saw carrying it full, a short time since. He went by the path beside The Old Bridge." I looked straight into Peter's eyes. He flushed and then went white.

"I did not see him," he said presently; "but if the sack is not yours I will keep it—*at least it is not high treason to have it in my possession*," and then without another word, he turned and left the house.

We all knew then that Peter had seen the episode of The Flag. Father said that we need not fear, that Peter was all right; but Jim thought differently and so did Mollie and Mother. I agreed with them. I did not like Peter. Jim and Mollie went home shortly after Peter left, and we prepared for bed.

CHAPTER II

THE HELLHOUNDS

I HAD just slipped off my tunic when I heard the baying of the hellhounds close by. I thought they might be getting into the goat pen, so I waited a moment, listening, and then I heard a scream—the scream of a woman in terror. It sounded down by the river near the goat pens, and mingled with it was the vicious growling and barking of the hellhounds. I did not wait to listen longer; but seized my knife and a long staff.

I ran out the front door, which was closest, and turned toward the pens in the direction of the hellhounds' deep growlings and the screams of the woman, which were repeated twice.

As I neared the pens and my eyes became accustomed to the outer darkness I made out what appeared to be a human figure resting partially upon the top of one of the sheds that formed a portion of the pen wall. The legs and lower body dangled over the edge of the roof and I could see three or four hellhounds leaping for it, while another, that had evidently gotten a hold, was hanging to one leg and attempting to drag the figure down.

As I ran forward I shouted at the beasts, and those that were leaping for the figure stopped and turned toward me. I knew something of the temper of these animals and that I might expect them to charge, for they were quite fearless of man ordinarily; but I ran forward toward them so swiftly and with such determination that they turned, growling, and ran off before I reached them; but not far.

The one that had hold of the figure succeeded in dragging it to earth just before I reached them and then it discovered me and turned, standing over its prey, with wide jaws and terrific fangs menacing me. It was a huge beast, almost as large as a full grown goat, and easily a match for several men as poorly armed as I. Under ordinary circumstances I should have given it plenty of room; but what was I to do when the life of a woman was at stake? I am an American, not a Kalkar—those swine would throw a woman to the hellhounds to save their own skins—and I had been brought up to revere woman in a world that considered her on a par with the cow, the nanny and the sow, only less valuable since the latter were not the common property of the state.

I knew then that death stood very near as I faced that frightful beast, and from the corner of an eye I could see its mates creeping closer. There was no time to think, even, and so I rushed in upon the hellhound with my staff and blade. As I did so, I saw the wide and terrified eyes of a young girl looking up at me from beneath the beast of prey. I had not thought to desert her to her fate before; but after that single glance I could not have done so had a thousand deaths confronted me.

As I was almost upon the beast it sprang for my throat, rising high upon its hind feet and leaping straight as an arrow. My staff was useless and so I dropped it, meeting the charge with my knife and a bare hand. By luck the fingers of my left hand found the creature's throat at the first clutch; but the impact of his body against mine hurled me to the ground beneath him and there, growling and struggling, he sought to close those snapping fangs upon me. Holding his jaws at arm's length I struck at his breast with my blade, nor did I miss him once. The pain of the wounds turned him crazy and yet, to my utter surprise, I found I still could hold him and not that alone; but that I could also struggle to my knees and then to my feet—still holding him at arm's length in my left hand.

I had always known that I was muscular; but until that moment I had never dreamed of the great strength that Nature had given me, for never before had I had occasion to exert the full measure of my powerful thews. It was like a revelation from above, and of a sudden I found myself smiling and in the instant a miracle occurred—all fear of these hideous beasts dissolved from my brain like thin air and with it fear of man as well. I, who had been brought out of a womb of fear into a world of terror, who had been suckled and nurtured upon apprehension and timidity—I, Julian 9th, at the age of twenty years, became in the fraction of a second utterly fearless of man or beast. It was the knowledge of my great power that did it—that and, perhaps, those two liquid eyes that I knew to be watching me.

The other hounds were closing in upon me when the creature in my grasp went suddenly limp. My blade must have found its heart. And then the others charged and I saw the girl upon her feet beside me, my staff in her hands, ready to battle with them.

"To the roof!" I shouted to her; but she did not heed. Instead, she stood her ground, striking a vicious blow at the leader as he came within range.

Swinging the dead beast above my head I hurled the carcass

at the others so that they scattered and retreated again, and then I turned to the girl and without more parley lifted her in my arms and tossed her lightly to the roof of the goat shed. I could easily have followed to her side and safety had not something filled my brain with an effect similar to that which I imagine must be produced by the vile concoction brewed by the Kalkars and which they drink to excess, while it would mean imprisonment for us to be apprehended with it in our possession. At least, I know that I felt a sudden exhilaration—a strange desire to accomplish wonders before the eyes of this stranger, and so I turned upon the four remaining hellhounds who had now bunched to renew the attack and without waiting for them, I rushed toward them. They did not flee, but stood their ground, growling hideously, their hair bristling upon their necks and along their spines, their great fangs bared and slavering; but among them I tore and by the very impetuosity of my attack I overthrew them. The first sprang to meet me and him I seized by the neck and clamping his body between my knees I twisted his head entirely around until I heard the vertebrae snap. The other three were upon me then, leaping and tearing; but I felt no fear. One by one I took them in my mighty hands and lifting them high above my head hurled them violently from me. Two only of the hellhounds returned to the attack, and these I vanquished with my bare hands, disdaining to use my blade upon such carrion.

It was then that I saw a man running toward me from up the river and another from our house. The first was Jim, who had heard the commotion and the girl's screams, and the other was my father. Both had seen the last part of the battle and neither could believe that it was I, Julian, who had done this thing. Father was very proud of me and Jim was, too, for he had always said that having no son of his own, Father must share me with him.

And then I turned toward the girl who had slipped from the roof and was approaching us. She moved with the same graceful dignity that was Mother's—not at all like the clumsy clods that belonged to the Kalkars, and she came straight to me and laid a hand upon my arm.

"Thank you," she said, "and God bless you! Only a very brave and powerful man could have done what you have done."

And then, all of a sudden, I did not feel brave at all, but very weak and silly, for all I could do was finger my blade and look at the ground. It was Father who spoke and the interruption helped to dispel my embarrassment.

"Who are you?" he asked, "and from where do you come? It is strange to find a young woman wandering about alone at night; but stranger still to hear one who dares invoke the forbidden Deity."

I had not realized until then that she had used His name; but when I did recall it I could not but glance apprehensively about to see if any others might be around who could have heard. Father and Jim I knew to be safe; for there was a common tie between our families that lay in the secret religious rites we held once each month. Since that hideous day that had befallen even before my father's birth—that day, which none dared mention above a whisper, when the clergy of every denomination, to the last man, had been murdered by order of The Twentyfour, it had been a capital crime to worship God in any form, whatsoever.

We took the girl to the house, and when my mother saw her and how young and beautiful she was and took her in her arms, the child broke down and sobbed and clung to Mother, nor could either speak for some time. In the light of the candle I saw that the stranger was of wondrous beauty. I have said that my mother was the most beautiful woman I had ever seen, and such is the truth; but this girl who had come so suddenly among us was the most beautiful girl. She was about nineteen, delicately molded and yet without weakness. There were strength and vitality apparent in every move she made as well as in the expression of her face, her gestures and her manner of speech. She was girlish, and at the same time filled one with an impression of great reserve strength of mind and character. She was very brown, showing exposure to the sun, yet her skin was clear—almost translucent. Her garb was similar to mine—the common garmenture of people of our class, both men and women. She wore the tunic and breeches and boots just as Mother and Mollie and the rest of us did; but somehow there was a difference—I had never before realized what a really beautiful costume it was. The band about her forehead was wider than was generally worn and upon it were sewn numerous tiny shells, set close together and forming a pattern—it was her only attempt at ornamentation; but even so it was quite noticeable in a world where women strove to make themselves plain rather than beautiful—some going even so far as to permanently disfigure their faces and those of their female offspring, while others, many, many others, killed the latter in infancy. Mollie had done so with two. No wonder that grown-ups never laughed and seldom smiled!

When the girl had quieted her sobs on Mother's breast, Father renewed his questioning; but Mother said to wait until morning, that the girl was tired and unstrung and needed sleep, and then came the question of where she was to sleep. Father said that he would sleep in the living room with me and that the stranger could sleep with Mother; but Jim suggested that she come home with him as he and Mollie had three rooms, as did we, and no one to occupy his living room; and so it was arranged, although I would rather have had her remain with us.

At first she rather shrank from going, until Mother told her that Jim and Mollie were good, kind-hearted people and that she would be as safe with them as with her own father and mother. At mention of her parents the tears came to her eyes and she turned impulsively toward my mother and kissed her, after which she told Jim that she was ready to accompany him.

She started to say good-bye to me and to thank me again; but, having found my tongue at last, I told her that I would go with them as far as Jim's house. This appeared to please her and so we set forth. Jim walked ahead and I followed with the girl, and on the way I discovered a very strange thing. Father had shown me a piece of iron once that pulled smaller bits of iron to it. He said that it was a magnet. This slender, stranger girl was certainly no piece of iron, nor was I a smaller bit of anything; but nevertheless, I could not keep away from her. I cannot explain it—however wide the way was, I was always drawn over close to her, so that our arms touched and once our hands swung together and the strangest and most delicious thrill ran through me that I had ever experienced.

I used to think that Jim's house was a long way from ours— when I had to carry things over there as a boy; but that night it was far too close—just a step or two and we were there.

Mollie heard us coming and was at the door, full of questionings, and when she saw the girl and heard a part of our story she reached out and took the girl to her bosom, just as Mother had. Before they took her in, the stranger turned and held out her hand to me.

"Good night," she said, "and thank you again, and once more, may God, our Father, bless and preserve you."

And I heard Mollie murmur: "The Saints be praised!" And then I turned homeward, treading on air.

CHAPTER III

BROTHER GENERAL OR-TIS

THE next day I set out as usual to peddle goat's milk. We were permitted to trade in perishable things on other than market days, though we had to make a strict accounting for all such bartering. I usually left Mollie until the last as Jim had a deep, cold well on his place where I liked to quench my thirst after my morning trip; but today Mollie got her milk fresh and first and early—about half an hour earlier than I was wont to start out.

When I knocked and she had bade me enter and saw who it was, she looked surprised at first, for just an instant, and then a strange expression came into her eyes—half amusement, half pity—and she rose and went into the kitchen for the milk jar. I saw her wipe the corners of her eyes with the back of one finger; but I did not understand why—not then.

The stranger girl had been in the kitchen helping Mollie, and the latter must have told her I was there, for she came right in and greeted me. It was the first good look I had had of her, for candle light is not brilliant at best. If I had been enthralled the evening before, there is no word in my limited vocabulary to express the effect she had on me by daylight. She—but it is useless, I cannot describe her!

It took Mollie a long time to find the milk jar, bless her, though it seemed short enough to me, and while she was finding it the stranger girl and I were getting acquainted. First she asked after Father and Mother and then she asked our names. When I told her mine she repeated it several times to herself in a low voice. "Julian 9th," she said, "Julian 9th!" and then she smiled up at me. "It is a nice name, I like it."

"And what is your name?" I asked.

"Juana," she said—she pronounced it Whanna; "Juana St. John."

"I am glad," I said, "that you like my name; but I like yours better." It was a very foolish speech, and it made me feel silly; but she did not seem to think it foolish, or if she did, she was too nice to let me know it. I have known many girls; but mostly they were homely and stupid. The pretty girls were seldom allowed in the market place—that is, the pretty girls of our class. The Kalkars permitted their girls to go abroad for they did not care who got them, as long as someone got them; but American fathers and mothers would rather slay their girls than send them to the market place, and the former often was done. The Kalkar girls, even those born of American mothers, were coarse and brutal in appearance—low-browed, vulgar, bovine. No stock can be improved, or even kept to its normal plane, unless high grade males are used.

This girl was so entirely different from any other that I had ever seen that I marveled that such a glorious creature could exist. I wanted to know all about her. It seemed to me that in some way I had been robbed of my right for many years that she should have lived and breathed and talked and gone her way without my ever knowing it, or her. I wanted to make up for lost time and so I asked her many questions.

She told me that she had been born and raised in the teivos just west of Chicago, which extended along the Desplaines River and embraced a considerable area of unpopulated country and scattered farms.

"My father's home is in a district called Oak Park," she said, "and our house was one of the few that remained from ancient times. It was of solid concrete and stood upon the corner of two roads—once it must have been a very beautiful place, and even time and war have been unable entirely to erase its charm. Three great poplar trees rose to the north of it beside the ruins of what my father said was once a place where motor cars were kept by the long dead owner. To the south of the house were many roses, growing wild and luxuriant, while the concrete walls, from which the plaster had fallen in great patches, were almost entirely concealed by the clinging ivy that reached to the very eaves.

"It was my home and so I loved it; but now it is lost to me forever. The Kash Guard and the tax collector came seldom— we were too far from the station and the market place, which lay southwest of us, on Salt Creek. But recently the new Jemadar Jarth appointed another commandant and a new tax collector. They did not like the station at Salt Creek and so they sought for a better location, and after inspecting the district they chose Oak Park, and my father's home being the most comfortable and substantial, they ordered him to sell it to The Twentyfour. You know what that means. They appraised it at a high figure— $50,000.00 it was, and paid him in paper money. There was nothing to do, and so we prepared to move. Whenever they had come to look at the house my mother had hidden me in a little cubbyhole on the landing between the second and third floors, placing a pile of rubbish in front of me; but the day that we were leaving to take a place on the banks of the Desplaines, where Father thought that we might live without being disturbed, the new commandant came unexpectedly and saw me.

" 'How old is the girl?' he asked my mother.

" 'Fifteen,' she replied, sullenly.

" 'You lie, you sow!' he cried angrily; 'she is eighteen if she is a day.'

"Father was standing there beside us and when the commandant spoke as he did to Mother I saw Father go very white and then, without a word, he hurled himself upon the swine and before the Kash Guard who accompanied him could prevent, Father had almost killed the commandant with his bare hands.

"You know what happened—I do not need to tell you. They killed my father before my eyes. Then the commandant gave my mother to one of his Kash Guard; but she snatched his bayonet from his belt and ran it through her heart before they could prevent. I tried to follow her example; but they seized me.

"I was carried to my own bedroom on the second floor of my father's house and locked there. The commandant said that he would come and see me in the evening and that everything would be all right with me. I knew what he meant and I made up my mind that he would find me dead.

"My heart was breaking for the loss of my father and mother and yet the desire to live was strong within me. I did not want to die—something urged me to live, and in addition was the teaching of my father and mother. They were both from Quaker stock and very religious. They educated me to fear God and to do no wrong by thought or violence to another, and yet I had seen my father attempt to kill a man and I had seen my mother slay herself. My world was all upset. I was almost crazed by grief and fear and uncertainty as to what was the right thing for me to do.

"And then darkness came and I heard someone ascending the stairway. The windows of the second story are too far from the ground for one to risk a leap; but the ivy is old and strong. The commandant was not sufficiently familiar with the place to have taken the ivy into consideration, and before the footsteps reached my door I had swung out of the window and clinging to the ivy made my way to the ground down the rough and strong old stem.

"That was three days ago. I hid and wandered—I did not know in what direction I went. Once an old woman took me in over night and fed me and gave me food to carry for the next day. I think that I must have been almost mad, for mostly the happenings of the past three days are only indistinct and jumbled fragments of memory in my mind. And then the hellhounds! Oh, how frightened I was! And then—you!"

I don't know what there was about the way she said it; but it seemed to me as though it meant a great deal more than she knew herself. Almost like a prayer of thanksgiving, it was, that she had at last found a safe haven of refuge—safe and permanent. Anyway I liked the idea.

And then Mollie came in and as I was leaving she asked me if I would come that evening, and Juana cried: "Oh, yes, do!" and I said that I would.

When I had finished delivering the goats' milk I started for home, and on the way I met old Samuels, the Jew. He made his living, and a scant one it was, by tanning hides. He was a most excellent tanner; but as nearly everyone else knew how to tan there were not many customers; but some of the Kalkars used to bring him hides to tan. They knew nothing of how to do any useful thing, for they were descended from a long line of the most ignorant and illiterate people in the Moon, and the moment they obtained a little power they would not even work at what small trades their fathers once had learned, so that after a generation or two they were able to live only off the labor of others. They created nothing, they produced nothing, they became the most burdensome class of parasites the world ever has endured.

The rich non-producers of olden times were a blessing to the world by comparison with these, for the former at least had intelligence and imagination—they could direct others and they could transmit to their offspring the qualities of mind that are essential to any culture, progress or happiness that the world ever may hope to attain.

So the Kalkars patronized Samuels for their tanned hides, and if they had paid him for them the old Jew would have waxed rich; but they either did not pay him at all or else mostly in paper money that did not even burn well, as Samuels used to say.

"Good morning, Julian," he called as we met. "I shall be

needing some hides soon, for the new commander of the Kash
Guard has heard of old Samuels and has sent for me and ordered
five hides tanned the finest that can be. Have you seen this Or-tis,
Julian?" He lowered his voice.

I shook my head negatively.

"Heaven help us!" whispered the old man. "Heaven help us!"

"Is he as bad as that, Moses?" I asked.

The old man wrung his hands. "Bad times are ahead, my son,"
he said. "Old Samuels knows his kind. He is not lazy like the last
one, and he is more cruel and more lustful; but about the hides.
I have not paid you for the last—they paid me in paper money;
but that I would not offer to a friend in payment for a last
year's bird's nest. Maybe that I shall not be able to pay you for
these new hides for a long time—it depends upon how Or-tis pays
me. Sometimes they are liberal—as they can afford to be with the
property of others; but if he is a half breed, as I hear he is, he
will hate a Jew and I shall get nothing. However, if he is pure
Kalkar it may be different—the pure Kalkars do not hate a Jew
more than they hate other Earth Men, though there is one Jew
who hates a Kalkar."

That night we had our first introduction to Or-tis. He came
in person; but I will tell how it all happened. After supper I
went over to Jim's. Juana was standing in the little doorway as
I came up the path. She looked rested now and almost happy.
The hunted expression had left her eyes and she smiled as I
approached. It was almost dusk, for the spring evenings were
still short; but the air was balmy and so we stood outside, talking.

I recited the little gossip of our district that I had picked up
during my day's work—The Twentyfour had raised the local
tax on farm products—Andrew Wright's woman had given birth
to twins, a boy and a girl; but the girl had died (no need of
comment here as most girl babies die) —Soor had said that he
would tax this district until we all died of starvation (pleasant
fellow, Soor)—one of the Kash Guard had taken Nellie Levy—
Hoffmeyer had said that next winter we would have to pay more
for coal—Dennis Corrigan had been sent to the mines for ten
years because he had been caught trading at night. It was all
alike, this gossip of ours—all sordid, or sad, or tragic; but then
life was a tragedy with us.

After awhile I took Juana over to our house to see my mother.
She liked the house very much. My father's father built it with
his own hands. It is constructed of stone taken from the ruins

of the old city—stone and brick. Father says that he thinks the
bricks are from an old pavement as we still see patches of these
ancient bricks in various localities. Nearly all our houses are
of this construction, for timber is scarce. The foundation and
the walls above the ground for about three feet are of rough
stones of various sizes and above this are the bricks. The stones
are laid so that some project farther than others and the effect
is odd and rather nice. The eaves are low and overhanging and
the roof is thatched. It is a nice house and Mother keeps it
scrupulously clean and meticulously neat within.

We had been talking for perhaps an hour, sitting in our living room—Father, Mother, Juana, and I—when the door was suddenly thrust open without warning and we looked up to see a
man in the uniform of a Kash Guard confronting us. Behind
him were others. We all rose and stood in silence. Two entered
and took posts on either side of the doorway and then a third
came in—a tall, dark man in the uniform of a commander and
we knew at once that it was Or-tis. At his heels were six more.

Or-tis looked at each of us and then singling out Father he
said: "You are Brother Julian 8th."

Father nodded. Or-tis eyed him for a moment and then his
gaze wandered to Mother and Juana and I saw a new expression
lessen the fierce scowl that had clouded his face from the moment of his entry. He was a large man, his nose was thin and
rather fine, his eyes cold, gray and piercing. He was very different from the fat swine that had preceded him—very different and
more dangerous; even I could see that. I could see a thin, cruel
upper lip and a full and sensuous lower. If the other had been
a pig, this one was a wolf and he had the nervous restlessness of
the wolf—and the vitality to carry out any wolfish designs his
crafty brain might entertain.

"So you are Brother Julian 8th!" he repeated. "I do not have
good reports of you. I have come for two reasons tonight. One
is to warn you that the Kash Guard is commanded by a different
sort of man from him whom I relieved. I will stand no trifling
and no treason. There must be unquestioned loyalty to the
Jemadar at Washington—every national and local law will be
enforced. Trouble makers and traitors will get short shrift. A
manifesto will be read in each market place Saturday—a manifesto that I have just received from Washington. Our great Jemadar has conferred greater powers upon the commanders of the
Kash Guard. You will come to me with all your grievances.

Where justice miscarries I shall be the court of last resort. The judgment of any court may be appealed to me.

"On the other hand, let wrongdoers beware, as under the new law any cause may be tried before a summary military court over which the commander of the Kash Guard must preside.

"And," continued Or-tis, "I have come for another reason—a reason that looks bad for you, Brother Julian; but we shall see what we shall see," and turning to the men behind him he issued a curt command: "Search the place!" That was all; but I saw, in memory, another man standing in this same living room— a man from beneath whose coat fell an empty sack when he raised an arm.

For an hour they searched that little three room house. For an hour they tumbled our few belongings over and over; but mostly they searched the living room and especially about the fireplace did they hunt for a hidden nook. A dozen times my heart stood still as I saw them feeling of the stones above the mantel.

We all knew what they sought—all but Juana—and we knew what it would mean if they found it. Death for Father and for me, too, perhaps, and worse for Mother and the girl. And to think that Johansen had done this awful thing to curry favor for himself with the new commander! I knew it was he—I knew it as surely as though Or-tis had told me. To curry favor with the commander! I thought that that was the reason then. God, had I but known his real reason!

Well, they searched for an hour and found nothing; but I knew that Or-tis was not satisfied that the thing he sought was not there, and toward the end of the search I could see that he was losing patience. He took direct charge at last and then when they had no better success under his direction he became very angry.

"Yankee swine!" he cried suddenly, turning upon Father; "you will find that you cannot fool a descendant of the great Jemadar Orthis as you have fooled the others—not for long. I have a nose for traitors—I can smell a Yank farther than most men can see one. Take a warning, take a warning to your kind— it will be death or the mines for every traitor in the teivos."

He stood then, in silence for a moment, glaring at Father and then his gaze moved to Juana, where she stood just behind my shoulder at the far side of the room.

"Who are you, girl?" he demanded. "Where do you live and what do you that adds to the prosperity of the community?"

"Adds to the prosperity of the community!" It was a phrase often on their lips, and it was always directed at us—a meaningless phrase, as there was no prosperity. We supported the Kalkars and that was their idea of prosperity. I suppose ours was to get barely sufficient to sustain life and strength to enable us to continue slaving for them.

"I live with Mollie Sheehan," replied Juana, "and help her care for the chickens and the little pigs, also I help with the house work."

"Mm-m," ejaculated Or-tis; "house work! That is good—I shall be needing someone to keep my quarters tidy. How about it, my girl? It will be easy work and I will pay you well—no pigs or chickens to slave for. Eh?"

"But I love the little pigs and chickens, I like to care for them," she pleaded, "and I am happy with Mollie—I do not wish to change."

"Do not wish to change, eh?" he mimicked her. She had drawn farther behind me now, as though for protection, and closer—I could feel her body touching mine. "Mollie can doubtless take care of her own pigs and chickens without help. If she has so many she cannot do it alone then she has too many, and we will see why it is that she is more prosperous than the rest of us—probably she should pay a larger income tax—we shall see."

"Oh, no!" cried Juana, frightened now on Mollie's account; "please, she has only a few, scarcely enough that she and her man may live after the taxes are paid."

"Then she does not need you to help her," said Or-tis with finality, a nasty sneer upon his lip. "You will come and work for me, girl!"

And then Juana surprised me—she surprised us all, and particularly Or-tis. Before, she had been rather pleading and seemingly a little frightened; but now she drew herself to her full height and with her chin in air looked Or-tis straight in the eye.

"I will not come," she said, haughtily; "I do not wish to." That was all.

Or-tis looked surprised. His soldiers, shocked. For a moment no one spoke. I glanced at Mother. She was not trembling as I had expected. Her head was up, too, and she was openly looking her scorn of the man. Father stood as he usually did before them, with his head bowed; but I saw that he was watching Or-tis out of the corners of his eyes and that his fingers were moving as might the fingers of hands fixed upon a hated throat.

"You will come," said Or-tis, a little red in the face now at this defiance. "There are ways," and he looked straight at me— and then he turned upon his heel and followed by his Kash Guard left the house.

CHAPTER IV

A FIGHT ON MARKET DAY

WHEN the door had closed upon them, Juana buried her face in her hands.

"Oh, what misery I bring everywhere," she sobbed. "To my father and mother I brought death and now to you all and to Jim and Mollie I am bringing ruin and perhaps death also. But it shall not be—you shall not suffer for me! He looked straight at you, Julian, when he made his threat. What could he mean to do? You have done nothing. But you need not fear. I know how I may undo the harm I have so innocently done."

We tried to assure her that we did not care—that we would protect her as best we could and that she must not feel that she had brought any greater burden upon us than we already carried; but she only shook her head and at last asked me to take her home to Mollie's.

She was very quiet all the way back, though I did my best to cheer her up.

"He cannot make you work for him," I insisted. "Even The Twentyfour, rotten as it is, would never dare enforce such an order. We are not yet entirely slaves."

"But I am afraid that he will find a way," she replied, "through you, my friend. I saw him look at you and it was a very ugly look."

"I do not fear," I said.

"I fear for you. No, it shall not be!" She spoke with such vehement finality that she almost startled me, and then she bade me good night and went in to Mollie's house and closed the door.

All the way back home I was much worried about her, for I did not like to see her unhappy.

As I approached the house I saw that the candle was still burning in the living room—I had left so hurriedly that I had given it no thought—and as I came closer I saw something else, too. I was walking very slowly, and in the soft dust of the pathway my soft boots made no sound, or I might not have seen what I did see—two figures, close in the shadow of the wall, peering through one of our little windows into the living room.

I crept stealthily forward until I was close enough to see that one was in the uniform of a Kash Guard while the other was clothed as are those of my class, and in the latter I recognized the stoop-shouldered, lanky figure of Peter Johansen. I was not at all surprised at this confirmation of my suspicions.

I knew what they were there for—hoping to learn the secret hiding place of The Flag—but I also knew that unless they already knew it, there was no danger of their discovering it from the outside since The Flag had been removed from its hiding place. So I hid and watched them for awhile, and then circled the house and entered from the front as though I did not know they were there, for it would never do to let them know that they had been discovered.

Taking off my clothes I went to bed, after putting out the candle. I do not know how long they remained—it was enough to know that we were being watched, and though it was not pleasant I was glad that we were forewarned. In the morning I told Father and Mother what I had seen. Mother sighed and shook her head.

"It is coming," she said. "I always knew that sooner or later it would come. One by one they get us—now it is our turn."

It was market day, and I went in with a few wethers, some hides and cheese. Father did not come along—in fact, I advised him not to as Soor would be there and also Hoffmeyer. One cheese I took as tribute to Soor. God, how I hated to do it! But both Mother and Father thought it best to propitiate the fellow, and I suppose they were right. A lifetime of suffering does not incline one to seek further trouble.

The market place was full, for I was a little late. There were many Kash Guards in evidence—more than usual. It was a warm day—the first really warm day we had had—and a number of men were sitting beneath a canopy at one side of the market place in front of Hoffmeyer's office. As I approached I saw that Or-tis was there, as well as Pthav the coal baron, and Hoffmeyer of course, with several others, including some Kalkar women and children. I recognized Pthav's woman—a renegade Yank who had gone to him willingly—and their little child, a girl of about six. The latter was playing in the dust in front of the canopy some hundred feet from the group, and I had scarcely recognized her when I saw that which made my heart almost stop beating for an instant.

Two men were driving a small bunch of cattle into the market place upon the other side of the canopy when suddenly I saw one of the creatures, a great bull, break away from the herd and with lowered head charge toward the tiny figure playing, unconscious of danger, in the dust. The men tried to head the beast off but their efforts were futile. Those under the canopy saw the child's danger at the same time that I did, and they rose and cried aloud in warning. Pthav's woman shrieked and Or-tis yelled lustily for the Kash Guard; but none hastened in the path of the infuriated beast to the rescue of the child.

I was the closest to her and the moment that I saw her danger I started forward; but even as I ran, there passed through my brain some terrible thoughts. She is Kalkar! She is the spawn of the beast Pthav and of the woman who turned traitor to her kind to win ease and comfort and safety! Many a little life has been snuffed out because of her father and his class! Would they save a sister or a daughter of mine!

I thought all these things as I ran; but I did not stop running —something within impelled me to her aid. It must have been simply that she was a little child and I the descendant of American gentlemen. No, I kept right on in the face of the fact that my sense of justice cried out that I let the child die.

I reached her just a moment before the bull did and when he saw me there between him and the child he stopped, and with his head down he pawed the earth, throwing clouds of dust about, and bellowed—and then he came for me; but I met him half way, determined to hold him off until the child escaped, if it were humanly possible for me to do so. He was a huge beast and quite evidently a vicious one, which possibly explained the reason for bringing him to market, and altogether it seemed to me that he would make short work of me; but I meant to die fighting.

I called to the little girl to run and then the bull and I came together. I seized his horns as he attempted to toss me and I exerted all the strength in my young body. I had thought that I had let the hellhounds feel it all that other night; but now I knew that I had yet more in reserve, for to my astonishment I held that great beast and slowly, very slowly, I commenced to twist his head to the left.

He struggled and fought and bellowed—I could feel the muscles of my back and arms and legs hardening to the strain that was put upon them; but almost from the first instant I knew that I was master. The Kash Guards were coming now, on the run, and I could hear Or-tis shouting to them to shoot the bull; but before they reached me I gave the animal a final mighty wrench so that he went down first upon one knee and then over on his side and there I held him until a sergeant came and put a bullet through his head.

When he was quite dead Or-tis and Pthav and the others approached—I saw them coming as I was returning to my wethers, my skins and my cheese. Or-tis called to me, and I turned and stood looking at him, as I had no mind to have any business with any of them that I could avoid.

"Come here, my man," he called.

I moved sullenly toward him a few paces and stopped again.

"What do you want of me?" I asked.

"Who are you?" He was eyeing me closely now. "I never saw such strength in any man. You should be in the Kash Guard. How would you like that?"

"I would not like it," I replied. It was about then, I guess, that he recognized me, for his eyes hardened. "No," he said, "we do not want such as you among loyal men." He turned upon his heel; but immediately wheeled toward me again. "See to it, young man," he snapped, "that you use that strength of yours and in good causes."

"shall use it wisely," I replied, "and in the best of causes." think Pthav's woman had intended to thank me for saving her child, and perhaps Pthav had, too, for they had both come toward me; but when they saw Or-tis' evident hostility toward me, they turned away, for which I was thankful. I saw Soor looking on with a sneer on his lips and Hoffmeyer eyeing me with that cunning expression of his.

I gathered up my produce and proceeded to that part of the market place where we habitually showed that which we had to sell, only to find that a man named Vonbulen was there ahead of me. Now there is an unwritten law that each family has its own place in the market. I was the third generation of Julians who had brought produce to this spot—formerly horses mostly, for we were a family of horsemen; but more recently goats, since the government had taken over the horse industry. Though Father and I still broke horses occasionally for The Twentyfour, we did not own or raise them any more.

Vonbulen had had a little pen in a far corner, where trade was not so brisk as it usually was in our section, and I could not understand what he was doing in ours, where he had three or four scrub pigs and a few sacks of grain. Approaching, I asked him why he was there.

"This is my pen now," he said. "Tax Collector Soor told me to use it."

"You will get out of it," I replied. "You know that it is ours—everyone in the teivos knows that it is and has been for many years. My grandfather built it and my family have kept it in repair. You will get out!"

"I will not get out," he replied truculently. He was a very large man and when he was angry he looked quite fierce, as he had large mustaches which he brushed upward on either side of his nose—like the tusks of one of his boars.

"You will get out or be thrown out," I told him; but he put his hand on the gate and attempted to bar my entrance.

Knowing him to be heavy minded and stupid I thought to take him by surprise, nor did I fail, as, with a hand upon the topmost rail, I vaulted the gate full in his face and letting my knees strike his chest I sent him tumbling backward into the filth of his swine. So hard I struck him that he turned a complete back somersault, and as he scrambled to his feet, his lips foul with oaths, I saw murder in his eye. And how he charged me! It was for all the world like the charge of the great bull I had just vanquished, except that I think that Vonbulen was angri̶̶̶̶ wisely a̶
the bull and not so good looking.   "I s̶
                                                                  I
His great fists were flailing about in a most terrifying m̶
ner, and his mouth was open just as though he intended eating me alive; but for some reason I felt no fear. In fact, I had to smile to see his face and his fierce mustache smeared with soft hog dung.

I parried his first wild blows and then stepping in close I struck him lightly in the face—I am sure I did not strike him hard, for I did not mean to—I wanted to play with him; but the result was as astonishing to me as it must have been to him, though not so painful. He rebounded from my fist fully three feet and then went over on his back again, spitting blood and teeth from his mouth.

And then I picked him up by the scruff of his neck and the seat of his breeches and lifting him high above my head I hurled him out of the pen into the market place, where, for the first time, I saw a large crowd of interested spectators.

Vonbulen was not a popular character in the teivos, and many were the broad smiles I saw on the faces of those of my class; but there were others who did not smile. They were Kalkars and half-breeds.

I saw all this in a single glance and then I returned to my work, for I was not through. Vonbulen lay where he had alighted and after him and onto him, one by one, I threw his sacks of grain and his scrub pigs and then I opened the gate and started out to bring in my own produce and livestock. As I did so, I almost ran into Soor, standing there eyeing me with a most malignant expression upon his face.

"What does this mean?" he fairly screamed at me.

"It means," I replied, "that no one can steal the place of a Julian as easily as Vonbulen thought."

"He did not steal it," yelled Soor. "I gave it to him. Get out! It is his."

"It is not yours to give," I replied. "I know my rights and no man shall take them from me without a fight. Do you understand me?" And then I brushed by him without another glance and drove my wethers into the pen. As I did so, I saw that no one was smiling any more—my friends looked very glum and very frightened; but a man came up from my right and stood by my side, facing Soor, and when I turned my eyes in his direction I saw that it was Jim.

Then I realized how serious my act must have seemed and I was sorry that Jim had come and thus silently announced that he stood with me in what I had done. No others came, although there were many who hated the Kalkars fully as much as we.

Soor was furious; but he could not stop me. Only The Twenty-four could take the pen away from me. He called me names and threatened me; but I noticed that he waited until he had walked a short distance away before he did so. It was as food to a starving man to know that even one of our oppressors feared me. So far, this had been the happiest day of my life.

I hurriedly got the goats into the pen and then, with one of the cheeses in my hand, I called to Soor. He turned to see what I wanted, showing his teeth like a rat at bay.

"You told my father to bring you a present," I yelled at the top of my lungs, so that all about in every direction heard and turned toward us. "Here it is!" I cried. "Here is your bribe!" and I hurled the cheese with all my strength full in his face. He went down like a felled ox and the people scattered like frightened rabbits. Then I went back into the pen and started to open and arrange my hides across the fence so that they might be inspected by prospective purchasers.

Jim, whose pen was next to ours, stood looking across the fence at me for several minutes. At last he spoke.

"You have done a very rash thing, Julian," he said; and then: "I envy you."

CHAPTER V

THE COURT MARTIAL

THAT afternoon I saw a small detachment of the Kash Guard crossing the market place. They came directly toward my pen and stopped before it. The sergeant in charge addressed me. "You are Brother Julian 9th?" he asked.

"I am Julian 9th," I replied.

"You had better be Brother Julian 9th when you are addressed by Brother General Or-tis," he snapped back. "You are under arrest—come with me!"

"What for?" I asked.

"Brother Or-tis will tell you if you do not know—you are to be taken to him."

So! It had come and it had come quickly. I felt sorry for Mother; but, in a way, I was glad. If only there had been no such person in the world as Juana St. John I should have been almost happy, for I knew Mother and Father would come soon, and as she had always taught me, we would be reunited in a happy world on the other side—a world in which there were no Kalkars or taxes—but then there was a Juana St. John and I was very sure of this world, while not quite so sure of the other which I had never seen.

There seemed no particular reason for refusing to accompany the Kash Guard. They would simply have killed me with their bullets, and if I went I might have an opportunity to wipe out some more important swine than they before I was killed—if they intended killing me. One never knows what they will do—other than that it will be the wrong thing.

Well, they took me to the headquarters of the teivos, way down on the shore of the lake; but as they took me in a large wagon drawn by horses it was not a tiresome trip, and as I was not worrying, I rather enjoyed it. We passed through many market places, for numerous districts lie between ours and headquarters, and always the people stared at me, just as I had stared at other prisoners being carted away to no one knew what fate. Sometimes they came back—sometimes they did not. I wondered which I would do.

At last we arrived at headquarters after passing through miles of lofty ruins where I had played and explored as a child. I was taken immediately into Or-tis' presence. He sat in a large room at the head of a long table and I saw that there were other men sitting along the sides of the table, the local representatives of that hated authority known as The Twentyfour, the form of government that the Kalkars had brought with them from the Moon a century before. The Twentyfour originally consisted of a committee of that number. Now, however, it was but a name that stood for power, for government and for tyranny. Jarth the Jemadar was, in reality, what his lunar title indicated—emperor. Surrounding him was a committee of twenty-four Kalkars; but as they had been appointed by him and could be removed by him at will, they were nothing more than his tools. And this body before which I had been haled had in our teivos the same power as The Twentyfour which gave it birth, and so we spoke of it, too, as The Twentyfour, or as the Teivos, as I at first thought it to be.

Many of these men I recognized as members of the teivos. Pthav and Hoffmeyer were there, representing our district, or misrepresenting it, as Father always put it, yet I was presently sure that this could not be a meeting of the teivos proper, as these were held in another building farther south—a magnificent pillared pile of olden times that the Government had partially restored, as they had the headquarters, which also had been a beautiful building in a past age, its great lions still standing on either side of its broad entranceway, facing toward the west.

No, it was not the teivos; but what could it be, and then it dawned upon me that it must be an arm of the new law that Or-tis had announced, and such it proved to be—a special military tribunal for special offenders. This was the first session, and it chanced to be my luck that I committed my indiscretion just in time to be haled before it when it needed someone to experiment on.

I was made to stand under guard at the foot of the table, and as I looked up and down the rows of faces on either side, I saw not a friendly eye—no person of my class or race—just swine, swine, swine. Low-browed, brute-faced men, slouching in their chairs, slovenly in their dress, uncouth, unwashed, unwholesome looking

—this was the personnel of the court that was to try me—for what?

I was soon to find out. Or-tis asked who appeared against me and what was the charge and then I saw Soor for the first time. He should have been in his district collecting his taxes; but he wasn't. No, he was here on more pleasant business. He eyed me malevolently and stated the charge: Resisting an officer of the law in the discharge of his duty, and assaulting same with a deadly weapon with intent to commit murder.

They all looked ferociously at me, expecting, no doubt, that I would tremble with terror, as most of my class did before them; but I couldn't tremble—the charge struck me as so ridiculous. As a matter of fact, I am afraid that I grinned. I know I did.

"What is it," asked Or-tis, "that amuses you so?"

"The charge," I replied.

"What is there funny about that?" he asked again—"men have been shot for less—men who were not suspected of treasonable acts."

"I did not resist an officer in the discharge of his duty," I said. "It is not one of a tax collector's duties to put a family out of its pen at the market place, is it?—a pen they have occupied for three generations? I ask you, Or-tis, is it?"

Or-tis half rose from his chair. "How dare you address me thus?" he cried.

The others turned scowling faces upon me, and beating the table with their dirty fists they all shouted and bellowed at me at once; but I kept my chin up as I had sworn to do until I died and I laughed in their faces.

Finally they quieted down, and again I put my question to Or-tis and I'll give him credit for answering it fairly. "No," he said, "only the teivos may do that—the teivos or the commandant."

"Then I did not resist an officer in the discharge of his duty"; I shot back at them, "for I only refused to leave the pen that is mine. And now another question. Is a cheese a deadly weapon?"

They had to admit that it was not. "He demanded a present from my father," I explained, "and I brought him a cheese. He had no right under the law to demand it, and so I threw it at him and it hit him in the face. I shall deliver thus every such illegal tithe that is demanded of us. I have my rights under the law and I intend to see that they are respected."

They had never been talked to thus before, and suddenly I realized that by merest chance I had stumbled upon the only way in which to meet these creatures. They were moral as well as physical cowards. They could not face an honest, fearless man— already they were showing signs of embarrassment. They knew that I was right, and while they could have condemned me had I bowed the knee to them they hadn't the courage to do it in my presence.

The natural outcome was that they sought a scape goat, and Or-tis was not long in finding one—his baleful eye alighted upon Soor.

"Does this man speak the truth?" he cried at the tax collector. "Did you turn him out of his pen—did he do no more than throw a cheese at you?"

Soor, a coward before those in authority over him, flushed and stammered.

"He tried to kill me," he mumbled lamely, "and he did almost kill Brother Vonbulen."

Then I told them of that—and always I spoke in a tone of authority and I held my ground. I did not fear them and they knew it. Sometimes I think they attributed it to some knowledge I had of something that might be menacing them—for they were always afraid of revolution. That is why they ground us down so.

The outcome of it was that I was let go with a warning—a warning that if I did not address my fellows as Brother I would be punished, and even then I gave the parting shot, for I told them I would call no man Brother unless he was.

The whole affair was a farce; but all trials were farces, only as a rule the joke was on the accused. They were not conducted in a dignified or proper manner as I imagine trials in ancient times to have been. There was neither order nor system.

I had to walk all the way home—another manifestation of justice—and I arrived there an hour or two after supper time. I found Jim and Mollie and Juana at the house, and I could see that Mother had been crying. She started again when she saw me —poor Mother. I wonder if it has always been such a terrible thing to be a mother; but no, it cannot have been, else the human race would long since have been extinct—as the Kalkars will rapidly make it anyway.

Jim had told them of the happenings in the market place—the episode of the bull, the encounter with Vonbulen and the matter of Soor. For the first time in my life, and the only time, I heard my Father laugh aloud. Juana laughed, too; but there was still an undercurrent of terror that I could feel, and which Mollie finally voiced.

"They will get us yet, Julian," she said; "but what you have done is worth dying for."

"Yes!" cried my father, "I can go to The Butcher with a smile on my lips after this. He has done what I always wanted to do; but dared not. If I am a coward I can at least thank God that there sprang from my loins a brave and fearless man."

"You are not a coward!" I cried and Mother looked at me and smiled. I was glad that I said that, then.

You may not understand what Father meant by "going to The Butcher"; but it is simple. The manufacture of ammunition is a lost art—that is, the high powered ammunition that the Kash Guard likes to use—and so they conserve all the vast stores of ammunition that were handed down from ancient times—millions upon millions of rounds—or they would not be able to use the rifles that were handed down with the ammunition. They use this ammunition only in cases of dire necessity, a fact which long ago placed the firing squad of old in the same class with flying machines and automobiles. Now they cut our throats when they kill us, and the man who does it is known as The Butcher.

I walked home with Jim and Mollie and Juana; but more especially Juana. Again I noticed that strange magnetic force which drew me to her, so that I kept bumping into her every step or two, and intentionally I swung my arm that was nearest to her in the hope that my hand might touch hers, nor was I doomed to disappointment, and at every touch I thrilled. I could not but notice that Juana made no mention of my clumsiness, nor did she appear to attempt to prevent our contact; but yet I was afraid of her—afraid that she would notice and afraid that she would not. I am good with horses and goats and hellhounds; but I am not much good with girls.

We had talked upon many subjects and I knew her views and beliefs and she knew mine, so when we parted, and I asked her if she would go with me on the morrow, which was the first Sunday of the month, she knew what I meant. She said that she would, and I went home very happy, for I knew that she and I were going to defy the common enemy side by side—that hand in hand we would face the grim reaper for the sake of the greatest cause on earth.

On the way I overtook Peter Johansen going in the direction of our home. I could see that he had no mind to meet me and he immediately fell to explaining lengthily why he was out at night, for the first thing I did was to ask him what strange business took him abroad so often lately after the sun had set.

I could see him flush even in the dark.

"Why," he exclaimed, "this is the first time in months that I have gone out after supper," and then something about the man made me lose my temper and I blurted out what was in my heart.

"You lie!" I cried. "You lie, you damned spy!"

And then Peter Johansen went white and suddenly whipping a knife from his clothes he leaped at me, striking wildly for any part of me that the blade might reach. At first he like to have got me, so unexpected and so venomous was the attack; but though I was struck twice on the arm and cut a little, I managed to ward the point from any vital part and in a moment I had seized his knife wrist. That was the end—I just twisted it a little —I did not mean to twist hard—and something snapped inside his wrist.

Peter let out an awful scream, his knife dropped from his fingers and I pushed him from me and gave him a good kick as he was leaving—a kick that I think he will remember for some time. Then I picked up his knife and hurled it as far as I could in the direction of the river, and went on my way toward home —whistling.

When I entered the house Mother came out of her room and putting her arms about my neck she clung closely to me.

"Dear boy," she murmured, "I am so happy, because you are happy. She is a dear girl and I love her as much as you do."

"What is the matter?" I asked. "What are you talking about?"

"I heard you whistling," she said, "and I knew what it meant —grown men whistle but once in their lives."

I picked her up in my arms and tossed her to the ceiling.

"Oh, Mother, dear!" I cried, "I wish it were true, and maybe it will be some day—if I am not too much of a coward; but not yet."

"Then why were you whistling?" she asked, surprised and a bit skeptical, too, I imagine.

"I whistled," I explained, "because I just broke the wrist of a spy and kicked him across the road."

"Peter?" she asked, trembling.

"Yes, Mother, Peter. I called him a spy and he tried to knife me."

"Oh, my son!" she cried. "You did not know. It is my fault, I should have told you. Now he will fight no more in the dark; but will come out in the open, and when he does that I am lost."

"What do you mean?" I asked.

"I do not mind dying," she said; "but they will take your father first, because of me."

"What do you mean?—I can understand nothing of what you are driving at."

"Then listen," she said. "Peter wants me. That is the reason he is spying on your father. If he can prove something on him, and Father is taken to the mines or killed, Peter will claim me."

"How do you know this?" I asked.

"Peter himself has told me that he wants me. He tried to make me leave your dear father and go with him, and when I refused he bragged that he was in the favor of the Kalkars and that he would get me in the end. He has tried to buy my honor with your father's life. That is why I have been so afraid and so unhappy; but I knew that you and Father would rather die than have me do that thing and so I have withstood him."

"Did you tell Father?" I asked.

"I dared not. He would have killed Peter and that would have been the end of us, for Peter stands high in the graces of the authorities."

"I will kill him," I said.

She tried to dissuade me, and finally I had to promise her that I would wait until I had provocation that the authorities might recognize—God knows I had provocation enough, though.

After breakfast the next day we set out singly and in different directions, as was always our custom on the first Sunday in each month. I went to Jim's first to get Juana, as she did not know the way, having never been with us. I found her ready and waiting and alone, as Jim and Mollie had started a few minutes before, and she was seemingly very glad to see me.

I told her nothing of Peter, as there is enough trouble in the world without burdening people with any that does not directly threaten them—each has plenty of his own. I led her up the river for a mile and all the while we watched to see if we were followed. Then we found a skiff, where I had hidden it, and crossed the river, and after hiding it again we continued on up for a half a mile. Here was a raft that I had made myself and on this we poled to the opposite shore; if any followed us they must have swum, for there were no other boats on this part of the river.

A mile west of the river is a thick forest of very old trees, and toward this I led Juana. At its verge we sat down, ostensibly to rest; but really to see if anyone was near who might have followed us or who could accidentally discover our next move.

There was no one in sight and so with light hearts we arose and entered the forest.

For a quarter of a mile we made our way along a winding path and then I turned to the left at a right angle, and entered thick brush where there was no trail. Always we did this, never covering the last quarter of a mile over the same route, lest we make a path that might be marked and followed.

Presently we came to a pile of brush wood beneath one edge of which was an opening into which, by stooping low, one might enter. It was screened from view by a fallen tree over which had been heaped broken branches. Even in winter time and early spring the opening in the brush beyond was invisible to the passers-by, if there had been any passers-by, which except upon rare occasions there were not. A man trailing lost stock might come this way; but no others, for it was a lonely and unfrequented spot. During the summer, the season of the year when there was the greatest danger of discovery, the entire brush pile and its tangled screen were hidden completely beneath a mass of wild vines, so that it was with difficult that we found it.

Into this opening I led Juana—taking her by the hand as one might a blind person, although it was not so dark within that she could not see perfectly every step she took. However, I took her by the hand, a poor excuse being better than none. The winding tunnel beneath the brush was a hundred yards long, perhaps —I wished then that it had been a hundred miles—it ended abruptly before a rough stone wall in which was a heavy door. Its oaken panels were black with age and streaked with green from the massive hinges that ran across its entire width in three places, while from the great lag screws that fastened them to the door, brownish streaks of rust ran down to mingle with the green and the black. In patches, moss grew upon it, so that all-in-all it had the appearance of great antiquity, though even the oldest among those who knew of it at all could only guess at its age— it had been there longer than they could recall. Above the door, carved in the stone, was a shepherd's crook and the words, *Dieu et mon droit.*

Halting before this massive portal I struck the panels once with my knuckles, counted five and struck again, once; then I counted three and, in the same cadence, struck three times. It was the signal for the day—never twice was it the same. Should one come with the wrong signal, and later force the door he would find only an empty room beyond.

Now the door opened a crack and an eye peered forth, then

it swung outward and we entered a long, low room lighted by burning wicks floating in oil. Across the width of the room were rough wooden benches and at the far end a raised platform upon which stood Orrin Colby, the blacksmith, behind an altar which was the sawn-off trunk of a tree, the roots of which, legend has it, still run down into the ground beneath the church, which is supposed to have been built around it.

CHAPTER VI

BETRAYED

THERE were twelve people sitting on the benches when we entered, so that with Orrin Colby, ourselves, and the man at the door we were sixteen in all. Colby is the head of our church, his great-grandfather having been a methodist minister. Father and Mother were there, sitting next to Jim and Mollie, and there were Samuels the Jew, Betty Worth, who was Dennis Corrigan's woman, and all the other familiar faces.

They had been waiting for us, and as soon as we were seated the services commenced with a prayer, everyone standing with bowed head. Orrin Colby always delivered this same short prayer at the opening of services each first Sunday of every month. It ran something like this:

> God of our fathers, through generations of persecution and cruelty in a world of hate that has turned against You, we stand at Your right hand, loyal to You and to our Flag. To us Your name stands for justice, humanity, love, happiness and right and The Flag is Your emblem. Once each month we risk our lives that Your name may not perish from the Earth. Amen!

From behind the altar he took a shepherd's crook to which was attached a flag like that in my father's possession, and held it aloft, whereat we all knelt in silence for a few seconds, then he replaced it and we arose. Then we sang a song—it was an old, old song that started like this: "Onward, Christian soldiers." It was my favorite song. Mollie Sheehan played a violin while we sang.

Following the song Orrin Colby talked to us—he always talked about the practical things that affected our lives and our future. It was a homely talk; but it was full of hope for better times. I think that at these meetings, once each month, we heard the only suggestions of hope that ever came into our lives. There was something about Orrin Colby that inspired confidence and hope. These days were the bright spots in our drab existence that helped to make life bearable.

After that we sang again and then Samuels, the Jew, prayed, and the regular service was over, after which we had short talks by various members of our church. These talks were mostly on the subject which dominated the minds of all—a revolution; but we never got any further than talking. How could we? We were probably the most thoroughly subjugated people the world ever had known—we feared our masters and we feared our neighbors. We did not know whom we might trust, outside that little coterie of ours, and so we dared not seek recruits for our cause although we knew that there must be thousands who would sympathize with us. Spies and informers were everywhere—they, The Kash Guard and The Butcher, were the agencies by which they controlled us; but of all, we feared most the spies and informers. For a woman, for a neighbor's house, and in one instance of which I know, for a setting of eggs, men have been known to inform on their friends—sending them to the mines or The Butcher.

Following the talks we just visited together and gossiped for an hour or two, enjoying the rare treat of being able to speak our minds freely and fearlessly. I had to re-tell several times my experiences before Or-tis' new court martial, and I know that it was with difficulty that they believed that I had said the things I had to our masters and come away free and alive. They simply could not understand it.

All were warned of Peter Johansen and the names of others under suspicion of being informers were passed around that we might all be on our guard against them. We did not sing again, for even on these days that our hearts were lightest they were too heavy for song. About two o'clock the pass signal for the next meeting was given out and then we started away singly or in pairs. I volunteered to go last, with Juana, and see that the door was locked, and an hour later, after the rest had gone, we started out about five minutes behind Samuels, the Jew.

Juana and I had emerged from the wood, when we noticed a man walking cautiously in the shade of the trees ahead of us. He seemed to be following someone and immediately there sprang to my thoughts the ever-near suspicion—spy.

The moment that he turned a bend in the pathway and was out of our sight Juana and I ran forward as rapidly as we could, that we might get a closer view of him, nor were we disappointed. We saw and recognized him, and we also saw whom he shadowed. It was Peter Johansen, carrying one arm in a sling, sneaking along behind Samuels.

Casting about in my mind for some plan to throw Peter off the track I finally hit upon a scheme which I immediately put into execution. I knew the way that the old man followed to and from church, and that presently he would make a wide detour that would bring him back to the river about a quarter of a mile below. Juana and I could walk straight to the spot and arrive long before Samuels did. And this we proceeded to do.

About half an hour after we reached the point at which we knew he would strike the river we heard him coming and withdrew into some bushes. On he came, all oblivious of the creature on his trail, and a moment later we saw Peter come into view and halt at the edge of the trees. Then Juana and I stepped out and hailed Samuels.

"Did you see nothing of them?" I asked in a tone of voice loud enough to be distinctly heard by Peter, and then before Samuels could reply I added: "We have searched far up the river and never a sign of a goat about—I do not believe that they came this way after all; but if they did the hellhounds will get them after dark. Come, now, we might as well start for home and give the search up as a bad job."

I had talked so much and so rapidly that Samuels had guessed that I must have some reason for it and so he held his peace, other than to say that he had seen nothing of any goats. Not once had Juana or I let our glances betray that we knew of Peter's presence, though I could not help but see him dodge behind a tree the moment that he saw us.

The three of us then continued on toward home in the shortest direction, and on the way I whispered to Samuels what we had seen. The old man chuckled, for he thought as I did that my ruse must have effectually baffled Johansen—unless he had followed Moses farther than we guessed.

Very cautiously during the ensuing week the word was passed around by means with which we were familiar that Johansen had followed Samuels from church; but as the authorities paid no more attention to Moses than before, we finally concluded that we had thrown Peter off the trail.

The Sunday following church we were all seated in Jim's yard under one of his trees that had already put forth its young leaves and afforded shade from the sun. We had been talking of homely things—the coming crops, the newborn kids, Mollie's little pigs. The world seemed unusually kindly. The authorities had not persecuted us of late—rather they had left us alone—a respite of two weeks seemed like heaven to us. We were quite sure by this time that Peter Johansen had discovered nothing, and our hearts were freer than for a long time past.

We were sitting thus in quiet and contentment enjoying a brief rest from our lives of drudgery, when we heard the pounding of horses' hoofs upon the hard earth of the path that leads down the river in the direction of the market place. Suddenly the entire atmosphere changed—relaxed nerves became suddenly taut; peaceful eyes resumed their hunted expression. Why? The Kash Guard rides.

And so they came—fifty of them, and at their head rode Brother General Or-tis. At the gateway of Jim's house they drew rein and Or-tis dismounted and entered the yard. He looked at us as a man might look at carrion; and he gave us no greeting, which suited us perfectly. He walked straight to Juana, who was seated on a little bench beside which I stood leaning against the bole of the tree. None of us moved. He halted before the girl.

"I have come to tell you," he said to her, "that I have done you the honor to choose you as my woman, to bear my children and keep my house in order."

He stood then looking at her and I could feel the hair upon my head rise, and the corners of my upper lip twitched—I know not why. I only know that I wanted to fly at his throat and kill him, to tear his flesh with my teeth—to see him die! And then he looked at me and stepped back, after which he beckoned to some of his men to enter. When they had come, he again addressed Juana, who had risen and stood swaying to and fro, as might one who has been dealt a heavy blow upon the head and half-stunned.

"You may come with me now," he said to her, and then I stepped between them and faced him, and again he stepped back a pace.

"She will not come with you now, or ever," I said, and my voice was very low—not above a whisper. "She is my woman—I have taken her!"

It was a lie—the last part; but what is a lie to a man who would commit murder in the same cause. He was among his men now—they were close around him and I suppose they gave him courage, for he addressed me threateningly.

"I do not care whose she is," he cried, "I want her and I shall have her. I speak for her now, and I speak for her when she is a widow. After you are dead I have first choice of her and traitors do not live long."

"I am not dead yet," I reminded him. He turned to Juana.

"You shall have thirty days as the law requires; but you can save your friends trouble if you come now—they will not be molested then and I will see that their taxes are lowered."

Juana gave a little gasp and looked around at us and then she straightened her shoulders and came close to me.

"No!" she said to Or-tis. "I will never go. This is my man—he has taken me. Ask him if he will give me up to you. You will never have me—alive."

"Don't be too sure of that," he growled. "I believe that you are both lying to me, for I have had you watched and I know that you do not live under the same roof. And you!" he glared at me. "Tread carefully, for the eyes of the law find traitors where others do not see them." Then he turned and strode from the yard. A minute later they were gone in a cloud of dust.

Now our happiness and peace had fled—it was always thus— and there was no hope. I dared not look at Juana after what I had said; but then, had she not said the same thing? We all talked lamely for a few minutes and then Father and Mother rose to go, and a moment later Jim and Mollie went indoors. I turned to Juana. She stood with her eyes upon the ground and a pretty flush upon her cheek. Something surged up in me—a mighty force, that I had never known, possessed me, and before I realized what it impelled me to do I had seized Juana in my arms and was covering her face and lips with kisses.

She fought to free herself; but I would not let her go.

"You are mine!" I cried. "You are my woman. I have said it —you have said. You are my woman. God, how I love you!"

She lay quiet then, and let me kiss her, and presently her arms stole about my neck and her lips sought mine in an interval that I had drawn them away, and they moved upon my lips in a gentle caress, that was yet palpitant with passion. This was a new Juana—a new and very wonderful Juana.

"You really love me?" she asked at last—"I heard you say it!"

"I have loved you from the moment I saw you looking up at me from beneath the hellhound," I replied.

"You have kept it very much of a secret to yourself then," she teased me. "If you loved me so, why did you not tell me? Were you going to keep it from me all my life, or—were you afraid? Brother Or-tis was not afraid to say that he wanted me—is my man, my Julian, less brave than he?"

I knew that she was only teasing me, and so I stopped her mouth with kisses and then: "Had you been a hellhound, or Soor, or even Or-tis," I said, "I could have told you what I thought of you; but being Juana and a little girl the words would not come. I am a great coward."

We talked until it was time to go home to supper and I took her hand to lead her to my house. "But first," I said, "you must tell Mollie and Jim what has happened, and that you will not be back. For a while we can live under my father's roof; but as soon as may be I will get permission from the teivos to take the adjoining land and work it and then I shall build a house."

She drew back and flushed. "I cannot go with you yet," she said.

"What do you mean?" I asked. "You are mine!"

"We have not been married," she whispered.

"But no one is married," I reminded her. "Marriage is against the law."

"My mother was married," she told me. "You and I can be married. We have a church and a preacher. Why cannot he marry us? He is not ordained because there is none to ordain him; but being the head of the only church that he knows of or that we know of, it is evident that he can be ordained only by God and who knows but that he already has been ordained!"

I tried to argue her out of it, as now that heaven was so near I had no mind to wait three weeks to attain it; but she would not argue—she just shook her head and at last I saw that she was right and gave in—as I would have had to do in any event.

I went to Pthav, who was one of our representatives in the teivos, and asked him to procure for me permission to work the vacant land adjoining my father's. The land all belonged to the community; but each man was allowed what he could work as long as there was plenty, and there was more than plenty for us all.

Pthav was very ugly—he seemed to have forgotten that I had saved his child's life—and said that he did not know what he could do for me—that I had acted very badly to General Or-tis and was in disfavor, beside being under suspicion in another matter.

"What has General Or-tis to do with the distribution of land by the teivos?" I asked. "Because he wants my woman will the teivos deny me my rights?"

Pthav's woman came in while I was talking and recognized me; but she said nothing to me other than to mention that the child had asked for me. Pthav scowled at this and ordered her from the room just as a man might order a beast around. It was nothing to me, though, as the woman was a renegade anyway.

Finally I demanded of Pthav that he obtain the concession for me unless he could give me some valid reason for refusing.

"I will ask it," he said, finally; "but you will not get it—be sure of that."

As I was leaving the house Pthav's woman stopped me. "I will do what I can for you," she whispered. She must have seen me draw away instinctively as from an unclean thing, for she flushed and then said: "Please don't! I have suffered enough. I have paid the price of my treachery; but know, Yank," and she put her lips close to my ear, "that at heart I am more Yank than I was when I did this thing. And," she continued, "I have never spoken a word that could harm one of you. Tell them that—please tell them! I do not want them to hate me so, and God of our Fathers, how I have suffered—the degradation, the humiliation—it has been worse than what you are made to suffer. The creatures are lower than the beasts of the forest. When his friends come he serves them food and drink and—me! Ugh! I could kill him, if I were not such a coward. I have seen and I know how they can make one suffer before death."

I could not but feel sorry for her, and I told her so. The poor creature appeared very grateful and assured me that she would aid me.

"I know a few things about Pthav that he would not want Ortis to know," she said, "and even though he beats me for it I will make him get the land for you."

Again I thanked her and departed, realizing that there were others worse off than we—that the closer one came to the Kalkars the more hideous life became.

At last the day came and we set out for the church. As before I took Juana, though she tried to order it differently; but I would not trust her to the protection of another. We arrived without mishap—sixteen of us—and after the religious services were over Juana and I stood before the altar and were married—much after the fashion of the ancients, I imagine.

Juana was the only one of us who was at all sure about the ceremony and it had been she who trained Orrin Colby—making him memorize so much that he said his head ached for a week. All I can recall of it is that he asked me if I would take her to be my lawfully wedded wife—I lost my voice and only squeaked a weak "yes"—and that he pronounced us man and wife, and then something about not letting anyone put asunder what God had joined together. I felt very much married and very happy, and then just as it was all nicely over and everybody was shaking hands with us there came a loud knocking at the door and the command: "Open, in the name of the law!"

We looked at one another and gasped. Orrin Colby put a finger to his lips for silence and led the way toward the back of the church where a rough niche was built in, containing a few shelves upon which stood several rude candle sticks. We knew our parts and followed him in silence, except one who went quickly about putting out the lights. All the time the pounding on the door became more insistent, and then we could hear the strokes of what must have been an ax beating at the panels. Finally, a shot was fired through the heavy wood and we knew that it was the Kash Guard.

Taking hold of the lower shelf Orrin pulled upward with all his strength with the result that all the shelving and woodwork to which it was attached slid upward revealing an opening beyond. Through this we filed, one by one, down a flight of stone steps into a dark tunnel. When the last man had passed I lowered the shelving to its former place, being careful to see that it fitted tightly.

Then I turned and followed the others, Juana's hand in mine. We groped our way for some little distance in the·stygian darkness of the tunnel until Orrin halted and whispered to me to come to him. I went and stood at his side while he told me what I was to do. He had called upon me because I was the tallest and the strongest of the men. Above us was a wooden trap. I was to lift this and push it aside.

It had not been moved for generations and was very heavy with earth and growing things above; but I put my shoulders to it and it had to give—either it or the ground beneath my feet and that could not give. At last I had it off and in a few minutes I had helped them all out into the midst of a dense wood. Again we knew our parts, for many times had we been coached for just such an emergency, and one by one the men scattered in different directions, each taking his woman with him.

Suiting our movements to a prearranged plan, we reached our homes from different directions and at different times, some arriving after sundown, to the end that were we watched, none might be sure that we had been upon the same errand or to the same place.

CHAPTER VII

THE ARREST OF JULIAN 8TH

A WEEK later, Pthav sent for me and very gruffly told me that the teivos had issued the permit for me to use the land adjoining that allotted to my father. As before, his woman stopped me as I was leaving.

"It was easier than I thought," she told me, "for Or-tis has angered the teivos by attempting to usurp all its powers and knowing that he hates you they were glad to grant your petition over his objection."

During the next two or three months I was busy building our home and getting my place in order. I had decided to raise horses and obtained permission from the teivos to do so—again over Or-tis' objections. Of course the government controlled the entire horse traffic; but there were a few skilled horsemen permitted to raise them, though at any time their herds could be commandeered by the authorities. I knew that it might not be a very profitable business; but I loved horses and wanted to have just a few—a stallion and two or three mares. These I could use in tilling my fields and in the heavier work of hauling, and at the same time I would keep a few goats, pigs and chickens to insure us a living.

Father gave me half his goats and a few chickens, and from Jim I bought two young sows and a boar. Later I traded a few goats to the teivos for two old mares that they thought were no longer worth keeping and that same day I was told of a stallion—a young outlaw—that Hoffmeyer had. The beast was five years old and so vicious that none dared approach him and they were on the point of destroying him.

I went to Hoffmeyer and asked if I could buy the animal—I offered him a goat for it, which he was glad to accept and then I took a strong rope and went to get my property. I found a beautiful bay with the temper of a hellhound. When I attempted to enter the pen he rushed at me with ears back and jaws distended; but I knew that I must conquer him now or never and so I met him with only a rope in my hand, nor did I wait for him. Instead, I ran to meet him and when he was in reach I struck him once across the face with the rope, at which he wheeled and let both hind feet fly out at me. Then I cast the noose that was at one end of the rope and caught him about the neck and for half an hour we had a battle of it.

I never struck him unless he tried to bite or strike me and finally I must have convinced him that I was master, for he let me come close enough to stroke his glossy neck, though he snorted loudly all the while that I did so. When I had quieted him a bit I managed to get a half hitch around his lower jaw and after that I had no difficulty in leading him from the pen. Once in the open I took the coils of my rope in my left hand and before the creature knew what I was about, had vaulted to his back.

He fought fair, I'll say that for him, for he stood on his feet; but for fifteen minutes he brought into play every artifice known to horse-kind for unseating a rider. Only my skill and my great strength kept me on his back and at that even the Kalkars who were looking on had to applaud my horsemanship.

After that it was easy. I treated him with kindness, something he had never known before, and as he was an unusually intelligent animal, he soon learned that I was not only his master but his friend, and from being an outlaw he became one of the kindest and most tractable animals I have ever seen, so much so in fact, that Juana used to ride him bareback.

I love all horses and always have; but I think I never loved any animal as I did Red Lightning, as we named him.

The authorities left us pretty well alone for some time because they were quarreling among themselves. Jim said there was an ancient saying about honest men getting a little peace when thieves fell out and it certainly fitted our case perfectly; but the peace didn't last forever and when it broke the bolt that fell was the worst calamity that had ever come to us.

One evening Father was arrested for trading at night and taken away by the Kash Guard. They got him as he was returning to the house from the goat pens and would not even permit him to bid good-bye to Mother. Juana and I were eating supper in our own house about three hundred yards away and never knew anything about it until Mother came running over to tell us. She said that it was all done so quickly that they had Father and were gone before she could run from the house to where they arrested him. They had a spare horse and hustled him onto it—then they galloped away toward the lake front. It seems strange that neither Juana nor I heard the hoof beats of the horses; but we did not.

I went immediately to Pthav and demanded to know why Father had been arrested; but he professed ignorance of the whole affair. I had ridden to his place on Red Lightning and from there I started to the Kash Guard barracks where the military prison is. It is contrary to law to approach the barracks after sunset without permission, so I left Red Lightning in the shadow of some ruins a hundred yards away and started on foot toward that part of the post where I knew the prison to be located. The latter consists of a high stockade around the inside of which are rude shelters upon the roofs of which armed guards patrol. The center of the rectangle is an open court where the prisoners exercise, cook their food, and wash their clothing—if they care to. There are seldom more than fifty confined here at a time as it is only a detention camp where they hold those who are awaiting trial and those who have been sentenced to the mines. The latter are usually taken away when there are from twenty-five to forty of them.

After I reached the stockade I was at a loss to communicate with my father, since any noise I might make would doubtless attract the attention of the guard; but finally, through a crack between two boards, I attracted the attention of a prisoner. The man came close to the stockade and I whispered to him that I wished to speak with Julian 8th. By luck I had happened upon a decent fellow, and it was not long before he had brought Father and I was talking with him, in low whispers.

He told me that he had been arrested for trading by night and that he was to be tried on the morrow. I asked him if he would like to escape—that I would find the means if he wished me to, but he said that he was innocent of the charge as he had not been off our farm at night for months and that doubtless it was a case of mistaken identity and that he would be freed in the morning.

I had my doubts; but he would not listen to escape as he argued that it would prove his guilt and then they would have him for sure.

"Where may I go," he asked, "if I escape? I might hide in the woods; but what a life! I could never return to your mother, and so sure am I that they can prove nothing against me that I would rather stand trial than face the future as an outlaw."

I think now that he refused my offer of assistance not because he expected to be released but rather that he feared that evil might befall me were I to connive at his escape. At any rate I did nothing, since he would not let me, and went home again with a heavy heart and dismal forebodings.

Trials before the teivos were public, or at least were supposed to be, though they made it so·uncomfortable for spectators that few, if any, had the temerity to attend; but under Jarth's new rule the proceedings of the military courts were secret and Father was tried before such a court.

CHAPTER VIII

I HORSEWHIP AN OFFICER

WE passed days of mental anguish—hearing nothing, knowing nothing—and then one evening a single Kash Guard rode up to Father's house. Juana and I were there with Mother. The fellow dismounted and knocked at the door—a most unusual courtesy from one of these. He entered at my bidding and stood there a moment looking at Mother. He was only a lad—a big, overgrown boy, and there was neither cruelty in his eyes nor the mark of the beast in any of his features. His mother's blood evidently predominated, and he was unquestionably not all Kalkar. Presently he spoke.

"Which is Julian 8th's woman?" he asked; but he looked at Mother as though he already guessed.

"I am," said Mother.

The lad shuffled his feet and caught his breath—it was like a stifled sob.

"I am sorry," he said, "that I bring you such sad news," and then we guessed that the worst had happened.

"The mines?" Mother asked him, and he nodded affirmatively.

"Ten years!" he exclaimed, as one might announce a sentence of death, for such it was. "He never had a chance," he volunteered. "It was a terrible thing. They are beasts!"

I could not but show my surprise that a Kash Guard should speak so of his own kind, and he must have seen it in my face.

"We are not all beasts," he hastened to exclaim.

I commenced to question him then and I found that he had been a sentry at the door during the trial and had heard it all.

There had been but one witness—the man who had informed on Father, and Father had been given no chance to make any defense.

I asked him who the informer was.

"I am not sure of the name," he replied; "he was a tall, stoop-shouldered man. I think I heard him called Peter."

But I had known even before I asked. I looked at Mother and saw that she was dry-eyed and that her mouth had suddenly hardened into a firmness of expression such as I had never dreamed it could assume.

"Is that all?" she asked.

"No," replied the youth, "it is not. I am instructed to notify you that you have thirty days to take another man, or vacate these premises," and then he took a step toward Mother. "I am sorry, Madam," he said. "It is very cruel; but what are we to do? It becomes worse each day. Now they are grinding down even the Kash Guard, so that there are many of us who—;" but he stopped suddenly as though realizing that he was on the point of speaking treason to strangers, and turning on his heel he quit the house and a moment later was galloping away.

I expected Mother to break down then; but she did not. She was very brave; but there was a new and terrible expression in her eyes—those eyes that had shone forth always with love. Now they were bitter, hate-filled eyes. She did not weep—I wish to God she had. Instead she did that which I had never known her to do before—she laughed aloud. Upon the slightest pretext, or upon no pretext at all, she laughed. We were afraid for her.

The suggestion dropped by the Kash Guard started in my mind a train of thought of which I spoke to Mother and Juana, and after that Mother seemed more normal for a while, as though I had aroused hope, however feeble, where there had been no hope before. I pointed out that if the Kash Guard was dissatisfied, the time was ripe for revolution, for if we could get only a part of them to join us there would surely be enough of us to overthrow those who remained loyal to The Flag. Then we would liberate all prisoners and set up a republic of our own such as the ancients had had.

It took time to develop my plan. I talked with everyone I could trust and found them all willing to join me when we had enough. In the meantime, I cared for my own place and Father's as well—I was very busy and time flew rapidly.

About a month after Father was taken away, I came home one day with Juana who had accompanied me up river in search of a goat that had strayed. We had found its carcass, or rather its bones, where the hellhounds had left them. Mother was not at our house, where she now spent most of her time, so I went over to Father's to get her. As I approached the door I heard sounds of an altercation and scuffling that made me cover the few remaining yards at a rapid run.

Without waiting to knock, as Mother had taught me always to do, I burst into the living room to discover Mother in the clutches of Peter Johansen. She was trying to fight him off; but he was forcing her slowly toward her bedroom, for he was a large and powerful man. He heard me just as I leaped for him and turning, grappled with me. He tried to hold me off with one hand then while he drew his knife; but I struck him in the face with one fist and knocked him from me, way across the room. He was up again in an instant, bleeding from nose and mouth, and back at me with his knife in his hand, slashing furiously. Again I struck him and knocked him down and when he arose and came again I seized his knife-hand and tore the weapon from him. He had no slightest chance against me, and he saw it soon, for he commenced to back away and beg for mercy.

"Kill him, Julian," said Mother; "kill the murderer of your father."

I did not need her appeal to influence me, for the moment that I had seen Peter there I knew my long awaited time had come to kill him. He commenced to cry then—great tears ran down his cheeks and he bolted for the door and tried to escape. It was my pleasure to play with him as a cat plays with a mouse.

I kept him from the door, seizing him and hurling him bodily across the room, and then I let him reach the window, through which he tried to crawl—and I permitted him to get so far that he thought he was about to escape and then I seized him again and dragged him back to the floor and lifting him to his feet I made him fight.

I struck him lightly in the face many times and then I laid him on his back across the table and kneeling on his chest I spoke to him, softly.

"You had my friend, old Samuels, murdered and my father, too, and now you come to befoul my mother. What did you expect, swine, but this? Have you no intelligence? You must have known that I would kill you—speak!"

"They said that they would get you today," he whimpered. "They lied to me. They went back on me. They told me that you would be in the pen at the barracks before noon. Damn them, they lied to me!"

So! that was how it was, eh? And the lucky circumstance of the strayed goat had saved me to avenge my father and succor my mother; but they would come yet. I must hurry or they might come before I was through, and so I took his head between my hands and bent his neck far back over the edge of the table until I heard his spine part—and that was the end of the vilest traitor who ever lived—one who professed friendship openly and secretly conspired to ruin us. In broad daylight I carried his body to the river and threw it in. I was past caring what they knew. They were coming for me and they would have their way with me whether they had any pretext or not; but they would have to pay a price for me, that I determined, and I got my knife and strapped it in its scabbard about my waist beneath my shirt; but they did not come—they had lied to Peter just as they lie to everyone.

The next day was market day and tax day, so I went to market with the necessary goats and produce to make my trades and pay my taxes. As Soor passed around the market place making his collections, or rather his levies, for we had to deliver the stuff to his place ourselves, I saw from the excited conversation of those in his wake that he was spreading alarm and consternation among the people of the commune.

I wondered what it might all be about, nor had I long to wait to discover, for he soon reached me. He could neither read nor write; but he had a form furnished by the government upon which were numbers that the agents were taught how to read and which stood for various classes of produce, live-stock and manufactures. In columns beneath these numbers he made marks during the month for the amounts of my trades in each item—it was all crude, of course, and inaccurate; but as they always over-charged us and then added something to make up for any errors they might have made to our credit, the government was satisfied, even if we were not.

Being able to read and write, as well as to figure, I always knew to a dot just what was due from me in tax and I always had an argument with Soor, from which Government emerged victorious every time.

This month I should have owed him one goat, but he de-manded three.

"How is that?" I asked.

"Under the old rate you owed me the equivalent of a goat and a half; but since the tax had been doubled under the new law you owe me three goats." Then it was I knew the cause of the excitement in other parts of the market place.

"How do you expect us to live if you take everything from us?" I asked.

"The government does not care whether you live or not," he replied, "as long as you pay taxes while you do live."

"I will pay the three goats," I said, "because I have to; but next market day I will bring you a present of the hardest cheese I can find."

He did not say anything, for he was afraid of me unless he was surrounded by Kash Guards; but he looked ugly.

The commander of the Kash Guard company must have noticed the crowd around us, for he rode straight toward me, alone. I would not give him the satisfaction of thinking that I feared him and so I stood there waiting.

The officer reined in before me.

"What are you doing here?" he barked.

"Minding my own business, as you had better do," I replied.

"You swine are becoming insufferable," he cried. "Get to your pen, where you belong—I will stand for no mobs and no insolence."

I just stood there looking at him; but there was murder in my heart. He loosened the bull-hide whip that hung at the pommel of his saddle.

"You have to be driven, do you?" He was livid with sudden anger and his voice almost a scream. Then he struck at me—a vicious blow—with the heavy whip—struck at my face. I dodged the lash and seized it, wrenching it from his puny grasp and then I caught his bridle and though his horse plunged and fought, I lashed the rider with all my strength a dozen times, before he tumbled from the saddle to the trampled earth of the market place.

Then his men were upon me and I went down from a blow on the head. They bound my hands while I was unconscious and then hustled me roughly into a saddle. I was half dazed during the awful ride that ensued—we rode to the military prison at the barracks and all the way that fiend of a captain rode beside me and lashed me with his bull-hide whip.

CHAPTER IX

REVOLUTION

THEN they threw me into the pen where the prisoners were kept, and after they had left I was surrounded by the other unfortunates incarcerated there. When they learned what I had done they shook their heads and sighed. It would be all over with me in the morning, they said—nothing less than The Butcher for such an offense as mine.

I lay upon the hard ground, bruised and sore, thinking not of my future but of what was to befall Juana and Mother if I too were taken from them, and the thought gave me new strength and made me forget my hurts, for my mind was busy with plans, mostly impossible plans, for escape—and vengeance. Vengeance was often uppermost in my mind.

Above my head at intervals, I heard the pacing of the sentry upon the roof. I could tell, of course, each time that he passed and the direction in which he was going. It required about five minutes for him to pass above me, reach the end of his post and return—that was when he went west. Going east he took but a trifle over two minutes. Therefore, when he passed me going west his back was toward me for about two and a half minutes; but when he went east it was only for about a minute that his face was turned from the spot where I lay.

Of course he could not see me while I lay beneath the shed; but my plan—the one I finally decided upon—did not include remaining in the shed. I had evolved several subtle schemes for escape; but finally cast them all aside and chose, instead, the boldest that occurred to me. I knew that at best the chances were small that I could succeed in any plan and therefore the boldest seemed as likely as any other and it at least had the advantage of speedy results—I would be free or I would be dead in a few brief moments after I essayed it.

I waited, therefore, until the other prisoners had quieted down and comparative silence in the direction of the barracks and the parade assured me that there were few abroad. The sentry came and went and came again upon his monotonous round. Now he was coming toward me from the east and I was ready, standing just outside the shed beneath the low eaves which I could reach by jumping. I heard him pass and gave him a full minute to gain the distance I thought necessary to drown the sounds of my attempt from his ears and then I leaped for the eaves, caught with my fingers and drew myself quickly to the roof.

I thought that I did it very quietly, but the fellow must have had the ears of a hellhound, for no more had I drawn my feet beneath me for the quick run across the roof than a challenge rang out from the direction of the sentry and almost simultaneously the report of a rifle.

Instantly all was pandemonium. Guards ran, shouting, from all directions, lights flashed in the barracks, rifles spoke from either side of me and from behind me, while from below rose the dismal howlings of the prisoners. It seemed then that a hundred men had known of my plan and been lying in wait for me; but I was launched upon it and even though I had regretted it, there was nothing to do but carry it through to whatever was its allotted end.

It seemed a miracle that none of the bullets struck me; but of course, it was dark and I was moving rapidly. It takes seconds to tell about it, but it required less than a second for me to dash across the roof and leap to the open ground beyond the prison pen. I saw lights moving west of me, and so I ran east toward the lake and presently the firing ceased as they lost sight of me, though I could hear sounds of pursuit. Nevertheless, I felt that I had succeeded and was congratulating myself upon the ease with which I had accomplished the seemingly impossible when there suddenly rose before me out of the black night the figure of a huge soldier pointing a rifle point blank at me. He issued no challenge nor asked any question—just pulled the trigger. I could hear the hammer strike the firing pin, but there was no explosion. I did not know what the reason was, nor did I ever know. All that was apparent was that the rifle missed fire and then he brought his bayonet into play while I was springing toward him.

Foolish man! But then he did not know that it was Julian 9th he faced. Pitifully, futilely he thrust at me and with one hand I seized the rifle and tore it from his grasp. In the same movement I swung it behind me and above my head, bringing it down with all the strength of one arm upon his thick skull. Like a felled ox he tumbled to his knees and then sprawled forward upon his face—his head crushed to a pulp. He never knew how he died.

Behind me I heard them coming closer and they must have seen me, for they opened fire again and I heard the beat of horses' hoofs upon my right and left. They were surrounding me upon three sides and upon the fourth was the great lake. A moment later I was standing upon the edge of the ancient breakwater while behind me rose the triumphant cries of my pursuers. They had seen me and they knew that I was theirs.

At least, they thought they knew so. I did not wait for them to come closer; but raising my hands above me I dove head foremost into the cool waters of the lake, and swimming rapidly beneath the surface I kept close in the shadows and headed north. I had spent much of my summer life in the water of the river so that I was as much at home in that liquid element as in air; but this of course, the Kash Guard did not know, for even had they known that Julian 9th could swim they could not at that time have known which prisoner it was who had escaped and so I think they must have thought what I wanted them to think—that I had chosen self-drowning to recapture.

However I was sure they would search the shore in both directions and so I kept to the water after I came to the surface and when I was sure that no one was directly above me I swam farther out until I felt there was little danger of being seen from shore, for it was a dark night. And thus I swam on until I thought I was opposite the mouth of the river, when I turned toward the west, searching for it. Luck was with me. I swam directly into it and a short distance up the sluggish stream before I knew that I was out of the lake; but even then I did not take to the shore, preferring to pass the heart of the ancient city before trusting myself to land.

At last I came out upon the north bank of the river, which is farthest from the Kash Guard barracks and made my way as swiftly as possible up stream in the direction of my home. Here, hours later, I found an anxious Juana awaiting me, for already she had heard what had transpired in the market place. I had made my plans and had soon explained them to Juana and Mother. There was nothing for them but to acquiesce, as only death could be our lot if we remained in our homes another day. I was astonished even, that they had not already fallen upon Juana and Mother. As it was, they might come any minute—there was no time to lose.

Hastily wrapping up a few belongings I took The Flag from

its hiding place above the mantel and tucked it in my shirt—
then we were ready. Going to the pens we caught up Red Lightning and the two mares and three of my best milk goats. These
latter we tied, and after Juana and Mother had mounted the
mares I laid one goat in front of each across a mare's withers
and the third before myself upon Red Lightning, who did not
relish the strange burden and gave me considerable trouble at
first.

We rode out up-river, leaving the pens open that the goats
might scatter and posibly cover our trail until we could turn
off the dusty path beyond Jim's house. We dared not stop to
bid Jim and Mollie good-bye, lest we be apprehended there by
our enemies and bring trouble to our good friends. It was a
sad occasion for poor Mother, leaving thus her home and those
dear neighbors who had been as close to her as her own people;
but she was as brave as Juana, nor once did either of them attempt to dissuade me from the wild scheme I had outlined to
them. Instead they encouraged me and Juana laid her hand upon
my arm as I rode beside her, saying: "I would rather that you
died thus than that we lived on as downtrodden serfs, without
happiness and without hope."

"I shall not die," I said, "until my work is done at least, and
then if die I must, I shall be content to know that I leave a
happier country for my fellow men to live in."

"Amen!" whispered Juana.

That night I hid them in the ruins of the old church which
we found had been partially burned by the Kalkars. For a
moment I held them in my arms—my mother and my wife—and
then I left them to ride toward the southwest and the coal mines.
The mines lie about fifty miles away—those to which our people
are sent—and west of south, according to what I had heard. I
had never been to them; but I knew that I must find the bed of
an ancient canal and follow it through the district of Joliet and
between fifteen and twenty miles beyond, where I must turn
south, and after passing a large lake, I would presently come to
the mines. I rode the balance of the night and into the morning
until I commenced to see people astir in the thinly populated
country through which I passed. Then I hid in a wood through
which a stream wound and here found pasture for Red Lightning and rest for myself. I had brought no food, leaving what
little bread and cheese we had brought from the house for
Mother and Juana. I did not expect to be gone over a week and I
knew that with goat's milk and what they had on hand in addi-

"I know," he said; "but the worm impaled upon the hook still struggles and hopes for life. Turn back, my son, we can do nothing against them."

"I shall not turn back," I whispered. "I shall not turn back."

"I will help you; but I cannot speak for the others."

We had spoken only when the sentry had been at a distance, falling into silence each time he approached the point where we stood. In the intervals of silence I could hear the growing restlessness of the prisoners and I guessed that what I had said to the first man was being passed around from mouth to mouth within until already the whole adjacent shed was seething with something akin to excitement. I wondered if it would arouse their spirit sufficiently to carry them through the next ten minutes. If it did, success was assured.

Father had told me all that I wanted to know—the location of the guard house and the barracks and the number of Kash Guard posted here—only fifty men to guard five thousand! How much more eloquently than words did this fact bespeak the humiliation of the American people and the utter contempt in which our scurvy masters held us—fifty men to guard five thousand!

And then I started putting my plan into execution—a mad plan which had only its madness to recommend it. The sentry approached and came opposite where I stood, and I leaped for the eaves as I had leaped for the eaves of the prison pen at Chicago, only this time I leaped from the outside where the eaves are closer to the ground and so the task was easier. I leaped for them and caught them, and then I scrambled up behind the sentry and before his dull wits told him that there was someone behind him I was upon his back and the same fingers that threw a mad bull closed upon his wind pipe. The struggle was brief— he died quickly and I lowered him to the roof. Then I took his uniform from him and donned it, with his ammunition belt, and I took his bayonetted rifle and started out upon his post, walking with slow tread and with my chin upon my breast as he had walked.

At the end of my post I waited for the sentry I saw coming upon the next and when he was close to me I turned back and he turned back away from me and then I wheeled and struck him an awful blow upon the head with my rifle. He died more quickly than the other—instantly, I should say.

I took his rifle and ammunition from him and lowered them inside the pen to waiting hands, and then I went on to the next sentry and the next, until I had slain five more and passed their rifles to the prisoners below and while I was doing this, five prisoners who had volunteered to Father climbed to the roof of the shed and stripped the dead men of their uniforms and donned them.

It was all done quietly and in the black night none might see what was going on fifty feet away. I had to stop when I came near to the guard house. There I turned back and presently slid into the pen with my accomplices who had been going among the other prisoners with Father, arousing them to mutiny. Now were most of them ready to follow me, for so far my plan had proven successful. With equal quietness we overcame the men at the guard house and then moved on in a silent body toward the barracks.

So sudden and so unexpected was our attack that we met with little resistance and we were almost five thousand to forty now. We swarmed in upon them like wild bees upon a foe and we shot them and bayonetted them until none remained alive. Not one escaped. And now we were flushed with success so that the most spiritless became a veritable lion for courage.

We who had taken the uniforms of the Kash Guard discarded them for our own garb as we had no mind to go abroad in the hated livery of our oppressors. That very night we saddled their horses with the fifty saddles that were there and fifty men rode the balance of the horses bareback—that made one hundred mounted men and the others were to follow on foot—on to Chicago. On to Chicago, was our first slogan.

We traveled cautiously, though I had difficulty in making them do so, so intoxicated were they with their first success. I wanted to save the horses and also I wanted to get as many men into Chicago as possible, so we let the weakest ride, though I had a time of it getting Red Lightning to permit another on his sleek back.

Some fell out upon the way, from exhaustion or from fear, for the nearer Chicago we approached the more their courage ebbed. The very thought of the feared Kalkars and their Kash Guards took the marrow from the hearts of many. I do not know that one may blame them, for the spirit of man can endure only so much and when it is broken only a miracle can mend it in the same generation.

We reached the ruined church a week from the day I left Mother and Juana there and we reached it with less than two thousand men, so rapid had been the desertions in the last few miles before we entered the district.

Father and I could scarcely wait to see our loved ones and so we rode on ahead to greet them, and inside the church we found three dead goats and a dying woman—my mother with a knife protruding from her breast. She was still conscious when we entered and I saw a great light of happiness in her eyes as they fell upon Father and upon me. I looked around for Juana and my heart stood still, fearing that I would not find her—and fearing that I would.

Mother could still speak, and as we leaned over her as Father held her in his arms she breathed a faint story of what had befallen them. They had lived in peace until that very day when the Kash Guard had stumbled upon them—a large detachment under Or-tis, himself. They had seized them to take them away; but Mother had had a knife hidden in her clothing and had utilized it, as we saw, rather than suffer the fate she knew awaited them. That was all, except that Juana had had no knife and Or-tis had carried her off.

I saw Mother die then, in Father's arms, and I helped him bury her after our men came and we had shown them what the beasts had done, though they knew well enough and had suffered themselves enough to know what was to be expected of the swine.

CHAPTER X

THE BUTCHER

WE went on then, Father and I filled with grief and bitterness and hatred even greater than we had known before. We marched toward the market place of our district, and on the way we stopped at Jim's and he joined us. Mollie wept when she heard what had befallen Mother and Juana, but presently she controlled herself and urged us on and Jim with us, though Jim needed no urging. She kissed him good-bye with tears and pride mingled in her eyes, and all he said was: "Good-bye, girl, keep your knife with you always."

And so we rode away with Mollie's "May the Saints be with you" in our ears. Once again we stopped at our abandoned goat pens, and there we dug up the rifle, belt and ammunition of the soldier Father had slain years before. These we gave to Jim. Before we reached the market place our force commenced to dwindle again—most of them could not brave the terrors of the Kash Guard upon which they had been fed in whispered story and in actual experience since infancy. I do not say that these men were cowards—I do not believe that they were cowards, and yet they acted like cowards. It may be that a lifetime of training had taught them so thoroughly to flee the Kash Guard that now no amount of urging could make them face it—the terror had become instinctive as is man's natural revulsion for snakes. They could not face the Kash Guard any more than some men can touch a rattler, even though it may be dead.

It was market day and the place was crowded. I had divided my force so that we marched in from two directions in wide fronts, about five hundred men in each party, and surrounded the market place. As there were only a few men from our district among us I had given orders that there was to be no killing other than that of Kash Guards until we who knew the population could pick out the right men.

When the nearest people first saw us they did not know what to make of it, so complete was the surprise. Never in their lives had they seen men of their own class armed and there were a hundred of us mounted. Across the plaza a handful of Kash Guard were lolling in front of Hoffmeyer's office. They saw my party first, as the other was coming up from behind them, and they mounted and came toward us. At the same moment I drew The Flag from my breast and waving it above my head, urged Red Lightning forward, shouting, as I rode: "Death to the Kash Guard! Death to the Kalkars!"

And then, of a sudden, the Kash Guard seemed to realize that they were confronted by an actual force of armed men and their true color became apparent—all yellow. They turned to flee, only to see another force behind them. The people had now caught the idea and the spirit of our purpose and they flocked around us, shouting, screaming, laughing, crying. "Death to the Kash Guard!" "Death to the Kalkars!" "The Flag!" I heard more than once, and "Old Glory!" from some who, like myself, had not been permitted to forget. A dozen men rushed to my side, and grasping the streaming banner pressed it to their lips while tears coursed down their cheeks. "The Flag! The Flag!" they cried. "The Flag of our fathers!"

It was then, before a shot had been fired, that one of the Kash Guard rode toward me with a white cloth above his head.

I recognized him immediately as the youth who had brought
the cruel order to Mother and who had shown sorrow for the
acts of his superiors.

"Do not kill us," he said, "and we will join with you. Many
of the Kash Guard at the barracks will join, too."

And so the dozen soldiers in the market place joined us, and
a woman ran from her house carrying the head of a man stuck
upon a short pole and she screamed forth her hatred against
the Kalkars—the hatred that was the common bond between us
all. As she came closer I saw that it was Pthav's woman and
the head upon the short pole was the head of Pthav. That was
the beginning—that was the little spark that was needed. Like
maniacs, laughing horribly, the people charged the houses of
the Kalkars and dragged them forth to death.

Above the shrieking and the groans and the din could be
heard shouts for The Flag and the names of loved ones who
were being avenged. More than once I heard the name of
Samuels the Jew—never was a man more thoroughly avenged
than he that day.

Dennis Corrigan was with us, freed from the mines, and
Betty Worth, his woman, found him there, his arms red to the
elbows with the blood of our oppressors. She had never thought
to see him alive, and when she heard his story, and of how they
had escaped she ran to me and nearly pulled me from Red
Lightning's back, trying to hug and kiss me.

It was she who started the people shouting for me until a
mad, swirling mob of joy-crazed people surrounded me. I tried
to quiet them, for I knew that this was no way in which to
forward our cause and finally I succeeded in winning a partial
silence and then I told them that this madness must cease, that
we had not yet succeeded, that we had won only a single small
district and that we must go forward quietly and in accordance
with a sensible plan if we were to be victorious.

"Remember," I admonished them, "that there are still thousands of armed men in the city and that we must overthrow
them all, and then there are other thousands that The Twenty-
four will throw in upon us, for they will not surrender this territory until they are hopelessly defeated from here to Washington—and that will require months and maybe years."

They quieted down a little then, and we formed plans for
marching immediately upon the barracks that we might take the
Kash Guard by surprise. It was about this time that Father
found Soor and killed him.

"I told you," said Father, just before he ran a bayonet through the tax collector, "that some day I would have my little joke, and this is the day."

Then a man dragged Hoffmeyer from some hiding place and the people literally tore him to pieces and that started the pandemonium all over again. There were cries of "On to the barracks!" and "Kill the Kash Guard!" followed by a concerted movement toward the lake front. On the way our numbers were increased by volunteers from every house—either fighting men and women from the houses of our class or bloody heads from the houses of the Kalkars, for we carried them all with us, waving above us upon the ends of poles, and at the head of all I rode with Old Glory, now waving from a tall staff.

I tried to maintain some semblance of order; but it was impossible and so we streamed along, screaming and killing, laughing and crying, each as the mood claimed him. The women seemed the maddest, possibly because they had suffered most, and Pthav's woman led them. I saw others there with one hand clutching a suckling baby to a bare breast while the other held aloft the dripping head of a Kalkar, an informer, or a spy. One could not blame them who knew the lives of terror and hopelessness they had led—they and their mothers before them.

We had just crossed the new bridge over the river into the heart of the great, ruined city when the Kash Guard fell upon us from ambush with their full strength. They were poorly disciplined; but they were armed, while we were not disciplined at all nor scarcely armed. We were nothing but an angry mob into which they poured volley after volley at close range. Men, women and babies went down and many turned and fled; but there were others who rushed forward and grappled hand to hand with the Kash Guard, tearing their rifles from them. We who were mounted rode among them. I could not carry The Flag and fight, so I took it from the staff and replaced it inside my shirt and then I clubbed my rifle and guiding Red Lightning with my knees I drove into them.

God of our Fathers, but it was a pretty fight. If I had known that I was to die the next minute I would have died gladly for the joy I had in those few minutes. Down they went before me, to right and to left, reeling from their saddles with crushed skulls and broken bodies, for wherever I hit them made no difference in the result—they died if they came within reach of my rifle, which was soon only a bent and twisted tube of bloody metal.

And so I rode completely through them with a handful of men behind me. We turned then to ride back over the crumbling ruins that were in this spot only mounds of debris, and from the elevation of one of these hillocks of the dead past, I saw the battle down by the river and a great lump came into my throat. It was all over—all but the bloody massacre. My poor mob had turned at last to flee, they were jammed and stuck upon the narrow bridge and the Kash Guard were firing volleys into that wedged mass of human flesh. Hundreds were leaping into the river only to be shot from the banks by the soldiers.

Twenty-five mounted men surrounded me—all that was left of my fighting force—and at least two thousand Kash Guards lay between us and the river. Even could we have fought our way back we could have done nothing to save the day or our own people. We were doomed to die; but we decided to inflict more punishment before we died.

I had in mind Juana in the clutches of Or-tis—not once had the frightful thought left my consciousness—and so I told them that I would ride to headquarters and search for her and they said that they would ride with me and that we would slay whom we could before the soldiers returned.

Our dream had vanished, our hopes were dead. In silence we rode through the streets toward the barracks. The Kash Guard had not come over to our side as we had hoped—possibly they would have come had we had some measure of success in the city; but there could be no success against armed troops for an undisciplined mob of men, women and children.

I realized too late that we had not planned sufficiently, yet we might have won had not someone escaped and ridden ahead to notify the Kash Guard. Could we have taken them by surprise in the barracks the outcome might have been what it had been in the market place through which we had passed. I had realized our weakness and the fact that if we took time to plan and arrange, some spy or informer would have divulged all to the authorities long before we could have put our plans into execution. Really, there had been no other way than to trust to a surprise attack and the impetuosity of our first blow.

I looked about among my followers as we rode along. Jim was there, but not Father—I never saw him again. He probably fell in the battle at the new bridge. Orrin Colby, blacksmith and preacher, rode at my side covered with blood—his own and Kash Guard. Dennis Corrigan was there, too.

We rode right into the barrack yard, for with their lack of

discipline and military efficiency they had sent their whole force against us with the exception of a few men who remained to guard the prisoners and a handful at headquarters building. The latter we overcame with scarce a struggle and from one whom I took prisoner I learned where the sleeping quarters of Or-tis were located.

Telling my men that our work was done I ordered them to scatter and escape as best they might; but they said that they would remain with me. I told them that the business I was on was such that I must handle it alone and asked them to go and free the prisoners while I searched for Juana. They said that they would wait for me outside and so we parted.

Or-tis' quarters were on the second floor of the building in the east wing and I had no difficulty in finding them. As I approached the door I heard the sound of voices raised in anger within and of rapid movement as though someone was running hither and thither across the floor. I recognized Or-tis' voice—he was swearing foully, and then I heard a woman's scream and I knew that it was Juana.

I tried the door and found it locked. It was a massive door, such as the ancients built in their great public buildings, such as this had originally been, and I doubted my ability to force it. I was mad with apprehension and lust for revenge, and if maniacs gain tenfold in strength when the madness is upon them, I must have been a maniac that moment, for when, after stepping back a few feet, I hurled myself against the door the shot bolt tore through the splintering frame and the barrier swung in upon its hinges with a loud bang.

Before me, in the center of the room, stood Or-tis with Juana in his clutches. He had her partially upon a table and with one hairy hand he was choking her. He looked up at the noise of my sudden entry, and when he saw me he went white and dropped Juana, at the same time whipping a pistol from its holster at his side. Juana saw me too, and springing for his arm dragged it down as he pulled the trigger, so that the bullet went harmlessly into the floor.

Before he could shake her off I was upon him and had wrenched the weapon from his grasp. I held him in one hand as one might a little child—he was utterly helpless in my grip—and I asked Juana if he had wronged her.

"Not yet," she said, "he just came in after sending the Kash Guard away. Something has happened. There is going to be a battle; but he sneaked back to the safety of his quarters," and then she seemed to notice for the first time that I was covered with blood. "There has been a battle!" she cried, "and you have been in it."

I told her that I had and that I would tell her about it after I had finished Or-tis. He commenced to plead and then to whimper. He promised me freedom and immunity from punishment and persecution if I would let him live. He promised never to bother Juana again and to give us his protection and assistance. He would have promised me the Sun and the Moon and all the little stars had he thought I wished them; but I wished only one thing just then and I told him so—to see him die.

"Had you wronged her," I said, "you would have died a slow and terrible death; but I came in time to save her and so you are saved that suffering."

When he realized that nothing could save him he began to weep and his knees shook so that he could not stand, and I had to hold him from the floor with one hand and with my other clenched I dealt him a single terrific blow between the eyes— a blow that broke his neck and crushed his skull—then I dropped him to the floor and took Juana in my arms.

Quickly, as we walked toward the entrance of the building, I told her of all that had transpired since we parted and that now she would be left alone in the world for awhile, until I could join her. I told her where to go and await me in a forgotten spot I had discovered upon the banks of the old canal on my journey to the mines. She cried and clung to me, begging to remain with me; but I knew it could not be, for already I could hear fighting in the yard below. We would be fortunate indeed if one of us escaped. At last she promised on condition that I would join her immediately, which, of course, I had intended doing as soon as I had the chance.

Red Lightning stood where I had left him before the door. A company of Kash Guard, evidently returning from the battle, were engaged with my little band that was slowly falling back toward the headquarters building. There was no time to be lost if Juana was to escape. I lifted her to Red Lightning's back from where she stooped and threw her dear arms about my neck, covering my lips with kisses.

"Come back to me soon," she begged, "I need you so—and it will not be long before there will be another to need you too."

I pressed her close to my breast. "And if I do not come back," I said, take this and give it to my son to guard as his fathers before him have," and I placed The Flag in her hands.

The bullets were singing around us and I made her go, watching her as the noble horse raced swiftly across the parade and disappeared among the ruins to the west. Then I turned to the fighting to find but ten men left to me. Orrin Colby was dead and Dennis Corrigan. Jim was left and nine others. We fought as best we could; but we were cornered now, for other guards were streaming onto the parade from other directions and our ammunition was expended.

They rushed us then—twenty to one—and though we did the best we could, they overwhelmed us. Lucky Jim was killed instantly; but I was only stunned by a blow upon the head.

That night they tried me before a court martial and tortured me in an effort to make me divulge the names of my accomplices; but there were none left alive that I knew of, even had I wished to betray them. As it was, I just refused to speak. I never spoke again after bidding Juana good-bye, other than the few words of encouragement that passed between those of us who remained fighting to the last.

Early the next morning I was led forth to The Butcher.

I recall every detail up to the moment the knife touched my throat—there was a slight stinging sensation followed instantly by—oblivion.

It was broad daylight when he finished—so quickly had the night sped—and I could see by the light from the east window of the room where we sat that his face looked drawn and pinched and that even then he was suffering the sorrows and disappointments of the bitter, hopeless life he had just described.

I rose to retire. "That is all?" I asked.

"Yes," he replied, "that is all of that incarnation."

"But you recall another?" I insisted. He only smiled as I was closing the door.

PART III

The Red Hawk

Being the Story of Julian 20th

CHAPTER I

THE DESERT CLANS

THE January sun beat hotly down upon me as I reined Red Lightning in upon the summit of a barren hill and looked down upon the rich land of plenty that stretched away below me as far as the eye could see toward the mighty sea that lay a day's ride, perhaps, to the westward—the sea that none of us had ever looked upon—the sea that had become as fabulous as a legend of the ancients during the almost four hundred years since the Moon Men had swept down upon us and overwhelmed the Earth in their mad and bloody carnival of revolution.

In the near distance the green of the orange groves mocked us from below, and great patches that were groves of leafless nut trees, and there were sandy patches toward the south that were vineyards waiting for the hot suns of April and May before they, too, broke into riotous, tantalizing green. And from this garden spot of plenty a curling trail wound up the mountainside to the very level where we sat gazing fiercely down upon this last stronghold of our foes. When the ancients built that trail it must have been wide and beautiful indeed, but in the centuries that have elapsed man and the elements have sadly defaced it. The rains have washed it away in places and the Kalkars have made great gashes in it to deter us, their enemies, from invading their sole remaining lands and driving them into the sea; and upon their side of the gashes they have built forts where they keep warriors always. And well for them that they do. It is so upon every pass that leads down into their country.

Since fell my great ancestor, Julian 9th, in the year 2122, at the end of the first uprising against the Kalkars, we have been driving them slowly back across the world. That was over three hundred years ago. For a hundred years they have held us here, a day's ride from the ocean. Just how far it is we do not know; but in 2408 my grandfather, Julian 18th, rode alone almost to the sea. He had won back almost to safety when he was discovered and pursued almost to the tents of his people. There was a battle, and the Kalkars who had dared invade our country were destroyed, but Julian 18th died of his wounds without being able to tell more than that a wondrous rich country lay between us and the sea, which was not more than a day's ride distant. A day's ride, for us, might be anything under a hundred miles.

We are desert people. Our herds range a vast territory where feed is scarce that we may be always near the goal that our ancestors set for us three centuries ago—the shore of the western sea into which it is our destiny to drive the remnants of our former oppressors. In the forests and mountains of Arizona there is rich pasture, but it is far from the land of the Kalkars where the last of the tribe of Or-tis make their last stand, and so we prefer to live in the desert near our foes, driving our herds great distances to pasture when the need arises, rather than to settle down in a comparative land of plenty, resigning the age-old struggle, the ancient feud between the house of Julian and the house of Or-tis.

A light breeze moves the black mane of the bright bay stallion beneath me. It moves my own black mane where it falls loose below the buckskin thong that encircles my head and keeps it from my eyes. It moves the dangling ends of the Great Chief's blanket where it is strapped behind my saddle. On the twelfth day of the eighth month of the year just gone this Great Chief's blanket covered the shoulders of my father, Julian 19th, from the burning rays of the summer's desert sun. I was twenty on that day and on that day my father fell before the lance of an Or-tis in the Great Feud and I became The Chief of Chiefs.

Surrounding me today, as I sit looking down upon the land of my enemies, are fifty of the fierce chieftains of the hundred clans that swear allegiance to the house of Julian. They are bronzed and, for the most part, beardless men. The insignias of their clans are painted in various colors upon their foreheads, their cheeks, their breasts. Ochre, they use and blue and white and scarlet. Feathers rise from the head bands that confine their hair—the feathers of the vulture, the hawk and the eagle. I, Julian 20th, wear a single feather. It is from a red-tailed hawk —the clan-sign of my family.

We are all garbed similarly. Let me describe The Wolf, and in his portrait you will see a composite of us all. He is a sinewy, well built man of fifty, with piercing, gray-blue eyes beneath straight brows. His head is well shaped, denoting great intelligence. His features are strong and powerful and of a certain fierce cast that might well strike terror to a foeman's heart—and does, if the Kalkar scalps that fringe his ceremonial blanket stand for aught. His breeches, wide below the hips and skin tight from above the knees down are of the skin of the buck deer. His soft boots, tied tight about the calf of each leg, are also of buck. Above the waist he wears a sleeveless vest of calfskin tanned with the hair on. The Wolf's is of fawn and white. Sometimes these vests are ornamented with bits of colored stone or metal sewn to the hide in various manners of design. From The Wolf's headband, just above the right ear, depends the tail of a timber wolf—the clan-sign of his family.

An oval shield, upon which is painted the head of a wolf, hangs about this chief's neck, covering his back from nape to kidneys. It is a stout, light shield—a hard wood frame covered with bull hide. Around its periphery have been fastened the tails of wolves. In such matters each man, with the assistance of his women folk, gives rein to his fancy in the matter of ornamentation. Clan-signs and chief-signs, however, are sacred. The use of one to which he is not entitled might spell death for any man. I say might, because we have no inflexible laws. We have few laws. The Kalkars were forever making laws, so we hate them. We judge each case upon its own merits, and we pay more attention to what a man intended doing than what he did.

The Wolf is armed, as are the rest of us, with a light lance about eight feet in length, a knife and a straight, two-edged sword. A short, stout bow is slung beneath his right stirrup leather and a quiver of arrows is at his saddle bow.

The blades of his sword and his knife and the metal of his lance tip come from a far place called Kolrado and are made by a tribe that is famous because of the hardness and the temper of the metal of its blades. The Utaws bring us metal, also, but theirs is inferior and we use it only for the shoes that protect our horses' feet from the cutting sands and the rocks of our hard and barren country.

The Kolrados travel many days to reach us, coming once in two years. They pass, unmolested, through the lands of many tribes because they bring what none might otherwise have and what we need in our never ending crusade against the Kalkars. That is the only thread that holds together the scattered clans and tribes that spread east and north and south beyond the ken of man. All are animated by the same purpose—to drive the last of the Kalkars into the sea.

From the Kolrados we get meager news of clans beyond them toward the rising sun. Far, far to the east, they say, so far that in a lifetime no man might reach it, lies another great sea, and that there, as here upon the world's western edge, a few Kalkars are making their last stand. All the rest of the world has been won back by the people of our own blood—by Americans.

We are always glad to see the Kolrados come, for they bring us news of other peoples, and we welcome the Utaws, too, though we are not a friendly people, killing all others who come among us, for fear, chiefly, that they may be spies sent by the Kalkars. It is handed down from father to son that this was not always so, and that once the people of the world went to and fro safely from place to place and that then all spoke the same language; but now it is different. The Kalkars brought hatred and suspicion among us, until now we trust only the members of our own clans and tribes.

The Kolrados, from coming often among us, we can understand, and they can understand us, by means of a few words and many signs, though when they speak their own language among themselves we cannot understand them, except for an occasional word that is like one of ours. They say that when the last of the Kalkars is driven from the world we must live at peace with one another, but I am afraid that that will never come to pass, for who would go through life without breaking a lance or dipping his sword point now and again into the blood of a stranger? Not The Wolf, I swear, nor no more The Red Hawk. By The Flag! I take more pleasure in meeting a stranger upon a lonely trail than in meeting a friend, for I cannot set my lance against a friend and feel the swish of the wind as Red Lightning bears me swiftly down upon the prey as I crouch in the saddle, nor thrill to the shock as we strike.

I am The Red Hawk. I am but twenty, yet the fierce chiefs of a hundred fierce clans bow to my will. I am a Julian—the twentieth Julian—and from this year, 2434, I can trace my line back five hundred and thirty-four years to Julian 1st, who was born in 1896. From father to son, by word of mouth, has been handed down to me the story of every Julian, and there is no blot upon the shield of one in all that long line, nor shall there be any blot upon the shield of Julian 20th. From my fifth year to my tenth I learned, word for word, as had my father before me, the deeds of my forebears, and to hate the Kalkars and the tribe of Or-tis. This, with riding, was my schooling. From ten to fifteen I learned to use lance and sword and knife, and on my sixteenth birthday I rode forth with the other men—a warrior.

As I sat there this day, looking down upon the land of the accursed Kalkars, my mind went back to the deeds of the 15th Julian, who had driven the Kalkars across the desert and over the edge of these mountains into the valley below just one hundred years before I was born, and I turned to The Wolf and pointed down toward the green groves and the distant hills and off beyond to where the mysterious ocean lay.

"For a hundred years they have held us here," I said. "It is too long."

"It is too long," replied The Wolf.

"When the rains are over The Red Hawk leads his people into the land of plenty."

The Rock raised his spear and shook it savagely toward the valley far below. The scalp-lock fastened just below its metal-shod tip trembled in the wind. "When the rains are over!" cried The Rock. His fierce eyes glowed with the fire of fanaticism.

"The green of the groves we will dye red with their blood," cried The Rattlesnake.

"With our swords, not our mouths," I said, and wheeled Red Lightning toward the east. The Coyote laughed and the others joined with him as we wound downward out of the hills toward the desert.

On the afternoon of the following day we came within sight of our tents where they were pitched beside the yellow flood of The River. Five miles before that we had seen a few puffs of smoke rise from the summit of a hill to the north of us. It told the camp that a body of horsemen was approaching from the west. It told us that our sentry was on duty and that doubtless all was well. At a signal my warriors formed themselves in two straight lines, crossing one another at their centers. A moment later another smoke signal arose informing the camp that we were friends and us that our signal had been rightly read.

Presently, in a wild charge, whooping and brandishing our spears, we charged down among the tents. Dogs, children and slaves scampered for safety, the dogs barking, the children and the slaves yelling and laughing. As we swung ourselves from our mounts before our tents, slaves rushed out to seize our bridle reins, the dogs leaped, growling, upon us in exuberant welcome, while the children fell upon their sires, their uncles or their brothers, demanding the news of the ride or a share in the spoils of conflict or chase. Then we went in to our women.

I had no wife, but there were my mother and my two sisters, and I found them awaiting me in the inner tent, seated upon a low couch that was covered, as was the floor, with the bright blankets that our slaves weave from the wool of sheep. I knelt and took my mother's hand and kissed it and then I kissed her upon the lips and in the same fashion I saluted my sisters, the elder first. It is custom among us; but it is also our pleasure, for we both respect and love our women. Even if we did not, we should appear to, if only for the reason that the Kalkars do otherwise. They are brutes and swine. We do not permit our women a voice in the councils of the men, but none the less do they influence our councils from the seclusion of their inner tents. It is indeed an unusual mother among us who does not make her voice heard in the council ring, through her husband or her sons, and she does it through the love and respect in which they hold her and not by scolding and nagging. They are wonderful, our women. It is for them and The Flag that we have fought the foe across a world for three hundred years. It is for them that we shall go forth and drive him into the sea.

As the slaves prepared the evening meal I chatted with my mother and my sisters. My two brothers, The Vulture and Rain Cloud, lay also at my mother's feet. The Vulture was eighteen, a splendid warrior, a true Julian. Rain Cloud was sixteen then, and I think the most beautiful creature I had ever seen. He had just become a warrior, but so sweet and lovable was his disposition that the taking of human life seemed a most incongruous calling for him, yet he was a Julian and there was no alternative. Everyone loved him and respected him too, even though he had never excelled in feats of arms for which he seemed to have no relish; but they respected him because they knew that he was brave and that he would fight as courageously as any of them, even though he might have no stomach for it. Personally, I considered Rain Cloud braver than I, for I knew that he would do well the thing he hated while I would be only doing well the thing I loved.

The Vulture resembled me in looks and the love of blood, so we left Rain Cloud at home to help guard the women and the children, which was no disgrace since it is a most honorable and sacred trust, and we went forth to the fighting when there was likely to be any, and when there wasn't we went forth and searched for it. How often have I ridden the trails leading in across our vast frontiers longing for sight of a strange horseman against whom I might bend my lance! We asked no questions then when we had come close enough to see the clan-sign of the stranger and to know that he was of another tribe and likely he was as keen for the fray as we, otherwise he would have tried to avoid us. We each drew rein at a little distance and set his lance, and each called aloud his name, and then with a mighty oath each bore down upon the other, and then one rode away with a fresh scalp-lock, and a new horse to add to his herd, while the other remained to sustain the vulture and the coyote.

Two or three of our great, shaggy hounds came in and sprawled among us as we lay talking with mother and the two girls, Nallah and Neeta. Behind my mother and sisters squatted three slave girls, ready to do their bidding, for our women do no labor. They ride and walk and swim and keep their bodies strong and fit that they may bear mighty warriors, but labor is beneath them as it is beneath us. We hunt and fight and tend our own herds, for that is not menial, but all other labor the slaves perform. We found them here when we came. They have been here always—a stolid, dark skinned people, weavers of blankets and baskets, makers of pottery, tillers of the soil. We are kind to them and they are happy. The Kalkars, who preceded us, were not kind to them—it has been handed down to them from father to son for over a hundred years that the Kalkars were cruel to them and they hate their memory, yet, were we to be driven away by the Kalkars, these simple people would remain and serve anew their cruel masters, for they will never leave their soil. They have strange legends of a far time when great horses of iron raced across the desert dragging iron tents filled with people behind them, and they point to holes in the mountain sides through which these iron monsters made their way to the green valleys by the sea, and they tell of men who flew like birds and as swiftly, but of course we know that such things were never true and are but the stories that the old men and the women among them told to the children for their amusement. However, we like to listen to them.

I told my mother of my plans to move down into the valley of the Kalkars after the rains. She was silent some time before replying.

"Yes, of course," she said; "you would be no Julian were you not to attempt it. At least twenty times before in a hundred years have our warriors gone down in force into the valley of the Kalkars and been driven back. I wish that you might have taken a wife and left a son to be Julian 21st before you set out upon this expedition from which you may not return. Think well of it, my son, before you set forth. A year or two will make no great difference. But you are The Great Chief and if you decide to go we can but wait here for your return and pray that all is well with you."

"But you do not understand, Mother," I replied. "I said that we are going to move down into the valley of the Kalkars after the rains. I did not say that we are coming back again. I did not say that you would remain here and wait for our return. You will accompany us. The tribe of Julian moves down into the valley of the Kalkars when the rains are over, and they take with them their women and their children and their tents and all their flocks and herds and every other possession that is movable, and—they do not return to live in the desert ever more."

She did not reply, but only sat in thought. Presently a man-slave came to bid us warriors to the evening meal. The women and the children eat this meal within their tents, but the warriors gather around a great, circular table, called The Council Ring.

There were a hundred of us there that night. Flares in the hands of slaves gave us light and there was light from the cooking fire that burned within the circle formed by the table. The others remained standing until I had taken my seat which was the signal that the eating might begin. Before each warrior was an earthenware vessel containing beer and another filled with wine, and there were slaves whose duty it was to keep these filled, which was no small task, for we are hearty men and great drinkers, though there is no drunkenness among us as there is among the Kalkars. Other slaves brought meat and vegetables— beef and mutton, both boiled and broiled, potatoes, beans and corn, and there were bowls of figs and dried grapes and dried plums. There were also venison and bear meat and fish. There was a great deal of talk and a great deal of laughter, loud and boisterous, for the evening meal in the home camp is always a gala event. We ride hard and we ride often and we ride long. Often we are fighting and much of the time away from home. Then we have little to eat and nothing to drink but water, which is often warm and unclean and always scarce in our country.

We sit upon a long bench that encircles the outer periphery

of the table and as I took my seat, the slaves, bearing platters of meat, passed along the inner rim of the table, and as they came opposite each warrior he rose, and leaning far across the board, seized a portion of meat with a thumb and finger and cut it deftly away with his sharp knife. The slaves moved in slow procession without pause and there was a constant gleam and flash of blades and movement and change of color as the painted warriors rose and leaned across the table, the firelight playing upon their beads and metal ornaments and the gay feathers of their headdresses. And the noise!

Pacing to and fro behind the warriors were two or three score shaggy hounds waiting for the scraps that would presently be tossed them—large, savage beasts bred to protect our flocks from coyote and wolf, hellhound and lion, and capable of doing it, too.

As the warriors fell to eating the din subsided, and at a word from me a youth at my elbow struck a deep note from a drum. Instantly there was silence.

"For a hundred years we have dwelt beneath the heat of this barren waste land while our foes occupied a flowering garden, their cheeks fanned by the cooling breezes of the sea. They live in plenty; their women eat of luscious fruits, fresh from the trees, while ours must be satisfied with the dried and wrinkled semblance of the real; ten slaves they have to do their labor for every one that we possess; their flocks and herds find lush pasture and sparkling water beside their masters' tents, while ours pick a scant existence across forty thousand square miles of sandy, rock-bound desert; but these things gall the soul of The Red Hawk least of all. The wine turns bitter in my mouth when in my mind's eye I look out across the rich valleys of the Kalkars and I recall that here alone in all the world that we know there flies not The Flag."

A great growl rose from the fierce throats. "Since my youth I have held one thought sacred in my breast against the day that the blanket of The Great Chief should fall upon my shoulders. That day has come and I but await the time that the rains shall be safely over before making of that thought a deed. Twenty times in a hundred years have the Julian warriors ridden down into the Kalkar country in force, but their women and their children and their flocks remained behind in the desert—an unescapable argument for their return.

"It shall not be so again. In April the tribe of Julian leaves the desert forever. With our tents and our women and all our flocks and herds we shall descend and live among the orange groves. This time there shall be no turning back. I, The Red Hawk, have spoken."

CHAPTER II

EXODUS

APRIL arrived and with it the clans, coming at my bidding. Soon there would be little danger of heavy rains in the coast valleys. To have been caught there in a week of rain with an army would have been fatal, for the mud is deep and sticky and our horses would have mired and the Kalkars fallen upon us and destroyed us. They greatly outnumber us, and so our only hope must lie in our mobility. We realize that we are reducing this by taking along our women and our flocks, but we believe that so desperate will be our straits that we must conquer, since the only alternative to victory must be death—death for us and worse for our women and children.

The clans have been gathering for two days and all are here—some fifty thousand souls, and of horses, cattle and sheep there must be a thousand thousand, for we are rich in live stock. In the past two months, at my orders, all our swine have been slaughtered and smoked, for we could not be hampered by them on the long desert march, even if they could have survived it.

There is water in the desert this time of year and some feed, but it will be a hard, a terrible march. We shall lose a great deal of our stock, one in ten, perhaps; The Wolf thinks it may be as high as five in ten. We shall start tomorrow an hour before sunset, making a short march of about ten miles to a place where there is a spring along the trail the ancients used. It is strange to see all across the desert evidence of the great work they accomplished. After five hundred years the location of their well graded trail, with its wide, sweeping curves, is plainly discernible. It is a narrow trail, but there are signs of another, much wider, that we discover occasionally. It follows the general line of the other, crossing it and recrossing it, without any apparent reason, time and time again. It is almost obliterated by drifting sand, or washed away by the rains of ages. Only where it is of a material like stone has it endured. The pains those ancients took with things! The time and men and effort they expended! And for what? They have disappeared and their works with them.

As we rode that first night Rain Cloud rode often at my side and, as usual, he was gazing at the stars.

"There is so much that we do not know," sighed Rain Cloud; "yet all that we can spare the time for is thoughts of fighting. I shall be glad when we have chased the last of the Kalkars into the sea, so that some of us may sit down in peace and think."

"It is handed down to us that the ancients prided themselves upon their knowledge, but what did it profit them? I think we are happier. They must have had to work all their lives to do the things they did and to know all the things they knew, yet they could eat no more, or sleep no more, or drink no more in a lifetime than can we. And now they are gone forever from the Earth and all their works with them and all their knowledge is lost."

"And presently we will be gone," said Rain Cloud.

"And we will have left as much as they to benefit those who follow," I replied.

"Perhaps you are right, Red Hawk," said Rain Cloud; "yet I cannot help wanting to know more than I do know."

The second march was also made at night and was a little longer than the first. We had a good moon and the desert night was bright. The third march was about twenty-five miles and the fourth a short one, only ten miles; and there we left the trail of the ancients and continued in a southwesterly direction to a trail that followed a series of springs that gave us short marches the balance of the way to a lake called Bear by our slaves. The way, of course, was all well known to us, and so we knew just what was ahead and dreaded the fifth march, which was a terrible one, by far the worst of them all. It lay across a rough and broken area of desert and crossed a range of barren mountains—for forty-five miles it wound its parched way from water hole to water hole. For horsemen alone it would have been but a hard march, but with cattle and sheep to herd across that waterless waste, it became a terrific undertaking. Every beast that was strong enough carried hay, oats or barley in sacks, for we could not depend entirely upon the sparse feed of the desert for so huge a caravan; but water we could not carry in sufficient quantities for the stock, transporting enough, however, on the longer marches to insure a supply for the women and all children under sixteen, and on the short marches enough for nursing mothers and children under ten.

We rested all day before the fifth march began, setting forth about three hours before sundown. From fifty camps in fifty parallel lines we started. Every man, woman and child was mounted. The women carried all children under five, usually seated astride a blanket on the horse's rump behind the mother. The rest rode alone. The bulk of the warriors and all the women and children set out ahead of the herds, which followed slowly behind, each bunch securely hemmed in by outriders and followed by a rear guard of warriors.

A hundred men on swift horses rode at the head of the column, and as the night wore on, gradually increased their lead until they were out of sight of the remainder of the caravan. Their duty was to reach the camp site ahead of the others and fill the water tanks that slaves had been preparing for the past two months. We took but few slaves with us, only a few personal attendants for the women and such others as did not wish to be separated from their masters and had chosen to accompany us. For the most part the slaves preferred to remain in their own country and we were willing to let them, since it made fewer mouths to feed upon the long journey and we knew that in the Kalkar country we should find plenty to take their places, as we would take those from the Kalkars we defeated.

The long, tiresome march was over at last. The years of thought that I had given it, the two months of preparation that had immediately preceded it, the splendid condition of all our stock, the training and the temper of my people bore profitable fruit and we came through without the loss of a man, woman or child, and with the loss of less than two in a hundred of our herds and flocks. The mountain crossing on that memorable fifth march took the heaviest toll, fully ten thousand head, mostly lambs and calves, falling by the trail side.

With two days out for rest, we came, at the end of the tenth march and the twelfth day, to the lake called Bear and into a rich mountain country, lush with feed and game. Here deer and wild goats and wild sheep abounded, with rabbit and quail and wild chicken and the beautiful wild cattle that the legends of our slaves say are descended from the domestic stock of the ancients.

It was not my plan to rest here longer than was necessary to fully restore the strength and spirits of the stock. Our horses were not jaded as we had had sufficient to change often. In fact we warriors had not ridden our warhorses once upon the journey. Red Lightning had trotted into the last camp fat and sleek.

To have remained here long would have been to have apprised

the enemy of our plans, for the Kalkars and their slaves hunt in these mountains which adjoin their land, and should a single hunter see this vast concourse of Julians, our coming would have been known throughout the valleys in a single day and our purpose guessed by all.

So, after a day of rest, I sent The Wolf and a thousand warriors westward to the main pass of the ancients with orders to make it appear that we were attempting to enter the valley there in force. For three days he would persist in this false advance and in that time I felt that I should have drawn all the Kalkar fighting men from the valley lying southwest of the lake of the Bear. My lookouts were posted upon every eminence that gave view of the valleys and the trails between the main pass of the ancients and that through which we should pour down from the Bear out into the fields and groves of the Kalkars.

The third day was spent in preparation. The last of the arrows were finished and distributed. We looked to our saddle leathers and our bridles. We sharpened our swords and knives once more and put keener points upon our lances. Our women mixed the war paint and packed our belongings again for another march. The herds were gathered in and held in close, compact bunches. Riders reported to me at intervals from the various lookouts and from down the trail to the edge of the Kalkar farms. No enemy had seen us, but that they had seen The Wolf and his warriors we had the most reassuring evidence in the reports from our outposts that every trail from south and west was streaming with Kalkar warriors converging upon the pass of the ancients.*

During the third day we moved leisurely down the mountain trails and as night fell our vanguard of a thousand warriors debouched into the groves of the Kalkars. Leaving four thousand warriors, mostly youths, to guard the women, the children, the flocks and the herds, I set out rapidly in a northwesterly direction toward the pass of the ancients at the head of full twenty thousand warriors.

Our war horses we had led all day as we came slowly out of the mountains riding other animals, and not until we were ready to start upon the twenty-five mile march to the pass of the ancients did we saddle and mount the fleet beasts upon which the fate of the Julians might rest this night. In consequence our horses were fresh from a two weeks' rest. Three hours of comparatively easy riding should see us upon the flanks of the enemy.

*Probably Cajon Pass.

The Rock, a brave and seasoned warrior, I had left behind to guard the women, the children and the stock. The Rattlesnake, with five thousand warriors, bore along a more westerly trail, after fifteen miles had been covered, that he might fall upon the rear of the enemy from one point while I fell upon them from another, and at the same time place himself between their main body, lying at the foot of the pass, and the source of their supplies and reinforcements.

With The Wolf, the mountains and the desert upon one side and The Rattlesnake and I blocking them upon the south and the southeast, the position of the Kalkars appeared to me to be hopeless.

Toward midnight I called a halt to await the report of scouts who had preceded us and it was not long before they commenced to come in. From them I learned that the camp fires of the Kalkars were visible from an eminence less than a mile ahead. I gave the signal to advance. Slowly the great mass of warriors moved forward. The trail dipped down into a little valley and then wound upward to the crest of a low ridge, where a few minutes later I brought Red Lightning to a halt. Before me spread a broad valley bathed in the soft light of moon and stars. Dark masses in the nearer foreground I recognized as orange groves even without the added evidence of the sweet aroma of their blossoms that was heavy on the still night air. Beyond, to the northwest, a great area was dotted with the glowing embers of a thousand dying camp fires. I filled my lungs with the cool, sweet air; I felt my nerves tingle; a wave of exaltation surged through me; Red Lightning trembled beneath me. After nearly four hundred years a Julian stood at last upon the threshold of complete revenge!

CHAPTER III

ARMAGEDDON

VERY quietly we crept down among the orange groves, nearer, ever nearer to the sleeping foe. Somewhere to the west of us, beneath the silvery moon, The Rattlesnake was creeping stealthily forward to strike. Presently the stillness of the night would be broken by the booming of his war drums and the hoarse war-cries of his savage horde. It would be the signal that would send The Wolf down from the mountain heights above them and The Red Hawk from the orange groves below them to sink fang and talon into the flesh of the hated Kalkars, and ever The Rattlesnake would be striking at their heels.

Silently we awaited the signal from The Rattlesnake. A thousand bowmen unslung their bows and loosened arrows in their quivers; swords were readjusted, their hilts ready to the hand; men spat upon their right palms that their lance grip might be the surer. The night dragged on toward dawn. The success of my plan depended upon a surprise attack while the foe slept. I knew that The Rattlesnake would not fail me, but something must have delayed him. I gave the signal to advance silently. Like shadows we moved through the orange groves and deployed along a front two miles in length, a thousand bowmen in the lead and behind these, line after line of lancers and swordsmen. Slowly we moved forward toward the sleeping camp. How like the lazy, stupid Kalkars that no sentries were posted at their rear. Doubtless there were plenty of them on the front exposed to The Wolf. Where they could see an enemy they could prepare for him, but they have not imagination enough to foresee aught. Only the desert and their great numbers have saved them from extermination during the past hundred years.

Scarce a mile away now we could catch occasional glimpses of the dying embers of the nearest fires, and then from the east there rolled across the valley the muffled booming of distant war drums. A momentary silence followed and then faintly, there broke upon our ears the war-cries of our people. At my signal our own drums shattered the silence that had surrounded us. It was the signal for the charge. From twenty thousand savage throats rose the awful cries of battle, twenty thousand pairs of reins were loosed and eighty thousand iron shod hoofs set the earth atremble as they thundered down upon the startled enemy, and from the heights above came the growl of the drums of The Wolf and the eerie howls of his painted horde.

It was dawn as we smote the camp. Our bowmen, guiding their mounts with their knees and the swing of their bodies, raced among the bewildered Kalkars, loosing their barbed shafts into the cursing, shrieking mob that fled before them only to be ridden down and trampled by their horses' feet.

Behind the bowmen came the lancers and the swordsmen thrusting and cutting at those who survived. From our left came the tumult of The Rattlesnake's assault and from far ahead and above us the sounds of battle proclaimed that The Wolf had fallen on the foe.

Ahead I could see the tents of the Kalkar leaders and toward these I spurred Red Lightning. Here would be the representatives of the house of Or-tis and here would the battle center. Ahead the Kalkars were forming in some semblance of order to check and repel us. They are huge men and ferocious fighters, but I could see that our surprise attack had unnerved them. They gave before us, before their chiefs could organize them for resistance, yet again and again they reformed and faced us. We were going more slowly now, the battle had become largely a matter of hand-to-hand combats; they were checking us, but they were not stopping us. So great were their numbers that even had they been unarmed it would have been difficult to force our horses through their massed ranks. Back of their front line they were saddling and mounting their horses, which those who had borne the brunt of our first onslaught had been unable to do. We had cut the lines to which their animals had been tethered and driven them, terrified, ahead of us to add to the confusion of the enemy. Riderless horses were everywhere, those of the Kalkars and many of our own, whose riders had fallen in battle. The tumult was appalling, for to the shrieks of the wounded and the groans of the dying were added the screams of stricken horses and the wild, hoarse war-cries of battle-maddened men, and underlying all, the dull booming of the war drums. Above us waved The Flag, and here were the drums and a massed guard of picked men. The Flag and the drums moved forward as we moved. And near me was the clan flag of my family with the red hawk upon it and with it were its drums. In all there were a hundred clan flags upon that field this day, and the drums of each rolled out, incessantly, defiance of the enemy.

Their horsemen now were rallied, and the dismounted men were falling back behind them and presently a Kalkar chief upon a large horse confronted me. Already was my blade red with their blood. I had thrown away my lance long since, for we were fighting in too close quarters for its effective use, but the Kalkar had his spear, and there was a little open space between us. In the instant he crouched and put spurs to his horse and bore down upon me.

He was a large man as most Kalkars are, for they have bred with that alone in mind for five hundred years, so that many of them are seven feet in height and over. He looked very fierce, did this fellow, with his great bulk and his little, blood-shot eyes. He wore a war bonnet of iron to protect his head from sword cuts and a vest of iron covered his chest against the thrusts of sword or lance, or the barbed tips of arrows. We Julians, or Americans, disdain such protection, choosing to depend upon our skill and agility, not hampering ourselves and our horses with the weight of all this metal.

My light shield was on my left forearm and in my right hand I grasped my two-edged sword. A pressure of my knees, an inclination of my body, a word in his pointed ear were all that was needed to make Red Lightning respond to my every wish, even though the reins hung loose upon his withers.

The fellow bore down upon me with a loud yell and Red Lightning leaped to meet him. The Kalkar's point was set straight at my chest and I had only a sword on that side to deflect it, and at that I think I might have done so had I cared to try, even though the Kalkar carries a heavy lance and this one was backed by a heavy man and a heavy horse. With my left hand I grasped Red Lightning's mane and at the instant that the Kalkar thought to see his point tear through my chest I swung from my saddle and lay flat against Red Lightning's near side, while the Kalkar and his spear brushed harmlessly past an empty saddle. Empty for but an instant though. Swinging back to my seat in the instant that I wheeled Red Lightning I was upon the Kalkar from the rear even as the fighting mass before him brought him to a halt. He was swinging to have at me again, but even as he faced me my sword swung down upon his iron bonnet, driving pieces of it through his skull and into his brain. A fellow on foot cut viciously at me at the instant I was recovering from the blow I had dealt the mounted Kalkar, so that I was able only to partially parry with my shield, with the result that his point opened up my right arm at the shoulder—a flesh wound, but one that bled profusely, though it did not stay the force of my return, which drove through his collarbone and opened up his chest to his heart.

Once again I spurred in the direction of the tents of the Or-tis, above which floated the red banners of the Kalkars, around which were massed the flower of the Kalkar forces; too thickly massed, perhaps, for most effective defense, since we were driving them in from three sides and packing them there as tightly as eggs in the belly of a she-salmon. But now they surged forward and drove us back by weight of numbers, and now we threw ourselves upon them again until they, in their turn, were forced to give the ground that they had won. Sometimes the force of our attack drove them to one side while at another point their warriors were pushing out into the very body of the massed clans, so that here and there our turning movements would cut off a detachment of the enemy, or again a score or more of our own men would be swallowed by the milling Kalkar horde, until as the day wore on, the great field became a jumbled mass of broken detachments of Julian and Kalkar warriors surging back and forth over a bloody shambles, the iron shoes of their reeking mounts trampling the corpse of friend and foe alike into the gory mire.

Once, late in the afternoon, during a lull in the battle, I sat looking about the chaos of the field. Red with our own blood from a score of wounds and with the blood of friend and foe, Red Lightning and I stood panting in the midst of the welter. The tents of the Or-tis lay south of us—we had fought half way around them—but they were scarce a hundred yards nearer for all those bitter hours of battle. Some of the warriors of The Wolf were near me, showing how far that old, grey chief had fought his way since dawn, and presently behind a mask of blood I saw the flashing eyes of The Wolf himself, scarce twenty feet away.

"The Wolf!" I cried and he looked up and smiled in recognition.

"The Red Hawk is red indeed," he bantered; "but his pinions are yet unclipped."

"And the fangs of The Wolf are yet undrawn," I replied.

A great Kalkar, blowing like a spent hound, was sitting his tired horse between us. At our words he raised his head. "You are The Red Hawk?" he asked.

"I am The Red Hawk," I replied.

"I have been searching for you these two hours," he said.

"I have not been far, Kalkar," I told him; "what would you of The Red Hawk?"

"I bear word from Or-tis the Jemadar."

"What word has an Or-tis for a Julian?" I demanded.

"The Jemadar would grant you peace," he explained.

I laughed. "There is only one peace which we may share together," I said, "and that is the peace of death—that peace I will grant him, and he will come hither and meet me. There is nothing that an Or-tis has the power to *grant* a Julian."

"He would stop the fighting while you and he discuss the terms of peace," insisted the Kalkar. "He would stop this bloody strife that must eventually annihilate both Kalkar and Yank." He used an ancient term which the Kalkars have applied to us for ages in

a manner of contempt, but which we have been taught to consider as an appellation of honor, though its very meaning is unknown to us and its derivation lost in antiquity.

"Go back to your Jemadar," I said, "and tell him that the world is not wide enough to support both Kalkar and Yank, Ortis and Julian; that the Kalkars must slay us to the last man or be slain."

He wheeled his horse toward the tent of the Or-tis and The Wolf bade his warriors let him pass. Soon he was swallowed by the close-packed ranks of his own people, and then a Kalkar struck at one of us from behind and the battle raged again.

How many men had fallen one might not even guess, but the corpses of warriors and horses lay so thick that the living mounts could but climb and stumble over them and sometimes barriers of them nearly man-high lay between me and the nearest foeman so that I was forced to jump Red Lightning over the gory obstacle to find new flesh for my blade. And then, slowly, night descended until man could not tell foe from friend, but I called to my tribesmen about me to pass along the word that we would not move from our ground that night, staying on for the first streak of dawn that would permit us to tell a Kalkar from a Yank.

All through the night we heard a considerable movement of men and horses among the Kalkars, and we judged that they were reforming for the dawn's attack, and then quite suddenly and without warning of any sort, we saw a black mass moving down upon us. It was the Kalkars—the entire body of them—and they rode straight for us, not swiftly, for the corpse-strewn, slipper ground prevented that, but steadily, overwhelmingly, like a great slow-moving river of men and horses. They swept into us and over us, or they carried us along with them. Their first line broke upon us in a bloody wave and went down and those behind passed over the corpses of those that had fallen. We hacked until our tired arms could scarce raise a blade shoulder high. Kalkar went down screaming in agony, but they could not halt, they could not retreat, for the great, ever-moving mass behind them pushed them onward, nor could they turn to right or left because we hemmed them in on both flanks, nor could they flee ahead for there, too, were we.

Borne on by this resistless tide I was carried with it. It surrounded me. It pinioned my arms at my sides. It crushed my legs. It even tore my sword from my hand. At times, when the foe ahead stemmed it for a moment, and the force behind continued

to push on, it rose in the center until horses were lifted from the ground, and then those behind sought to climb over the backs of those in front, until the latter were borne to earth and the others passed over their struggling forms, or the obstacle before gave way and the flood smoothed out and passed along again between the flashing banks of Julian blades, hewing, ever hewing, at the Kalkar stream. Never have I looked upon such a sight as the moon revealed that night—never in the memory or the tradition of man has there been such a holocaust. Thousands upon thousands of Kalkars must have fallen upon the edge of that torrent as it swept its slow way between the blades of my painted warriors, who hacked at the living mass until their arms fell numb at their sides, and then gave way to the eager thousands pressing from behind.

And ever onward I was borne, helpless to extricate myself from the sullen, irresistible flood that carried me southward down the broadening valley. The Kalkars about me did not seem to realize that I was an enemy, or notice me in any way, so intent were they upon escape. Presently we had passed the field of yesterday's thickest fighting, the ground was no longer strewn with corpses and the speed of the rout increased, and as it did so the massed warriors spread to right and left sufficiently to permit more freedom of individual action, still not enough to permit me to worm my way from the current.

That I was attempting to do so, however, was what attracted attention to me at first and then the single red hawk feather and my other trappings, so different from those of the Kalkars.

"A Yank!" cried one near me and another drew his sword and struck at me, but I warded the blow with my shield as I drew my knife, a pitiful weapon wherewith to face a swordsman.

"Hold!" cried a voice of authority near by. "It is he whom they call The Red Hawk, their chief. Take him alive to the Jemadar."

I tried to break through their lines, but they closed in upon me, and though I used my knife to good effect upon several of them they overbore me with their numbers, and then one of them must have struck me upon the head with the flat of his sword, for of a sudden everything went black, and of that moment I remember only reeling in my saddle.

CHAPTER IV

THE CAPITAL

WHEN I regained consciousness it was night again. I was lying upon the ground, out beneath the stars. For a moment I experienced a sense of utter comfort, but as my tired nerves awoke they spoke to me of pain and stiffness from many wounds, and my head throbbed with pain. I tried to raise a hand to it, and it was then that I discovered that my wrists were bound. I could feel the matted stiffness of my scalp, and I knew that it was caked with dried blood, doubtless from the blow that had stunned me.

In attempting to move, that I might ease my cramped muscles, I found that my ankles were fastened together as well as my wrists, but I managed to roll over, and raising my head a little from the ground I looked about and saw that I was surrounded by sleeping Kalkars and that we lay in a barren hollow ringed by hills. There were no fires, and from this fact and the barrenness and seclusion of the camp I guessed that we were snatching a brief rest in hiding from a pursuing foe.

I tried to sleep, but could do so only fitfully, and presently I heard men moving about and soon they approached and awakened the warriors sleeping near me. The thongs were removed from my ankles shortly thereafter, and Red Lightning was brought and I was helped into the saddle. Immediately after, we resumed the march. A glance at the stars showed me that we were moving west. Our way led through hills and was often rough, evidencing that we were following no beaten trail, but rather that the Kalkars were attempting to escape by a devious route.

I could only guess at the numbers of them, but it was evident that there was not the great horde that had set forth from the battlefield below the pass of the ancients. Whether they had separated into smaller bands, or the balance had been slain I could not even conjecture; but that their losses must have been tremendous I was sure. We traveled all that day, stopping only occasionally when there was water for the horses and the men. I was given neither food nor water, nor did I ask for either. I would die rather than ask a favor of an Or-tis. In fact, I did not speak all that day, nor did any of the Kalkars address me.

I had seen more Kalkars in the past two days than in all my life before and was now pretty familiar with the appearance of them. They range in height from six to eight feet, the majority of them being midway between these extremes. There is a great variety of physiognomy among them, for they are a half-caste race, being the result of hundreds of years of interbreeding between the original Moon Men and the women of the Earth whom they seized for slaves when they overran and conquered the world. Among them there is occasionally an individual who might pass anywhere for a Yank, in so far as external appearances are concerned; but the low, coarse, brutal features of the Kalkar preponderate.

They wear a white blouse and breeches of cotton woven by their slaves and long, woolen cloaks fabricated by the same busy hands. Their women help in this work as well as in the work of the fields, for the Kalkar women are no better than slaves, with the possible exception of those who belong to the families of the Jemadar and his nobles. Their cloaks are of red, with collars of various colors, or with borders or other designs to denote rank. Their weapons are similar to ours, but heavier. They are but indifferent horsemen. That, I think, is because they ride only from necessity and not, as we, from love of it.

That night, after dark, we came to a big Kalkar camp. It was one of the camps of the ancients, the first that I ever had seen. It must have covered a great area, and some of the huge stone tents were still standing. It was in these that the Kalkars lived or in dirt huts leaning against them. In some places I saw where the Kalkars had built smaller tents from the building materials salvaged from the ruins of the ancient camp, but as a rule they were satisfied with hovels of dirt, or the half-fallen and never-repaired structures of the ancients.

This camp lies about forty-five or fifty miles west of the battlefield, among beautiful hills and rich groves, upon the banks of what must once have been a mighty river, so deeply has it scoured its pathway into the earth in ages gone.*

I was hustled into a hut where a slave woman gave me food and water. There was a great deal of noise and excitement outside, and through the open doorway I could hear snatches of conversation as Kalkars passed to and fro. From what I heard, I gathered that the defeat of the Kalkars had been complete and that they were flying toward the coast and their principal camp,

*The camp described probably occupies the site of present-day Pasadena.

called The Capital, which the slave woman told me lay a few miles southwest. This, she said, was a wonderful camp, with tents reaching so high into the heavens that often the Moon brushed against their tops as she made her way through the sky.

They had released my hands, but my feet were still bound and two Kalkars squatted just outside the door of the hut to see that I did not escape. I asked the slave woman for some warm water to wash my wounds and she prepared it for me. Not only that, the kindly soul saw to my wounds herself, and after they had been cleansed she applied a healing lotion which greatly soothed them, and then she bound them as best she could. I felt much refreshed by this, and with the food and drink in me was quite happy, for had I not accomplished what my people had been striving after for a hundred years—a foothold on the western coast? This first victory had been greater than I had dared to hope, and if I could but escape and rejoin my people I felt that I could lead them to the waters of the ocean with scarce a halt while the Kalkars still were suffering the demoralization of defeat.

It was while I was thinking these thoughts that a Kalkar chief entered the hut. Beyond the doorway the score of warriors that had accompanied him, waited.

"Come!" commanded the Kalkar, motioning me to arise.

I pointed to my tethered ankles.

"Cut his bonds," he directed the slave woman.

When I was free, I arose and followed the Kalkar without. Here the guard surrounded me and we marched away between avenues of splendid trees such as I never had seen before, to a tent of the ancients, a partially ruined structure of imposing height that spread over a great area of ground. It was lighted upon the inside by many flares and there were guards at the entrance and slaves holding other flares.

They led me into a great chamber that must be much as the ancients left it, though I had seen from the outside that in other places the roof of the tent had fallen in and its walls were crumbling. There were many Kalkars in this place, and at the far end of the room, upon a platform, one sat alone on a huge, carved bench—a bench with a high back and arms.

I was led before this man. He had a thin face and a long, thin nose, and cruel lips and crafty eyes. His features, however, were good. He might have passed in any company as a full-blood Yank. My guard halted me in front of him.

"This is he, Jemadar," said the chief who had fetched me.

"Who are you?" demanded the Jemadar, addressing me.

His tone did not please me. It was unpleasant and dictatorial. I am not accustomed to that, even from equals, and a Julian has no superiors. I looked upon him as scum. Therefore I did not reply.

He repeated his question angrily. I turned to the Kalkar chief who stood at my elbow. "Tell this man that he is addressing a Julian," I said, "and that I do not like his manner. Let him ask for it in a more civil tone if he wishes information."

The eyes of the Jemadar narrowed angrily. He half rose from his bench. "A Julian!" he exclaimed. "You are all Julians—but you are *the* Julian. You are the Great Chief of the Julians. Tell me," his tone became suddenly civil, almost ingratiating, "is it not true that you are *the* Julian, The Red Hawk who led the desert hordes upon us?"

"I am Julian 20th, The Red Hawk," I replied; "and you?"

"I am Or-tis, the Jemadar," he replied.

"It has been long since an Or-tis and a Julian met," I said.

"Heretofore they always have met as enemies," he replied. "I have sent for you to offer peace and friendship. For five hundred years we have fought uselessly and senselessly because two of our forebears hated one another. You are the 20th Julian, I am the 16th Or-tis. Never before have we seen one another; yet we must be enemies. How silly!"

"There can be no friendship between a Julian and an Or-tis," I replied, coldly.

"There can be peace," he said, "and friendship will come later, maybe long after you and I are dead. There is room in this great, rich country for us all. Go back to your people. I will send an escort with you and rich presents. Tell them that the Kalkars would share their country with the Yanks. You will rule half of it and I will rule the other half. If the power of either is threatened, the other will come to his aid with men and horses. We can live in peace and our people will prosper. What say you?"

"I sent you my answer yesterday," I told him. "It is the same today—the only peace that you and I can share is the peace of death. There can be but one ruler for this whole country and he will be a Julian—if not I, the next in line. There is not room in all the world for both Kalkar and Yank. For three hundred years we have been driving you toward the sea. Yesterday we started upon the final drive that will not stop until the last of you has been driven from the world you ruined. That is my answer, Kalkar."

"Take him away," cried the Jemadar. "Send this message to

his people: I offer them peace on these terms—they may have all the country east and southeast of a straight line drawn from the pass of the ancients south to the sea; we will occupy the country to the west and northwest of that line. If they accept I will send back their Great Chief. If they refuse, he will go to The Butcher, and remind them that he will not be the first Julian that an Ortis has sent to The Butcher. If they accept, there are to be no more wars between our people."

They took me back then to the hut of the old slave woman and there I slept until early morning, when I was awakened by a great commotion without. Men were shouting orders and cursing as they ran hurriedly to and fro. There was the trampling of horses' feet, the clank and clatter of trappings of war. Faintly, as from a great distance, I heard presently a familiar sound and my blood leaped in answer. It was the war-cry of my people, and beneath it ran the dull booming of their drums.

"They come!" I must have spoken aloud, for the old slave woman turned toward me.

"Let them come," she said. "They cannot be worse than these others, and it is time that we changed masters. It has been long now since the rule of the ancients, who, it is said, were not unkind to us. Before them were other ancients, and before those still others. Always they came from far places, ruled us and went their way, displaced by others. Only we remain, never changing. Like the coyote, the deer and the mountains we have been here always. We belong to the land, we are the land—when the last of our rulers has passed away we shall still be here, as we were in the beginning—unchanged. They come and mix their blood with ours, but in a few generations the last traces of it have disappeared, swallowed up by the slow, unchanging flood of ours. You will come and go, leaving no trace; but after you are forgotten we shall still be here."

Now Kalkars entered the hovel. They came hurriedly and as hurriedly departed, taking me with them. My wrists were tied again and I was almost thrown upon Red Lightning's back. A moment later we were swallowed up by the torrent of horsemen surging toward the southwest.

Less than two hours later we were entering the greatest camp that man has ever looked upon. For miles we rode through it, our party now reduced to the score of warriors who guarded me. The others had halted at the outskirts of the camp to make a stand against my people and as we rode through the strange trails of the camp we passed thousands upon thousands of Kalkars rushing past us to defend The Capital.

We passed vast areas laid out in squares, as was the custom of the ancients, a trail upon each side of the square, and within, the grass-grown mounds that covered the fallen ruins of their tents. Now and again a crumbling wall raised its ruin above the desolation, or some more sturdily constructed structure remained almost intact except for fallen roof and floors. As we advanced, we encountered more and more of the latter, built of that strange, rock-like substance, the secret of which has vanished with the ancients.

My guard turned in beneath the high arched entrance of a mighty structure. From the filth of its spacious floor rose mighty columns of polished stone, richly variegated. The tops of the columns were carved and decorated in colors and in gold. The place was filled with horses, tied to long lines that stretched almost the length of the room, from column to column. At one end a broad flight of stone steps led upward to the second floor. After we had dismounted I was led up these steps. There were many Kalkars coming and going. We passed them as I was conducted along a narrow avenue of polished white stone upon either side of which were openings in the walls leading to other chambers.

Through one of these openings we turned into a large chamber, and there I saw again the Or-tis whom I had seen the night before. He was standing before one of the openings overlooking the trail below, talking with several of his nobles. One of the latter glanced up and saw me as I entered, calling the Jemadar's attention to me. Or-tis faced me. He spoke to one near him who stepped to another opening in the chamber and motioned to someone without. Immediately a Kalkar guard entered bringing a youth of one of my desert clans. At sight of me the young warrior raised his hand to his forehead in salute.

"I give you another opportunity to consider my offer of last night," said the Or-tis, addressing me. "Here is one of your own men who can bear your message to your people if you still choose to condemn them to a futile and bloody struggle and with it he will bear a message from me—that you go to The Butcher in the morning if your warriors do not retire and your chiefs engage to maintain peace hereafter. In that event you will be restored to your people. If you give me this promise yourself, you may carry your own message to the tribes of Julian."

"My answer," I replied, "is the same as it was last night, as it will be tomorrow." Then I turned to the Yank warrior. "If you are permitted to depart, go at once to The Vulture and tell him that my last command is that he carry The Flag onward to the sea. That is all."

The Or-tis was trembling with disappointment and rage. He laid a hand upon the hilt of his sword and took a step toward me; but whatever he intended, he thought better of it and stopped. "Take him above," he snapped to my guard; "and to The Butcher in the morning. I will be present," he said to me, "to see your head roll into the dust and your carcass fed to the pigs."

They took me from the chamber then and led me up and up along an endless stairway, or at least it seemed endless before we finally reached the highest floor of the great tent. There they pushed me into a chamber the doorway to which was guarded by two giant warriors.

Squatted upon the floor of the chamber, his back leaning against the wall, was a Kalkar. He glanced up at me as I entered, but said nothing. I looked about the bare chamber, its floor littered with the dust and debris of ages, its walls stained by the dirt and grease from the bodies that had leaned against it, to the height of a man. I approached one of the apertures in the front wall. Far below me, like a narrow buckskin thong, lay the trail filled with tiny people and horses no bigger than rabbits. I could see the pigs rooting in the filth—they and the dogs are the scavengers of the camp.

For a long time I stood looking out over what was to me a strange landscape. The tent in which I was confined was among the highest of the nearer structures of the ancients, and from its upper floor I could see a vast expanse of tent roofs, some of the structures apparently in an excellent state of preservation, while here and there a grass grown mound marked the site of others that had fallen. Evidences of fire and smoke were numerous and it was apparent that whatever the ancients had built of other materials than their enduring stone had long since disappeared, while many of the remaining buildings had been gutted by flame and left mere shells, as was attested by hundreds of smoke-blackened apertures within the range of my vision.

As I stood gazing out over distant hills beyond the limits of the camp I became aware of a presence at my elbow. Turning I saw that it was the Kalkar whom I had seen sitting against the wall as I entered the chamber.

"Look well, Yank," he said, in a not unpleasant voice, "for you have not long to look." He was smiling grimly. "We have a wonderful view from here," he continued; "on a clear day you can see the ocean and the island."

"I should like to see the ocean," I said.

He shook his head. "You are very near," he said, "but you will never see it. I should like to see it again, myself; but I shall not."

"Why?" I asked.

"I go with you to The Butcher in the morning," he replied, simply.

"You?"

"Yes, I."

"And why?"

"Because I am a true Or-tis," he replied.

"Why should they send an Or-tis to The Butcher?" I de- manded. "It is not strange that an Or-tis should send me, *the* Julian; but why should an Or-tis send an Or-tis?"

"He is not a true Or-tis who sends me," replied the man, and then he laughed.

"Why do you laugh?"

"Is it not a strange joke of Fate," he cried, "that sees *the* Julian and *the* Or-tis going to The Butcher together? By the blood of my sires! I think our feud be over, Julian, at least so far as you and I are concerned."

"It can never be over, Kalkar," I replied.

He shook his head. "Had my father lived and carried out his plans, I think it might have ended," he insisted.

"While an Or-tis and a Julian lived? Never!"

"You are young, and the hate that has been suckled into you and yours from your mothers' breasts for ages runs hot in your veins; but my father was old and he saw things as few of my kind, I imagine, ever have seen them. He was a kindly man and very learned, and he came to hate the Kalkars and the horrid wrong the first Or-tis did the world and our people when he brought them hither from the Moon, even as you and yours have hated them always. He knew the wrong and he wished to right it. Al- ready he had planned means whereby he might get into commu- nication with the Julians and join with them in undoing the crime that our ancestor committed upon the world. He was Jemadar, but he would have renounced his throne to be with his own kind again. Our blood strain is as clear as yours—we are Americans. There is no Kalkar or half-breed blood in our veins. There are perhaps a thousand others among us who have brought down their birthright unsullied. These he would have brought with him, for they all were tired of the Kalkar beasts.

"But some of the Kalkar nobles learned of the plan, and among them was he who calls himself Or-tis and Jemadar. He is the son of a Kalkar woman by a renegade uncle of mine. There is Or-tis blood in his veins, but a drop of Kalkar makes one all Kalkar, therefore he is no Or-tis.

"He assassinated my father, and then set out to exterminate every pure-blood Or-tis and all those other uncontaminated Americans who would not swear fealty to him. Some have done so to save their hides, but many have gone to The Butcher. In so far as I know, I am the last of the Or-tis line. There were two brothers and a sister, all younger than I. We scattered and I have not heard of them since, but I am sure that they are all dead.

"Yes, if my father had lived the feud might have been ended; but tomorrow The Butcher will end it. However, the other way would have been better. What think you, Julian?"

I stood meditating in silence for a long time. I wondered if, after all, the dead Jemadar's way would not have been better.

CHAPTER V

THE SEA

IT SEEMED strange indeed to me that I stood conversing thus amicably with an Or-tis. I should have been at his throat, but there was something about him that disarmed me, and after his speech I felt, I am almost ashamed to say, something of friendliness for him. He was an American after all, and he hated the common enemy. Was he responsible for the mad act of an ancestor dead now almost four hundred years? But the hate that was almost a part of my being would not down entirely—he was still an Or-tis. I told him as much. He shrugged his shoulders.

"I do not know that I can blame you," he said; "but what matters it? Tomorrow we shall both be dead. Let us at least call a truce until then."

He was a pleasant-faced young fellow, two or three years my senior, perhaps, with a winning way that disarmed malice. It would have been very hard to have hated this Or-tis.

"Agreed!" I said, and held out my hand. He took it and then he laughed.

"Thirty-four ancestors would turn over in their graves if they could see this," he cried.

We talked there by the opening for a long time, while in the trail below us constant streams of Kalkars moved steadily to the battle front. Faintly, from a great distance, came the booming of the drums.

"You beat them badly yesterday," he said. "They are filled with terror."

"We will beat them again today and tomorrow and the next day until we have driven them into the sea," I said.

"How many warriors have you?" he asked.

"There were full twenty-five thousand when we rode out of the desert," I replied proudly.

He shook his head dubiously. "They must have ten, twenty times twenty-five thousand," he told me.

"Even though they have forty times twenty-five thousand we shall prevail," I insisted.

"Perhaps you will, for you are better fighters; but they have so many youths growing into the warrior class every day. It will take years to wear them down. They breed like rabbits. Their women are married before they are fifteen, as a rule. If they have no child at twenty they are held up to scorn, and if they are still childless at thirty they are killed, and unless they are mighty good workers they are killed at fifty anyhow—their usefulness to the State is over."

Night came on. The Kalkars brought us no food or water. It became very dark. In the trail below and in some of the surrounding tents flares gave a weird, flickering light. The sky was overcast with light clouds. The Kalkars in the avenue beyond our doorway dozed. I touched the Or-tis upon the shoulder where he lay stretched beside me on the hard floor.

"What is it?" he whispered.

"I am going," I said. "Do you wish to come?"

He sat up. "How are you going?" he demanded, still in a low whisper.

"I do not know, nor how far I shall go; but I am going, if only far enough to cheat The Butcher."

He laughed. "Good! I will go with you."

It had taken me a long time to overcome the prejudices of heredity, and I had thought long before I could bring myself to ask an Or-tis to share with me this attempt to escape; but now it was done. I hoped I would not regret it.

I arose and moved cautiously toward the doorway. A wick, burning from the nozzle of a clay vessel filled with oil, gave forth a sickly light. It shone upon two hulking Kalkars nodding against the wall as they sat upon the stone floor of the avenue. My knife, of course, had been taken from me and I was unarmed; but here was a sword within my reach and another for the Or-tis. The hilt of one protruded from beneath the cloak of the nearer Kalkar. My hand, reaching forth, was almost upon it when he moved. I could not wait to learn if he was awaking or but moving in his sleep. I lunged for the hilt, grasped it and the fellow was awake. At the same instant the Or-tis sprang upon the other.

He whom I had attacked lumbered to his feet, clawing at the hand that had already half drawn his sword from its scabbard, and at the same time he set up a terrific yelling. I struck him on the jaw with my clenched fist. I struck him as hard as I could strike, as he loomed above me his full eight feet. The Or-tis was having a bad time with his man, who had seized him by the throat and was trying to draw a knife to finish him. The knife must have become stuck in its scabbard for a moment, or his long, red cloak was in the way. I do not know. I saw only a flash of it from the corner of my eye as my man stiffened and then sank to the floor. Then I wheeled upon the other, a naked blade in my hand. He threw the Or-tis aside when he saw me and whipped out his own sword, but he was too slow. As I ran my point into his heart I heard the sound of running footsteps ascending the stairway and the shouts of men. I handed the sword I carried to the Or-tis and snatched the other from the fellow I had just finished. Then I kicked the puny flare as far as I could kick it and called to the Or-tis to follow me. The light went out and together we ran along the dark avenue toward the stairway, up which we could hear the warriors coming in response to the cries of our late antagonists.

We reached the head of the stairs but a moment before the Kalkars appeared. There were three of them, and one carried a weak, smoking flare that did little but cast large, grotesque, dancing shadows upon wall and stair and reveal our targets to us without revealing us to them.

"Take the last one," I whispered to the Or-tis.

We leaned over the railing and as he smote the head of the last of the three I finished the second. The first, carrying the flare, turned to find himself facing two swords. He gave a shriek

and started down the avenue. That would not do. If he had kept
still we might have let him live, for we were in a hurry; but he
did not keep still and so we pursued him. He reminded me of a
comet as he fled through the dark with his tail of light, only it
was such a little tail. However, he was a little comet. He was a
fast comet, though, and we could not catch him until the end of
the avenue brought him to bay, then, in turning, he slipped and
fell. I was upon him in the same instant, but some fancy stayed
my blade when I might have run it through him. Instead I seized
him, before he could recover himself, and lifting him from the
floor I hurled him through the aperture at the end of the avenue.
He still clung to his lamp and as I leaned out above him he appeared a comet indeed, though he was quickly extinguished in
the courtyard far below.

The Or-tis chuckled at my elbow. "The stupid clod!" he ejaculated. "He clung to that flare even to death, when, had he
thrown it away and dodged into one of these many chambers he
could have eluded us and still lived."

"Perhaps he needed it to light his way to Hell," I suggested.

"They need no help in that direction," the Or-tis assured me,
"for they will all get there, if there be such a place."

We retraced our steps to the stairway again, but once more we
heard men ascending. The Or-tis plucked me by the sleeve.
"Come," he whispered; "it is futile to attempt escape in this
direction now that the guard is aroused. I am familiar with this
place. I have been here many times. If we have the nerve we may
yet escape. Will you follow me?"

"Certainly," I replied.

The corpses of two of our recent antagonists lay at our feet at
the head of the stairs, where we stood. Or-tis stooped and
snatched their cloaks and bonnets from them. "We shall need
these if we reach the ground—alive," he said. "Follow me closely."

He turned and continued along the corridor, presently entering a chamber at the left. Behind us we heard the Kalkars ascending the stairs. They were calling to their fellows above, from
whom they would never receive a reply; but they were evidently
coming slowly, for which we were both thankful.

Or-tis crossed the chamber to an aperture in the wall. "Below
is the courtyard," he said. "It is a long way down. These walls
are laid in uneven courses. An agile man might make his way
to the bottom without falling. Shall we try it? We can go down
close to these apertures and thus rest often, if we wish."

"You go on one side and I will go on the other," I told him.

He rolled the two cloaks and the bonnets into a bundle and dropped them into the dark void beneath, then we slid over the edge of the aperture. Clinging with my hands I found a foot-hold and then another below the first. The ledges were about half the width of my hand. Some of them were rounded by time and the weather. These did not afford a very good hold. However, I reached the aperture below without mishap and there, I am free to confess, I was glad to pause for a moment, as I was panting as though I had run a mile.

Or-tis came down in safety, too. "The Butcher appears less terrible," he said.

I laughed. "He would have it over quicker," I replied.

The next stage we descended two floors before we halted. I like to have slipped and fallen twice in that distance. I was wet with sweat as I took a seat beside my companion. I do not like to recall that adventure. It sends the shivers through me always, even now; but at last it was over—we reached the bottom together and donned the cloaks and the bonnets of the Kalkars. The swords, for which we had no scabbards, we slipped through our own belts, the cloaks hiding the fact that they were scabbardless.

The smell of horses was strong in our nostrils as we crept forward toward a doorway. All was darkness within as we groped forward to find that we were in a small chamber with a door at the opposite side. Nearly all the doors of the ancients have been destroyed, either by the fires that have gutted most of the buildings, by decay, or by the Kalkars that have used them for fuel; but there are some left—they are the metal doors, and this was one. I pushed it open enough to see if there was a light beyond. There was. It was in the great chamber on the first floor where the horses were tethered. It was not a brilliant light, but a sad, flickering light. Even the lights of the Kalkars are grimy and unclean. It cast a pallid luminance beneath it; elsewhere were heavy shadows. The horses, when they moved, cast giant shadows upon the walls and floor and upon the great, polished stone columns.

A guard loafed before the door that led to the trail in front of the tent. It was composed of five or six men. I suppose there were others in some nearby chamber. The doorway through which we peered was in shadow. I pushed it open far enough to admit our bodies and we slipped through. In an instant we were hidden from the sight of the guard, among the horses. Some of them moved restlessly as we approached them. If I could but find Red Lightning! I had searched along one line almost the full length of the chamber and had started along a second when I heard a low nicker close by. It was he! Love of The Flag! It was like finding my own brother.

In the slovenly manner of the Kalkars, the saddles and bridles lay in the dirt in the aisle behind the horses. Fortunately I found my own, more easily, of course, because it is unlke those of the Kalkars, and while I slipped them quietly upon Red Lightning, the Or-tis, selecting a mount haphazard, was saddling and bridling it.

After a whispered consultation, we led our horses to the rear of the room and mounted among the shadows, unobserved by the guard. Then we rode out from behind the picket lines and moved slowly toward the entrance, talking and laughing in what we hoped might appear an unconcerned manner, the Or-tis, riding on the side nearer the guard and a little in advance, that Red Lightning might be hidden from them, for we thought that they might recognize him more quickly than they would us.

As they saw us coming they ceased their chatter and looked up, but we paid no attention to them, riding straight on for the aperture that led into the trail outside the structure. I think we might have passed them without question had there not suddenly burst from the doorway of what was, I judge, the guard-room, an excited figure who shouted lustily to all within hearing of his voice.

"Let no one leave! The Julian and the Or-tis have escaped!" he screamed.

The guard threw themselves across the entrance and at the same instant I put spurs to Red Lightning, whipped out my sword, and bore down upon them, the Or-tis following my example. I cut at one upon my left front and Red Lightning bore down another beneath his iron hoofs. We were out upon the trail and the Or-tis was beside us. Reining to the left we bore south a few yards and then turned west upon another trail, the shouts and curses of the Kalkars ringing in our ears.

With free rein we let our mounts out to far greater speed than the darkness and the littered trail gave warrant, and it was not until we had put a mile behind us that we drew in to a slower gait. The Or-tis spurred to my side.

"I had not thought it could be done, Julian," he said; "yet here we ride, as free as any men in all the country wide."

"But still within the shadow of The Butcher," I replied.

"Listen! They are following hot-foot." The pounding of the hoofs of our pursuers' horses rose louder and louder behind us as we listened. Again we spurred on, but presently we came to a place where a ruined wall had fallen across the trail.

"May The Butcher get me!" cried the Or-tis, "that I should have forgotten that this trail is blocked. We should have turned north or south at the last crossing. Come, we must ride back quickly, if we are to reach it before they."

Wheeling, we put our mounts to the run back along the trail over which we had but just come. It was but a short distance to the cross trail, yet our case looked bad, for even in the darkness the pursuing Kalkars could now be seen, so close were they. It was a question as to which would reach the crossing first.

"You turn to the south," I cried to Or-tis, "and I will turn to the north. In that way one of us may escape."

"Good!" he agreed; "there are too many of them for us to stand and fight."

He was right—the trail was packed with them, and we could hear others coming far behind the van. It was like a young army. I hugged the left hand side of the trail and Or-tis the right. We reached the crossing not a second in advance of the leaders of the pursuit and Or-tis turned to the south and I to the north. Into the blackness of the new trail I plunged and behind me came the Kalkars. I urged Red Lightning on and he responded as I knew he would. It was madness to ride through the black night along a strange trail at such speed, yet it was my only hope. Quickly my fleet stallion drew away from the clumsy, ill-bred mounts of my pursuers. At the first crossing I turned again to the west and though here I encountered a steep and winding hill it was fortunately but a short ride to the top and after that the way was along a rolling trail, but mostly down hill.

The structures of the ancients that remained standing became fewer and fewer as we proceeded and in an hour they had entirely disappeared. The trail, however, was fairly well marked and after a single, short turn to the south it continued westward over rolling country in almost a straight line.

I had reduced my speed to conserve Red Lightning's strength, and as no sign of pursuit developed, I jogged along at a running walk, a gait which Red Lightning could keep up for hours without fatigue. I had no idea where the trail was leading me, and at the time I did not even know that it was bearing west (for the heavens were still overcast), though I judged that this must be the fact. My first thought was to put as much distance as possible between me and the Kalkar camp and at the first streak of dawn take to the hills and then work my way north and east in an attempt to rejoin my people.

And so I moved on, through country that was now level and now rolling, for the better part of three hours. A cool breeze sprang up and blew in my face. It had a damp freshness and a strange odor with which I was entirely unfamiliar. I was tired from my long exertions, from loss of sleep and from lack of food and water, yet this strange breeze revived me and filled me with new strength and life.

It had become very dark, although I knew that dawn must be near. I wondered how Red Lightning could pick his way through the utter blackness. This very thought was in my mind when he came to a sudden halt. I could see nothing, yet I could tell that Red Lightning had some good reason for his action. I listened and there came to my ears a strange, sullen roar— a deep pounding, such as I never had heard before. What could it be?

I dismounted to rest my beloved friend while I listened and sought for an explanation of this monotonously reiterated sound. At length I determined to await dawn before continuing. With the bridle reins about my wrist I lay down, knowing that if danger threatened, Red Lightning would warn me. In an instant I was asleep.

How long I slept I do not know—an hour, perhaps—but when I awoke it was daylight and the first thing that broke upon my sensibilities was the dull, monotonous booming, the pounding, pounding, pounding that had lulled me to sleep so quickly.

Never shall I forget the scene that burst upon my astonished eyes as I rose to my feet. Before me was a sheer cliff dropping straight away at my feet, upon the very verge of which Red Lightning had halted the previous night; and beyond, as far as the eye could reach, water—a vast expanse of water, stretching on and on and on—the sea! At last a Julian had looked upon it! It rolled up upon the sands below me, pounding, surging, booming. It rolled back again, resistless, restless, and, at once, terrifying and soothing. Terrifying in its immensity and mystery, soothing in the majestic rhythm of its restlessness.

CHAPTER VI

SAKU THE NIPON

HUNGRY and thirsty, Red Lightning and I set off up the canyon away from the sea, presently entering the first side-canyon* bearing in a northerly direction, for it was my desire to pass through these mountains in the hope of finding a valley running east and west, which I could follow back in the direction of my people.

We had proceeded only a short distance up the side-canyon when I discovered a spring of pure water and around it an abundance of fine pasture, and a moment later Red Lightning and I were drinking avidly from the same pool. Then I removed his saddle and bridle and turned him loose to browse upon the lush grasses, while I removed my clothing and bathed my body, which was, by now, sorely in need of it. I felt much refreshed and could I have found food should soon have been myself again; but without bow and arrows my chances seemed slight unless I were to take the time to construct a snare and wait for prey. This, however, I had no mind to do, since I argued that sooner or later I must run across human habitation, where, unless greatly outnumbered by armed men, I would obtain food.

For an hour I permitted Red Lightning to line his belly with nutritious grasses and then I called him to me, resaddled, and was on my way again up the wooded, winding canyon, following a well-marked trail in which constantly appeared the spoor of coyote, wolf, hellhound, deer and lion, as well as the tracks of domestic animals and the sandaled feet of slaves; but I saw no signs of shod horses to indicate the presence of Kalkars. The imprints of sandals might mark only the passage of native hunters, or they might lead to a hidden camp. It was this that I hoped.

I had wound upward for perhaps two or three miles when I came suddenly upon a little open meadow and the realization of

*Probably Rustic Canyon, which enters Santa Monica Canyon a short distance above the sea.

my wish, for there stood three of the pointed tents of slaves consisting of a number of poles leaning inward and lashed together
at the top, the whole covered by a crazy patchwork consisting
of the skins of animals sewn together. These tents, however, were
peculiar, in that they were very small.

As I came in sight of the camp I was discovered by a horde
of scrawny curs that came bristling and yapping toward me,
apprising their masters of the presence of a stranger. A head
appeared in the opening of one of the tents and was as quickly
withdrawn. I called aloud that I would speak with their chief
and then I waited through a full minute of silence. Receiving no
reply I called again, more peremptorily, for I am not accustomed
to waiting long for obedience.

This time I received a reply. "Go away, Kalkar," cried a
man's voice. "This is our country. Go away or we will kill you."

"But I am not a Kalkar. I have but just escaped them and
I have been long without food. I wish food and then I will go
on, for I am in search of my own people who are fighting the
Kalkars at the edge of their great camp to the east."

He stuck his head through the flap then and eyed me closely.
His face was small and much wrinkled, and he had a great
shock of stiff, black hair that stuck out in all directions and was
not confined by any band. I thought that he must still be sitting
or squatting upon the ground, so low was his head, but a moment later, when, evidently having decided to investigate my
claims more closely, he parted the flap and stepped out of the
tent, I was startled to see a man little more than three feet tall
standing before me. He was stark naked and carried a bow in
one hand and several arrows in the other. At first I thought he
might be a child, but his old and wrinkled face, as well as the
well-developed muscles moving beneath his brown skin, belied
that.

Behind him came two other men of about the same height
and simultaneously from the other two tents appeared six or
eight more of these diminutive warriors. They formed a semicircle
about me, their weapons in readiness.

"From what country do you come?" demanded the little
chief.

I pointed toward the east. "From the desert beyond your
farthest mountains," I replied.

He shook his head. "We have never been beyond our own
hills," he said.

It was most difficult to understand him, though I am familiar with the dialects of a score of tribes and the mongrel tongue that is employed by both the Kalkars and ourselves to communicate with the natives, yet we managed to make ourselves understood to one another.

I dismounted and approached them, my hand held out toward them as is the custom of my people in greeting friends, with whom we always clasp hands after an absence, or when meeting friendly strangers for the first time. They did not seem to understand my intentions and drew back, fitting arrows to their bows.

I dropped my hand and smiled, at a loss as how best to reassure them. The smile must have done it, for immediately the old man's face broke into a smile.

"You are not a Kalkar," he said; "they never smile at us." He lowered his weapon, his example being followed by the others. "Tie your horse to a tree. We will give you food." He turned toward the tents and called to the women to come out and prepare food.

I dropped my reins to the ground, which is all the tying that Red Lightning requires, and advanced toward the little men, and when I had thrown aside my Kalkar coat and bonnet they crowded around me with question and comment.

"No, he is not a Kalkar," said one. "His cloak and bonnet are Kalkar, but not his other garments."

"I was captured by the Kalkars," I explained, "and to escape I covered myself with this cloak which I had taken from a Kalkar that I killed."

A stream of women and children were now issuing from the tents, whose capacity must have been taxed beyond their limit. The children were like tiny toys, so diminutive were they, and, like their fathers and mothers, quite naked, nor was there among them all the sign of an ornament or decoration of any nature. They crowded around me, filled with good-natured curiosity, and I could see that they were a joyous, kindly little people; but even as I stood there encircled by them I could scarce bring myself to believe in their existence, rather thinking that I was the victim of a capricious dream, for never had I seen or heard of such a race of tiny humans. As I had this closer and better opportunity to study them, I saw that they were not of the same race as the slaves, or In-juns, but were of a lighter shade of brown, with differently shaped heads and slanting eyes. They were a handsome little people and there was about the children that which was at once laughable and appealing, so that one could not help but love them.

The women busied themselves making fire and bringing meat —a leg of venison, and flour for bread, with fresh fruits, such as apricots, strawberries and oranges. They chattered and laughed all the time, casting quick glances at me and then giggling behind their hands. The children and the dogs were always under foot, but no one seemed to mind them and no one spoke a cross word, and often I saw the men snatch up a child and caress it. They seemed a very happy people—quite unlike any other peoples who have lived long in a Kalkar country. I mentioned this fact to the chief and asked him how they could be so happy under the cruel domination of the Kalkars.

"We do not live under their rule," he replied. "We are a free people. When they attempted to harass us, we made war upon them."

"You made war upon the Kalkars?" I demanded, incredulously.

"Upon those who came into our hills," he replied. "We never leave the hills. We know every rock and tree and trail and cave, and being a very little people and accustomed to living always in the hills we can move rapidly from place to place. Long ago the Kalkars used to send warriors to kill us, but they could never find us, though first from one side and then from another our arrows fell among them, killing many. We were all about them but they could not see us. Now they leave us alone. The hills are ours from the great Kalkar camp to the sea and up the sea for many marches. The hills furnish us with all that we require and we are happy."

"What do you call yourselves?" I asked. "From where do you come?"

"We are Nipons," he replied. "I am Saku, chief of this district. We have always been here in these hills. The first Nipon, our ancestor, was a most honorable giant who lived upon an island far, far out in the middle of the sea. His name was Mik-do. He lives there now. When we die we go there to live with him. That is all."

"The Kalkars no longer bother you?" I asked.

"Since the time of my father's father they have not come to fight with us," replied Saku. "We have no enemies other than Raban, the giant, who lives on the other side of the hills. He comes sometimes to hunt us with his dogs and his slaves. Those whom he kills or captures, he eats. He is a very terrible creature, is Raban. He rides a great horse and covers himself with iron so that our arrows and our spears do not harm him. He is three times as tall as we."

I assumed that, after the manner of the ignorant, he was referring to an imaginary personification of some greatly feared manifestation of natural forces—storm, fire or earthquake, perhaps—probably fire, though, since his reference to the devouring of his people by this giant suggested fire, and so dismissed the subject from my mind.

As I ate, I questioned Saku concerning the trails leading back in the direction of my people. He told me that the trail upon which he was camped led to the summit of the hills, joining with another that led straight down into a great valley which he thought would lead me to my destination, but of that he was not sure, having only such knowledge of the extent of the valley as one might glean from viewing it from the summit of his loftiest hills. Against this trail, however, he warned me explicitly, saying that I might use it in comparative safety only to the summit, for upon the other side it led straight down past the great stone tent of Raban the giant.

"The safer way," he said, "is to follow the trail that winds along the summit of the hills, back toward the camp of the Kalkars—a great trail that was built in the time of Mik-do, and from which you can ride down into the valley along any one of many trails. Always you will be in danger of Raban until you have gone a day's march beyond his tent, for he rides far in search of prey; but at least you will be in less danger than were you to ride down the canyon in which he lives."

But Raban, the imaginary giant, did not worry me much, and though I thanked Saku for his warnings, and let him believe that I would follow his advice, I was secretly determined to take the shortest route to the valley beyond the hills.

Having finished my meal I thanked my hosts and was preparing to depart when I saw the women and children pulling down the tents to an accompaniment of much laughter and squealing while several of the men started up the canyon, voicing strange cries. I looked at Saku questioningly.

"We are moving up the canyon for deer," he explained, "and will go with you part of the way to the summit. There are many trees across the trail that would hinder you, and these we will move or show you a way around."

"Must you carry all this camp equipment?" I asked him, seeing the women struggling with the comparatively heavy hide tents, which they were rolling and tying into bundles, while others gathered the tent poles and bound them together.

"We will put them on our horses," he explained, pointing up the canyon.

I looked in the direction he indicated, to see the strangest creatures I had ever looked upon—a string of tiny, woolly horses that were being driven toward camp by the men who had recently gone up the canyon after them. The little animals were scarce half the height of Red Lightning and they moved at so slow a pace that they seemed scarce to move at all. They had huge bellies and most enormous ears set upon great, uncouth heads. In appearance they seemed part sheep, part horse and a great deal of the long-eared rabbit of the desert.

They were most docile creatures, and during the business of strapping the loads to them the children played about between their feet or were tossed to their backs, where they frolicked, while the sad-eyed, dejected creatures stood with drooping heads and waving ears. When we started upon the march, the children were all mounted upon these little horses, sometimes perched upon the top of a load, or again there would be three or four of them upon the back of a single beast.

It did not take me long to discover that Red Lightning and I had no place in this cavalcade, for if we went behind we were constantly trampling upon the heels of the slow-moving little horses, and if we went ahead we lost them in a few yards, and so I explained to Saku that my haste made it necessary for me to go on, but that if I came to any obstacle I could not surmount alone I would wait there for them to overtake me. I thanked him again for his kindness to me, and we exchanged vows of friendship which I believe were as sincere upon his part as they were upon mine. They were a happy, lovable little people and I was sorry to leave them.

Pushing rapidly ahead I encountered no insuperable obstacles and after a couple of hours I came out upon a wide trail at the summit of the hills and saw spread before me a beautiful valley extending far to the east and to the west. At my feet was the trail leading down past the imaginary tent of the imaginary Raban and toward this I reined Red Lightning.

I had not yet crossed the old trail of the ancients when I heard the sound of the flying feet of horses approaching from the west. Here the trail winds upwards and passes around the shoulder of a hill, and as I looked I saw a running horse come into view and at its heels another in hot pursuit. The rider of the second horse was evidently a Kalkar warrior, as a red robe whipped in the wind behind him, but the figure upon the leading animal I could not identify at first; but as they drew rapidly nearer, the streaming hair of its head suggested that it must be a woman.

A Kalkar up to his old tricks, I thought, as I sat watching them. So intent was the man upon his prey that he did not notice me until after he had seized the bridle rein of his quarry and brought both animals to a halt not a score of feet from me, then he looked up in surprise. His captive was looking at me, too. She was a girl with wide, frightened eyes—appealing eyes that even while they appealed were dulled by hopelessness, for what aid might she expect from one Kalkar against another, and, of course, she must have believed me a Kalkar.

She was a Kalkar woman, but still she was a woman, and so I was bound to aid her. Even had I not felt thus obligated by her sex I should have killed her companion in any event, for was he not a stranger in addition to being a Kalkar?

I let my Kalkar cloak slip to the ground and I tossed my Kalkar bonnet after it. "I am The Red Hawk!" I cried, as I drew the sword from my belt and touched Red Lightning with my spurs. "Fight, Kalkar!"

The Kalkar tried to bring his spear into play, but it was slung across his back and he couldn't unsling it in time, so he, too, drew a sword, and to gain time he reined his horse behind that of the girl; but she was master of her own mount now, and with a shake of her reins she had urged her horse forward, uncovering the Kalkar, and now he and I were face to face. He towered above me and he had the protection of his iron vest and iron bonnet, while I was without even the protection of a shield; but whatever advantage these things might have seemed to give him they were outweighed by the lightness and agility of Red Lightning and the freedom of my own muscles, unencumbered by heavy metal protections. His big, clumsy horse was ill-mannered, and on top of all else, the Kalkar's swordsmanship was so poor that it seemed ill befitting a brave warrior to take his almost defenseless life; but he was a Kalkar and there was no alternative. Had I found him naked and unarmed in bed and unconscious with fever, it would still have been my duty to dispatch him, though there had been no glory in it.

I could not, however, bring myself to the point of butchering him without appearing, at least, to give him a chance, and so I played with him, parrying his cuts and thrusts and tapping him now and then upon his iron bonnet and vest. This must have given him hope, for suddenly he drew off and then rushed

me, his sword swinging high above his head. The Flag! What
a chance he offered, blundering down upon me with chest and
belly and groin exposed, for his iron shirt could never stop a
Julian's point.

So wondrous awkward was his method of attack that I waited
to see the nature of his weird technique before dispatching him.
I was upon his left front and when he was almost upon me he
struck downward at me and to his left, but he could not think
of two things at once—me and his horse—and as he did not strike
quite far enough to the left his blade clove his mount's skull
between the ears, and the poor brute, which was rushing forward
at the time, fell squarely upon its face, and turning completely
over, pinioned its rider beneath its corpse. I dismounted to put
the man out of his misery, for I was sure he must be badly injured, but I found that he was stone dead. His knife and spear
I appropriated as well as his heavy bow and arrows, though I
was fearful as to my skill with the last weapons, so much lighter
and shorter are the bows to which I am accustomed.

I had not concerned myself with the girl, thinking, of course,
that during the duel she would take advantage of the opportunity to escape; but when I looked up from the corpse of the
Kalkar she was still there, sitting her horse a few yards away,
and eyeing me intently.

CHAPTER VII

BETHELDA

"WELL!" I exclaimed; "why have you not flown?"

"And where?" she demanded.

"Back to your Kalkar friends," I replied.

"It is because you are not a Kalkar that I did not fly," she
said.

"How do you know that I am no Kalkar," I demanded, "and
why, if I am not, should you not fly from me, who must be an
enemy of your people?"

"You called him 'Kalkar' as you charged him," she explained,
"and one Kalkar does not call another Kalkar that. Neither am
I a Kalkar."

I thought then of what the Or-tis had told me of the thousand

Americans who had wished to desert the Kalkars and join themselves with us. This girl must be of them, then.

"Who are you?" I asked.

"My name is Bethelda," she replied; "and who are you?"

She looked me squarely in the eyes with a fearless frankness that was anything but Kalkarian. It was the first time that I had had a good look at her. By The Flag! She was not difficult to look at. She had large, gray-green eyes and heavy lashes and a cheerful countenance that seemed even now to be upon the verge of laughter. There was something almost boyish about her and yet she was all girl. I stood looking at her for so long a time without speaking that a frown of impatience clouded her brow.

"I asked you who you are," she reminded me.

"I am Julian 20th, The Red Hawk," I replied, and I thought for an instant that her eyes went a little wider and that she looked frightened; but I must have been mistaken, for I was to learn later that it took more than a name to frighten Bethelda.

"Tell me where you are going," I said, "and I will ride with you, lest you be again attacked."

"I do not know where to go," she replied, "for wherever I go I meet enemies."

"Where are your people?" I demanded.

"I fear that they are all slain," she told me, a quiver in her voice.

"But where were you going? You must have been going somewhere."

"I was looking for a place to hide," she said. "The Nipons would let me stay with them if I could find them. My people were always kind to them. They would be kind to me."

"Your people were of the Kalkars, even though you say you are no Kalkar, and the Nipons hate them. They would not take you in."

"My people were Americans. They lived among the Kalkars, but they were not Kalkars. We lived at the foot of these hills for almost a hundred years and we often met the Nipons. They did not hate us, though they hated the Kalkars about us."

"Do you know Saku?" I asked.

"Since I was a little child I have known Saku, the Chief," she replied.

"Come, then," I said, "I will take you to Saku."

"You know him? He is near?"

"Yes, come!"

She followed me down the trail up which I had so recently

come and though I begrudged the time that it delayed me, I was glad that I might have her off my hands so easily and so quickly, for, of a certainty, I could not leave her alone and unprotected, nor could I take her upon my long journey with me, even could I have prevailed upon my people to accept her.

In less than an hour we came upon Saku's new camp, and the little people were surprised indeed to see me, and overjoyed when they discovered Bethelda, more than assuring me by their actions that the girl had been far from stating the real measure of the esteem in which the Nipons held her. When I would have turned to ride away they insisted that I remain until morning, pointing out to me that the day was already far gone and that being unfamiliar with the trails I might easily become lost and thus lose more time than I would gain. The girl stood listening to our conversation, and when I at last insisted that I must go because, having no knowledge of the trails anyway, I would be as well off by night as by day, she offered to guide me.

"I know the valley from end to end," she said. "Tell me where you would go and I will lead you there as well by night as by day."

"But how would you return?" I asked.

"If you are going to your people perhaps they would let me remain, for am I not an American, too?"

I shook my head. "I am afraid that they would not," I told her. "We feel very bitterly toward all Americans that cast their lot with the Kalkars—even more bitterly than we feel toward the Kalkars themselves."

"I did not cast my lot with the Kalkars," she said, proudly. "I have hated them always—since I was old enough to hate. If four hundred years ago my people chose to do a wicked thing is it any fault of mine? I am as much an American as you, and I hate the Kalkars more because I know them better."

"My people would not reason that way," I said. "The women would set the hounds on you and you would be torn to pieces." She shivered.

"You are as terrible as the Kalkars," she said, bitterly.

"You forget the generations of humiliation and suffering that we have endured because of the renegade Americans who brought the Kalkar curse upon us," I reminded her.

"We have suffered, too," she said, "and we are as innocent as you," and then, suddenly, she looked me squarely in the eyes. "How do you feel about it? Do you, too, hate me worse than as though I were a Kalkar? You saved my life, perhaps. You could do that for one you hate?"

"You are a girl," I reminded her, "and I am an American—a Julian," I added, proudly.

"You saved me only because I am a girl?" she insisted.

I nodded.

"You are a strange people," she said, "that you could be so brave and generous to one you hate and yet refuse the simpler kindness of forgiveness—forgiveness of a sin that we did not commit."

I recalled the Or-tis, who spoken similarly, and I wondered if, perhaps, they might not be right, but we are a proud people and for generations before my day our pride had been ground beneath the heel of the victorious Kalkar. Even yet the wound was still raw. And we are a stubborn people—stubborn in our loves and our hatreds. Already had I regretted my friendliness with the Or-tis, and now I was having amicable dealings with another Kalkar—it was difficult for me to think of them as other than Kalkars. I should be hating this one—I should have hated the Or-tis —but for some reason I found it not so easy to hate them.

Saku had been listening to our conversation, a portion of which at least he must have understood. "Wait until morning," he said, "and then she can at least go with you as far as the top of the hills and point out the way for you; but you will be wise to take her with you. She knows every trail, and it will be better for her to go with you to your own people. She is not Kalkar, and if they catch her they will kill her. Were she Kalkar we would hate her and chase her away; but though she is welcome among us it would be hard for her to remain. We move camp often, and often our trails lead where one so large as she might have difficulty in following, nor would she have a man to hunt for her, and there are times when we have to go without food because we cannot find enough even for our own little people."

"I will wait until morning," I said, "but I cannot take her with me—my people would kill her."

I had two motives in remaining over night. One was to go forth early in the morning and kill game for the little Nipons in payment for their hospitality and the other was to avail myself of the girl's knowledge of the trails, which she could point out from some lofty hill top. I had only a general idea of the direction in which to search for my people and as I had seen from the summit that the valley beyond was entirely surrounded by hills, I realized that I might gain time by waiting until morning, when the girl should be able to point out the route to the proper pass to my destination.

After the evening meal that night I kept up a fire for the girl, as the air was chill and she was not warmly clad. The little people had only their tents and a few skins for their own protection, nor was there room in the former for the girl, so already overcrowded were they. The Nipons retired to their rude shelters almost immediately after eating, leaving the girl and me alone. She huddled close to the fire and she looked very forlorn and alone. I could not help but feel sorry for her.

"Your people are all gone?" I asked.

"My own people—my father, my mother, my three brothers—all are dead, I think," she replied. "My mother and father I know are dead. She died when I was a little girl. Six months ago my father was killed by the Kalkars. My three brothers and I scattered, for we heard that they were coming to kill us, also. I have heard that they captured my brothers; but I am not sure. They have been killing many in the valley lately, for here dwell nearly all the pure descendants of Americans, and those of us who were thought to favor the true Or-tis were marked for slaughter by the false Or-tis.

"I had been hiding in the home of a friend of my father, but I knew that if I were found there, it would bring death to him and his family, and so I came away, hoping to find a place where I might be safe from them; but I guess there is no place for me—even my friends, the Nipons, though they would let me stay with them, admit that it would be a hardship to provide for me."

"What will you do?" I asked. Somehow I felt very sorry for her.

"I shall find some nearly inaccessible place in the hills and build myself a shelter," she replied.

"But you cannot live here in the hills alone," I remonstrated.

She shrugged her shoulders. "Where may I live, then?"

"For a little while, perhaps," I suggested, "until the Kalkars are driven into the sea."

"Who will drive them into the sea?" she asked.

"We," I replied, proudly.

"And if you do, how much better off shall I be? Your people will set their hounds upon me—you have said so yourself. But you will not drive the Kalkars into the sea. You have no conception of their numbers. All up and down the coast, days' journeys north and south, wherever there is a fertile valley, they have bred like flies. For days they have been coming from all directions, marching toward The Capital. I do not know why they congregate now, nor why only the warriors come. Are they threatened, do you think?" A sudden thought seemed to burst upon her. "It cannot be," she exclaimed, "that the Yanks have attacked them! Have your people come out of the desert again?"

"Yes," I replied. "Yesterday we attacked their great camp—today my warriors must have eaten their evening meal in the stone tents of the Kalkars."

"You mean The Capital?"

"Yes."

"Your forces have reached The Capital? It seems incredible. Never before have you come so far. You have a great army?"

"Twenty-five thousand warriors marched down out of the desert beneath The Flag," I told her, "and we drove the Kalkars from the pass of the ancients back to The Capital, as you call their great camp."

"You lost many warriors? You must have."

"Many fell," I replied; "thousands."

"Then you are not twenty-five thousand now, and the Kalkars are like ants. Kill them and more will come. They will wear you down until your few survivors will be lucky if they can escape back to their desert."

"You do not know us," I told her. "We have brought our women, our children, our flocks and herds down into the orange groves of the Kalkars and there we shall remain. If we cannot drive the Kalkars into the sea today we shall have to wait until tomorrow. It has taken us three hundred years to drive them this far, but in all that time we have never given back a step that we have once gained—we have never retreated from any position to which we have brought our families and our stock."

"You have a large family?" she asked.

"I have no wife," I replied as I rose to add fuel to the fire. As I returned with a handful of sticks I saw that she hugged closer to the blaze and that she shivered with the cold. I removed my Kalkar robe and threw it across her shoulders.

"No!" she cried, rising; "I cannot take it. You will be cold." She held it out toward me.

"Keep it," I said. "The night will be cold, and you cannot go until morning without covering."

She shook her head. "No!" she repeated. "I cannot accept favors from an enemy who hates me." She stood there, holding the red robe out toward me. Her chin was high and her expression haughty.

I stepped forward and took the robe, and as her hand dropped to her side I threw the woolen garment about her once more and held it there upon her slim figure. She tried to pull away from it, but my arm was about her, holding the robe in place, and as I guessed her intention, I pressed the garment more closely around her, which drew her to me until we stood face to face, her body pressed against mine. As I looked down into her upturned face our eyes met and for a moment we stood there as though turned to stone. I do not know what happened. Her eyes, wide and half frightened, looked up into mine, her lips were parted and she caught her breath once in what was almost a sob. Just for an instant we stood thus and then her eyes dropped and she bent her head and turned it half away and at the same time her muscles relaxed and she went almost limp in my arms. Very gently I lowered her to her seat beside the fire and adjusted the robe about her. Something had happened to me. I did not know what it was, but of a sudden nothing seemed to matter so much in all the world as the comfort and safety of Bethelda.

In silence I sat down opposite her and looked at her as though I never before had laid eyes upon her, and well might it have been that I never had, for, by The Flag! I had not seen her before, or else, like some of the tiny lizards of the desert, she had the power to change her appearance as they change their colors, for this was not the same girl to whom I had been talking a moment since—this was a new and wonderful creature of a loveliness beyond all compare. No, I did not know what had happened, nor did I care—I just sat there and devoured her with my eyes. And then she looked up and spoke four words that froze my heart in my bosom.

She looked up and her eyes were dull and filled with pain. Something had happened to her, too—I could see it. She was changed.

"I am an Or-tis," she said and dropped her head again.

I could not speak. I just sat there staring at the slender little figure of my blood enemy sitting, dejected, in the firelight. After a long time she lay down beside the fire and slept, and I suppose that I must have slept, too, for once, when I opened my eyes, the fire was out, I was almost frozen, and the light of a new day was breaking over rugged hill tops to the east.

I arose and rekindled the fire. After that I would get Red Lightning and ride away before she awakened; but when I had found him, feeding a short distance from the camp, I did not mount and ride away, but came back to the camp again—why, I do not know. I did not want to see her again ever, yet something ground I put spurs to Red Lightning and set out up the trail where the fresh imprint of horses' hoofs pointed the direction in which the murderers had gone. There were the tracks of several horses in the trail and among them one huge imprint fully twice the size of the dainty imprint of Red Lightning's shoe. While the feet of all the Kalkar horses are large this was by far the largest I had ever seen. From the signs of the trail I judged that not less than twenty horses were in the party and while at first I had ridden impetuously in pursuit, presently my better judgment warned me that I could best serve Bethelda through strategy, since it was obvious that one man could not, singlehanded, overthrow a score of warriors by force alone.

And now, therefore, I went more warily, though had I been of a mind to do so, I doubt that I could have much abated my speed, for there was a force that drove me on and if I let my mind dwell long on the possibility of the dangers confronting Bethelda I forgot strategy and cunning and all else save brute force and blood. Vengeance! It is of my very marrow, bred into me through generations that have followed its emblem, The Flag, westward along its bloody trail toward the sea. Vengeance and The Flag and The Julian—they are one. And here was I, Lord of Vengeance, Great Chief of the Julians, Protector of The Flag, riding hot-foot to save or avenge a daughter of the Or-tis! I should have flushed for shame, but I did not. Never had my blood surged so hot even to the call of The Flag. Could it be, then, that there was something greater than The Flag? No, that I could not admit; but possibly I had found something that imparted to The Flag a greater meaning for me.

CHAPTER VIII

RABAN

I CAME to the summit without overtaking them, but I could tell from the trail that they were not far ahead of me. The canyon trail is very winding and there is a great deal of brush, so that oftentimes a horseman a score of yards ahead of you is out of sight and the noise of your own mount's passage drowns that of the others. For this reason I did not know, as long as I was in the canyon, how close I might be to them; but when I reached the

drew me to her. She was awake and standing looking all abo
up and down the canyon, when I first saw her and I was sure th
there was an expression of relief in her eyes when she discovere
me. She smiled wistfully, and I could not be hard, as I shoulc
have been to a blood enemy.

I was friendly with her brother, I thought—why should I not
be friendly with her? Of course, I shall go away and not see her
again, but at least I may be pleasant to her while I remain. Thus
I argued and thus I acted.

"Good morning," I said, as I approached; "how are you?"

"Splendid!" she replied. "And how are you?" Her tones were
rich and mellow and her eyes intoxicated me like old wine. Oh,
why was she an enemy?

The Nipons came from their little tents. The naked children
scampered around, playing with the dogs, in an attempt to get
warm. The women built the fires around which the men huddled
while their mates prepared the morning meal.

After we had eaten, I took Red Lightning and started off down
the canyon to hunt and although I was dubious as to what results I should achieve with the heavy Kalkar bow, I did better
than I had expected, for I got two bucks, although the chase
carried me much farther from camp than I had intended going.

The morning must have been half spent as Red Lightning
toiled up the canyon trail beneath the weight of the two carcasses
and myself to the camp. I noticed that he seemed nervous as we
approached, keeping his ears pricked forward and occasionally
snorting, but I had no idea of the cause of his perturbation and
was only the more on the alert myself, as I always am when
warned by Red Lightning's actions that something may be amiss.

And when I came to the camp site I did not wonder that he
had been aroused, for his keen nostrils had scented tragedy long
before my dull senses could become aware of it. The happy,
peaceful camp was no more. The little tents lay flat upon the
ground and near them the corpses of two of my tiny friends—two
little, naked warriors. That was all. Silence and desolation
broded where there had been life and happiness a few short
hours before. Only the dead remained.

Bethelda! What had become of her? What had happened? Who
had done this cruel thing? There was but a single answer—the
Kalkars must have discovered this little camp and rushed it. The
Nipons that had not been killed doubtless escaped, and the Kalkars had carried Bethelda away, a captive.

Suddenly I saw red. Casting the carcasses of the bucks to the summit it was different. Then I could see farther in all directions. The murderers were not in sight upon the great highway of the ancients, and I rode swiftly to where the trail drops down upon the north side of the mountains to the great valley that I had seen the day before. There are fewer trees and lower brush upon this side, and below me I could see the trail at intervals as it wound downward and as I looked, I saw the first of a party of horsemen come into sight around the shoulder of a hill as they made their way down into the canyon.

To my right, a short distance, was a ridge leading from the summit downward and along the flank of the canyon into which the riders were descending. A single glance assured me that a few minutes of hard and rather rough riding would permit me to gain the canyon ahead of the riders and unseen by them, unless the brush proved heavier than it appeared or some impassable ravine intervened. At least the venture was worth essaying and so, not waiting for a longer inspection of the enemy, I whe   l and rode along the summit and out on the ridge whicl   loped would prove an avenue to such a position as I wishe   ittain, where I might carry out a species of warfare for w   ve are justly famous, in that we are adepts at it.

I found along the ridge a faint game trail and th   ollowed at reckless speed, putting Red Lightning down ste   clivities in a manner that must have caused him to thinl   mad, so careful am I ordinarily of his legs; but today 1   as inconsiderate of them as I was of my own life.

At one place the thing I most feared occurree   ep ravine cut directly through the ridge, the side nearer r   opping almost sheer to the bottom. There was some sligl   ting, however, part way down and Red Lightning never h   ed as I put him over the brink. Squatting on his haunche   s front legs stiff before him, he slid and stumbled downwa   gaining momentum as he went, until, about twenty feet fr   the bottom, we went over a perpendicular dirt cliff together, landing in the soft sand at the foot of it a bit shaken, but unhurt.

There was no time even for an instant's breathing spell. Before us was the steep acclivity of the opposite side and like a cat Red Lightning pawed and scrambled his way up, clinging motionless at times for an instant, his toes dug deep into the yielding earth, while I held my breath as Fate decided whether he should hold his own or slip back into the ravine; but at last we made it and once more were upon the summit of the ridge.

Now I had to go more carefully, for my trail and the trail of the enemy were converging and constantly the danger of apprehension increased. I rode now slightly below the brow of the ridge, hidden from whomever might be riding the trail along the opposite side, and presently I saw the mouth of the canyon to my right and below me and across it the trail along which the Kalkars must pass. That they had not already done so I was confident, for I had ridden hard and almost in a straight line, while they had been riding slowly when I saw them and the trail they were following wound back and forth at an easy grade.

Where the ridge ended in a steep declivity at the bottom of the canyon I drew rein and dismounted, and leaving Red Lightning hidden in the brush, made my way to the summit where, below me, the trail lay in full view for a distance of a hundred yards up the canyon and for half a mile below. In my left hand I carried the heavy Kalkar bow and in my right a bundle of arrows, while a score or more others protruded from my right boot. Fitting an arrow to my bow I waited.

Nor did I have long to wait. I heard the clank of accouterments, the thud of horses' feet, the voices of men, and a moment later the head of the little column appeared about the shoulder of a hill.

I had tried my Kalkar bow this morning upon the bucks and I was surer of it now. It is a good bow, the principal objection to it being that it is too cumbersome for a mounted warrior. It is very powerful, though, and carries its heavy arrows accurately to a great distance. I knew now what I could do with it. I waited until half a dozen riders had come into view, covering the spot at which they appeared, and as the next one presented himself I loosed my shaft. It caught the fellow in the groin, and coming from above, as it did, passed through and into his horse. The stricken animal reared and threw itself backward upon its rider; but that I only caught with the tail of my eye, for I was loosing another shaft at the man in front of him. He dropped with an arrow through his neck.

By now all was pandemonium. Yelling and cursing, the balance of the troop galloped into sight and with them I saw such a man as mortal eye may never have rested upon before this time and, let us pray, never may again. He sat a huge horse, which I instantly recognized as the fellow who had made the great imprints in the trail I had been following to the summit, and was himself a creature of such mighty size that he dwarfed the big Kalkars about him.

Instantly I saw in him the giant, Raban, whom I had thought

but the figment of Saku's imagination or superstition. On a horse at Raban's side rode Bethelda. For an instant I was so astonished by the size of Raban that I forgot my business upon the ridge, but only for an instant. I could not let drive at the giant for fear of hitting Bethelda, but I brought down in quick succession the man directly in front of him and one behind.

By now the Kalkars were riding around in circles looking for the foe, and they presented admirable targets, as I had known they would. By the blood of my fathers! But there is no greater sport than this form of warfare. Always outnumbered by the Kalkars we have been forced to adopt tactics aimed to harass the enemy and wear him down a little at a time. By clinging constantly to his flanks, by giving him no rest, by cutting off detachments from his main body and annihilating them, by swooping down unexpectedly upon his isolated settlements, by roving the country about him and giving battle to every individual we met upon the trails, we have driven him two thousand miles across the world to his last stand beside the sea.

As the Kalkars milled about in the canyon bottom I drove shaft after shaft among them, but never could I get a fair shot at Raban the giant, for always he kept Bethelda between us after he had located me, guessing, evidently, that it was because of her that I had attacked his party. He roared like a bull as he sought to urge his men up the ridge to attack me, and some did make the attempt, half-heartedly, prompted, no doubt, by fear of their master—a fear that must have been a little greater than fear of the unknown enemy above them; but those who started up after me never came far, for they and I soon discovered that with their heavy bow I could drive their heavy arrows through their iron vests as if they had been wool.

Raban, seeing that the battle was going against him, suddenly put spurs to his great mount and went lumbering off down the canyon, dragging Bethelda's horse after him, while those of his men who remained covered his retreat.

This did not suit me at all. I was not particularly interested in the Kalkars he was leaving behind, but in him and his captive, and so I ran to Red Lightning and mounted. As I reined down the flank of the ridge toward the canyon bottom I saw the Kalkars drawing off after Raban. There were but six of them left and they were strung out along the trail. As they rode they cast backward glances in my direction as though they were expecting to see a great force of warriors appear in pursuit. When they saw me they did not return to engage me, but continued after Raban.

I had reslung my bow beneath my right stirrup leather and replaced the few arrows in my quiver as Red Lighting descended the side of the ridge, and now I prepared my lance. Once upon the level trail of the canyon bottom I whispered a word into the pointed ear before me, couched my lance, and crouched in the saddle as the thirtieth descendant of the first Red Lightning flattened in swift charge.

The last Kalkar in the retreating column, rather than receive my spear through the small of his unprotected back, wheeled his horse, unslung his spear and awaited me in the middle of the trail. It was his undoing. No man can meet the subtle tricks of a charging lancer from the back of a standing horse, for he cannot swerve to one side or the other with the celerity oft necessary to elude the point of his foe's lance, or take advantage of what opening the other may inadvertently leave him, and doubly true was this of the Kalkar upon his clumsy, splay-footed mount. So awkward were the twain that they could scarcely have gotten out of their own way, much less mine, and so I took him where I would as I crashed into him, which was the chest, and my heavy lance passed through him, carrying him over his horse's rump, splintering as he fell to earth. I cast the useless stump aside as I reined Red Lightning in and wheeled him about. I saw the nearer Kalkar halted in the trail to watch the outcome of the battle, and now that he saw his companion go down to death and me without a lance he bore down upon me, and I guess he thought that he had me on the run, for Red Lightning was indeed racing away from him, back toward the fallen foe; but with a purpose in my mind that one better versed in the niceties of combat might have sensed. As I passed the dead Kalkar I swung low from my saddle and picked his lance from where it lay in the dust beside him, and then, never reducing our speed, I circled and came back to meet the rash one riding to his doom. Together we came at terrific speed, and as we approached one another I saw the tactics that this new adversary was bent upon using to my destruction and I may say that he used judgment far beyond the seeming capacity of his low forehead, for he kept his horse's head ever straight for Red Lightning's front with the intention of riding me down and overthrowing my mount, which, considering the disparity of their weights, he would certainly have accomplished had we met full on; but we did not. My reins lay on Red Lightning's withers. With a touch of my left knee I swung the red stallion to the right and passed my spear to my left hand, all in a fraction of the time it takes to tell it, and as we met I had the Kalkar helpless, for he was not expecting me upon his left hand, his heavy horse could not swerve with the agility of Red Lightning, and so I had but to pick my target and put the fellow out of his misery—for it must be misery to be a low creature of a Kalkar. In the throat my point caught him, for I had no mind to break another lance since I saw two more of the enemy riding toward me, and being of tough wood, the weapon tore out through the flesh as the fellow tumbled backward into the dust of the trail.

There were four Kalkars remaining between me and the giant who, somewhere down the canyon and out of sight now, was bearing Bethelda off, I knew not where or to what fate. The four were strung out at intervals along the trail and seemed undecided as to whether to follow Raban or wait and argue matters out with me. Perhaps they hoped that I would realize the futility of pitting myself against their superior numbers, but when I lowered my lance and charged the nearer of them, they must have realized that I was without discretion and must be ridden down and dispatched. Fortunately for me they were separated by considerable intervals and I did not have to receive them all at once. The nearer, fortified by the sound of his companions' galloping approach, couched his lance and came halfway to meet me, but I think much of his enthusiasm must have been lost in contemplation of the fate that he had seen overtake the others that had pitted their crude skill against me, for certainly there were neither fire nor inspiration in his attack, which more closely resembled a huge, senseless boulder rolling down a mountain side than a sentient creature of nerves and brain driven by lofty purposes of patriotism and honor.

Poor clod! An instant later the world was a better place in which to live, by at least one less Kalkar; but he cost me another lance and a flesh wound in the upper arm, and left me facing his three fellows, who were now so close upon me that there was no time in which to retrieve the lance fallen from his nerveless fingers. There was recourse only to the sword, and drawing, I met the next of them with only a blade against his long lance; but I eluded his point, closed with him and, while he sought to draw, clove him open from his shoulder to the center of his chest.

It took but an instant, yet that instant was my undoing, for the remaining two were already upon me. I turned in time to partially dodge the lance point of the foremost, but it caught me a glancing blow upon the head and that is the last that I remember of immediately ensuing events.

When next I opened my eyes I was jouncing along, lashed to a saddle, belly down across a horse. Within the circumscribed limits of my vision lay a constantly renewed circle of dusty trail and four monotonously moving, gray, shaggy legs. At least I was not on Red Lightning.

I had scarcely regained consciousness when the horse bearing me was brought to a stop, and the two accompanying Kalkars dismounted and approached me. Removing the bonds that held me to the saddle, they dragged me unceremoniously to the ground and when I stood erect they were surprised to see that I was conscious.

"Dirty Yank!" cried one and struck me in the face with his open palm.

His companion laid a hand upon his arm. "Hold, Tav," he expostulated; "he put up a good fight against great odds." The speaker was a man of about my own height and might have passed as a full blood Yank, though, as I thought at the time, doubtless he was a half-breed.

The other gestured his disgust. "A dirty Yank," he repeated. "Keep him here, Okonnor, while I find Raban and ask what to do with him." He turned and left us.

We had halted at the foot of a low hill upon which grew tremendous old trees and of such infinite variety that I marveled at them. There were pine, cypress, hemlock, sycamore and acacia that I recognized and many others the like of which I never before had seen, and between the trees grew flowering shrubs, and where the ground was open it was carpeted with flowers—great masses of color; and there were little pools choked with lilies, and countless birds and butterflies. Never had I looked upon a place of such wondrous beauty. Through the trees I could see the outlines of the ruins of one of the stone tents of the ancients sitting upon the summit of the low hill. It was toward this structure that he who was called Tav was departing from us.

"What place is this?" I asked the fellow guarding me, my curiosity overcoming my natural aversion to conversation with his kind.

"It is the tent of Raban," he replied. "Until recently it was the home of Or-tis the Jemadar—the true Or-tis. The false Or-tis dwells in the great tents of The Capital. He would not last long in this valley."

"What is this Raban?" I asked.

"He is a great robber. He preys upon all, and to such an extent has he struck terror to the hearts of all who have heard of him

that he takes toll as he will, and easily. They say that he eats the
flesh of humans, but that I do not know—I have been with him
but a short time. After the assassination of the true Or-tis I
joined him because he preys upon the Kalkars. He lived long in
the eastern end of the valley where he could prey upon the outskirts of The Capital and then he did not rob or murder the people of the valley; but with the death of Or-tis he came and took
this place and now he preys upon my people as well as upon the
Kalkars, but I remain with him since I must serve either him or
the Kalkars."

"You are not a Kalkar?" I asked, and I could believe it because
of his good old American name, Okonnor.

"I am a Yank; and you?"

"I am Julian 20th, The Red Hawk," I replied.

He raised his brows. "I have heard of you in the past few days,"
he said. "Your people are fighting mightily at the edge of The
Capital; but they will be driven back—the Kalkars are too many.
Raban will be glad of you if the stories they tell of him are true.
One is that he eats the hearts of brave warriors that fall into his
hands."

I smiled. "What is the creature?" I asked again. "Where orig-
inates such a breed?"

"He is only a Kalkar," replied Okonnor; "but even a greater
monstrosity than his fellows. He was born in The Capital, of
ordinary Kalkar parents, they say, and early developed a lust for
blood that has increased with the passing years. He boasts yet of
his first murder—he killed his mother when he was ten."

I shuddered. "And it is into the hands of such that a daughter
of the Or-tis has fallen," I said, "and you, an American, aided in
her capture."

He looked at me in startled surprise. "The daughter of an Or-
tis?" he cried.

"Of *the* Or-tis," I repeated.

"I did not know," he said. "I was not close to her at any time
and thought that she was but a Kalkar woman."

"What are you going to do? Can you save her?"

He drew his knife and cut the bonds that held my arms behind
me. "Hide here among the trees," he said, "and watch the Raban
until I return. It will be after dark, but I will bring help. This
valley is almost exclusively peopled by those who have refused to
intermarry with the Kalkars and have brought down their strain
unsullied from ancient times. There are almost a thousand fighting men of pure Yank blood within its confines. I should be able

to gather enough to put an end to Raban for all time, and if the danger of a daughter of Or-tis cannot move them from their shame and cowardice they are hopeless indeed."

He mounted his horse. "Quick!" he cried, "get among the trees."

"Where is my horse?" I called as he was riding away. "He was not killed?"

"No," he called back; "he ran off when you fell. We did not try to catch him." A moment later he disappeared around the west end of the hill and I entered the miniature forest that clothed it. Through the gloom of my sorrow broke one ray of happiness—Red Lightning lived.

About me grew ancient trees of enormous size with boles five or six feet in diameter and their upper foliage waving a hundred and more feet above my head. Their branches excluded the sun where they grew thickest and beneath them baby trees struggled for existence in the wan light, or hoary monsters, long fallen, lay embedded in leaf mold, marking the spot where some long dead ancient set out a tiny seedling that was to outlive all his kind.

It was a wonderful place in which to hide, though hiding is an accomplishment that we Julians have little training in and less stomach for. However, in this instance it was in a worthy cause—a Julian hiding from a Kalkar in the hope of aiding an Or-tis! Ghosts of nineteen Julians! To what had I brought my proud name? And yet I could not be ashamed. There was something stubbornly waging war against all my inherited scruples, and I knew that it was going to win—had already won. I would have sold my soul for this daughter of my enemy.

I made my way up the hill toward the ruined tent, but at the summit the shrubbery was so dense that I could see nothing. Rose bushes fifteen feet high and growing as thickly together as a wall hid everything from my sight. I could not even penetrate them. Near me was a mighty tree with a strange, feathery foliage. It was such a tree as I had never seen before, but that fact did not interest me so much as the discovery that it might be climbed to a point that would permit me to see above the top of the rose bushes.

What I saw included two stone tents not so badly ruined as most of those one comes across, and between them a pool of water —an artificial pool of straight lines. Some fallen columns of stone lay about it and the vines and creepers fell over its edge into the water, almost concealing the stone rim. As I watched, a group of men came from the ruin to the east through a great archway, the coping of which had fallen away. They were all Kalkars and among them was Raban. I had my first opportunity to view him closely. He was a most repulsive appearing creature. His great size might easily have struck with awe the boldest heart, for he stood a full nine feet in height and was very large in proportion about the shoulders, chest and limbs. His forehead was so retreating that one might with truth say he had none, his thick thatch of stiffly erect hair almost meeting his shaggy eyebrows. His eyes were small and set close to a coarse nose and all his countenance was bestial. I had not dreamed that a man's face could be so repulsive.

He was speaking to that one of my captors who had left me at the foot of the hill to apprise Raban of my taking—that fellow who struck me in the face while my hands were bound and whose name was Tav. He spoke in a roaring, bull-like voice which I thought at the time was, like his swaggering walk and his braggadocio, but a pose to strike terror in those about him. I could not look at the creature and believe that real courage lay within so vile a carcass. I have known many fearless men—The Vulture, The Wolf, The Rock and hundreds like them—and in each, courageousness was reflected in some outward physical attribute of dignity and majesty.

"Fetch him!" he roared at Tav. "Fetch him! I will have his heart for my supper," and after Tav had gone to fetch me, the giant stood there with his other followers, roaring and bellowing and always about himself and what he had done and what he would do. He seemed to me an exaggeration of a type I had seen before, wherein gestures simulate action, noise counterfeits courage, and wind passes for brains. The only impressive thing about him was his tremendous bulk and yet even that did not impress me greatly—I have known small men, whom I respected, that filled me with far greater awe. I did not fear him. I think only the ignorant could have feared him at all, and I did not believe all the pother about his eating human flesh. I am of the opinion that a man who really intended eating the heart of another would say nothing about it.

Presently Tav came running back up the hill. He was much excited, as I had known that he would be, even before he started off to fetch me.

"He is gone!" he cried to Raban. "They are both gone—Okonnor and the Yank. Look!" he held out the thongs that had fastened my wrists. "They have been cut. How could he cut them with his hands bound behind him? That is what I want to know. How could he have done it? He could not unless——"

"There must have been others with him," roared Raban. "They followed and set him free, taking Okonnor captive."

"There were no others," insisted Tav.

"Perhaps Okonnor freed him," suggested another.

So obvious an explanation could not have originated in the pea girth brain of Raban and so he said: "I knew it from the first—it was Okonnor. With my own hands I shall tear out his liver and eat it for breakfast."

Certain insects, toads and men make a lot of unnecessary noise, but the vast majority of other animals pass through life in dignified silence. It is our respect for these other animals that causes us to take their names. Who ever heard of a red hawk screeching his intentions to the world? Silently he soars above the treetops, and as silently he swoops and strikes.

CHAPTER IX

REUNION

THROUGH the conversation that I overheard between Raban and his minions I learned that Bethelda was imprisoned in the westerly ruin, but as Raban did not go thither during the afternoon I waited in the hope that fortune would favor me with a better opportunity after dark to attempt her liberation with less likelihood of interruption or discovery than would have been possible during the day, when men and women were constantly passing in and out of the easterly tent. There was the chance, too, that Okonnor might return with help and I did not want to do anything while that hope remained that might jeopardize Bethelda's chances for escape.

Night fell and yet there was no sign of Okonnor. Sounds of coarse laughter came from the main ruin and I could imagine that Raban and his followers were at meat, washing down their food with the fiery liquor of the Kalkars. There was no one in sight and so I determined to come out of my concealment and investigate the structure in which I believed Bethelda imprisoned. If I could release her, well and good; if not I could but wait for Okonnor.

As I was about to descend from the tree there came down with the wind from out of the canyon to the south a familiar sound— the nicker of a red stallion. It was music to my ears. I must answer it even though I chanced arousing the suspicion of the Kalkars. Just once my answering whistle rose sharp and clear above the noises of the night. I do not think the Kalkars heard it —they were making too much noise of their own within doors— but the eager whinny that came thinly down the night wind told me that two fine, slim ears had caught the familiar summons.

Instead of going at once to the westerly ruin I made my way down the hill to meet Red Lightning, for I knew that he might mean, in the end, success or failure for me—freedom or death for Bethelda. Already, when I reached the foot of the declivity, I faintly heard the pounding of his hoofs and, steadily increasing in volume, the loved sound rolled swiftly out of the darkness toward me. The hoof beats of running horses, the rolling of the war drums! What sweeter music in all the world?

He saw me, of course, before I saw him, but he stopped in a cloud of dust a few yards from me and sniffed the air. I whispered his name and called him to me. Mincingly he came, stopping often, stretching his long neck forward, poised always, ready for instant flight. A horse depends much upon his eyes and ears and nostrils, but he is never so fully satisfied as when his soft, inquisitive muzzle has nosed an object of suspicion. He snorted now, and then he touched my cheek with his velvet lip and gave a great sigh and rubbed his head against me, satisfied. I hid him beneath the trees at the foot of the hill and bade him wait there in silence.

From the saddle I took the bow and some arrows and following the route that Tav had taken to the top of the hill I avoided the hedge of roses and came presently before the south archway of the ruin. Beyond was a small central court with windows and doors opening upon it. Light from flares burning in some of the rooms partially illuminated the court, but most of it was in shadow. I passed beneath the arch and to the far end of the enclosure, where, at my right, I saw a window and a door opening into two rooms in which a number of Kalkars were eating and drinking at two long tables. I could not see them all. If Raban was there he was not within range of my vision.

It is always well to reconnoiter thoroughly before carrying out any plan of action and with this idea in mind I left the court by the way I had entered and made my way to the east end of the structure, intending to pass entirely around it and along the north side of the westerly ruin, where I hoped to find Bethelda and devise means for her rescue.

At the southeast corner of the ruin are three gigantic cypress trees, growing so closely together as to almost resemble a single huge tree, and as I paused an instant behind them to see what lay before me, I saw a single Kalkar warrior come from the building and walk out into the rank grass that grew knee high on a level space before the structure.

I fitted an arrow to my bow. The fellow had that which I craved—a sword. Could I drop him noiselessly? If he would turn I was sure of it, and turn he did as though impelled to it by my insistent wish. His back was toward me. I drew the shaft far back. The cord twanged as I released it, but there was no other sound, except the muffled thud as the arrow entered its victim's spine at the base of the brain. Mute, he died. No other was around. I ran forward and removed his sword belt, to which were attached both sword and knife.

As I arose and buckled the weapons about me, I glanced into the lighted room from which he had just come. It was the same that I had seen from the court upon the other side and directly adjoining it was the other room that I had seen. Now I could see all of them that I had not seen before. Raban was not there. Where was he? A cold terror ran suddenly through me. Could it be that in the brief interval that had elapsed while I went down to meet Red Lightning he had left the feast and gone to the westerly ruin? I ran swiftly across the front of the house and along the north side toward the other structure.

I stopped before it and listened. I heard the sound of voices! From whence came they? This was a peculiar structure, built upon a downward sloping hill, with one floor on a level with the hilltop, another above that level and a third below and behind the others. Where the various entrances were and how to find the right one I did not know. From my hiding place in the tree I had seen that the front chamber at the hill top level was a single apartment with a cavernous entrance that stretched the full width of the ruin, while upon the south side and to the rear of this apartment were two doors, but where they led I could not guess. It seemed best, however, to try these first and so I ran immediately to them and here the sounds of voices came more distinctly to me and now I recognized the roaring, bull-tones of Raban.

I tried the nearer door. It swung open and before me a flight of stairs descended and at the same time the voices came more loudly to my ears—I had opened the right door. A dim light flickered below as though coming from a chamber near the foot of the stairs. These were but instantaneous impressions to which I gave no conscious heed at the time, for almost as they flashed upon me I was at the foot of the stairs, looking into a large, high-ceiled chamber in which burned a single flare that but diffused the gloom sufficiently for me to see the figure of Raban towering above that of Bethelda, whom he was dragging toward the doorway by her hair.

"An Or-tis!" he was bellowing. "An Or-tis! Who would have thought that Raban would ever take the daughter of a Jemadar to be his woman? Ah, you do not like the idea, eh? You might do worse, if you had a choice, but you have none, for who is there to say 'no' to Raban the Giant?"

"The Red Hawk!" I said, stepping into the chamber.

The fellow wheeled, and in the flickering light of the dim flare I saw his red face go purple and from purple to white, or rather a blotchy semblance of dirty yellow. Blood of my fathers! How he towered above me, a perfect mountain of flesh! I am six feet in height and Raban must have been half again as tall, a good nine feet; but I swear he appeared all of twenty, and broad!

For a moment he stood in silence glaring at me as though overcome by surprise and then he thrust Bethelda aside and drawing his sword advanced upon me, bellowing and roaring as was his wont for the purpose, I presume, of terrifying me, and also, I could not help but think, to attract the attention and the aid of his fellows.

I came to meet him then and he appeared a mountain, so high he loomed; but with all his size I did not feel the concern that I have when meeting men of my own stature whose honor and courage merited my respect, and it is well that I had this attitude in mind to fortify me in the impending duel, for, by The Flag! I needed whatever of encouragement I might find in it. The fellow's height and weight were sufficient to overcome a mighty warrior had Raban been entirely wanting in skill, which he by no means was. He wielded his great sword with a master hand and because of the very cowardice which I attributed to him he fought with a frenzy wrought by fear, as a cornered beast fights.

I needed all my skill and I doubt that that alone would have availed me had it not been upborne and multiplied by love and the necessity for protecting the object of my love. Ever was the presence of Bethelda, the Or-tis, a spur and an inspiration. What blows I struck I struck for her, what I parried, it was as though I parried from her soft skin.

As we closed he swung mightily at me a cut that would have severed me in twain, but I parried and stooped beneath it at once, and found his great legs unguarded before me and ran my sword through a thigh. With a howl of pain, Raban leaped back, but I followed him with a jab of my point that caught him just beneath the bottom of his iron vest and punctured his belly. At that he gave forth a horrible shriek, and though sorely wounded began to wield his blade with a skill I had not dreamed lay in him. It was with the utmost difficulty that I turned his heavy sword, and I saved myself as many times by the quickness of my feet as by the facility of my blade.

And much do I owe, too, to the cleverness of Bethelda, who, shortly after we crossed swords, had run to the great fireplace and seized the flare from where it had reposed upon the stone shelf above, and ever after had kept just behind my shoulder with it, so that whatever advantage of light there might be lay with me. Her position was a dangerous one and I begged her to put herself at a safe distance, but she would not, and no more would she take advantage of this opportunity to escape.

Momentarily I had expected to see Raban's men rushing into the chamber, for I could not understand that his yells had not reached every ear within a mile or more, and so I fought the more desperately to be rid of him and on our way before they came. Raban, now panting for breath, had none left with which to yell and I could see that from exertion, terror, and loss of blood he was weakening.

It was now that I heard the loud voices of men without and the tramp of running feet. They were coming! I redoubled my efforts and Raban his—I to kill, he to escape death until succor came. From a score of wounds was he bleeding and I was sure that that in his abdomen alone must prove fatal; but still he clung to life tenaciously, and fought with a froth of blood upon his lips from a punctured throat.

He stumbled and went to one knee and as he staggered to rise I thought that I had him, when we heard the hurrying feet of men descending the stairs. Instantly Bethelda hurled the flare to the floor, leaving us in utter darkness.

"Come!" she whispered, laying a hand upon my arm. "There will be too many now—we must escape as they enter or we are both indeed lost."

The warriors were cursing at the doorway now and calling for lights.

"Who hides within?" shouted one. "Stand forth, a prisoner! We are a hundred blades."

Bethelda and I edged nearer the doorway, hoping to pass out among them before a light was made. From the center of the room came a deep groan from where I had left Raban, followed by a scuffling noise upon the floor and a strange gurgling. I came to the doorway, leading Bethelda by the hand. I found it choked with men.

"Aside!" I said. "I will fetch a light."

A sword point was shoved against my belly. "Back!" warned a voice behind the point. "We will have a look at you before you pass—another is bringing a light."

I stepped back and crossed my sword with his. Perhaps I could hew my way to freedom with Bethelda in the confusion of the darkness. It seemed our only hope, for to be caught by Raban's minions now, after the hurts I had inflicted upon him, would mean sure death for me and worse for Bethelda.

By the feel of our steel we fenced in the dark, but I could not reach him, nor he me, though I felt that he was a master swordsman. I thought that I was gaining an advantage when I saw the flicker of a light coming from the doorway at the head of the stairs. Someone was coming with a flare. I redoubled my efforts, but to no avail.

And then the light came and as it fell upon the warriors in the doorway I stepped back, astounded, and dropped my point. The light that revealed them illumined my own face, and at sight of it my antagonist voiced a cry of joy.

"Red Hawk!" he cried and seized me by the shoulder. It was The Vulture, my brother, and with him were The Rattlesnake and a hundred warriors of our own beloved clans. Other lights were brought and I saw Okonnor and a host of strange warriors in Kalkar trappings pushing down the stairway with my own, nor did they raise sword against one another.

Okonnor pointed toward the center of the chamber, and we looked and there lay Raban, the giant, dead. "The Red Hawk, Julian 20th," he said, turning to those crowding into the chamber behind him, "Great Chief of the Tribe of Julians—our chief!"

"And Jemadar of all America!" cried another voice and the warriors, crowding into the room, raised their swords and their hoarse voices in acclamation. And he who had named me thus pushed past them and faced me and I saw that he was no other than the true Or-tis with whom I had been imprisoned in The Capital and with whom I had escaped. He saw Bethelda and rushed forward and took her in his arms, and for a moment I was jealous, forgetting that he was her brother.

"And how has all this happened," I asked, "that Or-tis and Julian come here together in peace?"

"Listen," said my brother, "before you pass judgment upon us. Long has run the feud between Julian and Or-tis for the crime of a man dead now hundreds of years. Few enough are the Americans of pure blood that they should be separated by hate when they would come together in friendship. Came the Or-tis to us after escaping the Kalkars and told of your escape and of the wish of his father that peace be made between us, and he offered to lead us against the Kalkars by ways that we did not know and The Wolf took council with me and there was also The Rock, The Rattlesnake and The Coyote, with every other chief who was at the front, and in your absence I dissolved the feud that has lain between us and the chiefs applauded my decision. Then, guided by the Or-tis, we entered The Capital and drove the Kalkars before us. Great are their numbers, but they have not The Flag with them and they must fall.

"Then," he continued, "came word, brought by the little Nipons of the hills, that you were in the mountains near the tent of Raban the Giant and we came to find you, and on the way we met Okonnor with many warriors and glad were they of the peace that had been made, and we joined with them who were also riding against Raban to rescue the sister of the Or-tis. And we are here awaiting the word of The Great Chief. If it is for peace between the Julian and the Or-tis, we are glad; if it is for war our swords are ready."

"It is for peace, ever," I replied and the Or-tis came and knelt at my feet and took my hand in his.

"Before my people," he said, very simply, "I swear allegiance to Julian 20th, Jemadar of America."

CHAPTER X

PEACE

THERE was still much fighting to be done, for though we had driven the Kalkars from The Capital they held the country to the south and west and we could not be satisfied until we had driven them into the sea, and so we prepared to ride to the front again that very night, but before we left I wanted a word with Bethelda who was to remain here with a proper retinue and a sufficient guard in the home of her people. Leading Red Lightning I searched about the grounds around the ruins and at last I came upon her beneath a great oak tree that grew at the northeast corner of the structure, its mighty limbs outspreading above the ruin. She was alone and I came and stood beside her.

"I am going now," I said, "to drive your enemies and mine into the sea. I have come to say good-bye."

"Good-bye, Julian." She held out her hand to me.

I had come full of brave words and mighty resolve, but when I took that slim and tender hand in mine I could but stand there mute and trembling. I, Julian 20th, The Red Hawk, for the first time in all my life, knew fear. A Julian quailed before an Or-tis.

For a full minute I stood there trying to speak and could not, and then I dropped to my knee at the feet of my enemy and with my lips against her fair hand I murmured what I had been too great a coward to look into her eyes and say: "I love you!"

She raised me to my feet then and lifted her lips to mine and I took her into my arms and covered her mouth with kisses; and thus ended the ancient feud between Julian and Or-tis, that had endured four hundred years and wrecked a world.

Two years later and we had driven the Kalkars into the sea, the remnants of them flying westward in great canoes which they had built and launched upon a beauteous bay a hundred miles or more south of The Capital.

The Rain Cloud said that if they were not overcome by storms and waves they might sail on and on around the world and come again to the eastern shores of America, but the rest of us knew that they would sail to the edge of the Earth and tumble off and that would be the end of them.

We live in such peace now that it is difficult to find an enemy upon whom to try one's lance, but I do not mind much, since my time is taken with the care of my flocks and herds, the business of my people and the training of Julian 21st, the son of a Julian and an Or-tis, who will one day be Jemadar of all America over which, once more, there flies but a single flag—The Flag.

CATALOG OF DOVER BOOKS

Classics of Science

*OPTICKS, Sir Isaac Newton. An enormous storehouse of insights and discoveries on light, reflection, color, refraction, theories of wave and corpuscular propagation of light, optical apparatus, and mathematical devices which have recently been reevaluated in terms of modern physics and placed in the top-most ranks of Newton's work. Foreword by Albert Einstein. Preface by I. B. Cohen of Harvard U. 7 pages of portraits, facsimile pages, letters, etc. cxvi + 412pp. 5⅜ x 8. S205 Paperbound **$2.00**

A SURVEY OF PHYSICAL THEORY, M. Planck. Lucid essays on modern physics for the general reader by the Nobel laureate and creator of the quantum revolution. Planck explains how the new concepts came into being; explores the clash between theories of mechanics, electrodynamics, and thermodynamics; and traces the evolution of the concept of light through Newton, Huygens, Maxwell, and his own quantum theory, providing unparalleled insights into his development of this momentous modern concept. Bibliography. Index. vii + 121pp. 5⅜ x 8. T650 Paperbound **$1.15**

DE RE METALLICA, Georgius Agricola. Written over 400 years ago, for 200 years the most authoritative first-hand account of the production of metals, translated in 1912 by former President Herbert Hoover and his wife, and today still one of the most beautiful and fascinating volumes ever produced in the history of science! 12 books, exhaustively annotated, give a wonderfully lucid and vivid picture of the history of mining, selection of sites, types of deposits, excavating pits, sinking shafts, ventilating, pumps, crushing machinery, assaying, smelting, refining metals, making salt, alum, nitre, glass, and many other topics. This definitive edition contains all 289 of the 16th century woodcuts which made the original an artistic masterpiece. It makes a superb gift for geologists, engineers, libraries, artists, historians, and everyone interested in science and early illustrative art. Biographical, historical introductions. Bibliography, survey of ancient authors. Indices. 289 illustrations. 672pp. 6¾ x 10¾. Deluxe library edition. S6 Clothbound **$10.00**

CHARLES BABBAGE AND HIS CALCULATING ENGINES, edited by P. Morrison and E. Morrison. Friend of Darwin, Humboldt, and Laplace, Babbage was a leading pioneer in large-scale mathematical machines and a prophetic herald of modern operational research—true father of Harvard's relay computer Mark I. His Difference Engine and Analytical Engine were the first successful machines in the field. This volume contains a valuable introduction on his life and work; major excerpts from his fascinating autobiography, revealing his eccentric and unusual personality; and extensive selections from "Babbage's Calculating Engines," a compilation of hard-to-find journal articles, both by Babbage and by such eminent contributors as the Countess of Lovelace, L. F. Menabrea, and Dionysius Lardner. 11 illustrations. Appendix of miscellaneous papers. Index. Bibliography. xxxviii + ·3 pp. 5⅜ x 8. · T12 Paperbound **$2.00**

A SOURCE BOOK IN MATHEMATICS, D. E. Smith. English translations of the original papers that announced the great discoveries in mathematics from the Renaissance to the end of the 19th century: succinct selections from 125 different treatises and articles, most of them unavailable elsewhere in English—Newton, Leibniz, Pascal, Riemann, Bernoulli, etc. 24 articles trace developments in the field of number, 18 cover algebra, 36 are on geometry, and 13 on calculus. Biographical-historical introductions to each article. Two volume set. Index in each. Total of 115 illustrations. Total of xxviii + 742pp. 5⅜ x 8. T552 Vol I Paperbound **$1.85**
T553 Vol II Paperbound **$1.85**
The set, boxed **$3.50**

*THE WORKS OF ARCHIMEDES WITH THE METHOD OF ARCHIMEDES, edited by T. L. Heath. All the known works of the greatest mathematician of antiquity including the recently discovered METHOD OF ARCHIMEDES. This last is the only work we have which shows exactly how early mathematicians discovered their proofs before setting them down in their final perfection. A 186 page study by the eminent scholar Heath discusses Archimedes and the history of Greek mathematics. Bibliography. 563pp. 5⅜ x 8. S9 Paperbound **$2.00**

*THE THIRTEEN BOOKS OF EUCLID'S ELEMENTS, edited by T. L. Heath. This is the complete EUCLID — the definitive edition of one of the greatest classics of the western world. Complete English translation of the Heiberg text with spurious Book XIV. Detailed 150 page introduction discusses aspects of Greek and medieval mathematics: Euclid, texts, commentators, etc. Paralleling the text is an elaborate critical exposition analyzing each definition, proposition, postulate, etc., and covering textual matters, mathematical analyses, refutations, extensions, etc. Unabridged reproduction of the Cambridge 2nd εdition. 3 volumes. Total of 995 figures, 1426pp. 5⅜ x 8. S88, 89, 90 — 3 vol. set, Paperbound **$6.00**

CLASSICS OF CARDIOLOGY, F. A. Willius, T. E. Keys. Monumental collection of 52 papers by great researchers, physicians on the anatomy, physiology and pathology of the heart and the circulation, and the diagnosis and therapy of their diseases. These are the original writings of Harvey, Sénac, Auenbrugger, Withering, Stokes, Einthoven, Osler, and 44 others from 1628 to 1912. 27 of the papers are complete, the rest in major excerpts; all are in English. The biographical notes and introductory essays make this a full history of cardiology—with exclusively first-hand material. 103 portraits, diagrams, and facsimiles of title pages. Chronological table. Total of xx + 858pp. 5⅝ x 8⅜. Two volume set. S912 Vol I Paperbound **$2.00**
S913 Vol II Paperbound **$2.00**
The set **$4.00**

*A PHILOSOPHICAL ESSAY ON PROBABILITIES, P. Laplace. Without recourse to any mathematics above grammar school, Laplace develops a philosophically, mathematically and historically classical exposition of the nature of probability: its functions and limitations, operations in practical affairs, calculations in games of chance, insurance, government, astronomy, and countless other fields. New introduction by E. T. Bell. viii + 196pp. S166 Paperbound **$1.35**

*DIALOGUES CONCERNING TWO NEW SCIENCES, Galileo Galilei. A classic of experimental science which has had a profound and enduring influence on the entire history of mechanics and engineering. Galileo based this, his finest work, on 30 years of experimentation. It offers a fascinating and vivid exposition of dynamics, elasticity, sound, ballistics, strength of materials, and the scientific method. Translated by H. Crew and A. de Salvio. 126 diagrams. Index. xxi + 288pp. 5⅜ x 8. S99 Paperbound **$1.65**

DE MAGNETE, William Gilbert. This classic work on magnetism founded a new science. Gilbert was the first to use the word "electricity," to recognize mass as distinct from weight, to discover the effect of heat on magnetic bodies; invented an electroscope, differentiated between static electricity and magnetism, conceived of the earth as a magnet. Written by the first great experimental scientist, this lively work is valuable not only as an historical landmark, but as the delightfully easy to follow record of a perpetually searching, ingenious mind. Translated by P. F. Mottelay. 25 page biographical memoir. 90 fix. lix + 368pp. 5⅜ x 8. S470 Paperbound **$2.00**

*THE GEOMETRY OF RENÉ DESCARTES. The great work which founded analytic geometry. The renowned Smith-Latham translation faced with the original French text containing all of Descartes' own diagrams! Contains: Problems the Construction of Which Requires Only Straight Lines and Circles; On the Nature of Curved Lines; On the Construction of Solid or Supersolid Problems. Notes. Diagrams. 258pp. S68 Paperbound **$1.50**

Nature and Biology

THE AUTOBIOGRAPHY OF CHARLES DARWIN AND SELECTED LETTERS, edited by Francis Darwin. The personal record of the professional and private life of the author of "Origin of the Species," whose ideas have shaped our thinking as have few others. His early life; the historic voyage aboard the "Beagle," the furor surrounding evolution and his replies; revealing anecdotes; reminiscences by his son; letters to Henslow, Lyell, Hooker, Huxley, Wallace, Kingsley, and others; his thought on religion and vivisection. Appendix. Index. 365pp. 5⅜ x 8. T479 Paperbound **$1.65**

THE LIFE OF PASTEUR, R. Vallery-Radot. 13th edition of this definitive biography, cited in Encyclopaedia Britannica. Authoritative, scholarly, well-documented with contemporary quotes, observations; gives complete picture of Pasteur's personal life; especially thorough presentation of scientific activities with silkworms, fermentation, hydrophobia, inoculation, etc. Introduction by Sir William Osler. Index. 505pp. 5⅜ x 8. T632 Paperbound **$2.00**

LOUIS PASTEUR, S. J. Holmes. A brief, very clear, and warmly understanding biography of the great French scientist by a former Professor of Zoology in the University of California. Traces his home life, the fortunate effects of his education, his early researches and first theses, and his constant struggle with superstition and institutionalism in his work on microorganisms, fermentation, anthrax, rabies, etc. New preface by the author. T197 Paperbound **$1.00**

THE ORIGIN OF LIFE, A. I. Oparin. This is the first modern statement of the theory that life evolved from complex nitro-carbon compounds. A historical introduction covers theories of the origin of life from the Greeks to modern times and then the techniques of biochemistry as applied to the problem by Dr. Oparin. The exposition presupposes a knowledge of chemistry but can be read with profit by everyone interested in this absorbing question. "Easily the most scholarly authority on the question," NEW YORK TIMES. Bibliography. Index. xxv + 270pp. 5⅜ x 8. S213 Paperbound **$1.75**

FREE! All you do is ask for it!

A WAY OF LIFE, by Sir William Osler. An inspirational classic that has helped countless business and professional men since the beloved physician and philosopher first delivered it at Yale in 1913. In warm human terms Osler tells how he managed to make the most of every day by an edifying mental and physical regimen. Illustrated. **FREE**

STUDIES ON THE STRUCTURE AND DEVELOPMENT OF VERTEBRATES, Edwin S. Goodrich. This definitive study by the greatest modern comparative anatomist covers the skeleton, fins and limbs, head region morphology, skull, skeletal viseral arches and labial cartilages, middle ear and ear ossicles, visceral clefts and gills, subdivisions of body cavity, vascular, respiratory, excretory, and peripheral nervous systems of vertebrates from fish to the higher mammals. 754 pictures. 69 page biographical study by C. C. Hardy. Bibliography of 1186 references. "For many a day this will certainly be the standard textbook," Journal of Anatomy. Index. Two volumes total 906pp. 5⅜ x 8. 2 volume set S449-50 Paperbound **$5.00**

CATALOG OF DOVER BOOKS

HEREDITY AND YOUR LIFE, A. M. Winchester. Authoritative, concise explanation of human genetics, in non-technical terms. What factors determine characteristics of 'future generations, how they may be altered; history of genetics, application of knowledge to control health, intelligence, number of entire populations. Physiology of reproduction, chromosomes, genes, blood types, Rh factor, dominant, recessive traits, birth by proxy, sexual abnormalities, radiation, much more. Index. 75 illus. 345pp. 5⅜ x 8. **T598 Paperbound $1.45**

FROM MAGIC TO SCIENCE, Charles Singer. Great historian of science examines aspects of medical science from the Roman Empire through the Renaissance. Especially valuable are the sections on early herbals, probably the best coverage of this subject available, and on "The Visions of Hildegarde of Bingen" which are explained by physiological means. Also covered are Arabian and Galenic influences, astrology, the Sphere of Pythagoras, Leonardo da Vinci, Vesalius, Paracelsus, et al. Frequent quotations and translations. New introduction by the author. New unabridged, corrected edition. 158 unusual illustrations from classical and medieval sources. Index. xxvii + 365pp. 5⅜ x 8. **T390 Paperbound $2.00**

A SHORT HISTORY OF ANATOMY AND PHYSIOLOGY FROM THE GREEKS TO HARVEY, C. Singer. An intermediate history formerly entitled THE EVOLUTION OF ANATOMY, this work conveys the thrill of discovery as the nature of the human body is gradually clarified by hundreds of scientists from the Greeks to the Renaissance. Diogenes, Hippocrates, and other early workers, up to Leonardo da Vinci, Vesalius, Harvey, and others, with 139 illustrations from medieval manuscripts, classical sculpture, etc. Index. 221pp. 5⅜ x 8. **T389 Paperbound $1.75**

INTRODUCTION TO THE STUDY OF EXPERIMENTAL MEDICINE, Claude Bernard. The only major work of Claude Bernard now available in English, this classic records Bernard's efforts to transform physiology into an exact science. He examines the roles of chance and error and incorrect hypothesis in leading to scientific truth and describes many classic experiments on the action of curare, carbon monoxide, and other poisons, the functions of the pancreas, the glycogenic function of the liver, and many others. Introduction. Foreword by I. B. Cohen. xxv + 266pp. 5⅜ x 8. **T400 Paperbound $1.50**

A WAY OF LIFE AND OTHER SELECTED WRITINGS, Sir William Osler. Physician and humanist, Osler writes brilliantly on philosophy, religion, and literature in "The Student Life," "Books and Men," "Creators, Transmuters, and Transmitters," "The Old Humanities and the New Science," and the title essay. His medical history is equally acute in discussions of Thomas Browne, Gui Patin, Robert Burton, Michael Servetus, William Beaumont, Laënnec. 5 more of his best essays. 5 photographs. Introduction by G. L. Keynes, M.D., F.R.C.S. Index. xx + 278pp. 5⅜ x 8. **T488 Paperbound $1.50**

FRUIT KEY AND TWIG KEY TO TREES AND SHRUBS, W. M. Harlow. Bound together in one volume for the first time, these handy and accurate keys to fruit and twig identification are the only guides of their sort with photographs (up to 3 times natural size). "Fruit Key": Key to over 120 different deciduous and evergreen fruits. 139 photographs and 11 line drawings. Synoptic summary of fruit types. Bibliography. 2 Indexes (common and scientific names). "Twig Key": Key to over 160 different twigs and buds. 173 photographs. Glossary of technical terms. Bibliography. 2 Indexes (common and scientific names). Two volumes bound as one. Total of xvii + 126pp. 5⅝ x 8⅜. **T511 Paperbound $1.25**

TREES OF THE EASTERN AND CENTRAL UNITED STATES AND CANADA, W. M. Harlow. A revised edition of a standard middle-level guide to native trees and important escapes. More than 140 trees are described in detail, and illustrated with more than 600 drawings and photographs. Supplementary keys will enable the careful reader to identify almost any tree he might encounter. xiii + 288pp. 5⅜ x 8. **T395 Paperbound $1.35**

INSECT LIFE AND INSECT NATURAL HISTORY, S. W. Frost. A work emphasizing habits, social life, and ecological relations of insects, rather than more academic aspects of classification and morphology. Prof. Frost's enthusiasm and knowledge are everywhere evident as he discusses insect associations, and specialized habits like leaf-rolling, leaf-mining, and case-making, the gall insects, the boring insects, aquatic insects, etc. He examines all sorts of matters not usually covered in general works, such as: insects as human food, insect music and musicians, insect response to electric and radio waves, use of insects in art and literature. The admirably executed purpose of this book, which covers the middle ground between elementary treatment and scholarly monographs, is to excite the reader to observe for himself. Over 700 illustrations. Extensive bibliography. x + 524pp. 5⅜ x 8.
T517 Paperbound $2.25

COMMON SPIDERS OF THE UNITED STATES, J. H. Emerton. Here is a nature hobby you can pursue right in your own cellar! Only non-technical, but thorough, reliable guide to spiders for the layman. Over 200 spiders from all parts of the country, arranged by scientific classification, are identified by shape and color, number of eyes, habitat and range, habits, etc. Full text, 501 line drawings and photographs, and valuable introduction explain webs, poisons, threads, capturing and preserving spiders, etc. Index. New synoptic key by S. W. Frost. xxiv + 225pp. 5⅜ x 8.   T223 Paperbound **$1.35**

HOW TO KNOW THE FERNS, F. T. Parsons. Ferns, among our most lovely native plants, are all too little known. This modern classic of nature lore will enable the layman to identify any American fern he may come across. After an introduction on the structure and life of ferns, the 57 most important ferns are fully pictured and described (arranged upon a simple identification key). Index of Latin and English names. 61 illustrations and 42 full-page plates. xiv + 215pp. 5⅜ x 8.   T740 Paperbound **$1.25**

RACING PIGEONS, C. Osman. A complete, practical, up-to-date, and authoritative book on racing pigeons by a British expert. Covers the anatomy of the pigeon, the homing instinct, the pigeon's life cycle, food and feeding, lofts and aviaries, breeding winners, preparing for races, winning systems, common diseases, and much more. Indispensable for beginner and expert alike. 24 photographs by the author. 10 line drawings. Index. 192pp. 5⅛ x 7⅛.
T513 Clothbound **$3.00**

Psychology

YOGA: A SCIENTIFIC EVALUATION, Kovoor T. Behanan. A complete reprinting of the book that for the first time gave Western readers a sane, scientific explanation and analysis of yoga. The author draws on controlled laboratory experiments and personal records of a year as a disciple of a yoga, to investigate yoga psychology, concepts of knowledge, physiology, "supernatural" phenomena, and the ability to tap the deepest human powers. In this study under the auspices of Yale University Institute of Human Relations, the strictest principles of physiological and psychological inquiry are followed throughout. Foreword by W. A. Miles, Yale University. 17 photographs. Glossary. Index. xx + 270pp. 5⅜ x 8. T505 Paperbound **$1.65**

CONDITIONED REFLEXES: AN INVESTIGATION OF THE PHYSIOLOGICAL ACTIVITIES OF THE CEREBRAL CORTEX, I. P. Pavlov. Full, authorized translation of Pavlov's own survey of his work in experimental psychology reviews entire course of experiments, summarizes conclusions, outlines psychological system based on famous "conditioned reflex" concept. Details of technical means used in experiments, observations on formation of conditioned reflexes, function of cerebral hemispheres, results of damage, nature of sleep, typology of nervous system, significance of experiments for human psychology. Trans. by Dr. G. V. Anrep, Cambridge Univ. 235-item bibliography. 18 figures. 445pp. 5⅜ x 8.   S614 Paperbound **$2.25**

EXPLANATION OF HUMAN BEHAVIOUR, F. V. Smith. A major intermediate-level introduction to and criticism of 8 complete systems of the psychology of human behavior, with unusual emphasis on theory of investigation and methodology. Part I is an illuminating analysis of the problems involved in the explanation of observed phenomena, and the differing viewpoints on the nature of causality. Parts II and III are a closely detailed survey of the systems of McDougall, Gordon Allport, Lewin, the Gestalt group, Freud, Watson, Hull, and Tolman. Biographical notes. Bibliography of over 800 items. 2 indexes. 38 figures. xii + 460pp. 5½ x 8¾.
T253 Clothbound **$6.00**

SEX IN PSYCHO-ANALYSIS (formerly CONTRIBUTIONS TO PSYCHO-ANALYSIS), S. Ferenczi. Written by an associate of Freud, this volume presents countless insights on such topics as impotence, transference, analysis and children, dreams, symbols, obscene words, masturbation and male homosexuality, paranoia and psycho-analysis, the sense of reality, hypnotism and therapy, and many others. Also includes full text of THE DEVELOPMENT OF PSYCHO-ANALYSIS by Ferenczi and Otto Rank. Two books bound as one. Total of 406pp. 5⅜ x 8.
T324 Paperbound **$1.85**

BEYOND PSYCHOLOGY, Otto Rank. One of Rank's most mature contributions, focussing on the irrational basis of human behavior as a basic fact of our lives. The psychoanalytic techniques of myth analysis trace to their source the ultimates of human existence: fear of death, personality, the social organization, the need for love and creativity, etc. Dr. Rank finds them stemming from a common irrational source, man's fear of final destruction. A seminal work in modern psychology, this work sheds light on areas ranging from the concept of immortal soul to the sources of state power. 291pp. 5⅜ x 8.   T485 Paperbound **$1.75**

ILLUSIONS AND DELUSIONS OF THE SUPERNATURAL AND THE OCCULT, D. H. Rawcliffe. Holds up to rational examination hundreds of persistent delusions including crystal gazing, automatic writing, table turning, mediumistic trances, mental healing, stigmata, lycanthropy, live burial, the Indian Rope Trick, spiritualism, dowsing, telepathy, clairvoyance, ghosts, ESP, etc. The author explains and exposes the mental and physical deceptions involved, making this not only an exposé of supernatural phenomena, but a valuable exposition of characteristic types of abnormal psychology. Originally titled "The Psychology of the Occult." 14 illustrations. Index. 551pp. 5⅜ x 8.   T503 Paperbound **$2.00**

THE PRINCIPLES OF PSYCHOLOGY, William James. The full long course, unabridged, of one of the great classics of Western literature and science. Wonderfully lucid descriptions of human mental activity, the stream of thought, consciousness, time perception, memory, imagination, emotions, reason, abnormal phenomena, and similar topics. Original contributions are integrated with the work of such men as Berkeley, Binet, Mills, Darwin, Hume, Kant, Royce, Schopenhauer, Spinoza, Locke, Descartes, Galton, Wundt, Lotse, Herbart, Fechner, and scores of others. All contrasting interpretations of mental phenomena are examined in detail — introspective analysis, philosophical interpretation, and experimental research. "A classic," JOURNAL OF CONSULTING PSYCHOLOGY. "The main lines are as valid as ever," PSYCHOANALYTICAL QUARTERLY. "Standard reading . . . a classic of interpretation," PSYCHIATRIC QUARTERLY. 94 illustrations. 1408pp. 2 volumes. 5⅜ x 8.　　　Vol. 1, T381 Paperbound **$2.50**
　　　　　　　　　　　　　　　　　　　　　　　　　　　　　Vol. 2, T382 Paperbound **$2.50**

Puzzles, Mathematical Recreations

SYMBOLIC LOGIC and THE GAME OF LOGIC, Lewis Carroll. "Symbolic Logic" is not concerned with modern symbolic logic, but is instead a collection of over 380 problems posed with charm and imagination, using the syllogism, and a fascinating diagrammatic method of drawing conclusions. In "The Game of Logic" Carroll's whimsical imagination devises a logical game played with 2 diagrams and counters (included) to manipulate hundreds of tricky syllogisms. The final section, "Hit or Miss" is a lagniappe of 101 additional puzzles in the delightful Carroll manner. Until this reprint edition, both of these books were rarities costing up to $15 each. Symbolic Logic: Index. xxxi + 199pp. The Game of Logic: 96pp. 2 vols. bound as one. 5⅜ x 8.　　　　　　　　　　　　　T492 Paperbound **$1.50**

PILLOW PROBLEMS and A TANGLED TALE, Lewis Carroll. One of the rarest of all Carroll's works, "Pillow Problems" contains 72 original math puzzles, all typically ingenious. Particularly fascinating are Carroll's answers which remain exactly as he thought them out, reflecting his actual mental process. The problems in "A Tangled Tale" are in story form, originally appearing as a monthly magazine serial. Carroll not only gives the solutions, but uses answers sent in by readers to discuss wrong approaches and misleading paths, and grades them for insight. Both of these books were rarities until this edition, "Pillow Problems" costing up to $25, and "A Tangled Tale" $15. Pillow Problems: Preface and Introduction by Lewis Carroll. xx + 109pp. A Tangled Tale: 6 illustrations. 152pp. Two vols. bound as one. 5⅜ x 8.　　　　　　　　　　　　　　　T493 Paperbound **$1.50**

AMUSEMENTS IN MATHEMATICS, Henry Ernest Dudeney. The foremost British originator of mathematical puzzles is always intriguing, witty, and paradoxical in this classic, one of the largest collections of mathematical amusements. More than 430 puzzles, problems, and paradoxes. Mazes and games, problems on number manipulation, unicursal and other route problems, puzzles on measuring, weighing, packing, age, kinship, chessboards, joiners', crossing river, plane figure dissection, and many others. Solutions. More than 450 illustrations. vii + 258pp. 5⅜ x 8.　　　　　　　　　　　　　　　T473 Paperbound **$1.25**

THE CANTERBURY PUZZLES, Henry Dudeney. Chaucer's pilgrims set one another problems in story form. Also Adventures of the Puzzle Club, the Strange Escape of the King's Jester, the Monks of Riddlewell, the Squire's Christmas Puzzle Party, and others. All puzzles are original, based on dissecting plane figures, arithmetic, algebra, elementary calculus and other branches of mathematics, and purely logical ingenuity. "The limit of ingenuity and intricacy," The Observer. Over 110 puzzles. Full Solutions. 150 illustrations. vii + 225pp. 5⅜ x 8.
　　　　　　　　　　　　　　　　　　　　　　　　　　　　　T474 Paperbound **$1.25**

MATHEMATICAL RECREATIONS, M. Kraitchik. One of the most thorough compilations of unusual mathematical problems for beginners and advanced mathematicians. Historical problems from Greek, Medieval, Arabic, Hindu sources. 50 pages devoted to pastimes derived from figurate numbers, Mersenne numbers, Fermat numbers, primes and probability. 40 pages of magic, Euler, Latin, panmagic squares. 25 new positional and permutational games of permanent value: fairy chess, latruncles, reversi, jinx, ruma, lasca, tricolor, tetrachrome, etc. Complete rigorous solutions. Revised second edition. 181 illustrations. 333pp. 5⅜ x 8.
　　　　　　　　　　　　　　　　　　　　　　　　　　　　　T163 Paperbound **$1.75**

MATHEMATICAL EXCURSIONS, H. A. Merrill. Even if you hardly remember your high school math, you'll enjoy the 90 stimulating problems contained in this book and you will come to understand a great many mathematical principles with surprisingly little effort. Many useful shortcuts and diversions not generally known are included: division by inspection, Russian peasant multiplication, memory systems for pi, building odd and even magic squares, square roots by geometry, dyadic systems, and many more. Solutions to difficult problems. 50 illustrations. 145pp. 5⅜ x 8.　　　　　　　　　　　　T350 Paperbound **$1.00**

MAGIC SQUARES AND CUBES, W. S. Andrews. Only book-length treatment in English, a thorough non-technical description and analysis. Here are nasik, overlapping, pandiagonal, serrated squares; magic circles, cubes, spheres, rhombuses. Try your hand at 4-dimensional magical figures! Much unusual folklore and tradition included. High school algebra is sufficient. 754 diagrams and illustrations. viii + 419pp. 5⅜ x 8.　　　　　T658 Paperbound **$1.85**

Chess, Checkers, Games, Go

THE ADVENTURE OF CHESS, Edward Lasker. A lively history of chess, from its ancient beginnings in the Indian 4-handed game of Chaturanga, through to the great players of our day, as told by one of America's finest masters. He introduces such unusual sidelights and amusing oddities as Maelzel's chess-playing automaton that beat Napoleon 3 times. Major discussion of chess-playing machines and personal memories of. Nimzovich, Capablanca, etc. 5-page chess primer. 11 illustrations, 53 diagrams. 296pp. 5⅜ x 8.   S510 Paperbound **$1.45**

A TREASURY OF CHESS LORE, edited by Fred Reinfeld. A delightful collection of anecdotes, short stories, aphorisms by and about the masters, poems, accounts of games and tournaments, photography. Hundreds of humorous, pithy, satirical, wise, and historical episodes, comments, and word portraits. A fascinating "must" for chess players; revealing and perhaps seductive to those who wonder what their friends see in the game. 48 photographs (14 full page plates) 12 diagrams. xi + 306pp. 5⅜ x 8.   T458 Paperbound **$1.75**

FREE! All you do is ask for it!

HOW DO YOU PLAY CHESS? by Fred Reinfeld. A prominent expert covers every basic rule of chess for the beginner in 86 questions and answers: moves, powers of pieces, rationale behind moves, how to play forcefully, history of chess, and much more. Bibliography of chess publications. 11 board diagrams. 48 pages.   **FREE**

THE PLEASURES OF CHESS, Assiac. Internationally known British writer, influential chess columnist, writes wittily about wide variety of chess subjects: Anderssen's "Immortal Game;" only game in which both opponents resigned at once; psychological tactics of Reshevsky, Lasker; varieties· played by masters for relaxation, such as "losing chess;" sacrificial orgies; etc. These anecdotes, witty observations will give you fresh appreciation of game. 43 problems. 150 diagrams. 139pp. 5⅜ x 8.   T597 Paperbound **$1.25**

WIN AT CHESS, F. Reinfeld. 300 practical chess situations from actual tournament play to sharpen your chess eye and test your skill. Traps, sacrifices, mates, winning combinations, subtle exchanges, show you how to WIN AT CHESS. Short notes and tables of solutions and alternative moves help you evaluate your progress. Learn to think ahead playing the "crucial moments" of historic games. 300 diagrams. Notes and solutions. Formerly titled CHESS QUIZ. vi + 120pp. 5⅜ x 8.   T438 Paperbound **$1.00**

THE ART OF CHESS, James Mason. An unabridged reprinting of the latest revised edition of the most famous general study of chess ever written. Also included, a complete supplement by Fred Reinfeld, "How Do You Play Chess?", invaluable to beginners for its lively question and answer method. Mason, an early 20th century master, teaches the beginning and intermediate player more than 90 openings, middle game, end game, how to see more moves ahead, to plan purposefully, attack, sacrifice, defend, exchange, and govern general strategy. Supplement. 448 diagrams. 1947 Reinfeld-Bernstein text. Bibliography. xvi + 340pp. 5⅜ x 8.   T463 Paperbound **$1.85**

THE PRINCIPLES OF CHESS, James Mason. This "great chess classic" (N. Y. Times) is a general study covering all aspects of the game; basic forces, resistance, obstruction, opposition, relative values, mating, typical end game situations, combinations, much more. The last section discusses openings, with 50 games illustrating modern master play of Rubinstein, Spielmann, Lasker, Capablanca, etc., selected and annotated by Fred Reinfeld. Will improve the game of any intermediate-skilled player, but is so forceful and lucid that an absolute beginner might use it to become an accomplished player. 1946 Reinfeld edition. 166 diagrams. 378pp. 5⅜ x 8.   T646 Paperbound **$1.85**

LASKER'S MANUAL OF CHESS, Dr. Emanuel Lasker. Probably the greatest chess player of modern times, Dr. Emanuel Lasker held the world championship 28 years, independent of passing schools or fashions. This unmatched study of the game, chiefly for intermediate to skilled players, analyzes basic methods, combinations, position play, the aesthetics of chess, dozens of different openings, etc., with constant reference to great modern games. Contains a brilliant exposition of Steinitz's important theories. Introduction by Fred Reinfeld. Tables of Lasker's tournament record. 3 indices. 308 diagrams. 1 photograph. xxx + 349pp. 5⅜ x 8.   T640 Paperbound **$2.00**

CATALOG OF DOVER BOOKS

WIN AT CHECKERS, M. Hopper. (Formerly CHECKERS). The former World's Unrestricted Checker Champion discusses the principles cf the game, expert's shots and traps, problems for the beginner, standard openings, locating your best move, the end game, opening "blitzkrieg" moves, ways to draw when you are behind your opponent, etc. More than 100 detailed questions and answers anticipate your problems. Appendix. 75 problems with solutions and diagrams. Index. 79 figures. xi + 107pp. 5⅜ x 8.   **T363 Paperbound $1.00**

GAMES ANCIENT AND ORIENTAL, AND HOW TO PLAY THEM, E. Falkener. A connoisseur's selection of exciting and different games: Oriental varieties of chess, with unusual pieces and moves (including Japanese shogi); the original pachisi; go; reconstructions of lost Roman and Egyptian games; and many more. Full rules and sample games. Now play at home the games that have entertained millions, not on a fad basis, but for millennia. 345 illustrations and figures. iv + 366pp. 5⅜ x 8.   **T739 Paperbound $1.85**

GO AND GO-MOKU, Edward Lasker. A fascinating Oriental game, Go, is winning new devotees in America daily. Rules that you can learn in a few minutes—a wealth of combinations that makes it more profound than chess! This is an easily followed step-by-step explanation of this 2000-year-old game, beginning with fundamentals. New chapter on advanced strategy in this edition! Also contains rules for Go-Moku, a very easy sister game. 72 diagrams. xix + 215pp. 5⅜ x 8.   **T613 Paperbound $1.45**

Fiction

FLATLAND, E. A. Abbott. A science-fiction classic of life in a 2-dimensional world that is also a first-rate introduction to such aspects of modern science as relativity and hyperspace. Political, moral, satirical, and humorous overtones have made FLATLAND fascinating reading for thousands. 7th edition. New introduction by Banesh Hoffmann. 16 illustrations. 128pp. 5⅜ x 8.   **T1 Paperbound $1.00**

THE WONDERFUL WIZARD OF OZ, L. F. Baum. Only edition in print with all the original W. W. Denslow illustrations in full color—as much a part of "The Wizard" as Tenniel's drawings are of "Alice in Wonderland." "The Wizard" is still America's best-loved fairy tale, in which, as the author expresses it, "The wonderment and joy are retained and the heartaches and nightmares left out." Now today's young readers can enjoy every word and wonderful picture of the original book. New introduction by Martin Gardner. A Baum bibliography. 23 full-page color plates. viii + 268pp. 5⅜ x 8.   **T691 Paperbound $1.45**

THE MARVELOUS LAND OF OZ, L. F. Baum. This is the equally enchanting sequel to the "Wizard," continuing the adventures of the Scarecrow and the Tin Woodman. The hero this time is a little boy named Tip, and all the delightful Oz magic is still present. This is the Oz book with the Animated Saw-Horse, the Woggle-Bug, and Jack Pumpkinhead. All the original John R. Neill illustrations, 10 in full color. 287 pp. 5⅜ x 8.   **T692 Paperbound $1.45**

FIVE GREAT DOG NOVELS, edited by Blanche Cirker. The complete original texts of five classic dog novels that have delighted and thrilled millions of children and adults throughout the world with their stories of loyalty, adventure, and courage. Full texts of Jack London's "The Call of the Wild"; John Brown's "Rab and His Friends"; Alfred Ollivant's "Bob, Son of Battle"; Marshall Saunders's "Beautiful Joe"; and Ouida's "A Dog of Flanders." 21 Illustrations from the original editions. 495pp. 5⅜ x 8.   **T777 Paperbound $1.50**

The Space Novels of Jules Verne

TO THE SUN? and OFF ON A COMET!, Jules Verne. Complete texts of two of the most imaginative flights into fancy in world literature display the high adventure that have kept Verne's novels read for nearly a century. Only unabridged edition of the best translation, by Edward Roth. Large, easily readable type. 50 illustrations selected from first editions. 462pp. 5⅜ x 8.
T634 Paperbound $1.75

FROM THE EARTH TO THE MOON and ALL AROUND THE MOON, Jules Verne. Complete editions of 2 of Verne's most successful novels, in finest Edward Roth translations, now available after many years out of print. Verne's visions of submarines, airplanes, television, rockets, interplanetary travel; of scientific and not-so-scientific beliefs; of peculiarities of Americans; all delight and engross us today as much as when they first appeared. Large, easily readable type. 42 illus. from first French edition. 476pp. 5⅜ x 8.
T633 Paperbound $1.75

3 ADVENTURE NOVELS by H. Rider Haggard. Complete texts of "She," "King Solomon's Mines," "Allan Quatermain." Qualities of discovery, desire for immortality, search for the primitive, for what is unadorned by civilization, have kept these novels of African adventure excitingly alive to readers from R. L. Stevenson to George Orwell. 636pp. 5⅜ x 8.
T584 Paperbound $2.00

CATALOG OF DOVER BOOKS

THE CASTING AWAY OF MRS. LECKS AND MRS. ALESHINE, F. R. Stockton. A charming light novel by Frank Stockton, one of America's finest humorists (and author of "The Lady, or the Tiger?"). This book has made millions of Americans laugh at the reflection of themselves in two middle-aged American women involved in some of the strangest adventures on record. You will laugh, too, as they endure shipwreck, desert island, and blizzard with maddening tranquillity. Also contains complete text of "The Dusantes," sequel to "The Casting Away." 49 original illustrations by F. D. Steele. vii + 142pp. 5⅜ x 8.

T743 Paperbound **$1.00**

THREE PROPHETIC NOVELS OF H. G. WELLS. Complete texts of 3 timeless science fiction novels by the greatest master of the art, with remarkable prophecies of technological and social changes that are really taking place!—"When the Sleeper Wakes" (first printing in 50 years), "A Story of the Days to Come," and "The Time Machine" (only truly complete text available). Introduction by E. F. Bleiler. "The absolute best of imaginative fiction," N. Y. Times. 335pp. 5⅜ x 8.

T605 Paperbound **$1.45**

SEVEN SCIENCE FICTION NOVELS, H. G. Wells. Full unabridged texts of 7 science-fiction novels of the master. Ranging from biology, physics, chemistry, astronomy, to sociology and other studies, Mr. Wells extrapolates whole worlds of strange and intriguing character. "One will have to go far to match this for entertainment, excitement, and sheer pleasure . . ." NEW YORK TIMES. Contents: The Time Machine, The Island of Dr. Moreau, The First Men in the Moon, The Invisible Man, The War of the Worlds, The Food of the Gods, In The Days of the Comet. 1015pp. 5⅜ x 8.

T264 Clothbound **$3.95**

28 SCIENCE FICTION STORIES OF H. G. WELLS. Two full unabridged novels, MEN LIKE GODS and STAR BEGOTTEN, plus 26 short stories by the master science-fiction writer of all time! Stories of space, time, invention, exploration, future adventure—an indispensible part of the library of everyone interested in science and adventure. PARTIAL CONTENTS: Men Like Gods, The Country of the Blind, In the Abyss, The Crystal Egg, The Man Who Could Work Miracles, A Story of the Days to Come, The Valley of Spiders, and 21 more! 928pp. 5⅜ x 8.

T265 Clothbound **$3.95**

DAVID HARUM, E. N. Westcott. This novel of one of the most loveable, humorous characters in American literature is a prime example of regional humor. It continues to delight people who like their humor dry, their characters quaint, and their plots ingenuous. First book edition to contain complete novel plus chapter found after author's death. Illustrations from first illustrated edition. 192pp. 5⅜ x 8.

T580 Paperbound **$1.15**

GESTA ROMANORUM, trans. by Charles Swan, ed. by Wynnard Hooper. 181 tales of Greeks, Romans, Britons, Biblical characters, comprise one of greatest medieval story collections, source of plots for writers including Shakespeare, Chaucer, Gower, etc. Imaginative tales of wars, incest, thwarted love, magic, fantasy, allegory, humor, tell about kings, prostitutes, philosophers, fair damsels, knights, Noah, pirates, all walks, stations of life. Introduction. Notes. 500pp. 5⅜ x 8.

T535 Paperbound **$1.85**

Dover publishes books on art, music, philosophy, literature, languages, history, social sciences, psychology, handcrafts, orientalia, puzzles and entertainments, chess, pets and gardens, books explaining science, intermediate and higher mathematics mathematical physics, engineering, biological sciences, earth sciences, classics of science, etc. Write to:

Dept. catrr.
Dover Publications, Inc.
180 Varick Street, N. Y. 14, N. Y.